The yellowbacks... classics of popular fiction

The yellowjackets or yellowbacks were a great series of bestselling adventure and crime thrillers that had its origins in the mid to late 19th century following on from the 'penny dreadfuls'. They virtually began the mass market revolution of the early 20th century with a clear standard format and imprint/series livery (what would today be called branding). Hodder & Stoughton published the yellow jackets in two main series with series run dates of: 1923-1939 and later 1949-1957.

As the tagline ('where thrillers really began') on the back cover implies, the imprint and series focused on thrillers that were the bestsellers of their time. This current reissue or retro revival if you will, brings back many of these masterpieces, now classics in their own way and extends it further by including key titles from that period that were either great crime or thriller or even general commercial fiction (including sub-genres of noir, horror, gothic, romance, westerns etc) influences of their time. There are some perennial favourites and many rarities either lost or not easily available being revived in the current series. Writers and characters ranged from adventure heroes like Bulldog Drummond, Allan Quatermain, Richard Hannay or the Saint through thriller grandmasters Edgar Wallace and E. Phillips Oppenheim, crime and mystery maestros like Patricia Wentworth, GK Chesterton, Agatha Christie and the Detection club, to western and swashbucklers like Zane Grey, Max Brand, Captain Blood and even romance or general fiction classics like Hermina Black, Denise Robins, Marie Corelli or Stella Morton. These were books that had storytelling at their heart and always entertained.

The yellowbacks had both hardback (with varying design elements) and paperback (which built the series look) versions with the latter still carrying the imprint 'yellowjacket'. The current reissues pay tribute to both and use an amalgam of elements from both editions while retaining the complete yellow (or 'mustard-plaster') livery with the author's name in blue beveled type with a 'simulated emboss' effect and a white outer 'outline', and the book title in black. These reissues retain the distinctive size of the original mass market paperback and follow the three main category variations—the thrillers (crime, westerns, mystery, adventure) had blue lettering for the author's name, while Romance and 'softer general fiction had red; and other categories like humour had green.

For more detail and a full list of titles visit https://www.hachetteindia.com/home/yellowbacks

THE COMPLETE TRENT CASE BOOK

THE COMPLETE TRENT CASE BOOK

Edmund Clerihew Bentley, who generally published under the names E.C. Bentley or E. Clerihew Bentley, was a popular English novelist and humourist, and inventor of the clerihew, an irregular form of humorous verse on biographical topics. His best known one is

Sir Christopher Wren
Said, "I am going to dine with some men.
If anyone calls
Say I am designing St. Paul's".

Bentley's detective novel *Trent's Last Case* was much praised, (see back cover) and with its labyrinthine and mystifying plotting can be seen as the first truly modern mystery. It was adapted as a film in 1920, 1929, and 1952. The success of the work inspired him, after 23 years, to cowrite a sequel, *Trent's Own Case* (1936). There was also a book of Trent short stories, *Trent Intervenes* (1938).

From 1936 until 1949 Bentley was president of the Detection Club. He contributed to two crime stories for the club's radio serials broadcast in 1930 and 1931, which were published in 1983 as *The Scoop* and *Behind The Screen*. In 1950 he contributed the introduction to a Constable & Co. omnibus edition of Damon Runyon's "stories of the bandits of Broadway", which was republished in 1990 as *On Broadway*.

He died in 1956 in London at the age of 80. His son Nicolas Bentley was an illustrator.

G.K. Chesterton dedicated his popular detective novel on anarchist terrorism, *The Man Who Was Thursday*, to Edmund Clerihew Bentley, a school friend.

THE COMPLETE TRENT CASE BOOK

E. C. Bentley

hachette

The Complete Trent Case Book
Trent's Last case first published by Thomas Nelson and Sons, Ltd. in 1913 (published as *The Woman in Black* in the United States) *Trent's Own Case* written in collaboration with H. Warner Allen and first published by Constable.
 Trent Intervenes first published in book form in 1938 by Thomas Nelson and Sons, Ltd.

An Hachette UK Company www.hachetteindia.com

1

The texts in these editions in most cases have been reprinted as is, with minimal editorial changes and by and large no bowdlerizing for political correctness; though in some editions, a few words and phrases considered archaic, or those considered offensive now, along with archaic punctuation may have been modified in places to make the text more accessible to today's readers. The narratives, language, beliefs, social mores and/or cultural depictions, in these volumes are a reflection of their times and must be viewed as such. They may also contain certain cultural, racial and gender prejudices and stereotypes that may be outdated or clearly wrong then and wrong today; but their removal would be tantamount to claiming these prejudices never existed. The Publisher does not endorse or support those depictions or stereotypes; and these books have been made available for a discerning audience that will read it for entertainment value and a chronicle/record of popular fiction of past times.

Cover design by Priya Singh adapted from the original classic yellowjacket by Hodder & Stoughton.

Cover illustration by Ishan Trivedi.

Series note: Some of the books in the series (unless otherwise credited) may have cover or inside illustrations from the original yellowbacks or early editions, and while full restoration has been attempted, some images may be grainy or faded due to the condition of the original material. The end notes or bonus material or blurb details may have been sourced from the public domain or free use publications such as Wikipedia and attribution is hereby made also allowing similar free use reproduction from here. Sources requiring further specific attribution may write in and further detailing and/or corrections shall be made in subsequent printings/editions.

Reprint specifications may be subject to change including but not limited to finishes, paper, colour sections.

ISBN: 978-93-5731-143-4

Hachette Book Publishing India Pvt. Ltd.
4th & 5th Floors, Corporate Centre,
Plot No. 94, Sector 44, Gurugram - 122 003, India

Typeset in Electra LT STD 10/12.5 pt by Manipal Technologies Limited, Manipal

Printed and bound in India by Manipal Technologies Limited, Manipal

CONTENTS

I
TRENT'S LAST CASE

1

BAD NEWS

Between what matters and what seems to matter, how should the world we know judge wisely?

When the scheming, indomitable brain of Sigsbee Manderson was scattered by a shot from an unknown hand, that world lost nothing worth a single tear; it gained something memorable in a harsh reminder of the vanity of such wealth as this dead man had piled up—without making one loyal friend to mourn him, without doing an act that could help his memory to the least honour. But when the news of his end came, it seemed to those living in the great vortices of business as if the earth too shuddered under a blow.

In all the lurid commercial history of his country there had been no figure that had so imposed itself upon the mind of the trading world. He had a niche apart in its temples. Financial giants, strong to direct and augment the forces of capital, and taking an approved toll in millions for their labour, had existed before; but in the case of Manderson there had been this singularity, that a pale halo of piratical romance, a thing especially dear to the hearts of his countrymen, had remained incongruously about his head through the years when he stood in every eye as the unquestioned guardian of stability, the stamper-out of manipulated crises, the foe of the raiding chieftains that infest the borders of Wall Street.

The fortune left by his grandfather, who had been one of those chieftains on the smaller scale of his day, had descended to him with accretion through his father, who during a long life had quietly continued to lend money and never had margined a stock. Manderson, who had at no time known what it was to be without large sums to his hand, should have been altogether of that newer American plutocracy which is steadied by the tradition and habit of great wealth. But it was not so. While his nurture and education had taught him European ideas of a rich man's proper external circumstance; while they had rooted in him an instinct for quiet magnificence, the larger costliness which does not shriek of itself with a thousand tongues; there had been handed on to him nevertheless much of the Forty-Niner and financial buccaneer, his forebear. During that first period of his business career which had been called his early bad manner, he had been little more than a gambler of genius, his hand against every man's—an infant prodigy who brought to the enthralling pursuit of speculation a brain better endowed than any opposed to it. At St. Helena it was laid down that war is *une belle occupation*; and so the young Manderson had found the multitudinous and complicated dogfight of the Stock Exchange of New York.

Then came his change. At his father's death, when Manderson was thirty years old, some new revelation of the power and the glory of the god he served seemed to have come upon him. With the sudden, elastic adaptability of his nation he turned to steady labour in his father's banking business, closing his ears to the sound of the battles of the Street. In a few years he came to control all the activity of the great firm whose unimpeached conservatism, safety, and financial weight lifted it like a cliff above the angry sea of the markets. All mistrust founded on the performances of his youth had vanished. He was quite plainly a different man. How the change came about none could with authority say, but there was a story of certain last words spoken by his father, whom alone he had respected and perhaps loved.

He began to tower above the financial situation. Soon his name was current in the bourses of the world. One who spoke the name of Manderson called up a vision of all that was broad-based and firm in the vast wealth of the United States. He planned great combinations of capital, drew together and centralized industries of continental scope, financed with unerring judgment the large designs of state or of private enterprise. Many a time when he "took hold" to smash a strike, or to federate the ownership of some great field of labour, he sent ruin upon a multitude of tiny homes; and if miners or steelworkers or cattlemen defied him and invoked disorder, he could be more lawless and ruthless than they. But this was done in the pursuit of legitimate business ends. Tens of thousands of the poor might curse his name, but the financier and the speculator execrated him no more. He stretched a hand to protect or to manipulate the power of wealth in every corner of the country. Forcible, cold, and unerring, in all he did he ministered to the national lust for magnitude; and a grateful country surnamed him the Colossus.

But there was an aspect of Manderson in this later period that lay long unknown and unsuspected save by a few, his secretaries and lieutenants and certain of the associates of his bygone hurling time. This little circle knew that Manderson, the pillar of sound business and stability in the markets, had his hours of nostalgia for the lively times when the Street had trembled at his name. It was, said one of them, as if Blackbeard had settled down as a decent merchant in Bristol on the spoils of the Main. Now and then the pirate would suddenly glare out, the knife in his teeth and the sulphur matches sputtering in his hatband. During such spasms of reversion to type a score of tempestuous raids upon the market had been planned on paper in the inner room of the offices of Manderson, Colefax and Company. But they were never carried out. Blackbeard would quell the mutiny of his old self within him and go soberly down to his counting-house—humming a stave or two of "Spanish Ladies," perhaps, under his breath. Manderson would allow himself the harmless satisfaction, as soon as the time for action had gone by, of pointing out to some Rupert of the markets how a coup worth a million to the depredator might have been made. "Seems to me," he would say almost wistfully, "the Street is getting to be a mighty dull place since I quit." By slow degrees this amiable weakness of the Colossus became known to the business world, which exulted greatly in the knowledge.

At the news of his death panic went through the markets like a hurricane; for it came at a luckless time. Prices tottered and crashed like towers in an earthquake. For two days Wall Street was a clamorous inferno of pale despair. All over the United States, wherever speculation had its devotees, went a waft of ruin, a plague of suicide. In Europe also not a few took with their own hands lives that had become pitiably linked to the destiny of a financier whom most of them had never seen. In Paris a well known banker walked quietly out of the Bourse and fell dead upon the broad steps among the raving crowd of Jews, a phial crushed in his hand. In Frankfort one leapt from the cathedral top, leaving a redder stain where he struck the red tower. Men stabbed and shot and strangled themselves, drank death or breathed it as the air, because in a lonely corner of England the life had departed from one cold heart vowed to the service of greed.

The blow could not have fallen at a more disastrous moment. It came when Wall Street was in a condition of suppressed "scare"—suppressed, because for a week past the great interests known to act with or to be actually controlled by the Colossus had been desperately combating the effects of the sudden arrest of Lucas Hahn, and the exposure of his plundering of the Hahn banks. This bombshell, in its turn, had fallen at a time when the market had been "boosted" beyond its real strength. In the language of the place, a slump was due. Reports from the corn-hands had not been good, and there had been two or three railway statements which had been expected to be much better than they were. But at whatever point in the vast area of speculation the shudder of the threatened break had been felt, "the Manderson crowd" had stepped in and held the market up. All through the week the speculator's mind, as shallow as it is quick-witted, as sentimental as greedy, had seen in this the hand of the giant stretched out in protection from afar. Manderson, said the newspapers in chorus, was in hourly communication with his lieutenants in the Street. One journal was able to give in round figures the sum spent on cabling between New York and Marlstone in the past twenty-four hours; it told how a small staff of expert operators had been sent down by the post office authorities to Marlstone to deal with the flood of messages. Another revealed that Manderson, on the first news of the Hahn crash, had arranged to abandon his holiday and return home by the *Mauretania;* but that he soon had the situation so well in hand that he had determined to remain where he was.

All this was falsehood, more or less consciously elaborated by the finance editors, consciously initiated and encouraged by the shrewd businessmen of the Manderson group, who knew that nothing could better help their plans than this illusion of hero-worship—knew also that no word had come from Manderson in answer to their messages, and that Howard B. Jeffrey, of Steel and Iron fame, was the true organizer of victory. So they fought down apprehension through four feverish days, and minds grew calmer. On Saturday, though the ground beneath the feet of Mr Jeffrey yet rumbled now and then with Etna-mutterings of disquiet, he deemed his task almost done. The market was firm, and slowly advancing. Wall Street turned to its sleep of Sunday, worn out but thankfully at peace.

In the first trading hour of Monday a hideous rumour flew round the sixty acres of the financial district. It came into being as the lightning comes—a blink that seems to begin nowhere; though it is to be suspected that it was first whispered over the telephone—together with an urgent selling order—by some employee in the cable service. A sharp spasm convulsed the convalescent share-list. In five minutes the dull noise of the curb market in Broad Street had leapt to a high note of frantic interrogation. From within the hive of the Exchange itself could be heard a droning hubbub of fear, and men rushed hatless in and out. Was it true? asked every man; and every man replied, with trembling lips, that it was a lie put out by some unscrupulous "short" interest seeking to cover itself. In another quarter of an hour news came of a sudden and ruinous collapse of "Yankees" in London at the close of the Stock Exchange day. It was enough. New York had still four hours' trading in front of her. The strategy of pointing to Manderson as the saviour and warden of the markets had recoiled upon its authors with annihilating force, and Jeffrey, his ear at his private telephone, listened to the tale of disaster with a set jaw. The new Napoleon had lost his Marengo. He saw the whole financial landscape sliding and falling into chaos before him. In half an hour the news of the finding of Manderson's body, with the inevitable rumour that it was suicide, was printing in a dozen newspaper offices; but before a copy reached Wall Street the tornado of the panic was in full fury, and Howard B. Jeffrey and his collaborators were whirled away like leaves before its breath.

All this sprang out of nothing.

Nothing in the texture of the general life had changed. The corn had not ceased to ripen in the sun. The rivers bore their barges and gave power to a myriad engines. The flocks fattened on the pastures, the herds were unnumbered. Men laboured everywhere in the various servitudes to which they were born, and chafed not more than usual in their bonds. Bellona tossed and murmured as ever, yet still slept her uneasy sleep. To all mankind save a million or two of half-crazed gamblers, blind to all reality, the death of Manderson meant nothing; the life and work of the world went on. Weeks before he died strong hands had been in control of every wire in the huge network of commerce and industry that he had supervised. Before his corpse was buried his countrymen had made a strange discovery—that the existence of the potent engine of monopoly that went by the name of Sigsbee Manderson had not been a condition of even material prosperity. The panic blew itself out in two days, the pieces were picked up, the bankrupts withdrew out of sight; the market "recovered a normal tone."

While the brief delirium was yet subsiding there broke out a domestic scandal in England that suddenly fixed the attention of two continents. Next morning the Chicago Limited was wrecked, and the same day a notable politician was shot down in cold blood by his wife's brother in the streets of New Orleans. Within a week of its arising, "the Manderson story," to the trained sense of editors throughout the United States, was "cold." The tide of American visitors pouring through Europe made eddies round the memorial or statue of many a man who had died in poverty; and never thought of their most famous plutocrat. Like the poet who died in Rome, so young and poor, a hundred years ago, he was buried far away from his own land; but for all the men and women of Manderson's people who flock round the tomb of Keats in the cemetery under the Monte Testaccio, there is not one, nor ever will be, to stand in reverence by the rich man's grave beside the little church of Marlstone.

2

KNOCKING THE TOWN ENDWAYS

In the only comfortably furnished room in the offices of the Record, the telephone on Sir James Molloy's table buzzed. Sir James made a motion with his pen, and Mr Silver, his secretary, left his work and came over to the instrument.

"Who is that?" he said. "Who?... I can't hear you... Oh, it's Mr Bunner, is it?... Yes, but... I know, but he's fearfully busy this afternoon. Can't you... Oh, really? Well, in that case—just hold on, will you?"

He placed the receiver before Sir James. "It's Calvin Bunner, Sigsbee Manderson's right-hand man," he said concisely. "He insists on speaking to you personally. Says it is the gravest piece of news. He is talking from the house down by Bishopsbridge, so it will be necessary to speak clearly."

Sir James looked at the telephone, not affectionately, and took up the receiver. "Well?" he said in his strong voice, and listened. "Yes," he said. The next moment Mr Silver, eagerly watching him, saw a look of amazement and horror. "Good God!" murmured Sir James. Clutching the instrument, he slowly rose to his feet, still bending ear intently. At intervals he repeated: "Yes." Presently, as he listened, he glanced at the clock and spoke quickly to Mr Silver over the top of the transmitter. "Go and hunt up Figgis and young Williams. Hurry." Mr Silver darted from the room.

The great journalist was a tall, strong, clever Irishman of fifty, swart and black-moustached, a man of untiring business energy, well known in the world, which he understood very thoroughly, and played upon with the half-cynical competence of his race. Yet was he without a touch of the charlatan: he made no mysteries, and no pretences of knowledge, and he saw instantly through these in others. In his handsome, well-bred, well-dressed appearance there was something a little sinister when anger or intense occupation put its imprint about his eyes and brow; but when his generous nature was under no restraint he was the most cordial of men. He was managing director of the company which owned that most powerful morning paper, the *Record*, and also that most indispensable evening paper, the *Sun*, which had its offices on the other side of the street. He was, moreover, editor-in-chief of the *Record*, to which he had in the course of years attached the most variously capable personnel in the country. It was a maxim of his that where you could not get gifts, you must do the best you could with solid merit; and he employed a great deal of both. He was respected by his staff as few are respected in a profession not favourable to the growth of the sentiment of reverence.

"You're sure that's all?" asked Sir James, after a few minutes of earnest listening and questioning. "And how long has this been known?... Yes, of course, the police are; but the servants? Surely it's all over the place down there by now... Well, we'll have a try... Look here, Bunner, I'm infinitely obliged to you about this. I owe you a good turn. You know I mean what I say. Come and see me the first day you get to town... All right, that's understood. Now I must act on your news. Goodby."

Sir James hung up the receiver, and seized a railway timetable from the rack before him. After a rapid consultation of this oracle, he flung it down with a forcible word as Mr Silver hurried into the room, followed by a hard-featured man with spectacles, and a youth with an alert eye.

"I want you to jot down some facts, Figgis," said Sir James, banishing all signs of agitation and speaking with a rapid calmness. "When you have them, put them into shape just as quick as you can for a special edition of the *Sun*." The hard-featured man nodded and glanced at the clock, which pointed to a few minutes past three; he pulled out a notebook and drew a chair up to the big writing-table. "Silver," Sir James went on, "go and tell Jones to wire our local correspondent very urgently, to drop everything and get down to Marlstone at once. He is not to say why in the telegram. There must not be an unnecessary word about this news until the *Sun* is on the streets with it—you all understand. Williams, cut across the way and tell Mr Anthony to hold himself ready for a two-column opening that will knock the town endways. Just tell him that he must take all measures and precautions for a scoop. Say that Figgis will be over in five minutes with the facts, and that he had better let him write up the story in his private room. As you go, ask Miss Morgan to see me here at once, and tell the telephone people to see if they can get Mr Trent on the wire for me. After seeing Mr Anthony, return here and stand by." The alert-eyed young man vanished like a spirit.

Sir James turned instantly to Mr Figgis, whose pencil was poised over the paper. "Sigsbee Manderson has been murdered," he began quickly and clearly, pacing the floor with his hands behind him. Mr Figgis scratched down a line of shorthand with as much emotion as if he had been told that the day was fine—the pose of his craft. "He and his wife and two secretaries have been for the past fortnight at the house called White Gables, at Marlstone near Bishopsbridge. He bought it four years ago. He and Mrs Manderson have since spent a part of each summer there. Last night he went to bed about half past eleven, just as usual. No one knows when he got up and left the house. He was not missed until this morning. About ten o'clock his body was found by a gardener. It was lying by a shed in the grounds. He was shot in the head, through the left eye. Death must have been instantaneous. The body was not robbed, but there were marks on the wrists which pointed to a struggle having taken place. Dr. Stock, of Marlstone, was at once sent for, and will conduct the post-mortem examination. The police from Bishopsbridge, who were soon on the spot, are reticent, but it is believed that they are quite without a clue to the identity of the murderer. There you are, Figgis. Mr Anthony is expecting you. Now I must telephone him and arrange things."

Mr Figgis looked up. "One of the ablest detectives at Scotland Yard," he suggested, "has been put in charge of the case. It's a safe statement."

"If you like," said Sir James.

"And Mrs Manderson? Was she there?"

"Yes. What about her?"

"Prostrated by the shock," hinted the reporter, "and sees nobody. Human interest."

"I wouldn't put that in, Mr Figgis," said a quiet voice. It belonged to Miss Morgan, a pale, graceful woman, who had silently made her appearance while the dictation was going on. "I have seen Mrs Manderson," she proceeded, turning to Sir James. "She looks quite healthy and intelligent. Has her husband been murdered? I don't think the shock would prostrate her. She is more likely to be doing all she can to help the police."

"Something in your own style, then, Miss Morgan," he said with a momentary smile. Her imperturbable efficiency was an office proverb. "Cut it out, Figgis. Off you go! Now, madam, I expect you know what I want."

"Our Manderson biography happens to be well up to date," replied Miss Morgan, drooping her dark eyelashes as she considered the position. "I was looking over it only a few months ago. It is practically ready for tomorrow's paper. I should think the *Sun* had better use the sketch of his life they had about two years ago, when he went to Berlin and settled the potash difficulty. I remember it was a very good sketch, and they won't be able to carry much more than that. As for our paper, of course we have a great quantity of clippings, mostly rubbish. The sub-editors shall have them as soon as they come in. Then we have two very good portraits that are our own property; the best is a drawing Mr Trent made when they were both on the same ship somewhere. It is better than any of the photographs; but you say the public prefers a bad photograph to a good drawing. I will send them down to you at once, and you can choose. As far as I can see, the *Record* is well ahead of the situation, except that you will not be able to get a special man down there in time to be of any use for tomorrow's paper."

Sir James sighed deeply. "What are we good for, anyhow?" he inquired dejectedly of Mr Silver, who had returned to his desk. "She even knows Bradshaw by heart."

Miss Morgan adjusted her cuffs with an air of patience. "Is there anything else?" she asked, as the telephone bell rang.

"Yes, one thing," replied Sir James, as he took up the receiver. "I want you to make a bad mistake sometime, Miss Morgan—an everlasting bloomer—just to put us in countenance." She permitted herself the fraction of what would have been a charming smile as she went out.

"Anthony?" asked Sir James, and was at once deep in consultation with the editor on the other side of the road. He seldom entered the *Sun* building in person; the atmosphere of an evening paper, he would say, was all very well if you liked that kind of thing. Mr Anthony, the Murat of Fleet Street, who delighted in riding the whirlwind and fighting a tumultuous battle against time, would say the same of a morning paper.

It was some five minutes later that a uniformed boy came in to say that Mr Trent was on the wire. Sir James abruptly closed his talk with Mr Anthony.

"They can put him through at once," he said to the boy.

"Hullo!" he cried into the telephone after a few moments.

A voice in the instrument replied: "Hullo be blowed! What do you want?"

"This is Molloy," said Sir James.

"I know it is," the voice said. "This is Trent. He is in the middle of painting a picture, and he has been interrupted at a critical moment. Well, I hope it's something important, that's all!"

"Trent," said Sir James impressively, "it is important. I want you to do some work for us."

"Some play, you mean," replied the voice. "Believe me, I don't want a holiday. The working fit is very strong. I am doing some really decent things. Why can't you leave a man alone?"

"Something very serious has happened."

"What?"

"Sigsbee Manderson has been murdered—shot through the brain—and they don't know who has done it. They found the body this morning. It happened at his place near Bishopsbridge." Sir James proceeded to tell the hearer, briefly and clearly, the facts that he had communicated to Mr Figgis. "What do you think of it?" he ended.

A considering grunt was the only answer.

"Come now," urged Sir James.

"Tempter!"

"You will go down?"

There was a brief pause.

"Are you there?" said Sir James.

"Look here, Molloy," the voice broke out querulously, "the thing may be a case for me, or it may not. We can't possibly tell. It may be a mystery; it may be as simple as bread and cheese.

The body not being robbed looks interesting, but he may have been outed by some wretched tramp whom he found sleeping in the grounds and tried to kick out. It's the sort of thing he would do. Such a murderer might easily have sense enough to know that to leave the money and valuables was the safest thing. I tell you frankly, I wouldn't have a hand in hanging a poor devil who had let daylight into a man like Sig Manderson as a measure of social protest."

Sir James smiled at the telephone—a smile of success. "Come, my boy, you're getting feeble. Admit you want to go and have a look at the case. You know you do. If it's anything you don't want to handle, you're free to drop it. By the by, where are you?"

"I am blown along a wandering wind," replied the voice irresolutely, "and hollow, hollow, hollow all delight."

"Can you get here within an hour?" persisted Sir James.

"I suppose I can," the voice grumbled. "How much time have I?"

"Good man! Well, there's time enough—that's just the worst of it. I've got to depend on our local correspondent for tonight. The only good train of the day went half an hour ago. The next is a slow one, leaving Paddington at midnight. You could have the Buster, if you like"—Sir James referred to a very fast motor-car of his—"but you wouldn't get down in time to do anything tonight."

"And I'd miss my sleep. No, thanks. The train for me. I am quite fond of railway travelling, you know; I have a gift for it. I am the stoker and the stoked. I am the song the porter sings."

"What's that you say?"

"It doesn't matter," said the voice sadly. "I say," it continued, "will your people look out a hotel near the scene of action, and telegraph for a room?"

"At once," said Sir James. "Come here as soon as you can."

He replaced the receiver. As he turned to his papers again a shrill outcry burst forth in the street below. He walked to the open window. A band of excited boys was rushing down the steps of the *Sun* building and up the narrow thoroughfare toward Fleet Street. Each carried a bundle of newspapers and a large broadsheet with the simple legend:

MURDER OF
SIGSBEE
MANDERSON

Sir James smiled and rattled the money in his pockets cheerfully.

"It makes a good bill," he observed to Mr Silver, who stood at his elbow.

Such was Manderson's epitaph.

3

BREAKFAST

At about eight o'clock in the morning of the following day Mr Nathaniel Burton Cupples stood on the veranda of the hotel at Marlstone. He was thinking about breakfast. In his case the colloquialism must be taken literally; he really was thinking about breakfast, as he thought about every conscious act of his life when time allowed deliberation. He reflected that on the preceding day the excitement and activity following upon the discovery of the dead man had disorganized his appetite and led to his taking considerably less nourishment than usual. This morning he was very hungry, having already been up and about for an hour; and he decided to allow himself a third piece of toast and an additional egg; the rest as usual. The remaining deficit must be made up at luncheon, but that could be gone into later.

So much being determined, Mr Cupples applied himself to the enjoyment of the view for a few minutes before ordering his meal. With a connoisseur's eye he explored the beauty of the rugged coast, where a great pierced rock rose from a glassy sea, and the ordered loveliness of the vast tilted levels of pasture and tillage and woodland that sloped gently up from the cliffs toward the distant moor: Mr Cupples delighted in landscape.

He was a man of middle height and spare figure, nearly sixty years old, by constitution rather delicate in health, but wiry and active for his age. A sparse and straggling beard and moustache did not conceal a thin but kindly mouth; his eyes were keen and pleasant; his sharp nose and narrow jaw gave him very much of a clerical air, and this impression was helped by his commonplace dark clothes and soft black hat. The whole effect of him, indeed, was priestly. He was a man of unusually conscientious, industrious, and orderly mind, with little imagination. His father's household had been used to recruit its domestic establishment by means of advertisements in which it was truthfully described as a serious family. From that fortress of gloom he had escaped with two saintly gifts somehow unspoiled: an inexhaustible kindness of heart, and a capacity for innocent gaiety which owed nothing to humour. In an earlier day and with a clerical training he might have risen to the scarlet hat. He was, in fact, a highly regarded member of the London Positivist Society, a retired banker, a widower without children. His austere but not unhappy life was spent largely among books and in museums; his profound and patiently accumulated knowledge of a number of curiously disconnected subjects which had stirred his interest at different times had given him a place in the quiet, half-lit world of professors and curators and devotees of research; at their amiable, unconvivial dinner parties he was most himself. His favourite author was Montaigne.

Just as Mr Cupples was finishing his meal at a little table on the veranda, a big motor turned into the drive before the hotel. "Who is this?" he inquired of the waiter. "Id is der manager," said the young man listlessly. "He have been to meed a gendleman by der train."

The car drew up and the porter hurried from the entrance. Mr Cupples uttered an exclamation of pleasure as a long, loosely built man, much younger than himself, stepped from the car and mounted the veranda, flinging his hat on a chair. His high-boned, quixotic face wore a pleasant smile; his rough tweed clothes, his hair and short moustache were tolerably untidy.

"Cupples, by all that's miraculous!" cried the man, pouncing upon Mr Cupples before he could rise, and seizing his outstretched hand in a hard grip. "My luck is serving me today," the new-comer went on spasmodically. "This is the second slice within an hour. How are you, my best of friends? And why are you here? Why sit'st thou by that ruined breakfast? Dost thou its former pride recall, or ponder how it passed away? I am glad to see you!"

"I was half expecting you, Trent," Mr Cupples replied, his face wreathed in smiles. "You are looking splendid, my dear fellow. I will tell you all about it. But you cannot have had your own breakfast yet. Will you have it at my table here?"

"Rather!" said the man. "An enormous great breakfast, too—with refined conversation and tears of recognition never dry. Will you get young Siegfried to lay a place for me while I go and wash? I shan't be three minutes." He disappeared into the hotel, and Mr Cupples, after a moment's thought, went to the telephone in the porter's office.

He returned to find his friend already seated, pouring out tea, and showing an unaffected interest in the choice of food. "I expect this to be a hard day for me," he said, with the curious jerky utterance which seemed to be his habit. "I shan't eat again till the evening, very likely. You guess why I'm here, don't you?"

"Undoubtedly," said Mr Cupples, "you have come down to write about the murder."

"That is rather a colourless way of stating it," the man called Trent replied, as he dissected a sole. "I should prefer to put it that I have come down in the character of avenger of blood, to hunt down the guilty, and vindicate the honour of society.

That is my line of business. Families waited on at their private residences. I say, Cupples, I have made a good beginning already. Wait a bit, and I'll tell you." There was a silence, during which the new-comer ate swiftly and abstractedly, while Mr Cupples looked on happily.

"Your manager here," said the tall man at last, "is a fellow of remarkable judgment. He is an admirer of mine. He knows more about my best cases than I do myself. The *Record* wired last night to say I was coming, and when I got out of the train at seven o'clock this morning, there he was waiting for me with a motor-car the size of a haystack. He is beside himself with joy at having me here. It is fame." He drank a cup of tea and continued: "Almost his first words were to ask me if I would like to see the body of the murdered man—if so, he thought he could manage it for me. He is as keen as a razor. The body lies in Dr. Stock's surgery, you know, down in the village, exactly as it was when found. It's to be post-mortemed this morning, by the way, so I was only just in time. Well, he ran me down there to the doctor's, giving me full particulars about the case all the way. I was pretty well *au fait* by the time we arrived. I suppose the manager of a place like this has some sort of a pull with the doctor. Anyhow, he made no difficulties, nor did the constable on duty, though he was careful to insist on my not giving him away in the paper."

"I saw the body before it was removed," remarked Mr Cupples. "I should not have said there was anything remarkable about it, except that the shot in the eye had scarcely disfigured the face at all, and caused scarcely any effusion of blood, apparently. The wrists were scratched and bruised. I expect that, with your trained faculties, you were able to remark other details of a suggestive nature."

"Other details, certainly; but I don't know that they suggest anything. They are merely odd. Take the wrists, for instance. How was it you could see bruises and scratches on them?

I dare say you saw something of Manderson down here before the murder."

"Certainly," Mr Cupples said.

"Well, did you ever see his wrists?"

Mr Cupples reflected. "No. Now you raise the point, I am reminded that when I interviewed Manderson here he was wearing stiff cuffs, coming well down over his hands."

"He always did," said Trent. "My friend the manager says so. I pointed out to him the fact you didn't observe, that there were no cuffs visible, and that they had, indeed, been dragged up inside the coat-sleeves, as yours would be if you hurried into a coat without pulling your cuffs down. That was why you saw his wrists."

"Well, I call that suggestive," observed Mr Cupples mildly. "You might infer, perhaps, that when he got up he hurried over his dressing."

"Yes, but did he? The manager said just what you say. 'He was always a bit of a swell in his dress,' he told me, and he drew the inference that when Manderson got up in that mysterious way, before the house was stirring, and went out into the grounds, he was in a great hurry. 'Look at his shoes,' he said to me: 'Mr Manderson was always specially neat about his foot-wear. But those shoe-laces were tied in a hurry.' I agreed. 'And he left his false teeth in his room,' said the manager. 'Doesn't that prove he was flustered and hurried?' I allowed that it looked like it. But I said, 'Look here: if he was so very much pressed, why did he part his hair so carefully? That parting is a work of art. Why did he put on so much? for he had on a complete outfit of underclothing, studs in his shirt, sock-suspenders, a watch and chain, money and keys and things in his pockets.' That's what I said to the manager. He couldn't find an explanation. Can you?"

Mr Cupples considered. "Those facts might suggest that he was hurried only at the end of his dressing. Coat and shoes would come last."

"But not false teeth. You ask anybody who wears them. And besides, I'm told he hadn't washed at all on getting up, which in a neat man looks like his being in a violent hurry from the beginning. And here's another thing. One of his waistcoat pockets was lined with wash-leather for the reception of his gold watch. But he had put his watch into the pocket on the other side. Anybody who has settled habits can see how odd that is. The fact is, there are signs of great agitation and haste, and there are signs of exactly the opposite. For the present I am not guessing. I must reconnoitre the ground first, if I can manage to get the right side of the people of the house." Trent applied himself again to his breakfast.

Mr Cupples smiled at him benevolently. "That is precisely the point," he said, "on which I can be of some assistance to you." Trent glanced up in surprise, "I told you I half expected you. I will explain the situation. Mrs Manderson, who is my niece—"

"What!" Trent laid down his knife and fork with a clash. "Cupples, you are jesting with me."

"I am perfectly serious, Trent, really," returned Mr Cupples earnestly. "Her father, John Peter Domecq, was my wife's brother. I never mentioned my niece or her marriage to you before, I suppose. To tell the truth, it has always been a painful subject to me, and I have avoided discussing it with anybody. To return to what I was about to say: last night, when I was over at the house—by the way, you can see it from here. You passed it in the car." He indicated a red roof among poplars some three hundred yards away, the only building in sight that stood separate from the tiny village in the gap below them.

"Certainly I did," said Trent. "The manager told me all about it, among other things, as he drove me in from Bishopsbridge."

"Other people here have heard of you and your performances," Mr Cupples went on. "As I was saying, when I was over there last night, Mr Bunner, who is one of Manderson's two secretaries, expressed a hope that the *Record* would send you down to deal with the case, as the police seemed quite at a loss. He mentioned one or two of your past successes, and Mabel—my niece—was interested when I told her afterwards. She is bearing up wonderfully well, Trent; she has remarkable fortitude of character. She said she remembered reading your articles about the Abinger case. She has a great horror of the newspaper side of this sad business, and she had entreated me to do anything I could to keep journalists away from the place—I'm sure you can understand her feeling, Trent; it isn't really any reflection on that profession. But she said you appeared to have great powers as a detective, and she would not stand in the way of anything that might clear up the crime. Then I told her you were a personal friend of mine, and gave you a good character for tact and consideration of others' feelings; and it ended in her saying that, if you should come, she would like you to be helped in every way."

Trent leaned across the table and shook Mr Cupples by the hand in silence. Mr Cupples, much delighted with the way things were turning out, resumed:

"I spoke to my niece on the telephone only just now, and she is glad you are here. She asks me to say that you may make any inquiries you like, and she puts the house and grounds at your disposal. She had rather not see you herself; she is keeping to her own sitting-room. She has already been interviewed by a detective-officer who is there, and she feels unequal to any more. She adds that she does not believe she could say anything that would be of the smallest use. The two secretaries and Martin, the butler (who is a most intelligent man), could tell you all you want to know, she thinks."

Trent finished his breakfast with a thoughtful brow. He filled a pipe slowly, and seated himself on the rail of the veranda. "Cupples," he said quietly, "is there anything about this business that you know and would rather not tell me?"

Mr Cupples gave a slight start, and turned an astonished gaze on the questioner. "What do you mean?" he said.

"I mean about the Mandersons. Look here! Shall I tell you a thing that strikes me about this affair at the very beginning? Here's a man suddenly and violently killed, and nobody's heart seems to be broken about it, to say the least. The manager of this hotel spoke to me about him as coolly as if he'd never set eyes on him, though I understand they've been neighbours every summer for some years. Then you talk about the thing in the coldest of blood. And Mrs Manderson—well, you won't mind my saying that I have heard of women being more cut up about their husbands' being murdered than she seems to be. Is there something in this, Cupples, or is it my fancy? Was there something queer about Manderson? I travelled on the same boat with him once, but never spoke to him. I only know his public character, which was repulsive enough. You see, this may have a bearing on the case; that's the only reason why I ask."

Mr Cupples took time for thought. He fingered his sparse beard and looked out over the sea. At last he turned to Trent. "I see no reason," he said, "why I shouldn't tell you as between ourselves, my dear fellow. I need not say that this must not be referred to, however distantly. The truth is that nobody really liked Manderson; and I think those who were nearest to him liked him least."

"Why?" the other interjected.

"Most people found a difficulty in explaining why. In trying to account to myself for my own sensations, I could only put it that one felt in the man a complete absence of the sympathetic faculty. There was nothing outwardly repellent about him. He was not ill-mannered, or vicious, or dull—indeed, he could be remarkably interesting. But I received the impression that there could be no human creature whom he would not sacrifice in the pursuit of his schemes, in his task of imposing himself and his will upon the world. Perhaps that was fanciful, but I think not altogether so. However, the point is that Mabel, I am sorry to say, was very unhappy. I am nearly twice your age, my dear boy, though you always so kindly try to make me feel as if we were contemporaries—I am getting to be an old man, and a great many people have been good enough to confide their matrimonial troubles to me; but I never knew another case like my niece's and her husband's. I have known her since she was a baby, Trent, and I know—you understand, I think, that I do not employ that word lightly—I *know* that she is as amiable and honourable a woman, to say nothing of her other good gifts, as any man could wish. But Manderson, for some time past, had made her miserable."

"What did he do?" asked Trent, as Mr Cupples paused.

"When I put that question to Mabel, her words were that he seemed to nurse a perpetual grievance. He maintained a distance between them, and he would say nothing. I don't know how it began or what was behind it, and all she would tell me on that point was that he had no cause in the world for his attitude. I think she knew what was in his mind, whatever it was; but she is full of pride. This seems to have gone on for months. At last, a week ago, she wrote to me. I am the only near relative she has. Her mother died when she was a child; and after John Peter died I was something like a father to her until she married—that was five years ago. She asked me to come and help her, and I came at once. That is why I am here now."

Mr Cupples paused and drank some tea. Trent smoked and stared out at the hot June landscape.

"I would not go to White Gables," Mr Cupples resumed. "You know my views, I think, upon the economic constitution of society, and the proper relationship of the capitalist to the employee, and you know, no doubt, what use that person made of his vast industrial power upon several very notorious occasions. I refer especially to the trouble in the Pennsylvania coal-fields, three years ago. I regarded him, apart from all personal dislike, in the light of a criminal and a disgrace to society. I came to this hotel, and I saw my niece here. She told me what I have more briefly told you. She said that the worry and the humiliation of it, and the strain of trying to keep up appearances before the world, were telling upon her, and she asked for my advice. I said I thought she should face him and demand an explanation of his way of treating her. But she would not do that. She had always taken the line of affecting not to notice the change in his demeanour, and nothing, I knew, would persuade her to admit to him that she was injured, once pride had led her into that course. Life is quite full, my dear Trent," said Mr Cupples with a sigh, "of these obstinate silences and cultivated misunderstandings."

"Did she love him?" Trent inquired abruptly. Mr Cupples did not reply at once. "Had she any love left for him?" Trent amended.

Mr Cupples played with his tea-spoon. "I am bound to say," he answered slowly, "that I think not. But you must not misunderstand the woman, Trent. No power on earth would have persuaded her to admit that to anyone—even to herself, perhaps so long as she considered herself bound to him. And I gather that, apart from this mysterious sulking of late, he had always been considerate and generous."

"You were saying that she refused to have it out with him."

"She did," replied Mr Cupples. "And I knew by experience that it was quite useless to attempt to move a Domecq where the sense of dignity was involved. So I thought it over carefully, and next day I watched my opportunity and met Manderson as he passed by this hotel. I asked him to favour me with a few minutes' conversation, and he stepped inside the gate down there. We had held no communication of any kind since my niece's marriage, but he remembered me, of course. I put the matter to him at once and quite definitely. I told him what

Mabel had confided to me. I said that I would neither approve nor condemn her action in bringing me into the business, but that she was suffering, and I considered it my right to ask how he could justify himself in placing her in such a position."

"And how did he take that?" said Trent, smiling secretly at the landscape. The picture of this mildest of men calling the formidable Manderson to account pleased him.

"Not very well," Mr Cupples replied sadly. "In fact, far from well. I can tell you almost exactly what he said—it wasn't much. 'See here, Cupples, you don't want to butt in. My wife can look after herself. I've found that out, along with other things.' He was perfectly quiet—you know he was said never to lose control of himself—though there was a light in his eyes that would have frightened a man who was in the wrong, I dare say. But I had been thoroughly roused by his last remark, and the tone of it, which I cannot reproduce. You see," said Mr Cupples simply, "I love my niece. She is the only child that there has been in our—in my house. Moreover, my wife brought her up as a girl, and any reflection on Mabel I could not help feeling, in the heat of the moment, as an indirect reflection upon one who is gone."

"You turned upon him," suggested Trent in a low tone. "You asked him to explain his words."

"That is precisely what I did," said Mr Cupples. "For a moment he only stared at me, and I could see a vein on his forehead swelling—an unpleasant sight. Then he said quite quietly. 'This thing has gone far enough, I guess,' and turned to go."

"Did he mean your interview?" Trent asked thoughtfully.

"From the words alone you would think so," Mr Cupples answered. "But the way in which he uttered them gave me a strange and very apprehensive feeling. I received the impression that the man had formed some sinister resolve. But I regret to say I had lost the power of dispassionate thought. I fell into a great rage"—Mr Cupples's tone was mildly apologetic—"and said a number of foolish things. I reminded him that the law allowed a measure of freedom to wives who received intolerable treatment. I made some utterly irrelevant references to his public record, and expressed the view that such men as he were unfit to live. I said these things, and others as ill-considered, under the eyes, and very possibly within earshot, of half-a-dozen persons sitting on this veranda. I noticed them, in spite of my agitation, looking at me as I walked up to the hotel again after relieving my mind—for it undoubtedly did relieve it," sighed Mr Cupples, lying back in his chair.

"And Manderson? Did he say no more?"

"Not a word. He listened to me with his eyes on my face, as quiet as before. When I stopped he smiled very slightly, and at once turned away and strolled through the gate, making for White Gables."

"And this happened—?"

"On the Sunday morning."

"Then I suppose you never saw him alive again?"

"No," said Mr Cupples. "Or rather yes—once. It was later in the day, on the golf course. But I did not speak to him. And next morning he was found dead."

The two regarded each other in silence for a few moments. A party of guests who had been bathing came up the steps and seated themselves, with much chattering, at a table near them. The waiter approached. Mr Cupples rose, and, taking Trent's arm, led him to a long tennis-lawn at the side of the hotel.

"I have a reason for telling you all this," began Mr Cupples as they paced slowly up and down.

"Trust you for that," rejoined Trent, carefully filling his pipe again. He lit it, smoked a little, and then said: "I'll try and guess what your reason is, if you like."

Mr Cupples's face of solemnity relaxed into a slight smile. He said nothing.

"You thought it possible," said Trent meditatively—"may I say you thought it practically certain?—that I should find out for myself that there had been something deeper than a mere conjugal tiff between the Mandersons. You thought that my unwholesome imagination would begin at once to play with the idea of Mrs Manderson having something to do with the crime. Rather than that I should lose myself in barren speculations about this, you decided to tell me exactly how matters stood, and incidentally to impress upon me, who know how excellent your judgment is, your opinion of your niece. Is that about right?"

"It is perfectly right. Listen to me, my dear fellow," said Mr Cupples earnestly, laying his hand on the other's arm. "I am going to be frank. I am extremely glad that Manderson is dead. I believe him to have done nothing but harm in the world as an economic factor. I know that he was making a desert of the life of one who was like my own child to me. But I am under an intolerable dread of Mabel being involved in suspicion with regard to the murder. It is horrible to me to think of her delicacy and goodness being in contact, if only for a time, with the brutalities of the law. She is not fitted for it. It would mark her deeply. Many young women of twenty-six in these days could face such an ordeal, I suppose. I have observed a sort of imitative hardness about the products of the higher education of women today which would carry them through anything, perhaps. I am not prepared to say it is a bad thing in the conditions of feminine life prevailing at present. Mabel, however, is not like that. She is as unlike that as she is unlike the simpering misses that used to surround me as a child. She has plenty of brains; she is full of character; her mind and her tastes are cultivated; but it is all mixed up"—Mr Cupples waved his hands in a vague gesture—"with ideals of refinement and reservation and womanly mystery. I fear she is not a child of the age. You never knew my wife, Trent. Mabel is my wife's child."

The younger man bowed his head. They paced the length of the lawn before he asked gently: "Why did she marry him?"

"I don't know," said Mr Cupples briefly.

"Admired him, I suppose," suggested Trent.

Mr Cupples shrugged his shoulders. "I have been told that a woman will usually be more or less attracted by the most successful man in her circle. Of course we cannot realize how a wilful, dominating personality like his would influence a girl whose affections were not bestowed elsewhere; especially if he laid himself out to win her. It is probably an overwhelming thing to be courted by a man whose name is known all over the world. She had heard of him, of course, as a financial great power, and she had no idea—she had lived mostly among people of artistic or literary propensities—how much soulless inhumanity that might involve. For all I know, she has no adequate idea of it to this day. When I first heard of the affair the mischief was done, and I knew better than to interpose my unsought opinions. She was of age, and there was absolutely nothing against him from the conventional point of view. Then I dare say his immense wealth would cast a spell over almost any woman. Mabel had some hundreds a year of her own; just enough, perhaps, to let her realize what millions really meant. But all this is conjecture. She certainly had not wanted to marry some scores of young fellows who to my knowledge had asked her; and though I don't believe, and never did believe, that she really loved this man of forty-five, she certainly did want to marry him. But if you ask me why, I can only say I don't know."

Trent nodded, and after a few more paces looked at his watch. "You've interested me so much," he said, "that I had quite forgotten my main business. I mustn't waste my morning. I am going down the road to White Gables at once, and I dare say I shall be poking about there until midday. If you can meet me then, Cupples, I should like to talk over anything I find out with you, unless something detains me."

"I am going for a walk this morning," Mr Cupples replied. "I meant to have luncheon at a little inn near the golf course, The Three Tuns. You had better join me there. It's farther along the road, about a quarter of a mile beyond White Gables. You can just see the roof between those two trees. The food they give one there is very plain, but good."

"So long as they have a cask of beer," said Trent, "they are all right. We will have bread and cheese, and oh, may heaven our simple lives prevent from luxury's contagion, weak and vile! Till then, goodby." He strode off to recover his hat from the veranda, waved it to Mr Cupples, and was gone.

The old gentleman, seating himself in a deck-chair on the lawn, clasped his hands behind his head and gazed up into the speckless blue sky. "He is a dear fellow," he murmured. "The best of fellows. And a terribly acute fellow. Dear me! How curious it all is!"

4

HANDCUFFS IN THE AIR

A painter and the son of a painter, Philip Trent had while yet in his twenties achieved some reputation within the world of English art. Moreover, his pictures sold. An original, forcible talent and a habit of leisurely but continuous working, broken by fits of strong creative enthusiasm, were at the bottom of it. His father's name had helped; a patrimony large enough to relieve him of the perilous imputation of being a struggling man had certainly not hindered. But his best aid to success had been an unconscious power of getting himself liked. Good spirits and a lively, humorous fancy will always be popular. Trent joined to these a genuine interest in others that gained him something deeper than popularity. His judgment of persons was penetrating, but its process was internal; no one felt on good behaviour with a man who seemed always to be enjoying himself. Whether he was in a mood for floods of nonsense or applying himself vigorously to a task, his face seldom lost its expression of contained vivacity. Apart from a sound knowledge of his art and its history, his culture was large and loose, dominated by a love of poetry. At thirty-two he had not yet passed the age of laughter and adventure.

His rise to a celebrity a hundred times greater than his proper work had won for him came of a momentary impulse. One day he had taken up a newspaper to find it chiefly concerned with a crime of a sort curiously rare in England—a murder done in a railway train. The circumstances were puzzling; two persons were under arrest upon suspicion. Trent, to whom an interest in such affairs was a new sensation, heard the thing discussed among his friends, and set himself in a purposeless mood to read up the accounts given in several journals. He became intrigued; his imagination began to work, in a manner strange to him, upon facts; an excitement took hold of him such as he had only known before in his bursts of art-inspiration or of personal adventure. At the end of the day he wrote and dispatched a long letter to the editor of the *Record*, which he chose only because it had contained the fullest and most intelligent version of the facts.

In this letter he did very much what Poe had done in the case of the murder of Mary Rogers. With nothing but the newspapers to guide him, he drew attention to the significance of certain apparently negligible facts, and ranged the evidence in such a manner as to throw grave suspicion upon a man who had presented himself as a witness. Sir James Molloy had printed this letter in leaded type. The same evening he was able to announce in the *Sun* the arrest and full confession of the incriminated man.

Sir James, who knew all the worlds of London, had lost no time in making Trent's acquaintance. The two men got on well, for Trent possessed some secret of native tact which had the effect of almost abolishing differences of age between himself and others. The great rotary presses in the basement of the *Record* building had filled him with a new enthusiasm. He had painted there, and Sir James had bought at sight, what he called a machinery-scape in the manner of Heinrich Kley.

Then a few months later came the affair known as the Ilkley mystery. Sir James had invited Trent to an emollient dinner, and thereafter offered him what seemed to the young man a fantastically large sum for his temporary services as special representative of the *Record* at Ilkley.

"You could do it," the editor had urged. "You can write good stuff, and you know how to talk to people, and I can teach you all the technicalities of a reporter's job in half an hour. And you have a head for a mystery; you have imagination and cool judgment along with it. Think how it would feel if you pulled it off!"

Trent had admitted that it would be rather a lark. He had smoked, frowned, and at last convinced himself that the only thing that held him back was fear of an unfamiliar task. To react against fear had become a fixed moral habit with him, and he had accepted Sir James's offer.

He had pulled it off. For the second time he had given the authorities a start and a beating, and his name was on all tongues. He withdrew and painted pictures. He felt no leaning towards journalism, and Sir James, who knew a good deal about art, honourably refrained—as other editors did not—from tempting him with a good salary. But in the course of a few years he had applied to him perhaps thirty times for his services in the unravelling of similar problems at home and abroad. Sometimes Trent, busy with work that held him, had refused; sometimes he had been forestalled in the discovery of the truth. But the result of his irregular connection with the *Record* had been to make his name one of the best known in England. It was characteristic of him that his name was almost the only detail of his personality known to the public. He had imposed absolute silence about himself upon the Molloy papers; and the others were not going to advertise one of Sir James's men.

The Manderson case, he told himself as he walked rapidly up the sloping road to White Gables, might turn out to be terribly simple. Cupples was a wise old boy, but it was probably impossible for him to have an impartial opinion about his niece. But it was true that the manager of the hotel, who had spoken of her beauty in terms that aroused his attention, had spoken even more emphatically of her goodness. Not an artist in words, the manager had yet conveyed a very definite idea to Trent's mind. "There isn't a child about here that don't brighten up at the sound of her voice," he had said, "nor yet a grown-up, for the matter of that. Everybody used to look forward to her coming over in the summer. I don't mean that she's one of those women that are all kind heart and nothing else. There's backbone with it, if you know what I mean—pluck—any amount of go. There's nobody in Marlstone that isn't sorry for the lady in her trouble—not but what some of us may think she's lucky at the last of it." Trent wanted very much to meet Mrs Manderson.

He could see now, beyond a spacious lawn and shrubbery, the front of the two-storied house of dull-red brick, with the pair of great gables from which it had its name. He had had but a glimpse of it from the car that morning. A modern house, he saw; perhaps ten years old. The place was beautifully kept, with that air of opulent peace that clothes even the smallest houses of the well-to-do in an English countryside. Before it, beyond the road, the rich meadow-land ran down to the edge of the cliffs; behind it a woody landscape stretched away across a broad vale to the moors. That such a place could be the scene of a crime of violence seemed fantastic; it lay so quiet and well ordered, so eloquent of disciplined service and gentle living. Yet there beyond the house, and near the hedge that rose between the garden and the hot, white road, stood the gardener's toolshed, by which the body had been found, lying tumbled against the wooden wall.

Trent walked past the gate of the drive and along the road until he was opposite this shed. Some forty yards farther along the road turned sharply away from the house, to run between thick plantations; and just before the turn the grounds of the house ended, with a small white gate at the angle of the boundary hedge. He approached the gate, which was plainly for the use of gardeners and the service of the establishment. It swung easily on its hinges, and he passed slowly up a path that led towards the back of the house, between the outer hedge and a tall wall of rhododendrons. Through a gap in this wall a track led him to the little neatly built erection of wood, which stood among trees that faced a corner of the front. The body had lain on the side away from the house; a servant, he thought, looking out of the nearer windows in the earlier hours of the day before, might have glanced unseeing at the hut, as she wondered what it could be like to be as rich as the master.

He examined the place carefully and ransacked the hut within, but he could note no more than the trodden appearance of the uncut grass where the body had lain. Crouching low, with keen eyes and feeling fingers, he searched the ground minutely over a wide area; but the search was fruitless.

It was interrupted by the sound—the first he had heard from the house—of the closing of the front door. Trent unbent his long legs and stepped to the edge of the drive. A man was walking quickly away from the house in the direction of the great gate.

At the noise of a footstep on the gravel, the man wheeled with nervous swiftness and looked earnestly at Trent. The sudden sight of his face was almost terrible, so white and worn it was. Yet it was a young man's face. There was not a wrinkle about the haggard blue eyes, for all their tale of strain and desperate fatigue. As the two approached each other, Trent noted with admiration the man's breadth of shoulder and lithe, strong figure. In his carriage, inelastic as weariness had made it; in his handsome, regular features; in his short, smooth, yellow hair; and in his voice as he addressed Trent, the influence of a special sort of training was confessed. "Oxford was your playground, I think, my young friend," said Trent to himself.

"If you are Mr Trent," said the young man pleasantly, "you are expected. Mr Cupples telephoned from the hotel. My name is Marlowe."

"You were secretary to Mr Manderson, I believe," said Trent. He was much inclined to like young Mr Marlowe. Though he seemed so near a physical break-down, he gave out none the less that air of clean living and inward health that is the peculiar glory of his social type at his years. But there was something in the tired eyes that was a challenge to Trent's penetration; a habitual expression, as he took it to be, of meditating and weighing things not present to their sight. It was a look too intelligent, too steady and purposeful, to be called dreamy. Trent thought he had seen such a look before somewhere. He went on to say: "It is a terrible business for all of you. I fear it has upset you completely, Mr Marlowe."

"A little limp, that's all," replied the young man wearily. "I was driving the car all Sunday night and most of yesterday, and I didn't sleep last night after hearing the news—who would? But I have an appointment now, Mr Trent, down at the doctor's—arranging about the inquest. I expect it'll be tomorrow. If you will go up to the house and ask for Mr Bunner, you'll find him expecting you; he will tell you all about things and show you round. He's the other secretary; an American, and the best of fellows; he'll look after you. There's a detective here, by the way—Inspector Murch, from Scotland Yard. He came yesterday."

"Murch!" Trent exclaimed. "But he and I are old friends. How under the sun did he get here so soon?"

"I have no idea," Mr Marlowe answered. "But he was here last evening, before I got back from Southampton, interviewing everybody, and he's been about here since eight this morning. He's in the library now—that's where the open French window is that you see at the end of the house there. Perhaps you would like to step down there and talk about things."

"I think I will," said Trent. Marlowe nodded and went on his way. The thick turf of the lawn round which the drive took its circular sweep made Trent's footsteps as noiseless as a cat's. In a few moments he was looking in through the open leaves of the window at the southward end of the house, considering with a smile a very broad back and a bent head covered with short grizzled hair. The man within was stooping over a number of papers laid out on the table.

" 'Twas ever thus," said Trent in a melancholy tone, at the first sound of which the man within turned round with startling swiftness. "From childhood's hour I've seen my fondest hopes decay. I did think I was ahead of Scotland Yard this time, and now here is the largest officer in the entire metropolitan force already occupying the position."

The detective smiled grimly and came to the window. "I was expecting you, Mr Trent," he said. "This is the sort of case that you like."

"Since my tastes were being considered," Trent replied, stepping into the room, "I wish they had followed up the idea by keeping my hated rival out of the business. You have got a long start, too—I know all about it." His eyes began to wander round the room. "How did you manage it? You are a quick mover, I know; the dun deer's hide on fleeter foot was never tied; but I don't see how you got here in time to be at work yesterday evening. Has Scotland Yard secretly started an aviation corps? Or is it in league with the infernal powers? In either case the Home Secretary should be called upon to make a statement."

"It's simpler than that," said Mr Murch with professional stolidity. "I happened to be on leave with the missis at Halvey, which is only twelve miles or so along the coast. As soon as our people there heard of the murder they told me. I wired to the chief, and was put in charge of the case at once. I bicycled over yesterday evening, and have been at it since then."

"Arising out of that reply," said Trent inattentively, "how is Mrs Inspector Murch?"

"Never better, thank you," answered the inspector, "and frequently speaks of you and the games you used to have with our kids. But you'll excuse me saying, Mr Trent, that you needn't trouble to talk your nonsense to me while you're using your eyes. I know your ways by now. I understand you've fallen on your feet as usual, and have the lady's permission to go over the place and make inquiries."

"Such is the fact," said Trent. "I am going to cut you out again, Inspector. I owe you one for beating me over the Abinger case, you old fox. But if you really mean that you're not inclined for the social amenities just now, let us leave compliments and talk business." He stepped to the table, glanced through the papers arranged there in order, and then turned to the open roll-top desk. He looked into the drawers swiftly. "I see this has been cleared out. Well now, Inspector, I suppose we play the game as before."

Trent had found himself on a number of occasions in the past thrown into the company of Inspector Murch, who stood high in the councils of the Criminal Investigation Department. He was a quiet, tactful, and very shrewd officer, a man of great courage, with a vivid history in connection with the more dangerous class of criminals. His humanity was as broad as his frame, which was large even for a policeman. Trent and he, through some obscure working of sympathy, had appreciated one another from the beginning, and had formed one of those curious friendships with which it was the younger man's delight to adorn his experience. The inspector would talk more freely to him than to any one, under the rose, and they would discuss details and possibilities of every case, to their mutual enlightenment. There were necessary rules and limits. It was understood between them that Trent made no journalistic use of any point that could only have come to him from an official source. Each of them, moreover, for the honour and prestige of the institution he represented, openly reserved the right to withhold from the other any discovery or inspiration that might come to him which he considered vital to the solution of the difficulty. Trent had insisted on carefully formulating these principles of what he called detective sportsmanship. Mr Murch, who loved a contest, and who only stood to gain by his association with the keen intelligence of the other, entered very heartily into the game. In these strivings for the credit of the press and of the police, victory sometimes attended the experience and method of the officer, sometimes the quicker brain and livelier imagination of Trent, his gift of instinctively recognizing the significant through all disguises.

The inspector then replied to Trent's last words with cordial agreement. Leaning on either side of the French window, with the deep peace and hazy splendour of the summer landscape before them, they reviewed the case.

Trent had taken out a thin notebook, and as they talked he began to make, with light, secure touches, a rough sketch-plan of the room. It was a thing he did habitually on such occasions, and often quite idly, but now and then the habit had served him to good purpose.

This was a large, light apartment at the corner of the house, with generous window-space in two walls. A broad table stood in the middle. As one entered by the window the roll-top desk stood just to the left of it against the wall. The inner door was in the wall to the left, at the farther end of the room; and was faced by a broad window divided into openings of the casement type. A beautifully carved old corner-cupboard rose high against the wall beyond the door, and another cupboard filled a recess beside the fire-place. Some coloured prints of Harunobu, with which Trent promised himself a better acquaintance, hung on what little wall-space was unoccupied by books. These had a very uninspiring appearance of having been bought by the yard and never taken from their shelves. Bound with a sober luxury, the great English novelists, essayists, historians, and poets stood ranged like an army struck dead in its ranks. There were a few chairs made, like the cupboard and table, of old carved oak; a modern armchair and a swivel office-chair before the desk. The room looked costly but very bare. Almost the only portable objects were a great porcelain bowl of a wonderful blue on the table, a clock and some cigar boxes on the mantelshelf, and a movable telephone standard on the top of the desk.

"Seen the body?" inquired the inspector.

Trent nodded. "And the place where it lay," he said.

"First impressions of this case rather puzzle me," said the inspector. "From what I heard at Halvey I guessed it might be common robbery and murder by some tramp, though such a thing is very far from common in these parts. But as soon as I began my inquiries I came on some curious points, which by this time I dare say you've noted for yourself. The man is shot in his own grounds, quite near the house, to begin with. Yet there's not the slightest trace of any attempt at burglary. And the body wasn't robbed. In fact, it would be as plain a case of suicide as you could wish to see, if it wasn't for certain facts. Here's another thing; for a month or so past, they tell me, Manderson had been in a queer state of mind. I expect you know already that he and his wife had some trouble between them. The servants had noticed a change in his manner to her for a long time, and for the past week he had scarcely spoken to her. They say he was a changed man, moody and silent—whether on account of that or something else. The lady's-maid says he looked as if something was going to arrive. It's always easy to remember that people looked like that, after something has happened to them. Still, that's what they say. There you are again, then: suicide! Now, why wasn't it suicide, Mr Trent?"

"The facts so far as I know them are really all against it," Trent replied, sitting on the threshold of the window and clasping his knees. "First, of course, no weapon is to be found.

I've searched, and you've searched, and there's no trace of any firearm anywhere within a stone's throw of where the body lay. Second, the marks on the wrists, fresh scratches and bruises, which we can only assume to have been done in a struggle with somebody. Third, who ever heard of anybody shooting himself in the eye? Then I heard from the manager of the hotel here another fact, which strikes me as the most curious detail in this affair. Manderson had dressed himself fully before going out there, but he forgot his false teeth. Now how could a suicide who dressed himself to make a decent appearance as a corpse forget his teeth?"

"That last argument hadn't struck me," admitted Mr Murch. "There's something in it. But on the strength of the other points, which had occurred to me, I am not considering suicide. I have been looking about for ideas in this house, this morning. I expect you were thinking of doing the same."

"That is so. It is a case for ideas, it seems to me. Come, Murch, let us make an effort; let us bend our spirits to a temper of general suspicion. Let us suspect everybody in the house, to begin with. Listen: I will tell you whom I suspect. I suspect Mrs Manderson, of course. I also suspect both the secretaries— I hear there are two, and I hardly know which of them I regard as more thoroughly open to suspicion. I suspect the butler and the lady's-maid. I suspect the other domestics, and especially do I suspect the boot-boy. By the way, what domestics are there?' I have more than enough suspicion to go round, whatever the size of the establishment; but as a matter of curiosity I should like to know."

"All very well to laugh," replied the inspector, "but at the first stage of affairs it's the only safe principle, and you know that as well as I do, Mr Trent. However, I've seen enough of the people here, last night and today, to put a few of them out of my mind for the present at least. You will form your own conclusions. As for the establishment, there's the butler and lady's-maid, cook, and three other maids, one a young girl. One chauffeur, who's away with a broken wrist. No boy."

"What about the gardener? You say nothing about that shadowy and sinister figure, the gardener. You are keeping him in the background, Murch. Play the game. Out with him—or I report you to the Rules Committee."

"The garden is attended to by a man in the village, who comes twice a week. I've talked to him. He was here last on Friday."

"Then I suspect him all the more," said Trent. "And now as to the house itself. What I propose to do, to begin with, is to sniff about a little in this room, where I am told Manderson spent a great deal of his time, and in his bedroom; especially the bedroom. But since we're in this room, let's start here. You seem to be at the same stage of the inquiry. Perhaps you've done the bedrooms already?"

The inspector nodded. "I've been over Manderson's and his wife's. Nothing to be got there, I think. His room is very simple and bare, no signs of any sort that I could see. Seems to have insisted on the simple life, does Manderson. Never employed a valet. The room's almost like a cell, except for the clothes and shoes. You'll find it all exactly as I found it; and they tell me that's exactly as Manderson left it, at we don't know what o'clock yesterday morning. Opens into Mrs Manderson's bedroom—not much of the cell about that, I can tell you. I should say the lady was as fond of pretty things as most. But she cleared out of it on the morning of the discovery—told the maid she could never sleep in a room opening into her murdered husband's room. Very natural feeling in a woman, Mr Trent. She's camping out, so to say, in one of the spare bedrooms now."

"Come, my friend," Trent was saying to himself, as he made a few notes in his little book. "Have you got your eye on Mrs Manderson? Or haven't you? I know that colourless tone of the inspectorial voice. I wish I had seen her. Either you've got something against her and you don't want me to get hold of it; or else you've made up your mind she's innocent, but have no objection to my wasting my time over her. Well, it's all in the game; which begins to look extremely interesting as we go on." To Mr Murch he said aloud: "Well, I'll draw the bedroom later on. What about this?"

"They call it the library," said the inspector. "Manderson used to do his writing and that in here; passed most of the time he spent indoors here. Since he and his wife ceased to hit it off together, he had taken to spending his evenings alone, and when at this house he always spent 'em in here. He was last seen alive, as far as the servants are concerned, in this room."

Trent rose and glanced again through the papers set out on the table. "Business letters and documents, mostly," said Mr Murch. "Reports, prospectuses, and that. A few letters on private matters, nothing in them that I can see. The American secretary—Bunner his name is, and a queerer card I never saw turned—he's been through this desk with me this morning. He had got it into his head that Manderson had been receiving threatening letters, and that the murder was the outcome of that. But there's no trace of any such thing; and we looked at every blessed paper. The only unusual things we found were some packets of bank-notes to a considerable amount, and a couple of little bags of unset diamonds. I asked Mr Bunner to put them in a safer place. It appears that Manderson had begun buying diamonds lately as a speculation—it was a new game to him, the secretary said, and it seemed to amuse him."

"What about these secretaries?" Trent inquired. "I met one called Marlowe just now outside; a nice-looking chap with singular eyes, unquestionably English. The other, it seems, is an American. What did Manderson want with an English secretary?"

"Mr Marlowe explained to me how that was. The American was his right-hand business man, one of his office staff, who never left him. Mr Marlowe had nothing to do with Manderson's business as a financier, knew nothing of it. His job was to look after Manderson's horses and motors and yacht and sporting arrangements and that—make himself generally useful, as you might say. He had the spending of a lot of money, I should think. The other was confined entirely to the office affairs, and I dare say he had his hands full. As for his being English, it was just a fad of Manderson's to have an English secretary. He'd had several before Mr Marlowe."

"He showed his taste," observed Trent. "It might be more than interesting, don't you think, to be minister to the pleasures of a modern plutocrat with a large P. Only they say that Manderson's were exclusively of an innocent kind. Certainly Marlowe gives me the impression that he would be weak in the part of Petronius. But to return to the matter in hand." He looked at his notes. "You said just now that he was last seen alive here, 'so far as the servants were concerned.' That meant—?"

"He had a conversation with his wife on going to bed. But for that, the manservant, Martin by name, last saw him in this room. I had his story last night, and very glad he was to tell it. An affair like this is meat and drink to the servants of the house."

Trent considered for some moments, gazing through the open window over the sun-flooded slopes. "Would it bore you to hear what he has to say again?" he asked at length. For reply, Mr Murch rang the bell. A spare, clean-shaven, middle-aged man, having the servant's manner in its most distinguished form, answered it.

"This is Mr Trent, who is authorized by Mrs Manderson to go over the house and make inquiries," explained the detective. "He would like to hear your story." Martin bowed distantly. He recognized Trent for a gentleman. Time would show whether he was what Martin called a gentleman in every sense of the word.

"I observed you approaching the house, sir," said Martin with impassive courtesy. He spoke with a slow and measured utterance. "My instructions are to assist you in every possible way. Should you wish me to recall the circumstances of Sunday night?"

"Please," said Trent with ponderous gravity. Martin's style was making clamorous appeal to his sense of comedy. He banished with an effort all vivacity of expression from his face.

"I last saw Mr Manderson—"

"No, not that yet," Trent checked him quietly. "Tell me all you saw of him that evening—after dinner, say. Try to recollect every little detail."

"After dinner, sir?—yes. I remember that after dinner Mr Manderson and Mr Marlowe walked up and down the path through the orchard, talking. If you ask me for details, it struck me they were talking about something important, because I heard Mr Manderson say something when they came in through the back entrance. He said, as near as I can remember, 'If Harris is there, every minute is of importance. You want to start right away. And not a word to a soul.' Mr Marlowe answered, 'Very well. I will just change out of these clothes and then I am ready'—or words to that effect. I heard this plainly as they passed the window of my pantry. Then Mr Marlowe went up to his bedroom, and Mr Manderson entered the library and rang for me. He handed me some letters for the postman in the morning and directed me to sit up, as Mr Marlowe had persuaded him to go for a drive in the car by moonlight."

"That was curious," remarked Trent.

"I thought so, sir. But I recollected what I had heard about 'not a word to a soul,' and I concluded that this about a moonlight drive was intended to mislead."

"What time was this?"

"It would be about ten, sir, I should say. After speaking to me, Mr Manderson waited until Mr Marlowe had come down and brought round the car. He then went into the drawing-room, where Mrs Manderson was."

"Did that strike you as curious?"

Martin looked down his nose. "If you ask me the question, sir," he said with reserve, "I had not known him enter that room since we came here this year. He preferred to sit in the library in the evenings. That evening he only remained with Mrs Manderson for a few minutes. Then he and Mr Marlowe started immediately."

"You saw them start?"

"Yes, sir. They took the direction of Bishopsbridge."

"And you saw Mr Manderson again later?"

"After an hour or thereabouts, sir, in the library. That would have been about a quarter past eleven, I should say; I had noticed eleven striking from the church. I may say I am peculiarly quick of hearing, sir."

"Mr Manderson had rung the bell for you, I suppose. Yes? And what passed when you answered it?"

"Mr Manderson had put out the decanter of whisky and a syphon and glass, sir, from the cupboard where he kept them—"

Trent held up his hand. "While we are on that point, Martin, I want to ask you plainly, did Mr Manderson drink very much? You understand this is not impertinent curiosity on my part. I want you to tell me, because it may possibly help in the clearing up of this case."

"Perfectly, sir," replied Martin gravely. "I have no hesitation in telling you what I have already told the inspector. Mr Manderson was, considering his position in life, a remarkably abstemious man. In my four years of service with him I never knew anything of an alcoholic nature pass his lips, except a glass or two of wine at dinner, very rarely a little at luncheon, and from time to time a whisky and soda before going to bed. He never seemed to form an habit of it. Often I used to find his glass in the morning with only a little soda water in it; sometimes he would have been having whisky with it, but never much. He never was particular about his drinks; ordinary soda was what he preferred, though I had ventured to suggest some of the natural minerals, having personally acquired a taste for them in my previous service. He used to keep them in the cupboard here, because he had a great dislike of being waited on more than was necessary. It was an understood thing that I never came near him after dinner unless sent for. And when he sent for anything, he liked it brought quick, and to be left alone again at once. He hated to be asked if he required anything more. Amazingly simple in his tastes, sir, Mr Manderson was."

"Very well; and he rang for you that night about a quarter past eleven. Now can you remember exactly what he said?"

"I think I can tell you with some approach to accuracy, sir. It was not much. First he asked me if Mr Bunner had gone to bed, and I replied that he had been gone up some time. He then said that he wanted some one to sit up until 12:30, in case an important message should come by telephone, and that Mr Marlowe having gone to Southampton for him in the motor, he wished me to do this, and that I was to take down the message if it came, and not disturb him. He also ordered a fresh syphon of soda water. I believe that was all, sir."

"You noticed nothing unusual about him, I suppose?"

"No, sir, nothing unusual. When I answered the ring, he was seated at the desk listening at the telephone, waiting for a number, as I supposed. He gave his orders and went on listening at the same time. When I returned with the syphon he was engaged in conversation over the wire."

"Do you remember anything of what he was saying?"

"Very little, sir; it was something about somebody being at some hotel—of no interest to me. I was only in the room just time enough to place the syphon on the table and withdraw. As I closed the door he was saying, 'You're sure he isn't in the hotel?' or words to that effect."

"And that was the last you saw and heard of him alive?"

"No, sir. A little later, at half-past eleven, when I had settled down in my pantry with the door ajar, and a book to pass the time, I heard Mr Manderson go upstairs to bed. I immediately went to close the library window, and slipped the lock of the front door. I did not hear anything more."

Trent considered. "I suppose you didn't doze at all," he said tentatively, "while you were sitting up waiting for the telephone message?"

"Oh no, sir. I am always very wakeful about that time. I'm a bad sleeper, especially in the neighbourhood of the sea, and I generally read in bed until somewhere about midnight."

"And did any message come?"

"No, sir."

"No. And I suppose you sleep with your window open, these warm nights?"

"It is never closed at night, sir."

Trent added a last note; then he looked thoughtfully through those he had taken. He rose and paced up and down the room for some moments with a downcast eye. At length he paused opposite Martin. "It all seems perfectly ordinary and simple," he said. "I just want to get a few details clear. You went to shut the windows in the library before going to bed. Which windows?"

"The French window, sir. It had been open all day. The windows opposite the door were seldom opened."

"And what about the curtains? I am wondering whether anyone outside the house could have seen into the room."

"Easily, sir, I should say, if he had got into the grounds on that side. The curtains were never drawn in hot weather. Mr Manderson would often sit right in the doorway at nights, smoking and looking out into the darkness. But nobody could have seen him who had any business to be there."

"I see. And now tell me this. Your hearing is very acute, you say, and you heard Mr Manderson enter the house when he came in after dinner from the garden. Did you hear him re-enter it after returning from the motor drive?"

Martin paused. "Now you mention it, sir, I remember that I did not. His ringing the bell in this room was the first I knew of his being back. I should have heard him come in, if he had come in by the front. I should have heard the door go. But he must have come in by the window." The man reflected for a moment, then added, "As a general rule, Mr Manderson would come in by the front, hang up his hat and coat in the hall, and pass down the hall into the study. It seems likely to me that he was in a great hurry to use the telephone, so went straight across the lawn to the window—he was like that, when there was anything important to be done. He had his hat on, now I remember, and had thrown his greatcoat over the end of the table. He gave his order very sharp, too, as he always did when busy. A very precipitate man indeed was Mr Manderson; a hustler, as they say."

"Ah! he appeared to be busy. But didn't you say just now that you noticed nothing unusual about him?"

A melancholy smile flitted momentarily over Martin's face. "That observation shows that you did not know Mr Manderson, sir, if you will pardon my saying so. His being like that was nothing unusual; quite the contrary. It took me long enough to get used to it. Either he would be sitting quite still and smoking a cigar, thinking or reading, or else he would be writing, dictating, and sending off wires all at the same time, till it almost made one dizzy to see it, sometimes for an hour or more at a stretch. As for being in a hurry over a telephone message, I may say it wasn't in him to be anything else."

Trent turned to the inspector, who met his eye with a look of answering intelligence. Not sorry to show his understanding of the line of inquiry opened by Trent, Mr Murch for the first time put a question.

"Then you left him telephoning by the open window, with the lights on, and the drinks on the table; is that it?"

"That is so, Mr Murch." The delicacy of the change in Martin's manner when called upon to answer the detective momentarily distracted Trent's appreciative mind. But the big man's next question brought it back to the problem at once.

"About those drinks. You say Mr Manderson often took no whisky before going to bed. Did he have any that night?"

"I could not say. The room was put to rights in the morning by one of the maids, and the glass washed, I presume, as usual. I know that the decanter was nearly full that evening. I had refilled it a few days before, and I glanced at it when I brought the fresh syphon, just out of habit, to make sure there was a decent-looking amount."

The inspector went to the tall corner-cupboard and opened it. He took out a decanter of cut glass and set it on the table before Martin. "Was it fuller than that?" he asked quietly. "That's how I found it this morning." The decanter was more than half empty.

For the first time Martin's self-possession wavered. He took up the decanter quickly, tilted it before his eyes, and then stared amazedly at the others. He said slowly: "There's not much short of half a bottle gone out of this since I last set eyes on it—and that was that Sunday night."

"Nobody in the house, I suppose?" suggested Trent discreetly.

"Out of the question!" replied Martin briefly; then he added, "I beg pardon, sir, but this is a most extraordinary thing to me. Such a thing never happened in all my experience of Mr Manderson. As for the women-servants, they never touch anything, I can answer for it; and as for me, when I want a drink I can help myself without going to the decanters." He took up the decanter again and aimlessly renewed his observation of the contents, while the inspector eyed him with a look of serene satisfaction, as a master contemplates his handiwork.

Trent turned to a fresh page of his notebook, and tapped it thoughtfully with his pencil. Then he looked up and said, "I suppose Mr Manderson had dressed for dinner that night?"

"Certainly, sir. He had on a suit with a dress-jacket, what he used to refer to as a tuxedo, which he usually wore when dining at home."

"And he was dressed like that when you saw him last?"

"All but the jacket, sir. When he spent the evening in the library, as usually happened, he would change it for an old shooting-jacket after dinner, a light-coloured tweed, a little too loud in pattern for English tastes, perhaps. He had it on when I saw him last. It used to hang in this cupboard here"—Martin opened the door of it as he spoke—"along with Mr Manderson's fishing-rods and such things, so that he could slip it on after dinner without going upstairs."

"Leaving the dinner-jacket in the cupboard?"

"Yes, sir. The housemaid used to take it upstairs in the morning."

"In the morning," Trent repeated slowly. "And now that we are speaking of the morning, will you tell me exactly what you know about that? I understand that Mr Manderson was not missed until the body was found about ten o'clock."

"That is so, sir. Mr Manderson would never be called, or have anything brought to him in the morning. He occupied a separate bedroom. Usually he would get up about eight and go round to the bathroom, and he would come down sometime before nine. But often he would sleep till nine or ten o'clock. Mrs Manderson was always called at seven. The maid would take in tea to her. Yesterday morning Mrs Manderson took breakfast about eight in her sitting-room as usual, and everyone supposed that Mr Manderson was still in bed and asleep, when Evans came rushing up to the house with the shocking intelligence." '

"I see," said Trent. "And now another thing. You say you slipped the lock of the front door before going to bed. Was that all the locking-up you did?"

"To the front door, sir, yes; I slipped the lock. No more is considered necessary in these parts. But I had locked both the doors at the back, and seen to the fastenings of all the windows on the ground floor. In the morning everything was as I had left it."

"As you had left it. Now here is another point—the last, I think. Were the clothes in which the body was found the clothes that Mr Manderson would naturally have worn that day?"

Martin rubbed his chin. "You remind me how surprised I was when I first set eyes on the body, sir. At first I couldn't make out what was unusual about the clothes, and then I saw what it was. The collar was a shape of collar Mr Manderson never wore except with evening dress. Then I found that he had put on all the same things that he had worn the night before—large fronted shirt and all—except just the coat and waistcoat and trousers, and the brown shoes, and blue tie. As for the suit, it was one of half a dozen he might have worn. But for him to have simply put on all the rest just because they were there, instead of getting out the kind of shirt and things he always wore by day; well, sir, it was unprecedented. It shows, like some other things, what a hurry he must have been in when getting up."

"Of course," said Trent. "Well, I think that's all I wanted to know. You have put everything with admirable clearness, Martin. If we want to ask any more questions later on, I suppose you will be somewhere about."

"I shall be at your disposal, sir." Martin bowed, and went out quietly.

Trent flung himself into the armchair and exhaled a long breath. "Martin is a great creature," he said. "He is far, far better than a play. There is none like him, none, nor will be when our summers have deceased. Straight, too; not an atom of harm in dear old Martin. Do you know, Murch, you are wrong in suspecting that man."

"I never said a word about suspecting him." The inspector was taken aback. "You know, Mr Trent, he would never have told his story like that if he thought I suspected him."

"I dare say he doesn't think so. He is a wonderful creature, a great artist; but, in spite of that, he is not at all a sensitive type. It has never occurred to his mind that you, Murch, could suspect him, Martin, the complete, the accomplished. But I know it. You must understand, inspector, that I have made a special study of the psychology of officers of the law. It is a grossly neglected branch of knowledge. They are far more interesting than criminals, and not nearly so easy. All the time I was questioning him I saw handcuffs in your eye. Your lips were mutely framing the syllables of those tremendous words: 'It is my duty to tell you that anything you now say will be taken down and used in evidence against you.' Your manner would have deceived most men, but it could not deceive me."

Mr Murch laughed heartily. Trent's nonsense never made any sort of impression on his mind, but he took it as a mark of esteem, which indeed it was; so it never failed to please him. "Well, Mr Trent," he said, "you're perfectly right. There's no point in denying it, I have got my eye on him. Not that there's anything definite; but you know as well as I do how often servants are mixed up in affairs of this kind, and this man is such a very quiet customer. You remember the case of Lord William Russell's valet, who went in as usual, in the morning, to draw up the blinds in his master's bedroom, as quiet and starchy as you please, a few hours after he had murdered him in his bed. I've talked to all the women of the house, and I don't believe there's a morsel of harm in one of them. But Martin's not so easy set aside. I don't like his manner; I believe he's hiding something. If so, I shall find it out."

"Cease!" said Trent. "Drain not to its dregs the urn of bitter prophecy. Let us get back to facts. Have you, as a matter of evidence, anything at all to bring against Martin's story as he has told it to us?"

"Nothing whatever at present. As for his suggestion that Manderson came in by way of the window after leaving Marlowe and the car, that's right enough, I should say. I questioned the servant who swept the room next morning, and she tells me there were gravelly marks near the window, on this plain drugget that goes round the carpet. And there's a footprint in this soft new gravel just outside." The inspector took a folding rule from his pocket and with it pointed out the traces. "One of the patent shoes Manderson was wearing that night exactly fits that print; you'll find them," he added, "on the top shelf in the bedroom, near the window end, the only patents in the row. The girl who polished them in the morning picked them out for me."

Trent bent down and studied the faint marks keenly. "Good!" he said. "You have covered a lot of ground, Murch, I must say. That was excellent about the whisky; you made your point finely. I feel inclined to shout 'Encore!' It's a thing that I shall have to think over."

"I thought you might have fitted it in already," said Mr Murch. "Come, Mr Trent, we're only at the beginning of our inquiries, but what do you say to this for a preliminary theory? There's a plan of burglary, say a couple of men in it and Martin squared. They know where the plate is, and all about the handy little bits of stuff in the drawing-room and elsewhere. They watch the house; see Manderson off to bed; Martin comes to shut the window, and leaves it ajar, accidentally on purpose. They wait till Martin goes to bed at twelve-thirty; then they just walk into the library, and begin to sample the whisky first thing. Now suppose Manderson isn't asleep, and suppose they make a noise opening the window, or however it might be. He hears it; thinks of burglars; gets up very quietly to see if anything's wrong; creeps down on them, perhaps, just as they're getting ready for work. They cut and run; he chases them down to the shed, and collars one; there's a fight; one of them loses his temper and his head, and makes a swinging job of it. Now, Mr Trent, pick that to pieces."

"Very well," said Trent, "just to oblige you, Murch, especially as I know you don't believe a word of it. First: no traces of any kind left by your burglar or burglars, and the window found fastened in the morning, according to Martin. Not much force in that, I allow. Next: nobody in the house hears anything of this stampede through the library, nor hears any shout from Manderson either inside the house or outside. Next: Manderson goes down without a word to anybody, though Bunner and Martin are at hand. Next: did you ever hear in your long experience of a householder getting up in the night to pounce on burglars, who dressed himself fully, with underclothing, shirt, collar and tie, trousers, waistcoat and coat, socks and hard leather shoes; and who gave the finishing touches to a somewhat dandified toilet by doing his hair, and putting on his watch and chain? Personally, I call that over-dressing the part. The only decorative detail he seems to have forgotten is his teeth."

The inspector leaned forward thinking, his large hands clasped before him. "No," he said at last. "Of course there's no help in that theory. I rather expect we have some way to go before we find out why a man gets up before the servants are awake, dresses himself fully, and is murdered within sight of his house early enough to be cold and stiff by ten in the morning."

Trent shook his head. "We can't build anything on that last consideration. I've gone into the subject with people who know. I shouldn't wonder," he added, "if the traditional notions about loss of temperature and rigour after death had occasionally brought an innocent man to the gallows, or near it. Dr. Stock has them all, I feel sure; most general practitioners of the older generation have. That Dr. Stock will make an ass of himself at the inquest, is almost as certain as that tomorrow's sun will rise. I've seen him. He will say the body must have been dead about so long, because of the degree of coldness and *rigor mortis*. I can see him nosing it all in some textbook that was out of date when he was a student. Listen, Murch, and I will tell you some facts which will be a great hindrance to you in your professional career. There are many things that may hasten or retard the cooling of the body. This one was lying in the long dewy grass on the shady side of the shed. As for rigidity, if Manderson died in a struggle, or labouring under sudden emotion, his corpse might stiffen practically instantaneously; there are dozens of cases noted, particularly in cases of injury to the skull, like this one. On the other hand, the stiffening might not have begun until eight or ten hours after death. You can't hang anybody on *rigor mortis* nowadays, Inspector, much as you may resent the limitation. No, what we *can* say is this. If he had been shot after the hour at which the world begins to get up and go about its business, it would have been heard, and very likely seen, too. In fact, we must reason, to begin with, at any rate, on the assumption that he wasn't shot at a time when people might be awake; it isn't done in these parts. Put that time at 6:30 a.m. Manderson went up to bed at 11 p.m., and Martin sat up till 12:30. Assuming that he went to sleep at once on turning in, that leaves us something like six hours for the crime to be committed in; and that is a long time. But whenever it took place, I wish you would suggest a reason why Manderson, who was a fairly late riser, was up and dressed at or before 6:30; and why neither Martin, who sleeps lightly, nor Bunner, nor his wife heard him moving about, or letting himself out of the house. He must have been careful. He must have crept about like a cat. Do you feel as I do, Murch, about all this; that it is very, very strange and baffling?"

"That's how it looks," agreed the inspector.

"And now," said Trent, rising to his feet, "I'll leave you to your meditations, and take a look at the bedrooms. Perhaps the explanation of all this will suddenly burst upon you while

I am poking about up there. But," concluded Trent in a voice of sudden exasperation, turning round in the doorway, "if you can tell me at any time, how under the sun a man who put on all those clothes could forget to put in his teeth, you may kick me from here to the nearest lunatic asylum, and hand me over as an incipient dement."

5

POKING ABOUT

There are moments in life, as one might think, when that which is within us, busy about its secret affair, lets escape into consciousness some hint of a fortunate thing ordained. Who does not know what it is to feel at times a wave of unaccountable persuasion that it is about to go well with him?—not the feverish confidence of men in danger of a blow from fate, not the persistent illusion of the optimist, but an unsought conviction, springing up like a bird from the heather, that success is at hand in some great or little thing. The general suddenly knows at dawn that the day will bring him victory; the man on the green suddenly knows that he will put down the long putt. As Trent mounted the stairway outside the library door he seemed to rise into certainty of achievement.

A host of guesses and inferences swarmed apparently unsorted through his mind; a few secret observations that he had made, and which he felt must have significance, still stood unrelated to any plausible theory of the crime; yet as he went up he seemed to know indubitably that light was going to appear.

The bedrooms lay on either side of a broad carpeted passage, lighted by a tall end window. It went the length of the house until it ran at right angles into a narrower passage, out of which the servants' rooms opened. Martin's room was the exception:

it opened out of a small landing half-way to the upper floor. As Trent passed it he glanced within. A little square room, clean and commonplace. In going up the rest of the stairway he stepped with elaborate precaution against noise, hugging the wall closely and placing each foot with care; but a series of very audible creaks marked his passage.

He knew that Manderson's room was the first on the right hand when the bedroom floor was reached, and he went to it at once. He tried the latch and the lock, which worked normally, and examined the wards of the key. Then he turned to the room.

It was a small apartment, strangely bare. The plutocrat's toilet appointments were of the simplest. All remained just as it had been on the morning of the ghastly discovery in the grounds. The sheets and blankets of the unmade bed lay tumbled over a narrow wooden bedstead, and the sun shone brightly through the window upon them. It gleamed, too, upon the gold parts of the delicate work of dentistry that lay in water in a shallow bowl of glass placed on a small, plain table by the bedside. On this also stood a wrought-iron candlestick. Some clothing lay untidily over one of the two rush-bottomed chairs. Various objects on the top of a chest of drawers, which had been used as a dressing-table, lay in such disorder as a hurried man might make. Trent looked them over with a questing eye. He noted also that the occupant of the room had neither washed nor shaved. With his finger he turned over the dental plate in the bowl, and frowned again at its incomprehensible presence.

The emptiness and disarray of the little room, flooded by the sunbeams, were producing in Trent a sense of gruesomeness. His fancy called up a picture of a haggard man dressing himself in careful silence by the first light of dawn, glancing constantly at the inner door behind which his wife slept, his eyes full of some terror.

Trent shivered, and to fix his mind again on actualities opened two tall cupboards in the wall on either side of the bed. They contained clothing, a large choice of which had evidently been one of the very few conditions of comfort for the man who had slept there.

In the matter of shoes, also, Manderson had allowed himself the advantage of wealth. An extraordinary number of these, treed and carefully kept, was ranged on two long low shelves against the wall. No boots were among them. Trent, himself an amateur of good shoe-leather, now turned to these, and glanced over the collection with an appreciative eye. It was to be seen that Manderson had been inclined to pride himself on a rather small and well-formed foot. The shoes were of a distinctive shape, narrow and round-toed, beautifully made; all were evidently from the same last.

Suddenly his eyes narrowed themselves over a pair of patent-leather shoes on the upper shelf.

These were the shoes of which the inspector had already described the position to him; the shoes worn by Manderson the night before his death. They were a well-worn pair, he saw at once; he saw, too, that they had been very recently polished. Something about the uppers of these shoes had seized his attention. He bent lower and frowned over them, comparing what he saw with the appearance of the neighbouring shoes. Then he took them up and examined the line of junction of the uppers with the soles.

As he did this, Trent began unconsciously to whistle faintly, and with great precision, an air which Inspector Murch, if he had been present, would have recognized.

Most men who have the habit of self-control have also some involuntary trick which tells those who know them that they are suppressing excitement. The inspector had noted that when Trent had picked up a strong scent he whistled faintly a certain melodious passage; though the inspector could not have told you that it was in fact the opening movement of Mendelssohn's *Lied ohneWörter* in A Major.

He turned the shoes over, made some measurements with a marked tape, and looked minutely at the bottoms. On each, in the angle between the heel and the instep, he detected a faint trace of red gravel.

Trent placed the shoes on the floor, and walked with his hands behind him to the window, out of which, still faintly whistling, he gazed with eyes that saw nothing. Once his lips opened to emit mechanically the Englishman's expletive of sudden enlightenment. At length he turned to the shelves again, and swiftly but carefully examined every one of the shoes there.

This done, he took up the garments from the chair, looked them over closely and replaced them. He turned to the wardrobe cupboards again, and hunted through them carefully. The litter on the dressing-table now engaged his attention for the second time. Then he sat down on the empty chair, took his head in his hands, and remained in that attitude, staring at the carpet, for some minutes. He rose at last and opened the inner door leading to Mrs Manderson's room.

It was evident at a glance that the big room had been hurriedly put down from its place as the lady's bower. All the array of objects that belong to a woman's dressing-table had been removed; on bed and chairs and smaller tables there were no garments or hats, bags or boxes; no trace remained of the obstinate conspiracy of gloves and veils, handkerchiefs and ribbons, to break the captivity of the drawer. The room was like an unoccupied guest-chamber. Yet in every detail of furniture and decoration it spoke of an unconventional but exacting taste. Trent, as his expert eye noted the various perfection of colour and form amid which the ill-mated lady dreamed her dreams and thought her loneliest thoughts, knew that she had at least the resources of an artistic nature. His interest in this unknown personality grew stronger; and his brows came down heavily as he thought of the burdens laid upon it, and of the deed of which the history was now shaping itself with more and more of substance before his busy mind.

He went first to the tall French window in the middle of the wall that faced the door, and opening it, stepped out upon a small balcony with an iron railing. He looked down on a broad stretch of lawn that began immediately beneath him, separated from the house wall only by a narrow flower-bed, and stretched away, with an abrupt dip at the farther end, toward the orchard. The other window opened with a sash above the garden entrance of the library. In the farther inside corner of the room was a second door giving upon the passage; the door by which the maid was wont to come in, and her mistress to go out, in the morning.

Trent, seated on the bed, quickly sketched in his notebook a plan of the room and its neighbour. The bed stood in the angle between the communicating door and the sash-window, its head against the wall dividing the room from Manderson's. Trent stared at the pillows; then he lay down with deliberation on the bed and looked through the open door into the adjoining room.

This observation taken, he rose again and proceeded to note on his plan that on either side of the bed was a small table with a cover. Upon that farthest from the door was a graceful electric-lamp standard of copper connected by a free wire with the wall. Trent looked at it thoughtfully, then at the switches connected with the other lights in the room. They were, as usual, on the wall just within the door, and some way out of his reach as he sat on the bed. He rose, and satisfied himself that the lights were all in order. Then he turned on his heel, walked quickly into Manderson's room, and rang the bell.

"I want your help again, Martin," he said, as the butler presented himself, upright and impassive, in the doorway.

"I want you to prevail upon Mrs Manderson's maid to grant me an interview."

"Certainly, sir," said Martin.

"What sort of a woman is she? Has she her wits about her?"

"She's French, sir," replied Martin succinctly; adding after a pause: "She has not been with us long, sir, but I have formed the impression that the young woman knows as much of the world as is good for her—since you ask me."

"You think butter might possibly melt in her mouth, do you?" said Trent. "Well, I am not afraid. I want to put some questions to her."

"I will send her up immediately, sir." The butler withdrew, and Trent wandered round the little room with his hands at his back. Sooner than he expected, a small neat figure in black appeared quietly before him.

The lady's-maid, with her large brown eyes, had taken favourable notice of Trent from a window when he had crossed the lawn, and had been hoping desperately that the resolver of mysteries (whose reputation was as great below-stairs as elsewhere) would send for her. For one thing, she felt the need to make a scene; her nerves were overwrought. But her scenes were at a discount with the other domestics, and as for Mr Murch, he had chilled her into self-control with his official manner. Trent, her glimpse of him had told her, had not the air of a policeman, and at a distance he had appeared *sympathique*.

As she entered the room, however, instinct decided for her that any approach to coquetry would be a mistake, if she sought to make a good impression at the beginning. It was with an air of amiable candour, then, that she said, "Monsieur desire to speak with me." She added helpfully, "I am called Célestine."

"Naturally," agreed Trent with businesslike calm. "Now what I want you to tell me, Célestine, is this. When you took tea to your mistress yesterday morning at seven o'clock, was the door between the two bedrooms—this door here—open?"

Célestine became intensely animated in an instant. "Oh yes!" she said, using her favourite English idiom. "The door was open as always, Monsieur, and I shut it as always. But it is necessary to explain. Listen! When I enter the room of Madame from the other door in there—ah! but if Monsieur will give himself the pain to enter the other room, all explains itself." She tripped across to the door, and urged Trent before her into the larger bedroom with a hand on his arm. "See! I enter the room with the tea like this. I approach the bed. Before I come quite near the bed, here is the door to my right hand—open always—so! But Monsieur can perceive that I see nothing in the room of Monsieur Manderson. The door opens to the bed, not to me who approach from down there. I shut it without seeing in. It is the order. Yesterday it was as ordinary. I see nothing of the next room. Madame sleep like an angel—she see nothing. I shut the door. I place the plateau—I open the curtains—I prepare the *toilette*—I retire—voilà!" Célestine paused for breath and spread her hands abroad.

Trent, who had followed her movements and gesticulations with deepening gravity, nodded his head. "I see exactly how it was now," he said. "Thank you, Célestine. So Mr Manderson was supposed to be still in his room while your mistress was getting up, and dressing, and having breakfast in her boudoir?"

"*Oui, Monsieur.*"

"Nobody missed him, in fact," remarked Trent. "Well, Célestine, I am very much obliged to you." He reopened the door to the outer bedroom.

"It is nothing, Monsieur," said Célestine, as she crossed the small room. "I hope that Monsieur will catch the assassin of Monsieur Manderson. But I not regret him too much," she added with sudden and amazing violence, turning round with her hand on the knob of the outer door. She set her teeth with an audible sound, and the colour rose in her small dark face. English departed from her. "*Je ne le regrette pas du tout, du tout!*" she cried with a flood of words. "*Madame—ah! je me jetterais au feu pour Madame—une femme si charmante, si adorable! mais un homme comme Monsieur—maussade, boudeur, impassible! Ah, non!—de ma vie! J'enavais par-dessus la tête, de Monsieur! Ah! vrai! Est-ce insupportable, tout de même, qu'ilexiste des types comme ça? Jevousjure que—*"

"*Finissez ce chahut*, Célestine!" Trent broke in sharply. Célestine's tirade had brought back the memory of his student days with a rush. "*En voilà une scène! C'est rasant, voussavez. Fant rentier ga, Mademoiselle. Du reste, c'est bien imprudent, croyez- moi*. Hang it! have some common sense! If the inspector downstairs heard you saying that kind of thing, you would get into trouble. And don't wave your fists about so much; you might hit something. You seem," he went on more pleasantly, as Célestine grew calmer under his authoritative eye, "to be even more glad than other people that Mr Manderson is out of the way. I could almost suspect, Célestine, that Mr Manderson did not take as much notice of you as you thought necessary and right."

"*A peine s'il m'avait regardé!*" Célestine answered simply.

"*Ça, c'est un comblei*" observed Trent. "You are a nice young woman for a small tea-party, I don't think. A star upon your birthday burned, whose fierce, serene, red, pulseless planet never yearned in heaven, Célestine. *Mademoiselle*, I am busy. *Bonjour*. You certainly are a beauty!"

Célestine took this as a scarcely expected compliment. The surprise restored her balance. With a sudden flash of her eyes and teeth at Trent over her shoulder, the lady's-maid opened the door and swiftly disappeared.

Trent, left alone in the little bedroom, relieved his mind with two forcible descriptive terms in Célestine's language, and turned to his problem. He took the pair of shoes which he had already examined, and placed them on one of the two chairs in the room, then seated himself on the other opposite to this. With his hands in his pockets he sat with eyes fixed upon those two dumb witnesses. Now and then he whistled, almost inaudibly, a few bars. It was very still in the room. A subdued twittering came from the trees through the open window. From time to time a breeze rustled in the leaves of the thick creeper about the sill. But the man in the room, his face grown hard and sombre now with his thoughts, never moved.

So he sat for the space of half an hour. Then he rose quickly to his feet. He replaced the shoes on their shelf with care, and stepped out upon the landing.

Two bedroom doors faced him on the other side of the passage. He opened that which was immediately opposite, and entered a bedroom by no means austerely tidy. Some sticks and fishing-rods stood confusedly in one corner, a pile of books in another. The housemaid's hand had failed to give a look of order to the jumble of heterogeneous objects left on the dressing-table and on the mantelshelf—pipes, penknives, pencils, keys, golf-balls, old letters, photographs, small boxes, tins, and bottles. Two fine etchings and some water-colour sketches hung on the walls; leaning against the end of the wardrobe, unhung, were a few framed engravings. A row of shoes and boots was ranged beneath the window. Trent crossed the room and studied them intently; then he measured some of them with his tape, whistling very softly. This done, he sat on the side of the bed, and his eyes roamed gloomily about the room.

The photographs on the mantelshelf attracted him presently. He rose and examined one representing Marlowe and Manderson on horseback. Two others were views of famous peaks in the Alps. There was a faded print of three youths—one of them unmistakably his acquaintance of the haggard blue eyes—clothed in tatterdemalion soldier's gear of the sixteenth century. Another was a portrait of a majestic old lady, slightly resembling Marlowe. Trent, mechanically taking a cigarette from an open box on the mantelshelf, lit it and stared at the photographs. Next he turned his attention to a flat leathern case that lay by the cigarette-box.

It opened easily. A small and light revolver, of beautiful workmanship, was disclosed, with a score or so of loose cartridges. On the stock were engraved the initials "J. M."

A step was heard on the stairs, and as Trent opened the breech and peered into the barrel of the weapon, Inspector Murch appeared at the open door of the room. "I was wondering—" he began; then stopped as he saw what the other was about. His intelligent eyes opened slightly. "Whose is the revolver, Mr Trent?" he asked in a conversational tone.

"Evidently it belongs to the occupant of the room, Mr Marlowe," replied Trent with similar lightness, pointing to the initials. "I found this lying about on the mantelpiece. It seems a handy little pistol to me, and it has been very carefully cleaned, I should say, since the last time it was used. But I know little about firearms."

"Well, I know a good deal," rejoined the inspector quietly, taking the revolver from Trent's outstretched hand. "It's a bit of a specialty with me, is firearms, as I think you know, Mr Trent. But it don't require an expert to tell one thing." He replaced the revolver in its case on the mantelshelf, took out one of the cartridges, and laid it on the spacious palm of one hand; then, taking a small object from his waistcoat pocket, he laid it beside the cartridge. It was a little leaden bullet, slightly battered about the nose, and having upon it some bright new scratches.

"Is that the one?" Trent murmured as he bent over the inspector's hand.

"That's him," replied Mr Murch. "Lodged in the bone at the back of the skull. Dr. Stock got it out within the last hour, and handed it to the local officer, who has just sent it on to me. These bright scratches you see were made by the doctor's instruments. These other marks were made by the rifling of the barrel—a barrel like this one." He tapped the revolver. "Same make, same calibre. There is no other that marks the bullet just like this."

With the pistol in its case between them, Trent and the inspector looked into each other's eyes for some moments. Trent was the first to speak. "This mystery is all wrong," he observed. "It is insanity. The symptoms of mania are very marked. Let us see how we stand. We were not in any doubt, I believe, about Manderson having dispatched Marlowe in the car to Southampton, or about Marlowe having gone, returning late last night, many hours after the murder was committed."

"There is no doubt whatever about all that," said Murch, with a slight emphasis on the verb.

"And now," pursued Trent, "we are invited by this polished and insinuating firearm to believe the following line of propositions: that Marlowe never went to Southampton; that he returned to the house in the night; that he somehow, without waking Mrs Manderson or anybody else, got Manderson to get up, dress himself, and go out into the grounds; that he then and there shot the said Manderson with his incriminating pistol; that he carefully cleaned the said pistol, returned to the house and, again without disturbing anyone, replaced it in its case in a favourable position to be found by the officers of the law; that he then withdrew and spent the rest of the day in hiding—*with* a large motor-car; and that he turned up, feigning ignorance of the whole affair, at—what time was it?"

"A little after 9 p.m." The inspector still stared moodily at Trent. "As you say, Mr Trent, that is the first theory suggested by this find, and it seems wild enough—at least it would do if it didn't fall to pieces at the very start. When the murder was done Marlowe must have been fifty to a hundred miles away. He *did* go to Southampton."

"How do you know?"

"I questioned him last night, and took down his story. He arrived in Southampton about 6:30 on the Monday morning."

"Come off!" exclaimed Trent bitterly. "What do I care about his story? What do you care about his story? I want to know how you know he went to Southampton."

Mr Murch chuckled. "I thought I should take a rise out of you, Mr Trent," he said. "Well, there's no harm in telling you. After I arrived yesterday evening, as soon as I had got the outlines of the story from Mrs Manderson and the servants, the first thing I did was to go to the telegraph office and wire to our people in Southampton. Manderson had told his wife when he went to bed that he had changed his mind, and sent Marlowe to Southampton to get some important information from someone who was crossing by the next day's boat. It seemed right enough, but, you see, Marlowe was the only one of the household who wasn't under my hand, so to speak. He didn't return in the car until later in the evening; so before thinking the matter out any further, I wired to Southampton making certain inquiries. Early this morning I got this reply." He handed a series of telegraph slips to Trent, who read:

> "Person answering description in motor answering description arrived Bedford Hotel here 6:30 this morning gave name Marlowe left car hotel garage told attendant car belonged Manderson had bath and breakfast went out heard of later at docks inquiring for passenger name Harris on Havre boat inquired repeatedly until boat left at noon next heard of at hotel where he lunched about 1:15 left soon afterwards in car company's agents inform berth was booked name Harris last week but Harris did not travel by boat Burke inspector."

"Simple and satisfactory," observed Mr Murch as Trent, after twice reading the message, returned it to him. "His own story corroborated in every particular. He told me he hung about the dock for half an hour or so on the chance of Harris turning up late, then strolled back, lunched, and decided to return at once. He sent a wire to Manderson—'Harris not turned up missed boat returning Marlowe,' which was duly delivered here in the afternoon, and placed among the dead man's letters. He motored back at a good rate, and arrived dog-tired. When he heard of Manderson's death from Martin, he nearly fainted. What with that and the being without sleep for so long, he was rather a wreck when I came to interview him last night; but he was perfectly coherent."

Trent picked up the revolver and twirled the cylinder idly for a few moments. "It was unlucky for Manderson that Marlowe left his pistol and cartridges about so carelessly," he remarked at length, as he put it back in the case. "It was throwing temptation in somebody's way, don't you think?"

Mr Murch shook his head. "There isn't really much to lay hold of about the revolver, when you come to think. That particular make of revolver is common enough in England. It was introduced from the States. Half the people who buy a revolver today for self-defence or mischief provide themselves with that make, of that calibre. It is very reliable, and easily carried in the hip pocket. There must be thousands of them in the possession of crooks and honest men. For instance," continued the inspector with an air of unconcern, "Manderson himself had one, the double of this. I found it in one of the top drawers of the desk downstairs, and it's in my overcoat pocket now."

"Aha! so you were going to keep that little detail to yourself."

"I was," said the inspector; "but as you've found one revolver, you may as well know about the other. As I say, neither of them may do us any good. The people in the house—"

Both men started, and the inspector checked his speech abruptly, as the half-closed door of the bedroom was slowly pushed open, and a man stood in the doorway. His eyes turned from the pistol in its open case to the faces of Trent and the inspector. They, who had not heard a sound to herald this entrance, simultaneously looked at his long, narrow feet. He wore rubber-soled tennis shoes.

"You must be Mr Bunner," said Trent.

6

MR BUNNER ON THE CASE

"Calvin C. Bunnek, at your service," amended the new-comer, with a touch of punctilio, as he removed an unlighted cigar from his mouth. He was used to finding Englishmen slow and ceremonious with strangers, and Trent's quick remark plainly disconcerted him a little. "You are Mr Trent, I expect," he went on. "Mrs Manderson was telling me a while ago. Captain, good morning." Mr Murch acknowledged the outlandish greeting with a nod. "I was coming up to my room, and I heard a strange voice in here, so I thought I would take a look in." Mr Bunner laughed easily. "You thought I might have been eavesdropping, perhaps," he said. "No, sir; I heard a word or two about a pistol—this one, I guess—and that's all."

Mr Bunner was a thin, rather short young man with a shaven, pale, bony, almost girlish face, and large, dark, intelligent eyes. His waving dark hair was parted in the middle. His lips, usually occupied with a cigar, in its absence were always half-open with a curious expression as of permanent eagerness. By smoking or chewing a cigar this expression was banished, and Mr Bunner then looked the consummately cool and sagacious Yankee that he was.

Born in Connecticut, he had gone into a broker's office on leaving college, and had attracted the notice of Manderson, whose business with his firm he had often handled. The Colossus had watched him for some time, and at length offered him the post of private secretary. Mr Bunner was a pattern business man, trustworthy, long-headed, methodical, and accurate. Manderson could have found many men with those virtues; but he engaged Mr Bunner because he was also swift and secret, and had besides a singular natural instinct in regard to the movements of the stock market.

Trent and the American measured one another coolly with their eyes. Both appeared satisfied with what they saw. "I was having it explained to me," said Trent pleasantly, "that my discovery of a pistol that might have shot Manderson does not amount to very much. I am told it is a favourite weapon among your people, and has become quite popular over here."

Mr Bunner stretched out a bony hand and took the pistol from its case. "Yes, sir," he said, handling it with an air of familiarity; "the captain is right. This is what we call out home a Little Arthur, and I dare say there are duplicates of it in ten thousand hip pockets this minute. I consider it rather too light in the hand myself," Mr Bunner went on, mechanically feeling under the tail of his jacket, and producing an ugly-looking weapon. "Feel of that, now, Mr Trent—it's loaded, by the way. Now this Little Arthur—Marlowe bought it just before we came over this year to please the old man. Manderson said it was ridiculous for a man to be without a pistol in the twentieth century. So he went out and bought what they offered him, I guess—never consulted me. Not but what it's a good gun," Mr Bunner conceded, squinting along the sights. "Marlowe was poor with it at first, but I've coached him some in the last month or so, and he's practised until he is pretty good. But he never could get the habit of carrying it around. Why, it's as natural to me as wearing my pants. I have packed one for some years now, because there was always likely to be somebody laying for Manderson. And now," Mr Bunner concluded sadly, "they got him when I wasn't around. Well, gentlemen, you must excuse me. I am going into Bishopsbridge. There is a lot to do these days, and I have to send off a bunch of cables big enough to choke a cow."

"I must be off too," said Trent. "I have an appointment at the Three Tuns Inn."

"Let me give you a lift in the automobile," said Mr Bunner cordially. "I go right by that joint. Say, Cap, are you coming my way too? No? Then come along, Mr Trent, and help me get out the car. The chauffeur is out of action, and we have to do 'most everything ourselves except clean the dirt off her."

Still tirelessly talking in his measured drawl, Mr Bunner led Trent downstairs and through the house to the garage at the back. It stood at a little distance from the house, and made a cool retreat from the blaze of the midday sun.

Mr Bunner seemed to be in no hurry to get out the car. He offered Trent a cigar, which was accepted, and for the first time lit his own. Then he seated himself on the footboard of the car, his thin hands clasped between his knees, and looked keenly at the other.

"See here, Mr Trent," he said, after a few moments. "There are some things I can tell you that may be useful to you. I know your record. You are a smart man, and I like dealing with smart men. I don't know if I have that detective sized up right, but he strikes me as a mutt. I would answer any questions he had the gumption to ask me—I have done so, in fact—but I don't feel encouraged to give him any notions of mine without his asking. See?"

Trent nodded. "That is a feeling many people have in the presence of our police," he said. "It's the official manner, I suppose. But let me tell you, Murch is anything but what you think. He is one of the shrewdest officers in Europe. He is not very quick with his mind, but he is very sure. And his experience is immense. My forte is imagination, but I assure you in police work experience outweighs it by a great deal."

"Outweighs nothing!" replied Mr Bunner crisply. "This is no ordinary case, Mr Trent. I will tell you one reason why. I believe the old man knew there was something coming to him. Another thing: I believe it was something he thought he couldn't dodge."

Trent pulled a crate opposite to Mr Bunner's place on the footboard and seated himself. "This sounds like business," he said. "Tell me your ideas."

"I say what I do because of the change in the old man's manner this last few weeks. I dare say you have heard, Mr Trent, that he was a man who always kept himself well in hand. That was so. I have always considered him the coolest and hardest head in business. That man's calm was just deadly—I never saw anything to beat it. And I knew Manderson as nobody else did. I was with him in the work he really lived for. I guess I knew him a heap better than his wife did, poor woman. I knew him better than Marlowe could—he never saw Manderson in his office when there was a big thing on. I knew him better than any of his friends."

"Had he any friends?" interjected Trent.

Mr Bunner glanced at him sharply. "Somebody has been putting you next, I see that," he remarked. "No: properly speaking, I should say not. He had many acquaintances among the big men, people he saw 'most every day; they would even go yachting or hunting together. But I don't believe there ever was a man that Manderson opened a corner of his heart to. But what I was going to say was this. Some months ago the old man began to get like I never knew him before—gloomy and sullen, just as if he was everlastingly brooding over something bad, something that he couldn't fix. This went on without any break; it was the same downtown as it was up home, he acted just as if there was something lying heavy on his mind. But it wasn't until a few weeks back that his self-restraint began to go; and let me tell you this, Mr Trent"—the American laid his bony claw on the other's knee—"I'm the only man that knows it. With everyone else he would be just morose and dull; but when he was alone with me in his office, or anywhere where we would be working together, if the least little thing went wrong, by George! he would fly off the handle to beat the Dutch. In this library here I have seen him open a letter with something that didn't just suit him in it, and he would rip around and carry on like an Indian, saying he wished he had the man that wrote it here, he wouldn't do a thing to him, and so on, till it was just pitiful. I never saw such a change. And here's another thing. For a week before he died Manderson neglected his work, for the first time in my experience. He wouldn't answer a letter or a cable, though things looked like going all to pieces over there. I supposed that this anxiety of his, whatever it was, had got on to his nerves till they were worn out. Once I advised him to see a doctor, and he told me to go to hell. But nobody saw this side of him but me. If he was having one of these rages in the library here, for example, and Mrs Manderson would come into the room, he would be all calm and cold again in an instant."

"And you put this down to some secret anxiety, a fear that somebody had designs on his life?" asked Trent.

The American nodded.

"I suppose," Trent resumed, "you had considered the idea of there being something wrong with his mind—a break-down from overstrain, say. That is the first thought that your account suggests to me. Besides, it is what sometimes happens to your big business men in America, isn't it? That is the impression one gets from the newspapers."

"Don't let them slip you any of that bunk," said Mr Bunner earnestly. "It's only the ones who have got rich too quick, and can't make good, who go crazy. Think of all our really big men—the men anywhere near Manderson's size: did you ever hear of any one of them losing his senses? They don't do it—believe me. I know they say every man has his loco point," Mr Bunner added reflectively, "but that doesn't mean genuine, sure-enough craziness; it just means some personal eccentricity in a man... like hating cats... or my own weakness of not being able to touch any kind of fish-food."

"Well, what was Manderson's?"

"He was full of them—the old man. There was his objection to all the unnecessary fuss and luxury that wealthy people don't kick at much, as a general rule. He didn't have any use for expensive trifles and ornaments. He wouldn't have anybody do little things for him; he hated to have servants tag around after him unless he wanted them. And although Manderson was as careful about his clothes as any man I ever knew, and his shoes—well, sir, the amount of money he spent on shoes was sinful—in spite of that, I tell you, he never had a valet. He never liked to have anybody touch him. All his life nobody ever shaved him."

"I've heard something of that," Trent remarked. "Why was it, do you think?"

"Well," Mr Bunner answered slowly, "it was the Manderson habit of mind, I guess; a sort of temper of general suspicion and jealousy. They say his father and grandfather were just the same... Like a dog with a bone, you know, acting as if all the rest of creation was laying for a chance to steal it. He didn't really think the barber would start in to saw his head off; he just felt there was a possibility that he might, and he was taking no risks. Then again in business he was always convinced that somebody else was after his bone—which was true enough a good deal of the time; but not all the time. The consequence of that was that the old man was the most cautious and secret worker in the world of finance; and that had a lot to do with his success, too... But that doesn't amount to being a lunatic, Mr Trent; not by a long way. You ask me if Manderson was losing his mind before he died. I say I believe he was just worn out with worrying over something, and was losing his nerve."

Trent smoked thoughtfully. He wondered how much Mr Bunner knew of the domestic difficulty in his chief's household, and decided to put out a feeler. "I understood that he had trouble with his wife."

"Sure," replied Mr Bunner. "But do you suppose a thing like that was going to upset Sig Manderson that way? No, sir! He was a sight too big a man to be all broken up by any worry of that kind."

Trent looked half-incredulously into the eyes of the young man. But behind all their shrewdness and intensity he saw *a* massive innocence. Mr Bunner really believed a serious breach between husband and wife to be a minor source of trouble for a big man.

"What was the trouble between them, anyhow?" Trent inquired.

"You can search me," Mr Bunner replied briefly. He puffed at his cigar. "Marlowe and I have often talked about it, and we could never make out a solution. I had a notion at first," said Mr Bunner in a lower voice, leaning forward, "that the old man was disappointed and vexed because he had expected a child; but Marlowe told me that the disappointment on that score was the other way around, likely as not. His idea was all right, I guess; he gathered it from something said by Mrs Manderson's French maid."

Trent looked up at him quickly. "Celestine!" he said; and his thought was, "So that was what she was getting at!"

Mr Bunner misunderstood his glance. "Don't you think I'm giving a man away, Mr Trent," he said. "Marlowe isn't that kind. Celestine just took a fancy to him because he talks French like a native, and she would always be holding him up for a gossip. French servants are quite unlike English that way. And servant or no servant," added Mr Bunner with emphasis, "I don't see how a woman could mention such a subject to a man. But the French beat me." He shook his head slowly.

"But to come back to what you were telling me just now," Trent said. "You believe that Manderson was going in terror of his life for some time. Who should threaten it? I am quite in the dark."

"Terror—I don't know," replied Mr Bunner meditatively. "Anxiety, if you like. Or suspense—that's rather my idea of it. The old man was hard to terrify, anyway; and more than that, he wasn't taking any precautions—he was actually avoiding them. It looked more like he was asking for a quick finish—supposing there's any truth in my idea. Why, he would sit in that library window, nights, looking out into the dark, with his white shirt just a target for anybody's gun. As for who should threaten his life—well, sir," said Mr Bunner with a faint smile, "it's certain you have not lived in the States. To take the Pennsylvania coal hold-up alone, there were thirty thousand men, with women and children to keep, who would have jumped at the chance of drilling a hole through the man who fixed it so that they must starve or give in to his terms. Thirty thousand of the toughest aliens in the country, Mr Trent. There's a type of desperado you find in that kind of push who has been known to lay for a man for years, and kill him when he had forgotten what he did. They have been known to dynamite a man in Idaho who had done them dirt in New Jersey ten years before. Do you suppose the Atlantic is going to stop them? ... It takes some sand, I tell you, to be a big business man in our country. No, sir: the old man knew—had always known—that there was a whole crowd of dangerous men scattered up and down the States who had it in for him. My belief is that he had somehow got to know that some of them were definitely after him at last. What licks me altogether is why he should have just laid himself open to them the way he did—why he never tried to dodge, but walked right down into the garden yesterday morning to be shot at."

Mr Bunner ceased to speak, and for a little while both men sat with wrinkled brows, faint blue vapours rising from their cigars. Then Trent rose. "Your theory is quite fresh to me," he said. "It's perfectly rational, and it's only a question of whether it fits all the facts. I mustn't give away what I'm doing for my newspaper, Mr Bunner, but I will say this: I have already satisfied myself that this was a premeditated crime, and an extraordinarily cunning one at that. I'm deeply obliged to you. We must talk it over again." He looked at his watch. I have been expected for some time by my friend. Shall we make a move?"

"Two o'clock," said Mr Bunner, consulting his own, as he got up from the footboard. "Ten a.m. in little old New York. You don't know Wall Street, Mr Trent. Let's you and I hope we never see anything nearer hell than what's loose in the Street this minute."

7

THE LADY IN BLACK

The sea broke raging upon the foot of the cliff under a good breeze; the sun flooded the land with life from a dappled blue sky. In this perfection of English weather Trent, who had slept ill, went down before eight o'clock to a pool among the rocks, the direction of which had been given him, and dived deep into clear water. Between vast gray boulders he swam out to the tossing open, forced himself some little way against a coastwise current, and then returned to his refuge battered and refreshed. Ten minutes later he was scaling the cliff again, and his mind, cleared for the moment of a heavy disgust for the affair he had in hand, was turning over his plans for the morning.

It was the day of the inquest, the day after his arrival in the place. He had carried matters not much farther after parting with the American on the road to Bishopsbridge. In the afternoon he had walked from the inn into the town, accompanied by Mr Cupples, and had there made certain purchases at a chemist's shop, conferred privately for some time with a photographer, sent off a reply-paid telegram, and made an inquiry at the telephone exchange. He had said but little about the case to Mr Cupples, who seemed incurious on his side, and nothing at all about the results of his investigation or the steps he was about to take. After their return from Bishopsbridge,

Trent had written a long dispatch for the *Record* and sent it to be telegraphed by the proud hands of the paper's local representative. He had afterwards dined with Mr Cupples, and had spent the rest of the evening in meditative solitude on the veranda.

This morning as he scaled the cliff he told himself that he had never taken up a case he liked so little, or which absorbed him so much. The more he contemplated it in the golden sunshine of this new day, the more evil and the more challenging it appeared. All that he suspected and all that he almost knew had occupied his questing brain for hours to the exclusion of sleep; and in this glorious light and air, though washed in body and spirit by the fierce purity of the sea, he only saw the more clearly the darkness of the guilt in which he believed, and was more bitterly repelled by the motive at which he guessed. But now at least his zeal was awake again, and the sense of the hunt quickened. He would neither slacken nor spare; here need be no compunction. In the course of the day, he hoped, his net would be complete. He had work to do in the morning; and with very vivid expectancy, though not much serious hope, he awaited the answer to the telegram which he had shot into the sky, as it were, the day before.

The path back to the hotel wound for some way along the top of the cliff, and on nearing a spot he had marked from the sea level, where the face had fallen away long ago, he approached the edge and looked down, hoping to follow with his eyes the most delicately beautiful of all the movements of water—the wash of a light sea over broken rock. But no rock was there. A few feet below him a broad ledge stood out, a rough platform as large as a great room, thickly grown with wiry grass and walled in steeply on three sides. There, close to the verge where the cliff at last dropped sheer, a woman was sitting, her arms about her drawn-up knees, her eyes fixed on the trailing smoke of a distant liner, her face full of some dream.

This woman seemed to Trent, whose training had taught him to live in his eyes, to make the most beautiful picture he had ever seen. Her face of southern pallor, touched by the kiss of the wind with colour on the cheek, presented to him a profile of delicate regularity in which there was nothing hard; nevertheless the black brows bending down toward the point where they almost met gave her in repose a look of something like severity, strangely redeemed by the open curves of the mouth. Trent said to himself that the absurdity or otherwise of a lover writing sonnets to his mistress's eyebrow depended after all on the quality of the eyebrow. Her nose was of the straight and fine sort, exquisitely escaping the perdition of too much length, which makes a conscientious mind ashamed that it cannot help, on occasion, admiring the tip- tilted. Her hat lay pinned to the grass beside her, and the lively breeze played with her thick dark hair, blowing backward the two broad bandeaux that should have covered much of her forehead, and agitating a hundred tiny curls from the mass gathered at her nape. Everything about this lady was black, from her shoes of suede to the hat that she had discarded; lustreless black covered her to her bare throat. All she wore was fine and well put on. Dreamy and delicate of spirit as her looks declared her, it was very plain that she was long-practised as only a woman grown can be in dressing well, the oldest of the arts, and had her touch of primal joy in the excellence of the body that was so admirably curved now in the attitude of embraced knees. With the suggestion of French taste in her clothes, she made a very modern figure seated there, until one looked at her face and saw the glow and triumph of all vigorous beings that ever faced sun and wind and sea together in the prime of the year. One saw, too, a womanhood so unmixed and vigorous, so unconsciously sure of itself, as scarcely to be English, still less American.

Trent, who had halted only for a moment in the surprise of seeing the woman in black, had passed by on the cliff above her, perceiving and feeling as he went the things set down. At all times his keen vision and active brain took in and tasted details with an easy swiftness that was marvellous to men of slower chemistry; the need to stare, he held, was evidence of blindness. Now the feeling of beauty was awakened and exultant, and doubled the power of his sense. In these instants a picture was printed on his memory that would never pass away.

As he went by unheard on the turf the woman, still alone with her thoughts, suddenly moved. She unclasped her long hands from about her knees, stretched her limbs and body with feline grace, then slowly raised her head and extended her arms with open, curving fingers, as if to gather to her all the glory and overwhelming sanity of the morning. This was a gesture not to be mistaken: it was a gesture of freedom, the movement of a soul's resolution to be, to possess, to go forward, perhaps to enjoy.

So he saw her for an instant as he passed, and he did not turn. He knew suddenly who the woman must be, and it was as if a curtain of gloom were drawn between him and the splendour of the day.

* * *

During breakfast at the hotel Mr Cupples found Trent little inclined to talk. He excused himself on the plea of a restless night. Mr Cupples, on the other hand, was in a state of birdlike alertness. The prospect of the inquest seemed to enliven him. He entertained Trent with a disquisition upon the history of that most ancient and once busy tribunal, the coroner's court, and remarked upon the enviable freedom of its procedure from the shackles of rule and precedent. From this he passed to the case that was to come before it that morning.

"Young Bunner mentioned to me last night," he said, "when I went up there after dinner, the hypothesis which he puts forward in regard to the crime. A very remarkable young man, Trent. His meaning is occasionally obscure, but in my opinion he is gifted with a clear-headed knowledge of the world quite unusual in one of his apparent age. Indeed, his promotion by Manderson to the position of his principal lieutenant speaks for itself. He seems to have assumed with perfect confidence the control at this end of the wire, as he expresses it, of the complicated business situation caused by the death of his principal, and he has advised very wisely as to the steps I should take on Mabel's behalf, and the best course for her to pursue until effect has been given to the provisions of the will. I was accordingly less disposed than I might otherwise have been to regard his suggestion of an industrial vendetta as far-fetched. When I questioned him he was able to describe a number of cases in which attacks of one sort or another—too often successful—had been made upon the lives of persons who had incurred the hostility of powerful labour organizations. This is a terrible time in which we live, my dear boy. There is none recorded in history, I think, in which the disproportion between the material and the moral constituents of society has been so great or so menacing to the permanence of the fabric. But nowhere, in my judgment, is the prospect so dark as it is in the United States."

"I thought," said Trent listlessly, "that Puritanism was about as strong there as the money-getting craze."

"Your remark," answered Mr Cupples, with as near an approach to humour as was possible to him, "is not in the nature of a testimonial to what you call Puritanism—a convenient rather than an accurate term; for I need not remind you that it was invented to describe an Anglican party which aimed at the purging of the services and ritual of their Church from certain elements repugnant to them. The sense of your observation, however, is none the less sound, and its truth is extremely well illustrated by the case of Manderson himself, who had, I believe, the virtues of purity, abstinence, and self-restraint in their strongest form. No, Trent, there are other and more worthy things among the moral constituents of which I spoke; and in our finite nature, the more we preoccupy ourselves with the bewildering complexity of external apparatus which science places in our hands, the less vigour have we left for the development of the holier purposes of humanity within us. Agricultural machinery has abolished the festival of the Harvest Home. Mechanical travel has abolished the inn, or all that was best in it. I need not multiply instances. The view I am expressing to you," pursued Mr Cupples, placidly buttering a piece of toast, "is regarded as fundamentally erroneous by many of those who think generally as I do about the deeper concerns of life, but I am nevertheless firmly persuaded of its truth."

"It needs epigrammatic expression," said Trent, rising from the table. "If only it could be crystallized into some handy formula, like 'No Popery,' or 'Tax the Foreigner,' you would find multitudes to go to the stake for it. But you are planning to go to White Gables before the inquest, I think. You ought to be off, if you are to get back to the court in time. I have something to attend to there myself, so we might walk up together. I will just go and get my camera."

"By all means," Mr Cupples answered; and they set off at once in the ever-growing warmth of the morning. The roof of White Gables, a surly patch of dull red against the dark trees, seemed to harmonize with Trent's mood; he felt heavy, sinister, and troubled. If a blow must fall that might strike down that creature radiant of beauty and life whom he had seen that morning, he did not wish it to come from his hand. An exaggerated chivalry had lived in Trent since the first teachings of his mother; but at this moment the horror of bruising anything so lovely was almost as much the artist's revulsion as the gentleman's. On the other hand, was the hunt to end in nothing? The quality of the affair was such that the thought of forbearance was an agony. There never was such a case; and he alone, he was confident, held the truth of it under his hand. At least, he determined, that day should show whether what he believed was a delusion. He would trample his compunction underfoot until he was quite sure that there was any call for it. That same morning he would know.

As they entered at the gate of the drive they saw Marlowe and the American standing in talk before the front door. In the shadow of the porch was the lady in black.

She saw them, and came gravely forward over the lawn, moving as Trent had known that she would move, erect and balanced, stepping lightly. When she welcomed him on Mr Cupples's presentation her eyes of golden-flecked brown observed him kindly. In her pale composure, worn as the mask of distress, there was no trace of the emotion that had seemed a halo about her head on the ledge of the cliff. She spoke the appropriate commonplace in a low and even voice. After a few words to Mr Cupples she turned her eyes on Trent again.

"I hope you will succeed," she said earnestly. "Do you think you will succeed?"

He made his mind up as the words left her lips. He said, "I believe I shall do so, Mrs Manderson. When I have the case sufficiently complete I shall ask you to let me see you and tell you about it. It may be necessary to consult you before the facts are published."

She looked puzzled, and distress showed for an instant in her eyes. "If it is necessary, of course you shall do so," she said.

On the brink of his next speech Trent hesitated. He remembered that the lady had not wished to repeat to him the story already given to the inspector—or to be questioned at all. He was not unconscious that he desired to hear her voice and watch her face a little longer, if it might be; but the matter he had to mention really troubled his mind, it was a queer thing that fitted nowhere into the pattern within whose corners he had by this time brought the other queer things in the case. It was very possible that she could explain it away in a breath; it was unlikely that anyone else could. He summoned his resolution.

"You have been so kind," he said, "in allowing me access to the house and every opportunity of studying the case, that I am going to ask leave to put a question or two to yourself—nothing that you would rather not-answer, I think. May I?"

She glanced at him wearily. "It would be stupid of me to refuse. Ask your questions, Mr Trent."

"It's only this," said Trent hurriedly. "We know that your husband lately drew an unusually large sum of ready money from his London bankers, and was keeping it here. It is here now, in fact. Have you any idea why he should have done that?"

She opened her eyes in astonishment. "I cannot imagine," she said. "I did not know he had done so. I am very much surprised to hear it."

"Why is it surprising?"

"I thought my husband had very little money in the house. On Sunday night, just before he went out in the motor, he came into the drawing-room where I was sitting. He seemed to be irritated about something, and asked me at once if I had any notes or gold I could let him have until next day. I was surprised at that, because he was never without money; he made it a rule to carry a hundred pounds or so about him always in a note-case. I unlocked my escritoire, and gave him all I had by me. It was nearly thirty pounds."

"And he did not tell you why he wanted it?"

"No. He put it in his pocket, and then said that Mr Marlowe had persuaded him to go for a run in the motor by moonlight, and he thought it might help him to sleep. He had been sleeping badly, as perhaps you know. Then he went off with Mr Marlowe. I thought it odd he should need money on Sunday night, but I soon forgot about it. I never remembered it again until now."

"It was curious, certainly," said Trent, staring into the distance. Mr Cupples began to speak to his niece of the arrangements for the inquest, and Trent moved away to where Marlowe was pacing slowly upon the lawn. The young man seemed relieved to talk about the coming business of the day. Though he still seemed tired out and nervous, he showed himself not without a quiet humour in describing the pomposities of the local police and the portentous airs of Dr. Stock. Trent turned the conversation gradually toward the problem of the crime, and all Marlowe's gravity returned.

"Bunner has told me what he thinks," he said when Trent referred to the American's theory. "I don't find myself convinced by it, because it doesn't really explain some of the oddest facts. But I have lived long enough in the United States to know that such a stroke of revenge, done in a secret, melodramatic way, is not an unlikely thing. It is quite a characteristic feature of certain sections of the labour movement there. Americans have a taste and a talent for that sort of business. Do you know *Huckleberry Finn?*"

"Do I know my own name?" exclaimed Trent.

"Well, I think the most American thing in that great American epic is Tom Sawyer's elaboration of an extremely difficult and romantic scheme, taking days to carry out, for securing the escape of the nigger Jim, which could have been managed quite easily in twenty minutes. You know how fond they are of lodges and brotherhoods. Every college club has its secret signs and handgrips. You've heard of the Know-Nothing movement in politics, I dare say, and the Ku Klux Klan. Then look at Brigham Young's penny-dreadful tyranny in Utah, with real blood. The founders of the Mormon State were of the purest Yankee stock in America; and you know what they did. It's all part of the same mental tendency. Americans make fun of it among themselves. For my part, I take it very seriously."

"It can have a very hideous side to it, certainly," said Trent, "when you get it in connection with crime—or with vice—or even mere luxury. But I have a sort of sneaking respect for the determination to make life interesting and lively in spite of civilization. To return to the matter in hand, however; has it struck you as a possibility that Manderson's mind was affected to some extent by this menace that Bunner believes in? For instance, it was rather an extraordinary thing to send you posting off like that in the middle of the night."

"About ten o'clock, to be exact," replied Marlowe. "Though, mind you, if he'd actually roused me out of my bed at midnight I shouldn't have been very much surprised. It all chimes in with what we've just been saying. Manderson had a strong streak of the national taste for dramatic proceedings. He was rather fond of his well-earned reputation for unexpected strokes and for going for his object with ruthless directness through every opposing consideration. He had decided suddenly that he wanted to have word from this man Harris—"

"Who is Harris?" interjected Trent.

"Nobody knows. Even Bunner never heard of him, and can't imagine what the business in hand was. All I know is that when I went up to London last week to attend to various things I booked a deck-cabin, at Manderson's request, for a Mr George Harris on the boat that sailed on Monday. It seems that Manderson suddenly found he wanted news from Harris which presumably was of a character too secret for the telegraph; and there was no train that served; so I was sent off as you know."

Trent looked round to make sure that they were not overheard, then faced the other gravely. "There is one thing I may tell you," he said quietly, "that I don't think you know. Martin the butler caught a few words at the end of your conversation with Manderson in the orchard before you started with him in the car. He heard him say, 'If Harris is there, every moment is of importance.' Now, Mr Marlowe, you know my business here. I am sent to make inquiries, and you mustn't take offence. I want to ask you if, in the face of that sentence, you will repeat that you know nothing of what the business was."

Marlowe shook his head. "I know nothing, indeed. I'm not easily offended, and your question is quite fair. What passed during that conversation I have already told the detective. Manderson plainly said to me that he could not tell me what it was all about. He simply wanted me to find Harris, tell him that he desired to know how matters stood, and bring back a letter or message from him. Harris, I was further told, might not turn up. If he did, 'every moment was of importance.' And now you know as much as I do."

"That talk took place before he told his wife that you were taking him for a moonlight run. Why did he conceal your errand in that way, I wonder?"

The young man made a gesture of helplessness. "Why? I can guess no better than you."

"Why," muttered Trent as if to himself, gazing on the ground, "did he conceal it—from Mrs Manderson?" He looked up at Marlowe.

"And from Martin," the other amended coolly. "He was told the same thing."

With a sudden movement of his head Trent seemed to dismiss the subject. He drew from his breast pocket a letter-case, and thence extracted two small leaves of clean, fresh paper.

"Just look at these two slips, Mr Marlowe," he said. "Did you ever see them before? Have you any idea where they come from?" he added as Marlowe took one in each hand and examined them curiously.

"They seem to have been cut with a knife or scissors from a small diary for this year—from the October pages," Marlowe observed, looking them over on both sides. "I see no writing of any kind on them. Nobody here has any such diary so far as I know. What about them?"

"There may be nothing in it," Trent said dubiously. "Anyone in the house, of course, might have such a diary without you having seen it. But I didn't much expect you would be able to identify the leaves—in fact, I should have been surprised if you had."

He stopped speaking as Mrs Manderson came towards them. "My uncle thinks we should be going now," she said.

"I think I will walk on with Mr Bunner," Mr Cupples said as he joined them. "There are certain business matters that must be disposed of as soon as possible. Will you come on with these two gentlemen, Mabel? We will wait for you before we reach the place."

Trent turned to her. "Mrs Manderson will excuse me, I hope," he said. "I really came up this morning in order to look about me here for some indications I thought I might possibly find. I had not thought of attending the—the court just yet."

She looked at him with eyes of perfect candour. "Of course, Mr Trent. Please do exactly as you wish. We are all relying upon you. If you will wait a few moments, Mr Marlowe, I shall be ready."

She entered the house. Her uncle and the American had already strolled towards the gate.

Trent looked into the eyes of his companion. "That is a wonderful woman," he said in a lowered voice.

"You say so without knowing her," replied Marlowe in a similar tone. "She is more than that."

Trent said nothing to this. He stared out over the fields towards the sea. In the silence a noise of hobnailed haste rose on the still air. A little distance down the road a boy appeared trotting towards them from the direction of the hotel. In his hand was the orange envelope, unmistakable afar off, of a telegram. Trent watched him with an indifferent eye as he met and passed the two others. Then he turned to Marlowe. "Apropos of nothing in particular," he said, "were you at Oxford?"

"Yes," said the young man. "Why do you ask?"

"I just wondered if I was right in my guess. It's one of the things you can very often tell about a man, isn't it?"

"I suppose so," Marlowe said. "Well, each of us is marked in one way or another, perhaps. I should have said you were an artist, if I hadn't known it."

"Why? Does my hair want cutting?"

"Oh, no! It's only that you look at things and people as I've seen artists do, with an eye that moves steadily from detail to detail—rather looking them over than looking at them."

The boy came up panting. "Telegram for you, sir," he said to Trent. "Just come, sir."

Trent tore open the envelope with an apology, and his eyes lighted up so visibly as he read the slip that Marlowe's tired face softened in a smile.

"It must be good news," he murmured half to himself.

Trent turned on him a glance in which nothing could be read. "Not exactly news," he said. "It only tells me that another little guess of mine was a good one."

8

THE INQUEST

The coroner, who fully realized that for that one day of his life as a provincial solicitor he was living in the gaze of the world, had resolved to be worthy of the fleeting eminence. He was a large man of jovial temper, with a strong interest in the dramatic aspects of his work, and the news of Manderson's mysterious death within his jurisdiction had made him the happiest coroner in England. A respectable capacity for marshalling facts was fortified in him by a copiousness of impressive language that made juries as clay in his hands, and sometimes disguised a doubtful interpretation of the rules of evidence.

The court was held in a long, unfurnished room lately built on to the hotel, and intended to serve as a ball-room or concert-hall. A regiment of reporters was entrenched in the front seats, and those who were to be called on to give evidence occupied chairs to one side of the table behind which the coroner sat, while the jury, in double row, with plastered hair and a spurious ease of manner, flanked him on the other side. An undistinguished public filled the rest of the space, and listened, in an awed silence, to the opening solemnities. The newspaper men, well used to these, muttered among themselves. Those of them who knew Trent by sight assured the rest that he was not in the court.

The identity of the dead man was proved by his wife, the first witness called, from whom the coroner, after some inquiry into the health and circumstances of the deceased, proceeded to draw an account of the last occasion on which she had seen her husband alive. Mrs Manderson was taken through her evidence by the coroner with the sympathy which every man felt for that dark figure of grief. She lifted her thick veil before beginning to speak, and the extreme paleness and unbroken composure of the lady produced a singular impression. This was not an impression of hardness. Interesting femininity was the first thing to be felt in her presence. She was not even enigmatic. It was only clear that the force of a powerful character was at work to master the emotions of her situation. Once or twice as she spoke she touched her eyes with her handkerchief, but her voice was low and clear to the end.

Her husband, she said, had come up to his bedroom about his usual hour for retiring on Sunday night. His room was really a dressing-room attached to her own bedroom, communicating with it by a door which was usually kept open during the night. Both dressing-room and bedroom were entered by other doors giving on the passage. Her husband had always had a preference for the greatest simplicity in his bedroom arrangements, and liked to sleep in a small room. She had not been awake when he came up, but had been half-aroused, as usually happened, when the light was switched on in her husband's room. She had spoken to him. She had no clear recollection of what she had said, as she had been very drowsy at the time; but she had remembered that he had been out for a moonlight run in the car, and she believed she had asked whether he had had a good run, and what time it was. She had asked what the time was because she felt as if she had only been a very short time asleep, and she had expected her husband to be out very late. In answer to her question he had told her it was half-past eleven, and had gone on to say that he had changed his mind about going for a run.

"Did he say why?" the coroner asked.

"Yes," replied the lady, "he did explain why. I remember very well what he said, because—" she stopped with a little appearance of confusion.

"Because—" the coroner insisted gently.

"Because my husband was not as a rule communicative about his business affairs," answered the witness, raising her chin with a faint touch of defiance. "He did not—did not think they would interest me, and as a rule referred to them as little as possible. That was why I was rather surprised when he told me that he had sent Mr Marlowe to Southampton to bring back some important information from a man who was leaving for Paris by the next day's boat. He said that Mr Marlowe could do it quite easily if he had no accident. He said that he had started in the car, and then walked back home a mile or so, and felt all the better for it."

"Did he say any more?"

"Nothing, as well as I remember," the witness said. "I was very sleepy, and I dropped off again in a few moments. I just remember my husband turning his light out, and that is all. I never saw him again alive."

"And you heard nothing in the night?"

"No: I never woke until my maid brought my tea in the morning at seven o'clock. She closed the door leading to my husband's room, as she always did, and I supposed him to be still there. He always needed a great deal of sleep. He sometimes slept until quite late in the morning. I had breakfast in my sitting-room. It was about ten when I heard that my husband's body had been found." The witness dropped her head and silently waited for her dismissal.

But it was not to be yet.

"Mrs Manderson." The coroner's voice was sympathetic, but it had a hint of firmness in it now. "The question I am going to put to you must, in these sad circumstances, be a painful one;

but it is my duty to ask it. Is it the fact that your relations with your late husband had not been, for some time past, relations of mutual affection and confidence? Is it the fact that there was an estrangement between you?"

The lady drew herself up again and faced her questioner, the colour rising in her cheeks. "If that question is necessary," she said with cold distinctness, "I will answer it so that there shall be no misunderstanding. During the last few months of my husband's life his attitude towards me had given me a great deal of anxiety and sorrow. He had changed towards me; he had become very reserved, and seemed mistrustful. I saw much less of him than before; he seemed to prefer to be alone. I can give no explanation at all of the change. I tried to work against it; I did all I could with justice to my own dignity, as I thought. Something was between us, I did not know what, and he never told me. My own obstinate pride prevented me from asking what it was in so many words; I only made a point of being to him exactly as I had always been, so far as he would allow me. I suppose I shall never know now what it was." The witness, whose voice had trembled in spite of her self-control over the last few sentences, drew down her veil when she had said this, and stood erect and quiet.

One of the jury asked a question, not without obvious hesitation. "Then was there never anything of the nature of what they call words between you and your husband, ma'am?"

"Never." The word was colourlessly spoken; but everyone felt that a crass misunderstanding of the possibilities of conduct in the case of a person like Mrs Manderson had been visited with some severity.

Did she know, the coroner asked, of any other matter which might have been preying upon her husband's mind recently?

Mrs Manderson knew of none whatever. The coroner intimated that her ordeal was at an end, and the veiled lady made her way to the door. The general attention, which followed her for a few moments, was now eagerly directed upon Martin, whom the coroner had proceeded to call.

It was at this moment that Trent appeared at the doorway and edged his way into the great room. But he did not look at Martin. He was observing the well-balanced figure that came quickly toward him along an opening path in the crowd, and his eye was gloomy. He started, as he stood aside from the door with a slight bow, to hear Mrs Manderson address him by name in a low voice. He followed her a pace or two into the hall.

"I wanted to ask you," she said in a voice now weak and oddly broken, "if you would give me your arm a part of the way to the house. I could not see my uncle near the door, and I suddenly felt rather faint... I shall be better in the air... No, no; I cannot stay here—please, Mr Trent!" she said, as he began to make an obvious suggestion. "I must go to the house." Her hand tightened momentarily on his arm as if, for all her weakness, she could drag him from the place; then again she leaned heavily upon it, and with that support, and with bent head, she walked slowly from the hotel and along the oak-shaded path towards White Gables.

Trent went in silence, his thoughts whirling, dancing insanely to a chorus of "Fool! fool!" All that he alone knew, all that he guessed and suspected of this affair, rushed through his brain in a rout; but the touch of her unnerved hand upon his arm never for an instant left his consciousness, filling him with an exaltation that enraged and bewildered him. He was still cursing himself furiously behind the mask of conventional solicitude that he turned to the lady when he had attended her to the house and seen her sink upon a couch in the morning-room. Raising her veil, she thanked him gravely and frankly, with a look of sincere gratitude in her eyes. She was much better now, she said, and a cup of tea would work a miracle upon her. She hoped she had not taken him away from anything important. She was ashamed of herself; she thought she could go through with it, but she had not expected those last questions. "I am glad you did not hear me," she said when he explained. "But of course you will read it all in the reports. It shook me so to have to speak of that," she added simply; "and to keep from making an exhibition of myself took it out of me. And all those staring men by the door! Thank you again for helping me when I asked you... I thought I might," she ended queerly, with a little tired smile; and Trent took himself away, his hand still quivering from the cool touch of her fingers.

The testimony of the servants and of the finder of the body brought nothing new to the reporters' net. That of the police was as colourless and cryptic as is usual at the inquest stage of affairs of the kind. Greatly to the satisfaction of Mr Bunner, his evidence afforded the sensation of the day, and threw far into the background the interesting revelation of domestic difficulty made by the dead man's wife. He told the court in substance what he had already told Trent. The flying pencils did not miss a word of the young American's story, and it appeared with scarcely the omission of a sentence in every journal of importance in Great Britain and the United States.

Public opinion next day took no note of the faint suggestion of the possibility of suicide which the coroner, in his final address to the jury, had thought it right to make in connection with the lady's evidence. The weight of evidence, as the official had indeed pointed out, was against such a theory. He had referred with emphasis to the fact that no weapon had been found near the body.

"This question, of course, is all-important, gentlemen," he had said to the jury. "It is, in fact, the main issue before you. You have seen the body for yourselves. You have just heard the medical evidence; but I think it would be well for me to read you my notes of it in so far as they bear on this point, in order to refresh your memories. Dr. Stock told you—I am going to omit all technical medical language and repeat to you merely the plain English of his testimony—that in his opinion death had taken place six or eight hours previous to the finding of the body. He said that the cause of death was a bullet wound, the bullet having entered the left eye, which was destroyed, and made its way to the base of the brain, which was quite shattered. The external appearance of the wound, he said, did not support the hypothesis of its being self-inflicted, inasmuch as there were no signs of the firearm having been pressed against the eye, or even put very close to it; at the same time it was not physically impossible that the weapon should have been discharged by the deceased with his own hand, at some small distance from the eye. Dr. Stock also told us that it was impossible to say with certainty, from the state of the body, whether any struggle had taken place at the time of death; that when seen by him, at which time he understood that it had not been moved since it was found, the body was lying in a collapsed position such as might very well result from the shot alone; but that the scratches and bruises upon the wrists and the lower part of the arms had been very recently inflicted, and were, in his opinion, marks of violence.

"In connection with this same point, the remarkable evidence given by Mr Bunner cannot be regarded, I think, as without significance. It may have come as a surprise to some of you to hear that risks of the character described by this witness are, in his own country, commonly run by persons in the position of the deceased. On the other hand, it may have been within the knowledge of some of you that in the industrial world of America the discontent of labour often proceeds to lengths of which we in England happily know nothing. I have interrogated the witness somewhat fully upon this. At the same time, gentlemen, I am by no means suggesting that Mr Bunner's personal conjecture as to the cause of death can fitly be adopted by you. That is emphatically not the case. What his evidence does is to raise two questions for your consideration. First, can it be said that the deceased was to any extent in the position of a threatened man—of a man more exposed to the danger of murderous attack than an ordinary person? Second, does the recent alteration in his demeanour, as described by this witness, justify the belief that his last days were overshadowed by a great anxiety? These points may legitimately be considered by you in arriving at a conclusion upon the rest of the evidence."

Thereupon the coroner, having indicated thus clearly his opinion that Mr Bunner had hit the right nail on the head, desired the jury to consider their verdict.

9

A HOT SCENT

"Come in!" called Trent.

Mr Cupples entered his sitting-room at the hotel. It was the early evening of the day on which the coroner's jury, without leaving the box, had pronounced the expected denunciation of a person or persons unknown. Trent, with a hasty glance upward, continued his intent study of what lay in a photographic dish of enamelled metal, which he moved slowly about in the light of the window. He looked very pale, and his movements were nervous.

"Sit on the sofa," he advised. "The chairs are a job lot bought at the sale after the suppression of the Holy Inquisition in Spain. This is a pretty good negative," he went on, holding it up to the light with his head at the angle of discriminating judgment. "Washed enough now, I think. Let us leave it to dry, and get rid of all this mess."

Mr Cupples, as the other busily cleared the table of a confusion of basins, dishes, racks, boxes, and bottles, picked up first one and then another of the objects and studied them with innocent curiosity.

"That is called hypo-eliminator," said Trent, as Mr Cupples uncorked and smelt at one of the bottles. "Very useful when you're in a hurry with a negative. I shouldn't drink it, though, all the same. It eliminates sodium hypophosphite, but I shouldn't wonder if it would eliminate human beings too." He found a place for the last of the litter on the crowded mantelshelf, and came to sit before Mr Cupples on the table. "The great thing about a hotel sittingroom is that its beauty does not distract the mind from work. It is no place for the mayfly pleasures of a mind at ease. Have you ever been in this room before, Cupples? I have, hundreds of times. It has pursued me all over England for years. I should feel lost without it if, in some fantastic, far-off hotel, they were to give me some other sitting-room. Look at this table-cover; there is the ink I spilt on it when I had this room in Halifax. I burnt that hole in the carpet when I had it in Ipswich. But I see they have mended the glass over the picture of 'Silent Sympathy,' which I threw a boot at in Banbury. I do all my best work here. This afternoon, for instance, since the inquest, I have finished several excellent negatives. There is a very good dark-room downstairs."

"The inquest—that reminds me," said Mr Cupples, who knew that this sort of talk in Trent meant the excitement of action, and was wondering what he could be about. "I came in to thank you, my dear fellow, for looking after Mabel this morning. I had no idea she was going to feel ill after leaving the box; she seemed quite unmoved, and, really, she is a woman of such extraordinary self-command, I thought I could leave her to her own devices and hear out the evidence, which I thought it important I should do. It was a very fortunate thing she found a friend to assist her, and she is most grateful. She is quite herself again now."

Trent, with his hands in his pockets and a slight frown on his brow, made no reply to this. "I tell you what," he said after a short pause, "I was just getting to the really interesting part of the job when you came in. Come; would you like to see a little bit of high- class police work? It's the very same kind of work that old Murch ought to be doing at this moment. Perhaps he is; but I hope to glory he isn't." He sprang off the table and disappeared into his bedroom. Presently he came out with a large drawing-board on which a number of heterogeneous objects was ranged.

"First I must introduce you to these little things," he said, setting them out on the table. "Here is a big ivory paper-knife; here are two leaves cut out of a diary—my own diary; here is a bottle containing dentifrice; here is a little case of polished walnut. Some of these things have to be put back where they belong in somebody's bedroom at White Gables before night. That's the sort of man I am—nothing stops me. I borrowed them this very morning when everyone was down at the inquest, and I dare say some people would think it rather an odd proceeding if they knew. Now there remains one object on the board. Can you tell me, without touching it, what it is?"

"Certainly I can," said Mr Cupples, peering at it with great interest. "It is an ordinary glass bowl. It looks like a finger-bowl. I see nothing odd about it," he added after some moments of close scrutiny.

"I can't see much myself," replied Trent, "and that is exactly where the fun comes in. Now take this little fat bottle, Cupples, and pull out the cork. Do you recognize that powder inside it? You have swallowed pounds of it in your time, I expect. They give it to babies. Grey powder is its ordinary name—mercury and chalk. It is great stuff. Now, while I hold the basin sideways over a sheet of paper, I want you to pour a little powder out of the bottle over this part of the bowl—just here... Perfect! Sir Edward Henry himself could not have handled the powder better. You have done this before, Cupples, I can see. You are an old hand."

"I really am not," said Mr Cupples seriously, as Trent returned the fallen powder to the bottle. "I assure you it is all a complete mystery to me. What did I do then?"

"I brush the powdered part of the bowl lightly with this camel- hair brush. Now look at it again. You saw nothing odd about it before. Do you see anything now?"

Mr Cupples peered again. "How curious!" he said. "Yes, there are two large gray fingermarks on the bowl. They were not there before."

"I am Hawkshaw the detective," observed Trent. "Would it interest you to hear a short lecture on the subject of glass fingerbowls? When you take one up with your hand you leave traces upon it, usually practically invisible, which may remain for days or months. You leave the marks of your fingers. The human hand, even when quite clean, is never quite dry, and sometimes—in moments of great anxiety, for instance, Cupples—it is very moist. It leaves a mark on any cold smooth surface it may touch. That bowl was moved by somebody with a rather moist hand quite lately." He sprinkled the powder again. "Here on the other side, you see, is the thumbmark—very good impressions all of them." He spoke without raising his voice, but Mr Cupples could perceive that he was ablaze with excitement as he stared at the faint gray marks. "This one should be the index finger. I need not tell a man of your knowledge of the world that the pattern of it is a single-spiral whorl, with deltas symmetrically disposed. This, the print of the second finger, is a simple loop, with a staple core and fifteen counts. I know there are fifteen, because I have just the same two prints on this negative, which I have examined in detail. Look!"—he held one of the negatives up to the light of the declining sun and demonstrated with a pencil point. "You can see they're the same. You see the bifurcation of that ridge. There it is in the other. You see that little scar near the centre. There it is in the other. There are a score of ridge-characteristics on which an expert would swear in the witness-box that the marks on that bowl and the marks I have photographed on this negative were made by the same hand."

"And where did you photograph them? What does it all mean?" asked Mr Cupples, wide-eyed.

"I found them on the inside of the left-hand leaf of the front window in Mrs Manderson's bedroom. As I could not bring the window with me, I photographed them, sticking a bit of black paper on the other side of the glass for the purpose. The bowl comes from Manderson's room. It is the bowl in which his false teeth were placed at night. I could bring that away, so I did."

"But those cannot be Mabel's fingermarks."

"I should think not!" said Trent with decision. "They are twice the size of any print Mrs Manderson could make."

"Then they must be her husband's."

"Perhaps they are. Now shall we see if we can match them once more? I believe we can." Whistling faintly, and very white in the face, Trent opened another small squat bottle containing a dense black powder. "Lamp-black," he explained. "Hold a bit of paper in your hand for a second or two, and this little chap will show you the pattern of your fingers." He carefully took up with a pair of tweezers one of the leaves cut from his diary, and held it out for the other to examine. No marks appeared on the leaf. He tilted some of the powder out upon one surface of the paper, then, turning it over, upon the other; then shook the leaf gently to rid it of the loose powder. He held it out to Mr Cupples in silence. On one side of the paper appeared unmistakably, clearly printed in black, the same two fingerprints that he had already seen on the bowl and on the photographic plate. He took up the bowl and compared them. Trent turned the paper over, and on the other side was a bold black replica of the thumbmark that was printed gray on the glass in his hand.

"Same man, you see," Trent said with a short laugh. "I felt that it must be so, and now I know." He walked to the window and looked out. "Now I know," he repeated in a low voice, as if to himself. His tone was bitter. Mr Cupples, understanding nothing, stared at his motionless back for a few moments.

"I am still completely in the dark," he ventured presently. "I have often heard of this fingerprint business, and wondered how the police went to work about it. It is of extraordinary interest to me, but upon my life I cannot see how in this case Manderson's fingerprints are going—"

"I am very sorry, Cupples," Trent broke in upon his meditative speech with a swift return to the table. "When I began this investigation I meant to take you with me every step of the way. You mustn't think I have any doubts about your discretion if I say now that I must hold my tongue about the whole thing, at least for a time. I will tell you this: I have come upon a fact that looks too much like having very painful consequences if it is discovered by anyone else." He looked at the other with a hard and darkened face, and struck the table with his hand. "It is terrible for me here and now. Up to this moment I was hoping against hope that I was wrong about the fact. I may still be wrong in the surmise that I base upon that fact. There is only one way of finding out that is open to me, and I must nerve myself to take it." He smiled suddenly at Mr Cupples's face of consternation. "All right—I'm not going to be tragic any more, and I'll tell you all about it when I can. Look here, I'm not half through my game with the powder-bottles yet."

He drew one of the defamed chairs to the table and sat down to test the broad ivory blade of the paper-knife. Mr Cupples, swallowing his amazement, bent forward in an attitude of deep interest and handed Trent the bottle of lamp-black.

10

THE WIFE OF DIVES

Mrs Manderson stood at the window of her sitting-room at White Gables gazing out upon a wavering landscape of fine rain and mist. The weather had broken as it seldom does in that part in June. White wreathings drifted up the fields from the sullen sea; the sky was an unbroken gray deadness shedding pin-point moisture that was now and then blown against the panes with a crepitation of despair. The lady looked out on the dim and chilling prospect with a woeful face. It was a bad day for a woman bereaved, alone, and without a purpose in life.

There was a knock, and she called "Come in," drawing herself up with an unconscious gesture that always came when she realized that the weariness of the world had been gaining upon her spirit. Mr Trent had called, the maid said; he apologized for coming at such an early hour, but hoped that Mrs Manderson would see him on a matter of urgent importance. Mrs Manderson would see Mr Trent. She walked to a mirror, looked into the olive face she saw reflected there, shook her head at herself with the flicker of a grimace, and turned to the door as Trent was shown in.

His appearance, she noted, was changed. He had the jaded look of the sleepless, and a new and reserved expression, in which her quick sensibilities felt something not propitious, took the place of his half smile of fixed good-humour.

"May I come to the point at once?" he said, when she had given him her hand. "There is a train I ought to catch at Bishopsbridge at twelve o'clock, but I cannot go until I have settled this thing, which concerns you only, Mrs Manderson. I have been working half the night and thinking the rest; and I know now what I ought to do."

"You look wretchedly tired," she said kindly. "Won't you sit down? This is a very restful chair. Of course it is about this terrible business and your work as correspondent. Please ask me anything you think I can properly tell you, Mr Trent. I know that you won't make it worse for me than you can help in doing your duty here. If you say you must see me about something, I know it must be because, as you say, you ought to do it."

"Mrs Manderson," said Trent, slowly measuring his words, "I won't make it worse for you than I can help. But I am bound to make it bad for you—only between ourselves, I hope. As to whether you can properly tell me what I shall ask you, you will decide that; but I tell you this on my word of honour: I shall ask you only as much as will decide me whether to publish or to withhold certain grave things that I have found out about your husband's death, things not suspected by anyone else, nor, I think, likely to be so. What I have discovered—what I believe that I have practically proved—will be a great shock to you in any case. But it may be worse for you than that; and if you give me reason to think it would be so, then I shall suppress this manuscript," he laid a long envelope on the small table beside him, "and nothing of what it has to tell shall ever be printed. It consists, I may tell you, of a short private note to my editor, followed by a long dispatch for publication in the Record. Now you may refuse to say anything to me. If you do refuse, my duty to my employers, as I see it, is to take this up to London with me today and leave it with my editor to be dealt with at his discretion. My view is, you understand, that I am not entitled to suppress it on the strength of a mere possibility that presents itself to my imagination. But if I gather from you—and I can gather it from no other person—that there is substance in that imaginary possibility I speak of, then I have only one thing to do as a gentleman and as one who"—he hesitated for a phrase—"wishes you well. I shall not publish that dispatch of mine. In some directions I decline to assist the police. Have you followed me so far?" he asked with a touch of anxiety in his careful coldness; for her face, but for its pallor, gave no sign as she regarded him, her hands clasped before her, and her shoulders drawn back in a pose of rigid calm. She looked precisely as she had looked at the inquest.

"I understand quite well," said Mrs Manderson in a low voice. She drew a deep breath, and went on: "I don't know what dreadful thing you have found out, or what the possibility that has occurred to you can be, but it was good, it was honourable of you to come to me about it. Now will you please tell me?"

"I cannot do that," Trent replied. "The secret is my newspaper's, if it is not yours. If I find it is yours, you shall have my manuscript to read and destroy. Believe me," he broke out with something of his old warmth, "I detest such mystery-making from the bottom of my soul; but it is not I who have made this mystery. This is the most painful hour of my life, and you make it worse by not treating me like a hound. The first thing I ask you to tell me," he reverted with an effort to his colourless tone, "is this: is it true, as you stated at the inquest, that you had no idea at all of the reason why your late husband had changed his attitude toward you, and become mistrustful and reserved, during the last few months of his life?"

Mrs Manderson's dark brows lifted and her eyes flamed; she quickly rose from her chair. Trent got up at the same moment, and took his envelope from the table; his manner said that he perceived the interview to be at an end. But she held up a hand, and there was colour in her cheeks and quick breathing in her voice as she said: "Do you know what you ask, Mr Trent? You ask me if I perjured myself."

"I do," he answered unmoved; and he added after a pause: "You knew already that I had not come here to preserve the polite fictions, Mrs Manderson. The theory that no reputable person, being on oath, could withhold a part of the truth under any circumstances is a polite fiction." He still stood as awaiting dismissal, but she was silent. She walked to the window, and he stood miserably watching the slight movement of her shoulders until it subsided. Then with face averted, looking out on the dismal weather, she spoke at last clearly.

"Mr Trent," she said, "you inspire confidence in people, and I feel that things which I don't want known or talked about are safe with you. And I know you must have a very serious reason for doing what you are doing, though I don't know what it is. I suppose it would be assisting justice in some way if I told you the truth about what you asked just now. To understand that truth you ought to know about what went before—I mean about my marriage. After all, a good many people could tell you as well as I can that it was not... a very successful union. I was only twenty. I admired his force and courage and certainty; he was the only strong man I had ever known. But it did not take me long to find out that he cared for his business more than for me, and I think I found out even sooner that I had been deceiving myself and blinding myself, promising myself impossible things and wilfully misunderstanding my own feelings, because I was dazzled by the idea of having more money to spend than an English girl ever dreams of. I have been despising myself for that for five years. My husband's feeling for me... well, I cannot speak of that... what I want to say is that along with it there had always been a belief of his that I was the sort of woman to take a great place in society, and that I should throw myself into it with enjoyment, and become a sort of personage and do him great credit—that was his idea; and the idea remained with him after other delusions had gone. I was a part of his ambition. That was his really bitter disappointment, that I failed him as a social success. I think he was too shrewd not to have known in his heart that such a man as he was, twenty years older than I, with great business responsibilities that filled every hour of his life, and caring for nothing else—he must have felt that there was a risk of great unhappiness in marrying the sort of girl I was, brought up to music and books and unpractical ideas, always enjoying myself in my own way. But he had really reckoned on me as a wife who would do the honours of his position in the world; and I found I couldn't."

Mrs Manderson had talked herself into a more emotional mood than she had yet shown to Trent. Her words flowed freely, and her voice had begun to ring and give play to a natural expressiveness that must hitherto have been dulled, he thought, by the shock and self-restraint of the past few days. Now she turned swiftly from the window and faced him as she went on, her beautiful face flushed and animated, her eyes gleaming, her hands moving in slight emphatic gestures, as she surrendered herself to the impulse of giving speech to things long pent up.

"The people," she said. "Oh, those people! Can you imagine what it must be for anyone who has lived in a world where there was always creative work in the background, work with some dignity about it, men and women with professions or arts to follow, with ideals and things to believe in and quarrel about, some of them wealthy, some of them quite poor; can you think what it means to step out of that into another world where you have to be very rich, shamefully rich, to exist at all—where money is the only thing that counts and the first thing in everybody's thoughts—where the men who make the millions are so jaded by the work, that sport is the only thing they can occupy themselves with when they have any leisure, and the men who don't have to work are even duller than the men who do, and vicious as well; and the women live for display and silly amusements and silly immoralities; do you know how awful that life is? Of course I know there are clever people, and people of taste in that set, but they're swamped and spoiled, and it's the same thing in the end; empty, empty! Oh! I suppose I'm exaggerating, and I did make friends and have some happy times; but that's how I feel after it all. The seasons in New York and London—how I hated them! And our house-parties and cruises in the yacht and the rest—the same people, the same emptiness.

"And you see, don't you, that my husband couldn't have an idea of all this. His life was never empty. He did not live it in society, and when he was in society he had always his business plans and difficulties to occupy his mind. He hadn't a suspicion of what I felt, and I never let him know; I couldn't, it wouldn't have been fair. I felt I must do something to justify myself as his wife, sharing his position and fortune; and the only thing I could do was to try, and try, to live up to his idea about my social qualities... I did try. I acted my best. And it became harder year by year… I never was what they call a popular hostess, how could I be? I was a failure; but I went on trying... I used to steal holidays now and then. I used to feel as if I was not doing my part of a bargain—it sounds horrid to put it like that, I know, but it was so—when I took one of my old school-friends, who couldn't afford to travel, away to Italy for a month or two, and we went about cheaply all by ourselves, and were quite happy; or when I went and made a long stay in London with some quiet people who had known me all my life, and we all lived just as in the old days, when we had to think twice about seats at the theatre, and told each other about cheap dressmakers. Those and a few other expeditions of the same sort were my best times after I was married, and they helped me to go through with it the rest of the time. But I felt my husband would have hated to know how much I enjoyed every hour of those returns to the old life.

"And in the end, in spite of everything I could do, he came to know... He could see through anything, I think, once his attention was turned to it. He had always been able to see that I was not fulfilling his idea of me as a figure in the social world, and I suppose he thought it was my misfortune rather than my fault. But the moment be began to see, in spite of my pretending, that I wasn't playing my part with any spirit, he knew the whole story; he divined how I loathed and was weary of the luxury and the brilliancy and the masses of money just because of the people who lived among them—who were made so by them, I suppose. It happened last year. I don't know just how or when. It may have been suggested to him by some woman—for they all understood, of course. He said nothing to me, and I think he tried not to change in his manner to me at first; but such things hurt—and it was working in both of us. I knew that he knew. After a time we were just being polite and considerate to each other. Before he found me out we had been on a footing of—how can I express it to you?—of intelligent companionship, I might say. We talked without restraint of many things of the kind we could agree or disagree about without its going very deep... if you understand. And then that came to an end. I felt that the only possible basis of our living in each other's company was going under my feet. And at last it was gone.

"It had been like that," she ended simply, "for months before he died." She sank into the corner of a sofa by the window, as though relaxing her body after an effort. For a few moments both were silent. Trent was hastily sorting out a tangle of impressions. He was amazed at the frankness of Mrs Manderson's story. He was amazed at the vigorous expressiveness in her telling of it. In this vivid being, carried away by an impulse to speak, talking with her whole personality, he had seen the real woman in a temper of activity, as he had already seen the real woman by chance in a temper of reverie and unguarded emotion. In both she was very unlike the pale, self-disciplined creature of majesty that she had been to the world. With that amazement of his went something like terror of her dark beauty, which excitement kindled into an appearance scarcely mortal in his eyes. Incongruously there rushed into his mind, occupied as it was with the affair of the moment, a little knot of ideas... she was unique not because of her beauty but because of its being united with intensity of nature; in England all the very beautiful women were placid, all the fiery women seemed to have burnt up the best of their beauty; that was why no beautiful woman had ever cast this sort of spell on him before; when it was a question of wit in women, he had preferred the brighter flame to the duller, without much regarding the lamp. "All this is very disputable," said his reason; and instinct answered: "Yes, except that I am under a spell;" and a deeper instinct cried out: "Away with it!" He forced his mind back to her story, and found growing swiftly in him an irrepressible conviction. It was all very fine; but it would not do.

"I feel as if I had led you into saying more than you meant to say, or than I wanted to learn," he said slowly. "But there is one brutal question which is the whole point of my inquiry." He braced his frame like one preparing for a plunge into cold waters. "Mrs Manderson, will you assure me that your husband's change toward you had nothing to do with John Marlowe?"

And what he had dreaded came. "Oh!" she cried with a sound of anguish, her face thrown up and open hands stretched out as if for pity; and then the hands covered the burning face, and she flung herself aside among the cushions at her elbow, so that he saw nothing but her heavy crown of black hair, and her body moving with sobs that stabbed his heart, and a foot turned inward gracelessly in an abandonment of misery. Like a tall tower suddenly breaking apart she had fallen in ruins, helplessly weeping.

Trent stood up, his face white and calm. With a senseless particularity he placed his envelope exactly in the centre of the little polished table. He walked to the door, closed it noiselessly as he went out, and in a few minutes was tramping through the rain out of sight of White Gables, going nowhere, seeing nothing, his soul shaken in the fierce effort to kill and trample the raving impulse that had seized him in the presence of her shame, that clamoured to him to drag himself before her feet, to pray for pardon, to pour out words—he knew not what words, but he knew that they had been straining at his lips—to wreck his self-respect for ever, and hopelessly defeat even the crazy purpose that had almost possessed him, by drowning her wretchedness in disgust, by babbling with the tongue of infatuation to a woman with a husband not yet buried, to a woman who loved another man.

Such was the magic of her tears, quickening in a moment the thing which, as his heart had known, he must not let come to life. For Philip Trent was a young man, younger in nature even than his years, and a way of life that kept his edge keen and his spirit volcanic had prepared him very ill for the meeting that comes once in the early manhood of most of us, usually—as in his case, he told himself harshly—to no purpose but the testing of virtue and the power of the will.

11

HITHERTO UNPUBLISHED

My dear Molloy:—This is in case I don't find you at your office. I have found out who killed Manderson, as this dispatch will show. This was my problem; yours is to decide what use to make of it. It definitely charges an unsuspected person with having a hand in the crime, and practically accuses him of being the murderer, so I don't suppose you will publish it before his arrest, and I believe it is illegal to do so afterwards until he has been tried and found guilty. You may decide to publish it then; and you may find it possible to make some use or other before then of the facts I have given. This is your affair. Meanwhile, will you communicate with Scotland Yard, and let them see what I have written? I have done with the Manderson mystery, and I wish to God I had never touched it. Here follows my dispatch. P.T.

Marlstone, *June 16th.*

I begin this, my third and probably my final dispatch to the Record upon the Manderson murder, with conflicting feelings. I have a strong sense of relief, because in my two previous dispatches I was obliged, in the interests of justice, to withhold facts ascertained by me which would, if published then, have put a certain person upon his guard and possibly have led to his escape; for he is a man of no common boldness and resource. These facts I shall now set forth. But I have, I confess, no liking for the story of treachery and perverted cleverness which I have to tell. It leaves an evil taste in the mouth, a savour of something revolting in the deeper puzzle of motive underlying the puzzle of the crime itself, which I believe I have solved.

It will be remembered that in my first dispatch I described the situation as I found it on reaching this place early on Tuesday morning. I told how the body was found, and in what state; dwelt upon the complete mystery surrounding the crime, and mentioned one or two local theories about it; gave some account of the dead man's domestic surroundings; and furnished a somewhat detailed description of his movements on the evening before his death. I gave, too, a little fact which may or may not have seemed irrelevant: that a quantity of whisky much larger than Manderson habitually drank at night had disappeared from his private decanter since the last time he was seen alive. On the following day, the day after the inquest, I wired little more than an abstract of the proceedings in the coroner's court, of which a verbatim report was made at my request by other representatives of the Record. That day is not yet over as I write these lines; and I have now completed an investigation which has led me directly to the man who must be called upon to clear himself of the guilt of the death of Manderson.

Apart from the central mystery of Manderson's having arisen long before his usual hour to go out and meet his death, there were two minor points of oddity about this affair which, I suppose, must have occurred to thousands of those who have read the accounts in the newspapers: points apparent from the very beginning. The first of these was that, whereas the body was found at a spot not thirty yards from the house, all the people of the house declared that they had heard no cry or other noise in the night. Manderson had not been gagged; the marks on his wrists pointed to a struggle with his assailant; and there had been at least one pistol-shot. (I say at least one, because it is the fact that in murders with firearms, especially if there has been a struggle, the criminal commonly misses his victim at least once.) The odd fact seemed all the more odd to me when I learned that Martin the butler was a bad sleeper, very keen of hearing, and that his bedroom, with the window open, faced almost directly toward the shed by which the body was found.

The second odd little fact that was apparent from the outset was Manderson's leaving his dental plate by the bedside. It appeared that he had risen and dressed himself fully, down to his necktie and watch and chain, and had gone out of doors without remembering to put in this plate, which he had carried in his mouth every day for years, and which contained all the visible teeth of the upper jaw. It had evidently not been a case of frantic hurry; and even if it had been, he would have been more likely to forget almost anything than this denture. Anyone who wears such a removable plate will agree that the putting it in on rising is a matter of second nature. Speaking as well as eating, to say nothing of appearances, depends upon it.

Neither of these queer details, however, seemed to lead to anything at the moment. They only awakened in me a suspicion of something lurking in the shadows, something that lent more mystery to the already mysterious question how and why and through whom Manderson met his end.

With this much of preamble I come at once to the discovery which, in the first few hours of my investigation, set me upon the path which so much ingenuity had been directed to concealing.

I have already described Manderson's bedroom, the rigorous simplicity of its furnishing, contrasted so strangely with the multitude of clothes and shoes, and the manner of its communication with Mrs Manderson's room. On the upper of the two long shelves on which the shoes were ranged I found, where I had been told I should find them, the pair of patent leather shoes which Manderson had worn on the evening before his death. I had glanced over the row, not with any idea of their giving me a clue, but merely because it happens that I am a judge of shoes, and all these shoes were of the very best workmanship. But my attention was at once caught by a little peculiarity in this particular pair. They were the lightest kind of lace-up dress shoes, very thin in the sole, without toe-caps, and beautifully made, like all the rest. These shoes were old and well worn; but being carefully polished, and fitted, as all the shoes were, upon their trees, they looked neat enough. What caught my eye was a slight splitting of the leather in that part of the upper known as the vamp—a splitting at the point where the two laced parts of the shoe rise from the upper. It is at this point that the strain comes when a tight shoe of this sort is forced upon the foot, and it is usually guarded with a strong stitching across the bottom of the opening. In both the shoes I was examining this stitching had parted, and the leather below had given way. The splitting was a tiny affair in each case, not an eighth of an inch long, and the torn edges having come together again on the removal of the strain, there was nothing that a person who was not something of a connoisseur of shoe-leather would have noticed. Even less noticeable, and indeed not to be seen at all unless one were looking for it, was a slight straining of the stitches uniting the upper to the sole. At the toe and on the outer side of each shoe this stitching had been dragged until it was visible on a close inspection of the join.

These indications, of course, could mean only one thing—the shoes had been worn by someone for whom they were too small.

Now it was clear at a glance that Manderson was always thoroughly well shod, and careful, perhaps a little vain, of his small and narrow feet. Not one of the other shoes in the collection, as I soon ascertained, bore similar marks; they had not belonged to a man who squeezed himself into tight shoe-leather. Someone who was not Manderson had worn these shoes, and worn them recently; the edges of the tears were quite fresh.

The possibility of someone having worn them since Manderson's death was not worth considering; the body had only been found about twenty-six hours when I was examining the shoes; besides, why should anyone wear them? The possibility of someone having borrowed Manderson's shoes and spoiled them for him while he was alive seemed about as negligible. With others to choose from he would not have worn these. Besides, the only men in the place were the butler and the two secretaries. But I do not say that I gave those possibilities even as much consideration as they deserved, for my thoughts were running away with me, and I have always found it good policy, in cases of this sort, to let them have their heads. Ever since I had got out of the train at Marlstone early that morning I had been steeped in details of the Manderson affair; the thing had not once been out of my head. Suddenly the moment had come when the daemon wakes and begins to range.

Let me put it less fancifully. After all, it is a detail of psychology familiar enough to all whose business or inclination brings them in contact with difficult affairs of any kind. Swiftly and spontaneously, when chance or effort puts one in possession of the key-fact in any system of baffling circumstances, one's ideas seem to rush to group themselves anew in relation to that fact, so that they are suddenly rearranged almost before one has consciously grasped the significance of the key-fact itself. In the present instance, my brain had scarcely formulated within itself the thought, "Somebody who was not Manderson has been wearing these shoes," when there flew into my mind a flock of ideas, all of the same character and all bearing upon this new notion. It was unheard-of for Manderson to drink much whisky at night. It was very unlike him to be untidily dressed, as the body was when found—the cuffs dragged up inside the sleeves, the shoes unevenly laced; very unlike him not to wash when he rose, and to put on last night's evening shirt and collar and underclothing; very unlike him to have his watch in the waistcoat pocket that was not lined with leather for its reception. (In my first dispatch I mentioned all these points, but neither I nor anyone else saw anything significant in them when examining the body.) It was very strange, in the existing domestic situation, that Manderson should be communicative to his wife about his doings, especially at the time of his going to bed, when he seldom spoke to her at all. It was extraordinary that Manderson should leave his bedroom without his false teeth.

All these thoughts, as I say, came flocking into my mind together, drawn from various parts of my memory of the morning's inquiries and observations. They had all presented themselves, in far less time than it takes to read them as set down here, as I was turning over the shoes, confirming my own certainty on the main point. And yet when I confronted the definite idea that had sprung up suddenly and unsupported before me—"*It was not Manderson who was in the house that night*"—it seemed a stark absurdity at the first formulating. It was certainly Manderson who had dined at the house and gone out with Marlowe in the car. People had seen him at close quarters. But was it he who returned at ten? That question too seemed absurd enough. But I could not set it aside. It seemed to me as if a faint light was beginning to creep over the whole expanse of my mind, as it does over land at dawn, and that presently the sun would be rising. I set myself to think over, one by one, the points that had just occurred to me, so as to make out, if possible, why any man masquerading as Manderson should have done these things that Manderson would not have done.

I had not to cast about very long for the motive a man might have in forcing his feet into Manderson's narrow shoes. The examination of footmarks is very well understood by the police. But not only was the man concerned to leave no footmarks of his own: he was concerned to leave Manderson's, if any; his whole plan, if my guess was right, must have been directed to producing the belief that Manderson was in the place that night. Moreover, his plan did not turn upon leaving footmarks. He meant to leave the shoes themselves, and he did so. The maidservant had found them outside the bedroom door, as Manderson always left his shoes, and had polished them, replacing them on the shoe-shelves later in the morning, after the body had been found.

When I came to consider in this new light the leaving of the false teeth, an explanation of what had seemed the maddest part of the affair broke upon me at once. A dental plate is not inseparable from its owner. If my guess was right, the unknown had brought the denture to the house with him, and left it in the bedroom, with the same object as he had in leaving the shoes: to make it impossible that anyone should doubt that Manderson had been in the house and had gone to bed there. This, of course, led me to the inference that *Manderson was* dead *before the false Manderson came to the house*; and other things confirmed this.

For instance, the clothing, to which I now turned in my review of the position. If my guess was right, the unknown in Manderson's shoes had certainly had possession of Manderson's trousers, waistcoat, and shooting jacket. They were there before my eyes in the bedroom; and Martin had seen the jacket—which nobody could have mistaken—upon the man who sat at the telephone in the library. It was now quite plain (if my guess was right) that this unmistakable garment was a cardinal feature of the unknown's plan. He knew that Martin would take him for Manderson at the first glance.

And there my thinking was interrupted by the realization of a thing that had escaped me before. So strong had been the influence of the unquestioned assumption that it was Manderson who was present that night, that neither I nor, as far as I know, anyone else had noted the point. Martin had *not seen the man's face; nor had Mrs Manderson.*

Mrs Manderson (judging by her evidence at the inquest, of which, as I have said, I had a full report made by the *Record* stenographers in court) had not seen the man at all. She hardly could have done, as I shall show presently. She had merely spoken with him as she lay half asleep, resuming a conversation which she had had with her living husband about an hour before. Martin, I perceived, could only have seen the man's back, as he sat crouching over the telephone; no doubt a characteristic pose was imitated there. And the man had worn his hat, Manderson's broad-brimmed hat! There is too much character in the back of a head and neck. The unknown, in fact, supposing him to have been of about Manderson's build, had had no need for any disguise, apart from the jacket and the hat and his powers of mimicry.

I paused there to contemplate the coolness and ingenuity of the man. The thing, I now began to see, was so safe and easy, provided that his mimicry was good enough, and that his nerve held. These two points assured, only some wholly unlikely accident could unmask him.

To come back to my puzzling out of the matter as I sat in the dead man's bedroom with the telltale shoes before me. The reason for the entrance by the window instead of by the front door will already have occurred to anyone reading this. Entering by the door, the man would almost certainly have been heard by the sharp-eared Martin in his pantry just across the hall; he might have met him face to face.

Then there was the problem of the whisky. I had not attached much importance to it; whisky will sometimes vanish in very queer ways in a household of eight or nine persons; but it had seemed strange that it should go in that way on that evening. Martin had been plainly quite dumbfounded by the fact. It seemed to me now that many a man—fresh, as this man in all likelihood was, from a bloody business, from the unclothing of a corpse, and with a desperate part still to play—would turn to that decanter as to a friend. No doubt he had a drink before sending for Martin; after making that trick with ease and success, he probably drank more.

But he had known when to stop. The worst part of the enterprise was before him: the business—clearly of such vital importance to him, for whatever reason—of shutting himself in Manderson's room and preparing a body of convincing evidence of its having been occupied by Manderson; and this with the risk—very slight, as no doubt he understood, but how unnerving!—of the woman on the other side of the half-open door awaking and somehow discovering him. True, if he kept out of her limited field of vision from the bed, she could only see him by getting up and going to the door. I found that to a person lying in her bed, which stood with its head to the wall a little beyond the door, nothing was visible through the doorway but one of the cupboards by Manderson's bed-head. Moreover, since this man knew the ways of the household, he would think it most likely that Mrs Manderson was asleep. Another point with him, I guessed, might have been the estrangement between the husband and wife, which they had tried to cloak by keeping up, among other things, their usual practice of sleeping in connected rooms, but which was well known to all who had anything to do with them. He would hope from this that if Mrs Manderson heard him, she would take no notice of the supposed presence of her husband.

So, pursuing my hypothesis, I followed the unknown up to the bedroom, and saw him setting about his work. And it was with a catch in my own breath that I thought of the hideous shock with which he must have heard the sound of all others he was dreading most: the drowsy voice from the adjoining room.

What Mrs Manderson actually said, she was unable to recollect at the inquest. She thinks she asked her supposed husband whether he had had a good run in the car. And now what does the unknown do? Here, I think, we come to a supremely significant point. Not only does he—standing rigid there, as I picture him, before the dressing-table, listening to the sound of his own leaping heart—not only does he answer the lady in the voice of Manderson; he volunteers an explanatory statement. He tells her that he has, on a sudden inspiration, sent Marlowe in the car to Southampton; that he had sent him to bring back some important information from a man leaving for Paris by the steamboat that morning. Why these details from a man who had long been uncommunicative to his wife, and that upon a point scarcely likely to interest her? Why these details *about Marlowe?*

Having taken my story so far, I now put forward the following definite propositions: that between a time somewhere about ten, when the car started, and a time somewhere about eleven, Manderson was shot—probably at a considerable distance from the house, as no shot was heard; that the body was brought back, left by the shed, and stripped of its outer clothing; that at some time round about eleven o'clock a man who was not Manderson, wearing Manderson's shoes, hat, and jacket, entered the library by the garden window; and he had with him Manderson's black trousers, waistcoat, and motor-coat, the denture taken from Manderson's mouth, and the weapon with which he had been murdered; that he concealed these, rang the bell for the butler, and sat down at the telephone with his hat on and his back to the door; that he was occupied with the telephone all the time Martin was in the room; that on going up to the bedroom floor he quietly entered Marlowe's room and placed the revolver with which the crime had been committed—Marlowe's revolver—in the case on the mantelpiece from which it had been taken; and that he then went to Manderson's room, placed Manderson's shoes outside the door, threw Manderson's garments on a chair, placed the denture in the bowl by the bedside, and selected a suit of clothes, a pair of shoes, and a tie from those in the bedroom.

Here I will pause in my statement of this man's proceedings to go into a question for which the way is now sufficiently prepared:—

Who was the false *Manderson?*

Reviewing what was known to me, or might almost with certainty be surmised, about that person, I set down the following five conclusions:

(1) He had been in close relations with the dead man. In his acting before Martin and his speaking to Mrs Manderson he had made no mistake.
(2) He was of a build not unlike Manderson's, especially as to height and breadth of shoulder, which mainly determine the character of the back of a seated figure when the head is concealed and the body loosely clothed. But his feet were larger, though not greatly larger, than Manderson's.
(3) He had considerable aptitude for mimicry and acting—probably some experience too.
(4) He had a minute acquaintance with the ways of the Manderson household.
(5) He was under a vital necessity of creating the belief that Manderson was alive and in that house until sometime after midnight on the Sunday night.

So much I took as either certain or next door to it. It was as far as I could see. And it was far enough.

I proceed to give, in an order corresponding with the numbered paragraphs above, such relevant facts as I was able to obtain about Mr John Marlowe, from himself and other sources:—

(1) He had been Mr Manderson's private secretary, upon a footing of great intimacy, for nearly four years.
(2) The two men were nearly of the same height, about five feet eleven inches; both were powerfully built and heavy in the shoulder. Marlowe, who was the younger by some twenty years, was rather slighter about the body, though Manderson was a man in good physical condition. Marlowe's shoes (of which I examined several pairs) were roughly about one shoemaker's size longer and broader than Manderson's.
(3) In the afternoon of the first day of my investigation, after arriving at the results already detailed, I sent a telegram to a personal friend, a Fellow of a college at Oxford, whom I knew to be interested in theatrical matters, in these terms:

> PLEASE WIRE JOHN MARLOWE'S RECORD IN CONNECTION WITH ACTING AT OXFORD SOME TIME PAST DECADE VERY URGENT AND CONFIDENTIAL.

My friend replied in the following telegram, which reached me next morning (the morning of the inquest):—

> MARLOWE WAS MEMBER O.U.D.S. FOR THREE YEARS AND PRESIDENT 19—PLAYED BARDOLPH CLEON AND MERCUTIO EXCELLED IN CHARACTER ACTING AND IMITATIONS IN GREAT DEMAND AT SMOKERS WAS HERO OF SOME HISTORIC HOAXES.

I had been led to send the telegram which brought this very helpful answer by seeing on the mantelshelf in Marlowe's bedroom a photograph of himself and two others in the costume of Falstaff's three followers, with an inscription from The Merry Wives, and by noting that it bore the imprint of an Oxford firm of photographers.

(4) During his connection with Manderson, Marlowe had lived as one of the family. No other person, apart from the servants, had his opportunities for knowing the domestic life of the Mandersons in detail.

(5) I ascertained beyond doubt that Marlowe arrived at a hotel in Southampton on the Monday morning at 6:30, and there proceeded to carry out the commission which, according to his story, and according to the statement made to Mrs Manderson in the bedroom by the false Manderson, had been entrusted to him by his employer. He had then returned in the car to Marlstone, where he had shown great amazement and horror at the news of the murder.

These, I say, are the relevant facts about Marlowe. We must now examine fact number 5 (as set out above) in connection with conclusion number 5 about the false Manderson.

I would first draw attention to one important fact. *The only person who professed to have heard Manderson mention Southampton at all before he started in the car was Marlowe.* His story—confirmed to some extent by what the butler overheard—was that the journey was all arranged in a private talk before they set out, and he could not say, when I put the question to him, why Manderson should have concealed his intentions by giving out that he was going with Marlowe for a moonlight drive. This point, however, attracted no attention. Marlowe had an absolutely air-tight alibi in his presence at Southampton by 6:30; nobody thought of him in connection with a murder which must have been committed after 12:30—the hour at which Martin the butler had gone to bed. But it was the Manderson who came back from the drive who went out of his way to mention Southampton openly to two persons. *He even went so far as to ring up a hotel at Southampton and ask questions which bore out Marlowe's story of his errand.* This was the call he was busy with when Martin was in the library.

Now let us consider the alibi. If Manderson was in the house that night, and if he did not leave it until some time after 12:30, Marlowe could not by any possibility have had a direct hand in the murder. It is a question of the distance between Marlstone and Southampton. If he had left Marlstone in the car at the hour when he is supposed to have done so—between 10 and 10:30—with a message from Manderson, the run would be quite an easy one to do in the time. But it would be physically impossible for the car—a 15 h.p. four-cylinder Northumberland, an average medium-power car—to get to Southampton by half-past six unless it left Marlstone by midnight at latest. Motorists who will examine the road map and make the calculations required, as I did in Manderson's library that day, will agree that on the facts as they appeared there was absolutely no case against Marlowe.

But even if they were not as they appeared; if Manderson was dead by eleven o'clock, and if at about that time Marlowe impersonated him at White Gables; if Marlowe retired to Manderson's bedroom—how can all this be reconciled with his appearance next morning at Southampton? *He had to get out of the house, unseen and unheard, and away in the car by midnight.* And Martin, the sharp-eared Martin, was sitting up until 12:30 in his pantry, with the door open, listening for the telephone bell. Practically he was standing sentry over the foot of the staircase, the only staircase leading down from the bedroom floor.

With this difficulty we arrive at the last and crucial phase of my investigation. Having the foregoing points clearly in mind, I spent the rest of the day before the inquest in talking to various persons and in going over my story, testing it link by link. I could only find the one weakness which seemed to be involved in Martin's sitting up until 12:30; and since his having been instructed to do so was certainly a part of the plant, meant to clinch the alibi for Marlowe, I knew there must be an explanation somewhere. If I could not find that explanation, my theory was valueless. I must be able to show that at the time Martin went up to bed the man who had shut himself in Manderson's bedroom might have been many miles away on the road to Southampton.

I had, however, a pretty good idea already—as perhaps the reader of these lines has by this time, if I have made myself clear—of how the escape of the false Manderson before midnight had been contrived. But I did not want what I was now about to do to be known. If I had chanced to be discovered at work, there would have been no concealing the direction of my suspicions. I resolved not to test them on this point until the next day, during the opening proceedings at the inquest. This was to be held, I knew, at the hotel, and I reckoned upon having White Gables to myself so far as the principal immates were concerned.

So in fact it happened. By the time the proceedings at the hotel had been begun I was hard at work at White Gables. I had a camera with me. I made search, on principles well known to and commonly practised by the police, and often enough by myself, for certain indications. Without describing my search, I may say at once that I found and was able to photograph two fresh fingerprints, very large and distinct, on the polished front of the right-hand top drawer of the chest of drawers in Manderson's bedroom; five more (among a number of smaller and less recent impressions made by other hands) on the glasses of the French window in Mrs Manderson's room, a window which always stood open at night with a curtain before it; and three more upon the glass bowl in which Manderson's dental plate had been found lying.

I took the bowl with me from White Gables. I took also a few articles which I selected from Marlowe's bedroom, as bearing the most distinct of the innumerable fingerprints which are always to be found upon toilet articles in daily use. I already had in my possession, made upon leaves cut from my pocket diary, some excellent fingerprints of Marlowe's which he had made in my presence without knowing it. I had shown him the leaves, asking if he recognized them; and the few seconds during which he had held them in his fingers had sufficed to leave impressions which I was afterwards able to bring out.

By six o'clock in the evening, two hours after the jury had brought in their verdict against a person or persons unknown, I had completed my work, and was in a position to state that two of the five large prints made on the window-glasses, and the three on the bowl, were made by the left hand of Marlowe; that the remaining three on the window and the two on the drawer were made by his right hand.

By eight o'clock I had made at the establishment of Mr H. T. Copper, photographer, of Bishopsbridge, and with his assistance, a dozen enlarged prints of the fingermarks of Marlowe, clearly showing the identity of those which he unknowingly made in my presence and those left upon articles in his bedroom, and those found by me as I have described, and thus establishing the facts that Marlowe was recently in Manderson's bedroom, where he had in the ordinary way no business, and in Mrs Manderson's room, where he had still less. I hope it may be possible to reproduce these prints for publication with this dispatch.

At nine o'clock I was back in my room at the hotel and sitting down to begin this manuscript. I had my story complete.

I bring it to a close by advancing these further propositions: that on the night of the murder the impersonator of Manderson, being in Manderson's bedroom, told Mrs Manderson, as he had already told Martin, that Marlow was at that moment on his way to Southampton; that having made his dispositions in the room, he switched off the light, and lay in the bed in his clothes; that he waited until he was assured that Mrs Manderson was asleep; that he then arose and stealthily crossed Mrs Manderson's bedroom in his stocking feet, having under his arm the bundle of clothing and shoes for the body; that he stepped behind the curtain, pushing the doors of a window a little further open with his hands, strode over the iron railing of the balcony, and let himself down until only a drop of a few feet separated him from the soft turf of the lawn.

All this might very well have been accomplished within half an hour of his entering Manderson's bedroom, which, according to Martin, he did at about half-past eleven.

What followed your readers and the authorities may conjecture for themselves. The corpse was found next morning clothed—rather untidily. Marlowe in the car appeared at Southampton by half-past six.

I bring this manuscript to an end in my sitting-room at the hotel at Marlstone. It is four o'clock in the morning. I leave for London by the noon train from Bishopsbridge, and immediately after arriving I shall place these pages in your hands. I ask you to communicate the substance of them to the Criminal Investigation Department.

PHILIP TRENT.

12

EVIL DAYS

"I am returning the cheque you sent for what I did on the Manderson case," Trent wrote to Sir James Molloy from Munich, whither he had gone immediately after handing in at the Record office a brief dispatch bringing his work on the case to an unexciting close. "What I sent you wasn't worth one-tenth of the amount; but I should have no scruple about pocketing it if I hadn't taken a fancy—never mind why—not to touch any money at all for this business. I should like you, if there is no objection, to pay for the stuff at your ordinary space-rate, and hand the money to some charity which does not devote itself to bullying people, if you know of any such. I have come to this place to see some old friends and arrange my ideas, and the idea that comes out uppermost is that for a little while I want some employment with activity in it. I find I can't paint at all: I couldn't paint a fence. Will you try me as your Own Correspondent somewhere? If you can find me a good adventure I will send you good accounts. After that I could settle down and work."

Sir James sent him instruction by telegram to proceed at once to Kurland and Livonia, where Citizen Browning was abroad again, and town and countryside blazed in revolt. It was a roving commission, and for two months Trent followed his luck. It served him not less well than usual. He was the only correspondent who saw General Dragilew killed in the street at Volmar by a girl of eighteen. He saw burnings, lynchings, fusillades, hangings; each day his soul sickened afresh at the imbecilities born of misrule. Many nights he lay down in danger. Many days he went fasting. But there was never an evening or a morning when he did not see the face of the woman whom he hopelessly loved.

He discovered in himself an unhappy pride at the lasting force of this infatuation. It interested him as a phenomenon; it amazed and enlightened him. Such a thing had not visited him before. It confirmed so much that he had found dubious in the recorded experience of men.

It was not that, at thirty-two, he could pretend to ignorance of this world of emotion. About his knowledge let it be enough to say that what he had learned had come unpursued and unpurchased, and was without intolerable memories; broken to the realities of sex, he was still troubled by its inscrutable history. He went through life full of a strange respect for certain feminine weakness and a very simple terror of certain feminine strength. He had held a rather lukewarm faith that something remained in him to be called forth, and that the voice that should call would be heard in its own time, if ever, and not through any seeking.

But he had not thought of the possibility that, if this proved true some day, the truth might come in a sinister shape. The two things that had taken him utterly by surprise in the matter of his feeling towards Mabel Manderson were the insane suddenness of its uprising in full strength and its extravagant hopelessness. Before it came, he had been much disposed to laugh at the permanence of unrequited passion as a generous boyish delusion. He knew now that he had been wrong, and he was living bitterly in the knowledge.

Before the eye of his fancy the woman always came just as she was when he had first had sight of her, with the gesture which he had surprised as he walked past unseen on the edge of the cliff; that great gesture of passionate joy in her new liberty which had told him more plainly than speech that her widowhood was a release from torment, and had confirmed with terrible force the suspicion, active in his mind before, that it was her passport to happiness with a man whom she loved. He could not with certainty name to himself the moment when he had first suspected that it might be so. The seed of the thought must have been sown, he believed, at his first meeting with Marlowe; his mind would have noted automatically that such evident strength and grace, with the sort of looks and manners that the tall young man possessed, might go far with any woman of unfixed affections. And the connection of this with what Mr Cupples had told him of the Mandersons' married life must have formed itself in the unconscious depths of his mind. Certainly it had presented itself as an already established thing when he began, after satisfying himself of the identity of the murderer, to cast about for the motive of the crime. Motive, motive! How desperately he had sought for another, turning his back upon that grim thought, that Marlowe—obsessed by passion like himself, and privy perhaps to maddening truths about the wife's unhappiness—had taken a leaf, the guiltiest, from the book of Bothwell. But in all his investigations at the time, in all his broodings on the matter afterwards, he had been able to discover nothing that could prompt Marlowe to such a deed—nothing but that temptation, the whole strength of which he could not know, but which if it had existed must have pressed urgently upon a bold spirit in which scruple had been somehow paralyzed. If he could trust his senses at all, the young man was neither insane nor by nature evil. But that could not clear him. Murder for a woman's sake, he thought, was not a rare crime, heaven knew! If the modern feebleness of impulse in the comfortable classes, and their respect for the modern apparatus of detection, had made it rare among them, it was yet far from impossible. It only needed a man of equal daring and intelligence, his soul drugged with the vapours of an intoxicating intrigue, to plan and perform such a deed.

A thousand times, with a heart full of anguish, he had sought to reason away the dread that Mabel Manderson had known too much of what had been intended against her husband's life. That she knew all the truth after the thing was done he could not doubt; her unforgettable collapse in his presence when the question about Marlowe was suddenly and bluntly put had swept away his last hope that there was no love between the pair, and had seemed to him, moreover, to speak of dread of discovery. In any case, she knew the truth after reading what he had left with her; and it was certain that no public suspicion had been cast upon Marlowe since. She had destroyed his manuscript, then, and taken him at his word to keep the secret that threatened her lover's life.

But it was the monstrous thought that she might have known murder was brewing, and guiltily kept silence, that haunted Trent's mind. She might have suspected, have guessed something; was it conceivable that she was aware of the whole plot, that she connived? He could never forget that his first suspicion of Marlowe's motive in the crime had been roused by the fact that his escape was made through the lady's room. At that time, when he had not yet seen her, he had been ready enough to entertain the idea of her equal guilt and her co-operation. He had figured to himself some passionate *hystérique*, merciless as a cat in her hate and her love, a zealous abettor, perhaps even the ruling spirit in the crime.

Then he had seen her, had spoken with her, had helped her in her weakness; and such suspicions, since their first meeting, had seemed the vilest of infamy. He had seen her eyes and her mouth; he had breathed the woman's atmosphere. Trent was one of those who fancy they can scent true wickedness in the air. In her presence he had felt an inward certainty of her ultimate goodness of heart; and it was nothing against this that she had abandoned herself a moment, that day on the cliff, to the sentiment of relief at the ending of her bondage, of her years of starved sympathy and unquickened motherhood. That she had turned to Marlowe in her destitution he believed; that she had any knowledge of his deadly purpose he did not believe.

And yet, morning and evening the sickening doubts returned, and he recalled again that it was almost in her presence that Marlowe had made his preparations in the bedroom of the murdered man, that it was by the window of her own chamber that he had escaped from the house. Had he forgotten his cunning and taken the risk of telling her then? Or had he, as Trent thought more likely, still played his part with her then, and stolen off while she slept? He did not think she had known of the masquerade when she gave evidence at the inquest; it read like honest evidence. Or—the question would never be silenced, though he scorned it—had she lain expecting the footsteps in the room and the whisper that should tell her that it was done? Among the foul possibilities of human nature, was it possible that black ruthlessness and black deceit as well were hidden behind that good and straight and gentle seeming?

These thoughts would scarcely leave him when he was alone.

Trent served Sir James well, earning his pay, for six months, and then returned to Paris, where he went to work again with a better heart. His powers had returned to him, and he began to live more happily than he had expected among a tribe of strangely assorted friends, French, English, and American, artists, poets, journalists, policemen, hotel-keepers, soldiers, lawyers, business men, and others. His old faculty of sympathetic interest in his fellows won for him, just as in his student days, privileges seldom extended to the Briton. He enjoyed again the rare experience of being taken into the bosom of a Frenchman's family. He was admitted to the momentous confidence of *les jeunes*, and found them as sure that they had surprised the secrets of art and life as the departed *jeunes* of ten years before had been.

The bosom of the Frenchman's family was the same as those he had known in the past, even to the patterns of the wallpaper and movables. But the *jeunes*, he perceived with regret, were totally different from their forerunners. They were much more shallow and puerile, much less really clever. The secrets they wrested from the universe were not such important and interesting secrets as had been wrested by the old *jeunes*. This he believed and deplored until one day he found himself seated at a restaurant next to a too well-fed man whom, in spite of the ravages of comfortable living, he recognized as one of the *jeunes* of his own period. This one had been wont to describe himself and three or four others as the Hermits of the New Parnassus. He and his school had talked outside cafes and elsewhere more than solitaries do as a rule; but then, rules were what they had vowed themselves to destroy. They proclaimed that verse, in particular, was free. The Hermit of the New Parnassus was now in the Ministry of the Interior, and already decorated: he expressed to Trent the opinion that what France needed most was a hand of iron. He was able to quote the exact price paid for certain betrayals of the country, of which Trent had not previously heard.

Thus he was brought to make the old discovery that it was he who had changed, like his friend of the Administration, and that les *jeunes* were still the same. Yet he found it hard to say what precisely he had lost that so greatly mattered; unless indeed it were so simple a thing as his high spirits.

One morning in June, as he descended the slope of the Rue des Martyrs, he saw approaching a figure that he remembered. He glanced quickly round, for the thought of meeting Mr Bunner again was unacceptable. For some time he had recognized that his wound was healing under the spell of creative work; he though less often of the woman he loved, and with less pain. He would not have the memory of those three days reopened.

But the straight and narrow thoroughfare offered no refuge, and the American saw him almost at once.

His unforced geniality made Trent ashamed, for he had liked the man. They sat long over a meal, and Mr Bunner talked. Trent listened to him, now that he was in for it, with genuine pleasure, now and then contributing a question or remark. Besides liking his companion, he enjoyed his conversation, with its unending verbal surprises, for its own sake.

Mr Bunner was, it appeared, resident in Paris as the chief Continental agent of the Manderson firm, and fully satisfied with his position and prospects. He discoursed on these for some twenty minutes. This subject at length exhausted, he went on to tell Trent, who confessed that he had been away from England for a year, that Marlowe had shortly after the death of Manderson entered his father's business, which was now again in a flourishing state, and had already come to be practically in control of it. They had kept up their intimacy, and were even now planning a holiday for the summer. Mr Bunner spoke with generous admiration of his friend's talent for affairs. "Jack Marlowe has a natural big head," he declared, "and if he had more experience, I wouldn't want to have him up against me. He would put a crimp in me every time."

As the American's talk flowed on, Trent listened with a slowly growing perplexity. It became more and more plain that something was very wrong in his theory of the situation; there was no mention of its central figure. Presently Mr Bunner mentioned that Marlowe was engaged to be married to an Irish girl, whose charms he celebrated with native enthusiasm.

Trent clasped his hands savagely together beneath the table. What could have happened? His ideas were sliding and shifting. At last he forced himself to put a direct question.

Mr Bunner was not very fully informed. He knew that Mrs Manderson had left England immediately after the settlement of her husband's affairs, and had lived for some time in Italy. She had returned not long ago to London, where she had decided not to live in the house in Mayfair, and had bought a smaller one in the Hampstead neighbourhood; also, he understood, one somewhere in the country. She was said to go but little into society. "And all the good hard dollars just waiting for some one to spraddle them around," said Mr Bunner, with a note of pathos in his voice. "Why, she has money to burn—money to feed to the birds—and nothing doing. The old man left her more than half his wad. And think of the figure she might make in the world. She is beautiful, and she is the best woman I ever met, too. But she couldn't ever seem to get the habit of spending money the way it ought to be spent."

His words now became a soliloquy: Trent's thoughts were occupying all his attention. He pleaded business soon, and the two men parted with cordiality.

Half an hour later Trent was in his studio, swiftly and mechanically "cleaning up." He wanted to know what had happened; somehow he must find out. He could never approach herself, he knew; he would bring back to her the shame of that last encounter with him; it was scarcely likely that he would even set eyes on her. But her must get to know!... Cupples was in London, Marlowe was there... And, anyhow, he was sick of Paris.

Such thoughts came and went; and below them all strained the fibres of an unseen cord that dragged mercilessly at his heart, and that he cursed bitterly in the moments when he could not deny to himself that it was there. The folly, the useless, pitiable folly of it!

In twenty-four hours his feeble roots in Paris had been torn out. He was looking over a leaden sea at the shining fortress-wall of the Dover cliffs.

But though he had instinctively picked out the lines of a set purpose from among the welter of promptings in his mind, he found it delayed at the very outset.

He had decided that he must first see Mr Cupples, who would be in a position to tell him much more than the American knew. But Mr Cupples was away on his travels, not expected to return for a month; and Trent had no reasonable excuse for hastening his return. Marlowe he would not confront until he had tried at least to reconnoitre the position. He constrained himself not to commit the crowning folly of seeking out Mrs Manderson's house in Hampstead; he could not enter it, and the thought of the possibility of being seen by her lurking in its neighborhood brought the blood to his face.

He stayed at a hotel, took a studio, and while he awaited Mr Cupples's return attempted vainly to lose himself in work.

At the end of a week he had an idea that he acted upon with eager precipitancy. She had let fall some word at their last meeting of a taste for music. Trent went that evening, and thenceforward regularly, to the opera. He might see her; and if, in spite of his caution, she caught sight of him, they could be blind to each other's presence—anybody might happen to go to the opera.

So he went alone each evening, passing as quickly as he might through the people in the vestibule; and each evening he came away knowing that she had not been in the house. It was a habit that yielded him a sort of satisfaction along with the guilty excitement of his search; for he too loved music, and nothing gave him so much peace while its magic endured.

One night as he entered, hurrying through the brilliant crowd, he felt a touch on his arm. Flooded with an incredible certainty at the touch, he turned.

It was she: so much more radiant in the absence of grief and anxiety, in the fact that she was smiling, and in the allurement of evening dress, that he could not speak. She, too, breathed a little quickly, and there was a light of daring in her eyes and cheeks as she greeted him.

Her words were few. "I wouldn't miss a note of Tristan," she said, "nor must you. Come and see me in the interval." She gave him the number of the box.

13

ERUPTION

The following two months were a period in Trent's life that he has never since remembered without shuddering. He met Mrs Manderson half a dozen times, and each time her cool friendliness, a nicely calculated mean between mere acquaintance and the first stage of intimacy, baffled and maddened him. At the opera he had found her, to his further amazement, with a certain Mrs Wallace, a frisky matron whom he had known from childhood. Mrs Manderson, it appeared, on her return from Italy, had somehow wandered into circles to which he belonged by nurture and disposition. It came, she said, of her having pitched her tent in their hunting-grounds; several of his friends were near neighbours. He had a dim but horrid recollection of having been on that occasion unlike himself, ill at ease, burning in the face, talking with idiot loquacity of his adventures in the Baltic provinces, and finding from time to time that he was addressing himself exclusively to Mrs Wallace. The other lady, when he joined them, had completely lost the slight appearance of agitation with which she had stopped him in the vestibule. She had spoken pleasantly to him of her travels, of her settlement in London, and of people whom they both knew.

During the last half of the opera, which he had stayed' in the box to hear, he had been conscious of nothing, as he sat behind them, but the angle of her cheek and the mass of her hair, the lines of her shoulder and arm, her hand upon the cushion. The black hair had seemed at last a forest, immeasurable, pathless and enchanted, luring him to a fatal adventure... At the end he had been pale and subdued, parting with them rather formally.

The next time he saw her—it was at a country house where both were guests—and the subsequent times, he had had himself in hand. He had matched her manner and had acquitted himself, he thought, decently, considering—

Considering that he lived in an agony of bewilderment and remorse and longing. He could make nothing, absolutely nothing, of her attitude. That she had read his manuscript and understood the suspicion indicated in his last question to her at White Gables was beyond the possibility of doubt. Then how could she treat him thus amiably and frankly, as she treated all the world of men who had done her no injury?

For it had become clear to his intuitive sense, for all the absence of any shade of differentiation in her outward manner, that an injury had been done, and that she had felt it. Several times, on the rare and brief occasions when they had talked apart, he had warning from the same sense that she was approaching this subject; and each time he had turned the conversation with the ingenuity born of fear. Two resolutions he made. The first was that when he had completed a commissioned work which tied him to London he would go away and stay away. The strain was too great. He no longer burned to know the truth; he wanted nothing to confirm his fixed internal conviction but faith, that he had blundered, that he had misread the situation, misinterpreted her tears, written himself down a slanderous fool. He speculated no more on Marlowe's motive in the killing of Manderson. Mr Cupples returned to London, and Trent asked him nothing. He knew now that he had been right in those words—Trent remembered them for the emphasis with which they were spoken—"So long as she considered herself bound to him... no power on earth could have persuaded her." He met Mrs Manderson at dinner at her uncle's large and tomb-like house in Bloomsbury, and there he conversed most of the evening with a professor of archaeology from Berlin.

His other resolution was that he would not be with her alone.

But when, a few days after, she wrote asking him to come and see her on the following afternoon, he made no attempt to excuse himself. This was a formal challenge.

While she celebrated the rites of tea, and for some little time thereafter, she joined with such natural ease in his slightly fevered conversation on matters of the day that he began to hope she had changed what he could not doubt had been her resolve, to corner him and speak to him gravely. She was to all appearance careless now, smiling so that he recalled, not for the first time since that night at the opera, what was written long ago of a Princess of Brunswick: "Her mouth has ten thousand charms that touch the soul." She made a tour of the beautiful room where she had received him, singling out this treasure or that from the spoils of a hundred bric-à-brac shops, laughing over her quests, discoveries, and bargainings. And when he asked if she would delight him again with a favourite piece of his which he had heard her play at another house, she consented at once.

She played with a perfection of execution and feeling that moved him now as it had moved him before. "You are a musician born," he said quietly when she had finished, and the last tremor of the music had passed away. "I knew that before I first heard you."

"I have played a great deal ever since I can remember. It has been a great comfort to me," she said simply, and half turned to him smiling. "When did you first detect music in me? Oh, of course: I was at the opera. But that wouldn't prove much, would it?"

"No," he said abstractedly, his sense still busy with the music that had just ended. "I think I knew it the first time I saw you." Then understanding of his own words came to him, and turned him rigid. For the first time the past had been invoked.

There was a short silence. Mrs Manderson looked at Trent, then hastily looked away. Colour began to rise in her cheeks, and she pursed her lips as if for whistling. Then with a defiant gesture of the shoulders which he remembered, she rose suddenly from the piano and placed herself in a chair opposite to him.

"That speech of yours will do as well as anything," she began slowly, looking at the point of her shoe, "to bring us to what I wanted to say. I asked you here today on purpose, Mr Trent, because I couldn't bear it any longer. Ever since the day you left me at White Gables I have been saying to myself that it didn't matter what you thought of me in that affair; that you were certainly not the kind of man to speak to others of what you believed about me, after what you had told me of your reasons for suppressing your manuscript. I asked myself how it could matter. But all the time, of course, I knew it did matter. It mattered horribly. Because what you thought was not true." She raised her eyes and met his gaze calmly. Trent, with a completely expressionless face, returned her look.

"Since I began to know you," he said, "I have ceased to think it."

"Thank you," said Mrs Manderson; and blushed suddenly and deeply. Then, playing with a glove, she added, "But I want you to know what was true.

"I did not know if I should ever see you again," she went on in a lower voice, "but I felt that if I did I must speak to you about this. I thought it would not be hard to do so, because you seemed to me an understanding person; and besides, a woman who has been married isn't expected to have the same sort of difficulty as a young girl in speaking about such things when it is necessary. And then we did meet again, and I discovered that it was very difficult indeed. You made it difficult."

"How?" he asked quietly.

"I don't know," said the lady. "But yes—I do know. It was just because you treated me exactly as if you had never thought or imagined anything of that sort about me. I had always supposed that if I saw you again you would turn on me that hard, horrible sort of look you had when you asked me that last question—do you remember?—at White Gables. Instead of that you were just like any other acquaintance. You were just"—she hesitated and spread out her hands—"nice. You know. After that first time at the opera when *I* spoke to you I went home positively wondering if you had really recognized me. I mean, I thought you might have recognized my face without remembering who it was."

A short laugh broke from Trent in spite of himself, but he said nothing.

She smiled deprecatingly. "Well, I couldn't remember if you had spoken my name; and I though it might be so. But the next time, at the Iretons', you did speak it, so I knew; and a dozen times during those few days I almost brought myself to tell you, but never quite. I began to feel that you wouldn't let me, that you would slip away from the subject if I approached it. Wasn't I right? Tell me, please." He nodded. "But why?" He remained silent.

"Well," she said, "I will finish what I had to say, and then you will tell me, I hope, why you had to make it so hard. When I began to understand that you wouldn't let me talk of the matter to you, it made me more determined than ever. I suppose you didn't realize that I would insist on speaking even if you were quite discouraging. I dare say I couldn't have done it if I had been guilty, as you thought. You walked into my parlour today, never thinking I should dare. Well, now you see."

Mrs Manderson had lost all her air of hesitancy. She had, as she was wont to say, talked herself enthusiastic and in the ardour of her purpose to annihilate the misunderstanding that had troubled her so long she felt herself mistress of the situation.

"I am going to tell you the story of the mistake you made," she continued, as Trent, his hands clasped between his knees, still looked at her enigmatically. "You will have to believe it, Mr Trent; it is utterly true to life, with its confusions and hidden things and cross-purposes and perfectly natural mistakes that nobody thinks twice about taking for facts. Please understand that I don't blame you in the least, and never did, for jumping to the conclusion you did. You knew that I was estranged from my husband, and you knew what that so often means. You knew before I told you, I expect, that he had taken up an injured attitude towards me; and I was silly enough to try and explain it away. I gave you the explanation of it that I had given myself at first, before I realized the wretched truth; I told you he was disappointed in me because I couldn't take a brilliant lead in society. Well, that was true; he was so. But I could see you weren't convinced. You had guessed what it took me much longer to see, because I knew how irrational it was. Yes; my husband was jealous of John Marlowe; you divined that.

"Then I behaved like a fool when you let me see you had divined it; it was such a blow, you understand, when I had supposed all the humiliation and strain was at an end, and that his delusion had died with him. You practically asked me if my husband's secretary was not my lover, Mr Trent—I have to say it, because I want you to understand why I broke down and made a scene. You took that for a confession; you thought I was guilty of that, and I think you even thought I might be a party to the crime, that I had consented... That did hurt me; but perhaps you couldn't have thought anything else— I don't know."

Trent, who had not hitherto taken his eyes from her face, hung his head at the words. He did not raise it again as she continued. "But really it was simple shock and distress that made me give way, and the memory of all the misery that mad suspicion had meant to me. And when I pulled myself together again you had gone."

She rose and went to an escritoire beside the window, unlocked a drawer, and drew out a long, sealed envelope.

"This is the manuscript you left with me," she said. "I have read it through again and again. I have always wondered, as everybody does, at your cleverness in things of this kind." A faintly mischievous smile flashed upon her face, and was gone. "I thought it was splendid, Mr Trent—I almost forgot that the story was my own, I was so interested. And I want to say now, while I have this in my hand, how much I thank you for your generous, chivalrous act in sacrificing this triumph of yours rather than put a woman's reputation in peril. If all had been as you supposed, the facts must have come out when the police took up the case you put in their hands. Believe me, I understood just what you had done, and I never ceased to be grateful even when I felt most crushed by your suspicion."

As she spoke her thanks her voice shook a little, and her eyes were bright. Trent perceived nothing of this. His head was still bent. He did not seem to hear. She put the envelope into his hand as it lay open, palm upwards, on his knee. There was a touch of gentleness about the act which made him look up.

"Can you—" he began slowly.

She raised her hand as she stood before him. "No, Mr Trent; let me finish before you say anything. It is such an unspeakable relief to me to have broken the ice at last, and I want to end the story while I am still feeling the triumph of beginning it." She sank down into the sofa from which she had first risen. "I am telling you a thing that nobody else knows. Everybody knew, I suppose, that something had come between us, though I did everything in my power to hide it. But I don't think anyone in the world ever guessed what my husband's notion was. People who know me don't think that sort of thing about me, I believe. And his fancy was so ridiculously opposed to the facts. I will tell you what the situation was. Mr Marlowe and I had been friendly enough since he came to us. For all his cleverness—my husband said he had a keener brain than any man he knew—I looked upon him as practically a boy. You know I am a little older than he is, and he had a sort of amiable lack of ambition that made me feel it the more. One day my husband asked me what I thought was the best thing about Marlowe, and not thinking much about it I said, 'His manners.' He surprised me very much by looking .black at that, and after a silence he said, 'Yes, Marlowe is a gentleman; that's so,' not looking at me.

"Nothing was ever said about that again until about a year ago, when I found that Mr Marlowe had done what I always expected he would do—fallen desperately in love with an American girl. But to my disgust he had picked out the most worthless girl, I do believe, of all those whom we used to meet. She was the daughter of wealthy parents, and she did as she liked with them; very beautiful, well educated, very good at games—what they call a woman-athlete—and caring for nothing on earth but her own amusement. She was one of the most unprincipled flirts I ever knew, and quite the cleverest. Everyone knew it, and Mr Marlowe must have heard it; but she made a complete fool of him, brain and all. I don't know how she managed it, but I can imagine. She liked him, of course; but it was quite plain to me that she was playing with him. The whole affair was so idiotic, I got perfectly furious. One day I asked him to row me in a boat on the lake—all this happened at our house by Lake George. We had never been alone together for any length of time before. In the boat I talked to him. I was very kind about it, I think, and he took it admirably, but he didn't believe me a bit. He had the impudence to tell me that I misunderstood Alice's nature. When I hinted at his prospects—I knew he had scarcely anything of his own—he said that if she loved him he could make himself a position in the world. I dare say that was true, with his abilities and his friends—he is rather well connected, you know, as well as popular. But his enlightenment came very soon after that.

"My husband helped me out of the boat when we got back. He joked with Mr Marlowe about something, I remember; for through all that followed he never once changed in his manner to him, and that was one reason why I took so long to realize what he thought about him and myself. But to me he was reserved and silent that evening—not angry. He was always perfectly cold and expressionless to me after he took this idea into his head. After dinner he only spoke to me once. Mr Marlowe was telling him about some horse he had bought for the farm in Kentucky, and my husband looked at me and said, 'Marlowe may be a gentleman, but he seldom quits loser in a horse-trade.' I was surprised at that, but at that time—and even on the next occasion when he found us together—I didn't understand what was in his mind. That next time was the morning when Mr Marlowe received a sweet little note from the girl asking for his congratulations on her engagement. It was in our New York house. He looked so wretched at breakfast that I thought he was ill, and afterwards I went to the room where he worked, and asked what was the matter. He didn't say anything, but just handed me the note, and turned away to the window. I was very glad that was all over, but terribly sorry for him too, of course. I don't remember what I said, but I remember putting my hand on his arm as he stood there staring out on the garden; and just then my husband appeared at the open door with some papers. He just glanced at us, and then turned and walked quietly back to his study. I thought that he might have heard what I was saying to comfort Mr Marlowe, and that it was rather nice of him to slip away. Mr Marlowe neither saw nor heard him. My husband left the house that morning for the West while I was out. Even then I did not understand. He used often to go off suddenly like that, if some business project called him.

"It was not until he returned a week later that I grasped the situation. He was looking white and strange, and as soon as he saw me he asked me where Mr Marlowe was. Somehow the tone of his question told me everything in a flash.

"I almost gasped; I was wild with indignation. You know, Mr Trent, I don't think I should have minded at all if anyone had thought me capable of openly breaking with my husband and leaving him for somebody else. I dare say I might have done that. But that coarse suspicion... a man whom he trusted... and the notion of concealment. It made me see scarlet. Every shred of pride in me was strung up till I quivered, and I swore to myself on the spot that I would never show by any word or sign that I was conscious of his having such a thought about me. I would behave exactly as I always had behaved, I determined—and that I did, up to the very last. Though I knew that a wall had been made between us now that could never be broken down—even if he asked my pardon and obtained it—I never once showed that I noticed any change.

"And so it went on. I never could go through such a time again. My husband showed silent and cold politeness to me always when we were alone—and that was only when it was unavoidable. He never once alluded to what was in his mind; but I felt it, and he knew that I felt it. Both of us were stubborn in our different attitudes. To Mr Marlowe he was more friendly, if anything, than before—heaven only knows why. I fancied he was planning some sort of revenge; but that was only a fancy. Certainly Mr Marlowe never knew what was suspected of him. He and I remained good friends, though we never spoke of anything intimate after that disappointment of his; but I made a point of seeing no less of him than I had always done. Then we came to England and to White Gables, and after that followed—my husband's dreadful end."

She threw out her right hand in a gesture of finality. "You know about the rest—so much more than any other man," she added, and glanced up at him with quaint expression.

Trent wondered at that look, but the wonder was only a passing shadow on his thought. Inwardly his whole being was possessed by thankfulness. All the vivacity had returned to his face. Long before the lady had ended her story he had recognized the certainty of its truth, as from the first days of their renewed acquaintance he had doubted the story that his imagination had built up at White Gables, upon foundations that seemed so good... to him.

He said, "I don't know how to begin the apologies I have to make. There are no words to tell you how ashamed and disgraced I feel when I realize what a crude, cocksure blundering at a conclusion my suspicion was. Yes, I suspected—you! I had almost forgotten that I was ever such a fool. Almost—not quite. Sometimes when I have been alone I have remembered that folly, and poured contempt on it. I have tried to imagine what the facts were. I have tried to excuse myself."

She interrupted him quickly. "What nonsense! Do be sensible, Mr Trent. You had only seen me on two occasions in your life before you came to me with your solution of the mystery." Again the quaint expression came and was gone. "If you talk of folly, it really is folly for a man like you to pretend to a woman like me that I had innocence written all over me in large letters—so large that you couldn't believe very strong evidence against me after seeing me twice."

"What do you mean by 'a man like me'?" he demanded with a sort of fierceness. "Do you take me for a person without any normal instincts? I don't say you impress people as a simple, transparent sort of character—what Mr Calvin Bunner calls a case of open-work; I don't say a stranger might not think you capable of wickedness, if there was good evidence for it: but I say that a man who, after seeing you and being in your atmosphere, could associate you with the particular kind of abomination I imagined, is a fool—the kind of fool who is afraid to trust his senses... As for my making it hard for you to approach the subject, as you say, it is true. It was simply moral cowardice. I understood that you wished to clear the matter up; and I was revolted at the notion of my injurious blunder being discussed. I tried to show you by my actions that it was as if it had never been. I hoped you would pardon me without any words. I can't forgive myself, and I never shall. And yet if you could know—" He stopped short, and then added quietly: "Well, will you accept all that as an apology? The very scrubbiest sackcloth made, and the grittiest ashes on the heap... I didn't mean to get worked up," he ended lamely.

Mrs Manderson laughed, and her laugh carried him away with it. He knew well by this time that sudden rush of cascading notes of mirth, the perfect expression of enjoyment; he had many times tried to amuse her merely for his delight in the sound of it.

"But I love to see you worked up," she said. "The bump with which you always come down as soon as you realize that you are up in the air at all is quite delightful. Oh, we're actually both laughing. What a triumphant end to our explanations, after all my dread of the time when I should have it out with you. And now it's all over, and you know; and we'll never speak of it any more."

"I hope not," Trent said in sincere relief. "If you're resolved to be so kind as this about it, I am not high-principled enough to insist on your blasting me with your lightnings. And now, Mrs Manderson, I had better go. Changing the subject after this would be like playing puss-in-the-corner after an earthquake." He rose to his feet.

"You are right," she said. "But no! Wait. There is another thing—part of the same subject; and we ought to pick up all the pieces now while we are about it. Please sit down." She took the envelope containing Trent's manuscript dispatch from the table where he had laid it. "I want to speak about this."

His brows bent, and he looked at her questioningly. "So do I, if you do," he said slowly. "I want very much to know one thing."

"Tell me."

"Since my reason for suppressing that information was all a fantasy, why did you never make any use of it? When I began to realize that I had been wrong about you, I explained your silence to myself by saying that you could not bring yourself to do a thing that would put a rope round a man's neck, whatever he might have done. I can quite understand that feeling. Was that what it was? Another possibility I thought of was that you knew of something that was by way of justifying or excusing Marlowe's act. Or I thought you might have a simple horror, quite apart from humanitarian scruples, of appearing publicly in connection with a murder trial. Many important witnesses in such cases have to be practically forced into giving their evidence. They feel there is defilement in the shadow of the scaffold."

Mrs Manderson tapped her lips with the envelope without quite concealing a smile. "You didn't think of another possibility, I suppose, Mr Trent," she said.

"No." He looked puzzled.

"I mean the possibility of your having been wrong about Mr Marlowe as well as about me. No, no; you needn't tell me that the chain of evidence is complete. I know it is. But evidence of what? Of Mr Marlowe having impersonated my husband that night, and having escaped by way of my window, and built up an alibi. I have read your dispatch again and again, Mr Trent, and I don't see that those things can be doubted."

Trent gazed at her with narrowed eyes. He said nothing to fill the brief pause that followed. Mrs Manderson smoothed her skirt with a preoccupied air, as one collecting her ideas.

"I did not make any use of the facts found out by you," she slowly said at last, "because it seemed to me very likely that they would be fatal to Mr Marlowe."

"I agree with you," Trent remarked in a colourless tone.

"And," pursued the lady, looking up at him with a mild reasonableness in her eyes, "as I knew that he was innocent I was not going to expose him to that risk."

There was another little pause. Trent rubbed his chin, with an affectation of turning over the idea. Inwardly he was telling himself, somewhat feebly, that this was very right and proper; that it was quite feminine, and that he liked her to be feminine. It was permitted to her—more than permitted—to set her loyal belief in the character of a friend above the clearest demonstrations of the intellect. Nevertheless, it chafed him. He would have had her declaration of faith a little less positive in form. It was too irrational to say she "knew." In fact (he put it to himself bluntly), it was quite unlike her. If to be unreasonable when reason led to the unpleasant was a specially feminine trait, and if Mrs Manderson had it, she was accustomed to wrap it up better than any woman he had known.

"You suggest," he said at length, "that Marlowe constructed an alibi for himself, by means which only a desperate man would have attempted, to clear himself of a crime he did not commit. Did he tell you he was innocent?"

She uttered a little laugh of impatience. "So you think he has been talking me round. No, that is not so. I am merely sure he did not do it. Ah! I see you think that absurd. But see how unreasonable you are, Mr Trent! Just now you were explaining to me quite sincerely that it was foolishness in you to have a certain suspicion of me after seeing me and being in my atmosphere, as you said." Trent started in his chair. She glanced at him, and went on: "Now, I and my atmosphere are much obliged to you, but we must stand up for the rights of other atmospheres. I know a great deal more about Mr Marlowe's atmosphere than you know about mine even now. I saw him constantly for several years. I don't pretend to know all about him; but I do know that he is incapable of a crime of bloodshed. The idea of his planning a murder is as unthinkable to me as the idea of your picking a poor woman's pocket, Mr Trent. I can imagine you killing a man, you know... if the man deserved it and had an equal chance of killing you. I could kill a person myself in some circumstances. But Mr Marlowe was incapable of doing it, I don't care what the provocation might be. He had a temper that nothing should shake, and he looked upon human nature with a sort of cold magnanimity that would find excuses for absolutely anything. It wasn't a pose; you could see it was a part of him. He never put it forward, but it was there always. It was quite irritating at times... Now and then in America, I remember, I have heard people talking about lynching, for instance, when he was there. He would sit quite silent and expressionless, appearing not to listen; but you could feel disgust coming from him in waves. He really loathed and hated physical violence. He was a very strange man in some ways, Mr Trent. He gave one a feeling that he might do unexpected things—do you know that feeling one has about some people? What part he really played in the events of that night I have never been able to guess. But nobody who knew anything about him could possibly believe in his deliberately taking a man's life." Again the movement of her head expressed finality, and she leaned back in the sofa, calmly regarding him.

"Then," said Trent, who had followed this with earnest attention, "we are forced back on two other possibilities, which I had not thought worth much consideration until this moment. Accepting what you say, he might still conceivably have killed in self-defence; or he might have done so by accident."

The lady nodded. "Of course I thought of those two explanations when I read your manuscript."

"And I suppose you felt, as I did myself, that in either of those cases the natural thing, and obviously the safest thing, for him to do was to make a public statement of the truth, instead of setting up a series of deceptions which would certainly stamp him as guilty in the eyes of the law, if anything went wrong with them."

"Yes," she said wearily, "I thought over all that until my head ached. And I thought somebody else might have done it, and that he was somehow screening the guilty person. But that seemed wild. I could see no light in the mystery, and after a while I simply left it alone. All I was clear about was that Mr Marlowe was not a murderer, and that if I told what you had found out, the judge and jury would probably think he was. I promised myself that I would speak to you about it if we should meet again; and now I've kept my promise."

Trent, his chin resting on his hand, was staring at the carpet. The excitement of the hunt for the truth was steadily rising in him. He had not in his own mind accepted Mrs Manderson's account of Marlowe's character as unquestionable. But she had spoken forcibly; he could by no means set it aside, and his theory was much shaken.

"There is only one thing for it," he said, looking up. "I must see Marlowe. It worries me too much to have the thing left like this. I will get at the truth. Can you tell me," he broke off, "how he behaved after the day I left White Gables?"

"I never saw him after that," said Mrs Manderson simply. "For some days after you went away I was ill, and didn't go out of my room. When I got down he had left and was in London, settling things with the lawyers. He did not come down to the funeral. Immediately after that I went abroad. After some weeks a letter from him reached me, saying he had concluded his business and given the solicitors all the assistance in his power.

He thanked me very nicely for what he called all my kindness, and said goodby. There was nothing in it about his plans for the future, and I thought it particularly strange that he said not a word about my husband's death. I didn't answer. Knowing what I knew, I couldn't. In those days I shuddered whenever I thought of that masquerade in the night. I never wanted to see or hear of him again."

"Then you don't know what has become of him?"

"No; but I dare say Uncle Burton—Mr Cupples, you know—could tell you. Some time ago he told me that he had met Mr Marlowe in London, and had some talk with him. I changed the conversation." She paused and smiled with a trace of mischief. "I rather wonder what you supposed had happened to Mr Marlowe after you withdrew from the scene of the drama that you had put together so much to your satisfaction."

Trent flushed. "Do you really want to know?" he said.

"I ask you," she retorted quietly.

"You ask me to humiliate myself again, Mrs Manderson. Very well. I will tell you what I thought I should most likely find when I returned to London after my travels; that you had married Marlowe and gone to live abroad."

She heard him with unmoved composure. "We certainly couldn't have lived very comfortably in England on his money and mine," she observed thoughtfully. "He had practically nothing then."

He stared at her—"gaped," she told him some time afterwards. At the moment she laughed with a little embarrassment.

"Dear me, Mr Trent! Have I said anything dreadful? You surely must know... I thought everybody understood by now... I'm sure I've had to explain it often enough... if I marry again I lose everything that my husband left me."

The effect of this speech upon Trent was curious. For an instant his face was flooded with the emotion of surprise. As this passed away he gradually drew himself together, as he sat, into a tense attitude. He looked, she thought as she saw his knuckles grow white on the arms of the chair, like a man prepared for pain under the hand of the surgeon. But all he said, in a voice lower than his usual tone, was: "I had no idea of it."

"It is so," she said calmly, trifling with a ring on her finger. "Really, Mr Trent, it is not such a very unusual thing. I think I am glad of it. For one thing, it has secured me—at least since it became generally known—from a good many attentions of a kind that a woman in my position has to put up with as a rule."

"No doubt," he said gravely. "And... the other kind?"

She looked at him questioningly. "Ah!" she laughed. "The other kind trouble me even less. I have not yet met a man silly enough to want to marry a widow with a selfish disposition, and luxurious habits and tastes, and nothing but the little my father left me."

She shook her head, and something in the gesture shattered the last remnants of Trent's self-possession.

"Haven't you, by heaven!" he exclaimed, rising with a violent movement and advancing a step towards her. "Then I am going to show you that human passion is not always stifled by the smell of money. I am going to end the business—my business. I am going to tell you what I dare say scores of better men have wanted to tell you, but couldn't summon up what I have summoned up—the infernal cheek to do it. They were afraid of making fools of themselves. I am not. You have accustomed me to the feeling this afternoon." He laughed aloud in the rush of words, and spread out his hands. "Look at me! It is the sight of the century. It is one who says he loves you, and would ask you to give up very great wealth to stand at his side."

She was hiding her face in her hands. He heard her say brokenly: "Please... don't speak in that way."

He answered: "It will make a great difference to me if you will allow me to say all I have to say before I leave you. Perhaps it is in bad taste, but I will risk that; I want to relieve my soul;

it needs open confession. This is the truth. You have troubled me ever since the first time I saw you—and you did not know it—as you sat under the edge of the cliff at Marlstone, and held out your arms to the sea. It was only your beauty that filled my mind then. As I passed by you it seemed as if all the life in the place were crying out a song about you in the wind and the sunshine. And the song stayed in my ears; but even your beauty would be no more than an empty memory to me by now if that had been all. It was when I led you from the hotel there to your house, with your hand on my arm, that—what was it that happened? I only knew that your stronger magic had struck home, and that I never should forget that day, whatever the love of my life should be. Till that day I had admired as I should admire the loveliness of a still lake; but that day I felt the spell of the divinity of the lake. And next morning the waters were troubled, and she rose—the morning when I came to you with my questions, tired out with doubts that were as bitter as pain, and when I saw you without your pale, sweet mask of composure—when I saw you moved and glowing, with your eyes and your hands alive, and when you made me understand that for such a creature as you there had been emptiness and the mere waste of yourself for so long. Madness rose in me then, and my spirit was clamouring to say what I say at last now: that life would never seem a full thing again because you could not love me, that I was taken for ever in the nets of your black hair and by the incantation of your voice—"

"Oh, stop!" she cried, suddenly throwing back her head, her face flaming and her hands clutching the cushions beside her. She spoke fast and disjointedly, her breath coming quick. "You shall not talk me into forgetting common sense. What does all this mean? Oh, I do not recognize you at all—you seem another man. We are not children; have you forgotten that? You speak like a boy in love for the first time. It is foolish, unreal—I know that if you do not, I will not hear it. What has happened to you?" She was half sobbing. "How can these sentimentalities come from a man like you? Where is your self-restraint?"

"Gone!" exclaimed Trent, with an abrupt laugh. "It has got right away. I am going after it in a minute." He looked gravely down into her eyes. "I don't care so much now. I never could declare myself to you under the cloud of your great fortune. It was too heavy. There's nothing creditable in that feeling, as I look at it; as a matter of simple fact it was a form of cowardice—fear of what you would think, and very likely say—fear of the world's comment too, I suppose. But the cloud being rolled away, I have spoken, and I don't care so much. I can face things with a quiet mind now that I have told you the truth in its own terms. You may call it sentimentality or any other nickname you like. It is quite true that it was not intended for a scientific statement. Since it annoys you, let it be extinguished. But please believe that it was serious to me if it was comedy to you. I have said that I love you, and honour you, and would hold you dearest of all the world. Now give me leave to go."

But she held out her hands to him.

14

WRITING A LETTER

"If you insist," Trent said, "I suppose you will have your way. But I had much rather write it when I am not with you. However, if I must, bring me a tablet whiter than a star, or hand of hymning angel; I mean a sheet of note-paper not stamped with your address. Don't underestimate the sacrifice I am making. I never felt like correspondence in my life."

She rewarded him.

"What shall I say?" he inquired, his pen hovering over the paper. "Shall I compare him to a summer's day? What *shall* I say?"

"Say what you want to say," she suggested helpfully.

He shook his head. "What I want to say—what I have been wanting for the past twenty-four hours to say to every man, woman, and child I met—is 'Mabel and I are betrothed, and all is gas and gaiters.' But that wouldn't be a very good opening for a letter of strictly formal, not to say sinister, character. I have got as far as 'Dear Mr Marlowe.' What comes next?"

"I am sending you a manuscript," she prompted, "which I thought you might like to see."

"Do you realize," he said, "that in that sentence there are only two words of more than one syllable? This letter is meant to impress, not to put him at his ease. We must have long words."

"I don't see why," she answered. "I know it is usual, but why is it? I have had a great many letters from lawyers and business people, and they always begin: 'with reference to our communication,' or some such mouthful, and go on like that all the way through. Yet when I see them they don't talk like that. It seems ridiculous to me."

"It is not at all ridiculous to them." Trent laid aside the pen with an appearance of relief and rose to his feet. "Let me explain. A people like our own, not very fond of using its mind, gets on in the ordinary way with a very small and simple vocabulary. Long words are abnormal, and like everything else that is abnormal, they are either very funny or tremendously solemn. Take the phrase 'intelligent anticipation,' for instance. If such a phrase had been used in any other country in Europe, it would not have attracted the slightest attention. With us it has become a proverb; we all grin when we hear it in a speech or read it in a leading article; it is considered to be one of the best things ever said. Why? Just because it consists of two long words. The idea expressed is as commonplace as cold mutton. Then there's 'terminological inexactitude.' How we all roared, and are still roaring, at that! And the whole of the joke is that the words are long. It's just the same when we want to be very serious; we mark it by turning to long words. When a solicitor can begin a sentence with: 'pursuant to the instructions communicated to our representative,' or some such gibberish, he feels that he is earning his six-and-eightpence. Don't laugh! It is perfectly true. Now Continentals haven't got that feeling. They are always bothering about ideas, and the result is that every shopkeeper or peasant has a vocabulary in daily use that is simply Greek to the vast majority of Britons. I remember some time ago I was dining with a friend of mine who is a Paris cabman. We had dinner at a dirty little restaurant opposite the central post office, a place where all the clients were cabmen or porters. Conversation was general, and it struck me that a London cabman would have felt a little out of his depth. Words like 'functionary' and 'unforgettable' and 'exterminate' and 'independence' hurtled across the table every instant. And these were just ordinary, vulgar, jolly, red-faced cabmen. Mind you," he went on hurriedly, as the lady crossed the room and took up his pen, "I merely mention this to illustrate my point. I'm not saying that cabmen ought to be intellectuals. I don't think so; I agree with Keats—happy is England, sweet her artless cabmen, enough their simple loveliness for me. But when you come to the people who make up the collective industrial brain-power of the country... Why, do you know—"

"Oh, no, no, no!" cried Mrs Manderson. "I don't know anything at the moment, except that your talking must be stopped somehow, if we are to get any farther with that letter to Mr Marlowe. You shall not get out of it. Come!" She put the pen into his hand.

Trent looked at it with distaste. "I warn you not to discourage my talking," he said dejectedly. "Believe me, men who don't talk are even worse to live with than men who do. Oh, have a care of natures that are mute. I confess I'm shirking writing this thing. It is almost an indecency. It's mixing two moods to write the sort of letter I mean to write, and at the same time to be sitting in the same room with you."

She led him to his abandoned chair before the escritoire and pushed him gently into it. "Well, but please try. I want to see what you write, and I want it to go to him at once. You see, I would be contented enough to leave things as they are; but you say you must get at the truth, and if you must, I want it to be as soon as possible. Do it now—you know you can if you will—and I'll send it off the moment it's ready. Don't you ever feel that—the longing to get the worrying letter into the post and off your hands, so that you can't recall it if you would, and it's no use fussing any more about it?'

"I will do as you wish," he said, and turned to the paper, which he dated as from his hotel. Mrs Manderson looked down at his bent head with a gentle light in her eyes, and made as if to place a smoothing hand upon his rather untidy crop of hair. But she did not touch it. Going in silence to the piano, she began to play very softly. It was ten minutes before Trent spoke.

"If he chooses to reply that he will say nothing?"

Mrs Manderson looked over her shoulder. "Of course he dare not take that line. He will speak to prevent you from denouncing him."

"But I'm not going to do that anyhow. You wouldn't allow it—you said so; besides, I won't if you would. The thing's too doubtful now."

"But," she laughed, "poor Mr Marlowe doesn't know you won't, does he?"

Trent sighed. "What extraordinary things codes of honour are!" he remarked abstractedly. "I know that there are things I should do, and never think twice about, which would make you feel disgraced if you did them—such as giving anyone who grossly in suited me a black eye, or swearing violently when I barked my shin in a dark room. And now you are calmly recommending me to bluff Marlowe by means of a tacit threat which I don't mean; a thing which hell's most abandoned fiend did never, in the drunkenness of guilt—well, anyhow, f won't do it." He resumed his writing, and the lady, with an indulgent smile, returned to playing very softly.

In a few minutes more, Trent said: "At last I am his faithfully. Do you want to see it?" She ran across the twilit room, and turned on a reading lamp beside the escritoire. Then, leaning on his shoulder, she read what follows:

DEAR MR MARLOWE,—You *will perhaps remember that we met,* under unhappy *circumstances, in* June of last year *at Marlstone.*

On that occasion it was my duty, as representing a newspaper, to make an independent investigation of the circumstances of the death of the late Sigsbee Manderson. I did so, and I arrived at certain conclusions. You may learn from the enclosed manuscript, which was originally written as a dispatch for my newspaper, what those conclusions were. For reasons which it is not necessary to state I decided at the last moment not to make them public, nor to communicate them to you, and they are known to only two persons besides myself.

At this point Mrs Manderson raised her eyes quickly from the letter. Her dark brows were drawn together. "Two persons?" she said with a note of inquiry.

"Your uncle is the other. I sought him out last night and told him the whole story. Have you anything against it? I always felt uneasy at keeping it from him as I did, because I had led him to expect I should tell him all I discovered, and my silence looked like mystery-making. Now it is to be cleared up finally, and there is no question of shielding you, I wanted him to know everything. He is a very shrewd adviser, too, in a way of his own; and I should like to have him with me when I see Marlowe. I have a feeling that two heads will be better than one on my side of the interview."

She sighed. "Yes, of course, Uncle ought to know the truth. I hope there is nobody else at all." She pressed his hand. "I so much want all that horror buried—buried deep. I am very happy now, dear, but I shall be happier still when you have satisfied that curious mind of yours and found out everything, and stamped down the earth upon it all." She continued her reading.

Quite recently, however (the letter went on), *facts have come to my knowledge which have led me to change my decision.*

I do not mean that I shall publish what I discovered, but that I have determined to approach you *and ask you for a private statement. If you have anything to say which would place the matter in another light, I can imagine no reason why* you *should withhold it.*

I expect, then, to hear from you when and where I may call upon you; unless you would prefer the interview to take place at my hotel. In either case I desire that Mr Cupples, whom you will remember, and who has read the enclosed document, should be present also.—Faithfully yours,

PHILIP TRENT.

"What a very stiff letter!" she said. "Now I am sure you couldn't have made it any stiffer in your own rooms."

Trent slipped the letter and enclosure into a long envelope. "Yes," he said, "I think it will make him sit up suddenly. Now this thing mustn't run any risk of going wrong. It would be best to send a special messenger with orders to deliver it into his own hands. If he's away it oughtn't to be left."

She nodded. "I can arrange that. Wait here for a little."

When Mrs Manderson returned, he was hunting through the music cabinet, and she knelt on the carpet beside him. "Tell me something, Philip," she said.

"If it is among the few things that I know."

"When you saw Uncle last night, did you tell him about—about us?"

"I did not," he answered. "I remembered you had said nothing about telling anyone. It is for you—isn't it?—to decide whether we take the world into our confidence at once or later on."

"Then will you tell him?" She looked down at her clasped hands. "I wish you to tell him. Perhaps if you think you will guess why... There! That is settled." She lifted her eyes again to his, and for a time there was silence between them.

He leaned back at length in the deep chair. "What a world!" he said. "Mabel, will you play something on the piano that expresses mere joy, the genuine article, nothing feverish or like thorns under a pot, but joy that has decided in favour of the universe? It's a mood that can't last altogether, so we had better get all we can out of it."

She went to the instrument and struck a few chords while she thought. Then she began to work with all her soul at the theme in the last movement of the Ninth Symphony which is like the sound of the opening of the gates of Paradise.

15

DOUBLE CUNNING

An old oaken desk with a deep body stood by the window in a room that overlooked St. James's Park from a height. The room was large, furnished and decorated by someone who had brought taste to the work; but the hand of the bachelor lay heavily upon it. John Marlowe unlocked the desk and drew a long, stout envelope from the back of the well.

"I understand," he said to Mr Cupples, "that you have read this."

"I read it for the first time two days ago," replied Mr Cupples, who, seated on a sofa, was peering about the room with a benignant face. "We have discussed it fully."

Marlowe turned to Trent. "There is your manuscript," he said, laying the envelope on the table. "I have gone over it three times. I do not believe there is another man who could have got at as much of the truth as you have set down there."

Trent ignored the compliment. He sat by the table gazing stonily at the fire, his long legs twisted beneath his chair. "You mean, of course," he said, drawing the envelope towards him, "that there is more of the truth to be disclosed now. We are ready to hear you as soon as you like. I expect it will be a long story, and the longer the better, so far as I am concerned; I want to understand thoroughly. What we should both like, I think, is some preliminary account of Manderson and your relations with him. It seemed to me from the first that the character of the dead man must be somehow an element in the business."

"You were right," Marlowe answered grimly. He crossed the room and seated himself on a corner of the tall cushion-topped fender. "I will begin as you suggest."

"I ought to tell you beforehand," said Trent, looking him in the eyes, "that although I am here to listen to you, I have not as yet any reason to doubt the conclusions I have stated here." He tapped the envelope. "It is a defence that you will be putting forward—you understand that?"

"Perfectly." Marlowe was cool and in complete possession of himself, a man different indeed from the worn-out, nervous being Trent remembered at Marlstone a year and a half ago. His tall, lithe figure was held with the perfection of muscular tone. His brow was candid, his blue eyes were clear, though they still had, as he paused collecting his ideas, the look that had troubled Trent at their first meeting. Only the lines of his mouth showed that he knew himself in a position of difficulty, and meant to face it.

"Sigsbee Manderson was not a man of normal mind," Marlowe began in his quiet voice. "Most of the very rich men I met with in America had become so by virtue of abnormal greed, or abnormal industry, or abnormal personal force, or abnormal luck. None of them had remarkable intellects. Manderson delighted too in heaping up wealth; he worked incessantly at it; he was a man of dominant will; he had quite his share of luck; but what made him singular was his brain-power. In his own country they would perhaps tell you that it was his ruthlessness in pursuit of his aims that was his most striking characteristic; but there are hundreds of them who would have carried out his plans with just as little consideration for others if they could have formed the plans.

"I'm not saying Americans aren't clever; they are ten times cleverer than we are, as a nation; but I never met another who showed such a degree of sagacity and foresight, such gifts of memory and mental tenacity, such sheer force of intelligence, as there was behind everything Manderson did in his money-making career. They called him the 'Napoleon of Wall Street' often enough in the papers; but few people knew so well as I did how much truth there was in the phrase. He seemed never to forget a fact that might be of use to him, in the first place; and he did systematically with the business facts that concerned him what Napoleon did, as I have read, with military facts. He studied them in special digests which were prepared for him at short intervals, and which he always had at hand, so that he could take up his report on coal or wheat or railways, of whatever it might be, in any unoccupied moment. Then he could make a bolder and cleverer plan than any man of them all. People got to know that Manderson would never do the obvious thing, but they got no farther; the thing he did do was almost always a surprise, and much of his success flowed from that. The Street got rattled, as they used to put it, when it was known that the old man was out with his gun, and often his opponents seemed to surrender as easily as Colonel Crockett's coon in the story. The scheme I am going to describe to you would have occupied most men long enough. Manderson could have plotted the whole thing, down to the last detail, while he shaved himself.

"I used to think that his strain of Indian blood, remote as it was, might have something to do with the cunning and ruthlessness of the man. Strangely enough, its existence was unknown to anyone but himself and me. It was when he asked me to apply my taste for genealogical work to his own obscure family history that I made the discovery that he had in him a share of the blood of the Iroquois chief Montour and his French wife, a terrible woman who ruled the savage politics of the tribes of the wilderness two hundred years ago. The Mandersons were active in the fur trade on the Pennsylvania border in those days, and more than one of them married Indian women. Other Indian blood than Montour's may have descended to Manderson, for all I can say, through previous and subsequent unions; some of the wives' antecedents were quite untraceable, and there were so many generations of pioneering before the whole country was brought under civilization. My researches left me with the idea that there is a very great deal of the aboriginal blood present in the genealogical make-up of the people of America, and that it is very widely spread. The newer families have constantly intermarried with the older, and so many of them had a strain of the native in them—and were often rather proud of it, too, in those days. But Manderson had the idea about the disgracefulness of mixed blood, which grew much stronger, I fancy, with the rise of the Negro question after the war. He was thunderstruck at what I told him, and was anxious to conceal it from every soul. Of course I never gave it away while he lived, and I don't think he supposed I would; but I have thought since that his mixed mind took a turn against me from that time onward. It happened about a year before his death."

"Had Manderson," asked Mr Cupples, so unexpectedly that the others started, "any definable religious attitude?"

Marlowe considered a moment. "None that ever I heard of," he said. "Worship and prayer were quite unknown to him, so far as I could see, and I never heard him mention religion. I should doubt if he had any real sense of God at all, or if he was capable of knowing God through the emotions. But I understood that as a child he had a religious upbringing with a strong moral side to it. His private life was, in the usual limited sense, blameless. He was almost ascetic in his habits, except as to smoking. I lived with him four years without ever knowing him to tell a direct verbal falsehood, constantly as he used to practise deceit in other forms. Can you understand the soul of a man who never hesitated to take steps that would have the effect of hoodwinking people, who would use every trick of the markets to mislead, and who was at the same time scrupulous never to utter a direct lie on the most insignificant matter? Manderson was like that, and he was not the only one. I suppose you might compare the state of mind to that of a soldier who is personally a truthful man, but who will stick at nothing to deceive the enemy. The rules of the game allow it; and the same may be said of business as many business men regard it. Only with them it is always war-time."

"It is a sad world," observed Mr Cupples.

"As you say," Marlowe agreed. "Now I was saying that one could always take Manderson's word if he gave it in a definite form. The first time I ever heard him utter a downright lie was on the night he died; and hearing it, I believe, saved me from being hanged as his murderer."

Marlowe stared at the light above his head, and Trent moved impatiently in his chair. "Before we come to that," he said, "will you tell us exactly on what footing you were with Manderson during the years you were with him?"

"We were on very good terms from beginning to end," answered Marlowe. "Nothing like friendship—he was not a man for making friends—but the best of terms as between a trusted employee and his chief. I went to him as private secretary just after getting my degree at Oxford. I was to have gone into my father's business, where I am now, but my father suggested that I should see the world for a year or two. So I took this secretaryship, which seemed to promise a good deal of varied experience, and I had let the year or two run on to four years before the end came. The offer came to me through the last thing in the world I should have put forward as a qualification for a salaried post, and that was chess."

At the word Trent struck his hands together with a muttered exclamation. The others looked at him in surprise.

"Chess!" repeated Trent. "Do you know," he said, rising and approaching Marlowe, "what was the first thing I noted about you at our first meeting? It was your eye, Mr Marlowe. I couldn't place it then, but I know now where I had seen your eyes before. They were in the head of no less a man than the great Nikolay Korchagin, with whom I once sat in the same railway carriage for two days. I thought I should never forget the chess eye after that, but I could not put a name to it when I saw it in you. I beg your pardon," he ended suddenly, resuming his marmoreal attitude in his chair.

"I have played the game from my childhood, and with good players," said Marlowe simply. "It is an hereditary gift, if you can call it a gift. At the University I was nearly as good as anybody there, and I gave most of my brains to that and the O.U.D.S. and playing about generally. At Oxford, as I dare say you know, inducements to amuse oneself at the expense of one's education are endless, and encouraged by the authorities. Well, one day toward the end of my last term, Dr. Munro of Queen's, whom I had never defeated, sent for me. He told me that I played a fairish game of chess. I said it was very good of him to say so. Then he said: 'They tell me you hunt, too.' I said: 'Now and then.' He asked: 'Is there anything else you can do?' 'No,' I said, not much liking the tone of the conversation—the old man generally succeeded in putting people's backs up. He grunted fiercely, and then told me that inquiries were being made on behalf of a wealthy American man of business who wanted an English secretary. Manderson was the name, he said. He seemed never to have heard it before, which was quite possible, as he never opened a newspaper and had not slept a night outside the college for thirty years. If I could rub up my spelling—as the old gentleman put it—I might have a good chance for the post, as chess and riding and an Oxford education were the only indispensable points.

"Well, I became Manderson's secretary. For a long time I liked the position greatly. When one is attached to an active American plutocrat in the prime of life one need not have many dull moments. Besides, it made me independent. My father had some serious business reverses about that time, and I was glad to be able to do without an allowance from him. At the end of the first year Manderson doubled my salary. 'It's big money,' he said, 'but I guess I don't lose.' You see, by that time I was doing a great deal more than accompany him on horseback in the morning and play chess in the evening, which was mainly what he had required. I was attending to his houses, his farm in Ohio, his shooting in Maine, his horses, his cars, and his yacht. I had become a walking railway-guide and an expert cigar-buyer. I was always learning something.

"Well, now you understand what my position was in regard to Manderson during the last two or three years of my connection with him. It was a happy life for me on the whole. I was busy, my work was varied and interesting; I had time to amuse myself too, and money to spend. At one time I made a fool of myself about a girl, and that was not a happy time; but it taught me to understand the great goodness of Mrs Manderson." Marlowe inclined his head to Mr Cupples as he said this. "She may choose to tell you about it. As for her husband, he had never varied in his attitude towards me, in spite of the change that came over him in the last months of his life, as you know. He treated me well and generously in his unsympathetic way, and I never had a feeling that he was less than satisfied with his bargain—that was the sort of footing we lived upon. And it was that continuance of his attitude right up to the end that made the revelation so shocking when I was suddenly shown, on the night on which he met his end, the depth of crazy hatred of myself that was in Manderson's soul."

The eyes of Trent and Mr Cupples met for an instant.

"You never suspected that he hated you before that time?" asked Trent; and Mr Cupples asked at the same moment: "To what did you attribute it?"

"I never guessed until that night," answered Marlowe, "that he had the smallest ill-feeling toward me. How long it had existed I do not know. I cannot imagine why it was there. I was forced to think, when I considered the thing in those awful days after his death, and it was a case of a madman's delusion, that he believed me to be plotting against him, as they so often do. Some such insane conviction must have been at the root of it. But who can sound the abysses of a lunatic's fancy? Can you imagine the state of mind in which a man dooms himself to death with the object of delivering someone he hates to the hangman?"

Mr Cupples moved sharply in his chair. "You say Manderson was responsible for his own death?" he asked.

Trent glanced at him with an eye of impatience, and resumed his intent watch upon the face of Marlowe. In the relief of speech it was now less pale and drawn.

"I do say so," Marlowe answered concisely, and looked his questioner in the face. Mr Cupples nodded.

"Before we proceed to the elucidation of your statement," observed the old gentleman, in a tone of one discussing a point of abstract science, "it may be remarked that the state of mind which you attribute to Manderson—"

"Suppose we have the story first," Trent interrupted, gently laying a hand on Mr Cupples's arm. "You were telling us," he went on, turning to Marlowe, "how things stood between you and Manderson. Now will you tell us the facts of what happened that night?"

Marlowe flushed at the barely perceptible emphasis which Trent laid upon the word "facts." He drew himself up.

"Bunner and myself dined with Mr and Mrs Manderson that Sunday evening," he began, speaking carefully. "It was just like other dinners at which the four of us had been together. Manderson was taciturn and gloomy, as we had latterly been accustomed to see him. We others kept a conversation going. We rose from the table, I suppose, about nine. Mrs Manderson went to the drawing-room, and Bunner went up to the hotel to see an acquaintance. Manderson asked me to come into the orchard behind the house, saying he wished to have a talk. We paced up and down the pathway there, out of earshot from the house, and Manderson, as he smoked his cigar, spoke to me in his cool, deliberate way. He had never seemed more sane, or more well-disposed to me. He said he wanted me to do him an important service. There was a big thing on. It was a secret affair. Bunner knew nothing of it, and the less I knew the better. He wanted me to do exactly as he directed, and not bother my head about reasons.

"This, I may say, was quite characteristic of Manderson's method of going to work. If at times he required a man to be a mere tool in his hand, he would tell him so. He had used me in the same kind of way a dozen times. I assured him he could rely on me, and said I was ready. 'Right now?' he asked. I said of course I was.

"He nodded, and said—I tell you his words as well as I can recollect them—'Well, attend to this. There is a man in England now who is in this thing with me. He was to have left tomorrow for Paris by the noon-boat from Southampton to Havre. His name is George Harris—at least that's the name he is going by. Do you remember that name?' 'Yes,' I said, 'when I went up to London a week ago you asked me to book a cabin in that name on the boat that goes tomorrow. I gave you the ticket.' 'Here it is,' he said, producing it from his pocket.

" 'Now,' Manderson said to me, poking his cigar-butt at me with each sentence in a way he used to have, 'George Harris cannot leave England tomorrow. I find I shall want him where he is. And I want Bunner where he is. But somebody has got to go by that boat and take certain papers to Paris. Or else my plan is going to fall to pieces. Will you go?' I said, 'Certainly. I am here to obey orders.'

"He bit his cigar, and said: 'That's all right; but these are not just ordinary orders. Not the kind of thing one can ask of a man in the ordinary way of his duty to an employer. The point is this. The deal I am busy with is one in which neither myself nor anyone known to be connected with me must appear as yet. That is vital. But these people I am up against know your face as well as they know mine. If my secretary is known in certain quarters to have crossed to Paris at this time and to have interviewed certain people—and that would be known as soon as it happened—then the game is up.' He threw away his cigar-end and looked at me questioningly.

"I didn't like it much, but I liked failing Manderson at a pinch still less. I spoke lightly. I said I supposed I should have to conceal my identity, and I would do my best. I told him I used to be pretty good at make-up.

"He nodded in approval. He said: 'That's good. I judged you would not let me down.' Then he gave me my instructions. 'You take the car right now,' he said, 'and start for Southampton—there's no train that will fit in. You'll be driving all night. Barring accidents, you ought to get there by six in the morning. But whenever you arrive, drive straight to the Bedford Hotel and ask for George Harris. If he's there, tell him you are to go over instead of him, and ask him to telephone me here. It is very important he should know that at the earliest moment possible. But if he isn't there, that means he has got the instructions I wired today, and hasn't gone to Southampton. In that case you don't want to trouble about him any more, but just wait for the boat. You can leave the car at a garage under a fancy name—mine must not be given. See about changing your appearance—I don't care how, so you do it well. Travel by the boat as George Harris. Let on to be anything you like, but be careful, and don't talk much to anybody. When you arrive, take a room at the Hotel St. Petersbourg. You will receive a note or message there, addressed to George Hanis, telling you where to take the wallet I shall give you. The wallet is locked, and you want to take good care of it. Have you got that all clear?'

"I repeated the instructions. I asked if I should return from Paris after handing over the wallet. 'As soon as you like,' he said. 'And mind this—whatever happens, don't communicate with me at any stage of the journey. If you don't get the message in Paris at once, just wait until you do—days, if necessary. But not a line of any sort to me. Understand? Now get ready as quick as you can. I'll go with you in the car a little way. Hurry.'

"That is, as far as I can remember, the exact substance of what Manderson said to me that night. I went to my room, changed into day clothes, and hastily threw a few necessaries into a kit-bag. My mind was in a whirl, not so much at the nature of the business as at the suddenness of it. I think I remember telling you the last time we met"—he turned to Trent—"that Manderson shared the national fondness for doing things in a story-book style. Other things being equal, he delighted in a bit of mystification and melodrama, and I told myself that this was Manderson all over. I hurried downstairs with my bag and rejoined him in the library. He handed me a stout leather letter-case, about eight inches by six, fastened with a strap with a lock on it. I could just squeeze it into my side pocket. Then I went to get out the car from the garage behind the house.

"As I was bringing it round to the front a disconcerting thought struck me. I remembered that I had only a few shillings in my pocket.

"For some time past I had been keeping myself very short of cash, and for this reason—which I tell you because it is a vital point, as you will see in a minute. I was living temporarily on borrowed money. I had always been careless about money while I was with Manderson, and being a gregarious animal I had made many friends, some of them belonging to a New York set that had little to do but get rid of the large incomes given them by their parents. Still, I was very well paid, and I was too busy even to attempt to go very far with them in that amusing occupation. I was still well on the right side of the ledger until

I began, merely out of curiosity, to play at speculation. It's a very old story—particularly in Wall Street. I thought it was easy; I was lucky at first; I would always be prudent—and so on. Then came the day when I went out of my depth. In one week I was separated from my roll, as Bunner expressed it when I told him; and I owed money too. I had had my lesson. Now in this pass I went to Manderson and told him what I had done and how I stood. He heard me with a very grim smile, and then, with the nearest approach to sympathy I had ever found in him, he advanced me a sum on account of my salary that would clear me. 'Don't play the markets any more,' was all he said.

"Now on that Sunday night Manderson knew that I was practically without any money in the world. He knew that Bunner knew it too. He may have known that I had even borrowed a little more from Bunner for pocket-money until my next cheque was due, which, owing to my anticipation of my salary, would not have been a large one. Bear this knowledge of Manderson's in mind.

"As soon as I had brought the car round I went into the library and stated the difficulty to Manderson.

"What followed gave me, slight as it was, my first impression of something odd being afoot. As soon as I mentioned the word 'expenses' his hand went mechanically to his left hip pocket, where he always kept a little case containing notes to the value of about a hundred pounds in our money. This was such a rooted habit in him that I was astonished to see him check the movement suddenly. Then, to my greater amazement, he swore under his breath. I had never heard him do this before; but Bunner had told me that of late he had often shown irritation in this way when they were alone. 'Has he mislaid his note-case?' was the question that flashed through my mind. But it seemed to me that it could not affect his plan at all, and I will tell you why. The week before, when I had gone up to London to carry out various commissions, including the booking of a berth for Mr George Harris, I had drawn a thousand pounds for Manderson from his bankers, and all, at his request, in notes of small amounts. I did not know what this unusually large sum in cash was for, but I did know that the packets of notes were in his locked desk in the library, or had been earlier in the day, when I had seen him fingering them as he sat at the desk.

"But instead of turning to the desk, Manderson stood looking at me. There was fury in his face, and it was a strange sight to see him gradually master it until his eyes grew cold again. 'Wait in the car,' he said slowly. 'I will get some money.' We both went out, and as I was getting into my overcoat in the hall I saw him enter the drawing-room, which, you remember, was on the other side of the entrance hall.

"I stepped out onto the lawn before the house and smoked a cigarette, pacing up and down. I was asking myself again and again where that thousand pounds was; whether it was in the drawing-room; and if so, why. Presently, as I passed one of the drawing-room windows, I noticed Mrs Manderson's shadow on the thin silk curtain. She was standing at her escritoire. The window was open, and as I passed I heard her say, 'I have not quite thirty pounds here. Will that be enough?' I did not hear the answer, but next moment Manderson's shadow was mingled with hers, and I heard the chink of money. Then, as he stood by the window, and as I was moving away, these words of his came to my ears—and these at least I can repeat exactly, for astonishment stamped them on my memory:—'I'm going out now. Marlowe has persuaded me to go for a moonlight run in the car. He is very urgent about it. He says it will help me to sleep, and I guess he is right.'

"I have told you that in the course of four years I had never once heard Manderson utter a direct lie about anything, great or small. I believed that I understood the man's queer, skin-deep morality, and I could have sworn that if he was firmly pressed with a question that could not be evaded he would either refuse to answer or tell the truth. But what had I just heard? No answer to any question. A voluntary statement, precise in terms, that was utterly false. The unimaginable had happened. It was almost as if someone I knew well, in a moment of closest sympathy, had suddenly struck me in the face. The blood rushed to my head, and I stood still on the grass. I stood there until I heard his step at the front door, and then I pulled myself together and stepped quickly to the car. He handed me a banker's paper bag with gold and notes in it. 'There's more than you'll want there,' he said, and I pocketed it mechanically.

"For a minute or so I stood discussing with Manderson—it was by one of those *tours de force of* which one's mind is capable under great excitement—certain points about the route of the long drive before me. I had made the run several times by day, and I believe I spoke quite calmly and naturally about it. But while I spoke my mind was seething in a flood of suddenly born suspicion and fear. I did not know what I feared. I simply felt fear, somehow—I did not know how—connected with Manderson. My soul once opened to- it, fear rushed in like an assaulting army. I felt—I knew—that something was altogether wrong and sinister, and I felt myself to be the object of it. Yet Manderson was surely no enemy of mine. Then my thoughts reached out wildly for an answer to the question why he had told that lie. And all the time the blood hammered in my ears, 'Where is that money?' Reason struggled hard to set up the suggestion that the two things were not necessarily connected. The instinct of a man in danger would not listen to it. As we started, and the car took the curve into the road, it was merely the unconscious part of me that steered and controlled it, and that made occasional empty remarks as we slid along in the moonlight. Within me was a confusion and vague alarm that was far worse than any definite terror I ever felt.

"About a mile from the house, you remember, one passed on one's left a gate, on the other side of which was the golf course. There Manderson said he would get down, and I stopped the car. 'You've got it all clear?' he asked. With a sort of wrench I forced myself to remember and repeat the directions given me. 'That's O.K.' he said. 'Goodby, then. Stay with that wallet.' Those were the last words I heard him speak, as the car moved gently away from him."

Marlowe rose from his chair and pressed his hands to his eyes. He was flushed with the excitement of his own narrative, and there was in his look a horror of recollection that held both listeners silent. He shook himself with a movement like a dog's, and then, his hands behind him, stood erect before the fire as he continued his tale.

"I expect you both know what the back-reflector of a motorcar is."

Trent nodded quickly, his face alive with anticipation; but Mr Cupples, who cherished a mild but obstinate prejudice against motor-cars, readily confessed to ignorance.

"It is a small round or more often rectangular mirror," Marlowe explained, "rigged out from the right side of the screen in front of the driver, and adjusted in such a way that he can see, without turning round, if anything is coming up behind to pass him. It is quite an ordinary appliance, and there was one on this car. As the car moved on, and Manderson ceased speaking behind me, I saw in that mirror a thing that I wish I could forget."

Marlowe was silent for a moment, staring at the wall before him.

"Manderson's face," he said in a low tone. "He was standing in the road, looking after me, only a few yards behind, and the moonlight was full on his face. The mirror happened to catch it for an instant.

"Physical habit is a wonderful thing. I did not shift hand or foot on the controlling mechanism of the car. Indeed, I dare say it steadied me against the shock to have myself braced to the business of driving. You have read in books, no doubt, of hell looking out of a man's eyes, but perhaps you don't know what a good metaphor that is. If I had not known Manderson was there, I should not have recognized the face. It was that of a madman, distorted, hideous in the imbecility of hate, the teeth bared in a simian grin of ferocity and triumph; the eyes... In the little mirror I had this glimpse of the face alone. I saw nothing of whatever gesture there may have been as that writhing white mask glared after me. And I saw it only for a flash. The car went on, gathering speed, and as it went, my brain, suddenly purged of the vapours of doubt and perplexity, was as busy as the throbbing engine before my feet. I knew.

"You say something in that manuscript of yours, Mr Trent, about the swift automatic way in which one's ideas arrange themselves about some new illuminating thought. It is quite true. The awful intensity of ill-will that had flamed after me from those straining eyeballs had poured over my mind like a searchlight. I was thinking quite clearly now, and almost coldly, for I knew what—at least I knew whom—I had to fear, and instinct warned me that it was not a time to give room to the emotions that were fighting to possess me. The man hated me insanely. That incredible fact I suddenly knew. But the face had told me, it would have told anybody, more than that. It was a face of hatred gratified, it proclaimed some damnable triumph. It had gloated over me driving away to my fate. This too was plain to me. And to what fate?

"I stopped the car. It had gone about two hundred and fifty yards, and a sharp bend of the road hid the spot where I had set Manderson down. I lay back in the seat and thought it out. Something was to happen to me. In Paris? Probably—why else should I be sent there, with money and a ticket? But why Paris? That puzzled me, for I had no melodramatic ideas about Paris. I put the point aside for a moment. I turned to the other things that had roused my attention that evening. The lie about my 'persuading him to go for a moonlight run.' What was the intention of that? Manderson, I said to myself, will be returning without me while I am on my way to Southampton. What will he tell them about me? How account for his returning alone, and without the car? As I asked myself that sinister question there rushed into my mind the last of my difficulties: 'Where are the thousand pounds?' And in the same instant came the answer: 'The thousand pounds are in my pocket.'

"I got up and stepped from the car. My knees trembled and I felt very sick. I saw the plot now, as I thought. The whole of the story about the papers and the necessity of their being taken to Paris was a blind. With Manderson's money about me, of which he would declare I had robbed him, I was, to all appearance, attempting to escape from England, with every precaution that guilt could suggest. He would communicate with the police at once, and would know how to put them on my track. I should be arrested in Paris, if I got so far, living under a false name, after having left the car under a false name, disguised myself, and travelled in a cabin which I had booked in advance, also under a false name. It would be plainly the crime of a man without money, and for some reason desperately in want of it. As for my account of the affair, it would be too preposterous.

"As this ghastly array of incriminating circumstances rose up before me, I dragged the stout letter-case from my pocket. In the intensity of the moment, I never entertained the faintest doubt that I was right, and that the money was there. It would easily hold the packets of notes. But as I felt it and weighed it in my hands it seemed to me there must be more than this. It was too bulky. What more was to be laid to my charge? After all, a thousand pounds was not much to tempt a man like myself to run the risk of penal servitude. In this new agitation, scarcely knowing what I did, I caught the surrounding strap in my fingers just above the fastening and tore the staple out of the lock. Those locks, you know, are pretty flimsy as a rule."

Here Marlowe paused and walked to the oaken desk before the window. Opening a drawer full of miscellaneous objects, he took out a box of odd keys, and selected a small one distinguished by a piece of pink tape.

He handed it to Trent. "I keep that by me as a sort of morbid memento. It is the key to the lock I smashed. I might have saved myself the trouble, if I had known that this key was at that moment in the left-hand side pocket of my overcoat. Manderson must have slipped it in, either while the coat was hanging in the hall or while he sat at my side in the car. I might not have found the tiny thing there for weeks: as a matter of fact I did find it in two days after Manderson was dead, but a police search would have found it in five minutes. And then I—I with the case and its contents in my pocket, my false name and my sham spectacles and the rest of it—I should have had no explanation to offer but the highly convincing one that I didn't know the key was there."

Trent dangled the key by its tape idly. Then: "How do you know this is the key of that case?" he asked quickly.

"I tried it. As soon as I found it I went up and fitted it to the lock. I knew where I had left the thing. So do you, I think, Mr Trent. Don't you?" There was a faint shade of mockery in Marlowe's voice.

"*Touché*," Trent said, with a dry smile. "I found a large empty letter-case with a burst lock lying with other odds and ends on the dressing-table in Manderson's room. Your statement is that you put it there. I could make nothing of it." He closed his lips.

"There was no reason for hiding it," said Marlowe. "But to get back to my story. I burst the lock of the strap. I opened the case before one of the lamps of the car. The first thing I found in it I ought to have expected, of course, but I hadn't." He paused and glanced at Trent.

"It was—" began Trent mechanically, and then stopped himself. "Try not to bring me in any more, if you don't mind," he said, meeting the other's eye. "I have complimented you already in that document on your cleverness. You need not prove it by making the judge help you out with your evidence."

"All right," agreed Marlowe. "I couldn't resist just that much. If you had been in my place you would have known before I did that Manderson's little pocket-case was there. As soon as I saw it, of course, I remembered his not having had it about him when I asked for money, and his surprising anger. He had made a false step. He had already fastened his note-case up with the rest of what was to figure as my plunder, and placed it in my hands. I opened it. It contained a few notes as usual, I didn't count them.

"Tucked into the flaps of the big case in packets were the other notes, just as I had brought them from London. And with them were two small wash-leather bags, the look of which I knew well. My heart jumped sickeningly again, for this, too, was utterly unexpected. In those bags Manderson kept the diamonds in which he had been investing for some time past. I didn't open them; I could feel the tiny stones shifting under the pressure of my fingers. How many thousands of pounds' worth there were there I have no idea. We had regarded Manderson's diamond-buying as merely a speculative fad. I believe now that it was the earliest movement in the scheme for my ruin. For anyone like myself to be represented as having robbed him, there ought to be a strong inducement shown. That had been provided with a vengeance.

"Now, I thought, I have the whole thing plain, and I must act. I saw instantly what I must do. I had left Manderson about a mile from the house. It would take him twenty minutes, fifteen if he walked fast, to get back to the house, where he would, of course, immediately tell his story of robbery, and probably telephone at once to the police in Bishopsbridge. I had left him only five or six minutes ago; for all that I have told you was as quick thinking as I ever did. It would be easy to overtake him in the car before he neared the house. There would be an awkward interview. I set my teeth as I thought of it, and all my fears vanished as I began to savour the gratification of telling him my opinion of him. There are probably few people who ever positively looked forward to an awkward interview with Manderson; but I was mad with rage. My honour and my liberty had been plotted against with detestable treachery. I did not consider what would follow the interview. That would arrange itself.

"I had started and turned the car, I was already going fast toward White Gables, when I heard the sound of a shot in front of me, to the right.

"Instantly I stopped the car. My first wild thought was that Manderson was shooting at me. Then I realized that the noise had not been close at hand. I could see nobody on the road, though the moonlight flooded it. I had left Manderson at a spot just round the corner that was now about a hundred yards ahead of me. After a minute or so, I started again, and turned the corner at a slow pace. Then I stopped again with a jar, and for a moment I sat perfectly still.

"Manderson lay dead a few steps from me on the turf within the gate, clearly visible to me in the moonlight."

Marlowe made another pause, and Trent, with a puckered brow, inquired, "On the golf course?"

"Obviously," remarked Mr Cupples. "The eighth green is just there." He had grown more and more interested as Marlowe went on, and was now playing feverishly with his thin beard.

"On the green, quite close to the flag," said Marlowe. "He lay on his back, his arms were stretched abroad, his jacket and heavy overcoat were open; the light shone hideously on his white face and his shirt-front; it glistened on his bared teeth and one of the eyes. The other... you saw it. The man was certainly dead. As I sat there stunned, unable for the moment to think at all, I could even see a deep dark line of blood running down from the shattered socket to the ear. Close by lay his soft black hat, and at his feet a pistol.

"I suppose it was only a few seconds that I sat helplessly staring at the body. Then I rose and moved to it with dragging feet; for now the truth had come to me at last, and I realized the fullness of my appalling danger. It was not only my liberty or my honour that the maniac had undermined. It was death that he had planned for me; death with the degradation of the scaffold. To strike me down with certainty, he had not hesitated to end his life; a life which was, no doubt, already threatened by a melancholic impulse to self-destruction; and the last agony of the suicide had been turned, perhaps, to a devilish joy by the thought that he dragged down my life with him. For as far as I could see at the moment my situation was utterly hopeless. If it had been desperate on the assumption that Manderson meant to denounce me as a thief, what was it now that his corpse denounced me as a murderer?

"I picked up the revolver and saw, almost without emotion, that it was my own. Manderson had taken it from my room, I suppose, while I was getting out the car. At the same moment I remembered that it was by Manderson's suggestion that I had had it engraved with my initials to distinguish it from a precisely similar weapon which he had of his own.

"I bent over the body and satisfied myself that there was no life left in it. I must tell you here that I did not notice, then or afterwards, the scratches and marks on the wrists, which were taken as evidence of a struggle with an assailant. But I have no doubt that Manderson deliberately injured himself in this way before firing the shot; it was a part of his plan.

"Though I never perceived that detail, however, it was evident enough as I looked at the body that Manderson had not forgotten, in his last act on earth, to tie me tighter by putting out of court the question of suicide. He had clearly been at pains to hold the pistol at arm's length, and there was not a trace of smoke or of burning on the face. The wound was absolutely clean, and was already ceasing to bleed outwardly. I rose and paced the green, reckoning up the points in the crushing case against me.

"I was the last to be seen with Manderson. I had persuaded him—so he had lied to his wife and, as I afterwards knew, to the butler—to go with me for the drive from which he never returned. My pistol had killed him. It was true that by discovering his plot I had saved myself from heaping up further incriminating facts—flight, concealment, the possession of the treasure. But what need of them, after all? As I stood, what hope was there? What could I do?"

Marlowe came to the table and leaned forward with his hands upon it. "I want," he said very earnestly, "to try to make you understand what was in my mind when I decided to do what I did. I hope you won't be bored, because I must do it. You may both have thought I acted like a fool. But after all the police never suspected me. I walked that green for a quarter of an hour, I suppose, thinking the thing out like a game of chess. I had to think ahead and think coolly; for my safety depended on upsetting the plans of one of the longest-headed men who ever lived. And remember that, for all I knew, there were details of the scheme still hidden from me, waiting to crush me.

"Two plain courses presented themselves at once. Either of them, I thought, would certainly prove fatal. I could, in the first place, do the completely straightforward thing: take back the dead man, tell my story, hand over the notes and diamonds, and trust to the saving power of truth and innocence. I could have laughed as I thought of it. I saw myself bringing home the corpse and giving an account of myself, boggling with sheer shame over the absurdity of my wholly unsupported tale, as I brought a charge of mad hatred and fiendish treachery against a man who had never, as far as I knew, had a word to say against me. At every turn the cunning of Manderson had forestalled me. His careful concealment of such a hatred was a characteristic feature of the stratagem; only a man of his iron self-restraint could have done it. You can see for yourselves how every fact in my statement would appear, in the shadow of Manderson's death, a clumsy lie. I tried to imagine myself telling such a story to the counsel for my defence. I could see the face with which he would listen to it; I could read in the lines of it his thought, that to put forward such an impudent farrago would mean merely the disappearance of any chance there might be of a commutation of the capital sentence.

"True, I had not fled. I had brought back the body; I had handed over the property. But how did that help me? It would only suggest that I had yielded to a sudden funk after killing my man, and had no nerve left to clutch at the fruits of the crime; it would suggest, perhaps, that I had not set out to kill but only to threaten, and that when I found that I had done murder the heart went out of me. Turn it which way I would, I could see no hope of escape by this plan of action.

"The second of the obvious things that I might do was to take the hint offered by the situation, and to fly at once. That too must prove fatal. There was the body. I had no time to hide it in such a way that it would not be found at the first systematic search. But whatever I should do with the body, Manderson's not returning to the house would cause uneasiness in two or three hours at most. Martin would suspect an accident to the car, and would telephone to the police. At daybreak the roads would be scoured and inquiries telegraphed in every direction. The police would act on the possibility of there being foul play. They would spread their nets with energy in such a big business as the disappearance of Manderson. Ports and railway termini would be watched. Within twenty-four hours the body would be found, and the whole country would be on the alert for me—all Europe, scarcely less; I did not believe there was a spot in Christendom where the man accused of Manderson's murder could pass unchallenged, with every newspaper crying the fact of his death into the ears of all the world. Every stranger would be suspect; every man, woman, and child would be a detective. The car, wherever I should abandon it, would put people on my track. If I had to choose between two utterly hopeless courses, I decided, I would take that of telling the preposterous truth.

"But now I cast about desperately for some tale that would seem more plausible than the truth. Could I save my neck by a lie? One after another came into my mind; I need not trouble to remember them now. Each had its own futilities and perils; but every one split upon the fact—or what would be taken for fact—that I had induced Manderson to go out with me, and the fact that he had never returned alive. Notion after notion I swiftly rejected as I paced there by the dead man, and doom seemed to settle down upon me more heavily as the moments passed. Then a strange thought came to me.

"Several times I had repeated to myself half-consciously, as a sort of refrain, the words in which I had heard Manderson tell his wife that I had induced him to go out. 'Marlowe has persuaded me to go for a moonlight run in the car. He is very urgent about it.' All at once it struck me that, without meaning to do so, I was saying this in Manderson's voice.

"As you found out for yourself, Mr Trent, I have a natural gift of mimicry. I had imitated Manderson's voice many times so successfully as to deceive even Bunner, who had been much more in his company than his own wife. It was, you remember"—Marlowe turned to Mr Cupples—"a strong, metallic voice, of great carrying power, so unusual as to make it a very fascinating voice to imitate, and at the same time very easy. I said the words carefully to myself again, like this—" he uttered them, and Mr Cupples opened his eyes in amazement—"and then I struck my hand upon the low wall beside me. 'Manderson never returned alive,' I said aloud. 'But Manderson *shall* return alive!'

"In thirty seconds the bare outline of the plan was complete in my mind. I did not wait to think over details. Every instant was precious now. I lifted the body and laid it on the floor of the car, covered with a rug. I took the hat and the revolver. Not one trace remained on the green, I believe, of that night's work. As I drove back to White Gables my design took shape before me with a rapidity and ease that filled me with a wild excitement. I should escape yet! It was all so easy if I kept my pluck. Putting aside the unusual and unlikely, I should not fail. I wanted to shout, to scream!

"Nearing the house I slackened speed, and carefully reconnoitred the road. Nothing was moving. I turned the car into the open field on the other side of the road, about twenty paces short of the little door at the extreme corner of the grounds. I brought it to rest behind a stack. When, with Manderson's hat on my head and the pistol in my pocket, I had staggered with the body across the moonlit road and through that door, I left much of my apprehension behind me. With swift action and an unbroken nerve I thought I ought to succeed."

With a long sigh Marlowe threw himself into one of the deep chairs at the fireside and passed his handkerchief over his damp forehead. Each of his hearers, too, drew a deep breath, but not audibly.

"Everything else you know," he said. He took a cigarette from a box beside him and lighted it. Trent watched the very slight quiver of the hand that held the match, and privately noted that his own was at the moment not so steady.

"The shoes that betrayed me to you," pursued Marlowe after a short silence, "were painful all the time I wore them, but I never dreamed that they had given anywhere. I knew that no footstep of mine must appear by any accident in the soft ground about the hut where I laid the body, or between the hut and the house, so I took the shoes off and crammed my feet into them as soon as I was inside the little door. I left my own shoes, with my own jacket and overcoat, near the body, ready to be resumed later. I made a clear footmark on the soft gravel outside the French window, and several on the drugget round the carpet. The stripping off of the outer clothing of the body, and the dressing of it afterwards in the brown suit and shoes, and putting the things into the pockets, was a horrible business; and getting the teeth out of the mouth was worse. The head—but you don't want to hear about it. I didn't feel it much at the time. I was wriggling my own head out of a noose, you see. I wish I had thought of pulling down the cuffs, and had tied the shoes more neatly. And putting the watch in the wrong pocket was a bad mistake. It had all to be done so hurriedly.

"You were wrong, by the way, about the whisky. After one stiffish drink I had no more; but I filled up a flask that was in the cupboard and pocketed it. I had a night of peculiar anxiety and effort in front of me, and I didn't know how I should stand it. I had to take some once or twice during the drive. Speaking of that, you give rather a generous allowance of time in your document for doing that run by night. You say that to get to Southampton by half-past six in that car, under the conditions, a man must, even if he drove like a demon, have left Marlstone by twelve at latest. I had not got the body dressed in the other suit, with tie and watch-chain and so forth, until nearly ten minutes past; and then I had to get to the car and start it going. But then I don't suppose any other man would have taken the risks I did in that car at night, without a headlight. It turns me cold to think of it now.

"There's nothing much to say about what I did in the house. I spent the time after Martin had left me in carefully thinking over the remaining steps in my plan, while I unloaded and thoroughly cleaned the revolver, using my handkerchief and a penholder from the desk. I also placed the packets of notes, the note-case, and the diamonds in the roll-top desk, which

I opened and relocked with Manderson's key. When I went upstairs it was a trying moment, for though I was safe from the eyes of Martin, as he sat in his pantry, there was a faint possibility of somebody being about on the bedroom floor. I had sometimes found the French maid wandering about there when the other servants were in bed. Bunner, I knew, was a deep sleeper. Mrs Manderson, I had gathered from things I had heard her say, was usually asleep by eleven; I had thought it possible that her gift of sleep had helped her to retain all her beauty and vitality in spite of a marriage which we all knew was an unhappy one. Still it was uneasy work mounting the stairs, and holding myself ready to retreat to the library again at the least sound from above. But nothing happened.

"The first thing I did on reaching the corridor was to enter my room and put the revolver and cartridges back in the case. Then I turned off the light and went quietly into Manderson's room.

"What I had to do there you know. I had to take off the shoes and put them outside the door, leave Manderson's jacket, waistcoat, trousers, and black tie, after taking everything out of the pockets, select a suit and tie and shoes for the body, and place the dental plate in the bowl, which I moved from the washing- stand to the bedside, leaving those ruinous fingermarks as I did so. The marks on the drawer must have been made when I shut it after taking out the tie. Then I had to lie down in the bed and tumble it. You know all about it—all except my state of mind, which you couldn't imagine and I couldn't describe.

"The worst came when I had hardly begun my operations: the moment when Mrs Manderson spoke from the room where I supposed her asleep. I was prepared for it happening; it was a possibility; but I nearly lost my nerve all the same. However...

"By the way, I may tell you this: in the extremely unlikely contingency of Mrs Manderson remaining awake, and so putting out of the question my escape by way of her window, I had planned simply to remain where I was a few hours, and then, not speaking to her, to leave the house quickly and quietly by the ordinary way. Martin would have been in bed by that time. I might have been heard to leave, but not seen. I should have done just as I had planned with the body, and then made the best time I could in the car to Southampton. The difference would have been that I couldn't have furnished an unquestionable alibi by turning up at the hotel at 6:30. I should have made the best of it by driving straight to the docks, and making my ostentatious inquiries there. I could in any case have got there long before the boat left at noon. I couldn't see that anybody could suspect me of the supposed murder in any case; but if anyone had, and if I hadn't arrived until ten o'clock, say, I shouldn't have been able to answer: 'It is impossible for me to have got to Southampton so soon after shooting him.' I should simply have had to say I was delayed by a breakdown after leaving Manderson at half-past ten, and challenged anyone to produce any fact connecting me with the crime. They couldn't have done it. The pistol, left openly in my room, might have been used by anybody, even if it could be proved that that particular pistol was used. Nobody could reasonably connect me with the shooting so long as it was believed that it was Manderson who had returned to the house. The suspicion could not, I was confident, enter anyone's mind. All the same, I wanted to introduce the element of absolute physical impossibility; I knew I should feel ten times as safe with that. So when I knew from the sound of her breathing that Mrs Manderson was asleep again, I walked quickly across her room in my stocking feet, and was on the grass with my bundle in ten seconds. I don't think I made the least noise. The curtain before the window was of soft, thick stuff and didn't rustle, and when I pushed the glass doors farther open there was not a sound."

"Tell me," said Trent, as the other stopped to light a new cigarette, "why you took the risk of going through Mrs Manderson's room to escape from the house. I could see when I looked into the thing on the spot why it had to be on that side of the house; there was a danger of being seen by Martin, or by some servant at a bedroom window, if you got out by a window on one of the other sides. But there were three unoccupied rooms on that side; two spare bedrooms and Mrs Manderson's sitting-room. I should have thought it would have been safer, after you had done what was necessary to your plan in Manderson's room, to leave it quietly and escape through one of those three rooms... The fact that you went through her window, you know," he added coldly, "would have suggested, if it became known, various suspicions in regard to the lady herself. I think you understand me."

Marlowe turned upon him with a glowing face. "And I think you will understand me, Mr Trent," he said in a voice that shook a little, "when I say that if such a possibility had occurred to me then, I would have taken any risk rather than make my escape by that way... Oh, well!" he went on more coolly, "I suppose that to anyone who didn't know her, the idea of her being privy to her husband's murder might not seem so indescribably fatuous. Forgive the expression." He looked attentively at the burning end of his cigarette, studiously unconscious of the red flag that flew in Trent's eyes for an instant at his words and the tone of them.

That emotion, however, was conquered at once. "Your remark is perfectly just," Trent said with answering coolness. "I can quite believe, too, that at the time you didn't think of the possibility I mentioned. But surely, apart from that, it would have been safer to do as I said; go by the window of an unoccupied room."

"Do you think so?" said Marlowe. "All I can say is, I hadn't the nerve to do it. I tell you, when I entered Manderson's room I shut the door of it on more than half my terrors. I had the problem confined before me in a closed space, with only one danger in it, and that a *known* danger: the danger of Mrs Manderson. The thing was almost done; I had only to wait until she was certainly asleep after her few moments of waking up, for which, as I told you, I was prepared as a possibility. Barring accidents, the way was clear. But now suppose that I, carrying Manderson's clothes and shoes, had opened that door again and gone in my shirt-sleeves and socks to enter one of the empty rooms. The moonlight was flooding the corridor through the end window. Even if my face was concealed, nobody could mistake my standing figure for Manderson's. Martin might be going about the house in his silent way. Bunner might come out of his bedroom. One of the servants who were supposed to be in bed might come round the corner from the other passage—I had found Célestine prowling about quite as late as it was then. None of these things was very likely; but they were all too likely for me. They were uncertainties. Shut off from the household in Manderson's room I knew exactly what I had to face. As I lay in my clothes in Manderson's bed and listened for the almost inaudible breathing through the open door, I felt far more ease of mind, terrible as my anxiety was, than I had felt since I saw the dead body on the turf. I even congratulated myself that I had had the chance, through Mrs Manderson's speaking to me, of tightening one of the screws in my scheme by repeating the statement about my having been sent to Southampton."

Marlowe looked at Trent, who nodded as who should say that his point was met.

"As for Southampton," pursued Marlowe, "you know what I did when I got there, I have no doubt. I had decided to take Manderson's story about the mysterious Harris and act it out on my own lines. It was a carefully prepared lie, better than anything I could improvise. I even went so far as to get through a trunk call to the hotel at Southampton from the library before starting, and ask if Harris was there. As I expected, he wasn't."

"Was that why you telephoned?" Trent inquired quickly.

"The reason for telephoning was to get myself into an attitude in which Martin couldn't see my face or anything but the jacket and hat, yet which was a natural and familiar attitude. But while I was about it, it was obviously better to make a genuine call. If I had simply pretended to be telephoning, the people at the exchange could have told you at once that there hadn't been a call from White Gables that night."

"One of the first things I did was to make that inquiry," said Trent. "That telephone call, and the wire you sent from Southampton to the dead man to say Harris hadn't turned up, and you were returning—I particularly appreciated both those."

A constrained smile lighted Marlowe's face for a moment. "I don't know that there's anything more to tell. I returned to Marlstone and faced your friend the detective with such nerve as I had left. The worst was when I heard you had been put on the case—no, that wasn't the worst. The worst was when I saw you walk out of the shrubbery the next day, coming away from the shed where I had laid the body. For one ghastly moment I thought you were going to give me in charge on the spot. Now I've told you everything, you don't look so terrible."

He closed his eyes, and there was a short silence. Then Trent got suddenly to his feet.

"Cross-examination?" inquired Marlowe, looking at him gravely.

"Not at all," said Trent, stretching his long limbs. "Only stiffness of the legs. I don't want to ask any questions. I believe what you have told us. I don't believe it simply because I always liked your face, or because it saves awkwardness, which are the most usual reasons for believing a person, but because my vanity will have it that no man could lie to me steadily for an hour without my perceiving it. Your story is an extraordinary one; but Manderson was an extraordinary man, and so are you. You acted like a lunatic in doing what you did; but I quite agree with you that if you had acted like a sane man you wouldn't have had the hundredth part of a dog's chance with a judge and jury. One thing is beyond dispute on any reading of the affair: you are a man of courage."

The colour rushed into Marlowe's face, and he hesitated for words. Before he could speak Mr Cupples arose with a dry cough.

"For my part," he said, "I never supposed you guilty for a moment." Marlowe turned to him in grateful amazement, Trent with an incredulous stare. "But," pursued Mr Cupples, holding up his hand, "there is one question which I should like to put."

Marlowe bowed, saying nothing.

"Suppose," said Mr Cupples, "that someone else had been suspected of the crime and put upon trial. What would you have done?"

"I think my duty was clear. I should have gone with my story to the lawyers for the defence, and put myself in their hands."

Trent laughed aloud. Now that the thing was over, his spirits were rapidly becoming ungovernable. "I can see their faces!" he said. "As a matter of fact, though, nobody else was ever in danger. There wasn't a shred of evidence against anyone. I looked up Murch at the Yard this morning, and he told me he had come round to Bunner's view, that it was a case of revenge on the part of some American blackhand gang. So there's the end of the Manderson case. Holy, suffering Moses! What an ass a man can make himself when he thinks he's being preternaturally clever!" He seized the bulky envelope from the table and stuffed it into the heart of the fire. "There's for you, old friend! For want of you the world's course will not fail. But look here! It's getting late—nearly seven, and Cupples and

I have an appointment at half-past. We must go. Mr Marlowe, goodby." He looked into the other's eyes. "I am a man who has worked hard to put a rope round your neck. Considering the circumstances, I don't know whether you will blame me. Will you shake hands?"

16

THE LAST STRAW

"What was that you said about our having an appointment at half-past seven?" asked Mr Cupples as the two came out of the great gateway of the pile of flats. "Have we such an appointment?"

"Certainly we have," replied Trent. "You are dining with me. Only one thing can properly celebrate this occasion, and that is a dinner for which I pay. No, no! I asked you first. I have got right down to the bottom of a case that must be unique—a case that has troubled even my mind for over a year—and if that isn't a good reason for standing a dinner, I don't know what is. Cupples, we will not go to my club. This is to be a festival, and to be seen in a London club in a state of pleasurable emotion is more than enough to shatter any man's career. Besides that, the dinner there is always the same, or, at least, they always make it taste the same, I know not how. The eternal dinner at my club hath bored millions of members like me, and shall bore; but tonight let the feast be spread in vain, so far as we are concerned. We will not go where the satraps throng the hall. We will go to Sheppard's."

"Who is Sheppard?" asked Mr Cupples mildly, as they proceeded up Victoria Street. His companion went with an unnatural lightness, and a policeman, observing his face, smiled indulgently at a look of happiness which he could only attribute to alcohol.

"Who is Sheppard?" echoed Trent with bitter emphasis. "That question, if you will pardon me for saying so, Cupples, is thoroughly characteristic of the spirit of aimless inquiry prevailing in this restless day. I suggest our dining at Sheppard's, and instantly you fold your arms and demand, in a frenzy of intellectual pride, to know who Sheppard is before you will cross the threshold of Sheppard's. I am not going to pander to the vices of the modern mind. Sheppard's is a place where one can dine. I do not know Sheppard. It never occurred to me that Sheppard existed. Probably he is a myth of totemistic origin. All I know is that you can get a bit of saddle of mutton at Sheppard's that has made many an American visitor curse the day that Christopher Columbus was born... Taxi!"

A cab rolled smoothly to the curb, and the driver received his instructions with a majestic nod.

"Another reason I have for suggesting Sheppard's," continued Trent, feverishly lighting a cigarette, "is that I am going to be married to the most wonderful woman in the world. I trust the connection of ideas is clear."

"You are going to marry Mabel!" cried Mr Cupples. "My dear friend, what good news this is! Shake hands, Trent; this is glorious! I congratulate you both from the bottom of my heart. And may I say—I don't want to interrupt your flow of high spirits, which is very natural indeed, and I remember being just the same in similar circumstances long ago—but may I say how earnestly I have hoped for this? Mabel has seen so much unhappiness, yet she is surely a woman formed in the great purpose of humanity to be the best influence in the life of a good man. But I did not know her mind as regarded yourself. Your mind I have known for some time," Mr Cupples went on, with a twinkle in his eye that would have done credit to the worldiest of creatures. "I saw it at once when you were both dining at my house, and you sat listening to Professor Peppmiiller and looking at her. Some of us older fellows have our wits about us still, my dear boy."

"Mabel says she knew it before that," replied Trent, with a slightly crestfallen air. "And I thought I was acting the part of a person who was not mad about her to the life. Well, I never was any good at dissembling. I shouldn't wonder if even old Peppmiiller noticed something through his double convex lenses. But however crazy I may have been as an undeclared suitor," he went on with a return to vivacity, "I am going to be much worse now. As for your congratulations, thank you a thousand times, because I know you mean them. You are the sort of uncomfortable brute who would pull a face three feet long if you thought we were making a mistake. By the way, I can't help being an ass tonight; I'm obliged to go on blithering. You must try to bear it. Perhaps it would be easier if I sang you a song—one of your old favourites. What was that song you used always to be singing? Like this, wasn't it?" He accompanied the following stave with a dexterous clog-step on the floor of the cab:

> *There* was an *old nigger, and he had a wooden leg.*
> *He had no tobacco, no tobacco could he beg.*
> *Another old nigger was as cunning as a fox,*
> *And he always had tobacco in his old tobacco-box.*

Now for the chorus!

> *Yes, he always had tobacco in his old tobacco-box.*

But you're not singing! I thought you would be making the welkin ring."

"I never sang that song in my life," protested Mr Cupples. "I never heard it before."

"Are you sure?" inquired Trent doubtfully. "Well, I suppose I must take your word for it. It is a beautiful song, anyhow: not the whole warbling grove in concert heard can beat it. Somehow it seems to express my feelings at the present moment as nothing else could; it rises unbidden to the lips. Out of the fullness of the heart the mouth speaketh, as the Bishop of Bath and Wells said when listening to a speech of Mr Balfour's."

"When was that?" asked Mr Cupples.

"On the occasion," replied Trent, "of the introduction of the Compulsory Notification of Diseases of Poultry Bill, which ill-fated measure you of course remember. Hullo!" he broke off, as the cab rushed down a side street and swung round a corner into a broad and populous thoroughfare, "we're there already." The cab drew up.

"Here we are," said Trent, as he paid the man, and led Mr Cupples into a long, panelled room set with many tables and filled with a hum of talk. "This is the house of fulfilment of craving, this is the bower with the roses around it. I see there are three bookmakers eating pork at my favourite table. We will have that one in the opposite corner."

He conferred earnestly with a waiter, while Mr Cupples, in a pleasant meditation, warmed himself before the great fire. "The wine here," Trent resumed, as they seated themselves, "is almost certainly made out of grapes. What shall we drink?"

Mr Cupples came out of his reverie. "I think," he said, "I will have milk and soda water."

"Speak lower!" urged Trent. "The headwaiter has a weak heart, and might hear you. Milk and soda water! Cupples, you may think you have a strong constitution, and I don't say you have not, but I warn you that this habit of mixing drinks has been the death of many a robuster man than you. Be wise in time. Fill high the bowl with Samian wine, leave soda to the Turkish hordes. Here comes our food." He gave another order to the waiter, who ranged the dishes before them and darted away. Trent was, it seemed, a respected customer. "I have sent," he said, "for wine that I know, and I hope you will try it. If you have taken a vow, then in the name of all the teetotal saints drink water, which stands at your elbow, but don't seek a cheap notoriety by demanding milk and soda."

"I have never taken any pledge," said Mr Cupples, examining his mutton with a favourable eye. "I simply don't care about wine. I bought a bottle once and drank it to see what it was like, and it made me ill. But very likely it was bad wine. I will taste some of yours, as it is your dinner, and I do assure you, my dear Trent, I should like to do something unusual to show how strongly I feel on the present occasion. I have not been so delighted for many years. To think," he reflected aloud as the waiter filled his glass, "of the Manderson mystery disposed of, of the innocent exculpated, and your own and Mabel's happiness crowned—all coming upon me together! I drink to you, my dear friend." And Mr Cupples took a very small sip of the wine.

"You have a great nature," said Trent, much moved. "Your outward semblance doth belie your soul's immensity. I should have expected as soon to see an elephant conducting at the opera as you drinking my health. Dear Cupples! May his beak retain ever that delicate rose-stain!—No, curse it all!" He broke out, surprising a shade of discomfort that flitted over his companion's face as he tasted the wine again. "I have no business to meddle with your tastes. I apologize. You shall have what you want, even if it causes the headwaiter to perish in his pride."

When Mr Cupples had been supplied with his monastic drink, and the waiter had retired, Trent looked across the table with significance. "In this babble of many conversations," he said, "we can speak as freely as if we were on a bare hillside. The waiter is whispering soft nothings into the ear of the young woman at the pay-desk. We are alone. What do you think of the interview of this afternoon?" He began to dine with an appetite.

Without pausing in the task of cutting his mutton into very small pieces Mr Cupples replied: "The most curious feature of it, in my judgment, was the irony of the situation. We both held the clue to that mad hatred of Manderson's which Marlowe found so mysterious. We knew of his jealous obsession; which knowledge we withheld, as was very proper, if only in consideration of Mabel's feelings. Marlowe will never know of what he was suspected by that person. Strange! Nearly all of us, I venture to think, move unconsciously among a network of opinions, often quite erroneous, which other people entertain about us. I remember, for instance, discovering quite by accident some years ago that a number of people of my acquaintance believed me to have been secretly received into the Church of Rome. This absurd fiction was based upon the fact, which in the eyes of many appeared conclusive, that I had expressed myself in talk as favouring the plan of a weekly abstinence from meat. Manderson's belief in regard to his secretary probably rested upon a much slighter ground. It was Mr Bunner, I think you said, who told you of his rooted and apparent hereditary temper of suspicious jealousy... With regard to Marlowe's story, it appeared to me entirely straightforward, and not, in its essential features, especially remarkable, once we have admitted, as we surely must, that in the case of Manderson we have to deal with a more or less disordered mind."

Trent laughed loudly. "I confess," he said, "that the affair struck me as a little unusual."

"Only in the development of the details," argued Mr Cupples. "What is there abnormal in the essential facts? A madman conceives a crazy suspicion; he hatches a cunning plot against his fancied injurer; it involves his own destruction. Put thus, what is there that any man with the least knowledge of the ways of lunatics would call remarkable? Turn now to Marlowe's proceedings. He finds himself in a perilous position from which, though he is innocent, telling the truth will not save him. Is that an unheard-of situation? He escaped by means of a bold and ingenious piece of deception. That seems to me a thing that might happen every day, and probably does so." He attacked his now unrecognizable mutton.

"I should like to know," said Trent, after an alimentary pause in the conversation, "whether there is anything that ever happened on the face of the earth that you could not represent as quite ordinary and commonplace by such a line of argument as that."

A gentle smile illuminated Mr Cupples's face. "You must not suspect me of empty paradox," he said. "My meaning will become clearer, perhaps, if I mention some things which do appear to me essentially remarkable. Let me see... Well, I would call the life history of the liver-fluke, which we owe to the researches of Poulton, an essentially remarkable thing."

"I am unable to argue the point," replied Trent. "Fair science may have smiled upon the liver-fluke's humble birth, but I never even heard it mentioned."

"It is not, perhaps, an appetizing subject," said Mr Cupples thoughtfully, "and I will not pursue it. All I mean is, my dear Trent, that there are really remarkable things going on all round us if we will only see them, and we do our perceptions no credit in regarding as remarkable only those affairs which are surrounded with an accumulation of sensational detail."

Trent applauded heartily with his knife-handle on the table, as Mr Cupples ceased and refreshed himself with milk and soda water. "I have not heard you go on like this for years," he said. "I believe you must be almost as much above yourself as I am. It is a bad case of the unrest which men miscall delight. But much as I enjoy it, I am not going to sit still and hear the Manderson affair dismissed as commonplace. You may say what you like, but the idea of impersonating Manderson in those circumstances was an extraordinarily ingenious idea."

"Ingenious—certainly!" replied Mr Cupples. "Extraordinarily so—no! In those circumstances (your own words) it was really not strange that it should occur to a clever man. It lay almost on the surface of the situation. Marlowe was famous for his imitation of Manderson's voice; he had a talent for acting; he had a chess-player's mind; he knew the ways of the establishment intimately. I grant you that the idea was brilliantly carried out; but everything favoured it. As for the essential idea, I do not place it, as regards ingenuity, in the same class with, for example, the idea of utilizing the force of recoil in a discharged firearm to actuate the mechanism of ejecting and reloading. I do, however, admit, as I did at the outset, that in respect of details the case had unusual features. It developed a high degree of complexity."

"Did it really strike you in that way?" inquired Trent with desperate sarcasm.

"The affair became complicated," went on Mr Cupples, unmoved, "because after Marlowe's suspicions were awakened, a second subtle mind came in to interfere with the plans of the first. That sort of duel often happens in business and politics, but less frequently, I imagine, in the world of crime."

"I should say never," Trent replied; "and the reason is, that even the cleverest criminals seldom run to strategic subtlety. When they do, they don't get caught, since clever policemen have if possible less strategic subtlety than the ordinary clever criminal. But that rather deep quality seems very rarely to go with the criminal make-up. Look at Crippen. He was a very clever criminal as they go. He solved the central problem of every clandestine murder, the disposal of the body, with extreme neatness. But how far did he see through the game? The criminal and the policeman are often swift and bold tacticians, but neither of them is good for more than a quite simple plan. After all, it's a rare faculty in any walk of life."

"One disturbing reflection was left on my mind," said Mr Cupples, who seemed to have had enough of abstractions for the moment, "by what we learned today. If Marlowe had suspected nothing and walked into the trap, he would almost certainly have been hanged. Now how often may not a plan to throw the guilt of murder on an innocent person have been practised successfully? There are, I imagine, numbers of cases in which the accused, being found guilty on circumstantial evidence, have died protesting their innocence. I shall never approve again of a death sentence imposed in a case decided upon such evidence."

"I never have done so, for my part," said Trent. "To hang in such cases seems to me flying in the face of the perfectly obvious and sound principle expressed in the saying that 'you never can tell.' I agree with the American jurist who lays it down that we should not hang a yellow dog for stealing jam on circumstantial evidence, not even if he has jam all over his nose. As for attempts being made by malevolent persons to fix crimes upon innocent men, of course it is constantly happening. It's a marked feature, for instance, of all systems of rule by coercion, whether in Ireland or Russia or India or Korea; if the police cannot get hold of a man they think dangerous by fair means, they do it by foul. But there's one case in the State Trials that is peculiarly to the point, because not only was it a case of fastening a murder on innocent people, but the plotter did in effect what Manderson did; he gave up his own life in order to secure the death of his victims. Probably you have heard of the Campden Case."

Mr Cupples confessed his ignorance and took another potato.

"John Masefield has written a very remarkable play about it," said Trent, "and if it ever comes on again in London, you should go and see it, if you like having the fan-tods. I have often seen women weeping in an undemonstrative manner at some slab of oleomargarine sentiment in the theatre. By George! what everlasting smelling-bottle hysterics they ought to have if they saw that play decently acted! Well, the facts were that John Perry accused his mother and brother of murdering a man, and swore he had helped them to do it. He told a story full of elaborate detail, and had an answer to everything, except the curious fact that the body couldn't be found; but the judge, who was probably drunk at the time—this was in Restoration days—made nothing of that. The mother and brother denied the accusation. All three prisoners were found guilty and hanged, purely on John's evidence. Two years after, the man whom they were hanged for murdering came back to Campden. He had been kidnapped by pirates and taken to sea. His disappearance had given John his idea. The point about John is, that his including himself in the accusation, which amounted to suicide, was the thing in his evidence which convinced everybody of its truth. It was so obvious that no man would do himself to death to get somebody else hanged. Now that is exactly the answer which the prosecution would have made if Marlowe had told the truth. Not one juryman in a million would have believed in the Manderson plot."

Mr Cupples mused upon this a few moments. "I have not your acquaintance with that branch of history," he said at length, "in fact, I have none at all. But certain recollections of my own childhood return to me in connection with this affair. We know from the things Mabel told you what may be termed the spiritual truth underlying this matter; the insane depth of jealous hatred which Manderson concealed. We can understand that he was capable of such a scheme. But as a rule it is in the task of penetrating to the spiritual truth that the administration of justice breaks down. Sometimes that truth is deliberately concealed, as in Manderson's case. Sometimes, I think, it is concealed because simple people are actually unable to express it, and nobody else divines it. When I was a lad in Edinburgh the whole country went mad about the Sandyford Place murder."

Trent nodded. "Mrs M'Lachlan's case. She was innocent right enough."

"My parents thought so," said Mr Cupples. "I thought so myself when I became old enough to read and understand that excessively sordid story. But the mystery of the affair was so dark, and the task of getting at the truth behind the lies told by everybody concerned proved so hopeless, that others were just as fully convinced of the innocence of old James Fleming. All Scotland took sides on the question. It was the subject of debates in Parliament. The press divided into two camps, and raged with a fury I have never seen equalled. Yet it is obvious, is it not?—for I see you have read of the case—that if the spiritual truth about that old man could have been known there would have been very little room for doubt in the matter. If what some surmised about his disposition was true, he was quite capable of murdering Jessie M'Pherson and then casting the blame on the poor feeble-minded creature who came so near to suffering the last penalty of the law."

"Even a commonplace old dotard like Fleming can be an unfathomable mystery to all the rest of the human race," said Trent, "and most of all in a court of justice. The law certainly does not shine when it comes to a case requiring much delicacy of perception. It goes wrong easily enough over the Flemings of this world. As for the people with temperaments who get mixed up in legal proceedings, they must feel as if they were in a forest of apes, whether they win or lose. Well, I dare say it's good for their sort to have their noses rubbed in reality now and again. But what would twelve red-faced realities in a jury-box have done to Marlowe? His story would, as he says, have been a great deal worse than no defence at all. It's not as if there were a single piece of evidence in support of his tale. Can't you imagine how the prosecution would tear it to rags? Can't you see the judge simply taking it in his stride when it came to the summing up? And the jury—you've served on juries, I expect—in their room, snorting with indignation over the feebleness of the lie, telling each other it was the clearest case they ever heard of, and that they'd have thought better of him if he hadn't lost his nerve at the crisis, and had cleared off with the swag as he intended. Imagine yourself on that jury, not knowing Marlowe, and trembling with indignation at the record unrolled before you—cupidity, murder, robbery, sudden cowardice, shameless, impenitent, desperate lying! Why, you and I believed him to be guilty until—"

"I beg your pardon! I beg your pardon!" interjected Mr Cupples, laying down his knife and fork. "I was most careful, when we talked it all over the other night, to say nothing indicating such a belief. I was always certain that he was innocent."

"You said something of the sort at Marlowe's just now. I wondered what on earth you could mean. Certain that he was innocent! How can you be certain? You are generally more careful about terms than that, Cupples."

"I said 'certain,' " Mr Cupples repeated firmly.

Trent shrugged his shoulders. "If you really were, after reading my manuscript and discussing the whole thing as we did," he rejoined, "then I can only say that you must have totally renounced all trust in the operations of the human reason; an attitude which, while it is bad Christianity and also infernal nonsense, is oddly enough bad Positivism too, unless I misunderstand that system. Why, man—"

"Let me say a word," Mr Cupples interposed again, folding his hands above his plate. "I assure you I am far from abandoning reason. I am certain he is innocent, and I always was certain of it, because of something that I know, and knew from the very beginning. You asked me just now to imagine myself on the jury at Marlowe's trial. That would be an unprofitable exercise of the mental powers, because I know that I should be present in another capacity. I should be in the witness-box, giving evidence for the defence. You said just now: 'If there were a single piece of evidence in support of his tale.' There is, and it is my evidence. And," he added quietly, "it is conclusive." He took up his knife and fork and went contentedly on with his dinner.

The pallor of sudden excitement had turned Trent to marble while Mr Cupples led laboriously up to this statement. At the last word the blood rushed to his face again, and he struck the table with an unnatural laugh. "It can't be!" he exploded. "It's something you fancied, something you dreamed after one of those debauches of soda and milk. You can't really mean that all the time I was working on the case down there you knew Marlowe was innocent."

Mr Cupples, busy with his last mouthful, nodded brightly. He made an end of eating, wiped his sparse moustache, and then leaned forward over the table. "It's very simple," he said. "I shot Manderson myself."

"I am afraid I startled you," Trent heard the voice of Mr Cupples say. He forced himself out of his stupefaction like a diver striking upward for the surface, and with a rigid movement raised his glass. But half of the wine splashed upon the cloth, and he put it carefully down again untasted. He drew a deep breath, which was exhaled in a laugh wholly without merriment. "Go on," he said.

"It was not murder," began Mr Cupples, slowly measuring off inches with a fork on the edge of the table. "I will tell you the whole story. On that Sunday night I was taking my before-bedtime constitutional, having set out from the hotel about a quarter past ten. I went along the field path that runs behind White Gables, cutting off the great curve of the road, and came out on the road nearly opposite that gate that is just by the eighth hole on the golf course. Then I turned in there, meaning to walk along the turf to the edge of the cliff, and go back that way. I had only gone a few steps when I heard the car coming, and then I heard it stop near the gate. I saw Manderson at once. Do you remember my telling you I had seen him once alive after our quarrel in front of the hotel? Well, this was the time. You asked me if I had, and I did not care to tell a falsehood."

A slight groan came from Trent. He drank a little wine, and said stonily, "Go on, please."

"It was, as you know," pursued Mr Cupples, "a moonlight night, but I was in shadow under the trees by the stone wall, and anyhow they could not suppose there was anyone near them. I heard all that passed just as Marlowe has narrated it to us, and I saw the car go off towards Bishopsbridge. I did not see Manderson's face as it went, because his back was to me, but he shook the back of his left hand at the car with extraordinary violence, greatly to my amazement. Then I waited for him to go back to White Gables, as I did not want to meet him again. But he did not go. He opened the gate through which I had just passed, and he stood there on the turf of the green, quite still. His head was bent, his arms hung at his sides, and he looked somehow—rigid. For a few moments he remained in this tense attitude, then all of a sudden his right arm moved swiftly, and his hand was at the pocket of his overcoat. I saw his face raised in the moonlight, the teeth bared, and the eyes glittering, and all at once I knew that the man was not sane. Almost as quickly as that flashed across my mind, something else flashed in the moonlight. He held the pistol before him, pointing at his breast.

"Now I may say here I shall always be doubtful whether Manderson really meant to kill himself then. Marlowe naturally thinks so, knowing nothing of my intervention. But I think it quite likely he only meant to wound himself, and to charge Marlowe with attempted murder and robbery.

"At that moment, however, I assumed it was suicide. Before I knew what I was doing I had leapt out of the shadows and seized his arm. He shook me off with a furious snarling noise, giving me a terrific blow in the chest, and presenting the revolver at my head. But I seized his wrists before he could fire, and clung with all my strength—you remember how bruised and scratched they were. I knew I was fighting for my own life now, for murder was in his eyes. We struggled like two beasts, without an articulate word, I holding his pistol-hand down and keeping a grip on the other. I never dreamed that I had the strength for such an encounter. Then, with a perfectly instinctive movement—I never knew I meant to do it—I flung away his free hand and clutched like lightning at the weapon, tearing it from his fingers. By a miracle it did not go off. I darted back a few steps, he sprang at my throat like a wild cat, and I fired blindly in his face. He would have been about a yard away, I suppose. His knees gave way instantly, and he fell in a heap on the turf.

"I flung the pistol down and bent over him. The heart's action ceased under my hand. I knelt there staring, struck motionless; and I don't know how long it was before I heard the noise of the car returning.

"Trent, all the time that Marlowe paced that green, with the moonlight on his white and working face, I was within a few yards of him, crouching in the shadow of the furze by the ninth tee. I dared not show myself. I was thinking. My public quarrel with Manderson the same morning was, I suspected, the talk of the hotel. I assure you that every horrible possibility of the situation for me had rushed across my mind the moment I saw Manderson fall. I became cunning. I knew what I must do. I must get back to the hotel as fast as I could, get in somehow unperceived, and play a part to save myself. I must never tell a word to anyone. Of course I was assuming that Marlowe would tell everyone how he had found the body. I knew he would suppose it was suicide; I thought everyone would suppose so.

"When Marlowe began at last to lift the body, I stole away down the wall and got out into the road by the clubhouse, where he could not see me. I felt perfectly cool and collected. I crossed the road, climbed the fence, and ran across the meadow to pick up the field path I had come by that runs to the hotel behind White Gables. I got back to the hotel very much out of breath."

"Out of breath," repeated Trent mechanically, still staring at his companion as if hypnotized.

"I had had a sharp run," Mr Cupples reminded him. "Well, approaching the hotel from the back I could see into the writingroom through the open window. There was nobody in there, so I climbed over the sill, walked to the bell and rang it, and then sat down to write a letter I had meant to write the next day. I saw by the clock that it was a little past eleven. When the waiter answered the bell I asked for a glass of milk and a postage stamp. Soon afterwards I went up to bed. But I could not sleep."

Mr Cupples, having nothing more to say, ceased speaking. He looked in mild surprise at Trent, who now sat silent, supporting his bent head in his hands.

"He could not sleep," murmured Trent at last in a hollow tone. "A frequent result of over-exertion during the day. Nothing to be alarmed about." He was silent again, then looked up with a pale face. "Cupples, I am cured. I will never touch a crime-mystery again. The Manderson affair shall be Philip Trent's last case. His high-blown pride at length breaks under him." Trent's smile suddenly returned. "I could have borne everything but that last revelation of the impotence of human reason. Cupples, I have absolutely nothing left to say, except this: you have beaten me. I drink your health in a spirit of self-abasement. And you shall pay for the dinner."

II
TRENT'S OWN CASE

1

SOUTHWARD BOUND

"I ought to be going," Philip Trent said. "I've got an appointment, as I told you, and I mustn't be late. You go on dining, Slick—have some of the *crevettes* Waldorf; they will bring the roses into your cheeks. If I come round with the car tomorrow about ten, will you be more or less ready?"

"Less, I expect," Slick Patmore grumbled. "That is, if this ghastly weather doesn't change in the night. A two-hours' run through drizzle and chill is not my idea of a morning's pleasure."

"It's bound to change in the night," Trent assured him. "The only question is how many times it will change. That's the exciting thing about a variable climate like ours; and it is at its best in April, as everybody knows. Oh to be in England, now that April's there, and whoever wakes in England is entirely unaware whether it is going to rain cats and dogs or be gay with sunshine, birds and blossoms. Besides, it isn't a question of pleasure for you and me tomorrow. It is duty, Slick, duty whose stern behest impels us to the deed of going to see Julian Pickett married."

"And drink his health in what old Blinky Fisher imagines to be champagne," Patmore added, moodily helping himself, to another glass of La Tour-Figeac.

"Why shouldn't he have an imagination, just because he is a Canon of Glasminster?" Trent asked. "He'll need it, I should say, when he gives away his niece to Julian, and has to pretend that he has some sort of responsibility for a girl of the present time. Ha! I can see it now. 'Who giveth this woman?' Come on, Blinky; to what green altar, O mysterious priest, lead'st thou that heifer? Probably he will have mislaid his spectacles, and will try to give Julian away."

"Didn't you say you had an appointment?" Patmore hinted.

Trent, descending the staircase of the Cactus Club, stood in the doorway and lighted a cigarette as he nerved himself to the task of going to see his favourite aunt off on the boat-train to New-haven. It is a part of our island heritage, he mused, that at such times as we are on the point of leaving the country the weather is usually pretty beastly. As God tempers the wind to the shorn lamb, so the Briton about to uproot himself from the native soil is upheld and solaced by the thought that the climate he is going to cannot possibly be so objectionable. An erroneous thought, perhaps; but what thoughts (he asked himself) are not so? This particular evening, at least, was quite noxious enough to warrant the rosiest anticipations of what it was going to be like anywhere across the Channel. Fortunate indeed was Aunt Judith!

As he looked out across Piccadilly, the air was full of a yellowish drizzle that had not character enough to be a fog. Behind the Green Park railings the trees showed vague drab outlines suggesting the scenery of a hell where the ache of dull depression reigned rather than any pain. Everywhere was that thin and scanty slime which modern cities dignify by the noble name of mud.

Trent glanced at the clock in the porter's office. He had told Patmore the truth, and nothing but the truth; not the whole truth, which, after all, nobody ever tells, if only because there is not time. He had an appointment, and he must not be late, since the 8:20 from Victoria waited for no man; but the fact that he intended to be there a quarter of an hour beforehand, and the reasons for that decision, would not have interested his friend. Although Trent had, like most of us, a strong distaste for prolonged farewells, he knew that Aunt Judith expected the decent observance of any social rite; and fifteen minutes appeared to him to hit the happy mean between the over-assiduous and the perfunctory. During the brief drive to the station he might tax his brain—fond hope!—for some happy and original form of goodby.

As he buttoned his overcoat, the slamming of the door of a motor-car came from without. The swing-door of the entrance was pushed half open, and a tall man, roaring with laughter, paused with his foot on the threshold, and spoke over his shoulder. "*Gute Nacht, du alte gute Kerl,*" he called, "*und herzlichen Dank.*"

"*Ach Quatsch!*" a harsh voice barked in reply as the car rolled away. "*Wiederseh'n!*"

The new-comer pushed through the doors and moved with long strides across the hall. Trent knew the man well enough; so well as to want no conversation with him. A completely unashamed and unscrupulous egotist is not as a rule the best of company, even if one has not, as Trent had, a personal reason for objecting to his existence. There was, too, always the strong possibility that Eugene Wetherill would not try to be the best of company. The habits of that brilliant man of letters included a tendency to be gratuitously offensive, and Trent had had more than one unpleasant encounter with him before.

Turning his head as he reached the stairway, Wetherill caught sight of Trent and raised a hand in recognition. "You're looking damnably serious," he observed with a wolfish grin. "It isn't the sight of me, I hope, that has banished the winning smile. Forget your trouble, dear friend. All may yet be well.

Forget our little disagreements in the past. Drown your sorrow with me at the bar—it's astonishing what a lot can be drowned in one small absinthe cocktail."

"Thanks, but I've got to go," Trent said. He added, "You don't look as if you had anything much to drown. If I look serious, you look quite pleased."

"So I am." Wetherill laughed as he removed his broad-brimmed black hat and white scarf so that it could be seen he was in evening dress beneath his overcoat. "Much pleased. Nothing to drown, as you remark with that infallible discernment of yours; so I shall have that drink purely as a matter of principle—not with any sordid utilitarian purpose. Pleased! I should think I am pleased. I did a good stroke of business yesterday, dear friend, and I haven't got over it yet." He paused a moment, as if recollecting himself; then he went on: "Whenever that happens, I have an unreasonable impulse to forgive the world for being what it is, and mankind for being what they are."

"Including Eugene Wetherill, I hope," Trent suggested sympathetically. "You ought not to be too hard on yourself, you know—it's a fatal tendency. Fight it. Don't let it master you. I've got to tear myself away now, but remember my words." He hurried through the doorway and down the greasy pavement in the direction of Piccadilly.

Wetherill, he thought, was certainly in a state of high satisfaction about something. The expression of contempt which he usually wore was probably, like all the rest of his external appearance, a carefully studied effect; but this evening it had yielded place to a look of genuine pleasure, and Trent wondered what might be the cause of it. Anything that pleased Wetherill would be quite likely to have a very different effect upon more normal minds; and Trent happened to know—as a good many people, unfortunately, knew—of one stroke of business done by Wetherill with which few men would have cared to soil their hands. But that had been months ago; this was evidently something recent, and it was curious that Wetherill had plainly hesitated to say what it was. He was anything but secretive as a rule about his own affairs, even the most discreditable; he liked posing as a paragon of immorality. It was difficult to reckon with a man who boasted of having destroyed his own self-respect,

A massive policeman loomed up at the corner of Charles Street.

"Not a nice night, Officer," Trent remarked.

"That it isn't, sir," rumbled the constable in a tone suggesting that the grimy mist had found its way beneath his heavy waterproofs and permeated all his being. "There's some that seem to enjoy it, though. See those runners coming up the other side of the way? Gawd! Sooner them than me. Funny amusement, isn't it, sir, on a night like this?"

"Splendid for them, really," Trent said. "When they've had a rub down and a change they'll be as happy as so many kings of the Persians. It is youth, Officer—youth footing swift to the dawn, or to the Polytechnic, or somewhere delightful. We ought to envy them."

Pushing on past the scattered procession of bedraggled lads in shorts and singlets who were jogging along in twos and threes at the edge of the pavement, Trent found the cab-rank he sought.

As he sat in the taxi, Trent's thoughts turned back to the interview with old James Randolph which had preceded his dinner at the Cactus Club. It had been, he reflected, shorter than he had anticipated; shorter and even more unpleasant. Nobody could be expected to enjoy the discovery that one of his secrets, and a decidedly humiliating one at that, was shared by another person not at all well disposed towards him. Still, Randolph's uncontrollable rage had seemed rather excessive for the occasion; he stood, after all, to lose nothing in either purse or repute so long as he behaved himself. And as to that there could be no doubt. Trent's threat of exposure had obviously been quite effective. Whether Randolph's denials of any dishonourable purpose were sincere or not, the man was certainly frightened now, and would conduct himself accordingly. Any scandal about the Tiara of Megabyzus would be a deadly blow to the old man's inflated self-esteem. In short, Aunt Judith could be fully reassured before she left. If she were to do so with any remaining uneasiness about Eunice, it would spoil the trip to which she had looked forward so eagerly.

All his life Trent had been strongly attached to his aunt, that unusual old lady. This was a great moment in the life of Miss Judith Yates. She was leaving England for the first time in nearly forty years. Brought up in the twilight of the Victorian era, she had seen in her youth not a little of the world abroad; but the time had come when an over-confident brother had flung away most of the family fortune in some concern floated by a yet more hopeful financier. Thenceforward she had lived in the country on very small means, uncomplaining—indeed, singularly happy. She kept in touch with a wide circle of friends, many of them moving in the midst of affairs; she heard all that was made public, and a good deal that was not, of the world's events, and the seamy side of high life and politics was pretty well known to her. Her prim appearance masked an exceedingly active, well-furnished and seasoned mind. Sometimes, to her amusement, modern young women imagined that they had shocked her; actually, Miss Yates in her time had contemplated with calm breaches of convention more startling than anything coming within their philosophy. She asked only that there should be something about the trespass that was worth considering; it was at pettiness and worthlessness that she drew the line. The closest bond of affection in her fife, indeed, was a friendship, quite casually begun, with Eunice Faviell, the most brilliant of the younger generation of actresses, whose private history centred in a liaison that was no secret to the world she lived in.

A few months earlier she had come into a legacy, and had decided at once to see something, while health remained to her, of the European world again. "I mean," she had told Trent, "to travel in luxury, and to go on travelling until the money is spent." The journey now in prospect was a visit to friends in Rome, and she had declared herself as excited as when she went to her first dance, ready to savour every moment and every incident...

It was by a chance that she was taking the Dieppe route. She had meant to enjoy the comforts of the shorter crossing; but as it happened, a commission that she had given to her nephew Philip could not be carried out until the evening of her day of departure. So, with memories of having been a good sailor, she had decided to take the night service.

It was this errand that had taken Trent to his acrimonious interview with James Randolph; and he was reviewing now, as the taxi took him to Victoria, the grounds of his conviction that the job had been well and truly done. Aunt Judith, he knew, had eyes of the sharpest, and would guess only too readily that all was not well if she showed any sign of uncertainty.

Arrived at the terminus, with a little more margin of time than he had planned, he proceeded to the boat-train platform, stopping by the way to make a purchase at the flower-shop within the precincts. To his surprise, Aunt Judith was not to be seen. She had, of course, her place reserved; but Trent, knowing well her habits of mind, and knowing too that it was the first time in her life that she would be travelling in a first-class Pullman, had assumed that the longer she took over the preliminaries the greater her pleasure would be.

As he turned back, however, from his search for a non-existent Pullman in the forward end of the train, he saw his aunt supervising the transfer of hand luggage to a seat in a rearward section. She must have followed close upon his footsteps through the barrier. As he approached, she was conferring with the Pullman attendant, and that occupational optimist was giving a favourable view of the prospect for the Channel crossing. Trent presented his tribute of exuberant carnations.

"Oh! That is kind of you, Philip. My favourite flower! And exactly what was wanted for the finishing touch to this stage of the adventure. My dear, you cannot imagine how I feel about it. Everything is so different from what it used to be—I mean everything in the way of getting abroad." Aunt Judith certainly appeared to be enjoying to the full the excitement that she had tasted in anticipation. Her eyes were bright, and her cheek had an unaccustomed flush.

Trent came at once to the point that was uppermost in his mind. "You will be glad to hear that it is all settled about Eunice. I saw Randolph this evening, as I had arranged, and I made quite sure that he won't trouble her again. You know, Aunt Ju, I could see you didn't feel quite confident about it when I told you I knew how to get a really binding promise out of the old man. Well, that is what I've done; you can set your mind at rest. I couldn't explain to you how I was going to manage it, and I can't now. I told him, you see, that I would keep quiet about it, as long as he lived at least; it was a bargain. But it's all right."

"It is such a relief to know that, Philip." Miss Yates buried her nose in the carnations gratefully. "You are quite right, I couldn't help being a little worried until it was quite certain."

"All the same," Trent went on, "it looks as if I am booked for a bit of a row with Eunice about it. It seems you wrote to her saying you had told me what had been going on, and you were letting me loose on the old man. She doesn't like it. I got a note from her yesterday, and it wasn't a nice note, though knowing what she is it didn't altogether surprise me."

There was a slight but perceptible elevation of Miss Yates's chin. "What do you mean, Phil, by knowing what she is?"

"Now don't get up in arms, Aunt Ju. Of course I didn't mean..."

"My dear boy, I am not up in arms, but..."

"Well, call it a partial mobilization then. You can't bear to hear a hint of criticism of Eunice, everybody knows that. It's how I feel myself about her, for that matter. But there's no harm in saying I wasn't surprised to be told that her private affairs were none of my damned business, and that she would be obliged if I would keep my nose out of them, and that she was perfectly capable of looking after herself... with more to the same effect."

Miss Yates, smiling, laid a neatly gloved hand on his arm. "If that's all you mean, Phil, by saying you know what she is, why of course you do... it's common knowledge that Eunice has a good allowance of spirit. I dare say you have heard things in that tone of voice from her before. So have I, sometimes. So has your wife, though she is a much older friend than you are. None of us take it too tragically, I am sure. We all know..."

"What she is. Wasn't that what you were going to say, Aunt Ju? So there we are again at the starting-point of our misunderstanding, and we find ourselves in complete agreement—just like foreign ministers in an official communiqué."

"Yes; only we really are, my dear. Now I will confess to you, Phil, that I thought it quite possible she might write you something like that, and I hoped that you would disregard it. She has always insisted on managing her own life just as she likes, and making a hash of it in any way she chooses—which she has done, goodness knows."

Trent nodded. "Goodness does know, indeed. Speaking of that," he added, "I saw Wetherill for a moment just before I started to come here. He was looking extremely well, I'm sorry to say. I never set eyes on that fellow without wanting to murder him."

"I wish you would, Pm sure," Miss Yates said with intense feeling. "Though there's no way of doing it that wouldn't be too good for him."

"Yes; and another thing against it is that it's a game two can play at. He could give me points at it. Wetherill is not the convenient sort of villain who will always take a licking from the hero without doing anything about it. He is fit to take care of himself in any sort of a scrap, he's afraid of nobody, and he loves a row. It's a fact, you know, that he killed a man in a duel at La Spezia, after being wounded twice."

"I expect he cheated," Miss Yates said. "I never cared much for La Spezia, and now I shall like it less. Wetherill ought to have lived in Italy of the fifteenth century, along with the Sforzas and the other Renaissance wild animals."

"So he ought," Trent agreed. "But he has always left undone the things that he ought to have done."

"She has had nothing to do with him for some time now—she told me so. But that has happened before, and it never lasts. I do wish," Miss Yates said fretfully, "Eunice could have managed to take that sort of interest in any other man. There were enough for her to choose from, goodness knows! and a number of them very decent fellows, I have no doubt. There was that young doctor friend of yours, I forget his name—"

"Bryan Fairman, you mean."

"Yes. I never met him, but I always thought it would be nice for her to be married to a friend of yours and Mabel's, and I knew from the way you both used to speak of him that he was the right sort. What makes it all the more irritating is, she has always been very fond of him in a way."

"I don't know," Trent said, "how many times she has refused to marry him—both of them have lost count, I should think—but I dare say she always did it in the most affectionate terms.

Poor Aunt Ju! You never realized what you were letting yourself in for when you decided to become a mother to a girl like Eunice Faviell."

Miss Yates smiled whimsically. "When I decided! It was Eunice who made up her mind to adopt me—you know it was. Why she did, I don't suppose she knows herself." Miss Yates turned the discussion to her plans of travel, and to the changes wrought in Rome since the eighteen nineties. Trent's own arrangements for the immediate future came under review. Early next day he was going down to Glasminster to attend the wedding of Julian Pickett. Perhaps Aunt Judith remembered Julian. Of course Aunt Judith did. He was the young fellow who had had a limp ever since a tiger bit him somewhere in the Himalayas.

"In the gluteus maximus," Trent murmured.

"I knew it was somewhere like that," Aunt Judith said. "Yes; and the day you brought him to see me he rolled up a sheet of music and made a noise like a panther through it, so that Elizabeth dropped the tea-tray in the pantry, and had to be given sal volatile."

At 8:15 Miss Yates was installed in her place, continuing the conversation through the open window. At 8:19% a man carrying a kit-bag hurried past the barrier. He fled to the first-class Pullman, and leapt in just as the train began to move. He was standing in the doorway, with the attendant hauling in his bag, when he chanced to turn and look Trent straight in the face.

Trent, whose casual glance had seen in him only an unknown individual in a big coat over brown tweeds, and a soft hat well pulled down, uttered an exclamation. "Bryan! By Jove, you nearly missed it!"

"Phil! You here!" With a wild gesture the man leaned from the receding coach. "Why the devil..." The rest of his shout was drowned in the rumble as the train gathered speed. Trent, in his astonishment, barely remembered to reply to his aunt's wave from the window.

What could be the meaning of Bryan Fairman's state of agitation? Why had his friend, usually so strictly self-controlled, looked and acted like a demoralized and desperate man?

2

A LITTLE SHEET OF PAPER

Miss Yates, for her part, had not perceived this brief scene of recognition, and she applied herself now, very contentedly, to the taking of things as they came. She observed that, as the train drew out of the station and gathered speed, there was a change in the atmosphere of the carriage. Passengers who had been painfully absorbed by long-drawn-out farewells pulled themselves together. They became more jaunty and less self-conscious. They were on the threshold of something like another existence, in which for a time they would be freed from the conventions of their environment and from neighbourly inquisition. Consciously or unconsciously, they hoped to be really rather more themselves. Moreover, they were southward bound, leaving fog and drizzle behind them. There was the sense of relief which doctors have in mind when they use the tactful expression "change of scene."

With a smile, Miss Yates settled herself in her place and looked round the carriage. There was a slight touch of luxury about it all which she found extremely soothing. The menu did not look exceedingly inviting, but to her there was a certain sense of adventure about dining in the train. And the man was so delightfully polite, particularly after she had ordered herself half a bottle of burgundy.

As dinner was served, she began unobtrusively to take note of her fellow-travellers, and build up for herself an imaginary picture of their lives. For Miss Yates had a keen curiosity about all strangers with whom she came in contact, and it amused her to fit each of them with a personal history. Sometimes she enjoyed the additional pleasure of contrasting her guesses with the later-appearing facts.

She had little hesitation in measuring up the tall, straight-backed, distinguished man, carefully dressed and with well-tended grey moustache, who sat nearest to her, reading a magazine. Not quite military, she decided; a more thoughtful type. Something diplomatic, undoubtedly; perhaps a newly-appointed ambassador or minister. Her conjecture would not have pleased the object of it, who prided himself on looking every inch a soldier. He was in fact a very eminent professor of history, on his way to Tunis, where he hoped to establish new facts about the battle of Thapsus that would blast the reputation of another eminent historian, whom he had been after for years.

Miss Yates was not much nearer the mark in placing the well-groomed young man of magnificent physique who came next under her eye. She thought the slight crookedness *of his nose* rather added to his attractiveness; too regular features often went, she had found, with an undesirable vanity in men. Some people might think his chest and shoulders over-developed, but that was often the case with rowing men, who were usually very nice boys; and Miss Yates thought of this youth as a Cambridge undergraduate going to join his parents abroad. His clothes were certainly quite right. At dinner he displayed a very healthy appetite, and drank only a little mineral water, while he happily studied a letter which Miss Yates surmised to be from a girl. She wondered what the young man could have been doing to his left ear.

The state of that organ, alas! was none of the young man's doing. Miss Yates was looking at the beginnings of what is known as a cauliflower ear, the work of Baker Isaacs of Hoxton; and the youth himself was Gunner Brand, formerly heavy-weight champion of the army, holder of the Abingdon Belt, winner of a series of lucrative professional battles, and looking forward to a contest for the world title in three months' time. He was on the way to join his trainer at their camp in Cap d'Antibes, and was now reading and re-reading a long letter from his fiancée, whose equal the world did not, in his opinion, contain.

Miss Yates was less at fault in her judgment of the neighbouring couple. Her quick glance took in a multitude of details of expression and turnout. The very pretty girl she set down unhesitatingly, and quite correctly, as a vain, selfish and bad-hearted fool. Her manner to the waiters as the train dinner was served appealed to Miss Yates as the very acme of the sort of *hauteur* represented in American films of English high-life. The young man, evidently her lately married husband, was a weak but not unamiable fool. Their whole appearance bespoke considerable wealth; and Miss Yates reflected, not for the first time, on the dangerous extent to which complete worthlessness is represented among the rich.

She understood best of all, perhaps, the kind of man who had so narrowly escaped missing the train. She liked his face, with its clean-cut lines and cloven chin. About thirty, she said to herself; an earnest type; a trained mind and a worker; perhaps a doctor; normally well controlled, but now showing signs of illness and all but ungovernable agitation. There was something reckless and haunted about his appearance. The term "Byronic" occurred to Miss Yates's unmodern mind. Was he, perhaps, suffering from a broken heart? Miss Judith believed in broken hearts, though she had learned that they can be broken in more ways than one. Certainly this man was desperately worried about something. He ate but little at dinner, and he drank a whole bottle of champagne without any visible improvement of his spirits. His hand shook as he raised his glass. Miss Yates wondered if he were flying from justice; but she could not think him an evil-doer.

As soon as he had finished his wine, he called on the waiter to clear the table at which he was sitting alone. The table clear, he planted on it his kit-bag and opened it. Miss Yates observed that on the top of its contents lay a number of paper packages, each secured with an elastic band; and of these the man proceeded to make one compact parcel, wrapped in a sheet of newspaper and tied with string. Replacing this in the bag, he next took from it a handful of sheets of paper, which he laid on the table before him.

Snapping the bag as if he was shutting up in it a guilty secret, he turned to writing busily in pencil. From where she sat Miss Judith could follow the ebb and flow of his inspiration. He would cover some sheets with a big scrawling hand, then suddenly shake his head critically, and seem to begin all over again.

"Can he be an author?" Miss Yates asked herself. "But surely no one could compose at that rate. And he doesn't look like a literary man. A journalist, perhaps—but would a journalist be in such a dither over his work? He may be preparing a speech—but then he looks like the kind of man who would always know what he wanted to say, and would say it in plain words."

As Miss Yates toyed with these speculations, the man wrote on. At length, rejecting yet another draft, he paused and considered; then scribbled what appeared to be a much briefer document. As he threw down his pencil, his glance met that of Miss Yates: and the blue eyes seemed to look right through her, focussed on something far beyond. So, at least, she hoped; for she saw him shudder violently before she turned her gaze away, with a sense as if she were spying on something that she had no right to see.

Vaguely she looked round the carriage, and remarked that the passengers were preparing for the arrival at Newhaven. Some with a half-furtive air were stowing cigarettes or tobacco from their bags in their pockets, with a view to the eluding of the French Customs. Others even more shamefaced were gulping down tablets and cachets of the drugs guaranteed to defy the demon of seasickness.

Miss Yates began to follow their example and prepare for transit to the boat. She had no fear of seasickness and no tobacco to conceal, but she got ready her tickets and passport. Her eyes wandered back to the agitated traveller. He had folded his final copy and placed it in a long envelope. The rest of his writing he folded into a wad, which he thrust beneath the fastenings of the newspaper-covered packet that Miss Yates had already observed.

As the train drew up at the platform he was the first to leave the Pullman; and Miss Yates noticed that as he started from his chair a piece of thin paper was wafted from it, unseen by him, to the floor of the carriage. It was unmistakably a leaf torn from an engagement-block, being headed by a printed date in thick capitals, with pencilled jottings below. So much Miss Yates could not but notice as she bent to pick it up; but the man was already heading a stream of travellers passing out, and she saw nothing of him as she stepped to the platform.

"But certainly," she thought, "he will be crossing to Dieppe, and I shall see him on the boat."

There, indeed, he was, already striding rapidly up and down the upper deck on the starboard side. Miss Yates attended first to the stowing of her own hand luggage. The turmoil of cargo-shifting and the casting-off of moorings ended at length; the steamer began to plough its steady way towards France. It was then that Miss Yates approached the man who had so much engaged her sympathy.

"When you left the train, sir," she said without any nervous preliminary, "you left this little sheet of paper which had fallen from your seat to the floor. I thought it might be something of importance, so I had better return it to you."

The man gazed at her a little wildly; then at the leaf which she was holding out to him. His eyes narrowed as he examined it in the half-light of the deck lamps; then he looked away, his face contorted as if with fear or keen anxiety.

Suddenly he turned to Miss Yates squarely. "You have made a mistake, ma'am," he said, in a shaking voice. "Very kind indeed of you to take the trouble, but that paper is not mine. I never saw it before. Many thanks all the same." He jerked a bow at her and immediately resumed his uneasy pacing of the deck.

Miss Yates was naturally taken aback. Why the man should so reject her good offices she was unable to conceive. The paper had unquestionably fallen from his chair. More than that—she had seen him, with a perplexed and frowning brow, intently studying that very paper more than once during the progress of his writing. Indignation might have overcome her; but Miss Yates was one of those who will always find excuses for anyone seeming so distressed and overwrought as did this fellow-passenger. She felt the agreeable thrill of a mystery as she carefully tucked the disowned scrap of writing in a pocket of her handbag.

The voyagers, for the most part, settled themselves for the crossing in the saloons and cabins, for the night was wet and cold. Miss Yates, in a glow of freedom and adventure, was resolved to lose none of the sensations proper to travel; she preferred to seclude herself with a rug in the shelter of one of the boats. That end of the deck might well have appeared deserted to the man who had so aroused her interest, when next she saw him. Emerging from one of the deck-houses, he resumed his pacing to and fro; and she noted that he now carried the shapeless package under his arm. Soon he paused beside the rail; and he quitted it with a nervous start when one of the crew passed by on some errand.

A minute later, what Miss Yates was half-expecting happened. The mysterious traveller again approached the rail, and furtively dropped overboard whatever it was that he was carrying. That done, he disappeared below; and Miss Yates saw no more of him until the disembarkation at Dieppe. She noted that he was among the first to pass out of the Customs shed; but neither on the Paris train nor elsewhere did she again set eyes on the man who had so surprisingly disowned the little sheet of paper.

Not until half an hour later did Miss Yates, having savoured the pleasure of skimming the first French newspaper she had seen for many years, think again of the leaflet which she had tried to restore to its possessor. Turning from the lively polemics of the *Homme Trompé*, which she had found more than a little bewildering, she began to review the details of the puzzle which had so much intensified the happiness of her release from the daily round of life in Farnham. The scrap of paper, now! If its possessor chose to deny his right to it, it was surely for anybody's reading.

Miss Yates drew the paper from her handbag and noted at once that it was headed by that same day's date. But what she read next, in a firm and legible pencilling, gave her a surprise far more thrilling than she had yet known in the brief affair of the mysterious passenger to Dieppe.

Heads jerked round, and startled looks were turned upon the quiet little Englishwoman, as she exclaimed aloud: "Good gracious!"

3

DEATH OF A PHILANTHROPIST

To Chief Inspector Gideon Bligh's experienced eye the scene explained itself—up to a point. That able officer stood in the centre of the late James Randolph's bedroom on the upper floor of No. 5, Newbury Place, known to a simpler age as Newbury Mews. This was a small enclosure, approached by archways from the streets at either end of it, in one of the purlieus of Park Lane; No. 5 being the nearest to Bullingdon Street of the neat row of stables and coach-houses, converted now to the uses of well-to-do human habitation.

Mr Bligh stroked with one great hand his prematurely bald cranium while he considered the position. His appearance always commanded respect. He was tall and loosely built. His cleanshaven face, with its massive, vigorous features, wore habitually a stern expression. His skin, slightly tanned, was otherwise colourless.

In the doorway stood a police-sergeant, closely attentive to the proceedings of the man from headquarters. He had already put his superior in possession of the facts learned since the police had been called to the place by telephone, just after midnight; he had mentioned the points of interest so far disclosed-in examination of the bedroom, and what he regarded as "a queer piece of evidence" in the sitting-room below it. The time now was half past eight in the morning.

The body had been left by the police-surgeon as he had found it, lying prone before the dressing-table. The old man had been shot from behind and killed instantly, the bullet entering below the left shoulder-blade. He had been at the time—whether it mattered or not—in a peculiarly defenceless posture; for, being fully dressed in day clothes, he had been in the act of taking off his coat. The left sleeve was half-way down the arm, and the right had just slipped from the shoulder, so that the arms were for the moment pinioned. Clearly he had not believed himself to be in danger of any sort of attack. He had placed the contents of his pockets on the table before the looking-glass. Assuming him to have been still facing the table at the moment of his death, the murderer would have been standing at or near the doorway of the room—possibly outside the open door.

The room, kept in a state of speckless neatness, was somewhat scantily furnished; but Inspector Bligh knew enough of such matters to perceive that the few movables were articles of value—probably, seeing what had been the dead man's reputation as a connoisseur, of great value.

Randolph, it was evident, had been about to dress for dinner. His evening clothes were neatly set out on two chairs. What he had carried in his pockets lay in a small disorderly heap before the looking-glass—a case containing notes to the value of seven pounds; a handful of coins; a watch with its slender chain of gold and platinum links; an eye-glass case; a leather key-case; a few letters, being ordinary business communications; a pencil; and, incongruous among these other articles, a champagne cork.

The inspector examined this last with some interest. Certainly it was an odd thing for Randolph to have been carrying, as appearances suggested, on his person. Had it been used, perhaps, to sheathe the end of some sharp-pointed object? The officer satisfied himself that this was not so. The cork was flawless and compact, to all appearances in just that condition in which it had left the bottle; it was branded "Felix Poubelle 1884." The inspector rubbed his chin as he considered these facts; but he found himself unable to attach to them any significance at all.

Close to this pile of personal oddments lay the separated parts of a safety razor, lacking a blade. The other materials for shaving, as Mr Bligh soon ascertained, lay among the articles on a shelf in the bathroom adjoining. They had not been recently used. On the same shelf lay the little case belonging to the razor, and within it were two new blades in their unbroken envelopes. Curious, then, was the presence of the razor alone, unscrewed and bladeless, on the dressing-table.

The inspector turned now to a small chest of drawers against the wall hard by the door opening from the passage. On the embroidered blue linen "runner" covering its top stood a water-bottle, half-empty, and a tumbler from which, it appeared, water had been drunk. A glance showed that the inevitable fingerprints had been left on both of these—probably Randolph's own prints, the inspector reflected sadly. Still, you couldn't be sure. Murderers were not—so ran Mr Bligh's train of thought—like criminals as a rule. All the regular crooks knew about fingerprints; and none of them were deliberate killers. Murderers were apt to be quite respectable; at least to know nothing of the ways of criminals or of the police either. But again, you couldn't be sure.

Leaving this point for later investigation, he turned next to the fireplace. Randolph, the police had learned, had always a good coal fire burning in this during the cold weather. Yesterday's fire had long burnt itself out, and the inspector raked through the ashes with the small poker that lay to hand. Nothing, however, rewarded his search.

His eye travelled now over the floor of the room, and came to rest where, beneath the window, there lay a quantity of crumpled brown paper and tangled string, marring the extreme tidiness of the surroundings. A moment's examination showed that several packets, fastened with sealed cord, had been opened, their contents removed, and the covers flung down carelessly. From the appearance of these relics Mr Bligh judged them to have been slim parcels containing letters or documents of some kind, each parcel conspicously marked with a number in soft black pencil. The string in each case, the seals being unbroken, had been cut with an instrument of peculiar sharpness, as the perfectly clean division of the strands made plain.

The inspector's eyes narrowed as his deft fingers smoothed these crumpled wrappings into their original shapes—shells emptied, now, of so much perhaps explosive matter. Had Randolph been shot for the sake of what was in these packets? Was that the murderer's intended spoil? Letters, or papers? Not money or valuables, certainly; enough of those had been left on the dressing-table. And what kind of letters or papers were worth the taking of a man's life? Apart from secret treaties and other materials of thrilling fiction, which Mr Bligh did not take very seriously, he knew of one kind which had, not seldom, been considered worth that price of guilt and peril.

But surely old James Randolph, that busy architect of good works, could have had no interest in blackmail. Scotland Yard knew of some little peculiarities of his—it knows so much about so many public characters, little as they dream of it. But there was nothing savouring of illegality. Besides, the man had been for years immensely wealthy, and the sources of his wealth were no secret. There could have been no temptation to one of the most sordid of crimes.

Setting aside this difficulty for the time, Mr Bligh poked about diligently among the brown paper and string; and on the carpet beneath them he soon discovered a safety-razor blade. His lips pursed themselves in a silent whistle. Here, no doubt, was the instrument chosen hastily for the opening of the packets—a blade taken from the razor where it had been placed in readiness for use. Bending down, the inspector noted that this was a blade of the make that went with the unscrewed razor on the dressing-table; a duplicate of the two in unopened envelopes in the razor-case.

If, thought Mr Bligh, the man who cut strings with this blade has left no fingerprints, it can only have been because he was careful not to do so. The inspector used his own pocketknife to raise the little slip of steel from the carpet, and place it beside the waterbottle and tumbler already destined for expert examination.

His eyes now began to search the wall at this part of the room, and he discovered at once the small keyhole of a built-in safe—a safe of a primitive type, as Mr Bligh's experience suggested.

It was as he noted this that heavy and hasty footsteps were heard on the stairs, and the excited red face of a young constable appeared over the shoulder of the sergeant in the doorway. The formula which Mr Bligh had employed so many hundreds of times in the earliest phase of his career rose again to his lips. "Now then," he said gruffly, "what's all this?"

"This is the man posted at the street door," the sergeant explained in the tone of one inured to the follies of inexperience. "What is it, Clarkson?"

"I've just found this, sir, in the corner of the passage, just inside the entrance," the young man said. "I thought it might be important." He held out a green tie-on luggage-label, the string of which had somehow been snapped. "It's a dark spot just there, and this label is much the same shade as the carpet. The door opens into a narrow passage, as you know, sir, and it would be awkward going out in a hurry with a bag of any size. This label may have caught against something, and come off without it being noticed, if the man was a bit flurried—so I thought, sir."

The inspector, who had listened to this with wooden impassivity, now took the label in his hand. It was inscribed, in a shaky but sufficiently legible script, "Bryan Fairman, passenger to Dieppe."

"Dieppe, eh?" Mr Bligh said thoughtfully. "I wonder." He spoke sharply to the attentive sergeant. "Get me the Yard on the phone at once." The apparatus stood on one of the two small tables flanking the bed; and the sergeant jumped to it.

"Very good, Clarkson," the inspector said. "This may very possibly have a bearing on the case. I am acting on it now. You can go back to your post." He took the telephone instrument in hand.

In a few moments he was in touch with a colleague at headquarters, and giving swift instructions that inquiry should be made whether a passenger giving the name of Bryan Fairman had travelled by the night-boat reaching Dieppe that morning. The French police, he said, should be asked to co-operate to the extent of keeping this man, if identified, under observation, supposing that he had remained in Dieppe. If not, it would be of great assistance if his movements could be traced, as a serious charge might be brought against him.

Mr Bligh rang off.

4

NOT HARD OF HEARING

"And now," Inspector Bligh said to his subordinate, "for a look at the sitting-room, and that queer piece of evidence, as you call it."

He led the way downstairs to the room beneath the bedroom. It was an apartment of less bare appearance than the other, an effect of more luxurious comfort being produced at once by the deep-piled, patternless grey carpet which covered the whole extent of the floor from wall to wall. Two low-backed, thick-cushioned armchairs flanked an old-fashioned fireplace. One of these, the one having its back towards the window, had between it and the wall a table just large enough to hold a grey-enamelled telephone instrument, a London telephone directory, and an orderly pile of journals and printed documents. There were an oval centre table and, before the window, a small writing-table; both, as the inspector correctly guessed, "pieces" of great price. At right angles to this last an inviting double-ended sofa stood backed against the wall; beside it, rising a modest two feet from the floor, was a narrow bookcase. In the bedroom there had not been a book to be seen. The bookcase here appeared to be occupied entirely by works of reference, from the austerity of Bradshaw, Baedeker and Whitaker to the more engaging appeal of a tall row of art-sales annuals.

Mr Bligh spent little time in examining the room and its contents as a whole. All appeared to be in precisely the state of undisturbed neatness that a man of rigidly orderly habits would require in his own establishment. It was the writing-table to which a gesture from the police-sergeant directed his special attention. Upon it was trimly laid out the usual array of writing materials, with a small open-fronted cabinet of Chinese lacquer, on the shelves of which were arranged in various sizes, note-paper, sheets of blank paper, cards and envelopes.

Upon the flat top of the cabinet stood an upright engagement-block. It had a separate leaf, with a sentence of Scripture at the foot, allotted to each day, and the leaves were set loosely so as to be turned over on metal rings as each day passed. On the leaf which now met the eye, two afternoon appointments at City addresses were noted, followed by the words, "5:30. T. Searle to call," presumably referring to some visitor expected by Randolph at his own house. The leaf so exposed was that for the day which had just begun; not, as would have been natural, the leaf for the previous day, the day of the crime. That leaf was missing, and vestiges of paper showed that it had been torn roughly from the file. Handling the block delicately, the inspector satisfied himself that this was the only leaf that had been so removed.

The block, he knew, had not been touched during the first police examination of the premises some hours before, when the signs of a leaf having been torn away had been noted. He considered the fact with bent brows. Someone, before or after the murder, had been tampering with this record of Randolph's arrangements, and tampering to some purpose. The fingers of Mr Bligh's left hand drummed lightly on his hairless skull—an indication with him of restrained excitement.

"You were right," he observed to the gratified sergeant. "This is important. I don't know, though, that I should call it queer when a murderer destroys the only direct evidence of his having been on the spot. And now I want to see this man Raught. Send him to me in here."

Randolph's manservant, who had been told to stay in his bedroom adjoining the sitting-room, soon presented himself—a lean, small, dark-visaged individual with a furtive eye. A shifty-looking character at the best of times, thought the inspector; and now looking sick and frightened. Mr Bligh stared hard at him for a few moments; then said with a quietness that seemed only to add to the man's discomfort: "So your name is Simon Raught."

"Yes, sir."

"You were the late Mr Randolph's personal servant, and you always slept on the premises when he was staying here. That right?"

"Yes, sir."

"Any other servants?"

"Not here, sir. Mr Randolph kept his establishment at his place in Yorkshire, where he lived most of the time. Besides me, there's only a woman, Mrs Barley, to look after this place. She has a doorkey and her job is to keep the place tidy, all the year round. Mr Randolph liked to have it kept so that he could come to London any time without notice, and find it ready for occupation. So long as he did find it ready—which I must say he always did—Mrs Barley could arrange her time to suit herself. When we were here, I used always to get the breakfast and do the bedrooms myself."

Mr Bligh, still bending on Raught a gaze which he continued to avoid meeting, said gently: "It isn't exactly your place as valet, is it, to do that sort of thing?"

"I didn't consider that, sir—not in dealing with Mr Randolph," Raught said. He swallowed nervously, and went on: "I didn't mind what I did for him, owing everything to him, as you might say."

The inspector grunted sceptically. "What about this Mrs Barley?" he asked. "Oughtn't she to be here this morning?"

"I don't know when she'll be coming in, sir," Raught declared. "She had been here when we got down from Yorkshire day before yesterday, and she was here yesterday morning for an hour. But as soon as she hears of what's happened, she'll be along quick enough, you may be sure of that."

"What do you know about her?"

"She's a perfectly respectable woman, sir, I need 'ardly say. Before her husband died—a carpenter, I believe he was—they rented one of Mr Randolph's cottages in Humberstone. I have 'eard that Barley got into bad company, sir, and got himself into some sort of trouble, which Mr Randolph 'elped him out of; but there was never anything against Mrs Barley. Since he died, she's been living with her sister, who keeps a boarding-house used by foreigners mostly, I've been told—in Bayswater it is, Oldbury Terrace, I forget the number."

The inspector took down these particulars in his notebook; then referred to an earlier entry.

"When you were first questioned this morning, you mentioned a secretary."

"Mr Verney; yes, sir. He's the gentleman that had the management of all Mr Randolph's charities and that—his good works, as you may say. When Mr Randolph was staying here—"

"When did he stay here? How much time did he spend here?"

"There was nothing regular about it, sir. Every few weeks—I couldn't put it any nearer than that; sometimes it was more frequent—we would come down for two or three days. Or we might go back to Brinton the next day. This time we came the day before yesterday, the Tuesday."

"Well, now about Mr Verney."

"He was often up at Brinton, sir, the place in Yorkshire; but he didn't live there. He had rooms here in London, in Purvis Crescent, No. 36—off Willesley Road; I believe he spends a lot of time running the Randolph Institute, sir, in Kilburn—a sort of club, that is, for young men and boys. Whenever we were here, Mr Verney would come in, having his own door-key, to talk business. I should have expected to see him here before this, sir."

Mr Bligh took another note; then once more he fixed the man before him with an intimidating eye.

"And where do you say you were last night, when your employer was murdered?"

Raught repeated the account of his movements of which the inspector had already learned the substance. It had been the valet's half day off, as it always was on Wednesdays. He had not gone out until a little before 6:30, when he had done so after laying out Mr Randolph's clothes for a dinner which he was to have attended. Raught, on leaving, had gone straight to the Three Tuns in Rowington Street, where he had spent some time, and had afterwards visited the Running Stag in Gooch Street. He had often "used" both places while in London, and was well known. Miss Whicker at the Tuns and Archie at the Stag could bear out his statement. Raught had then joined his sister, Mrs Livings, and her husband at the Pilatus restaurant in Warsaw Street at 7:30. After dinner they had gone on to Battersea, where his relations lived, and had visited the Parthenon Cinema, where a film called "The Two-Gun Terror" was being shown. After that he had had a drink at his brother-in-law's place, and come back to Newbury Place just before twelve o'clock. He was not expected to be back, he explained, before midnight, Mr Randolph being "very human" in that respect.

"And then?" Mr Bligh inquired in his uncomfortably colourless tone.

Raught had gone upstairs to see if his master had returned. He had found the bedroom door wide open, the lights on, and his master lying dead on the floor before the dressing-table; it had given him "such a turn, sir, as I never had in my life." He had "felt" at once that Mr Randolph was dead. There couldn't be any mistake about it, the valet said, looking at him as he lay "all of a heap." He had, therefore, rung up the police immediately, being careful to leave everything just as it was. He had seen, when he came in, no signs of any stranger having been about the place. In reply to a question, Raught declared that he had not touched the body, or even examined it closely, his nerves being "all to pieces." Then how had he known that it was murder, and a case for calling in the police? Raught had not known; he had only "supposed it must be that."

Inspector Bligh now resumed his silent study of Raught's unprepossessing face. The valet, his eyes wandering in all directions, pulled out a handkerchief and squeezed it between his palms. Suddenly the question was shot at him:

"Weren't you in trouble a few years ago?"

"Well, sir," Raught said with that shade of candour peculiar to those found out, "there was a small matter of false pretences—"

"Blackmail, don't you mean?" the inspector asked grimly. "I thought I remembered your face—it's a kind I see a lot of."

Raught licked his lips and took on an injured expression. "Truly, sir, it wasn't blackmail. What would be the use of my telling you a lie? I was in a bit of a 'ole, sir—through betting, it was. I was in Mr Randolph's service at that time, and with your memory, sir, you may recollect he gave evidence of my good character while I was with him—no man could have acted kinder. I got six months, and when I came out he took me into his service again. Not many gentlemen would have done as much—saving me from drifting from bad to worse, as you may say. I would have given my life for him, sir."

Raught's cry from the heart did not impress the inspector, to whose accustomed ear it had not a genuine ring. Nor did he think much of the man's alibi. The police surgeon had thought it probable that Randolph's death had taken place not earlier than seven o'clock and not later than ten. Unless both Miss Whicker and Archie should prove able to time their customer's coming and going with some accuracy, there was room enough in Raught's tale for him to move about in, before keeping his verifiable appointment in Warsaw Street.

Setting that matter aside for the time being, the inspector opened another line.

"Do you know anything about any person having an appointment to see your master yesterday evening, or any person who might have been coming here that evening for any reason?"

"Well, sir, the only appointment Mr Randolph had made—to my knowledge, that is—was at six o'clock, with Mr Trent, the artist, who had been at Brinton painting his portrait some time ago."

The inspector smiled faintly. "Ha! So Mr Trent, the artist, had an appointment at six. Why? Wasn't Mr Randolph satisfied with the portrait done by Mr Trent, the artist?"

"Oh! It wasn't that at all, sir—quite the contrary. Everyone thought highly of the portrait, and I believe Mr Randolph's intention in asking Mr Trent to call was to arrange about having another portrait done, or I should say a copy, like, of the first one. It was to be hung in the hall of the Institute, sir, the place I mentioned just now. Mr Verney was very keen about it, and though Mr Randolph was not so at first, he came to approve of the idea, sir."

"Hm! Very natural he should." Mr Bligh gazed thoughtfully out of the window. "It was to be a copy, yes? For the Institute—I see. You're sure it was for the Institute?"

"Oh yes, sir. Mr Verney was very anxious they should have it. They were speaking of it when Mr Verney was at Brinton last week, sir, and Mr Randolph said he would write a note to Mr Trent at once."

The inspector suddenly turned his eye on Raught once more. "Not hard of hearing, are you?" he observed agreeably; and as the colour flooded the man's pale face he added: "Ytm're sure you haven't forgotten any other little details of this private conversation between your master and his secretary? No? All right. Then Mr Trent called at six?"

"It was just six, sir, when I opened the door to him," Raught said subduedly. "It was accidental, sir, as you may say, me being here when he called, because on Wednesdays my time is supposed to be my own .after three o'clock. But you know, sir, what the weather was like all yesterday, and I hadn't anything to do with myself before meeting my sister and her husband at seven thirty, and so I had a bit of a sleep in the afternoon, and then there was my best suit wouldn't be none the worse for a pressing, and what with one thing—"

"Never mind all that," Mr Bligh snapped. "You were still here at six—is that it?"

"Yes, sir. And when I went to answer the bell, Mr Randolph was just coming out of the sitting-room to answer it himself; and he says: 'Oh! You're here still,' he says. 'Well, if that's Mr Trent at the door,' he says, 'show him in here,' he says. So I showed Mr Trent in."

"And then what did they talk about?"

"I could not say, sir."

"You didn't listen, I suppose," Mr Bligh remarked dispassionately, "because you knew all about it beforehand. Well; what next?"

"After about a quarter of an hour I heard the sitting-room door open, and Mr Randolph calls to me to show Mr Trent out again, which I did. And that's all I know, sir, about anyone calling on Mr Randolph yesterday, because I went out for the evening myself a little later, and never come back again till near twelve, like I told you."

Mr Bligh considered for a few moments, still fixing the unhappy Raught with a baleful eye.

"You say you were out of here," he summed up at last, "by not later than 6:30. And your master had a dinner appointment in the City. You have told the sergeant here that the dinner was for eight o'clock, and that Mr Randolph would usually send for a taxi when keeping appointments of that kind. Is that right?"

"Quite right, sir. He never had his own car in London."

"Hm! Time enough," the inspector muttered; then: "What do you know about a person called Bryan Fairman?"

Raught appeared sincerely surprised at the question. "I suppose that would be Dr Fairman, sir?"

"I shouldn't wonder," Mr Bligh grunted. "Who is he?"

"I believe, sir, he is one of the doctors at the mental 'ospital at Claypoole, which is named after Mr Randolph, and kept up as you probably know, sir, entirely at his expense." (Mr Bligh nodded.) "I have seen Dr Fairman once, when he was dining at Brinton one evening. I think he had been asked over, sir, to speak about the work he was doing at the mental 'ospital."

"You think!" Mr Bligh remarked with devastating emphasis. "You heard what he and Mr Randolph were talking about—that's what you mean. Well, you've seen Dr Fairman. What kind of a man is her to look at? Tall or short? Dark or fair? Give me a description."

Raught, in evident relief at the thought of some other person having attracted the notice of the police, took a moment for consideration. "I saw him only the once, sir, and that would be about three months ago, as near as I can fix it. But I remember him as a gentleman of what you might call medium size, rather thin, with black hair and a little moustache, a bit pale in the face."

"About what age? Does he wear glasses?"

"I should say somewhere in the thirties, sir. I didn't see him wearing glasses; he seemed to me like a keen-sighted man, his eye being sort of piercing, as they say, when he looked at you. I can't think of anything else special about him, except his acting a bit nervous-like—jerky in his movements, if you know what I mean, sir."

"What about his expression? Pleasant?"

" 'Ardly that, sir. I should call it severe—not unpleasant I don't mean, not that at all, but as if he wouldn't laugh very easy. If I may say so," Raught added with an air of cringing slyness, "Dr Fairman's expression is a little bit like your own, sir."

"Not unpleasant, eh?" Mr Bligh said. "Well, you ought to know. Now then; apart from his appearance, what else do you know about Dr Fairman?"

"Nothing, sir, only what I've heard mentioned in talk sometimes between Mr Randolph and other parties when—"

"When your ear happened to be in the neighbourhood of the keyhole," Mr Bligh suggested pleasantly.

"No, sir," the valet said, as one making patient allowance for the working of a suspicious temperament. "In my position, sir, people's conversation often comes to my ears without me having to listen for it, even in a big 'ouse like Brinton. And as for a small place like this, you can see for yourself, sir, I'd be bound to hear a good deal of what was being talked about unless it was meant to be private—what with doors left open, or me going in and out about my work. And if I know anything about Mr Randolph," Raught added with the first touch of genuine feeling that the inspector had noted in him, "anything he wanted to be kept private would be kept private."

"And no blooming error," Mr Bligh prompted him with the ghost of a smile.

"You take the words out of my mouth, sir," Raught said. "But I only mean that the old man—Mr Randolph, I should say—was no fool, if he was kind-hearted to a fault, as the saying is. I do know this, sir—if he wanted to see anybody here without the chance of being overheard, it was his habit to make an appointment for the Wednesday evening, which has always been my time off, and open the door to them himself."

"No fool, as you say," the inspector observed drily.

Raught ignored this offensive interjection. "As for what was said about Dr Fairman, his name has come up in conversation more than once between Mr Randolph and Mr Verney. Mr Verney seemed to think a lot of some special job Dr Fairman was doing at the mental 'ospital; what it was I can't say. I thought Mr Randolph didn't seem to think quite so much of it—spoke of it a bit short-like. Once, I remember, he said that the worst of these loony-doctors—"

"Did he say 'loony-doctors'?" Mr Bligh cut in.

The valet hesitated. "He did not, sir; but he used some expression which the meaning of it was obviously that. And he said that the worst of them was that when they often got a bee in their bonnets themselves—that he *did* say, I'll swear to it."

The inspector smiled another wintry smile. "I said you were not hard of hearing," he commented. "Did anything more about this Dr Fairman come to your ears?"

"Nothing that I can recall, sir."

Mr Bligh sighed gently. At this hour the much-wanted Fairman, if he had caught the night-boat, as appearances suggested, might still be at his destination in Dieppe. On the other hand, his true destination was more than likely to be elsewhere, and he might be receding each moment farther beyond the reach of the English law's long arm. The inspector strode to the sitting-room telephone, and soon was in touch with the same official to whom he had spoken before. He repeated briefly, for transmission to Dieppe, Raught's description of the suspect, and asked that inquiries about him should be made immediately at the Randolph Mental Hospital at Claypoole, where he was one of the medical staff.

"Now then," he resumed, turning to the valet who stood uneasily awaiting his attention, "before you went out, you left your master's evening clothes ready for him?"

"Yes, sir."

"Did you put out his razor?"

"No, sir. I never knew him need to shave in the evening. I had left the razor on the shelf in the bathroom, with the other shaving things."

"Was there a blade in the razor?"

"I had put in a new blade ready for next morning, sir. Mr Randolph liked to have a new one every day."

"And when you found his body, did you see the razor lying on the dressing-table?"

"No, sir. I was too much upset to notice anything of that sort."

"You didn't even see that there was a lot of brown paper and string on the floor?"

Raught dropped his eyes. "Now you mention it, sir, I did notice that—an untidy mess lying under the window, as if someone had been opening parcels. It slipped my memory sir—truly it did. And I never touched it."

The inspector grunted. He had the impression that the valet was meeting all these inquiries with as much frankness as was in his nature. "Do you know," he asked, "if your master kept any valuables in his bedroom?"

The man hesitated. "None, sir, to my knowledge, except studs and links and that. But I—I fancy he had a safe set in the wall by the window."

Mr Bligh's face hardened. "Yah!" he said ungracefully. "You fancy! Don't you know?"

"Well, sir," Raught said unhappily, "I *have* seen a keyhole."

"Of course you have," the inspector said brutally. "And the edges of the door too. The question is whether you know what was behind it."

"That I don't indeed, sir," the valet protested. "And it was never opened in my presence."

Mr Bligh still surveyed him with a disparaging eye. "Now, Raught," he said, "what can you tell me about this?" He indicated the engagement-block standing on the Chinese cabinet. "Is that the usual place for it?"

The valet appeared genuinely startled. "It certainly is not, sir," he declared with emphasis. "That thing—I never remember seeing it there before. I have seen it often enough, and anyone could tell what it was for, sir, of course. Mr Randolph would often jot down an appointment on it when I was about. But he wasn't ever communicative-like about his engagements—not that they were any business of mine. And this block, sir, was always treated like something specially private-like. He would always lock it away in a drawer of the writing-table—never once have I seen it left standing about like this. Most peculiar it is, to anyone knowing Mr Randolph's ways." He shook his head portentously.

"Well, that's that," the inspector remarked after a moment's rubbing of his chin. "Now come upstairs," he directed curtly. Raught's leaden complexion became visibly less healthy as he was shepherded into the room where the body still lay.

"Now, here's another peculiar thing I want your opinion about." Mr Bligh pointed to the small heap of articles on the dressingtable. "Did Mr Randolph usually put the contents of his pockets here?"

"Yes, sir. He always dressed here. There is no separate dressingroom."

"And have you ever seen anything of this sort among his personal effects?" The inspector, watching the man's face, indicated the champagne cork. "Can you think of any reason why he should have carried it about with him?"

Raught looked blankly at his questioner. "In the five years I have been with Mr Randolph, sir, I have never seen a cork among his things. It's funny it should be that kind of a cork, too. He didn't seem ever to care for sparkling wines. At home—at the place in Yorkshire, that is—he never touched them, though he kept champagne for his guests."

"Well," the inspector said sharply, "he might have had someone to lunch or dinner here, and given 'em champagne or something of the sort. You'd have known about that, I suppose."

The valet shook his head decisively. "He never had lunch or dinner here, sir; let alone entertaining. When in London, he would have his meals mostly at the Lansdowne Club—that was where I had to ring him up in case of anything pressing. An egg and a bit of toast and a cup of tea in the morning—that is all the food I have ever known him take here. It wasn't a 'ome, sir, not in any sense of the word. I had to cater for myself, that being allowed for in the wages—generous too. As for yesterday and the day before, he was out to lunch and dinner as usual. It's true I wasn't here at dinner-time being out for the evening; but I can answer for it there wasn't enough in the place for what you might call a proper meal. And the only drink ever kept here was some brandy and bottles of seltzer, which Mr Randolph would sometimes have a drop of before going to bed. Besides," Raught went on after a brief pause, "he certainly intended dining out last night, sir—the Tabarders' Company dinner it was to be—and he never missed anything to do with the Tabarders'."

Mr Bligh looked interested. "Didn't he?" he said. "And why was that?"

"Why, you see, sir," Raught explained, "Mr Randolph was a very large contributor to the Company's charities—very munificent indeed, sir, I have heard; and he naturally liked the position it used to give him at their public occasions."

Mr Bligh nodded. "Of course," he said. "Anybody would. And so," he added quickly, "you knew all about it being the Tabarders' dinner-night, though you never saw what was written on the block, and Mr Randolph was never, I think you said, communicative- like about his engagements. Not only that; you knew all about how he felt on the subject of the Tabarders' dinner. You seem to know a lot more than you pretend, Raught."

The valet's tottering self-control gave way at this. He wrung his hand together, and it was with a sobbing voice that he broke out in a suddenly degenerated speech: "That's it! That's the way! Leading of a man on till you get 'im in a corner, and set 'im up against himself. I ain't told you nothing but what's gospel, and you come making me out a liar. Why shouldn't I know it was the Tabarders' dinner-night? I got ears, ain't I? Even if he didn't say nothing to me, I 'eard him talking about it to Mr Verney 'alf a dozen times, if you want to know; and as for 'im likin' to be made a fuss of, and to be told 'e was a-runnin' over with the milk of 'uman kindness—ain't we got a reg'lar staff of servants down at Brinton, and don't they talk over the guvnor and his little ways? Not 'alf!" Raught exclaimed with lachrymose fervour. "Crool, that's what it is, a-badgerin' a man what ain't done nothing but his dooty about this 'ere business—sendin' for the pleece as I did, and a-dealin' with 'em honest and truthful. A chap what's once gone wrong ain't ever give a chance." Here the valet's emotion overcame him, and he mopped his eyes in wordless misery.

"There, that's enough of that," Mr Bligh said heartlessly. "You've told me a lot more, my lad, than I'd have got out of you if I'd been soft with you. Now about this safe." He took up the key-case, and held out its contents in silence.

"This 'ere's the key of the street door downstairs," whimpered Raught. "I know that because I've got one that's the same. I don't know nothing about any of the others, I wish I may—"

"That'll do," the inspector snapped. He picked out without hesitation the key to fit the lock in the wall, and soon the interior of a small and shallow safe was exposed—completely empty. His eyes travelled to the small pile of wrappings still lying almost beneath the safe, and again his fingers caressed his hairless scalp.

5

TRENT IS TAKEN ABACK

Trent stood at the sitting-room window of his small house in St. John's Wood, gazing at the sky and meditating on the enviable life lived by such men as old Blinky Fisher, in such lovely and well-tended retreats as the Cathedral Close at Glasminster. It was the evening of the day after his leave-taking of Aunt Judith at Victoria. He had driven down to Glasminster with his friend Patmore that morning, had surveyed the spectacle of Julian Pickett—looking rather more unnerved than a big-game hunter should—being married to a young woman who did not seem at all formidable; had foregathered with a number of old friends at the house of Canon Fisher, and had returned as he had gone.

The effect on his spirit had been, as he had known it would be, to discontent him with any way of life but that of the "mild, monastic faces, in quiet collegiate cloisters." Being not particularly pious, far from learned, and delighting in the society of his fellow men, Trent never came in contact with the life of piety, erudition and seclusion without yearning to be a part of it. It was, as he put it to himself in a familiar phrase of godliness and scholarship, too damned silly for words.

"What a wonderful sunset, Mrs McOmish!" Trent said.

His housekeeper, who was laying the table for his solitary dinner, glanced briefly at the flaming sky. "I've seen waur," she said. She was a person whose words, thought usually of the driest, were as usually highly charged with unspoken significance. In this case, Mrs McOmish contrived to convey the strongly held opinion that nothing was to be gained by encouraging either this sunset, or sunsets as a class.

Trent shook his head. "Sophisticated!" he said sadly. "To you, Mrs McOmish, all nature is old, outmoded stuff, I suppose. The sublime, unapproachable self-sufficiency of art—that is your whole creed."

"No the whole," Mrs McOmish replied guardedly. "I dinna ken what a' that means aboot airt, and it may be pairt of the confession of the United Presbyterian Kirk, but there's a guid deal else forbye, I assure ye."

"I shouldn't wonder," Trent said absently. "But a truce to theology, Mrs McOmish. We were talking animatedly about the sunset, and you were just going to recall to me those moving lines in which Sir Walter Scott describes a similar phenomenon in the neighbourhood of the Trossachs. But what says another poet, Mrs McOmish; the one who uttered nothing base, though occasionally something silly? It is, he observed, a beauteous evening, calm and free—"

"Weel, we a' ken there's nae chairge for it," Mrs McOmish admitted.

"The holy time is quiet as a nun, breathless with adoration—"

"It's a peety," Mrs McOmish commented with some severity, "he couldna appreciate the weather without being popish aboot it. There's a gentleman turning in at the gate, Mr Trent. Is it a friend of yours? Is it like he'll be staying to dinner?"

Trent looked at the tall, quietly dressed young man who was approaching the house. "I know who it is," he said, "though he is a good deal changed in his looks. He doesn't give me the idea that dinner would agree with him just now—had some kind of a shock, I should think. Now,"—Trent went nearer to the window—"what on earth can it be that he's picking up from the path?"

Mrs McOmish, an elbow clasped in either hand, also came to overlook the proceedings of the visitor. "It might be a wee piece of coal," she opined, with more display of interest than she usually permitted herself. "We had the new coal in three days syne. It's terrible good luck to pick up a wee piece of coal—or what is better still, an auld rusty nail. Only the nail maun be crookit, ye ken. Oh ay, it's a nail; he's putting it in his inside pouch. Twenty years, and mair, I've keepit a rusty nail I found just by the Tammas Coats statue in Dunn Square—Oh preserve us! What a loup he gave, Mr Trent, seeing ye at the window!"

"His nerves must be in a shocking state," Trent said. "There's never been anything frightening about me, has there, Mrs Mc-Omish? The beasts that roam over the plain my form with indifference see; let alone the private secretaries of Congregationalist millionaires. Well, if he wants to see me, will you show him into the studio? It isn't so maddeningly tidy in there." And Trent walked to the door communicating with that scene of his labours.

"I wouldna wonder!" the housekeeper said grimly. "Ye've been in it a full half hoor since ye came back." She went out to admit the visitor.

"Mr Verney to see you, sir," Mrs McOmish soon announced in what she would have described as an English voice.

Mr Verney, whose age might have been guessed at twenty-seven or thereabouts, was a person of somewhat damaged aspect, for he looked harassed and distraught to the last degree. But there was nothing weak in the essence of his appearance. His frame was spare and athletic, his carriage erect, and in his fresh-coloured eagle-featured face there was a pair of restless bright-blue eyes that did not give an impression of spiritual sloth.

It was he who spoke the first words as his hand met Trent's in a rather perfunctory salutation.

"What do you think," he said earnestly, "of this terrible news?"

"What do you mean?" Trent said. "I haven't heard of any terrible news, believe me, my dear fellow. I only hope it's not too bad—for you."

Verney stared at him intensely. "How can you have missed it?" he demanded, with a puzzled look in his very expressive eyes. "It's been in all the early afternoon papers—it's all over the town. Or do you mean that old James Randolph's death doesn't distress you at all?"

Trent was thoroughly taken aback, and for the best of reasons. Himself, at a little after six o'clock the evening before, he had left the same James Randolph not only alive but in a furiously bad temper, a picture of choleric vitality. "Randolph-dead!" he said blankly. "Why, did he have a stroke or something?"

"A bullet was what killed him, Trent," Verney said coldly. "I can't conceive—"

"Oh! he was shot!" A light broke over Trent's mind. "Now I understand. You see, Verney, I drove down to Glasminster to a wedding this morning, and I've only just got back after all the merrymaking. If anyone had heard of it down there, it wasn't mentioned in my hearing. But the early editions! They all had it, of course—I see that now. But you know how they like to keep you guessing. On the way back, I should think I saw a score of bills saying that a well-known millionaire had been found shot. I didn't care if fifty millionaires, each more well-known than the last, had been found shot. It never occurred to me that it was Randolph. My dear fellow, what a shocking thing! It must have been a bad blow for you, being what you were to him. Tell me what happened."

"That's just what I can't tell you," Verney said in a dull tone. He sat with hands clasped between his knees, and stared at the floor. "All I know is he was shot by someone last night in his bedroom at Newbury Place, when nobody else was there—it's the evening his manservant always had free every week. The man found his master lying dead when he came home, and at once sent for the police. You cannot imagine the shock the news was to me—I didn't even know Randolph was in London. The first I heard of it was when a C.I.D. man called on me early this morning, to see if I knew anything that could give them a line. All I could say was that the old man hadn't an enemy in the world, as far as I knew. And I said the last I had seen of Randolph had been last week, when I was staying at Brinton Lodge, having various matters to talk over with him; and that then he had seemed quite at ease and free from any anxiety. Since I heard the news I've been living in a sort of bad dream. I had a very real feeling for the old man; more like veneration than anything else. And this means more of a chaotic smash-up than you can very well imagine. At last I took to walking aimlessly about the streets, just to take the edge off my nerves; and when I found myself near your place, I thought I would look in for a talk. I suppose you had not seen Randolph lately?"

Trent looked at his visitor consideringly. What he had just been told by Verney made one thing clear: he, Trent, must have been one of the last persons to see Randolph before his being murdered. And he had strong reasons for wishing that interview of his with the old man to remain a private affair. It had concerned the reputation of a woman for whom he had a deep regard; and it had been of a decidedly unpleasant, not to say scandalous, nature. The less said about it the better, in Trent's judgment; above all, to those with whom Randolph had left an honourable memory. As for the police, of course they must be told; for one thing, the information would set a limit in one direction on the time during which the murder had been committed. But Trent saw no reason for taking Verney into his confidence.

"It is some time since I saw him," Trent therefore replied, with more truth than candour. "It's no use offering you a drink, is it?" he asked; and Verney shook his head. "Very often a cigarette helps you to pull yourself together," Trent went on. "You look all to pieces. Try one of these."

Verney looked up gratefully. "Thanks, I will," he said, extending a shaking hand towards the box held out to him, "I know all about tobacco and what it can do to you, though it's long enough since I smoked any." He lit a Virginia cigarette and inhaled deeply. "You see, the first year at Oxford I used to smoke a lot too much, as so many freshers do. Then, when I began to have dreams of a Blue, I dropped it altogether.'

"And you got your reward, I dare say."

Verney smiled, in momentary forgetfulness of the day's bad news. "Do you take an interest in that sort of thing? Yes: three-mile; also cross-country running, since we are on the subject."

"No, I know nothing about it," Trent said; "but as soon as you spoke of dreaming of a Blue, I could see that your dream had probably come true. You look like a Blue. When Nokes outdares Stokes in azure feats, you know, it often marks him for life."

Verney's dejection again took possession of him. "Well, it came in useful when I began working for Randolph," he said. "The boys' club part of the job was what always appealed to me most. You know about the Randolph Institute, I dare say. Nothing sectarian; just educational and social and athletic. I love it—in fact, I spend most of my time there, because there's a room I use as a sort of general office for all Randolph's charitable affairs. And of course, having a bit of a record in athletics gave me more influence with the lads than almost anything else could have done. Then my being a non-smoker was a good thing too, you see. You can hardly imagine the state that many of these young fellows get their respiratory tracts into with eternally smoking cheap fags. And as for running, there's simply nothing like it for our sort of lads, so long as they're sound physically—hard exercise in the open air, easy to fit in after the day's work, and costs next to nothing."

"It's good for you," Trent said. "You get all the exercise you need, I expect."

"All I need—yes. But to tell you the truth," Verney said, rather in the manner of one confessing to a secret vice, "since I began playing golf about five years ago, I prefer a round of that to any other open-air sport I know—and I have had a pretty good experience. Whenever I can manage it, I go off for a game to Matcham. It's not a good course, and you often can't get a caddy, but then I never want one; and it is the cheapest golf I know this side of London, which is what I have to consider. How I wish—but it is no use talking about that. As far as keeping fit goes, I have every opportunity, as you say. There's nothing like running, above all, for that."

"There's a good deal, no doubt," Trent said, "in having that sort of thing managed by someone who knows all about it."

"Yes," Verney said simply, "there is, of course. The boys have their committee; but they leave the whole show to me really, and I'm rather proud of the way our fellows have come forward since I took over. Last January the Randolph Athletic Club was runner- up in the Middlesex cross-country team championship, and challenged Southgate Harriers pretty closely. We provided the first two men home in that event, and we won the junior race easily. And now, I suppose"—he tossed the end of his cigarette into the fire—"the Kilburn Institute's all over and done with."

Trent felt a moment of keen sympathy, for Verney's whole manner was that of a heartbroken man.

"Do you mean that his death really means the end of all that work?" he asked. "Wasn't there any endowment? Or surely there would be some provision in his will for the keeping-up of the various organizations he had started—what was that phrase he was so fond of using?—for the benefit of the community. I should think, from what I've heard, that the shutting-up of that Institute would pretty well amount to a social disaster for that part of London. It ought not to be possible."

"Well, it is," Verney said, as he accepted another cigarette. "You see, Trent, old Randolph had a rather strange side to his character as a public benefactor. He made a great fortune fairly early in life, and he devoted almost the whole of his income to charities and public objects. He continued to heap up more money; but I think it was because he could hardly help it. The real hobby of his life was to attend personally to all his enormous expenditure on charities and public objects. Sometimes he would give a great sum for some special purpose; but when he did that, it was always in the way of capital expenditure. He would build and equip a sanatorium, say, for some town or some big charitable institution; but he would never settle anything on it. He might, and usually did, put his name down year by year for a contribution to its upkeep; but he used to say he started a place like that as an opportunity for charity on the part of other people."

Trent nodded. "That's not unusual, I know," he said. "But how about places like the Institute? I always understood that was entirely his own private show, maintained by him exclusively. He surely can't have left it high and dry, so to speak."

"That is just what I was coming to," Verney said. "The position of the Institute was just as you say—he held it in his own hands entirely, financing it as if it were a part of his own household. And he had other establishments on just the same footing, like the Randolph Infant Orphanage at Bishopsbridge, or the Randolph Mental Hospital at Claypoole. He was very proud of them, too, and saw to their being the best run places of their kind in the country. They cost him something, Trent; I'm telling you, and I know. But they never had a penny of funds of their own; and whatever Randolph parted with in any sort of way, he always would know what happened to it. He couldn't seem to bear the idea of anyone else controlling wealth that he had amassed—that was at the bottom of it. And I don't see that you could find fault with that, seeing that he did devote all those vast sums to other people, and put himself to a vast amount of trouble in looking after the spending of the money. But the unfortunate consequence is that now—" he raised a hand, palm-downwards, and brought it down sharply on the arm of his chair.

Trent stared at him. "You don't mean to say he's made no bequests to these places that he created, and lavished money on, and that made up a large part of his reputation?"

Verney arose and crossed his arms. "I mean this," he said harshly. "Randolph made no bequests at all. He left no will."

6

AN ARREST HAS BEEN MADE

There was a momentary silence as Trent took in this amazing statement and its implications.

"The man who murdered Randolph," Verney said, "has probably killed half a dozen invaluable charities and other good works stone dead with that same bullet. Besides that, he has dried up completely a great stream of benevolence that spread itself out in all directions. For I am convinced that there is no will; and if there is no will, what is to happen to the Randolph fortune, and to the causes that it supported, heaven alone knows. Somebody will inherit, I suppose; but there will be delay, and who can answer for what he will do with the money? He may prefer horse-racing, or yachting, or play-producing, or any other way of getting rid of money by the cartload. One thing is practically certain; he won't live on a few thousands a year, and devote the rest to well-directed benevolence.

"Another thing," Verney went on, holding up an expository finger. "There may be rival claimants, and a dispute dragging on indefinitely; for as far as I know Randolph had no near relations. You may have heard that he had a son, an only son, who disappeared from home when he was about sixteen, and has never been heard of since. The old man did everything possible to find out what had happened to him, but no trace of him was ever found and he was given up for dead long ago. But there may be other relatives. You see what a disaster the whole thing is likely to be, apart from the personal loss of such a man, and such an influence for good.

"There is one detail," Verney went on after a moment's pause, "of interest to you. Randolph was very anxious that you should paint a replica of the Tabarders' portrait of him, to be hung in the hall of the Institute. Did you hear about that?"

"I had a note from him about it," Trent said, "but nothing was settled."

"Well, it never will be now," Verney said; and then broke out desperately: "I tell you, Trent, the shock and the horror of this business, and the prospect of so much wreckage, have driven me pretty nearly insane." And Verney sunk his head between his hands, his fingers clutching his hair.

Trent, while his lips took a dubious twist, put a hand on the young man's shoulder. "Better not meet trouble half-way," he said. "After all, the whole thing depends on your belief that Randolph had made no will. What grounds are there for thinking that he could have been guilty of such an amazing piece of imprudence as that? It's really hardly credible."

Verney, without looking up, shrugged his shoulders. "The grounds for thinking so are good enough, unfortunately. The fact is that, at the time of his death, he was really thinking, for the first time, about putting his affairs in order. His lawyers had been dropping hints for a long time that it was high time he made a will. I told him so myself, too, more than once—it was my obvious duty to do so, I thought, though a very unpleasant one. Whenever I did, he made it quite clear that there was no will as yet. He used to say there was time enough, that he was good for many years yet. But he hated the subject being mentioned—didn't like the idea of dying, I suppose, like many other people; though if any living being had a right to feel confident about his prospects in the next world, Randolph had.

And then at last he did begin to consider the thing seriously. Several times he said things that showed me he was thinking about the disposal of his estate. And then, before he had got to the point of doing anything definite, he was struck down."

Trent thought for a few moments before saying: "Still, he may have made a will earlier in life—when he was married, for instance. Men usually do, I believe."

Verney made a gesture of impatience. "He may—yes; when he was a comparatively poor man with no great philanthropic interests to think about. But if he did, I think he would have mentioned it; and anyhow, it's not to be supposed that the terms of any such will would prevent everything getting into the sort of hopeless mess that I'm thinking about. Then, apart from his own foundations, there are all the causes that had expectations as regards Randolph's estate—had a right to have them, I mean, seeing that for years he had been a regular and generous supporter of them."

"What sort of things do you mean?" Trent asked. "Never having been a philanthropic millionaire, it would interest me to know how it all works—if you won't think I'm being irreverent to say so."

Verney looked into vacancy, as one assembling his ideas. "Why," he said, "to put it the simplest way, there must have been dozens of secretaries and chairmen of committees trying, at odd times, to sound me discreetly about what Randolph's testamentary dispositions were. There's the Humberstone General Infirmary; and the Humberstone Endowed Schools Foundation; and the Moss Lane Congregational Church of the same place; and the London Missionary Society; and the British and Foreign Bible Society; and the Yorkshire Congregational Union; and the Congregational Pastors Retiring Fund; and Leeds University; and the Scalbridge United Independent College; and the National Lifeboat Institution; and the Harrowby Seamen's Institute; and the Dewsby Deaf and Dumb

Institute; and—oh! I could name another dozen or more that have a direct interest in what happens to Randolph's estate."

"Thanks! Thanks!" Trent said smiling. "You needn't go on, Verney, I see how it is. I'd no idea your field of work was such an extensive one. It's no business of mine, of course, but I'm afraid this is going to be a serious thing for you personally."

Again Verney shrugged. "It will send me hunting another job, after over two years of such a job as I shall never get again. But I'm not worrying about that just now. I want," he said savagely, "to see the man who killed Randolph taken and hanged—the cowardly brute who shot a defenceless old man in the back, and cut short a life that was given up to works of mercy and humanity. I suppose they'll run the fellow down, Trent—you understand these things. It's not likely he'll escape, do you suppose?"

"No, not likely," Trent said. "It does happen of course, now and then. But you have to give the police a reasonable allowance of time when a murder has been undiscovered for a good many hours, as I gather from what you tell me."

Verney nodded. "Yes, naturally. I suppose it must depend on the traces left behind by the murderer—the weapon, footprints, fingerprints, the kind of thing one reads about."

"If he was careful," Trent pointed out, "he need not have left any traces at all. Criminals often don't; but they may easily get found out all the same. Do you remember exactly what it was that was given out to the papers this morning?"

"I've got one here." Verney produced a folded copy of the Sun from his coat pocket. "There you are—it's little enough."

Below an array of headlines, and a portrait of a clean-shaven, hard-looking old man, Trent read as follows:—

At an early hour this morning the police were called to No. 5, Newbury Place, Mayfair, the London residence of Mr James Randolph, the millionaire whose long record of charitable activities and public beneficence has made his name honoured throughout the country.

He had been shot through the heart, the body lying on the floor of the bedroom, where he had, it is presumed, been dressing before attending the banquet of the Tabarders' Company.

His absence from the banquet caused surprise, as he was a member of the Court of the Company, and was to have spoken to the toast of the guest of honour on this occasion, the Home Secretary. On inquiry at Tabarders' Hall this morning, we learn that several attempts were made during the evening to call Mr Randolph's house by telephone, but that the calls were unanswered.

Mr Randolph's valet, the only servant sleeping on the premises, was, in fact, out for the evening; and it was by him that the body was discovered on his returning to the house, when he immediately telephoned the police.

No. 5 Newbury Place is one of a row of mews converted into five small residences, all tenanted by persons of social position. Such a house was well adapted to the simple way of life preferred by the late Mr Randolph, for he spent but little time in London, and lived as a rule at Brinton Lodge, his country house in the neighbourhood of Humberstone, Yorks.

"So that's all," Trent remarked. "Most of that was written up in the Sun office, after they'd made their own inquiries. There's hardly anything at all about the crime itself, is there?"

"Hardly anything," Verney agreed. "But I suppose it's all that was given out. The other evening papers have just the same; not a syllable more. I've looked carefully."

Trent considered the other's haggard face for a moment in silence. "Well, the officer who saw you this morning," he suggested, "didn't he tell you anything more? By the way, it's the kind of case they would put Bligh onto, I should think, if his hands aren't too full already. Was your visitor a tall, powerful-looking sort of bloke with a head like a billiard-ball?"

"That was his name," Verney said with a faint smile, "and your description fits him nicely. No, he hadn't a word more to tell me than there is in that paper. It was I who was expected to do the telling—whether I knew of anyone who could conceivably have had any ill-will against Randolph, or whether he had seemed at all upset or unusual in his manner lately, or whether I knew what he kept in the safe in the bedroom; and so on. And to all of that my answer was no, and no, and no. The inspector also wanted to know how I had been spending my own time that evening."

Trent laughed. "Of course," he said. "That's the routine."

"So he was good enough to assure me," Verney said, with an answering gleam of grim amusement. "Fortunately I was able to satisfy him that my time had been fully occupied, in the presence of other people. It was the Institute Athletic Club's weekly grind that evening, you see. I never miss running with the boys, and after changing, I stayed on with them in Kilburn, till half past ten, as I usually do. And now I must be off. It's been a relief to talk the thing over."

Trent rang the bell. "You might wait and see the latest edition," he said. "It's usually delivered here before this time."

Mrs McOmish appeared at the door, a copy of the *Sun* in her outstretched hand. "If it's the paper you want—" she said.

But her speech was cut short by an exclamation from Trent, who had already caught sight of the line of capitals strung along the top of the first page. He seized the paper from her and read aloud to Verney the brief paragraph which had been added, in heavy type, to the matter which he had already seen dealing with the Newbury Place murder.

"It is understood," he read, "that an arrest has already been made in connection with this abominable crime."

7

ON A PLATE WITH PARSLEY ROUND IT

Verney had taken his leave, and Trent had noted that he was properly impressed—not to say astounded—by the fact, if fact it were, of the swift success of the official hunt for Randolph's murderer. Trent had busied himself at once in procuring copies of all the latest editions and comparing their statements; then, after a meditative dinner, he had rung up a certain number in Bloomsbury, and proposed himself for a private and friendly call upon Chief Inspector Bligh, whom he was lucky enough to find at the other end of the wire.

The number of Trent's friends among the metropolitan police, in its various grades, was small, but his relation with them was entirely one of mutual liking; and there was none with whom he was on easier terms than Mr Bligh, an officer of unusual parts, whose range of interests went considerably beyond his notable equipment of expert professional knowledge. In particular, he had made a hobby, and owned a considerable library, of the history of the Civil War in the United States.

It was nine o'clock when Trent found the inspector deeply engaged with book and pipe in his comfortable bachelor quarters.

"Sorry to spoil your evening," Trent said as he placed his hat on a chair.

"You won't," Mr Bligh assured him. "If I'd thought you were likely to, I'd have told them downstairs to set the dog on you, instead of bringing up the drinks for you. Help yourself." And he waved a vast hand towards the tray with its convivial contents on the plush-covered table.

Trent took the armchair facing his host's, and began the filling of a pipe. "Oh blessings on his kindly face and on his absent hair!" he said. "I've interrupted your reading, anyhow. What is the book, I wonder? But need I ask? It is the Life, Campaigns, Letters, Opinions and Table-talk of General Joseph Eggleston Johnston, the Victor of Pumpkin Creek."

"There's no such book," Mr Bligh retorted positively; "and," he added after a moment's thought, "there wasn't any such battle. What I was reading was Bernard Shaw—my favourite author."

"Another bond between us!" Trent exclaimed. "And what draws you so especially to Shaw?"

The inspector patted affectionately the volume lying on his knee. "Shaw," he declared, "is the literature of escape. That isn't," he added, in answer to Trent's bewildered gaze, "my own expression."

"You relieve my feelings," Trent gasped, "more than I can say."

"No," the inspector said reminiscently. "That was the phrase used about Shaw by the man who first brought him to my notice. I had to interrogate a prisoner some years ago about a certain matter. A confirmed criminal, he was. They used to call him Pantomime Joe, on account of the cheek he used to give everybody from the dock. Why, if I've heard a judge say once that his court wasn't a music hall, when Joe was on his trial, I've heard it half a dozen times. Joe was an educated man, and it was no surprise to me, when I visited him in his cell, to find him reading a book from the prison library. He showed it to me—*Plays Pleasant*, by G. B. Shaw. 'What's this?' I said. He grinned at me. 'This is the literature of escape, Blighter,' he says, using a silly nickname he and his sort have always had for me. I thought that sounded a funny sort of reading to be put in the hands of a man who spent half his time in gaol, but he explained his meaning."

"And what can that have been?" Trent wondered.

"Why," the inspector said, "Joe meant, and I agree with him, that Shaw takes you right out of the beastly realities of life. I can tell you, after a hard day at our job, with all the spite, and greed, and cruelty, and filthy-mindedness that we get our noses rubbed in, it's like coming out into the fresh country air to sit down to one of Shaw's plays. Nobody half-witted, nobody brutal, nobody to make you sick. And if he ever does try to give you anybody who is a rotten bad lot, he doesn't come within miles of the real thing. And there's never a dull moment. Every dam' character has something to say; even the stupidest ones. Everybody scores off everybody else. Who ever had the luck to listen to anything like it in real life? I tell you, it's a different world."

Trent nodded his appreciation of this. "But," he said, after a brief silence, "it was the world we live in that I wanted to consult you about."

"The Randolph murder," Mr Bligh said. "I know; you said so on the phone. And you have been painting his portrait, staying at Brinton to do it. And last week the man who runs the Randolph Institute said it would be a good idea to have a replica of it to hang up there. And Randolph was persuaded to agree, and wrote asking you to call at Newbury Place yesterday evening at six, which you did. And then he talked to you about doing the replica. And then you left, about six fifteen—so that you were one of the last persons to see the old man alive. Well! You've got something to tell me that I don't know, I hope."

Trent gazed at him as if in awe. "I don't think," he said humbly, "there can be anything you don't know. You have forgotten for the moment, perhaps, that he and I had a little disagreement, and I declined to do the job. Apart from that, I have nothing to add to your summary of the proceedings. How do you do it, Inspector? I may have an open countenance, but I hardly think you can have read all that in my face. Were you up the chimney listening to us, or what?"

Mr Bligh smiled grimly. "Information received—that's what we usually call it," he said. "As for listening, Simon Raught, Randolph's man, does all of that that's required when he's on the premises. Most of what I've mentioned he happened to hear, quite accidentally, last week at Brinton; and as for your visit, of course, he told me all about that."

"Of course," Trent agreed. "Be told, sweet Bligh, and let who will be clever; hear useful things, not deduce them, all day long. All the same, you will not persuade me that all that perfectly good information fell into your lap, as it were, when you were not noticing. I have seen Simon Raught only a few times—in fact, he never got as far as telling me his Christian name, as he evidently did with you—but he did not strike me as one who, when in trouble, would insist that all his secrets should be sung even into thine own soft-conchéd ear. I won't inquire how you got all that out of him—there are various ways and means, I know. The thing I really wanted to ask you when I came here appears not to be in any doubt. The case is in your hands, as I hoped it might be."

"Good guess," the inspector remarked sardonically.

"And you ask if I have anything to tell you—about Randolph as he was at our interview, I suppose you mean? No, I haven't. He said nothing about anyone coming to see him after I had gone. He didn't say anything about expecting to be shot, and he didn't look as if he was. He seemed just as usual, in excellent health, and perfectly satisfied with himself."

"Hm! That doesn't help much," Mr Bligh said. "Well, why did you want to see me about the case, then? We all understood you had gone out of the amateur sleuthing business long ago."

"Just because I happened to know Randolph, and to know some things about him that interested me—things I had heard before I made his acquaintance through painting his portrait, and things I have learnt since. And only this afternoon I was told a good deal by his secretary, Verney, whom I had met at Randolph's house last January. He had already been giving you information, I gathered, earlier in the day."

The inspector nodded. "But not a lot that I didn't know. There was that about his having left no will, of course, which seems to be the case. But bless you! That's not an unheard-of thing, even with the general run of wealthy people; and old James Randolph was not exactly an ordinary character."

"That's just it. I know how very far from ordinary he was, and that's why I'm interested. Besides, one of the reasons why I went out of business, as you call it, was that my wife has a morbid distaste for crime; but just now she is in the Cotswolds. I am alone and free, like the man in Chesterton; shameless, anarchic, infinite."

"I don't know about anarchic and infinite," Mr Bligh said pointedly. "Well," he added, assuming an expression *of* regretful sympathy, "I'm more sorry than I can say, but there's no need to let the thing trouble your ingenious brain any further, my lad. We've got the man."

"The papers have been told so—I saw that. And that is why I came to you; to hear more."

"The papers have been told nothing of the sort," Mr Bligh said testily. "They've found out for themselves that an arrest has been made, and they may possibly have found out that the man arrested was connected with one of Randolph's concerns, and had just been sacked. But they've said nothing about its being the man who shot Randolph, because of course they daren't;

and in fact he hasn't been charged with that. All the same, he's the man."

"He is, is he?" Trent looked into the other's rugged face. "Swift work, with a vengeance. You're certain about having got the man? Is the case really, so to speak, in the bag already?"

Mr Bligh's smile was grim. "In closest confidence, as usual, I don't mind telling you that I have clear evidence of the man's having been in Randolph's house in the evening, when Randolph was there alone. I have also—"

"Yes," Trent murmured. "An 'also' would seem to be in order."

"Also," the inspector went on, after blowing a couple of elaborate smoke-rings, "I have the man's written and signed confession that he murdered Randolph."

Trent fell back in his chair, while Mr Bligh resumed his pipe and gazed dreamily at a corner of the ceiling.

"That seems to have made you think a bit," he remarked after a moment, cannily observant of a slight frown on his guest's usually untroubled countenance. "I shouldn't wonder if you had been working up some valuable theory of your own about the case. If you have, let's hear it. A good laugh's the best tonic in the world. Come on! Am I right?"

"Very often, I dare say," Trent said, with a swift return to his accustomed manner. "Not now. I never had the slightest notion of a theory about the case. I only heard of it three hours ago. But I do take an interest in it as I told you, and I thought, with my well-known helpfulness, that you might like to have a talk about it, and even let me have a look at the scene of the crime; but now, perhaps, everything being as you tell me, you'd rather not."

Mr Bligh rubbed his chin. "I don't know about that," he said slowly. Then, after a few moments' consideration, he added: "It's like this. The evidence is all there. I've told you, roughly, what it is. But there are some queer things about the case all the same, and we might as well have a yarn about it."

"Just what I should like. You know it's safe to talk to me."

"If it wasn't, my lad, you wouldn't be here." A chuckle agitated the crumpled expanse of Mr Bligh's waistcoat. "Well, you've seen what little there is in the papers, of course."

"Certainly; and it's very little indeed. Can you tell me one thing, for instance, that they don't mention—just how Randolph was shot?"

"He was shot through the heart from behind, probably from the direction of the door of the bedroom, when he was just taking his coat off. It looks as if it was done by someone who had come to see him by appointment, and whom he had let in himself, the valet being out for the evening. The bullet was fired from a Webley .455, probably fitted with a silencer."

"Ah!" Trent received this information with a thoughtful brow. "So that's how it was. And you're telling me that nobody knows this as yet but the police—and the surgeon, of course."

"Well, the man who murdered him knows it, I suppose," the inspector observed.

"Yes, I'm capable of supposing that myself," Trent rejoined. "And now that we have arrived at that point, who did murder him?"

"We haven't arrived at that point." Mr Bligh, it was clear, was taking an innocent pleasure in saving up the climax of his tale. "Let's take things in their order. First, there were the obvious possibilities to be thought of."

"The servants, you mean."

"You've read in the paper that there was only one, a manservant, sleeping in the place. He was out for the evening, and found the body when he came home; then informed the police by phone immediately. So he said."

Trent nodded. "Raught—yes, I know him. And you put him through it, of course."

"I thought," the inspector said dubiously, "I had wrung him pretty dry; but one couldn't be certain. Still, he'd got a reasonable enough story about having left the place just after you left it, to spend his evening off with some relations; and he hadn't any motive that lay on the surface. He declared that when he found the body, he was in too much of a dither even to make out how Randolph had been killed. It might be true; but naturally I didn't set him aside. The only other servant is a charlady, Mrs Barley, who kept the place in order when Randolph wasn't staying there. I saw her too this morning—a simple soul, she is. I thought to myself, I miss my guess if she knows anything whatever about the crime—or about anything else worth mentioning. Then, as you know, I saw Verney, the secretary, who was always about the place when Randolph was in London; and he gave me a satisfactory account of his movements on the evening of the murder."

"Movements," Trent murmured. "An admirable word. Bend against Primrose Hill thy breast, dash down like torrent from its crest, with short and springing footstep pass the Marble Arch and Hamilton Place. Not a very good rhyme, that."

"The account he gave was rather more detailed," Mr Bligh said coldly. "After the run, which you appear to know about, he stayed at the Randolph Institute till ten thirty, and was in his rooms off Maida-vale five minutes later. All that's been checked. As for motive, all he seems to have got by the crime is the loss of a good job."

"Like Raught—yes," Trent said. "And now, if I may ask a question—you know what weapon was used. You've got it, I suppose."

"Why should you suppose anything of the kind?" the inspector retorted. "It's not usual for murderers to leave the weapon lying about, is it?"

"It's not usual for them to confess," Trent pointed out; and Mr Bligh grunted morosely. "I only thought," Trent went on, "he might have led gently up to the confession, as it were, by not taking away the revolver."

"Well, we haven't got it, that's all," Mr Bligh snapped. "But we know what make it was, and what calibre, by looking at the bullet and the breech-markings on it—nothing easier, as it happens, with that type. As for where it is, all I can say is that it's more likely than not to be lying somewhere on the floor of the Channel; but that's nothing better than a guess."

"What I want to know," Trent persisted, "is why this Webley should be visiting the bottom of the monstrous world, since the murderer has confessed."

The inspector rubbed his chin once more. "Well, of course, so do I. But come! We're getting in advance of the story. If you do want to know what really happened, you must let me tell it my own way."

He proceeded to give Trent a brief account of his investigation on the scene of the crime. He told of the empty safe; of the signs of documents having been stolen; of the fingerprints on the carafe and tumbler, and on the razor-blade found on the carpet; of the champagne cork; of the leaf missing from the engagement-block in the sitting-room.

Trent, who had listened in closely attentive silence, interposed at this point.

"An engagement-block!" he said. "And was that in a position where it could easily be seen?"

"Anybody could see it. The cabinet it stood on was on top of the writing-table, just in front of the window. What about it?"

"Only that I feel certain that it wasn't there when I saw the old man in that room at six o'clock. I noticed that dwarf cabinet, too—it is a beautiful little thing."

"Hm! Yes." Mr Bligh again fingered his chin. "That does happen to be one of the funny points. Because Raught, the manservant, says positively that it never was left lying about, that Randolph was always most careful to keep it locked away. Still, of course, he may have had it out to refer to, some time before he was shot."

"So he may. And then, of course, the man who came to see him, and whose name was on the block as having an appointment with him, very cunningly tore off that leaf and took it away; thus destroying a piece of direct evidence that he had been there that evening."

"Yes."

"After which he rushed off and bunged in a confession of having been there, and having shot Randolph. Changeable sort of bloke!" The inspector sighed wearily. "I know, I know. And Randolph may have torn off the leaf himself, for some reason. But look here! There's one more thing I haven't mentioned yet. When I saw it, it looked to me like a fatal blunder; and so it would have been, if the damfool hadn't gone and—but never mind that just now, I am telling you things as they happened." He went on to describe the last of the morning's finds, the luggage-label picked up in the hallway; and when he repeated the name written on the label, Trent made a movement of uncontrollable surprise.

"Bryan Fairman!" he exclaimed.

"That's what I said. He's the man who did it," Mr Bligh added.

"Do you mean to say he is the man whom you know to have been at Randolph's place when he was shot, and who has confessed to the murder? Why, I know him!"

"Is there anybody in this blasted case that you don't know?" I the inspector asked plaintively. "Anyhow, if you know Bryan Fairman, you know a damned nuisance—him and his confession!"

"I suppose you might call a murderer that," Trent admitted. "But really, Inspector, this is incredible. Fairman is one of my oldest friends. Do you remember when we were talking about Eunice Faviell some time ago, and the way so many men go crazy about her? I mentioned to you that a great friend of mine was one of those victims. I was speaking of this same Fairman.

I have known him half my life, and of all the men that I should call sound citizens, he is about the most blameless. Why, I saw him only last night—" and here Trent broke off, realizing suddenly the possible significance of that meeting.

The inspector's eyelids narrowed. "Yes?" he said gently.

"He was catching the 8:20 at Victoria," Trent said slowly. "He very nearly missed it. And that's the boat-train for Dieppe—I was seeing somebody off by it. But good Lord! Bryan Fairman! You know, it's quite impossible to believe—"

"Wait till you hear all there is to believe," Mr Bligh advised him. "There's plenty. To begin with, 'Passenger to Dieppe' was written on the label, as I was just going to tell you. Well, all that did for me was to give me someone to go after; which of course I did. If he was going to Dieppe by the night-boat, as seemed most likely, it was a thousand to one he was on his way to somewhere much further off, and had had a good many hours' start on his journey, whatever it was—because the boat gets there in the small hours. But on the off-chance of Dieppe being his real destination, I had him looked for there; and sure enough I soon got news of him—and a lot of it. The first information was that Dr Bryan Fairman, complete with passport, had come by the boat and taken a room at the Hotel Beau-Rivage. He left there about nine thirty this morning, after taking nothing but a cup of coffee. Then it came through that an Englishman carrying a kit-bag had been seen hanging about in a place called the Impasse de la *Chimère*, in the outskirts of the town, looking as if he had lost something. What on earth he can have wanted there the French police haven't the least idea; they say they have made every possible inquiry—and they are pretty good at that, as you know—and they cannot imagine what he was after in that spot."

"That is remarkable, too," Trent said thoughtfully. "If the French police could not get any information they were looking for from local householders or concierges, it should mean that there wasn't anything for them to get. And as for my friend Fairman being seen wandering about in the environs of Dieppe, it simply doesn't make sense to me. He studied for a year at the *Salpêtrière* in Paris, and as far as I know that is all the experience of France that he has. What else did you hear about him?"

"In the same place," the inspector proceeded, "there is an inn, and Fairman had some more coffee there before he went away. The man who keeps the place says that the Englishman looked sick, and a bit dotty."

"Did he really say that?" Trent inquired with keen interest.

"His words were, as reported to us," replied the inspector, who numbered a practical, working knowledge of French among his professional merits, "that the man seemed to be '*souffrant*' and '*un peu toqué*' and, if you can make that mean anything but what I said, you're welcome. Well, as I was about to tell you when interrupted, the next thing seen of Fairman, he was booking a return passage by the afternoon boat back to Newhaven. One of our men on duty at the port recognized him by the description which we had phoned across; also by the initials on his kit-bag. So our chap took a passage too, to keep him under observation. And then, dammit! What do you suppose the crazy fool did? The boat hadn't much more than cleared the harbour when he walked to the rail, climbed over it, and was in the act of jumping overboard when Sergeant Hewett grabbed him by the jacket and pants, and hung onto him until the crew came and dragged him inboard again. Quite a scrap they had of it, Hewett says—he's got a lovely black eye, and a mouth like a pound of liver with a slit in it. Then Hewett took him in charge for attempting suicide; and that's what we're holding him for at the present moment."

Trent looked his amazement. "Fairman tried to drown himself!' And then you say—"

"Wait a bit," the inspector said. "You must let me tell it my own way. Shortly after Fairman had been brought home and charged, a letter was received at the Yard which he had posted at Newhaven just before the boat left for Dieppe. It contained nothing but a confession of his having shot Randolph—short, but definite enough. I've got a copy of it here."

Mr Bligh got to his feet, and opened a dispatch-case that lay on a side-table. He took from it a typewritten document.

"Before you look at this I may tell you the result of our inquiries at Claypoole, which had already been received in London. Fairman bore an excellent character, though he was rather reserved; didn't get on with people very easily I gather. He was said to be entirely devoted to his work at the mental hospital. He was carrying on some sort of research there in addition to his ordinary duties, and had been showing signs of overwork. Then a month ago he got influenza pretty badly; and he seems to have returned to his job when he was still rather the worse for wear.

"The next thing was that he was suddenly sacked from the hospital staff, with six months' salary in lieu of notice. He got a letter to that effect yesterday morning, which he showed to one of his colleagues. The letter gave no reason; and the writer of it, the medical superintendent, Dr Dallow, tells our people plainly that he is not obliged to explain his action, and will not do so, the hospital being a purely privately managed institution. That, of course, was this morning, when he had no idea of why the police were showing this sudden interest in Fairman—when we knew nothing ourselves, for the matter of that, except that Fairman's label had been found on the scene of the crime.

"We are informed that Fairman, after getting his notice, had an interview with Dallow, which didn't last long, and that he came away from it looking haggard and desperate. He left the hospital about three o'clock, carrying his kit-bag, not having said a word to anyone. He was seen by a porter at the station, who knew him, to take the 3:10 up-train, which is due to arrive at St. Pancras at 7:30. I may say here that among the things found upon him, after his arrest, was a crumpled sheet of paper with Randolph's London address on it. Now then, how does all that look to you?"

"Bad," Trent said, looking at the floor. "I don't see how it could look very much worse."

"Not any worse at all," Mr Bligh rejoined, "when you know that Randolph had absolute control of the entire management of the hospital."

"Well, I did happen to know that, and that's why I agree about the badness. Dallow, of course, may talk about refusing to give his reasons; but he would have to sing a different tune if he was subpoenaed as a witness."

Mr Bligh rubbed his hands. "You're right there. There's another thing, too, that he would be asked to explain—what was the subject of the interview he had with Randolph at Brinton at 5 p.m. three days before the murder? I got that by looking back through the engagement-block. Well, we're agreed, I take it, that Randolph was responsible for the sacking. As a matter of fact, he had a bit of a down on Fairman for some reason or other—Raught, the valet, gave me that point. Well, now, to get on—all this I've been telling you is the result of inquiries made at the Claypoole end this morning. It was dictated to the Yard over the phone, and most of it was in my hands by lunch-time. As for what followed his arrival in London, we've only his own account—a bit sketchy, but definite enough as far as it goes. Here you are."

Trent took the typescript that the inspector now held out to him. "Pretty smart work," he observed glumly. "Activity on all fronts, London, Claypoole and Dieppe—with a naval engagement, so to speak, thrown in. You start on the job after an early breakfast, and it's all done up in a parcel just when it's getting to be time for a nice hot cup of tea."

Mr Bligh emitted a depreciative grunt. "I don't say the machine didn't run smoothly. It did—and a bit too slick for my taste, though you may think it a funny thing for me to say, perhaps. I don't care about it so much when things all come my way on the run, as if I was a bally magnet or something. Dammit! It's like having the case handed to me on a plate with parsley round it; and the more I've thought of it the less I like it."

Trent nodded. "I think I know what you mean. You feel that Destiny may have got a section of lead pipe concealed behind its back, ready to land you one unexpectedly on the cervical region."

"Something like that," the inspector grumbled. "It's the sort of thing that's happened before. And yet—but you run your eye over that paper, and let's hear what you think of it."

Trent turned his attention to the neatly-typed sheet in his hand, and read what follows:

In the train. London—Newhaven.
9:20 p.m.

This evening I shot and killed James Randolph. I went to his house in Newbury Place at about 7:45, as near as I can guess. There was no one else in the house. We had a violent quarrel, and it ended in my shooting him. I filled a glass with water from the carafe on the chest of drawers and drank the water. I then left the house and took a cab to Victoria, where I caught the 8:20 express to Newhaven, as I had intended. I am going to cross to Dieppe.

I prefer not to give my reasons for anything that I have done.

BRYAN FAIRMAN

After reading and re-reading this brief document Trent looked up with raised brows and met his host's expectant eye.

"Interesting, isn't it?" the inspector asked drily. "Prefers not to give his reasons for murdering a man, but doesn't mind mentioning that he had a drink of water after doing him in. Tells us he had arranged to escape from the country after shooting his victim; then changes his mind, doubles back on his tracks, and tries to drown himself on the way home. What infernal sense can you make of it?"

Trent, thrusting his fingers through his hair, stared a few moments into vacancy. "I suppose it's a silly suggestion," he said at length, "but have you considered the idea that he is trying to shield someone else?"

"Yes, of course. The confession, and the leaf missing from the block, and the care he takes to fix the thing on himself, suggested that to me at once. But it really doesn't hold water. To begin with, accusing yourself of a murder you didn't do is a pretty large order, however anxious you may be to do anybody a good turn. On the other hand, genuine confessions of murder are common enough. Then again, he had a motive of his own—resentment at the way he had been treated. Many a man has been bumped off for less than what had been done to Fairman. And besides all that, how are you going to fit the shielding idea in with this unaccountable flying visit to Dieppe, and his returning home again immediately afterwards, and his attempting suicide? No: I say again, what sense can you make of it?"

Trent glanced again through the paper in his hand. "Certainly," he said, "it leaves a good deal to the imagination. But—" he paused a moment—"I haven't had time to consider it, of course, but I don't see how this confession, open to criticism as it may be, makes such a devil of a lot of difference."

The cloud of chagrin on Mr Bligh's features grew heavier. "In a way it makes very little difference. There's a strong enough case against him already. We know he had a motive. And we know he was there about the time when Randolph was shot. His fingerprints have been taken, and they correspond with those on the glass that he is so careful to mention."

"And, of course, with those on the razor-blade too."

"No, they don't," the inspector said shortly. "That's just one of those points that I was afraid, at the time, were going to give a lot of trouble. The fingerprint artist found a lot of Randolph's and the valet's marks, naturally, and he found some—not only on the water-bottle and glass—which have now been identified as Fairman's. But he found marks on that razor-blade that don't belong to any of the three; and he didn't find those marks on any other article in the whole place. Raught says it was a new blade, only taken out of its envelope that morning. If so, somebody else had been handling that blade; had taken it out of the razor, as the appearances suggest, to cut open those packages."

"What does Fairman say about it?"

"Nothing. He refused to answer any questions, or say a word of any sort, from the moment he was arrested. Soon after he was charged, he had a complete nervous collapse—I don't think I told you that—and at present he is in the prison infirmary, quite unfit for interrogation or anything else. That's the doctor's report; and so the whole case is hung up until he is well enough for us to get on with it. We shall ask for an adjournment at the inquest, of course—we should have done in any case."

Trent rose to his feet and began to pace the room. "You can understand," he said, "that all this is very painful to me. To hear of his being in that state, after all the rest that has happened—well, I won't talk about it. Now look here. The case you've got against Fairman is a stiff one, even without his confession—I know that. But I could see from the start that you were not quite satisfied, and I suppose those unidentified fingerprints on the razorblade are among the points that don't seem to you to fit in. They don't to me."

"That's right," the inspector said. "They certainly don't seem to fit in—not at the first glance, that is. Like those missing papers. All the same, I have got an idea about those prints, and the papers too. Tell me, how much have you seen of Raught, old Randolph's servant?"

"I have stayed as a guest at Brinton three times, when Randolph was sitting to me for his portrait. Raught used to look after me, as he did after his master."

"And how did he strike you?"

"You mean in the role of a gentleman's gentleman?"

Mr Bligh grinned assent.

"Well, of course, it was comic," Trent said. "Raught is an intelligent, clear-headed sort of fellow, I suppose you'd agree—" the inspector nodded assent—"but he's got the words 'wrong 'un' written all over him in large capitals. There's a sort of greasiness about the man—I don't mean on the surface, but showing through from his soul."

Mr Bligh grunted. "Well, whatever that may mean, I happened to spot him as a man who had done time; remembered his face the minute I set eyes on him. But without that, he's obviously a good many notches below the class of a gentleman's servant. I put him down as one of the old man's reclamation cases. Anyway, my notion is that when Raught came home last night he had a pal with him. Perhaps they were going to have a spot or two of the old man's brandy, if he'd gone to bed. Then Raught found him lying dead; and they may have decided to have a go at the safe before the police were sent for. Or perhaps it was his friend who insisted on doing it. I didn't like the way Raught answered when I questioned him about that safe—pretending he wasn't sure if there really was a safe. If that was what happened, or something like it, the strings on those packages may have been cut by the man who was with Raught, and the prints on that blade were his. Then he cleared off with all the papers, and anything else there may have been that looked useful, before Raught rang up the station."

Trent leaned back and contemplated his friend with an admiring eye. "It's no wonder that you've got on in your profession," he said. "All that might have happened, no doubt—or it mightn't."

The inspector knocked his pipe out into a large ashtray presided over by a spotted china dog of melancholy appearance. "Well," he said, "it fits the facts, and it's suggested by experience, that's all; and it doesn't really matter. As far as the murder goes, we had got Fairman nailed to a board. And then, when everything was going nicely, he pitches in this blasted confession."

Trent rose, and made ready to take his leave. "But I still don't see," he said slowly, "why Fairman's confession should have cast such a shadow over the smiling prospect."

"You still don't see!" Mr Bligh's tone expressed weary resignation. "Look at it again—look at the damfool thing again. And consider how the man has acted all through."

Trent re-read the typescript in his hand, and then again met his friend's exasperated eye. "You mean—?"

"I mean unsound mind," the inspector rasped. "Not just nervous breakdown, but lunacy—and a silly end to what I thought looked like being a respectable bit of work."

8

THE WHITE FLOWER OF A BLAMELESS LIFE

Trent, as he walked homewards that night after taking leave of Inspector Bligh, thought over all the pitifulness of the policial tragedy now being faced by that officer. All that keen directive energy, that rapid working of a high-powered routine, to end in the arrest of a lunatic! But much more was he distressed by this dreadful news of one between whom and himself an old and deep attachment existed. He was completely convinced that the Fairman whom he knew was incapable of such a crime. The shooting of the old man in the back was an added detail of incredibility. But all this could but make more inevitable the conclusion that Fairman, if guilty, must be mentally deranged. His conduct, as the inspector insisted so strongly, had not been that of a man in his right mind.

As for the facts that might account for such a collapse, they were not in much doubt. Randolph's capricious dislike of the young doctor must be, as Mr Bligh had suggested, at the bottom of it. Trent remembered well an evening, some months before, when both he and Fairman had been Randolph's guests at Brinton. It had been evident then that the two did not take any pleasure in each other's company. The old man had seemed to be merely amusing himself, in a strange way, by pretending to be unable to believe in, or even understand, the lines of research in mental disease to which Fairman had devoted himself at the Claypoole Hospital. It appeared to Trent quite understandable that Fairman, with body and brain still depressed by the poison of influenza, had completely lost his balance under the shock of sudden separation from the work he lived for. One thing more Trent remembered with a shade of discomfort. Fairman had known of the old man's unpleasant advances to Eunice Faviell; for Trent himself had mentioned this in a quite recent letter to Fairman, adding that he knew how to put a stop to it, and intended doing so.

It was while Trent was reviewing this situation over an early breakfast the next morning that he was called to the telephone, and a sepulchral voice, the voice of Inspector Bligh, came to his ear.

"Is that Monteagle 3474?"

"Nothing less," Trent answered. "And I know who it is speaking. Why is it, Inspector, that you always talk on the telephone as if life was dead and so was light?"

"I wish to God," Mr Bligh retorted in accents yet more hollow, "you could be serious for a few minutes."

"I am not feeling particularly playful, as a matter of fact. Pure from the night and splendid for the day, of course, but not exactly frivolous. However, if I sound so, don't take it too much to heart," Trent urged. "Remember that if I appear untouched by solemn thought my nature is not therefore less divine. Besides, I can always be serious to oblige a friend. Let us see—it's just a quarter past eight. I can be perfectly serious most of the morning. At twelve o'clock Admiral Sir Densmore ffinch—you know, the man with two little effs and one leg—comes to sit for his portrait. He is one of the most amusing talkers I ever met. Until then, I can be as serious as an outbreak of cholera. What was it you were going to tell me?"

"You said last night," Mr Bligh answered, "you would like to have a look at the scene of the crime in Newbury Place. Well—there's nothing against your doing that if I'm responsible for you. But you will find that the only remaining bird has flown. I'm there now."

Trent hesitated a moment. "Do you mean Raught, the manservant?"

"Yes; he's gone."

"Really? Like a summer-dried fountain, when our need was the sorest? Well, well! So Raught has hopped it."

"If you prefer to use that low expression," the inspector answered, "he has. Another vulgar way of putting it is that he has beaten it while the beating was good; for I came here to arrest him this morning."

"What for? Do you mean you've got evidence of that theory of yours about Raught and Charles, his friend, going through the safe?"

A cavernous chuckle came over the wire. "Come along if you want to, and you can hear all the revolting details."

When Trent arrived at the little abode in Newbury Place, a salute from the attendant constable showed him that he was expected. No signs of life appeared on the ground floor. He mounted the stairs to find Inspector Bligh, accompanied by a long-faced sergeant, engaged in measuring distances on the thick-carpeted floor of the bedroom.

"That'll do for the present, Mills," the inspector said; and his subordinate, taking the hint, shut up his notebook and withdrew.

"Raught," Mr Bligh began without preliminary, "cleared out during the night. There was a constable posted at the door, of course; but it seems that our friend simply got out of the window of his bedroom, which is on the ground floor, crossed the small yard there, climbed over the wall into Torrington

Alley, then walked down either to Wigram Street at the one end or Bullingdon Street at the other, and was off on his way through London to Lord knows where. He was lucky not to be seen coming out from the alley; but probably he listened in the yard for the passing of the constable who goes through the alley at intervals, and gave him time to get well away on his beat."

"And why did Raught give you the slip?"

Mr Bligh drew from his breast pocket a long envelope. "He had his reasons all right. This letter, addressed to the commissioner, was delivered at the Yard by the last post last night. It was forwarded by Randolph's solicitors, who ought to have known enough to send it by special messenger as soon as they heard of the murder. As it was, they took their time about posting it—probably a firm who know nothing about criminal business. This was what they sent."

Trent took in hand the letter, which bore a date of three years earlier, and was written, as he saw at once, in Randolph's clear but somewhat crabbed hand. It ran as follows:

> Sir,
>
> Your attention should be directed to my valet, Simon Raught.
>
> He is a man whom I have befriended by taking him into my service again after he had served a sentence of imprisonment. In addition to that, my silence has saved him from the consequences of a more serious crime. Attached to this letter is a confession, signed by him, of the part he played in the Maidstone bankrobbery in 19—, when a watchman and a policeman were seriously injured.
>
> How the facts came to my knowledge is my own affair. I threatened Raught with the disclosure of them unless he signed this confession, but it is not my intention to make use of it personally. I have always been in favour of reclaiming by personal influence rather than punishing the

criminal, but I do not—though I have done my best with Raught—conceal from myself that with men like him some deterrent influence cannot wisely be neglected. He is, I am afraid, still a dangerous man when exposed to temptation. I have told him that his confession is a security for his good behaviour, and will not be brought up against him so long as he remains faithful to me.

I have accordingly instructed my solicitors that this letter, with Raught's confession enclosed, is to be destroyed unopened at my death, unless I should die by violence or in suspicious circumstances, in which case it is to be forwarded to you.

Yours, etc.,
JAMES M. RANDOLPH

"And what," the inspector asked grimly, "do you think of that?" "To begin with," Trent said, "there seems to be rather an overplus of letters to Scotland Yard, and an unusual amount of confessing, in this simple little case."

Mr Bligh snorted impatiently. "You can see for yourself," he snapped, "that Randolph's letter was written long ago, and Raught's confession has nothing on earth to do with this murder."

Trent sighed. "I stand rebuked. I was only wondering at the ways of coincidence. And this confession, as you say, can have nothing to do with a murder committed by Bryan Fairman. Where is Raught's confession, by the way?"

"They're checking up on it at the Yard. It's quite plain and circumstantial, signed by Raught, and with the signature properly witnessed. But you see, of course, that if his confession has no bearing on the murder, it has all the bearing in the world on my suggestion that he, and probably a pal of his, went through the documents in the safe- after finding Randolph's body. Raught hoped the confession would be found among them. Then when they realized it wasn't there, the friend walked off with the papers, whatever they were, and Raught, instead of walking off too, rang up the police."

Trent frowned. "I think I see. He knew his confession was hanging over him somewhere, and that if he ran off that night, leaving the murder to be discovered and reported by somebody else, everything would point to his having shot Randolph himself. He couldn't expect, of course, that the real murderer, after getting away, would proceed to inform against himself, as Fairman has done."

"Exactly. He had the sense to see that if his confession reached the police, and he was arrested here without any trouble, and got a long sentence for the Maidstone crime, that would be more comfortable than being tracked down and tried for his master's murder, with an excellent chance of swinging for it. And then, you see, next day, he soon saw that no serious suspicion was attached to him; and he heard in the evening that an arrest had been made. That being so, it seemed to Raught that he had nothing to answer for but that old business at Maidstone, so he decided he might as well give us the slip if he could. A near thing it was, too."

"And what chance has he of keeping out of your clutches?"

Mr Bligh laughed shortly. "Not a great deal. We've had his photo and fingerprints since that false-pretences job that he did time for. We know where his relatives live. He'll be well looked out for everywhere. But never mind about him now. I wanted to show you over the ground here, and to have a little more talk with you about Randolph."

Showing Trent over the ground involved a close examination of all the clues already picked up by the inspector, and described by him in the evening before. Trent, who knew that his friend had no superior in this kind of skill, followed his explanation with close interest and keen questioning. Despite Mr Bligh's conjectures, the razor-blade appeared to Trent as the strangest detail of the whole affair, with its fingermarks that were unmatched among all the numerous other prints brought out on the spot by the police expert. The champagne cork, too, he felt, had a mysterious fascination of its own, if it was true that Randolph had no taste for that beverage.

"All right," said Mr Bligh, on hearing these comments. "You can have the prints to turn over in your mind if you like." He turned to his dispatch-case. "Here's a duplicate enlargement of the photos of the finger and thumb that you can take, and if you make anything of them, I'll be glad to hear of it. What we make of them is that they aren't in the Criminal Record Office at Scotland Yard, and that the man who made them is probably not over ninety, and that he may not be an engineer's fitter, and that if he had any one of a number of nasty skin diseases, it hadn't spread to that finger and thumb. Isn't that useful? And here's the cork. I can't part with that, but you can take an eyeful of it, and make a note of what's stamped on it; and if you find that Felix Poubelle 1884 made the marks on the razor-blade, we shall begin to know where we are, of course."

Unmoved by this ponderous pleasantry, Trent carefully examined the cork, found it to be in perfect condition, and made a note of the brand, which, he reflected privately, was of a certain interest in itself.

"And now," the inspector said, "can we hit on any useful line by having a further talk about the old man, as you say you knew something about him? Suppose we go down to the sitting-room and make ourselves comfortable."

He led the way to the room downstairs, and took his seat in the corner of the sofa by the bookcase, producing a pipe and pouch as he did so.

"There's the engagement-block, with the leaf torn off, as I told you," he said with a wave of his pipe. Trent inspected the block with interest, carefully turning back the leaves with his fingertips; and he noted with surprise that the name of

Wetherill was put down for an appointment at 4:30 on the day before that of the crime. There was, so far as he knew, only one Wetherill; and what he could have had to do with Randolph passed conjecture. But the fact seemed pointless; and he joined Mr Bligh on the sofa.

"Let's come back, to start with," the inspector said, "to this amazing letter of his about Raught." He held the document out to Trent, who took and glanced through it once more.

"The character of Randolph seems to have been opening out like a flower in the sunbeams since his decease," he remarked. "Here's a piece of benevolence that nobody ever suspected. For once in a way, he did goodby stealth and would have blushed to find it fame."

"Blushing might have been one of the things that happened to him," Mr Bligh allowed. "But if this precious business had become known during his lifetime, he would have done his blushing in quod. 'My silence has saved him,' you observe. Randolph didn't mind compounding a felony."

"Not if he was going to be dead when it came out. But there were a lot of things Randolph didn't mind, it seems. He didn't mind keeping a man about him who dreaded and hated him. He didn't intend to let him go—'so long as he remains faithful to me,' the letter says. Then again, he didn't mind doing his best to smash a blameless young man of science merely because, as far as I can make out, he had taken a dislike to him. It may have been just that and nothing more. Fairman is one of those tight-lipped chaps—I mean that he has a physical habit of always keeping his mouth shut, unless he is using it for any purpose, and a moral habit of not talking unless he has got something to say. There are lots of people who don't like that—you may have noticed it. Especially people who are rather by way of getting themselves looked up to as little tin gods. They expect an ingratiating expression, or at least one of awed respect. Fairman, I should say, is quite incapable of either."

"Well, so am I!" the inspector said, not without complacency, as he completed the filling of his pipe. "I hope so, anyhow."

"Yes, but it is your business to be feared rather than loved, don't you see? It isn't Fairman's. Still, perhaps I'm all wrong; it may be just my imagination extending itself. The point is that Fairman was fired, presumably by Randolph's orders, without any reason given. And Randolph being dead, and Fairman out of his mind, as I agree he seems to be, it seems possible we shall never get at the whole inner history of the affair. But as regards Randolph's personality, which you wish that we should talk about, there surely must be very different opinions about that. Most people seem to have thought of him as an altruistic saint in the baffling disguise of a North-country business man. That I could understand in people who knew nothing about him except his record as a public benefactor; but that secretary of his, Verney, who I suppose was as close as anyone to him, talks about him in just the same way. Yet I didn't think he showed himself any more pleasant to Verney than to anyone else down at Brinton, during the times I was staying there to paint the old man's portrait."

"How do you mean?"

"Well, to begin with," Trent said, "the first time I met Verney there, not realizing what his position in the establishment was, I asked him if I hadn't seen him a few years before in the *cercle privé* at Monte Carlo, where I was having a mild flutter at the tables. I said this in Randolph's hearing. Verney assured me that I was mistaken, that he had never been near Monaco in his life. All the same, it struck me Randolph was a little abrupt in his manner to Verney after that. Then again it struck me he probably always was like that—I'd never heard him speak to Verney before. And really he was unpleasant, more or less, to everyone about him. He wasn't what I should call very agreeable in his dealings with me. I don't believe he knew how to be."

"Preferred to love his fellow men at a distance," the inspector observed reflectively. "No doubt it's easier. And you may say that, in a way, it flows a profit. Raught, the valet, told me the old man got a lot of satisfaction out of his reputation for benevolence all round. I'd heard that about him before; and after all, it's not very surprising."

Trent smiled wryly. "The charity that doesn't begin at home. Still, it was charity—what people call charity, anyhow; and a solid article enough, in Randolph's case... You know, I suppose, that he had an only son, who ran away from home when he was a lad."

Mr Bligh gave a grunt of assent.

"Why he ran away," Trent said, "I don't know, and perhaps nobody does. But I heard that he had never turned up, though everything possible was done to find him."

"Everything possible!" Mr Bligh exclaimed. "Well, I can tell you one thing possible that wasn't done, because I happen to know. The police were never asked to take a hand in tracing him. They were never even informed that he was missing. Officially, they've never heard of it to this day. And that reminds me of a funny thing. About a year ago, I should say it was, we got to know, in a round-about sort of way—it doesn't matter how—"

"It came to your ears, say," Trent suggested.

"Well, it did come to our ears," the inspector said defiantly, "that Randolph was employing a certain private inquiry agency—"

"Not the one that is run by ex-Chief Inspector Targett, I suppose?"

"Never you mind which it was. He was employing them to trace the whereabouts of any persons nearly related to him."

"Was he? That's very interesting," Trent said. "It looks as if he really was thinking seriously about putting his affairs in order, as Verney believes. But I gather that they didn't find the long-lost son."

"They did not. And no wonder, after more than twenty years. But they found another relative—however," Mr Bligh broke off, with an oblique glance at Trent, "all that is no business of mine or yours. We were talking of the disappearance of his son, which there never was any secret about. It caused a lot of talk, as you may suppose, because Randolph at that time was already getting to be a well-known man in the North, and when his servants began putting the story about, it soon became common knowledge. There wasn't any doubt about the fact. The lad's mother died when he was seventeen, working as an apprentice with an engineering firm; and soon after that he told his friends at the works that he had had enough of living at home, and was going to clear out. The next day he was gone; and Randolph would never say anything but that the boy had chosen to leave him, and no doubt would turn up again when he'd had enough of fending for himself. Well, he never did; and that's all I know about it."

"It's a queer story," Trent said thoughtfully. "One could imagine that that home, where charity didn't begin, may have been a little difficult to endure; but the boy must have had hard stuff in him to go away like that and stay away, when he had a well-to-do parent who was bound to provide for him."

The inspector nodded. "Yes, a queer story, as you say. But all of Randolph's life was a queer story. You've heard, perhaps, that he laid the foundations of his fortune as an owner of slum property in Humberstone—yes, and used to collect the rents himself, long after he was well enough off to pay other people to do his dirty work. House property, shrewd speculation in land values, here, there and everywhere—that's how he became a wealthy man. He understood the business, and he had the reputation of never making a mistake. He was chairman of two big real estate companies. Then he took to laying out his money in other directions, and was always getting richer, they say—in spite of all his enormous outlay on charities and public objects. But we've got to remember, of course, that he spent precious little on his own comfort and tastes. Look at this little hutch for a London house, for instance. And though I suppose keeping up Brinton cost him something, it must have been a trifle out of an income like his."

"Don't forget," Trent said, "his position as a donor to art collections and museums. That must have helped to keep the money moving, if you like. I know more about that than I do about his philanthropy, and I don't believe there has ever been anything quite like it. I don't know when he began to take an interest in pictures and art in general, but by the time *I got* the commission to paint his portrait he had come to know a lot more about the buying and selling end of it than I shall ever do. I don't believe, though, that he really had the stuff of a connoisseur in him. He had collected very little on his own account. Although what he had got at Brinton was all absolutely first-class—and in this midget of a place too, for that matter—he didn't give me the idea of being keen on it at all. What he certainly must have done was to get the best possible advice about his purchases."

"I've heard, of course," Mr Bligh said, "about his fad of giving things to foreign art galleries. Some of us have got a pretty good notion of what lay behind it. But I don't know anything about how it was done—it isn't my line of country."

"Well, I can tell you this much. There's hardly a national collection in Europe that he hasn't presented with something they were delighted to get hold of. Sometimes the gift would be cleverly selected for its particular interest to the nation concerned, like the Dante manuscript he gave to the Victor Emmanuel Library. Sometimes it would be a thing that any museum in the world would welcome, like that little Rembrandt, called *The Alchemist*, that he chose to present to the Pinakothek. He's been doing it for many years now, and all the curators and librarians and blokes of that description—

why, their ears used to go up with a click when his name was mentioned."

"Funny," the inspector commented, absorbedly probing the bowl of his pipe with a penknife. "Because of course he got nothing out of it."

Trent scowled at him thoughtfully. "What have you got in that pure mind of yours?" he demanded.

Mr Bligh reached back to the bookshelf that skirted the wall at his right hand. "Did you ever take a look at his record in 'Who's Who'?" he asked, turning the pages of that dropsical tome. "Here we are. There's pretty near a column about him, consisting mainly of—what do you think?"

Trent shook his head. "I give it up."

"Orders," the inspector said. "Decorations—all foreign ones. Legion of Honour, Red Eagle, Crown of Italy, ditto Sweden, Daneborg, Redeemer, Rising Sun, Star of Roumania, St. Vladimir, and lots more. He must have had a truckload of them. The big swells, I've noticed, don't put down all these things, as a rule; but Randolph was missing nothing."

Trent took the volume, and glanced over the impressive proofs of the regard in which James Mewburn Randolph had been held by foreign governments.

"Rather like collecting stamps," he remarked.

"But rather more costly," Mr Bligh rejoined. "You see the meaning of it, don't you? Every one of those little tributes represents a jolly expensive contribution to the art galleries and museums of the civilized world—or those parts of it that have official jewelry to hand out as a slight token of their esteem. Also there had probably to be a little palm-oil, or a lot, distributed here and there—you know how it is. Randolph would have wanted to be sure of getting his quid before parting with the *quo*. He was fond of recognition, as we've heard already."

"And yet," Trent mused, "he never had an English handle to his name. He could have got it easily enough long ago. Perhaps he thought it was rather a distinction for a man in his position not to be a Sir Somebody Something."

Mr Bligh laughed shortly. "Not he! It was just his wanting it so badly that started the whole of this chasing after foreign distinctions. At least, that's what I've been told. Anyhow, there's no doubt that he wanted a knighthood many years ago. One of the assistant-commissioners knew all about it at the time, and I heard it from him. The first time Randolph let it be known that he thought a knighthood was about due, and that he was ready to stump up, there was a hitch somewhere—possibly the list was a bit too long already. Or possibly one of the Prime Minister's private secretaries didn't like Randolph. You never know. Anyhow, he was told he'd have to wait till next time. Randolph was furious; and it didn't improve his temper when the list was made public, and he found in it two new knights that he'd had personal dealings with, and the best you could say of them was that they'd managed never to be caught with their hands in the till, so to speak."

"And sometimes through the mirror blue the knights come riding two and two," Trent murmured.

"I don't know anything," the inspector said, "about riding through mirrors—a dangerous amusement, I should say. Well, Randolph's idea was that if he wasn't good enough for the English order of knighthood, he would show them that he could get recognition enough in other quarters. And so he did."

Trent nodded; then looked hard at his companion, who returned his gaze with professional stolidity. "Well, what's on your mind?" he asked at length.

"All this about Randolph's deep interest in other people's art collections reminds me," Trent said, "of a rather quaint experience I had a few years ago. In a way, it led up to that bit of a row I had with Randolph, as I told you, shortly before he was murdered. I was going to mention the subject of this row in any case, because it raises a question that may be of interest to you. It's this. Did you ever hear of Randolph being—let me put it as delicately as possible—a bit of an old goat in his later years? My little trouble with him seemed to point to that; and isn't it just possible that his apparently aimless persecution of Fairman, and Fairman's very extreme method of resenting it, may have had behind them a quarrel of the same kind—a kind that Fairman wouldn't want to say anything about?"

The inspector pursed up his mouth dubiously. "Hm! *Cherchez la femme*, eh?" he said slowly. "Well, Randolph had been in the public eye, you know, for a good many years, and there was a lot of talk about him one way and another, but I never heard anything of what they call immoral mentioned about him; and you bet there would have been plenty, if there had ever been the slightest foundation for it, or even suspicion."

"I suppose there would," Trent agreed. "And yet I happen to know that he had been making himself objectionable to a certain woman of my acquaintance."

"How objectionable?"

"I'll tell you just as much as I know, and you will tell me, perhaps, that I jumped to a conclusion. I have an aunt who is a rather remarkable old lady, and she and my friend Miss Tanville-Tankerton, if you will allow me to call her so, are on very intimate terms. There's about thirty years' difference in age between them, and they've sort of adopted each other. Now she told my aunt that she had received from Randolph some notes which had very much distressed and upset her. I couldn't think why they should, because she is in a way a public character, and she gets lots of letters from unknown asses who admire her, and she is not a fool—"

"Are you talking about Miss Faviell?" Mr Bligh asked.

"How did you know?"

"You didn't wrap it up very much. I remember you telling me some time ago that she was an old friend of your wife's and that you knew her very well; and now you mention a lady who is a popular favourite, and has a fan mail, and has the pleasure of your acquaintance. Not so difficult! A good job for you, too, I should say, being a friend of Miss Faviell's. There has never been anyone like her in my time. And so," the inspector went on, with another swift sidelong glance at Trent, "she had been receiving letters that distressed her from old Randolph. I wonder what can have been in them."

"When you look sideways like that," Trent observed, "it means that you know something the other fellow doesn't know. You did it before, when we were talking about Randolph's missing relatives. I don't care about them; they can miss as much as they like; but I am interested in this odd business of the letters Eunice Faviell received from Randolph. I can't imagine how you could know anything about them, but perhaps you do, and it is something it wouldn't be good for me to hear."

"I never even heard about them until this minute," Mr Bligh said. "As for me and my looks, don't you get fancying things. What was in the letters?"

"She wouldn't tell my aunt what was in them."

Mr Bligh grunted several grunts, each grunt eloquent of a profundity of experience. "Just so," he remarked. "So your aunt suspected the worst. Very natural."

"I thought so. And when the old lady told me of this in confidence, asked me if I could do anything about it, I said to her: 'Watch me!' or words to that effect. Because, you see, I happened to know something that I could use to choke him off that or any other game. So I saw him, and I did use it."

The inspector, to all appearance quite unmoved, regarded him benevolently. "You're a very fair blackmailer for your age, I must say," he observed. "But if I may ask, what did the old chap say?"

Trent frowned with a shade of annoyance. "All that he said," he admitted, "goes to justify those admirably produced grunts of yours. He denied indignantly that he had ever had any evil designs on the lady, and said he had only wanted to do her a kindness. Also, that what he had written to her was none of my damned business. So all I could say was, of course, that if there was any more of his worrying her, I would tell the world the story of the Tiara of Megabyzus."

"Of course," the inspector agreed. "No gentleman could say less. And what in suffering cats is the story of the Tiara of Megabyzus?"

"It's one," Trent said, "which, as you have not already heard it, I will now proceed to relate."

He then recounted the experience which is described in the following chapter.

9

THE TIARA OF MEGABYZUS

It happened in the course of a long tramp in France with which Trent was refreshing his spirit after a long spell of work extending through a breathless London summer. It was now mid-September, and for a fortnight he had carried his knapsack through Lorraine and Burgundy, keeping up our national reputation for lunacy by marching long distances without being compelled to do so, avoiding cities, and halting for food and sleep at small country inns where an Englishman was as unfamiliar a sight as a crocodile.

Trent did not mind being the object of a curiosity that was always friendly; and when his entertainers politely hinted, as they sometimes did, that his way of taking his pleasure was beyond all understanding, he would try to explain the method that was in his madness. He was storing up health in abundance. He delighted in the beauty of the land, which, as commonly happens, had escaped the notice of its inhabitants. Moreover, most of the inns where he stayed were adapted to the needs of the French commercial traveller; a being who is by no means easy to please in the matter of creature comforts, and at the same time prefers, like most of his nation, to get value for money. Everywhere there was excellent cooking, drinkable wine, and clean accommodation; good living at about one-third of the cost of bad living in England—a point which Trent would refrain from making, in defence of his sanity, until after he had received his bill.

The harvest of the grapes had begun, and Trent, as a wayfarer through the *Côte d'Or*, had more than once been allowed to assist in those beautifully simple preliminary processes, carried out at the side of the vineyard itself, which have their result in the noblest wines known to our civilization. He had stood with others round the open tub, rammer in hand, and taken his part in squashing down the sweet-smelling mixture of grapes, stalks, dust, spiders, "et tout *le bazar*"—as one of his *vigneron* friends had crisply put it—with which the great vessel had just been half-filled by the gatherers.

Now he was marching into higher altitudes and a keener air. It was the Jura. As he passed through its crowded folds of mountain land, two sounds were never out of his ears; the dull tinkling of the bells borne by the collared cattle, and the noise of the waterfalls. Trent knew his France, its people, their manners and language, very well; but this corner of the country was new to him. Wild of aspect as it was, he found that it was run upon business lines. The more dense grew the cow-population of the countryside, the more difficult it became to get the midday glass of milk that Trent considered to be due to him in the midst of a pastoral landscape. It had all been carted off, still warm, to the local cheese-and-butter factory.

So he came at length to Lons, the chief town of the Department, and decided in favour of a break of routine, and a few days' stay in that small capital among the mountains; for it was the ideal centre for expeditions into a new and fascinating kind of country. Like the habitat of the Snark, it "consisted of chasms and crags" very largely, clothed with dark forests and filled with the music of cascades. Trent found the capital itself, however, when he explored it that afternoon, to be very much the type of such centres throughout the land of France. It possessed its *Hôtel de Ville, Palais de Justice,* Museum, Theatre, and main street flanked by arcades. In the middle of the *Place de la Liberté* was a fine statue of a general in a commanding attitude, who had been born in Lons. Trent was unable to recall the exploits, or even the name, of General Le-courbe; but it was evident that he had been one of the Napoleonic galaxy, and no part of France easily forgets a soldier of the Empire whom it can call a son. In the *Promenade de la Chevalerie* was a yet finer statue, in a yet more commanding attitude, of Rouget de Lisle, who had been born near Lons, represented in the act of declaiming the Marseillaise.

It was, Trent reflected, a general rule that the more eventless and humdrum the French provincial centre, the more flamboyant and exciting its statues were likely to be. He wished that the same principle of compensation could have been observed in the planning of English country towns; but reminded himself that it would be difficult to raise exciting statues to the memory of men who, however incontestably great, had not usually been very exciting characters. It was while these frivolities floated through his mind, as he stood contemplating the upflung right arm and impressive top-boots of Rouget de Lisle, that the capital of the Jura suddenly began to belie the reputation already attached to it by Trent as a place where nothing, excepting famous Frenchmen, ever happened.

The head of a column of marching infantry—of the 5th battalion of *Chasseurs*—turned into the Promenade, on the way to their quarters at the edge of the town. They looked workmanlike and formidable, though a little neglectful of their personal appearance. As they came on, dogs barked, pigeons fluttered up from the roadway, carts drew aside with drivers shouting inexcusable epithets at their horses, and the attention of some workmen at the top of a high building was momentarily distracted from their task.

It was before this building that Trent was standing. At the time of the enlivening appearance of the military, he had been watching the hoisting of bricks to the roof, by means of a pulley, from a dray beside the curb. Now he was appreciating, with the eye of a painter, the intensely Gallic aspect of a plump gentleman with a fuzzy, forked beard, tinted eyeglasses, and a general appearance of vivacity combined with dignity, who had halted a few yards away at the first sound of the rhythmic marching of the troops.

As the column approached, the idle squeaking of the workmen's pulley overhead was suddenly changed to a strident scream of friction. Trent, glancing upward, had barely time to make one jump at the plump gentleman, thrust him violently backwards, and leap aside himself, before a great round basket full of bricks, with a length of chain attached to it, hurtled to the ground on the spot where the plump gentleman had been standing.

The plump gentleman, after a moment's whirling fandango on the pavement, came to rest in a sitting position against the wall of the building; and the young men in the ranks, it is regrettable to have to say, laughed very heartily at the incident as they swung by.

In spite of the shock which he had received, the plump gentleman took in the situation instantaneously. He bounded up like a football, and rushing at Trent, seized his hands and wrung them. "*Intrépide!*" he panted. "You have saved my life at the risk of your own! Those cursed animals above there all but killed the two of us!"

The plump gentleman then replaced his tinted glasses, which were swinging from his right ear at the end of a little chain, and turned to the pressing business of hurling denunciations, prefaced by the term "Assassins!," at the cursed animals on the roof. They in their turn could be seen to shrug copiously, with apologetic and explanatory gestures. A considerable crowd had already gathered, discussing the affair in loud voices; and then two policemen, cleaving the throng from opposite directions with shouts of "*Allô! Allô!*," proceeded to take the names and addresses of all concerned. There was, in short, a scene.

When order had been restored, Trent's new friend passed an arm affectionately through his, and led the way to a neighbouring restaurant, the *Plat d'Argent*. In the forepart of this establishment a number of citizens had already entered on a prolonged preface to the evening meal with apéritifs and conversation; for it was by this time nearly six o'clock. Trent was delighted with the cordiality of the plump gentleman who, the moment they were installed behind the marble-topped table on the red plush settee, produced a formidable visiting-card with a self-introductory bow. "The man who owes you his life," he observed, touching himself on the chest with the fingertips of both hands, then slightly extending them palms upwards.

It appeared that the name of the man in question was M. Calixte Dupont, and that he resided at the *Villa du Puits* in the *Rue des Hirondelles*. Trent, with an apology, inscribed his own name and address on the back of the card; whereupon M. Dupont presented him with another. He read off aloud what Trent had written very much as an Englishman would have read it. "Aha!" he exclaimed, beaming with satisfaction, "I can read English, even speak English if I must. I have lived and worked two years in your colossal London. But you, my friend, you speak our tongue with such a facility! No English for me, if you permit."

M. Dupont proceeded, after consulting Trent, to order two glasses of export-cassis and a packet of Maryland cigarettes. "You dine here with me," he insisted, "at seven o'clock. One eats better nowhere in Lons, and I come here every Sunday. It would be a pity if the saver of my life could not swallow a morsel at my expense."

In answer to his host's inquiries, Trent explained the reason of his presence in Lons. "You are travelling on foot!" cried M. Dupont. "That is England!" Trent remarked that it was, perhaps, even more characteristic of Germany as he had known it. "It is quite possible," M. Dupont said with an air of detachment. "The Germans do not possess much interest for me." What did interest him was to hear of Trent's wanderings through France on this and earlier occasions, and to know that he was familiar with the region where M. Dupont had done his military service.

When Trent revealed that he was an artist by calling, M. Dupont's pleasure in his company was redoubled. He also, he declared, was an artist. Who had a better right to the name than a designer and artificer in a craft more ancient even than the painter's—that of the jeweler? Jewelers of the first order, said M. Dupont—modestly leaving it to be implied that he was in that class—had something in common with the architects of past time; their work remained for the admiration and delight of mankind, but those works were without signature, the name of the artist was unknown. M. Dupont could not estimate, he said, the number of his own masterpieces in their kind that were now in the possession of rich people everywhere. For the world of the jeweler, he remarked, had no frontiers.

By this time, the hour named by M. Dupont for dinner was close at hand, and he led his guest into the spacious room set apart for more serious refreshment. Trent begged his host to do him the kindness of choosing both the food and the wine; and M. Dupont, not unwilling to prove his quality as a gourmet, did. so. The dinner was excellent. The wine—*Château Châlon*, followed by an admirable *Vin d'Aibois*—was equal to it. As it proceeded, M. Dupont became more and more communicative. He spoke with animation of the jeweler's craft, and Trent, who liked nothing more than listening to other people's "shop," kept the flow going with question and comment.

It was when the stage of coffee and brandy had been reached that M. Dupont began to show signs of having something deeper to disclose, as well as of having enjoyed the lion's share of three bottles of wine. He looked carefully round, drew himself a little closer to his guest, and raised a forefinger with a glance of profound significance.

The restaurant was well-filled, and the conversation of those present was conducted in a key that favoured the imparting of confidences.

M. Dupont began by hinting that his present state of comfortable retirement in the place of his birth was not entirely due to his own thriftiness. He had always made his economies, he admitted—and Trent recognized that this was the utmost length to which a Frenchman could bring himself to go in speaking of his private means—but there was another source of income. It was due to the amiable generosity—here M. Dupont looked sideways at his guest with raised eyebrows—of one of Trent's own countrymen. On Trent confessing to a discreet interest in this statement, M. Dupont plunged into his story.

Some six years before, when he was at the height of his reputation as a craftsman, he had been approached privately by a certain archaeologist, who had the reputation of being eccentric as well as wealthy. This client required, and was willing to pay well for, an original piece in the style of the earliest known examples of ancient Persian jewelry. It was, M. Dupont pointed out, a task for an artist par excellence. Any capable artificer, supplied with the very costly materials needed, could make a passable copy of some existing piece of the period. What was asked of M. Dupont's talent was something of entirely new design, in which the style, the very spirit, of that period of ornamental art had been captured. He had consulted long with his new client, and had spent many hours with him in examining the best examples, before the decision was made that the work should take the form of a tiara. One had designed then, and effectively created, a tiara—a beautiful and sumptuous piece, despite its archaic quality. For what purpose it was wanted M. Dupont was not told, nor was it for him to inquire. He was well enough paid.

It was at this time that M. Dupont had received an offer of engagement, on irresistibly tempting terms, in the service of a London firm. He had accepted it without hesitation, and for two years his more intimate contacts with the life of France had been broken. Then, while taking a brief holiday in Paris, he had visited the Louvre to refresh his memory of the triumphs of his craft housed there. What had been his amazement to find, in the place of honour among the objects of Persian art of the fifth century, B.C., his own chef *d'oeuvre!* It had been expertly treated so as to reproduce the ravages of time; but its creator could swear to every least detail of the Tiara of Megabyzus, as the piece was now officially entitled. It had been presented to the museum, as the inscription showed, by an English benefactor, Mr James M. Randolph.

M. Dupont had lost no time in making inquiries. He learnt that Mr Randolph's gift, when offered to the Louvre, had been simply described as what it appeared to be, without any account of how it came into the owner's possession. The museum authorities knew well enough that objects of art of this kind were often brought to market by persons who preferred not to say how they had been acquired; that the looting of ancient tombs, for example, had enriched many public as well as private collections in Europe. All that concerned the Louvre was the genuineness of the piece; and upon that the museum experts, after the closest examination, were in no doubt. It was assuredly authentic. It was accepted with gratitude; it was placed in the position in which M. Dupont had seen it; and the French government's sense of the donor's generosity was manifested by his investment with a commandership of the Legion of Honour.

"Is not that a pretty little history?" M. Dupont asked of his guest. "But wait! Listen! That is only the beginning."

M. Dupont's inquiries in Paris, he continued, had shown further that, at the time of his visit, a spirited squabble over the genuineness of the tiara had only just died down. A certain Dr von Rieseneck—whom M. Dupont described pithily as a *saligaud d'Allemand*—had raised his voice from the archæological recesses of the Kaiser Friedrich Museum, asserting that the tiara was a forgery; a marvellously clever piece of work, but a forgery. The details of the dispute, said M. Dupont, would not interest Trent. Enough to say that the Louvre experts, and other French archæologists as one man, had leapt to the defence of the Tiara of Megabyzus.

A furious controversy had raged for months, in the course of which Dr von Rieseneck's son, a lieutenant in the army, had fought an inconclusive duel with one French savant, and had assaulted another whom he did not consider socially competent to measure swords with him. The whole affair had ended—perhaps one might say fortunately—in the mental breakdown of Dr von Rieseneck. As an expert, he had been formidable. As a lunatic, he was harmless, and the champions of the tiara were left in possession of the field.

What was M. Dupont to do? As an honest man, he had thought it his duty to inform Mr Randolph that he had been imposed upon.

On his return to his work in London he had written to Mr Randolph asking, in discreet terms, for an interview. He had seen Mr Randolph, and had told him the plain facts. Mr Randolph had been overwhelmed. "I told him, moreover," said M. Dupont, again cocking a sideways eye at Trent, "that I was not without the inquietude that this dispute over the tiara might be renewed; and I asked him to give me his advice as to the course which I should pursue."

Mr Randolph had reflected for some little time. He had looked M. Dupont in the eyes, *"d'un regard indéchiffrable."* He had then said that the fact of Dr von Rieseneck's affliction was not unknown to him; that he had, indeed, received from that personage a number of obviously insane letters, not only abusing him but threatening him in the most violent terms.

Mr Randolph had then gone on to say, with an appearance of choosing his words carefully, that in his own opinion no good purpose would be served by doing anything at the present time which might have humiliating results for France. That, however, was a view which he could not presume to urge upon M. Dupont, who was the best judge of his own responsibility. Apart from that, he had a proposition to make to M. Dupont. He had given such remarkable proofs, in this affair, of his talent and flair in his own department of art, that Mr Randolph would ask him to become his private adviser in all matters of that particular sort for the future. He hoped that M. Dupont's other engagements would permit of his acting in that capacity. If so, he would propose M. Dupont's acceptance of a retaining fee of a certain sum per annum, to be paid quarterly.

At this point in his narrative, M. Dupont made an artistic pause, and lighted a fresh cigarette.

"I hope," Trent said, with a gravity to match that with which M. Dupont had described this dignified transaction, "that the amount mentioned was such as you could consider."

"Since I am still in receipt of it!" M. Dupont replied simply. "It is paid regularly by Mr Randolph's bankers. So far, he has had no occasion to consult me; but I remain always at his disposal."

"And the controversy?" Trent inquired. "Has it arisen again as you were led to anticipate?"

"Circumstances intervened to prevent it," M. Dupont answered gravely. "Shortly after my interview with your amiable compatriot, an object of inestimable value was stolen from the Louvre. One might have imagined that the theft of da Vinci's superb masterpiece, a few years earlier, would have made the custodians more vigilant. But no! The Tiara of Megabyzus disappeared. Who knows," M. Dupont said sadly, finishing his third glass of brandy, "if it will ever again be restored to the world?"

By now the restaurant was nearly empty, and Trent hinted that it was time for a weary traveller's retirement to his hotel and to bed. M. Dupont vainly urged his guest to join him in taking another little glass; and he took one himself while checking his bill and counting the change. He walked to the door with elaborate steadiness; but once he was outside, the keen air of the mountains began to affect him slightly. "I live quite near here, my friend," he said, supporting himself with a hand on one of the *terrasse* tables.

Trent begged to be allowed the pleasure of accompanying him so far; and M. Dupont gratefully took his arm. "*Nous sortons,*" he remarked solemnly, "*des—des portes de Trézène.*" Taking up at that point the very long speech in *Phedre* in which Theramenes describes the death of Hippolytus, M. Dupont went on to declaim, with thickening speech but unfailing memory, the noble lines of Racine, as they made their somewhat wavering way to the *Rue des Hirondelles.* He did not cease, nor let go of Trent's upholding arm, as they entered the front garden gate of an ugly little house painted dove-colour. Having now reached the couplet—

Excusez ma douleur; cette image cruelle
Sera pour moi de pleurs une source éternelle

—M. Dupont burst into tears. He produced his latch-key, not without difficulty, and Trent obligingly opened the door for him. M. Dupont embraced him, saluted him on either cheek, and stumbled into a lamp-lit passage smelling strongly of furniture polish.

Trent, as he went his way to the *Hotel des Cascades,* wondered how much of the evening's talk M. Dupont would remember next morning; and how he would feel about what he did remember.

Such was the unusual story which Trent summarized for the benefit of Inspector Bligh as that officer smoked his pipe in attentive silence in the sitting-room at Newbury Place.

"I didn't give Randolph all of what I've told you," he concluded. "In fact, I merely mentioned that I happened to know the exact truth about the tiara and the origin of it. I said that if I saw fit to do so I could and would make it public. That was quite enough to shake him badly; I could see that. And what do you think of the pretty little history, as my French friend called it?"

Mr Bligh took the pipe from his mouth and stopped the tobacco with an out-size forefinger. "It goes to show," he observed, "that I was right when I said the old man didn't mind compounding a felony. Very interesting! I've never come across anything in that line of forgery myself—it's not up my street at all. But of course I know there's a great deal of it done. I dare say if all the truth was known..."

At this point he was interrupted by a sharp knock at the door.

"Here!" shouted Mr Bligh.

Sergeant Mills appeared. "There's a man at the door, sir," he said, "wanting to see the officer in charge of the case."

"Well! Who is he?"

"He sent in this card, sir." The sergeant held out a slip of pasteboard about the size of a post card.

"Joshua B. Waters," the inspector read aloud. "Private cars for hire. Chauffeur driven and self drive. Private ambulances with trained attendants. New car sales, all makes. 146, Kemble Street, Salisbury." He looked at Trent. "And who the devil is Waters, I wonder?"

"Waters on a starry night are beautiful and fair," Trent remarked thoughtfully.

"I wouldn't say this Waters looked that way—not by daylight," the sergeant said, with no trace of expression on his long face. "But if you look at the back of the card, sir, you'll see he's pencilled another name."

Mr Bligh looked at the back of the card.

"Well... I... am... damned!" he said slowly.

Trent, catching the card from his outstretched hand, read the name, "James Randolph."

10

A MATTER OF TEMPERAMENTS

Trent and the inspector caught each other's eye in a glance of amazement on the entrance of the personage who, at Mr Bligh's brusque order, was now shown into the room. He was a vigorous man whose age might be guessed at forty, short and compact of figure, and well-dressed in the police rather than the Savile-row sense of that term. His whole appearance bespoke the sturdily independent provincial who had got on in life, and of whom the world was at liberty to think exactly what it chose. But it was the face that had so undisguisably astonished Trent and the police- officer; a clean-shaven face, square, hard and ruddy, blunt-nosed, and with eyes glinting shrewdly between narrowed lids.

The new-comer took note of their surprise with grim amusement; then, glancing from one to the other, made the obvious choice. "You are Inspector Bligh?" he asked; and received the curt reply: "That is my name."

"I carry my credentials in my looks—it's easy to see that," the square-faced man remarked with a faint trace of Northern accent. "Yes, gentlemen, I am the old man's son; the only son who ran away from home."

Mr Bligh, his gaze still dwelling on the features of the claimant to the name of Randolph, took hold of the situation.

"I am very sorry, Mr Randolph," he said, "you should be returning under such tragic circumstances. When you speak of yourself as the son who ran away, I understand you to mean that you never have returned until now—never made it up with your father, in fact. That must make it all the more painful for you."

The hard face betrayed no emotion. "No man likes to hear of his own flesh and blood being murdered. As for our not having made it up, that's right enough. Since I was a lad, my father and I never set eyes on each other, or took any notice of each other's existence. I heard no more about him than anybody might do who reads the papers, and for all he knew about me I might have been dead and buried years ago. I suppose it would sound well for me to say I never expected to return to his roof under such tragic circumstances, as you put it. But I am no hand at saying what I don't mean. I have always known there wasn't likely to be any going back while my father was alive. When I let him know I meant to leave home, he told me I could go if I wanted to, and come back when I had learned some sense, but I needn't think he would ever send for me. Both of us were pretty hard chaps, so that settled it."

James Randolph, while offering this abridgement of a chapter of family history, had placed his hat on the table and serenely seated himself in one of the armchairs before the fireplace. Now, with a hand on either knee, he looked from one to the other of his hearers.

Trent's knowledge of his friend told him that, for all his expressionless face, Mr Bligh was not unfavourably impressed by the manner of this unusual self-introduction.

"Well, Mr Randolph," he said with a trace of a smile, "there can't be much doubt about who your father was, I should say; I never saw such a likeness. Barring a few lines in the face, which you'll get in time, you're his living image. Put on one of his square- topped bowlers, and carry that little bag he always took about with him, and anybody would think it was the old gentleman himself. But you say you are in favour of frankness, and you've shown that you are; so you won't object to me speaking frankly too. Your statement that you are the legitimate son of the late Mr Randolph will have to be legally made good, if you are counting on deriving any benefit from your claim. Of course you know that."

"I do, of course," Randolph said. "There won't be any difficulty about that, though. As for my getting any benefit from being my father's son, the Lord knows I haven't counted on it; but you never can tell what may happen, so I have always been in a position to prove my identity if I wanted to do so. And from what I hear now," James Randolph added coolly, "it seems there is a chance of something that you might call benefit coming my way. So here I am, and here I stay, until we've got it straightened out about how I stand. I've left my business in good hands, and I am in no hurry."

Mr Bligh looked at him with pursed lips. "What you should do first, Mr Randolph, is to get in touch with your father's solicitors. I can give you the name and address. Perhaps that was what was in your mind in calling here."

"Oh no," Randolph said, with some hint of a self-satisfied grin that made him for the first time seem quite human and very Yorkshire. "That wasn't in my mind. I've learnt to know my way about the world a bit, Inspector. When I read the news in the paper yesterday afternoon, I saw my solicitor in Salisbury, who knows me by the name of Waters. I got him to telephone his London agents to find out who were the late Mr Randolph's solicitors in London; and I soon got the information. I came up by car yesterday evening, put up at the Woburn Hotel, and called on the firm first thing this morning. When I asked if they could see Mr James Randolph, I hadn't any difficulty in obtaining an interview."

"No," the inspector said with a grin, "I suppose not. Then I take it you have come here to see me about the investigation of the crime, and possibly give me some help."

James Randolph nodded briefly, "Ay, that's it. I don't know about giving help, seeing that it's twenty-five years since I had anything to do with my father. But I would like to hear about the investigation, if you agree with me that I am entitled to do so; and what prospect there is of bringing the man who did this thing to justice. Any differences there may have been between my father and me were in the family, and nobody else's business. If I had cause for what I did, it didn't extend to wishing him any harm in his old age. As my father's son, I want to see the man who killed him taken, and made to pay the price."

Mr Bligh stroked his knees thoughtfully. "I should like," he said, "to know first of all just how we stand—or how you stand, to put it plainly, Mr Randolph. Have you any- objection to telling me briefly what I suppose you have been telling Muirhead & Soames this morning? You could speak quite freely before this gentleman, Mr Trent, who is a friend of mine, and sometimes gives me his assistance as confidential adviser."

Trent, hearing with suitable gravity this rather ambiguous account of his position, exchanged nods with James Randolph, who said: "I don't mind if I do. I've nought to be ashamed of, according to my view, and I don't worry much about other people's views. Well, then—I'll say just this much about my father, that he was never an easy man to live with. He had very strict notions about conduct. He had some fault to find with pretty near everything that anybody did. It was part of his belief that those who did wrong ought to suffer for the good of their own souls, and that it was his Christian duty to see that they did suffer, if he was in a position to do so. Naturally, his own family got the full benefit of that."

"And they were not grateful?" Trent suggested.

"They were weak, sir—that is how my father would have put it," Randolph returned composedly. "His sister, who lived with him until she made a marriage that he strongly disapproved of, must have been a bit like me; she went out of his life and stayed out, and her name was never mentioned in his household. My mother was the best of mothers to me, and it fair gives me the creeps to think what my boyhood would have been without her; but she couldn't please my father. Her health was not good, and she had a nurse to help look after me. After mother died, my old nurse stayed on, and she was always next door to a mother to me; but it wasn't long before she married, and then I couldn't stick it any longer. So there you have the story of why I left home.

"I told nobody where I was going when I went away from Humberstone. What I did was go straight to Salisbury, where my old nurse and her husband were living, to see if they could give me a job. His name was Waters, the same as you've seen it on that card I sent in. He had started a small motor-car business, as I knew, and I was a pretty good mechanic after a couple of years in Townrow's works. Waters was a right good chap, and besides, he would have done anything to please his wife. He agreed to give me a trial, and to say nought about who I was. It was given out that I was a nephew of his, of the same name. I wouldn't take anything but my keep at the start, but after six months I was getting decent pay, and earning it. Between us, we built up that business. Waters took me into partnership, and when he died I carried on under the old name, as I am doing now."

Mr Bligh glanced at Randolph's trade card. "So I see. A fine business, I should think, Mr Randolph, in these times." His tone expressed an amiable interest.

Randolph shot him a glance that was not quite so amiable. "The business is all right," he said bluffly.

"It means everything to a business," Mr Bligh reflected, "to have a man at the head of it who started at the foot of the ladder. You know how to pick your men, for one thing. And I expect you're a first-class driver yourself, Mr Randolph."

"The name of Waters," Randolph declared, "used to be pretty well known on the track at one time. But I have given all that up long ago. No time for it."

"Did you bring Mrs Randolph to London with you?"

"I have never married," Randolph said. "No time for that neither. Old Aggie—that's my partner's widow, my old nurse—she's living with me and looking after me still. There, gentlemen; now you know all about me, or as much as need be anyhow."

Randolph, still seated squarely in his chair, now pulled out a large handkerchief and blew his nose sonorously, as if sounding a challenge to all incredulity and suspicion. Trent, observing the gesture, once more exchanged significant looks with the inspector, who proceeded at once to make the comment for which the speaker appeared to be waiting.

"And so that is the account you have given to the lawyers, Mr Randolph," he said. "A plain enough solution of the puzzle about your disappearance. Well, well! It's all very simple when you know. You said something about being able to prove your identity, I think, if anyone should raise the question of your legitimate parentage. I suppose you are relying on the testimony of your old nurse."

"Ay! And there's more than that," Randolph said. "I brought several things away with me when I left home, in case they might be useful. There's the birth and baptism certificates that were taken out when I first went to Freyne Park School—my mother gave me them. And there's the silver mug I had when I was christened, with my name and the date engraved on it. And there's the Bible that was given me when I had learnt to read, with an inscription signed by my father—'from his attached father, James M. Randolph,' it says. And there's a photograph of my mother and father, taken when they were first married, which she gave me—there's something written on it," Randolph added after a moment's hesitation, "and signed by her. All those things I brought with me when I drove up from Salisbury yesterday evening, and I left them with the solicitors this morning. Taken together with the family likeness I bear, they pretty well settled the matter, and I have asked Muirhead & Soames to go ahead and get my position legally established."

The inspector nodded. "I gather, Mr Randolph, you have heard your father is believed to have left no will."

"So I have been told; and nobody more surprised about it than me. When I heard of his death, I thought he would have left a will of course, and if so there might or might not be something in my favour. 'Twasn't as if he had cast me off and disowned me, you see; none so bad as that. And you never know, anyhow. So I thought the sooner I came forward in my lawful name the better. I'm none so sure as yet, mind you, that there is no will, though the lawyers say they had often urged him to make one and he had always put off doing so. But however that may turn out, I mean to stand on my rights if I have got any." Randolph closed his lips inflexibly; then added with a change to an easier manner, "And now, if you're satisfied, Inspector, what do you say to letting me know what the police inquiries have led to, and what it means when the papers say an arrest has taken place?"

At this point Trent rose to go, for the hour of the appointment which he had mentioned to Mr Bligh was by this time not far off. James Randolph, who seemed now to be comfortably conscious of a certain mastery of the situation, gave him a curt but friendly farewell.

As a taxi took him homeward, Trent thought of Randolph with a sympathy which, to all appearances, was the last emotion that he desired to awaken in his fellow-men. The brief and trite intimations he had given of the sort of life lived in his father's household had developed in Trent's fertile fancy to a tragic history of watchful, self-righteous rigour and of spirits broken or stunted by unending frustration. It was curious—Trent had seen the same oddity before—how, despite a feeling in the child which must have been at best one of dogged resentment and rebellion, he had derived from his father not only a remarkable likeness in face and physique, but similarities of bearing, gait and gesture such as no merely conscious imitation could ever have produced. The inspector, as Trent had noted, had been as much struck as himself by the way that this was shown even in such trifles as the posture of sitting in a chair or the management of a handkerchief. The parentless and untaught kitten, crouched with twitching tail by the mouse-hole, did not give more telling proofs of heredity.

An hour of work at the portrait of Sir Densmore flinch, and of drafts on that veteran's fund of scandalous recollection, drove Trent's thoughts away from the Randolph affair; but they returned to it refreshed as he sat at a solitary luncheon. It was long enough since he had resolved to have no more to do, in a quasiprofessional way, with problems of crime. But the murder of a man whom he had known, and who had aroused his interest as a human curiosity, could not be disregarded; and the utterly unexpected appearance of an old friend in the character of the self-confessed criminal had given the keenest edge to Trent's reviving taste for that grimly fascinating business.

Bryan Fairman, he was still convinced, was quite incapable of deliberate homicide, to say nothing of shooting a man in the back. But there had always been—Trent now admitted it to himself—something in the make-up of Fairman not inconsistent with the idea that he might, in a state of extreme nervous tension, be guilty of fatal violence. The air of cool reserve that marked him in ordinary social relations, and made him a man of few friendships and no popularity, cloaked a nature of the most sensitive kind. He would have treated with disgust the suggestion of his being what is called temperamental; but he was, in his own way, nothing else. That was to be seen in the intensity of his devotion, quite hopeless as it had always been, to Eunice Faviell; but that was another aspect of the matter. Trent, as one of the few who knew Fairman thoroughly, could name some things that raised his temper to a white heat and strained his steely self-control to bursting-point. Cruelty was among those things; so was injustice; so, too, was the self-satisfied and, as it were, studied obtuseness that threw an ignorant contempt upon all pioneer work in the spacious world of scientific research. There could be little doubt that Randolph had been guilty of the first two—that the cutting off of Fairman from the research that he lived for had been his work; and the old man had, to Trent's own knowledge, made a deliberate display of the third. All this, taken along with the self-evident truth that Fairman's illness had told upon his mental condition, made it far from difficult to believe that he had called upon Randolph in a dangerous temper.

Trent, pacing up and down his studio as he turned these unacceptable thoughts over in his mind, felt in his pocket for a pipe; and along with it he turned out the thin cards on which were printed the enlarged photographs of the fingermarks found on the razor-blade in Randolph's bedroom. He looked at them with scant attention as he recalled the ingenious attempt of Inspector Bligh to fit these unidentified traces into his picture of what had happened on the night of the crime. It was long ago—Trent could not think how long, but certainly a number of years—that he had made a careful study of the system used by the police in the preserving and classifying of fingerprints. For practice in the use of it, he had for some time amused himself by taking impressions of the fingers of any of his friends who would submit to that rather messy operation. In this branch of knowledge, he told himself, he had grown decidedly rusty. Looking at these well-marked prints of a finger and thumb, he had no more than a vague recollection of the dactyloscopic terms to be used in describing them. He turned to rummage in one of the drawers of a tall cabinet, and soon pulled out a bundle of photographs fastened by an elastic band. He spread them on the table. Each consisted of a set of prints marked with a name, and with the characteristics of each print noted against it by his own hand in small but clear red-ink script. Neat work, he reflected; a waste of time, but neat enough. Ah! yes; that was the word for which he had been searching his memory—the word "ulnar." The forefingerprint on the blade showed an ulnar loop, with—he numbered the ridge-marks delicately with a fine pencil-point—seventeen counts. A very ordinary sort of pattern; there were many such, he could see, in his collection. But the unknown print had something else about it; a small white line dividing four of the ridges immediately to the left of the delta. The scar of a cut? No; there was no displacement or puckering of the ridges. What was the term for it? He shuffled through his own photographs rapidly. Yes; that was it! A crease.

And then Trent exploded in an oath, and the blood rushed to his head as he stared in consternation at the print from which he had read that harmless little word. He caught up the police photograph, and with shaking hands compared the two minutely. There could be no doubt or question. Here were two forefinger-prints exactly alike in every detail, even to the tiniest particulars brought out in each ridge by the process of enlargement. He turned to the thumbprint on his own card, and again compared the two. They were identically similar—of course!

Trent collapsed into a chair and wiped the beads of sweat from his forehead. He felt as if he were in the crisis of a nightmare. The thing was madness; it didn't make sense. But this was no dream; the cold facts were there. He strove to put a check on the racing tumult of his thoughts; the facts were there.

This, then, was the answer of experience to his resolve, so well kept until now, to have no more to do with mysteries of crime. His personal contacts with old James Randolph had tempted him to the extent of seeking information, at least, about the course of the official inquiry. Then the discovery of an old and close friend's incrimination in the affair had moved him to an absorbed and deeply distressful interest. And now this bewildering complication, this direct suggestion of something far worse than the revengeful act of a man mentally unhinged, had arisen as a challenge to the full exercise of such ingenuity and imagination as Trent had given formerly to problems of the sort. He could do no less than take that challenge up, and by his own way arrive at the truth, if possible, about this baffling case.

The most direct and swiftest approach would be by means of a personal appeal to Bryan Fairman, that he should consent to clothe with as much detail as he could the outline of what had happened, or been seen or heard, that night at Newbury Place. His statement, it was clear, had been deliberately made as bare and uninforming as was consistent with his purpose. But the making of any such appeal, Trent saw at once, was out of the question. Even if Fairman had been in a condition to reply to questions, he had the right to keep his own counsel if he had so determined, and he was not a man who could easily be made to see better reasons than his own, even by the closest friend. But Fairman was ill and unapproachable; the police themselves could not question him, and leave to speak with him in such a state would never be given to anyone applying merely as a friend of the accused.

It seemed to Trent that there was one line of inquiry, not altogether without promise, lying open. He had been struck at once—more so than Inspector Bligh had appeared to be—by the statement of the Dieppe police, that they had been completely unable to discover any reason why a foreigner, "*souffrant et un peu toqué,*" should have betaken himself to a certain quarter of their town, and there appeared to be in search of something.

Trent knew his France, as has been said, pretty well. He had lived two years there, for the most part in Paris, and at other times had explored many of the towns and countrysides. He was well aware that some acquaintance with the private affairs of every household was an object which every local police headquarters, for the soundest of public motives, set before itself, and was usually able to attain to its own satisfaction; so that a hand could be laid on the recorded facts at need. Fairman, whatever his state of mind, must certainly have had some purpose in travelling straight to a particular neighbourhood in Dieppe when he left England—in going thither, and in looking about for something which, it was alleged, he had failed to find. The Dieppe police, so Mr Bligh had said, declared themselves absolutely at a loss to account for such actions on Fairman's part, although they had made every possible inquiry.

It might be true. The Dieppe police might, on the other hand, have the soundest of public motives for being unable to find any clue to the proceedings of Fairman on this occasion. Trent could recall more than one case in which much more extraordinary facts had completely baffled the intelligence of officials who were certainly in a position to discover the truth if discovery had been their object. He reminded himself, indeed, that it was not an unheard-of thing for the French police to go to quite remarkable lengths with the purpose of making the truth undiscoverable by other people. On the whole, he was disposed to think that, as there was obviously more in Fairman's proceedings at Dieppe than met the eye, there might well be more than met the eye in the official inability to supply a clue to them.

At least there was something to be done in the way of search for the unguessable truth; and the next afternoon saw Trent setting foot on the quay in the old Avant Port of Dieppe.

11

IMPASSE

"Impasse de la Chimère." Trent said the words over to himself, relishing their hint of mystery, as he walked out of Dieppe harbour on his quest. Such a name, he thought, must lend some glamour of magic to the blindest of alleys.

Like all places worth finding, the Impasse de la Chimère was hard to find. Trent had to consult several passers-by before he discovered that the way to the Impasse ran down an old-fashioned narrow side street off a tram-bedevilled, motor-ridden road. From that side street another even narrower turned on the left.

He had the impression of walking into loneliness and the unknown. The grey houses were mute and mysterious; the streets were empty. At last "Impasse de la Chimère" caught his eye, rudely carved and half defaced by time, at the corner of a narrow passage down which a cart might just be able to pass with hubs scraping the wall on either side. It was a place of emptiness, for the alley ran straight for fifty yards or so between high and formidable walls above which showed the branches of ancient trees. The uneven cobbles of the roadway might have been laid in the days of the Grand Monarque.

Suddenly the alley turned right and opened out with a sweep on either hand. On the right was a gate surmounted by a battered nondescript animal in stone, which might well be the Chimera that gave its name to the Impasse. The house that lay behind it, visible through the iron gateway, was evidently a place of dignity and tradition. Unhonoured by any name on the gate-post, it was distinguished, convict-like, by a number, 7A, on an ugly little enamelled plaque set crookedly on the wall by a careless workman. Why the authorities of the town should have bestowed on the largest house in the Impasse this number-letter combination, as though there were not enough whole numbers in the universe, was a riddle to which Trent saw no answer. There were, in fact, four houses, 1, 3, 5 and 7A, with no gaps to account for the even numbers or the missing 7.

Musing on the high degree of success with which the fundamental logic of the Latins is concealed from the inquiring stranger, Trent went forward. A little wind sighed in the burgeoning branches overhead. The sense of desertion became almost unbearable. He thought with a shiver of the words:—

> Where no one comes
> Or hath come since the making of the world.

Further along from the gateway of the Chimera was another opening in the long containing wall, closed by a wooden gate. This was much the worse for wear, and through the chinks in it could be caught a glimpse of a smaller house, detached from its neighbour, but much resembling it in architectural style and in the traces of age. On the gate-post, below the official 5, was carved the curious name "Pavilion de l'Ecstase," and above the gate was a rough wooden notice daubed with whitewash, announcing "Villa à Louer."

As Trent stood gloomily considering the poetic contrast between these two inscriptions, a miracle happened; one of those miracles which so often pass unnoticed, though they change the whole face of nature. The Sun coming out from behind a cloud shot a sudden shaft into the Impasse de la Chimère, and a great splotch of colour blazed up beyond the gates he had been studying. A huge round pumpkin, a *potiron*, all red and gold, with a chunk cut mathematically out of it, flamed like fire outside a modest shop that was No. 3 of the Impasse, and an adjacent pile of withered oranges, a few green apples and some miscellaneous vegetables became a scene of splendour.

Trent's depression vanished. He thought no more of the loneliness, the grey mouldering gates and walls, the atmosphere of decay and desolation which had chilled him for the moment. He turned away from the Pavilion de l'Ecstase. The glory of the pumpkin had opened his eyes to the truth that the end of the Impasse was as inviting as the approach to it had been dismal. An ancient inn, one wing of it adjoining the fruiterer's shop, was built right across the dead end of the alley and round its other side in the shape of an E without the centre stroke; and this alluring hostelry bore the name of Hôtel du Petit Univers et de la Chimère. "Cuisine Bourgeoise, Vins de Touraine et d'Anjou, Quetsch de Lorraine, Armagnac Vieux," were among its promised attractions, and Trent succeeded in deciphering a prehistoric notice—"*Ici on loge à pied et à cheval.*"

Here it was, no doubt, that Fairman had taken his cup of coffee as mentioned in the brief report from the Dieppe police, before returning to the steamboat quay. It was clearly the place for beginning his own inquiries, and surely they could have no pleasanter starting-point.

"Here goes," he said to himself, "for the Hotel of the Little Universe. And there is Gargantua himself to welcome me! What more could the god of travellers have done for me?"

Gargantua had, in fact, appeared at the door in the shape of an enormous man wearing a cook's cap. His face was round and red and merry, and the leather belt around his middle would have girt two men of average corpulence.

Trent, taking off his hat, addressed this being courteously in the being's own language. "Sir," he said, "I have come from across the sea to greet you in the name of the Cure de Meudon. For surely you are a Tourangeau of the country of Rabelais." As he spoke, he pointed to the notice "Vins de Touraine."

Gargantua was quite unmoved by the extravagance of this greeting. With a gesture of his great arms he bade Trent enter, saying simply, "Welcome. Monsieur is right, I am of Chinon. We have good wine."

The Hotel of the Little Universe and of the Chimera was such an inn as wise men hope to find at the end of the world. Its rooms were long and low, shaped by an eccentric magician with a sense of humour and a taste for complicated geometry. Here and there the darkness of old oak was lightened by the gleam of burnished copper.

Trent found himself in a room half dining-room, half café. A tall fair woman with handsome impassive features and dark eyes was sitting behind the caisse. Trent had resolved that for that night at any rate he would be "lodged on foot" at this fantastic inn, and when he made his intention known, the lady, whom Gargantua addressed as Louise, laid aside her knitting and led him up a crazy zigzag staircase to the chief bedroom. This was a chamber with a matrimonial four-poster, an uneven floor and walls broken by a variety of unexpected bulges and angles. The air was stuffy, but pleasantly burdened with the scent of *pot-pourri*. He opened the window and looked out into a wilderness of trees and shrubs, surrounding a grey villa that must have been gay and smiling in the days of the Pompadour, though now in the abandonment of its shuttered windows it looked desolate enough.

"*Tiens*!" exclaimed Trent, "is that the Pavilion de l'Ecstase?"

There was no reply. Surprised at the silence, he turned round to find Louise already leaving the room, forgetful of the busy politeness with which she had dwelt upon the qualities of her best bedchamber. Had she made this sudden retreat to avoid his question? He repeated it as he followed her down the headlong stairs, and she mumbled something that sounded like "*Mais oui, Monsieur*." She made it clear that the Pavilion de l'Ecstase was not a subject that she intended to discuss. Her attention was absorbed first in sending the maid to prepare Trent's room for his occupation, then in despatching the boot-boy to bring his bag from the station *consigne*.

Trent fell into talk with Gargantua in the café. It soon appeared that his name in this incarnation was Alphonse Legros, known to his intimates as "*Le Joufflu*" from his cherubic cheeks. His wife was a Lorrainer and responsible for the Quetsch, the liqueur made from her father's plums. Trent called for a Pernod, and had no difficulty in persuading his host to take thought for the good of the house.

"Welcome to the Hotel of the Little Universe," said Gargantua, raising his glass, when a merry, black-eyed maid had busied herself about them.

Trent banished for the moment his natural curiosity about the oddly-named Pavilion, and his deeper concern with the events that had brought him to Dieppe. He addressed himself to the immediate and pleasing mystery of the name of this inn, the Hotel of the Little Universe and of the Chimera. Certainly the Chimera—a fabulous mongrel of lion, goat and dragon, if Trent remembered rightly—might reasonably adorn the escutcheon of some noble family; and the name, no doubt, was taken from that unidentifiable monster in weathered stone which stood above the gateway of the neighbouring *château*. But the Petit Univers! On the sign, he recalled, these words were painted in above "de la Chimère" as though they were a later addition. Gargantua could never have thought for himself of anything so philosophically satisfying and cosy.

"Monsieur Garg...," he began, "I mean Monsieur Legros, your very good health; and would you mind telling me, in the name of Rabelais and all other livers of the good life, what fly had bitten you when you named your inn the Little Universe?"

Gargantua scratched his head. "It was an idea," he said. "An idea of Monsieur le Comte. In the old times it was just the Hotel de la Chimere, like the Impasse and like the Maison de la Chimere, the great house that belongs to the count. That was good enough for me and my father. But one day—perhaps it was five years ago, or seven... when was it, Louise?"

Louise was back behind the *caisse*, silent and inscrutable, her knitting-needles flying with incredible speed.

"It was the year of the great storm," she said calmly, "when your brother's vintage was ruined by the hail."

Gargantua nodded. "That was it. Not a drop of decent wine did they make on the Loire that year. Happily the next year made up for it. I still have some bottles of Chinon and Rochecorbon of that year behind the faggots. It was a good year both for red and white. Perhaps Monsieur will like to taste them."

Monsieur certainly would, but for the moment his interest was monopolized by the Little Universe.

With an effort Gargantua resumed his tale.

"One day in 19—... now was it in the spring or summer?"

Trent mildly suggested that perhaps it didn't matter.

"Well, anyhow, Monsieur le Comte came to me and said '*Eh, le Joufflu*'—it is like that he calls me—'I am going to diminish your rent.' I was all taken aback; not but what it had been hard enough to make both ends meet, what with the dearness of life and the taxes. *Oui, Monsieur le Comte est gentil, mais il a des idées, quoi?*"

Gargantua talked warily of the count's ideas as though they were dangerous, almost disreputable, possessions.

Trent waited patiently for Gargantua to unfold his story. He was clearly not a man to be hurried.

"*Enfin,* he diminished the rent by ten per cent, and in return I called the hotel 'The Little Universe and the Chimera.' *Ça lui faisait plaisir. Voilà.*"

He evidently considered the problem to be adequately explained.

"But," asked Trent, "did he not say why he had chosen so strange an appellation?"

Gargantua shrugged his shoulders. "*Monsieur le Comte a des idées,*" he repeated, as though that explained everything. "He had a fancy to eat in a hotel that was called the Hotel of the Little Universe. For, mark you, he often eats at that very table in the corner. It was something to do with a book he had written. Yes, Monsieur le Comte is not proud, though he has written books and one can see his name in the newspapers... *Hélas!*"

Gargantua shook his head and sighed heavily.

Madame Louise clucked sharply, like a hen, from behind the caisse, and laid her fingers on her lips, frowning heavily.

Her husband pulled himself together. "Yes, the Comte d'Astalys is well known as a savant, a *psycho... psychosophe...* What is it, Louise?"

"*Psychologue,*" Louise said with pursed lips, "but it would be well for us to mind our own business. It is not for us to inquire into the ideas of Monsieur le Comte."

"No indeed," said Gargantua. "Least of all after the misfortune..."

Louise cut him short with a serpentine hiss. "Alphonse, will you stop chattering and look after your customers? There is Monsieur Gautier waiting for you to receive him, and no one to take his hat and coat."

Gargantua rose, and Trent had perforce to possess his soul in patience. He was evidently on the track of some obscure affair—perhaps some scandal—about which these two good folk were, for their own reasons, unwilling to talk; and in this might lie the key to the secret of Fairman's visit to the Impasse de la Chimère.

The newcomer, Monsieur Gautier, a lean stooping man with a short beard and big spectacles over bloodshot eyes, the violet ribbon of the academic palms in his buttonhole, sat down on the *banquette* at the table next to Trent's. He was, it appeared, a neighbouring bookseller, therefore a man of learning, and peculiarly gifted, as it occurred suddenly to Gargantua, to explain to this inquisitive foreigner the count's "ideas" about the name of the hotel. So Trent and Monsieur Gautier were made acquainted with each other; they shook hands, and the bookseller was persuaded to have an aperitif with the visitor, who in his turn accepted a cigarette from the new friend whom Gargantua addressed as *Hégésippe*.

Then Monsieur Gautier, after sipping his Amer Picon—that formidable brown drink of which, according to legend, a single undiluted drop will burn a neat round hole in a shirt cuff and on which the average Frenchman thrives nevertheless—tried to expound to Trent the count's ideas of the Little Universe.

"The Comte d'Astalys, whose family has owned the Maison de la Chimère and the houses of the Impasse for many generations—"

"That includes the Pavilion de l'Ecstase?" asked Trent.

A curious expression passed over the bookseller's face, and he raised his eyebrows fractionally.

"Yes, but it used to be known as the Pavilion de la Chimère," he said shortly; and went on, as if in haste to pass over an awkward subject. "The Astalys family has always been famous for its love of curious learning. It was said the Count Balthazar, the alchemist and magician, first added the Chimera to their coat of arms. He made a great fortune, ascribed by less lucky people to the black art and to unholy intimacy with the devil, and built the Maison de la Chimère. The present count has followed the family tradition in his search for knowledge.

The nature of consciousness has been his special interest. He studied hypnotism, and experimented with narcotic drugs."

Monsieur Gautier quite frankly disapproved of such researches. In his opinion the less a man knew about artificial paradises the better. He admitted, however, that the knowledge acquired by the count had proved of practical utility, since it had given him a high position in the poison-gas department of G.Q.G. during the war. Later the count had been fascinated by the new-born science of psychology, and had published certain monographs and treatises—*bouquins,* Monsieur Gautier called them—which had won for him a considerable reputation among experts.

"Je ne suis pas psychologue pour deux sous," said the bookseller, emphasizing the remark with a wave of his long artistic hands, "I am of the old school, the generation which saw 1870. For me, this life, my country, *noire belle Fiance,* are the only realities, and after death nothing. But M. le Comte has ideas. His researches have led him into strange paths, and sometimes he does me the honour to argue with me in my shop, when we turn over the pages of the latest books. Once he wrote a little book which he called 'L'Univers Particulier,' and it was thence that he took the name of the Little Universe, that private world which each one of us inhabits, and from which he can never escape."

"Now I understand," Trent exclaimed. "I have read it. It was translated into English under the title of 'The Private Universe.' "

A dim recollection of that book had been in the background of his mind ever since he had seen the curious name of the hotel. He had thought it notable, in particular, for the charm of its author's personality, which had found a haunting expression even through the dark glass of translation. The bookseller's evident affection and respect for one with whose ideas he profoundly disagreed made it natural that the count should be just such a man. The book had been published by one of those firms that specialize in works dealing with magic, astrology and the occult in general. Not that there had been anything occult or magical in "The Private Universe." It was no more than a development of Berkeley and Kant, maintaining that things in themselves we can never know, so that a man lives in a private universe of his own, of which he alone is the centre, though he may hold much of it in common with his fellows—the purpose of existence, then, must be the development of consciousness. The main part of the book was concerned with a series of experiments with narcotics and excitants which have the power *of* modifying consciousness either for good or ill, transforming the private universe into a hell of nightmares, or enriching and extending its content beyond this three-dimensional existence.

"But," said Trent, "the author's name... I have forgotten, but surely it was not d'Astalys?"

"The count has never written under his own name. His pseudonym is Pierre Deffaux. It was a strange book, and to my mind a dangerous book. As I said, *je n'aime pas les paradis artificiels*. Alas! events have proved me right."

"I have not read the count's book," said Gargantua suddenly and unnecessarily, just as Trent was about to ask the meaning of the bookseller's last words. "I read only the *Petit Parisien*."

M. Gautier shook his head with a gentle smile and went on. "For the count, dreams were as real as life, and the idea has served him ill."

He stopped abruptly. Once again the fringe of a dangerous subject had been reached.

Trent, to encourage him, repeated in a low voice the lines:

"Le seul rêve intéresse;
Vivre sans rêve, qu'est-ce?
Moi, j'aime la Princesse
Lointaine."

"It was no far-away princess," said M. Gautier sadly. "In fact, Monsieur"—and then again Trent was tantalized by an interruption. A tubby little man with a close-clipped beard and extraordinarily bright beady eyes bounced into the café with a boisterous "*Bonjour* Madame Louise; *bonjour, le Joufflu; bonjour, la compagnie.*" He was evidently a chartered buffoon, for he made a great ceremony of kissing the hand of Madame, whose statuesque serenity was for an instant broken by a smile. The newcomer was hailed affectionately as Bibi by Le Joufflu and M. Gautier, and after the indispensable formality of hand-shaking all round had been accomplished, he was presented to Trent as Monsieur William Rond-de-Cuir.

Trent, as he shook Bibi's hand, thought his ears must have played him false. William, camouflaged as Viyiamm, is not uncommon among the French in preference to Guillaume; but Rond- de-Cuir was a most unlikely surname, being a contemptuous sobriquet for a quill-driver or clerk, derived from the circular leather cushion on which in France he is wont to sit. Bibi saw the puzzlement on Trent's face, and produced from his pocket-book with a flourish of modest self-satisfaction an enormous card, bearing the inscription:

WILLIAM ROND-DE-CUIR.
(G. Dumanet.)
Rédacteur à la Gazette de la Manche.
Echotier et Courrieriste.

Bibi leaned across the table, and with a fat stumpy forefinger, stained with ink and tobacco, directed Trent's attention to "William."

"Viyiamm," he said, "Engleesh. It is like that—William Rond-de-Cuir—that I sign my *echoes* in the *Gazette de la*

Manche; but to all the world in the Café of the Little Universe I am Bibi, just Bibi tout court."

Trent, as in honour bound, brought out in exchange the miserable little slip of pasteboard which serves an Englishman as visiting card. He was duly impressed by the importance of Bibi's description. As "*échotier*," he would be responsible for the miscellaneous notes that brightened the front page of his paper. No doubt they would be humorous over such a signature, and Bibi clearly tried to live up to his job. For payment he would have the right to insert a number of blatant advertisements, scarcely disguised in the form of news, and would make what he could out of the advertisers. As "*courriériste*" he probably produced a Paris letter, extracted and more or less cunningly worked up from the Paris papers. As redacteur he would certainly be alive to the slightest breath of scandal in his town, and he was therefore just the man Trent needed.

Trent, however, found himself forgotten. Bibi challenged the bookseller to a game of "*trictrac*," otherwise backgammon. This was an amusement which Trent had attempted only in his boyhood, and then with a minimum of enthusiasm; but in the Café of the Little Universe, the only athletic sport that Douglas Jerrold ever mastered was taken as seriously as cricket or football. Every evening—so Le Joufflu informed Trent in an undertone—Bibi and Hégésippe duelled desperately for the price of their drinks.

A waiter, appearing suddenly in a condition which suggested that he had just risen from bed after sleeping in his dress clothes, produced the necessary apparatus. The antagonists plunged into their combat. For the moment it evidently would be mere waste of time to talk to either of the players; so Trent tried a new opening with Le Joufflu, who was watching the game with the eye of an *aficionado* at a bullfight.

Monsieur Legros," he said, "did you see one of my compatriots here the other day in the early morning—a rather thin, dark-haired fellow, about my own age? I believe he took some coffee here. He was ill, poor chap, and—"

Trent stopped. This time, it was only too clear, he had really put the cat among the pigeons. Le Joufflu blew his nose violently, and gulped as if he had swallowed an emetic. M. Gautier, who had overheard the fateful question, kept on shaking the dice box as if eventually it might provide an answer. Bibi screwed round his head like a bird, so that his shiny little eyes might gimlet into Trent's, and inquired casually: "Is Monsieur of the police—of the English police, *bien entendu*?"

"*Mais non, jamais de la vie.*"

"Then perhaps Monsieur is of the press?"

"Well," Trent said cautiously, "I have not the honour of being *échotier* and *courriériste,* like M. Rond-de-Cuir." He bowed ceremoniously. "But it is true that I have written for the London papers—for the *Record* and the Sun."

Bibi beamed, and jumped up to shake hands with Trent all over again. "*Mon cher confrère,* I understand perfectly. I ought to have recognized your name. We in Dieppe know well your London newspapers. Believe me, I am entirely at your disposal for all the information you may need, and I am sure that I can count on your discretion—*le secret professionel*, quoi?"

Trent replied that Bibi could rely on his honour and secrecy.

"Mon cher confrère, I am sure of it... but excuse me an instant while I restore the confidence of my fat friend here."

He took Le Joufflu by the arm and led him off to the caisse, where an animated conversation sotto voce began between the two men and Louise. M. Gautier was left gazing at the abandoned backgammon board, in obvious fear that Trent would ask him some unanswerable question. However, he was not left long alone and in doubt. Madame Louise, who seemed to regard him as a wiser counsellor than the volatile Bibi, beckoned to him imperiously, and he joined the others. The muttered conversation went on, to be wound up by Bibi in a loud voice: *"C'est convenu. Faut pas s'en faire. Je m'en occupe. Comptez sur moi."*

Bibi and Hégésippe returned to their backgammon. Other *habitués* began to come into the *café*, and there was a general orgy of handshaking, greetings and introductions. Trent began to think that the stars in their courses were fighting against him, and despaired of ever obtaining the information that Bibi had promised him.

Suddenly Bibi bent forward and whispered in his ear, "*Mon cher confrère,* do not disquiet yourself. You can depend on me, but you will understand that my friends are alarmed—the police, you know—and the affair is already *classé*. I have promised that we will not discuss it under this roof, so that they will be responsible for nothing. On ne veut pas *d'histoires*."

What Bibi could mean by saying that the affair was already pigeonholed passed Trent's understanding; but it was clear that the little man wanted to be helpful.

"Monsieur Bibi..."

"Not Monsieur Bibi to a confrere—Bibi tout court."

"All right," Trent said laughing, "Bibi; but have you not the same reason as they have to avoid *histoires*?"

"Me, my confrere," Bibi said with a sublime gesture, "I am a journalist, and I fear no one."

"Then, my dear colleague, I invite you to do me the honour of dining with me tonight, and since we cannot dine here, I ask you to choose the best place in the town."

12

THE COUNT EXPLAINS

An hour later Trent found himself sitting opposite a Bibi all smiles and satisfaction, his stout chest napkin-swathed from collar downwards. The restaurant was unpretentious, but the little journalist guaranteed both cuisine and cellar to be worthy of all respect.

Any mention of the affair that had brought them together was tactfully avoided by Trent until his guest had reached a second glass of Meursault 1906 with the *moules marinières.* Bibi smacked his lips, murmuring that this was real wine, with something to bite on. It was not often that he tasted such nectar.

"And now," Trent said, "will you explain to me, my dear friend, why we have to dine here like two conspirators? What is this terrible secret that you dare not even whisper to me under the roof of the Hotel of the Little Universe? What on earth could you say to me or I say to you that would bring disaster on the heads of your friends Le Joufflu, Madame Louise, and apparently M. Gautier as well?"

"But surely you understand," Bibi exclaimed in a tone which suggested that he had somewhat overrated Trent's intelligence. "There is the tobacco shop of Madame Louise's niece. There is Gautier's desire for the violet rosette. Even Le Joufflu has hopes of the *poireau* (leek), as he won the *soufflé* prize in the last *Concours de la Cuisine* at the Casino, and the deputy has promised him a coup de piston. Anyhow none of them want to have *histoires* concerning M. le Comte."

"Name of a name!" Trent exploded, "what have I to do with the tobacco shop of Madame Louise's niece? How could I prevent M. Gautier's promotion to officer d'*Académic*? How could I stand between Le Joufflu and the green and yellow ribbon? Why should anyone have a row with the count because of me? Have I stumbled into the middle of a secret of State?"

Bibi was obviously dismayed at the extent of Trent's ignorance. He took another sip of his Meursault, with brow wrinkled in thought, before he replied by another question.

"*Mon cher confrère*, will you be so obliging as to tell me quite frankly why you came to the Impasse de la Chimère?"

"Very willingly," Trent said. "In fact, I have tried already to tell your friend Le Joufflu, who refused to hear. Listen then. A few days ago a friend of mine, a certain Dr Fairman, came over to Dieppe by the night-boat. For some mysterious reason he visited the Impasse de la Chimère, and returned by the next steamer. On the way back he tried to jump overboard, and was arrested on a charge of attempting suicide."

"Ah yes'." Bibi said. "Over there you arrest people for trying to suicide themselves. Pity you cannot punish them when their crime is successful. *Ça, c'est bien anglais.*"

"That is true; but unfortunately there is another charge hanging over my friend—a charge of murder, the murder of a certain millionaire called Randolph. So far, you understand, he has not been accused of this crime; but there are some mysterious features about the affair which he has not explained, and declares that he will not explain. One of them is this short visit to Dieppe. Now, your police here say that he was seen hanging about the Impasse de la Chimère during the time between the two boats. I have come here to see whether I could not find some clue to the truth which Fairman persists in holding back."

"Yes," Bibi said, "I have heard of the Randolph murder, of course. As for your friend's visit to the Impasse, certainly the police were making inquiries there after he left, and making everybody anxious. But it is equally certain, in my opinion, that they had a pretty good idea of why he came there. That is why Madame Louise and her husband did not want me to tell you anything. Surely, my friend, you yourself must have imagined that your Dr Fairman's visit might have some connection with the affair of the Pavilion de l'Ecstase and the scandal of the Fatal Woman."

Bibi had dropped his voice impressively, though there was not a soul within earshot; for the restaurant was empty and the waiter was occupying himself with the Romanée St. Vivant 1904 which was to follow the Meursault.

"I assure you," Trent said earnestly, "I have never in my life heard a whisper even of the Pavilion de l'Ecstase or of the scandal of the Fatal Woman."

Bibi dropped his knife and fork, raised his hands and let them fall in a gesture of hopeless amazement.

"*Ça m'épate*! I know the affair was hushed up and shelved with what might seem indecent haste; but I thought the great press of London was so well informed that nothing was concealed from it."

Trent feared he might be shattering one of Bibi's idols, but he was compelled to confess that, so far as he knew, not one word had been published in England about the matters so thrillingly described.

Bibi would not allow his disappointment at the shortcomings of the London press to interfere with his enjoyment of this heavensent dinner. The poulet en casserole was a dream, and as for the Romanée St. Vivant, of which the first glass had been poured, he kissed his fingers at it in an ecstasy of appreciation.

"The good God," he said piously, "might no doubt have made a better wine, if He had so desired, but I very much doubt if He did. Fancy craving after an artificial paradise, when the natural juice of the grape is there to gladden the heart of man.

"I gather, *mon cher confrère*," he went on after an interval of blissful silence, "that it is your mission to pursue your own private inquiries about your Dr Fairman's object in coming to Dieppe. It is not your intention to write sensational articles about an unfortunate affair that has been shelved and suppressed?"

"You are right. My only purpose on this occasion is to discover what my unhappy friend was doing in Dieppe, and I give you my word of honour that I will not write a single word about this intriguing affair."

"*Tant mieux*," said Bibi. He breathed the sigh of the replete. "It would not do to reopen this scabrous case. It might be fatal to the government at a moment of crisis, and it would certainly be detrimental to the hopes of my good friends, to which I have already alluded."

He took another sip of his Burgundy, and cast aside the flippant waggishness which was the make-up of William Rond-de-Cuir. He leant forward across the table and started to tell his story.

"Count d'Astalys as a young man was very serious. He had great talent and devoted himself to his studies. His name first became known through his researches into the effects of *protoxide d'azote* on consciousness."

"Stop," said Trent. "What is *protoxide d'azote?*"

"I'm not a chemist like the count, but I happen to know that it is the gas dentists use to make their patients happy when their teeth are being drawn—*gaz hilarant*, in fact."

"Ah! laughing gas, we call it. Yes, I believe it is nitrous oxide, or something of the kind. I forgot that azote means nitrogen."

"*Peut-êtie bien*," Bibi said vaguely. "I only know about it because the dentist once gave me gas, and I met the count when I was still quite green in the face and felt queer. He gave me something to restore me, and told me that long ago, when it was first discovered, people used to give laughing-gas parties for their guests to take a whiff of it, and enjoy the most exquisite sensations. To begin with, it seemed quite innocent. People did not remember their sensations. Then some savant found out that it was *très excitant, quoi?*"

Trent did not need Bibi's wink to explain the rather special significance of the "*excitant*," which has betrayed not a few blameless English gentlewomen into shocking respectable French families.

"And so, it appears, those parties came to a sudden end. But all that, of course, did not prevent the count from going on with his experiments. In the war he was called to G.Q.G. after the first German gas attack, and was one of the chiefs of the poison gas department. After the war he returned to his experiments. He is not only a savant but also a philosopher, and Henri Poincaré and Bergson have both stayed at the Maison de la Chimère."

"Your count seems a versatile fellow."

"Then unhappily he became interested in that new science they call psychology. Ça *l'a détraqué*. I do not know myself what this psychology is, but it seems to be a machin Boche with its Freuds and its Jungs."

"Not so Boche as that," Trent protested. "Freud is an Austrian and Jung a Swiss."

"What differences does that make? Anyhow, psychology was the count's ruin. He fell in love."

"What on earth had psychology to do with his falling in love?"

"All his life he had been *tellement sage et sérieux*. Up to then he had never *jété sa gourme*—not a woman in his life."

"To my mind," observed Trent, "our English phrase about sowing wild oats is more picturesque than your French idiom, which I gather refers to an equine disease, or the rash of an infectious illness. Anyhow, what is the connection between his psychology and his love?"

"He fell in love with the Fatal Woman, the woman of the affair of the Pavilion de l'Ecstase, Marise Sylvain, the daughter of Raymond Sylvain the psychologist. He would never have met her but for his acquaintance with Sylvain—there is your connection! The count was forty-five, very gentle, studious and serious. She was twenty-two, *trés* rusée, hard and immoral. He brought her back to the great dull Maison de la Chimère, and she was bored. Everyone in Dieppe knew it; for she was seen everywhere with her young men from Paris, and her bathing-dresses were the scandal of the place. The count went back to his experiments, but he was no longer rich. He had spent a fortune on Marise."

"It is not an uncommon story."

"No, the count had married a Parisienne, and had to take the consequences."

Like other provincial bourgeois, Bibi regarded the frivolous women of the capital with a coveting hatred.

"Worse followed. There was no divorce. The count lived with his chemicals and books in the Maison de la Chimere. They say he still loved her. The countess spent most of her time in Paris, and when she came to Dieppe, she brought with her a band of Parisians who *faisaient la noce* in the Pavilion de la Chimère. It was she who gave this name to the Pavilion de la Chimère. Then she turned to politics and politicians. She made the conquest of..."

Bibi bent forward and whispered to Trent the name of a very well known personage who was still a member of the Cabinet.

"By this time she and the count were riddled with debts. All the gay parties had to be paid for. Then she had the idea of dealing in *les paradis artificiels*, in the strange drugs which her husband discovered and composed. Mind you, it was not a traffic in ordinary dope—cocaine, morphia, hashish and so on. They were drugs of which the law knew nothing, drugs that played mysterious tricks with the brain, and sometimes in the orgy led through ecstasy and transport to death."

Trent murmured to himself a favourite passage of *The Odyssey*.

"Straightway she cast into the wine they were drinking a drug that stayed all pain and wrath and brought forgetfulness of every evil. Whoso should drink it down, not all that day would he let a tear drop down his cheeks, no, not though his father and mother should lie dead before him, or though before his face men should put to the sword his brother or the son of his soul and his eyes should behold it."

Carried away by the swing of the Homeric hexameter, Trent rolled out the Greek lines as though he expected Bibi to understand them. Bibi, prepared for any madness from an Englishman, listened and looked at his host inquiringly.

"Golden Helen," Trent explained, "poured out for Telemachus a draught of Nepenthe and Forgetfulness. She was the first to dispense the artificial paradise."

"Oh, I know that," Bibi said surprisingly. "The *Odyssey* is one of my favourite books."

"The deuce it is! Do you read it in Greek?"

"Alas, no!" said Bibi, "but I read it in *Provençal*."

Then to take his revenge he began to declaim at Trent.

> *"Alor, Elano, chato de Jupitèr, aguè uno autro pensado e tout d'un tèrms vuejè dins lou vin que bevien lou trassegun que douno la demembranço di mau. Aquèu qu'aurié begu d'aquèu boucoun pourrié pas toumba 'no lagremo de tout un jour, emai fuguèsson mort si paire e maire, emai davans éu fuguèsson mata pèr lou fèrri soun fraire o soun fiéu bèn ama, e quand meme de sis iue vesènt lou veirié."*

Bibi looked at Trent with a twinkle in his bright eyes, and an air of satisfaction suggestive of the schoolboy who has got successfully through his repetition, and feels that he is on even terms with his master.

"It was something like that, I know. I never saw Marise d'Astalys without thinking of Golden Helen, so lovely and so fatal. Charloun's translation of *The Odyssey* has been one of my bedside books ever since I can remember. You see my mother is of the Camargue, and when she married my father and came to the North, she taught me her language, and made me talk it with her. But come! *Mon cher confrère*, we are talking not of Helen, but of Marise d'Astalys, who trafficked with her beauty and strange drugs in this twentieth century."

"Surely," Trent said, "the count was not involved in this traffic."

"No, he lived in a world of dreams. He shut his eyes to his wife's lovers. He was too gentle to deal with such a woman. She went her way, while he worked in the Maison de la Chimère with his servant Robert, trying to forget. It came out afterwards that Robert, whom he trusted, stole the drugs and passed them on to Lucette, the countess' maid, a *Parisienne* and a bad one, too."

Bibi paused for a time to attend to his dinner. Then he took up his parable again.

"In Dieppe people gossiped more and more, but it was some time before the scandal became public. First there were some deplorable cases in Paris among the countess' acquaintances, cases that puzzled both the doctors and the police. One of her lovers—he was said to have ruined himself for her—went mad, actually and permanently mad, and the doctors could find nothing to account for his condition. Other rich young men who had made fools of themselves—*des fils à papa, quoi?*—became mentally unhinged, and died equally mysteriously.

"So it happened that the police were already keeping an eye on the d'Astalys, when the scandal of the Pavilion de l'Ecstase broke out. She was at the Pavilion with the minister whom I have already named, several deputies, and heaven knows what women. They were to inhale some new gas which was to produce raptures beyond description. So there was another orgy.

"At four o'clock in the morning a policeman on duty outside the Impasse de la Chimère—his name is Jules Duphot—had a vision. He saw dancing over the cobbles, singing as she went, a very pretty girl clothed in nothing but a pair of slippers. Jules could not believe his eyes, though I suspect he tried to. Then he threw his cloak over the shameless hussy and marched her off to the *poste*.

"The lady turned out to be Madame Cloclo, *danseuse nue* of the Casino de Paris, so she was habituated to the situation, but when she came to the police station she began to laugh, and she laughed and she laughed as though she were being tickled until she fainted from exhaustion. They had to take her off to the hospital. And that was not the worst.

"About the same disreputable hour, some frightened servant called Dr Lambert by telephone to the Pavilion de l'Ecstase. He found a terrible state of affairs. The minister and the countess were lying unconscious on a divan; a deputy was groaning in agony on: the floor, and a half-a-dozen more men and women were in the same state. The doctor called the police. They started by arresting everyone, but by that time the minister had come to. There were, as I have said, several deputies and another minister's wife concerned as well.

"Now this happened at an unfortunate moment. It was one of those periods when everyone feels that the Republic itself is in danger. This scandal therefore had to be hushed up at any cost—one more straw, and the régime was fichu. Only a few paragraphs appeared in the press, and in them the truth was veiled by innuendo. As for us here in Dieppe, no one desired to do the count a bad turn, but Dr Lambert told his wife what he had seen at the Pavilion de l'Ecstase; and that was very foolish. Just imagine for yourself the stories that began to fly about the town; for Madame Lambert is bavarde. However, at last the gossip died down. The countess disappeared, and they say she is now in Africa with a *marchand de comestibles*."

Trent had listened to this savoury chapter of political history with keen attention. "I am afraid," he now said, "your story rather complicates than simplifies my problem. It does not in the least explain why Fairman should have dashed off to the Place de la Chimère. A serious, sober-minded man of science such as he is would be the last person in the world to take part in a drug-orgy or wallow in an artificial paradise."

"There I fear I cannot help you. I do not know your friend. Was he perhaps one of the countess's lovers?"

"Assuredly not. He was and is the victim of an unhappy love affair in England."

Bibi shrugged his shoulders. "Well, you understand, after what I have said, that the minister involved in the scandal would be favourably disposed towards any of us here who were by way of knowing the facts, and were willing to assist in keeping them dark. His influence would be at their disposal in any little matter of obtaining that which governments have to bestow. But on the other hand, what would have happened to those modest ambitions I mentioned to you, which mean so much to my good friends, if the scandal had been revived through indiscreet words let fall by any of them? And then, out of the blue, appears your friend Fairman. When Le Joufflu looked out of his window in the morning, he saw him wandering about like a ghost. He came to the inn and ordered coffee, and then he began to ask questions about where the Comte d'Astalys was to be found."

As Bibi said the words, Trent struck the table with his open hand. "Good!" he exclaimed. "Then that point is definitely settled at least. Fairman came here to find the Comte d'Astalys. He knew him, or he knew about him. You are quite sure that he mentioned d'Astalys's name?"

Bibi regarded him open-eyed. "But naturally, certainly! Was it not his mentioning that name that caused Le Joufflu, amiable as he is, to treat your friend with so little sympathy? I have heard all about it from his own lips. He told Dr Fairman, not too politely, that the château was shut up, and that he had no idea where the family had gone. As a matter of fact, the count had gone to Paris some time before, and the countess had disappeared, of course, with her *marchand de comestibles*. It took more than coffee to restore your Englishman, but after a cognac or two, he tottered away. Then the trouble began again. The police arrived later in the day. They questioned everyone in the neighbourhood about the movements of the mysterious stranger; they took notes of what he had said to Le Joufflu, and what Le Joufflu had replied. It looked as if the scandal was being disinterred. However, nothing more happened that day, or the next day. Then, when we are beginning to feel at our ease again, you suddenly appear on the scene and put the wind up us again."

Trent, summoning the waiter, gave another order, then turned to his guest with an apologetic smile. "I understand now why my curiosity was so unwelcome. I am still, however, as far away as ever from a solution to my difficulty. It is established now that my friend came here with the object of seeing the Count d'Astalys; but why? If they know each other, the count himself might perhaps help me. Is he still in Paris?"

"No, I believe he came back to the Maison de la Chimère this morning. But as you can imagine, he does not receive visitors."

"I must get hold of him somehow. He is my only hope."

Bibi, flushed and important, was now engaged in smelling with manifest satisfaction a glass of old cognac, and he seemed to gain inspiration from its bouquet.

"We of the press," he remarked, "are not accustomed to be balked of our interviews, and professional solidarity demands that I should help you. I have an idea. The count, when he is in Dieppe, strolls every morning along the Grande Rue before lunch. All through the scandal he kept up that habit, and never seemed to notice that people in the street looked at him curiously. He drops in at Gautier's shop to look at his books and talk. They have great arguments, he and Hegesippe. Now tomorrow morning I will take you to Gautier's shop, and if the count is there, you will introduce yourself to him. Of course you will know nothing of what I have told you tonight, but are only occupied with the case of your compatriot. Your tact will do the rest."

Trent jumped at the offer, and the rest of the evening was spent in less serious conversation inspired by an excellent dinner.

That night Trent, in his *pot-pourri*-scented bedroom, pleasantly haunted by the ghosts of centuries, tried to set his thoughts in order. He sat by the open window, looking out on the Pavilion de l'Ecstase, which wore an ethereal and less desolate appearance in the moonlight. It had been built for pleasure, but for a delight that was fastidious and delicate. Drugs and madness—in a way the scandal of the Pavilion de l'Ecstase was commonplace enough; but it was typical of France that it should have been mixed up with politics, and that private vice and folly such as every country knows should have become a question of state.

And when all the sordid tale was told, the matter of Randolph's death and the circumstances surrounding it remained as obscure as ever. Well, perhaps Count d'Astalys might be able to throw some light on it. Trent got into bed and slept.

There was an atmosphere of peace in the Librairie Gautier. The books of today inhabited the outer precincts of the temple;

the latest books from Paris, waiting there to have their pages turned without consideration of purchase. Gautier himself passed lovingly from one to the other with the fastidious taste of the connoisseur, happy to discuss them with any visitor capable of appreciating their merits and shortcomings.

Thither Bibi led Trent on the morning of the following day. Hégésippe was not pleased to see them, though it was as impossible for him to be discourteous in his own shop as for an Arab chief to forget the law of hospitality. He feared for his coveted violet rosette, for it seemed only too possible that this inconvenient foreigner might rake up the scandal that had been so carefully buried. Yet his wariness vanished like frost under the sun when he found that Trent had an eye for a beautiful book.

> *"Il pleure dans mon cœur,*
> *Comme il pleut sur la ville,"*

Trent read from an edition of Verlaine that lay on the counter. "And they say that there is no lyric poetry in French! What a joy it is to read such words on a perfect page!"

Tire bookseller, with his gentle features transfigured by the love of his life—his expression reminded Trent of the White Knight—led him away to see edition after edition that ranged from a startling *Aphrodite* of Pierre Louys to a dignified, yet humorous and confidential Montaigne. Hégésippe's quiet enthusiasm had so far captivated Trent that he started when Bibi touched him on the shoulder and murmured in his ear: "*Violà Monsieur le Comte: je me sauve.*" Bibi shook Trent's hand and shot off; saluting a newcomer, as he went, with a flourish of his hat and "*Bonjour, Monsieur le Comte.*"

Against the light Trent perceived the outline of a very tall stooping figure. The bookseller darted towards the entrance, muttering phrases of welcome. They came forward together, and there was a moment of awkward silence; for Gautier showed no intention of presenting his English visitor. Trent seized the bull by the horns.

"Monsieur le Comte," he said, "allow me to introduce myself." He held out his card. "I believe you may be able to tell me something that is of vital importance to a friend of mine, who is, I have reason to believe, a friend of yours, Dr Bryan Fairman. It may be a matter of life and death."

The count had drawn back at first with an involuntary movement of annoyance, but at the name of Fairman his manner changed. Taking Trent's card, he stretched out his hand to him and said, "I am at your disposal, Monsieur. The friends of Fairman are my friends. Let me show you a place where we can speak privately."

He led the way to a windowed recess at the back of the shop.

The count now stood so that the light fell upon his face. Trent, as a painter of human subjects, was fascinated by the lustrous eyes, set deep under shaggy brows above an eagle nose and a long ragged white moustache. They were greyish-green eyes, the pupil neatly bordered with a dark band, and gave an extraordinary impression of gazing not outwards but inwards. At Trent's first words there had been a hint of fear, or at least uneasiness, in their regard, as though the soul behind them had peeped out at the external world and disliked the prospect; but almost at once their serenity returned.

"You may possibly have heard," Trent said, "of the murder of Mr Randolph, a well-known English philanthropist, a few days ago in London. Dr Fairman appears to have been in some way connected with that crime; there is even some danger of his being accused as guilty of it."

Count d'Astalys held up his hands. "Fairman a murderer! *C'est inconcevable!* No, Monsieur, I have heard nothing about it. I never read newspapers."

"I too," Trent said, "could not believe that he was guilty of such a crime, and that is why I have come to ask your help, since I can get none from Fairman himself. It seems just possible that you may know something which will explain his extraordinary conduct."

He proceeded to state briefly the facts of Fairman's involvement in the crime, though he made no mention of what he had learned in confidence from Inspector Bligh—that the police had Fairman's own confession in their hands. "The night of the murder," he went on, "he came over to Dieppe. Next morning he was seen in the Impasse de la Chimere, and I have been informed that he was asking for you by name. Finding you to be not at home, he went back to England by the next boat, and on the way he was arrested when on the point of committing suicide by jumping overboard. He refused to give any explanation of his actions, or indeed to say a word of any sort; and at present he is too ill to be seen by his friends."

The count shook his head sadly, and pressed his hands over his eyes. "I am more deeply grieved than I can express," he said, "to hear what you tell me. But I fear I can be of very little help. I cannot imagine why he should have come to seek me out in these terrible circumstances. Believe me, Monsieur, I am much attached to our friend. For a year we occupied the same rooms when we were studying in Paris, and I learned to know him as well as one man can know another. I admired above all things his integrity and fearless logic. Anything I could do for him I would do, even though it cost me much; but I am obliged to confess myself at a loss."

"Perhaps," Trent hazarded, "from your special knowledge of our friend's character you may be able to lay your hand on the spring of such unaccountable behaviour. I thought I knew him well, but you may know him better."

"If it comes to that intangible thing, character," the count said, "all I can say is that I am morally certain he could never be an ordinary murderer; that is, he could never have killed for personal advantage or for passion. But—" he hesitated a moment—"it is not altogether impossible that if the cold, hard reason which he had made his god had ordained his own death or that of any other person, he might have carried out its behests, however unwillingly. I must tell you a little about the intellectual footing on which we stood. You know, of course, what sort of philosophy Fairman has always held."

"I think I understand what you mean," Trent said. "Science without art or religion, intellect without emotion. It is a hard master. It is apt, also, to betray those who submit to it. Fairman discovered that emotion can make demands which cannot be rejected."

The count smiled faintly. "That does not surprise me. Upon this matter Fairman and I always differed, though we were the better friends for our differences'. There is one truth, and countless reflections of it. Neither of us ever tried to impose his truth on the other. My philosophy has brought me trouble and to spare, but Fairman's common-sense and materialism seem to have landed him in scarcely less difficulty. Always from the beginning he was a pure scientist, holding that mind was a mere function of body, and believing that it was the visible external which conditioned the invisible within. He had to see and touch things before he could believe in their existence. He never swerved from his principle, and in all the remarkable work he did among the insane he regarded his patients as machines, though all that did not prevent him from being the kindest and most considerate of men.

"I, on the other hand, have always found it harder to believe in the reality of the seen than in that of the unseen. I have never felt sure of the solidity of external objects, but I have no doubts about the existence of my own thoughts and feelings. It was this opposition between our outlooks that made us such great friends and enabled us to do valuable work together...

"I need not speak of Fairman's career. You will know more of it than I do. My turn of mind, my truth, led me along a different path. All my interest lay in the inner world, and when I was tempted out of it I paid bitterly for the adventure. But I have never lost interest in my old friend, and at rare intervals we have exchanged letters—enough for me to perceive that he had changed in his opinions no more than myself. And there, Monsieur, you have all that I can tell you about Fairman's ideas and character. It appears to me, and I regret it much, to throw little light upon your enigma of conduct."

Trent did not attempt to conceal his disappointment. "I thank you, M. le Comte, for listening to my appeal," he said. "It was no more than a forlorn hope after all; but I could not help building upon it. Unhappily I am now thrown back upon a theory which suggested itself to me at the outset, or rather was suggested to me by the police themselves. I confess that I have fought against accepting it."

"I understand you too well," the count said, "though I hesitated to say the word to a friend of my friend's. You believe he may have lost his reason. The possibility is only too apparent on the facts as you have stated them to me."

"That is my anxiety," Trent said. "Well, there is no more for me to say or to do here. Very soon, I hope, I shall receive permission to visit Fairman, and I shall then be able to form a more definite idea of his state of mind. Once again, M. le Comte, many thanks; and goodby. I return to England by the boat which leaves in a few hours from now."

13

FELIX POUBELLE 1884

It was in a mood of keen disappointment and increased perplexity that Trent returned from Dieppe. Without realizing it fully, he had built much upon the hope of picking up there some clue to Bryan Fairman's personal involvement in the Randolph case. But neither in the reticence that prevailed at the Hôtel du Petit Univers, in the highly-seasoned gossip of William Rond-de-Cuir, nor in the philosophic frankness of the Comte d'Astalys had he found any help. What the count had had to say had merely added force to the simplest but most tragic explanation of the affair; and if Inspector Bligh, Trent himself at one time, and finally the count—with all his knowledge of Fairman's character, and attachment to him as a friend—had felt that the idea of Fairman's madness had to be entertained, the argument for that most unacceptable solution was undeniably a strong one.

Yet it was still clear to Trent, and perhaps to him alone—since the monstrous suggestion of the prints on the razor-blade was known to no other person—that there was too much simplicity; about that solution. There was still the possibility that Fairman had acted as he had done with the purpose of shielding another person. This had been officially considered, and had been set aside for what seemed sound reasons; but Trent, for his part, did not feel so sure. Certainly, it did not account for all the facts; but why should it do so? Trent asked himself the question as one passionately interested in proving the innocence of his friend; a motive which could not be said to actuate Inspector Bligh and the great institution he represented.

There remained one curiosity about the evidence available in the Randolph affair—not an outstanding challenge to detective ingenuity, by any means; yet still, a detail that from the first Trent had felt to need explaining. This was the champagne cork found among the contents of the dead man's pockets. One might imagine a dozen ways in which it might have found its way into that random collection; only they would not be plausible ways. One might think of it as a talisman or luck-bringer, kept for just the same reason as moved people like Mrs McOmish, or Verney the secretary, to cherish rusty nails found in the street. But Randolph had, emphatically, not been the sort of man to do that sort of thing. Was it, then, one of the many incongruous objects supposed to have the occult power of warding off lumbago, or catarrh, or epilepsy? Was it a memento of some crapulous orgy of the Association for Moral and Social Hygiene? Or a passport to secret conclaves of the Protestant Truth Society? None of these things seemed to have about them much intrinsic probability; but Trent could think of nothing more simple and satisfying.

Again, the brand on the cork constituted a small problem in itself. Without aspiring to any height of connoisseurship, Trent had always been interested in wine and the curious lore of it; he numbered some acknowledged experts among his friends; and he knew enough to realize, as soon as Mr Bligh had shown him the cork in question, that "Felix Poubelle 1884" must be something decidedly out of the common at this time of day. Anything strange in this affair was worth looking into, he thought; and there was no difficulty about the first step at least. He would seek counsel from an expert whose knowledge of wines, and therefore of corks, was unrivalled. William Clerihew, the renowned and erudite wine-merchant of Fountain Court, was the obvious man.

The house of Clerihew Bros and Co. inspected, purchased and offered rare and ancient wines with a reverent dignity which made precious stones seem commonplace by comparison. The shop was an oasis of peace in the noise and mercenary bustle of the West End. Its panelling and its ancient floors, which dived capriciously in any plane but the horizontal, the collection of quaint historic wine-bottles, and the unequalled excellence of the wines that were tasted within its precincts, made it a place apart. While the rest of London was demolishing the old and masking the beauties of the past under the unsightly dulness of modernity, Mr Clerihew had been quietly busy preserving the traditional simplicity of his premises, and rescuing from the overlay of later bad taste the peculiar charm of the original building.

There, next morning, in the tranquillity of a forgotten world, Trent played with a glass of fine dry sherry as he talked with his friend, who, as he told him, was growing with the passage of time more than ever like Vandyke's portrait of Jacobus van der Geest. Soon Trent turned the conversation to the subject of corks.

"Corks!" said William Clerihew with a prefatory cough. (He was not altogether indifferent to the sound of his own voice.) "They are almost as interesting as wine itself. The life of the wine is the life of the cork. There is a fascination in the brave cork which has preserved the beauty of an ancient wine for half a century or more against the assaults of its countless enemies. If only we could discover one of the secrets of the cork, it would be worth a king's ransom. Why does a cork, carefully chosen and to all appearances worthy of its high destiny, every now and then turn traitor, and infect the wine under its charge with the taste and smell of corruption? Does the evil come from within the bottle or without, or does it lie dormant in the cork itself? Science has no answer. Thousands and thousands of pounds are wasted on corked wine, and thousands and thousands of pounds have been expended on researches to discover the microbe—if it is a microbe—but it eludes the microscope, the filter and every device known to chemistry."

Clerihew was launched on a favourite subject. Trent began to suggest that it was not quite from that point of view that he was interested in corks; and instantly his friend's eloquence took another direction.

"Ah! You are thinking of the history of the cork, of course. So far as I know, the ancient Greeks did not use corks for their wines. On the other hand, the Romans used them sometimes as stoppers for their amphoræ—you know your Horace—perhaps for those small glass amphoræ of rare wines of which Petronius speaks. In the Dark Ages the cork was forgotten, like nearly everything else. For centuries wine was drunk from the wood, and the bottle started life as a glass jug to convey the wine from the wood to the table. Legend has it that Dom Perignon, a monk of Hautvillers in Champagne, discovered at the end of the seventeenth century the use of the cork as a stopper for wine-bottles, and by its virtue enriched the world with sparkling Champagne. It is more flattering, I think, to the learning of the worthy Benedictine to suppose that he remembered his Horace, and simply re-introduced the Roman use of the bark of the cork-oak."

Clerihew paused for breath, and Trent seized the fleeting opportunity.

"It is, in point of fact, about a Champagne cork that I want to consult you." He described with as much exactitude as possible the cork that had been found among the contents of Randolph's pockets.

"Clearly, an excellent cork," the wine-merchant said. "The graceful shape—the texture grown firm with years of perpetual pressure. As for the brand—" he paused, savouring his memories of a great vintage as lovingly as if they had been the wine itself.

"Felix Poubelle 1884, a beautiful wine, a wine to be remembered, a wine of great character and delicacy which even now, in its old age, is superb. It contained, I believe, an unusually high proportion of white grapes. You know how largely the black grapes enter into the composition of most Champagnes... Of course it is very old now; but to my mind a great Champagne rises to its noblest heights when through the alchemy of time it has laid aside the thoughtless effervescence of youth, that suspicion of vulgarity... "

A vague gesture completed the sentence, and Trent hastened to put the practical question which was the object of his visit.

"Are there, do you know, any restaurants in London where you can find a Felix Poubelle 1884 on the wine-list?"

Clerihew shook his head pensively.

"I have a few bottles myself, but you are not likely to find it on the list of any restaurant. Old Champagnes are among the rarest of wines. They are too expensive; a huge amount of capital lies idle while they are aging, and then only the bottles with the best corks survive. No; old Champagnes are no wines for the ordinary restaurant keeper. He would hardly put Felix Poubelle 1884 on his list—most customers would think it was far too old." Again he shook his head; then added, "But there are three, perhaps four, old-fashioned restaurants where you might find a stray bottle or two in the cellars."

Trent's look of disappointment vanished. "My dear Will!" he exclaimed. "My oracle and prophet! Let me into the secret of those few and, I fear, costly places of refreshment."

Clerihew mentioned the names of four restaurants; all small, all exclusive, and all outrageously dear.

"Hm! I thought as much," Trent said. "None of them is exactly the sort of place I pick when I have a trifling foolish banquet towards. They don't give bread with one fish-ball, as the song says. Well, William, you see my idea. Randolph, as I told you, seems to have had this cork in his pocket on the day he was murdered. I am interested, as the police are, in the question of who killed him. It seems to me just possible that some light may be thrown on that, if we can find out where that cork came from, and why he was carrying it about with him. He probably got it at lunch that day, because his man says he never knew him to have a cork in his possession before; and he did go out to lunch somewhere, though where is not known. Now if there was anybody with him at lunch, I should like to meet him, and hear what he may have to say about it, and what they discussed over the walnuts and the wine. Also, merely as a matter of curiosity, I should value any suggestion he might have to make as to why any person, being of sound mind, should walk off after his meal with a champagne cork."

Clerihew considered a few moments. "Yes; I suppose it might be worth following up. And as for the explanation you say you would value—I can give you one myself, for what it is worth. It is not worth much, I should say."

"William! You are a wonder." Trent raised his glass of sherry. "Here's to the long life and prosperity of the Amalgamated Federation of Cork-Snatchers, coupled with the name of Mr Clerihew, who will now address the meeting on the present position and immediate aims of that ancient institution."

A reminiscent smile hovered on Clerihew's lips. "I put a champagne cork in my pocket one evening," he said, "and carried it away, for a special reason. The truth of it is that I had lost my temper. Perhaps Mr Randolph had that cork in his pocket because he too had lost his temper." He smiled again as he offered this enlightening suggestion.

Trent struck the arm of his chair lightly. "Of course!" He exclaimed. "Why didn't I think of that before? When you lose your temper, you put a cork in your pocket—a quaint and widespread custom, traceable ultimately to the nature-worship and marriage ritual of the Solomon Islanders, as mentioned in *The Golden Bough*. The cork may be used to bite on, so as to prevent the teeth from grinding; or it may be forced down your enemy's throat; or it may be burnt, so that you can black his face like a seaside nigger's. Yes; a cork is clearly the very thing for an angry man. Its possibilities are endless."

"All right," Clerihew said equably. "I know what I'm talking about, and it is an explanation, though very likely it isn't the right one. You asked me to tell you, didn't you? Now can you tell me, first, whether Mr Randolph knew anything about wine? He had a cellar, I suppose, at that place of his in Yorkshire."

"Yes," Trent said, "he had; and he looked after it carefully, too. He told me so himself, when I was staying there; and certainly what I had was good. He drank very little wine himself; but he told me—as he would, of course—that he believed in doing a thing well, if you did it at all. He got his wine from Hughes & Saunders."

"Very good people," Clerihew observed with amiable condescension. "It is possible he may have heard from them what I am going to tell you now—though mind you, it isn't everybody, even in the trade, that knows it." And the wine-merchant proceeded to impart that esoteric knowledge for which he had so carefully prepared the way.

Armed with this information, Trent set forth on the quest of Felix Poubelle 1884. His first visit was to that mysterious little place known as L'Ecrevisse Souffrante, hidden shyly in the basement of a large building near the markets. There he was received with empressement by the French headwaiter and his henchmen, who bustled about him; but their solicitude was ill-rewarded, for he refused to remove his coat until he had inspected the wine-list. Waiters fluttered about with the bill of fare; but as it was early for a London luncheon, some minutes passed before the *sommelier* could be brought up from even lower depths than the dining-room, presumably from his beloved cellars.

While waiting, Trent spoke more in sorrow than in anger to the headwaiter and his satellites.

"I should not have thought that a restaurant of such repute would have fallen into this senseless habit of expecting its guests to choose their food before they decide on their wine. Do people buy a frame and then pick out a picture to match it? This cart-before-the-horse idea is heart-breaking. I have come here especially in search of a certain wine—a Champagne in fact. If you have it, I shall order a meal planned to bring out its finest qualities. If not, I shall just say goodby."

The subordinate waiters—Italians for the most part—were most sympathetic, because they had only the vaguest idea what Trent was talking about; but even they showed signs of relief when the wine-waiter, hastily adjusting his chain of office, appeared.

He had caught the word Champagne, and his resentment at being disturbed by a guest who lunched too early was mollified; for Champagne sounded like a good tip. He was grey-haired, with the white whiskers proper to his office; and he appeared to belong to that nameless tribe which talks all languages equally fluently and incorrectly, but has none of its own.

Trent put the wine-list aside after a brief inspection. "These wines are no use to me," he said. "Have you no Champagnes such as your special customers might ask for—wines that are not on the list? Felix Poubelle 1884, for instance?"

"Excuse, Señor, ze vine of Champagna ees not goot ven eet ees alt. Dopo tventi anni eet perds eets gleam and becommt as you say in Engleesh plat."

"I did not come here," Trent said with severity, "for a lecture on Champagne. I want a bottle of Felix Poubelle 1884, and if you have not got it I will go elsewhere."

The wine-waiter was "ver' sorry"; all the waiters were in the same condition. Trent departed from the Suffering Crayfish.

He was no more fortunate at the Huître aux Perles. The oyster might have pearls, but it had no Felix Poubelle 1884.

Thence he took a taxi to a restaurant known as Porter's. It was famous for its English cooking and its English waiters, but the official who presided over the wine was French. He almost wept on Trent's shoulder in the joy of finding a client who ordered his wine before his food.

"Ah!" he said, "Monsieur will perhaps take Bourgogne."

His face fell when Trent asserted his intention of drinking Champagne. He, as least, had no respect for customers who ordered that beverage. Trent noticed the change in the man's manner, and was the more authoritative in his examination of the wine-list.

Again there was no sign of Felix Poubelle 1884.

With reproachful sadness he shook his head. "I expected better of you than this. I must have a really old Champagne. Indeed there is only one wine I fancy at the moment—Felix Poubelle 1884."

A look of amazement passed over the waiter's face.

"Felix Poubelle 1884! By an extraordinary hazard, Monsieur, we have three bottles; but it has not been on the list for years."

Before Trent could say another word, the sommelier had bustled off. Trent, feeling that he had reached his goal, sat down and ordered himself a meal fit to celebrate the occasion. In a minute or two the precious bottle was presented for inspection. Trent's reputation went up when, after assuring himself that the bottle was really cold, he said he would have it at cellar temperature.

"I suppose," he remarked to the waiter, "you don't often sell any Champagne as old as this."

Again the waiter's eyebrows threatened to mingle with his hair. "It is very curious, Monsieur, but I sold a bottle of this same wine only last week, although it was years since it had been asked for. Monsieur knows, it is easy to see, how remarkable this wine is, but there are few others who would think so—few, in effect, capable of judging it. For almost everyone it is too old; they require what you call the kick, *n'est-ce-pas?*" He snapped his fingers illustratively; then added with tolerant pity, "They know no better."

"Certainly there are not many of us acquainted with this wine at least," Trent said, refraining from the admission that he had never tasted it in his life. "It is even possible that your client of last week was an acquaintance of mine. What was he like?"

The wine-waiter's lips, eyebrows and shoulders co-operated ably to suggest a certain distaste. "He was old—much more old than Monsieur, *d'un air bourru*, the eyes hard; if I dare say so, not very sympathetic. But he knew something about wine. He said to me that if he must drink Champagne he would have an old wine, and I mentioned this as the best."

Trent looked at him reflectively. "Yes; that must have been my man. You describe him to the life. And I think there was—was there not?—some slight unpleasantness on that occasion."

The waiter busied himself in silence with the opening of the bottle. He handed Trent the cork—own brother, as he could see, to the one which Inspector Bligh had shown him. Then he said, "*Eh bien*, it is clear that Monsieur has heard all about that."

"My only reason for coming here," Trent said coolly, "was that I knew the gentleman in question had had a bottle of this wine."

The waiter nodded as he completed the filling of Trent's glass. "Yes; it is true, there was a little incident. You see, your friend had taken a private room, and the service was in charge of an English waiter—the personnel is English here, as Monsieur probably knows—a little man who is quite ignorant on the subject of wine. I do not as a rule attend the private rooms myself. When the old gentleman spoke of Champagne, this waiter had the presumption to recommend a sparkling wine—Monsieur knows what I mean—not a Champagne, but a wine of fantasy."

"I do indeed know what you mean—some cheap white wine With carbonic acid gas pumped into it to make it fizz."

"*Parfaitement,* Monsieur. In this country there are people who drink such wine. It is less dear, of course. But your friend was much annoyed—and he was right—at the suggestion that he should drink Silver Foam, as it is called. *Et voilà toute l'histoire!*"

Trent was already occupied with the spoonful of caviar which had just been set before him. "Not quite all the story, perhaps," he suggested quietly. "Was there not a question of a cork?"

The waiter looked away. "I do not understand, Monsieur."

"I am not sure of that. Listen; I am going to imagine for you what happened. This acquaintance of mine was annoyed, not only because the wine with the lyrical name was recommended to him—but because he knew why it was recommended. And you know also, naturally."

The waiter's mobile face expressed a blank bewilderment.

"It is a bad custom," Trent went on, "but it is not, after all, the fault of the restaurants or their personnel. It was the Champagne firms who began it. Competition between them was so keen that one of them started the practice of paying a commission on each cork which a waiter could produce to the company's agent. Then they all had to do the same. Then—since we live in an age of business organization—a cork-exchange was formed for collecting the corks and disbursing the commissions. But a time came when all that defeated itself."

Here the waiter permitted himself a restrained smile as his wandering eye met Trent's; but he remained silent.

"The firm which concocts the stuff called Silver Foam pays a higher bonus than is paid upon any true Champagne cork.

That is why your English waiter dwelt upon the merits of that superb liquid. And if the client happened to know about this nefarious traffic, that is why he was enraged. That is why he sent, perhaps, for the *sommelier*, and obtained from him the excellent advice to try Felix Poubelle 1884. And that, finally, is why he put the cork in his pocket as soon as the culpable waiter had opened the bottle."

The waiter cast aside his embarrassment and faced Trent with a candid brow. "Certainly," he said, "Monsieur is well informed. It is not to be denied that this deplorable system exists, and that it may lead to bêtises sometimes. The gentleman pocketed the cork for that reason, no doubt. I am very sorry."

"I am not so sorry," Trent said, "since it has led me to your establishment, where I hope to obtain certain information. I must explain that the gentleman of whom we have been speaking is dead, murdered. He was named Mr James Randolph, and as you may have read in the papers, he was killed on the night of Wednesday last—the day when he had luncheon here."

"Mon Dieu!" The waiter exclaimed with starting eyes. He slapped his forehead. "I saw his photograph in the papers, but I did not recall the face. I can see now that it was the same. *Mon Dieu!*"

"The police-officer who is in charge of the case," Trent went on quickly, "is one of my friends, and I am giving him my assistance in the inquiry. I am trying to learn what I can about this luncheon, because it may have some importance—one cannot say. Now you can, if you will, tell me certain things—you can see that, in the circumstances, no harm will be done if you do so. In the first place, if Mr Randolph had a private room, presumably he did not lunch alone."

The waiter hesitated and looked uncomfortable. "Monsieur, you understand that in our profession it is necessary to be very discreet. But in the circumstances, as Monsieur says, I will speak frankly. One must assist the law, after all; and if there should be an official inquiry—"

"You can count upon that," Trent assured him, "if I should not be satisfied with what I can learn now."

"Well then, Mr Randolph had, in fact, a lady with him."

"A lady! That's interesting. Can you describe the lady for me?"

"Ah! That, as Monsieur says, is very interesting. If I do not deceive myself, it was a very well-known lady, a lady whose photograph everyone has seen in the papers, a lady whom I myself have seen on the stage more than once."

Trent fell back in his seat. Here was another totally unexpected and disabling blow. "Do you mean that Mr Randolph was here with Miss Eunice Faviell?"

"I am sure of it, Monsieur."

Trent, rallying his senses, rewarded the man generously and went on with a meal for which he now had little appetite, while he considered the new and apparently senseless turn thus given to the affair. If Eunice had been the old man's guest at this place, in conditions of privacy which pointed to some sort of intimate relations at least, what became of all the fuss made about his disagreeable advances to her? What sort of a figure was cut by the chivalrous character who had been called upon to protect her, and had embraced the task with such generous ardour—by Philip Trent, in fact? He was not by nature sensitive about his personal dignity, but the man has yet to be born who enjoys being made to look a fool without knowing why. He did not like it; and he liked still less that it should be done by a woman whom he had always believed to be incapable of deceit or secretiveness. The Eunice Faviell whom he had learned to know so well was impulsive, impatient, headstrong, emotionally uncontrolled, but he had never met with a character more open and straightforward.

Whatever might lie behind all this, his next step was decided for him by logic and inclination alike. He must see Eunice as soon as might be. Before leaving Porter's he had, through the good offices of the wine-waiter, a few words with the "little Englishman" who had attended on Randolph and his guest. The man, his memory refreshed by half a crown, could only say that he too had recognized Miss Faviell; that she had appeared to be on ordinarily good terms with her host until the end of the meal, when she had hurried away by herself, and apparently in a very bad temper; and that what he had heard of the conversation between the two, while he was in the room, seemed to be about theatrical matters.

When Trent, at a neighbouring post office, rang up Eunice Faviell's flat in Ovington Street he was answered by her maid. Miss Faviell was not at home. She had been away since Thursday afternoon last. She had refused to say more than that she was going out of town, and did not wish any letters to be forwarded.

14

GENIUS MUST LIVE

This was not the first time, to Trent's knowledge, that Eunice Faviell had gone away, cutting her communications with the world for a time. Her disappearances usually had to do with the study of a difficult part; and for all he knew, that might be the reason in this case. He hoped devoutly, at least, that it was so. Each new turn taken by the Randolph affair gave it an appearance more sinister as well as more incomprehensible.

He could be sure of one thing. If Eunice had really meant to vanish for the time being, she was fully capable of doing it so effectively that any attempt to get on her track was far from hopeful. She could, and on occasion did, make herself quite unrecognizable with a few touches to her appearance and a change of manner; and she had a singular flair, moreover, for places where it was most unlikely that anyone known to the world had ever been seen or heard of by the natives.

Yet Trent could not accept the possibility of being unable to get in touch with her. For him there could be no question of leaving unturned any stone that might conceal a grain of the truth about the Randolph murder. Eunice had certainly been among the last persons to see and speak with Randolph; and she had done so in circumstances that were more than strange. Trent would have felt it wholly unpardonable, in any ordinary case, to interfere with her desire for privacy: he did not feel so now.

As he walked slowly westwards through Leicester Square an idea came to him. It was not an agreeable one; but he could not let any personal preference sway him while such an inquiry as this was on foot. If Eunice had intended her place of retreat to be generally unknown, there was one person at least to whom it might have been disclosed. Trent determined to see if anything could be got out of one who headed the list of the few people that he cordially disliked; and he set out at once to find him.

He was fortunate at the first cast. The big smoking-room at the Cactus Club was well filled, but there was a little island of empty chairs by the window in one corner. In the midst of this emptiness sat Eugene Wetherill. His tongue and reputation would make a void round him in the most crowded rooms; nor did that trouble him at all. He found a pleasure in his unpopularity, which he accepted as the sincerest possible tribute from the groundlings to a superior spirit.

Genius is often strangely housed. Wetherill's success with women was counted by the gossips as a wonder of the world, for he was atrociously ugly. The coarse black hair had retreated far from his bulging forehead. The heavy, ill-shaped nose and the thick lips made an effect of grossness not redeemed by the clipped beard and moustache, with their hint of Elizabethan swagger. One of his frosty grey eyes had a repulsive inward cast; but there was no common fire—often even a touch of madness—in the glance that shot out from beneath the bushy, overhanging eyebrows. His voice was harsh and disagreeable. What beauty the man had was in his tall and well-built frame, kept by constant exercise in athletic condition.

As Trent, sighting his quarry, walked through the room, he was hailed by several acquaintances who offered him a seat on a chairarm or space on a sofa; but with a cheerful salute he made his way to the corner. Wetherill, who was studying a small notebook through the monocle that was a part of his pose, looked up as he approached and greeted him with surprising affability.

"Ah! Trent," he said. "The very man I wanted to see."

Trent could not imagine why Wetherill should want to see him, unless it were for the simple pleasure of inflicting his society on a man who did not desire it. That was a feeling which Trent had never tried to conceal, and he had marked it often enough by a discourtesy which would have led most men to ignore his existence for the future. But their occasional meetings had always left him with an exasperating sense that no word of his could make the slightest dent on Wetherill's impenetrable armour of self-esteem. Incivility, irony, laughter itself were powerless against a prodigious vanity that offered them not the smallest loop-hole. The worst of it was that Wetherill in his way was a poetic genius; as playwright and prosaist he had at command a beauty of imagery and a power of word-magic that carried all before them. His critics might say that behind all that felicity in externals there was nothing but a rubble of demoded hedonism; they could not deny the glamour of the façade.

Trent stretched his long legs in an armchair beside Wetherill and took a cigarette-case from his pocket. "The last time we met," he said as he proffered the case, "I was in too much of a hurry to have a drink with you. Will you have one with me now?"

Wetherill met his eye with a faint smile that told more plainly than any words his mistrust of this hospitality; then, with a rasping laugh, he took a cigarette and opened a line of conversation which, as instinct truly told him, would make short work of Trent's patience. "To be a splendid sinner," he said, "a man should deny himself. The great lover must be an ascetic, having little to do with drink or nicotine. I never taste alcohol, unless it is to take possession now and then of the soul of a noble wine, that blushes like a virgin."

"When I saw you last," Trent said briefly, "you were talking about having an absinthe cocktail."

"As for tobacco," Wetherill went on, precisely as if Trent had made no remark at all, "the extent of my abstinence is never to smoke anything that I have paid for myself. I allow myself the dissipation of one of your cigarettes."

"You may be a great sinner," Trent admitted. "I remember Saint Augustine insisted that he was one, so you are probably correct. Anyhow, you do your best, by all accounts, and which of us can do more? As for love—how much does a caterpillar know of the beauty of a rose?"

Wetherill grinned delightedly, displaying a row of great teeth as white as an animal's. "An excellent line!" He exclaimed. "You surpass yourself, dear friend. People often do when talking to me, I have observed." He reopened his notebook. "Do you mind if I write that down for my own use?—you can stand it me instead of a drink." He scribbled with his pencil. "My memory is the one thing about me that does not satisfy me. There! It is recorded—a really nasty remark. My compliments! Men," he added reflectively, "are always jealous of me; and no wonder. But pardon me, I haven't yet said why I wanted to see you. What do you know about this Randolph case? It interests me. The last time I saw you, in the lobby downstairs, was the very day after I had got a good, round, comfortable sum of money out of the old man."

Trent looked hard at Wetherill, who met his gaze with complete equanimity.

"I remember you said something about having done a good stroke of business. And that time we met was the same evening that Randolph was murdered. How could you have got his cheque through in time?"

"There was no cheque, dear friend. Among the lessons life has taught me is the truth that, in some transactions, the actual money in the pocket is better than a cheque. A cheque takes time to be cleared. The drawer may be visited by a second thought, and stop the cheque. Or other things may happen. Once—it is a long time ago now—I won a quite acceptable sum, nearly £400 in English money, from a young countryman of ours in a pleasant little game of baccarat at Ostend. I took his cheque; I knew he was a rich man, and that he would not repudiate a debt of honour. What happened? He left the club that night driving his own car; he had had too much to drink; he dashed his brains out running into a lamppost on the digue; the cheque was useless; and his executors refused to pay a gambling debt. No, dear friend; I took no cheque from Randolph. At my suggestion, we drove round to his bank, where he handed me the sum in notes; and within the hour I had paid them into my own account at Henson's. But this is wandering from our subject. Tell me, why did this fellow Fairman shoot the old man?"

Trent affected an astonishment that he was far from feeling. He had foreseen what turn gossip must inevitably take. "Fairman shoot him! What do you mean? He has never been accused of it, as far as I know."

Raising a long, well-tended hand, Wetherill shook his head reproachfully. "Give me credit for a little intelligence, dear friend. I am sure—everyone is sure, for that matter—that though they are detaining Fairman on a charge of attempting suicide, they are really holding him for the murder. And you have your friends in the police, as we all know. I assume you are better informed than the rest of us. Why did he do it?"

"Well, if my opinion matters so much," Trent said unpleasantly, "I don't believe he did, whatever you think or the police think. Why are you so anxious to take his guilt for granted? I didn't know you had ever even met him."

"I never saw him in my life; though of course I cannot help knowing that he fosters a hopeless passion for a certain friend of ours, which she is not in a position, alas! to return." Wetherill polished his eyeglass, then placed it in his eye and gazed tranquilly at Trent as he went on, "I could quite understand his murdering me; but why Randolph? I am really curious. So would Eunice be, I am sure; for she has a high regard for him."

Trent felt the blood rising in his face; and Wetherill's smile showed that he had observed it. He mastered his feelings and asked quietly, "Did you never see the old man again after you had got your money?"

"Never again, dear friend. It was not I who did the deed, if your thoughts are taking that direction. Curiously enough, though, I did threaten to kill him; I did so just before we parted. You see, after I had got the money, he saw fit to make himself very disagreeable to me; and as I was really quite seriously displeased by what he said—it was not a simple matter of deliberate rudeness, my dear Trent, such as I find merely amusing—I told him that one of these days I would shoot him like a dog.. How these quaint old phrases leap to the lips when one is deeply moved! Yes, I told him that." Wetherill, who had not failed to note the effect on Trent's temper of his assumption of Fairman's guilt, added lazily, "I should have smiled, I think, if I could have foreseen that Fairman was going to shoot him for me."

Trent disregarded the thrust. "You are being very frank about it. That means, I suppose, that your own position is quite secure—I mean, that you can give a satisfactory account of the way you spent your time on the evening Randolph was murdered?"

Wetherill raised his hands. "What language you pick up, dear friend, from that Scotland Yard set! 'Give a satisfactory account...' Soon you will be telling me that I am not obliged to make any statement, but that anything I may say... and the rest of the jargon. You know, you would look rather well in a dark blue helmet, Trent; it would go with your eyes, and lend just that little needed touch of austerity to your expression. Well,

I will tell you. I stayed a few minutes only at the club here after our meeting; then I returned to my rooms to work until daybreak. I was having a fearful struggle—indeed, it continues still—with the last act of my *Crucifixion of Aphrodite.* No," Wetherill continued musingly, "I did not kill Randolph; but if I had really felt that there lay any advantage for me in doing so, how perfect might I not have made the crime? The criminal, you will say, always makes a mistake—a senseless catchword, surely. It is those who are detected, and only they, who make mistakes. As well say that a meteor is always visible, although space is known to be swarming with lightless bodies. If with my imagination I can create a world of my own, could I not devise an insoluble criminal problem? But pardon me; this is soliloquy. My dear Trent, I have answered your questions; you have evaded my one question to you. I will put another, a grossly practical one. Do you happen to have heard anything about the terms of Randolph's will?"

Trent, who was far from being impressed by Wetherill's conversational fopperies, could not help being taken aback by the direct simplicity of this inquiry; nor could he guess what might lie behind it. He was disagreeably reminded, moreover, that the direct and simple question which he himself had come there to ask of Wetherill had not yet been put to him, and that his shameless allusion to his relations with Eunice Faviell had made it more than ever difficult to turn to him for that information. He answered, then, with equal plainness, "I understand that he died intestate."

"He did!" Wetherill sat up with the first manifestation of unaffected interest that he had yet given. "Dear friend, are you sure of what you say?" He stared at Trent with an evidently genuine anxiety.

"There isn't any doubt about it. He was just about to make a will when he was killed, but he never did so. That is what his lawyers say. But what has it got to do with you, Wetherill? Did you hope that he admired you to the extent of putting you down for a substantial legacy? Or did you think you had wormed your way into his affections by threatening to shoot him?"

Wetherill, his eyes half closed in deep consideration, only waved a hand vaguely, and for a few moments was silent. At last he said, "Forgive me, dear friend. I was obliged to arrange my ideas on hearing what you tell me. It is good news to me; not a disappointment by any means, but an unexpected piece of good fortune. On the strength of it, I have just made up my mind to a very serious step. I am going to marry Eunice; and you, if you will, shall be the first to congratulate her."

Astonishment and disgust went near to overcoming Trent's resolve to keep his temper. He drew a deep breath, then said, "I haven't the least idea what all this means."

Wetherill, still thoughtful, fingered his moustache. "No, I suppose you haven't," he replied coolly. "But when I say that, dear friend, don't imagine that I look upon you as a fool. On the contrary, you have the very uncommon talent of being able to defeat my utmost efforts to infuriate you. No: you could not know what all this means. But you can make your mind easy about the main thing. I really am going to marry Eunice."

"I don't believe it," Trent said bluntly. "You are assuming too much. She has had nothing to do with you for some time, I know. All her friends believe she has done with you for good and all," he added somewhat inexactly; then, looking Wetherill candidly in the eyes, "How she could ever bring herself to associate with such a ruffian as you are is quite incomprehensible to me."

Wetherill turned to polishing his eyeglass once more. "Naturally," he said. "You do not understand women, dear friend. That is a commonplace remark, I know; the sort of thing one alderman might say to another alderman. But it is true of you, just as it would incontestably be true of the other alderman. Perhaps you are to be envied your ignorance; who can say? As for my being a ruffian—do you know, dear friend,

I rather like your choice of an epithet? So many men, and so many women, have done their best to find searing names for me; but none of them ever hit upon anything at all apt and significant. Really, the subject is an interesting one. When I am likened to one of the lower animals, or to some inferior social type, by some dolt whose neck I could break with one hand, I naturally am not impressed; and I always have the feeling, too, that my denouncer is not satisfied with his own efforts. But I wander from the point. Forgive me again, dear friend; with you I become loquacious. You were speaking of Eunice having done with me. You misconceive the situation—deliberately, perhaps. It was I who had done with Eunice. Now, however, I intend to marry her—make her an honest woman, as the saying is. You cannot disapprove of that."

"You think not?" Trent asked. "I assure you, I have disapproved of much less revolting brutalities of yours. If I believed what you say was possible, I should not only disapprove of it; I should do my best to prevent it. But I don't believe it."

Wetherill smilingly waved his doubts aside. "Well, dear friend, you shall see, and you may do your best. This evening I shall write to her." tie eyed Trent through his glass with an air of gentle amusement. "She shall receive my wholly honourable proposal at your own house."

Trent was startled out of his self-command. "What the devil do you mean by that?" he exclaimed, thrusting back his chair.

"Yes, at your house," Wetherill drawled, flicking a trace of cigarette-ash from his sleeve. "I had a letter from her this morning, dated from Didbury Manor House, which is your property, I think."

Trent stared at him in silence as he took in this breath-taking statement. He knew enough of Wetherill's ways to understand that he was speaking the truth. He knew that his wife, now staying at the Manor House, was a devoted friend of Eunice Faviell. But he had heard nothing from her of this visit; and he felt, not for the first time, that he was getting the worst of an interview that was entirely of his own seeking. But at least the sole object of it was attained. Without asking, he had learned where Eunice was to be found.

"She was writing to me about—shall I say, a matter of business?" Wetherill went on, as if helpfully anxious to end an awkward pause in the conversation. "A disagreeable letter, too, I confess. But that has happened before; I disregard it; her heart will triumph before long, as it always does. By the way, her letter was concerned with our lamented Randolph—so much I may tell you. That also, I see, takes you aback; it is a day of little surprises for you, dear friend. How very visibly you react to such emotions—quite like the French poet, who likened his heart, you remember, to a suspended lute. '*Aussitôt qu'on y touche, il résonne.*' You don't think, do you," he went on musingly, "that Eunice herself murdered that old man? You seem determined to believe that the obvious man didn't. She can be very pettish, as we both know. That way she has of flying out at you suddenly—it is among the first of her charms. You recollect how Faust felt when Margaret snapped his nose off at their first meeting.

> *Wie sie kurz angebunden* war,
> *Das ist nun zum Entzücken gar!*

There have been moments when she would have liked to kill me, I am sure."

What Wetherill had said of Trent's difficulty in hiding his emotions was, as he knew, true enough. He had turned white, and felt chilled to the heart, as this suggestion was airily put forward. But it was in a tone of hard contempt that he said, "If you are so fond of *Faust*, let me remind you of what he said to the Witch in her kitchen—'You talk like a chorus of a hundred thousand idiots.' Nobody but an imbecile could imagine that

Eunice Faviell had anything to do with Randolph's death; and I'll do you the justice to assume that you don't seriously think so yourself. For one thing, she had no reason whatever to desire his death."

Wetherill put his fingertips together and leaned back in his chair, as if prepared for some intellectual diversion. "Well, perhaps we should distinguish. To desire a person's death is one thing; to be glad to hear of a person's death is, no doubt, not quite the same. I happen to know that Eunice must have been glad to hear of Randolph's."

"Why?" Trent felt, and sounded, explosive.

"Because, dear friend, his death made her a very rich woman." Wetherill gazed pleasantly out of the window, as if the chimneypots on the other side of Down Street made the loveliest of prospects.

Trent felt as if his senses were leaving him at this last mad turn of the conversation. He put a hand to his forehead, and asked weakly, "Would you mind explaining?"

"Not in the least," Wetherill said affably. "It is not a secret—at least, it soon will cease to be. Eunice Faviell is old James Randolph's niece, the daughter of his only sister with whom he quarrelled who knows how many years ago? I have it on the best authority—Randolph's own. He told me on the occasion of our last meeting, the time when I lightened his plethoric purse as I have mentioned already. He said he had discovered that Eunice was his next-of-kin, and that by his will she would inherit the greater part of his fortune."

Trent thrust his hands into his pockets and laughed long and heartily. "Is this the last of your revelations?" he inquired. "Not that it matters, really. I think I have lost the capacity to be surprised any more; my sense of the marvelous is completely worn out. Tell me that you have just been admitted to holy orders. Tell me that the president of the Jockey Club is a Chinaman. Tell me I've got a tail. Nothing can astonish me now. But there is one thing I should like to hear. I can still feel curiosity. If he had been keeping this fact about Eunice Faviell dark, what was it that led him to confide in you?"

Wetherill shook his head sadly. "I fear he told me in order to make himself unpleasant to me. I mentioned to you that he had done so, I think."

"Still," Trent remarked, "I can imagine simpler ways of hurting your feelings than telling you somebody else was his niece. And as for the money, I don't suppose you positively object to the idea of her having it." He was talking somewhat at random, while he tried privately to read a meaning into this amazing news and what had gone before it.

Did Eunice know of this? If she knew, how long had she known? Did it account for the mysterious rendezvous at Porter's? Was it the decent explanation of the affectionate interest in her which the old man had shown, and which she, not knowing the truth, had treated as the objectionable advances of an elderly amorist? But as for Wetherill, if he had believed for a week past that Eunice was to be Randolph's heir, why had he waited so long after Randolph's death before making up his mind to marry Randolph's money? And why, again, why had Wetherill been told by Randolph, who could not have been expecting to die, and so make Eunice "a rich woman," for years to come?

Wetherill was prepared, however, to help him out of this last difficulty. His peculiar taste for publishing his own iniquities was strong in him.

"I will tell you," he said after a brief pause, "why Randolph chose to confide in me, as you express it. You may find it an interesting story. You see, the transaction between us was the selling to him of a book of mine, an unpublished work of which he had heard, no doubt, when making his inquiries about Eunice."

A light broke over Trent's mind. "I see," he said slowly. "You mean the book you wrote so as to blackmail Eunice. That savoury part of the story is pretty well known."

"Very likely," Wetherill said. "But don't be misled into disparaging *The Broken Wing*, dear friend. It is a masterpiece, in some ways the finest piece of work I have ever done, a possession for ever. When Eunice had read it, she was good enough to pay me as much as she could to have it suppressed; but if she had given me a million, it would have been monstrous in me to deprive the world permanently of such a work of art."

"But you took her money."

"Dear friend, I had to have money. Genius must live, you will allow; and to live in any tolerable sense of the word, it must have luxury. In any case, it is bound by the rules of its own nature, and by no others. And it is thanks to me, remember, that Eunice's own genius has unfolded itself."

"Your other reasons for taking her money don't surprise me at all," Trent said. "I have heard that sort of cackle pretty often, and sometimes from people who really were artists. But I can't pass that last one. Eunice Faviell was what she was, and is, long before she was unfortunate enough to meet you, or acted in any of your plays."

Wetherill's dignity was unruffled. "Eunice knows, if others affect not to know, what she owes to me. That is why she gave me all that she could scrape together. All the same, it was foolish of her, I allow, to wish to have *The Broken Wing* suppressed. By that romance I have given her immortality; not as she would have it, perhaps, but in the figures of a woman, a great artist, struggling pitifully against a destroying and remorseless love, and against the advance of the years. It is a study—"

Trent cut him short. "I can't stand more than a certain amount of that sort of thing. We will take it as said, if you don't mind. The question is where Randolph came into the matter."

"Why," Wetherill explained with agreeable candour, "he came in, most fortunately, just about the time when all the money from Eunice was spent. He had heard about the book. He sent for me, and offered to buy it from me. At the time

I had no idea of his real motive, for Eunice's name was not mentioned by either of us. He named a quite considerable sum that he was ready to pay for the copyright. I named a larger one; we came to an agreement; and later in the day I returned to his house with the manuscript, and made over my rights to him in a document which he had ready. In my innocence I thought that he desired the credit of giving the work to the world on his own responsibility; and a lot of money in hand was of more importance to me just then than the prospect of royalties. You can understand that, I am sure."

"Perfectly. But I am still waiting to hear why he told you about Eunice's relationship to him."

"You shall hear, dear friend. When he had got the manuscript and the agreement, and when the money had been handed over to me, he informed me politely that he did not mean to publish the book, but to keep it for his own purposes. It was then that I allowed myself to lose my temper. I lashed him with words in a way that I very seldom do. He smiled, and appeared to be highly pleased. I threatened to kill him; he seemed even more delighted. Then he told me, as if it were the most natural thing in the world, that he had discovered Eunice Faviell to be his nearest living relative, and that most of his money would go to her at his death.

"I was surprised, as you may imagine, by this introduction of a name which neither of us had pronounced until that moment. I said, however, with perfect truth, that I was charmed to hear this news. How should I not be? I told myself that nothing could suit me better than to have Eunice for my own in the character of an heiress on such a scale, and with a millionaire to look to, in the meantime, for maintenance in conditions suitable to that character. I promised myself that I would take steps to bring us together again without delay."

"Yes; I can quite see all that," Trent said with ready sympathy. "Quite a glimpse of paradise for you—sponging for the rest of your life on a woman with money who is an incurable fool about you."

Wetherill held up a hand as if in gentle reproof. "These are words," he returned mildly. "Do not forget, dear friend, what I said about the necessities of genius. Let me resume. He had informed me that Eunice was his next-of-kin and destined heiress. I was dwelling in imagination on the agreeable prospect so disclosed. And then what did that wicked old man—that prodigy of coarse and bat-eyed prejudice—proceed to say?"

"I wonder."

"He said that he intended to put an end to all connection between Eunice and myself. He said this with plain and undisguised enjoyment, as if he were savouring some delightful essence. I was—I admit it—struck dumb with amazement and indignation; and he went on to make his meaning clear. He said that by the terms of his will Eunice would inherit nothing whatever, and that she would get nothing from him during his lifetime, unless she promised now to break off all relations with me immediately, and kept strictly to that undertaking for the future."

Wetherill paused, as if to let all the baseness of this atrocity sink in.

"And from his way of putting it," he went on, "I was led to assume that his will was already made, and there was an end of my hopes. And so there would have been, if he had lived long enough to carry out his monstrous intentions. The black-hearted old scoundrel! After leading me up to the very height of Pisgah! Well, I have my share of philosophy. When I left him, I put the idea of Eunice completely out of my mind. After all, I had extracted from him a sum large enough to meet my wants for some considerable time, and I was by so much the better off. And now, today, dear friend, imagine my feelings—the sudden glow of renewed and established happiness—when you told me that Randolph had died intestate after all!" He spread his hands abroad with a superb gesture.

"I see! I see!" Trent exclaimed hilariously. "That was why you sat up so abruptly when you heard the glad news. As you say, I can imagine your feelings. Eunice gets the lot, you grab Eunice, and love leads the rebel discords up the sacred mount. Lord! It's enough to make a cat laugh!" He exploded in a shout of mirth that caused many in the room to turn round inquisitively in their chairs.

"Your imitation of a cat is not a flattering one," Wetherill said. He had turned suddenly pale, and his voice was a little unsteady. "May I know what amuses you?"

Trent rose to his feet and turned to go. "Why, you ass! Randolph's only son has turned up, complete with proofs of his identity. Eunice Faviell will never get a farthing."

15

EUNICE MAKES A CLEAN BREAST OF IT

Trent had discovered the Cotswold country as a very young man, newly land-conscious, when it had appealed to him with an irresistible compulsion. There are some places which, seen for the first time, yet seem to strike a chord of recollection. "I have been here before," we think to ourselves, "and this is one of my true homes." It is no mystery for those philosophers who hold that all which we shall see, with all which we have seen and are seeing, exists already in an eternal now; that all those places are home to us which in the pattern of our life are twisting, in past, present and future, tendrils of remembrance round our heart-strings.

Trent, in his travels, had often chanced upon a house, a town or a stretch of country, unknown to him in terms of normal experience, which claimed him as its own with unerring certainty. As it had once been on a magic day in Tuscany, driving up to Montalcino, so with that counterscarp of the Cotswolds overlooking the vale of Evesham. So he had set his heart on a long, grey, stone-tiled house, flanked by shaped yews, which stood on a terrace cut in the brow of the steep hill, with woods and fields and villages stretching away below to the barrier of the Malvern Hills, and a glimpse of the Welsh mountains beyond.

Along the ridge of the hill ran a Roman road—Old Campden Lane, the people called it—lonely between the low stone walls that bounded the fields. So broad it was that a dozen four-horse chariots might have been driven abreast along it; and in summer it was thigh-deep with flowers and feathery grasses. The highest point was crowned by a cluster of tall beeches, a landmark known far and wide as Cromwell's Clump, from which, said legend, Cromwell had watched and directed a battle in the plain below, but Oliver was a modern interloper among the warlike spirits haunting the spot. For the beeches edged the rampart of a Roman camp; and that had been raised on the foundations of some far more ancient native stronghold.

What a man desires whole-heartedly enough, it is said, he will surely attain. Not long after Trent's marriage, the house that he coveted fell to his lot with the smoothness of destiny; for it fell vacant and was put up for sale at a time when he was prosperous enough to become its owner.

On the day following his interview with Eugene Wetherill, Trent drove swiftly across the bare wolds until the country broke away before him, and the road plunged headlong down past a wood of lofty trees. A sharp left-hand turn brought him into the drive of the Manor House, and he steered his car into the garage among the farm buildings.

As he closed the garage doors a small figure dashed down the few steps from the terrace before the house, and then, checking itself, paced gravely towards him. It was a small, round-eyed boy of about six years old, arrayed in a bead-bedizened red shirt and a bristling fillet of feathers, his cheeks and forehead barred with streaks of what Trent divined to be lipstick, his left hand grasping a wooden hatchet.

"How!" said this apparition, raising the right hand in a solemn gesture.

"I beg your pardon," Trent said blankly.

"How!" The child repeated; adding by way of explanation, "Stamping Bull great chief!"

"Oh ah! Yes, of course," Trent answered, calling on his memories. He raised his own hand. "How! The pale-face from the regions of the morning gives greeting to Stamping Bull and all his tribe."

"That's better," said the great chief, with an ear-embracing grin. "Stamping Bull glad to see pale-face. Pale-face just in time for lunch—bear's paw, buffalo-hump. Stamping Bull heap hungry!"

"Can Stamping Bull tell me," Trent asked, "if the pale-face squaw is—er—among his people?"

"Laughing Tortoise in the wigwam," replied the chief with dignity. " 'Nother pale-face squaw too—name Spring Cabbage, came last week, heap lovely." Here the noble savage changed the conversation abruptly. "Stamping Bull heap cruel, love kill, love scalp!" He screeched, and rushed off up the steps brandishing his tomahawk, while Trent followed at a slower pace.

Another voice, the voice of Eunice Faviell, hailed him from the edge of the terrace. "Philip," she called, I'm here incognita and I don't know you. Go away.

Trent looked up into the small, vivacious face, now twisted in the exaggeration of a scowl. "Is this gratitude?" he asked. "Is it justice? I fight a lady's battles for her, play Perseus to her Andromeda, and all the thanks I get is that she forbids me my own house, and tries to look like Medusa."

"What do you mean, Phil?" There was a catch of anxiety in her voice now that did not sound like joking. "Perseus—didn't he kill the dragon that was worrying Andromeda?"

"That's it—teasing her unmercifully. But you must not take my Perseus literally any more than your own Andromeda. After all, you were not chained to a rock with nothing on, waiting to be eaten—at least, if you were, your press agent has been neglecting his work. All I did was to draw the dragon's teeth, clip his claws, unbarb his tail, and domesticate him generally—

and then he was quite unnecessarily slain. Dragons, you know, are never just killed; always slain. Just as Douglases are always doughty, and paynims are always false."

"Don't talk nonsense, Phil; it isn't any good. I am frightened, I tell you."

Eunice Faviell was a creature of instinct who, in life, fell as naturally into the parts ordained for her as into those she played in the theatre. She was far from belonging to the country by taste or habit, yet here she had the air of being country born and bred. The tweeds she wore, with a burning spot of orange at the throat, made her somewhat a part of the landscape; her thrilling voice was tuned to the peace of the hills and woods. For all the distress and disquiet that showed in her face, she looked younger than art could make her look in town. When Mabel Trent appeared, dragged forcibly out of the house by Stamping Bull to join them, her dark and regular beauty gave much more of the effect of metropolitan life than was suggested by the woman who seldom entered into any other frame of existence. Trent's eye rejoiced a moment in the picture made by the two vivid and contrasted personalities in their setting of the grey house behind, the dark green of the yews on either side; then he mounted the steps to be with them, and embraced his wife as one clinging to her for protection.

"Mabel," he said, "you at least will not drive me away as if I were a verminous leper loitering with intent to commit a felony. What is this person doing here? She has been telling me to get to hell out of this, or words to that effect, though anyone can see that I am dying of hunger and thirst. Stamping Bull: will you kindly tell the women in the wigwam that the pale-face would like a fire-water and soda, as he is feeling rather like a wounded buffalo, after his long journey over the trackless prairie."

"Yes, Bull," his mother said. "Tell Maggie to bring it to your father out here."

"Fire-water for my great white father," repeated the chief; and dashed into the house with a yell.

"Why didn't you let me know you were coming, Phil?" Mabel Trent said. "Luckily you are just in time for lunch; and you won't be starved, because Eunice has eaten hardly anything since she came. You need feeding, too; you are looking thinner." She traced two lines of inanition on his cheeks with a slim forefinger. "You have been worrying, or overworking—"

"Or painting the town red," Eunice suggested. "Those are the lines of reckless dissipation, my girl, not the results of pining away because he is separated from you, as you are trying to suggest."

"They're the same thing," Trent explained. "When I attempt from love's sickness to fly, the first thing I do is to hurl myself into an ocean of drink and debauchery, of course. And if it comes to why-didn't-yous, why didn't you warn me that you had an actress in the house?"

"Because she wouldn't let me. She rang up last week saying she wanted to get away from everybody and everything, and would I give her a roof over her head? So I said I should like nothing better; and when she came she made me vow I would say nothing about her being here, not even to you. So I thought if she was slightly mad, it would be safest to humour her; especially as it didn't matter in the slightest to you or anybody else."

At this point a sturdy and smiling parlourmaid emerged with Trent's refreshment, announcing that luncheon would be served in a few minutes; and Eunice, remarking that it was time she became tactful, disappeared into the house.

Mabel looked after her with a troubled eye. "You know, my dear, I'm afraid it's something serious. I've known Eunice most of my life, and I've never seen her in such a state as she was when she came down last Friday, looking worried and scared and worn out. I have done what I could for her, and she seems much better, but you can see for yourself there is something wrong. I haven't asked her what it is, but she would have told me by this time if she was going to. And it is rather alarming when she insists on nobody being told she is here, not even you. Perhaps it is a good thing you didn't say you were coming—she might have rushed off to avoid meeting you. I can't understand it. Do you think you can induce her to say anything?"

"I mean to have a good try," Trent said. "I've come here on purpose to do that. And I'm glad you did as she asked about not telling me. She has had a bad shock of some sort, evidently, and raising objections would have made her worse."

"I knew you would say so. It's just what I felt myself."

Trent saw to it, with the able assistance of his little son, that luncheon should not be a too serious affair.

"When I saw you last," he said to his wife, "our child was going through a stage of being an animal—any sort of animal, so long as it was fierce. He was a fierce chimpanzee when I saw you off in the train, and he had been a fierce antelope just before that. Now, I gather, he is a Choctaw."

"Not Choctaw—Pottawattamie," the chief corrected him with some asperity. "Choctaw no good, heap chickenheart, eat snake. Ugh!"

"You can thank Eunice for all that," Mabel said. "As if he and his little friends were not savages enough already, she has taught him to be the complete redskin. She has dressed him, and painted him, and made him what he calls a bonnet of chicken-feathers, and taught him an entirely new language—including strange names for everybody in the house. She is packed with information on the subject."

"It is about the only thing I ever learnt properly at school," Eunice said, "and I always had a good memory."

"We both went through it at school," Mabel said. "Only all of us wanted to be braves, of course, and as I was one of the smallest girls I had to be a squaw, and I didn't take so much interest, I suppose."

"Your heart wasn't in it; you were born civilized. It all comes of having a French grandfather," Eunice said. "You have finished your coffee, Phil, haven't you? Do you mind if I borrow him for a time, Mabel? I want to talk to him about my troubles."

As they made their way to a seat above the house looking out over the plain, Eunice said, "I meant that; I do want to talk about my troubles. Now that you are here, and we have got into the old atmosphere, it seems idiotic that I should ever have thought of keeping them from you, or keeping out of your way. I really wasn't quite in my right senses last week; that's the only excuse. Let us just sit here and take in the peacefulness of it for a little; then you can start by asking me questions, if you don't mind."

"Well, why did you disappear like this?" Trent said at length. "You don't like people interesting themselves in your affairs as a rule—I seem to remember you hinted something of the sort to me in a note a week ago—but when you actually ask me to pry into them, I hope it is because I may be of some good. We are delighted to have you here on any terms—I needn't tell you that—but I can't cure myself of wanting to be helpful where you are concerned."

"I know that," she said, looking into the distance. "You are not the inquisitive kind, and I don't believe you care a damn how I behave myself. Nor does Mabel; only she wouldn't call it a damn. I suppose that is really the reason why I am here—I don't mean her not swearing, but not caring. There is nobody else I should have dreamed of planting myself on like this—nobody except Judith, that is; and she is abroad."

"That is almost the definition of any friendship that is worth while—that we don't care a damn how you behave yourself. Not that you have tested us very severely."

"Well," she said, "I will tell you. I wanted to get away out of sight if I could. I was afraid. If only Judith had been in England, I should have gone to her, and she would have told me what to do. But there was Mabel."

"There was me too," Trent observed. "In other words, there was I also; and in London—within your very grasp, as it were."

"Yes, I know; but you were mixed up in the very thing I was trying to escape from. You see, it was when I saw about Randolph's death, and poor old Bryan trying to commit suicide, that I felt I couldn't face things any longer. I wanted to get away from the police."

Trent coughed dubiously. "That isn't very easy—certainly not for an amateur. If they want you, they probably won't be long in catching up with you. But why on earth should they?"

"But surely you can guess! I know Judith told you about my being pestered by letters from Randolph which I didn't understand—at least, I thought I did understand them, and I resented them much more than I do that sort of nuisance as a rule. I never answered them, and he still went on, begging me to see him, because he had something of the greatest importance to say, that it concerned my whole future—hinting that I should never know troubles and uncertainties again—it was all that sort of thing. And when a rich old man writes to a woman in my position in that sort of prose style, she knows well enough what to think. Or she thinks she does. And who wouldn't?"

"You are trying to tell me," Trent suggested, "that you got him wrong?"

"Well, you will see. I am going to make a clean breast of it. But what I was saying was that I told Judith, and Judith told you; and then she wrote that you were going to have a row with Randolph, and that you could put a stop to it. I didn't see how you could; and anyhow I objected to having that sort of thing about me passed round without my leave; and so, as usual,

I went in off the deep end, and wrote you a perfectly beastly letter. At least, I meant it to be—I don't remember what I said."

"Oh, it was. You succeeded admirably. I was raked from stem to stern. Poking my nose into what was none—"

"Don't be a cad, Phil. You know how sorry I am; don't rub it in. I always am sorry after making a pig of myself; but I was a very special pig to write like that to you. But that isn't the worst. You see, some time before that I had been writing to Bryan—one of those letters about nothing in particular that we exchange from time to time—and I said something, not seriously at all, about the old man bothering me with silly letters. It was all mixed up with a lot of other personal chatter, and I never thought about it again—until—until I heard the news about Randolph, and about Bryan too. People were saying he must have done it; I heard it everywhere. Can you imagine what I felt?"

Trent digested this information with a clouded brow; for he himself had written to Fairman about that same "bothering." He could indeed imagine how Eunice felt; imagine, too, how much worse she would feel if she could know that their friend had confessed to the murder. But that could be told to no one without breach of a confidence that he had always been very careful to respect. Even if it were otherwise, what would be the good of turning Eunice's fears to certainty?—for so she would inevitably take it.

"You understand, don't you?" she said miserably. "If Bryan did it, it may have been all my fault. Of course I know it would be idiotic to go off and kill a person for a thing like that; but all the same, it is the sort of thing that would make Bryan perfectly furious, and I was an utter fool ever to have mentioned it to him. That is why I was frightened. That is why I dreaded the police asking me questions. Everything I could say would have been against him. Even if I said nothing, they might have found my letter—he may have kept it."

"That's highly probable, I should say," Trent admitted with a wry smile.

"But, Phil, do you believe he did it? Tell me what you really think, whatever it is."

"All I can tell you is that I don't know what to think. That isn't just a way of speaking; I really don't. There are too many infernal complications about the case; things I can make nothing of. What I can say is that I am working on the line that Bryan is not guilty. But it is going to take me all my time to get him out of the mess, if I ever do."

Eunice clapped her hands. "What, have you turned detective again? And you hope to get him out of the mess? Bless you, my dear, you can't say fairer than that! If I know that you are working at the thing, and doing all you can for him, it makes me feel—oh, I can't tell you how much better!"

"Yes," he said, "I have relapsed. Meet Philip Trent, the celebrated werewolf, who has been a man for some years, and is now a sleuth-hound once more. But I didn't want to be. I was dragged into it."

"You mean Bryan being suspected."

"That was only one thing. Among the other things was the discovery that Miss Eunice Faviell was floating vaguely around the outskirts of the case. I found that out before you told me. In fact, that's why I am here."

She stared at him.

"I am not asking whether you murdered Randolph yourself," he reassured her, "because something in your manner tells me that you would be rather put out if I suggested such a thing. But you have been very much annoyed with him. And you were, I gather, very much annoyed with him again only a few hours before he was found shot. And besides that, there is the little matter of wealth beyond the dreams of avarice. Didn't Randolph tell you that his death would make you inordinately rich, whether he made a will or not?"

"Good heavens!" Eunice gasped. "Then you mean—but I never thought of that side at all! You mean they might get to suspecting *me?*"

"Not necessarily that; but putting you on the list of possibles. In fact, I rather think you are there already. The last time I saw the officer in charge of the case he was taking a sort of faint interest in you that I couldn't quite account for. I can see now, from other things he said, what was in his mind. I didn't know then about your being Randolph's niece, and having expectations from his death; but *he* knew, and the old badger didn't tell me. I am sure he knew."

"And you have found it out for yourself."

"No I haven't," Trent said tartly. "I never had the slightest notion of it, or of your being related to the old man. I was told all that yesterday—told by Eugene Wetherill, who knew a lot more about the whole thing than I did. For instance, he knew where you were, and was kind enough to tell me. I was quite interested to hear that."

"Devil!" Eunice murmured, as if confiding a secret to the landscape. "I mean you," she added, glancing at Trent.

"Never mind about what species I belong to," Trent said warmly. "It is no joke to get nipped in the machinery in a case of this kind, and I didn't like the idea of its happening to you, especially when I had already got Bryan and—er—other people to bother about. So if there is nothing against it, could you clear up one little point for me?"

"Of course I will if I can," she said. "I told you I was going to make a clean breast of it, you know, and I haven't really begun yet. I don't feel so much like running away from the whole beastly business, now I know you are taking a hand. What is your one little point?"

"Perhaps it is hardly worth mentioning," Trent said apologetically. "It's this. After complaining bitterly about the way Randolph was persecuting you, and blasting the poor old chap's reputation, and generally behaving like Lucrece in the clutches of Tarquin—"

"I don't know what that means," she said, "but it sounds improper."

"Well, anyhow, after kicking up all that fuss, how did it happen that you were having a cosy little tête-à-tête luncheon with him on the same day that he was murdered? You see, I am putting it in simple terms; the kind of terms it would be discussed in if the facts were to become generally known. Come on then, Eunice; how about it?"

She sighed whimsically. "Yes; this affair has certainly got you going again. So you know about that, do you?—when it was, and where it was, and what I was wearing, and how late I was for it, and what flowers there were on the table, and what the waiter's first name was, and what we had to drink—"

Trent mentioned what they had had to drink.

She nodded; then said reflectively: "When I was learning my job, acting in the sort of places you never saw in your life, the public were very fond of those plays in which heroes were heroes, and villains were villains, and comic men were comic, and people were always getting tied down on railway lines, or turned out in the snow with their babies, or melting the heart of the prison governor by saying 'I am inno-scent!' What you have just said is the cue for me to clutch you by the wrist and whisper through my clenched teeth, 'How much do you know?' I shan't do it, though, because I don't care how much you know. I want you to know the whole thing, so I may as well tell it from the start, though you evidently know a lot of it already."

"You'll tell me the whole thing," Trent emphasized.

"Cross me 'eart," Eunice said vulgarly; and told her tale.

She had first met Randolph about a year before, at a vast hotel in Scotland, to which she had taken Miss Yates as her guest for a brief visit. He had appeared a short time after their arrival; they had fallen into conversation with him, and he had done his not very successful best to make himself agreeable. Eunice had been struck by the fact that he made no reference at all to her work in the theatre—"though every one knew who I was, of course," she said simply. Once he had mentioned that a portrait of him was to be painted, and had asked her if there was any artist whom she believed in for that sort of work. He said she must often have had her own portrait painted; which was the nearest he ever went to making a complimentary speech. Eunice told him that the right man for him was Philip Trent. "I tried," she said, "to give him the impression that you were a most extraordinary genius, whose work would be fought for by collectors for ages to come. I heard afterwards that you had landed the job; but I was too much of a lady to ask you for the usual ten per cent." Soon afterwards they had left the hotel, and Eunice had seen no more of him.

It was soon after this that unpleasant things had begun to happen to her professionally. Something seemed to have happened to her prestige—"with the accent on the press." An important group of papers did not hide their disappointment with her work in one new play; of another they had nothing good to say. Faintly malicious paragraphs in gossip columns reached her from the press-cutting bureau; it was hinted that her reputation was being somewhat severely strained.

"You don't know," she said to Trent, "what a difference that kind of thing makes to anyone who is before the public. It is like something poisonous in the air. I told myself it wasn't going to kill me; it couldn't really shake my position, even, so long as it wasn't widespread. I knew I was as good as I had ever been, and I knew the public knew it. But I hated it like sin all the same. And just when it was beginning to worry me, I found I had to provide a considerable sum of money. It wasn't anything to do with the theatre; simply a private affair. It was utterly unexpected and very painful, and there was no getting out of it—not if I was ever to hold up my head again. But it's no use talking to you about it, because you don't know, and I can't explain."

Trent did, on the contrary, know very well, but he had no desire at all to discuss the matter of Wetherill's infamous book, and the blackmailing use he had made of it. If Eunice, in her innocence, believed that transaction to be a secret from all the world, so much the better. So he merely said, "All right; go ahead. You were saying you had to find a sum of money."

"It took everything I had," she said, "and as much as I could raise. That hit me pretty hard; but I got it done and over, and there was an American tour being fixed up for me that would have pulled things straight again. Then that fell through. I really began to feel as if the gods had got a grudge against me. Still, I have always been able to earn my living, and soon I was on my feet again with the name part in Northmour's play. It was just then that I began to receive those letters from Randolph that I was telling you about. I suppose the reason why they upset me so much was just because, from what I had seen of him, they seemed so utterly unnatural and out of character. I have met with a good many nasty old men in my time, and though I could imagine Randolph being a brute in all sorts of ways, I had simply never thought of him in that particular way—no more than I should of the Cobden Statue in Hampstead Road. So I got more and more wrought up, and first I let slip something about it to Bryan, like a chattering fool, and then I relieved my feelings by telling Judith all about it, and then—well, what happened then really did surprise me."

"Do you mean that Randolph flung off the mask, and revealed that he was quite respectable after all?"

"Yes, if that's all that being respectable means. I got a letter from him saying he had hoped to make everything plain in a personal interview, but I must have misunderstood his earlier letters. He said that two years before he had commissioned a firm of inquiry agents to find out whether any relations of his were alive, because he felt it was time he made up his mind what was to happen to his money, or something like that. The agents had found no trace of his son; but they had got on the trail of his only sister Caroline, and they had established the fact that she was my mother, who died when I was nineteen. He gave a few details that showed there was no doubt about it. He said his sister had left home to marry an actor named Hunt. Well, I had always known that was my father's real name; and I had known there was some sort of row about the marriage, because my mother had never let slip a single word about any of her relations in my hearing, and she would never tell me what her maiden name had been. Neither would my father, even when he wasn't sober, which was pretty often.

"Randolph's letter mentioned the place where I was born, and gave the addresses where my parents had lived since then, and—oh! There was a lot more, but what it all came to was that I was certainly the old man's niece. And that wasn't at all a pleasant surprise, I can tell you. For one thing, I hated the idea of my parents' history being nosed out like that. You see, Phil, my father had some lovable qualities, and had a splendid appearance, and was quite a good actor with a reputation of his own in the provinces; but he had serious weaknesses, and he died soon after he was forty. After that my mother kept a boarding-house in Portsmouth, and she did well enough out of that to keep us decent, and send me to a good school. But she was what they call soured, I suppose. I never saw her look happy, and though she was never unkind to me, she was not exactly a doting parent. The long and the short of it is that I was an unhappy kid, and I have always thought about my early years as little as possible. Then here came somebody I hardly knew, and didn't much like, full of information about my parentage and childhood, and proving himself to be an uncle who I didn't even know existed."

Trent, as he listened to Eunice's tale, reflected that there were not, perhaps, very many women supporting themselves in an arduous calling who would have been seriously displeased by the discovery of a millionaire uncle looking about him for someone to inherit his wealth. But Eunice, as he knew, had always been one of those who seem able to steer a more or less happy course through life without troubling themselves about money. Not that she was one of the Skimpole family of that tribe; for she was devoted to her art, was a tireless worker, and for years had enjoyed such success that she might have laid the foundations of a fortune by now if she had been so inclined. As it was, though she valued her independence as much as life itself, she had never done anything to secure it in the pecuniary sense. She was generous and careless in the extreme. Sometimes she would make the pleasing discovery that there was a respectable balance to her credit at the bank; sometimes she was deep enough in debt to have alarmed a less mercurial spirit. She trusted to luck and to her genius to make ends meet; and when they even overlapped, it was not for long.

"That was what his letter told me," she said, "and it ended by asking me to have lunch with him and talk things over on a certain day when he would be next in London—that was last Wednesday, of course; the last day of his life." She raised her shoulders in a movement of distress, and for a moment her eyes closed.

"So that is the explanation of your meeting with him," Trent said quietly. "A good deal of what I have been hearing and finding out is fitting itself together now—not all of it, unfortunately, but a lot. Do you care to tell me what happened when you saw him?"

"I want to tell you," she said. "It was the worst part of the whole business. I wrote back to him at Brinton accepting his invitation. I didn't want to, but I didn't see how I could decently do anything else. After all, it was perfectly natural he should do what he had done; it was natural he should want to see me; and I had been doing him an injustice, though I still didn't blame myself at all for that. So I accepted; and on the day, I met him as you know. He was quite frank and pleasant at the start; talked about my mother a little, and told me I was much more like my father—which I knew better than he did—and said that in his old age his being alone in the world had begun to trouble him for the first time. Then he spoke of the time when we had met in Scotland, and he confessed that he had gone to that hotel knowing I was to be there, because he wanted to see what kind of a person I was."

Trent nodded. "I rather thought that might be so," he observed. "But you say that was about a year ago. I suppose he liked the look of you then—it's usual to like the look of you. Why, I wonder, was he such a devilish long time about taking action? I should have expected him to bring the family tree to your notice without delay, after satisfying himself that you were all his fancy painted you."

Eunice's look hardened. "Well, you didn't understand my uncle, that's all," she said. "Not many men would understand him, I should think—or I should hope. You will soon see why he took his time. After speaking of that time in Scotland, he went on to asking about my career. That gave me something to talk about, which I was glad of; and I told him how I had started, and how I had got on—a regular autobiography. He took it all in, but looking a little bit grim, I thought; and then he asked me how I had been doing lately. So I told him, quite frankly, it was the worst year I had had since I qualified as a star. Then he put questions, and I told about the way the Westlake papers had been crabbing me, and how my American tour had failed to materialize for some reason; and I said I had lost a lot of money, for me, in a private venture—by which I meant that unpleasant affair I mentioned to you without telling you what it was. Randolph wanted to know about that, and I told him I preferred not to discuss it.

"And then, Phil, I got the jolt that he had been saving up for me. He said to me something like this: 'Well, my dear, you see you can't reckon on the stage as a means of support all your life. You have had a good innings, but it looks to me as if your reputation was beginning to decline, and unless you have saved money your future is uncertain, to say the least of it. But I am your near relative. I am a rich man. I wish to place you in the position in life you are entitled to, as my niece, and I propose to leave you the bulk of my estate by will. But there are conditions attached to this; and one of them is that you give up the stage, which I regard as an immoral and disreputable way of earning a living. I would rather see anyone I cared for dead at my feet than winning success in the theatre.' "

Eunice, who had put the whole of her talent into this impersonation of the dour old man, and reproduced his very accents with startling effect, now shook back her clipped hair and turned a wide smile on Trent."How did that go with you?" she asked. "It has made me feel much better, anyhow. I can't swear to the actual words, except 'immoral and disreputable way of earning a living,' and the 'dead at my feet' gag; but I swear I got the general sense of it right. And perhaps you can imagine how it got me going! I was bursting! But I didn't let myself explode. I simply said I didn't want his money, that I had got on without it before and could get on without it for the future. I said I was used to looking out for myself, and was quite ready to take my chance, and that I preferred it anyhow.

"The next minute I was very glad I hadn't let my temper get the better of me, because he turned white with rage, and if it gets to being thoroughly unpleasant I always think it's a much better arrangement if the other party starts it. He told me that I was a fool, that everybody wanted money. He said, if I had had money I should never have taken to this vagabond existence—those were his very words, my dear. So I just looked at him—like this—as if he was a bad smell, but as if I supposed he couldn't help being a bad smell. That made him madder, of course. He said I might talk about taking my chance, but that I hadn't any chance, and he could see to it that I didn't get one. He said he didn't mind telling me that it was he who had worked it so as to make the Westlake papers give me the bird, and get my American tour messed up, but that that was only the start, just to show me what a rotten game the stage was, and if I wanted any more I could have plenty."

"You are giving me, as you say, his very words," Trent suggested.

"Of course not—don't be aggravating, Phil. I'm merely putting what he said into ordinary English. He said he did not withdraw the proposal he had made me, because he meant to have his way. He said he knew it wouldn't be long before I came to him with my pride humbled, and that then I should have to agree to another condition which he hadn't mentioned yet. At that I looked snootier still, and he looked as if he was going to have a fit. He said the other condition was that I should have to break off my association with Eugene Wetherill and any other blackguards I might be mixed up with. Well, when he went as far as that, I just got up and began to put on my cloak. Then he went on that I was much too unreserved in all my relations with men, according to the reports he had received; and he had the damned insolence to mention Bryan's name."

"Oho! He mentioned Bryan, did he? That," Trent said, "sheds a bright light on another of the enigmas. I wondered what he could possibly have got against Bryan."

"He would hate any man he came across who was half-way decent," Eunice said viciously. "Now here's the last thing. He said that before I went there was just one thing more for me to bear in mind. I won't tell you what that thing was, Phil, because it is a private matter. I hadn't the ghost of a notion he knew anything about it, and hearing him speak of it nearly knocked me out. I'll just say this much: he had bought—something—from Eugene, which he had had to pay a high price for, he said; and if I drove him to making use of it, he would do so. I'm sorry I can't make it plainer. And by the way, plain wasn't the word for the language I used to Eugene when I wrote to him about it a few days ago."

"Well, all that doesn't matter," Trent said. "It was something Randolph was going to hold over you. He had a taste for that sort of thing, it appears."

"If I had had anything to hold over him just then—something hard and heavy—there would have been an end of his tastes," Eunice said. "That last threat of his was the worst thing he had said yet. Just at that moment the waiter came into the room, and I grabbed up my bag and legged it without another word. God knows what I should have said if I had opened my mouth—probably I should have been like the girls in the novels, who hear themselves saying words they didn't even know they had ever heard. Well, there you are, Phil; that is the whole story. Pretty, isn't it?" Eunice shut her eyes, stretched out her feet and dropped her arms limply, in the manner adopted by boxers in the intervals between rounds.

"And you heard nothing more from him?" Trent inquired, realising that his own breath was coming quicker under the effect of Eunice's torrent of impetuous speech.

"Not a peep—nor a line either, if you mean writing. There wasn't much time for anything, was there? When I left him, I was in such a fury I hadn't room for anything else; but when I had cooled off, I began to think about the prospect for me, and you can guess how I felt about it. When you know a man with a disposition like that is going to use all his power to smash you, it's no merry jest, believe me. I couldn't study my new part. I couldn't sleep. It was well on into the next day before I could pull myself together and get back my pluck. And then, as soon as I went out, I heard the news of Randolph having been shot. If that had been all, it would have been—well, I won't say an answer to prayer; like a reprieve when one's just going to be hanged, let's say. But what the papers had about Bryan simply shattered me, as I told you. The only thing I could think of was getting away right out of things, and trying to get my balance again."

Trent took off his hat and fanned himself with it. "You have made it so exciting," he said, "that I feel all hot and agitated. By the way, there's one thing I can tell you that comes into the story. You are not in any danger of inheriting the old man's money. His prodigal son has turned up, and as far as I can see, he will get every farthing of what is left when the Chancellor of the Exchequer has had his whack. So you, my dear, will be just where you were before the band began to play."

"Praise the Lord for that!" Eunice said with fervour. "It's all I ask." She got up and stretched her arms abroad. "Mabel and that innocent child of yours have done me more good than I thought possible; but having got that long, long story off my chest with you has really completed the good work, I believe—that, and knowing you are once more upon the war-path, as Stamping Bull would say. Now, what my vocal cords chiefly need is rest." She took his arm. "I won't say another word till I have got outside at least two cups of tea. Lead me to it."

16

THE WHISPERED WORD

A long day's work in the studio had followed upon Trent's return from Didbury, and diverted his mind from the tormenting doubts that arose at every turn in the labyrinth of the Randolph case. He had dined late, and now, after an hour with a pipe and a volume of Boswell, he sat thinking of the next move to be made in his adopted task of running down the truth that eluded him so persistently. There was little question, in fact, what that move should be. He had heard that morning that leave for him to visit Bryan Fairman in the prison infirmary at Newhaven had been granted, that Fairman wished to see him, and would probably be fit for the interview in two days' time. If his friend meant now at last to clear up the mystification brought about by his crazy-seeming avowal of guilt and subsequent dogged silence, it was idle to go on with guess-work in the meantime. The best to be done was to consider the points on which Fairman, it might be hoped, would shed some light.

It was still in the studio, the centre of his private life, that Trent was turning over these things in his mind. Outside, he knew, the weather was heavy and windless; and he was roused at length to consciousness of the fact that some slight noise, hard to account for in such conditions, had for some time been coming from the direction of the French window opening upon the garden.

He listened now with attention. This was a gentle tapping on the window-glass—a few light taps; then an interval of a quarter of a minute or more; then a few light taps again. No dog or cat could produce such sounds. A twig moved by the breeze might do it; but there was no branch close to the window, nor any breeze to stir it if there had been. Heavy rain had fallen earlier in the evening, and Trent thought of the possibility of water dripping from some gutter or cornice. But the tapping, almost certainly, had been upon the surface of the window.

The noise made itself heard again; and Trent went to the window quickly, twitched the curtains aside, unfastened and threw open the glass doors. The night was moonless, and no gleam penetrated from the lamp-lit road on the far side of the house. Outside the path of radiance shed from the open window, it was too dark in the garden even to distinguish the outline of trees against the sky. The air was heavy with the smell of wet soil. There was little fault to be found, Trent thought, with the night as a night. There was as much of nature's healing gift of darkness as could fairly be expected within the limits of St. Marylebone, and the life of the earth was to be felt stirring in the warm dampness: Only there had been that noise.

Trent, loving, as ever, the mere sound of the words, began murmuring to himself:

Deeping into that darkness peering, long I stood there wondering, fearing,

Doubting, dreaming dreams no mortal ever dared to dream before; But the silence was unbroken, and the stillness gave no token, And the only word there spoken was the whispered word...

"Guv'nor!"

The whispered word came from the black shadows under the wall to the right.

"Guv'nor," the husky voice repeated. "Can I 'ave a word with you... for Gord's sake?"

There was a pleading urgency in the whisper. Trent, deciding that he was really awake, and ready always to welcome and fall in with the unusual, answered quietly, "Who's that?"

"Are you alone, sir?"

The question was asked in a slightly improved accent; and Trent, now vaguely conscious of having heard the voice before, answered "Yes."

"You aren't one to give an unfortunate man away, sir, I'm sure."

"You'll have to leave that to me," Trent said. "You have no business to be here, you know. Who are you, and what's it all about?"

There was a rustle from the hidden bushes, and a small man came hesitantly into the lighted space on the lawn. He was dressed in a chauffeur's uniform. As he stepped forward he removed his peaked cap, and for a moment his furtive eye met Trent's.

There was a brief silence. "I know you, of course," Trent then said. "You are Raught, the late Mr Randolph's manservant; you attended to me when I was staying at Brinton. I can't think why you should want to have a word with me, but if it's important I've no objection. The police haven't brought any charge against you, I believe, but they are looking for you—I suppose you know that."

"I do indeed, sir," Raught said. "That's the only reason for my calling on you in this—this irregular sort of way, sir, which I hope you'll have the kindness to overlook it. I didn't dare risk standing in the light at the door, nor being seen by anybody in the house except yourself. I dodged in by the passage beside the house, sir, when there was nobody about in the road, and tapped on the window where I could see you between the curtains. If you please, sir, might I ask you a question or two? It's vital to me, or I wouldn't have thought of troubling you." Raught, squeezing his cap in his hands, again turned his roving glance to Trent's face.

"Why should you suppose," Trent said, "that I am able to answer questions that are vital to you? That is what I don't understand."

Raught nodded. "Course you wouldn't, sir. Well, I made up my mind before I came here that I should have to tell you all about it. Here's the first thing, sir—I know you have been visiting the house in Newbury Place, and I know the inspector in charge of the case was there at the same time. You were there for over an hour, sir. You must have been talking over the case; and if you did, you probably heard what I want to know about, sir. I'm not asking you to do anything wrong, sir; only to do a man a kindness who has had cruel bad luck, and has been treated hard for years on end, sir."

Trent, in his little personal experience of Raught, had found nothing likeable about the man, but what he had lately learned made him pretty sure that there was truth in these last words. The appeal was one of a sort hard for him to resist; moreover, the wish to find out what lay behind all this was insuppressible.

"Let my heart be still a moment, and this mystery explore," he said. "Do you know, Raught, it's astonishing how you fit into the scheme of that fine poem that I was recalling just now, when you suddenly addressed me out of the shadows as 'Guv'nor'—that one word, as if your soul in that one word you did outpour. You are even a little like a raven—more than you are like a bird of paradise, anyhow. And you thrill me, fill me with fantastic terrors never felt before. Come inside and explain them."

"Thank you kindly, sir." Raught stepped over the threshold and, glancing apprehensively at the door, took up a position by the table.

"I can't offer you a bust of Pallas to perch on," Trent said apologetically, "but there's one on the shelf there of George Robey which I did myself, and my friends tell me it's not a bad likeness. If you don't care about it, sit anywhere you like. You need not worry about anyone coming in to interrupt us at this hour. My family is ninety miles away, roughly, and the housekeeper who is looking after me is probably asleep and dreaming of Paisley. If she should happen to look in on us, I shall tell her I am thinking of engaging you as a model for my picture of Apollo being cast out of Olympus."

Raught, who had seated himself uneasily on the edge of the model-throne, half rose at this suggestion.

"No, no; stay where you are. I'll make it Ulysses relating the story of his woes to Alcinous. I'll be Alcinous; and to start with, I think, I should like to hear how you come to know so much about my recent movements."

Raught licked his lips and passed a hand over his cheeks and chin. "Well, sir, it's a little bit awkward in a way. I mean, it isn't only myself that is concerned in that part of the story. You would always act honourable, sir, I'm sure."

"I hope so, Raught."

"The fact is, sir, during our visits to London last year and since, I formed the acquaintance of the cook at No. 46, Bullingdon Street; Sir Hector Findhorn's place, that is. She is a widow, Mrs Leather by name, and an attachment sprung up, as they say, between me and her. We used to go to the pictures and that, when I had my time off, and she had altered hers to be the same as mine. Besides that, we could see something of each other at odd times easy enough, the two houses being so close. You see, sir, No. 46 is just at the corner of Newbury Place, and the windows at the back—on the upper floors, that is—look right out over it; I mean, over Mr Randolph's and the other four houses in the row. I am telling you this, sir, because you will see why when I come to it."

"I am beginning to see something already, I believe," Trent said. "The Randolph house was under observation when I went there—is that it?"

"Yes, sir—asking your pardon for the liberty. I am telling you the whole thing, like I said. It was me that saw you, when I was watching from one of the top back rooms at No. 46."

Trent gazed at the man in delighted astonishment. "When you were watching? Do you mean to say that on the morning after you disappeared from Mr Randolph's place, giving the police the slip, you were hiding in that house at the corner, almost under their noses?"

"Yes, sir. You see, sir, Sir Hector Findhorn and his family have gone abroad for some months, and they left the house to be took care of by Mrs Leather, like they have done often before, her being a thoroughly reliable person and used to looking after herself. When we came down from Yorkshire this time, I asked Mrs Leather to go out with me on the Wednesday evening, but she was not feeling well enough for it, her digestion being out of order, which she suffers from at times. So I phoned up my sister, Mrs Livings, and arranged to have a bit of dinner with her and her husband, and see a show; and that was what we did, and so I told the police when they wanted to know about where I was on the evening of the murder. Only there was one thing I didn't mention, sir."

Trent had a lively recollection of the reserve with which Mr Bligh had repeated Raught's account of his doings. "Perhaps," he suggested, lighting a cigarette, "they wouldn't be surprised to hear that."

"You're right, sir," Raught declared with feeling. "Treating a man like dirt, and trying to make him give himself away, the way they do. The only thing I kept back was something that wasn't of no consequence whatever, but they were certain to be nasty about it. What I mean is, after I left the house for the evening, a little before 6:30 it was, I went first to make a call on

Mrs Leather, to see how she was getting on; and there I stayed with her till it was time for me to be on my way, in her room that's on the top floor, looking out over Newbury Place, like I told you."

At this point Trent, who had been observing the man with close attention, caught a stealthy glance suddenly directed at his face. Raught, plainly disconcerted at catching his attentive eye, continued hurriedly.

"After that I went on to meet the Livingses in Soho, stopping for a drink at a couple of places on the way; and I told the inspector that and everything else that happened, perfectly truthful, right up to the time of me coming home and finding the body and sending for the police. I am giving you all this perfectly straight, sir, which I hope you don't doubt it."

"Well, I do rather," Trent said gently, "if you really insist on knowing. It is just an idea of mine and I may be wrong; but isn't there some other little thing that you are, as you say, keeping back—something, perhaps, that happened during that short time you were with Mrs Leather. Your manner just now gave me that impression."

The colour came into Raught's pale face, and he looked sulky. "You're taking me up wrong, sir. There was something happened then, like you say, and I was going to speak of it, I was truly. But it hadn't anything to do with my own story, and the reason for me asking you to help me with a bid of information. I wanted you to get it straight, first of all, how I come to be keeping out of the way at No. 46."

"All right, tell it that way," Trent agreed. "It's your constructive scheme, not mine. But you did give such an excellent imitation of a man wondering whether to come quite clean or not, that for a moment I was quite deceived."

Raught's air of resentment was not completely banished by this ingratiating speech, but he took up his tale.

"You see, sir, when I found Mr Randolph lying there dead it gave me such a shock as I never had before. I was too much flurried to think, and I took it for granted, like, that he had been murdered—it all looked that way, somehow. And I knew, sir, that if he had been murdered it might be very awkward for me. I don't only mean that I should be one of the parties under suspicion from the start, before any inquiries being made. There was something besides that."

"Do you mean," Trent asked, "that you wouldn't be able to account quite fully for the way you had spent your time unless you explained about your visit to Mrs Leather, and that that would put Mrs Leather in a very unpleasant position, and that even then Mrs Leather might not be very useful as an entirely unsupported witness to an alibi for you. In the circumstances, of course, she might not—one sees that. Very awkward, as you say. You two were falcons taken in a snare, condemned to do the flitting of the bat."

"No, sir, that wasn't the awkwardness I meant. All the same, it is true I never told them about my having been at No. 46 that evening, nor anything about me and Mrs Leather. Where was the good, if my telling about it wasn't going to put me in a safe position? And besides, sir—I don't deceive you—I did have the idea that No. 46 would be a useful place for me—in case I *should* want to get away and lie low for a bit. I knew I could always go there, so long as the family was away."

"Yes, I see," Trent said. "You kept that card up your sleeve. And then, on the night after the night of the murder, you played it."

"Yes, sir. I only had to get out of my room-window and over the wall at the end of the yard, into the alley that runs behind there. Then I walked down to Bullingdon Street and round to No. 46, and there I went down the basement steps and pushed the bell at the servants' entrance three times, like I always did. Mrs Leather got up and let me in, and there I have been ever since, sir, not having ventured out until tonight. She lent me their chauffeur's second-best uniform, what he left behind in his room. It alters my appearance a bit, especially the cap."

Trent laughed. "It all seems so simple. Good generalship always does. But—forgive my curiosity—why did you decide to do that, after staying at home when you had found the body, and informing the police, like a good citizen?"

Once more Raught smoothed his chin and cheeks with a nervous hand. "Why there, sir, we come to the point; I mean the reason for me calling on you tonight. You see, when I told you that Mr Randolph being murdered made it very awkward for me, I wasn't thinking of Mrs Leather and her relations with me being brought into it. There was something much more serious, I am sorry to say."

Trent pitched his cigarette into the fire. "I know there was. Now you have come to it, Raught, I'll tell you—I heard all about it from Inspector Bligh."

"You did, sir?" Raught scrambled to his feet and stood trembling. "About the—the job at the Maidstone bank?"

"They have got your signed statement. It was forwarded to the police by Mr Randolph's solicitors. They received it on the morning after your disappearance."

With a weary sigh Raught sat down again, his head bowed and his hands clasped between his knees. So he remained for a few moments; then, raising his eyes and staring straight before him, he poured out upon the memory of his late employer a muttered stream of curses and foul language that surpassed everything in Trent's fairly wide anathematical experience.

At length Raught was silent, and Trent went to the sideboard at the far end of the studio. "Have a drink," he said. "It might do your mouth good. I won't say I know how you feel, because I've never even wanted to be as eloquent as that, but if I ever had I couldn't have done anything approaching it." He handed a tumbler to Raught, who accepted it thankfully. "Cigarette, too? That's better. There's a lot of nonsense talked about swearing by people who don't really understand the subject, don't you think? I mean, you may often read about some expert keeping it up for minutes on end without repeating himself. Now you certainly did wonders, but I should say it wasn't more than thirty seconds before you ran dry, and even then you used the same word nine times."

Raught restored himself with a deep draught, and put down the tumbler beside him. "I'm very much obliged to you, sir, for this, and for not minding me forgetting myself. It is a good thing to know the worst, they say, but it did knock me out for the moment. Now you know, sir, the question I wanted to ask of you, and you have answered it before me asking it. I wanted to know if that bank job was hanging over me still; that and the confession I was forced to sign. If you could have told me nothing was known about it, I should have gone away from here a happier man than what I have been for many a day—or for years if it comes to that. I did hope it might have been mislaid or destroyed, or that it was among the missing papers took out of the safe. Well, I might have known the old... might have known Mr Randolph better.

"You see what I meant, sir, when I said the murder might make it very awkward for me. If that paper I signed was to fall into the hands of the police, it would fix suspicion on me quite definite as a dangerous character, with a grudge against the old man for making me sign it. And they would be sure to think I had gone to the safe hoping to find the confession there, and that I had somehow made away with the lot of them when I didn't find it. And as you say yourself, sir, I hadn't got an alibi that would hold water. So I made up my mind the one thing I could do to make things worse would be to run off and try to disappear after finding the body. And I thought if I informed the police at once and told them a straight story it would look best for me, and I should maybe get off with a prosecution for that old job at Maidstone."

Trent nodded appreciatively. "You put that very well. And you know, it's remarkable what mind-readers the police are—that is exactly what Chief-Inspector Bligh thought you thought."

"Blast him!" Raught said savagely.

"And he thought that when you found next day that you were not being seriously suspected, and that another person had been arrested, you decided to have a try at disappearing, and to risk whether your confession of the Maidstone job turned up or not, because your running off would make no difference in the case of a crime that you had confessed to."

Raught scowled bitterly. "Well, he got me right. And there's just where it is, sir. You see what it means to me, their having got that statement of mine. It means that even if they don't get their hands on me I shall have to go on hiding and dodging, and trying to change my appearance; and wherever I may get to, no chance of any sort of job but the lowest of the low, being without a character. That's what I have got to face, sir. Well, there it is." He got to his feet slowly.

"I am sorry for you," Trent said in all sincerity. "I am sorry for everyone who has put himself within reach of the criminal law; in fact, I have been sorry before now for men who had a good deal more against them than you seem to have, and who had had a more bearable time of it than you."

"Well, sir," Raught said, "you didn't make the law—I know that; and me going wrong at the start wasn't none of your doing. You have treated me decent, too, like I thought you would; more decent than many a man would have done. Now, sir, there's one thing more."

"You mean the thing that happened while you were looking in on Mrs Leather. It must be something worth mentioning, I suppose."

"You can tell that, sir, when you hear it. All I ask is, if you do anything about it, you won't bring me in. I have put myself in your hands, sir, trusting to you to act honourable."

"All right."

"Well, sir, it was like this. When I went to see Mrs Leather, immediately after leaving Mr Randolph's, I stayed a little over half an hour. We heard it strike seven at St. Chad's, and a few minutes after that I said to her I would have to go. We were in that top room, like I told you. It was dark outside, of course, and as I got up to leave I happened to glance down through the window, and I saw somebody at the door of No. 5. It was a gentleman just going in the door. I only saw him for a moment, sir, against the light coming from inside the passage; then the door shut, and that was all I saw. But that I did see, sir, as plain as what I see you now. I didn't think nothing about it then, because I knew Mr Randolph would sometimes have people to see him when I was not on the premises. I just went downstairs and out by the basement entrance in Bullingdon Street. And that's all about it, sir."

As he listened to this brief recital, Trent felt the excitement of his quest thrilling every nerve and muscle, and it was with an effort that he spoke now in his usual tone.

"That was at a few minutes past seven. And you say it was a gentleman you saw. Why do you call him a gentleman? Because of the way he was dressed?"

"Yes, sir; partly that, and partly the way he carried himself. He looked—well, I don't know, sir. He looked class, as they say."

"I know what you mean; but damn it! You say you only saw him for a moment. And if he was just going in at the door, he would have had his back to you, I suppose. Could you see him by some light from the street as well as the light from inside?"

"There's the lamp at the entrance to Newbury Place, the far end of it, sir. But I couldn't hardly have told what he looked like at all, not by that. I just saw the outline of him, quite plain, in the open doorway, as he stepped in. He was in evening dress, sir, with a top hat and dark overcoat, and I could see the top of a white muffler above his coat."

"And nothing of his face at all, then?"

"No, sir."

"Well, what else did you notice about him? Was he tall and thin, or short and fat? Was he knock-kneed, or humpbacked, or bat-eared, or anything else that would give a touch of character to his rear elevation?"

"Not short, sir, I should say. That's about all I can say, seeing him only for a second."

"Hm! Portrait of a gentleman. Unmeasured in height, undistinguished in form, his breath it was lightning, his voice it was storm. As for his hair and complexion, he may have been a nigger for all we know. If one could have that little face of his painted upon a background of pale gold, such as the Tuscan's early art prefers, how much trouble it would save. By the way, what about Mr Randolph? Did you see anything of him on this occasion?"

"No, sir; but anyone letting a person in by that door could easy not be seen. The entrance is that narrow, you remember, sir, he would have to stand back against the wall, almost behind the door, to let a visitor pass in. I've done it so often, sir; I know."

For a few moments Trent digested this information in silence; then asked, "Was this man carrying a bag?"

"That I'm sure he wasn't, sir. Anything of any size, if he was carrying it, I should have seen, with him standing out against the light that way. I should say he hadn't anything in his hands at all, sir."

"Three ringing cheers!" Trent exclaimed. "This gets better and better. Evening dress, not short, no face and no bag! In a few deft strokes we have the man before us. Anything else you can remember? What about his tall hat, for instance? Was it a shiny one, or was it one of the collapsible sort?"

"That I couldn't say, sir. All I saw of him was just a glimpse, like, before the door shut."

Trent considered again. "The door shut. It would, of course. But not of its own accord, surely. Did the gentleman shut it, or did somebody else?"

"I couldn't see that, sir; it all happened so quick. But you remind me of one thing, sir—the door was shut very quiet."

"Then did it shut with a slam, as a rule?"

"Well, sir, anyone letting himself out would have to slam it—it shuts, a bit hard that way. But from inside you could shut it quite quiet if you liked. And speaking of being quiet, sir; that reminds me of something else, which I remember I passed a remark about it to Mrs Leather at the time. We had the window open at the top, the room being very warm from the stove; and we thought it was funny that neither of us had heard this gentleman's footsteps going up to No. 5. Being so close, we should be able to hear anyone walking on the flagstones in Newbury Place, without it was a cat or dog."

Raught took up his cap, and moved to the open window. "I won't keep you up any longer, sir. It's time I was on my way."

"You have certainly given me enough to think about," Trent said. "By the way, Raught, before you go, I should like to know one thing. Perhaps you are the only person who can tell me, as you were the late Mr Randolph's valet."

"What's that, sir?"

"Had he always used the same make of safety razor?"

"No, sir. Most of the time I was with him he used an Oswego razor, an old one with the plating rather worn. Then he took to using a Bok, a more up-to-date make, sir."

"And that was not very long ago?"

"Only a few weeks, sir. How did you know?"

"I didn't know; I only hoped." Trent laughed shortly and unpleasantly. "A safety razor can be a dangerous thing. Speaking of that, Raught, I think you said the police would have you listed now as a dangerous character. Are you a dangerous character?"

For the first time Raught looked him directly in the face, and his expression hardened. "I might be, for them as interferes with me. I don't mean to be took, not if I can help it. As for you, sir, you have treated me right, and I thank you. Goodnight, sir."

He went out into the shadows.

17

FINE BODY OF MEN

Raught, as he made his way homewards to his place of refuge at the corner of Newbury Place, was in a dangerous temper. Always an unstable character, he had lived of late through days of desperate anxiety, a crushing culmination to the years of ceaseless chafing and smothered hatred in Randolph's service. With lack of occupation, self-pity had wholly taken possession of him, encouraged as it was by the affection of the woman who had befriended him. He knew now that what he had dreaded had happened in fact; that the old man's malevolence, even after death, had denounced him for the Maidstone crime of long ago. As he went through the half darkness of the lamp-lit streets, deserted almost entirely at this hour, he brooded over his hard luck. What chance had he ever been given? Raught, for that matter, like many another in cases like his, was far from grasping fully how bad his luck had been, how little the chance that life had offered. Neglect and harshness had marked him in infancy; there had been nothing at any time to tell against the effect of them. But in all of the past that he remembered and could understand there had been more than enough to be stored up as matter for savage resentment, for the soul-sick criminal's conviction that he owes the world no more than such repayment as he can make in its own coin.

The small figure, for all its scowling brow, moved with an assumed jauntiness of carriage. Raught knew well enough that he must not have the appearance of a hunted man; he was living up as he best could to the chauffeur's uniform that clothed him. He was a skilled man in a good job, a man with a character and prospects; he was nobody's football. It was well done, and the one or two policemen whom he passed had no more than a glance for him.

Even less reason, it seemed, was there to look for any trouble from the solitary person to be seen as Raught turned up the long westward side of Purbeck Square. The tall man who was approaching him from the other end of the line of solid Georgian houses was, to any experienced eye, a slightly intoxicated gentleman. His clothes and bearing, the just perceptible deviation from the straight line in his walk, the occasional pause to gaze attentively at nothing in particular, could easily be made out in the lamplight. They told their own story; and it was one with which Raught had no fault to find. He was less afraid of gentlemen than of most other kinds of men; for instinct told him that, however detestable a gentleman's personal character might be, he was usually not inclined to be censorious or even inquisitive about the conduct of his fellow-creatures. As for the condition in which this particular gentleman was, Raught made the natural assumption that, in what was evidently an early stage of it, tipsiness would conduce to an amiability that was even more to be approved than indifference.

But in this assumption Raught was ill-advised. There are some natures which are too complex to conform to any recognized standard of behaviour; which are, in other words, unpleasant natures. This was eminently true of the person whom Raught was now able to recognize as they approached each other, both coming under the white beams of a street lamp. It was Eugene Wetherill, on his way home from a private place of resort where gambling was the principal attraction, and champagne figured as a popular sub-motive. Wetherill had done, for once in a way, pretty well at both sources of entertainment. He was in merry mood; and it was among his peculiarities, when in that mood, to be disposed to make himself a nuisance. He was far from being fighting drunk—a state in which he sometimes was, and in which he was never less than a violent and dangerous brute; but he was feeling mischievous.

The recognition was mutual. On the two recent occasions when Wetherill had been admitted by Raught to the little establishment in Newbury Place, each had so far fallen in with prevalent public feeling as to dislike the other at sight. The second time, when Raught had dropped the visitor's hat in taking it from him, Wetherill had cursed him peevishly, and had been silently cursed in return in language much less printable. Now, as Raught was about to pass him by with a studiously blank expression, Wetherill suddenly shot out an arm and gripped the little man's shoulder.

"Well, well! See who's here!" He crowed. "Murdered millionaire's damned ugly-looking devil of a manservant, disappeared in highly s'picious cir'mstances. Where you going to, my pretty maid? You know you're wanted by police? Damn queer taste to want you I must say; but police always had rotten taste—famous for it. Fine body of men, admiration and envy of civilized world, but as for their taste—simply 'plorable, no other word for it! Mind you, goes to my heart to say this, but fact must be faced—simply 'plorable."

Raught tried vainly to shake off the vigorous grasp. "You leave me alone," he growled. "Let go of my shoulder, blast you! I don't know you, and I don't know what you're talking about."

"Says he doesn't know me," Wetherill lamented, shaking his head in sorrowful reproof. "Cutting me in the street, openly and ost'ashously. Modelling yourself on Beau Brummel—I know you! Tell your 'stinguished friends at White's—met that damn feller Wetherill—I looked all round him, and there was an end of him. Stuck up, that's what you are—just because you disappear in highly s'picious cir'mstances, and wanted by police. All right—not going to force my society on anybody." He suddenly raised his voice to a loud shout. "Police can have you... Police!"

"You let me go, or you'll be sorry," Raught muttered, pouring out a stream of obscenity as he struggled to wrench himself free. The man was now blind with rage and quite reckless.

"Police!" roared Wetherill again.

"Have it then!" Raught darted his right hand to a breast pocket, and thrust the nose of an automatic against his tormentor's epigastrium. There was a dull report, and Wetherill, with a deep cough, dropped to the pavement and lay still.

Instantly a whistle was blown from the end of the square, at the corner from which Raught had come.

"Go on! Blow your—flute!" Raught screamed. He kicked the body viciously. "You won't bring him back!" He fired a wild shot towards the uniformed figure that was now to be seen coming up at a run, and took to his heels in the opposite direction.

Half-way down Lapworth Street, turning at a right angle out of Purbeck Square, the black cat in residence at No. 38 was sitting upon the steps, submitting with dignified condescension to being tickled behind the ears by Constable Mavor. Such attention to any small animal was automatic with that officer. What was really occupying his mind at the moment was his chance of being included in the divisional first eleven at the opening of the season. The time had come for it, he thought; he had given his proofs. If they had any sense they ought to play him for his bowling alone, good enough as he was all round; and this, as he was happily conscious, was not merely his own idea, but an opinion widely held even among his seniors.

But Constable Mavor had another and yet more serious interest in life—the desire for advancement in his career. It was never far from his thoughts. He had devoted his capable and alert intelligence to those studies of police technique and the operation of the law which were a part of the routine of the force; and he had notions of his own. When his chance came, he would, he believed, be fully prepared for it.

All this side of Mayor's nature was startled into tense activity by a distant shout, "Police!" from round the corner in Purbeck Square. The black cat, from whose ears his hand had been withdrawn as abruptly as if they were red-hot, stared after him with cool disdain as he departed at a brisk, athletic trot, pulling out his watch and noting the time as he went. Mavor was ready for business.

There was another shout, and then a sound that opened Mavor's eyes more wide, and brought a new light into them. It was that flat report for which American experts in homicide have coined the expressive word "Ker-bap!"; and it was followed immediately by the deep buzzing chord of a police whistle. As Mavor quickened his pace, he pressed his helmet firmly down on his head, shifted the strap slightly on his chin to get the maximum tension, and drew his baton.

Another shot sounded; and then round the corner from the square, now some twenty yards away, a small man came pelting straight towards him. As the fugitive raised his hand with a menacing yell, Mavor could see the glint of lamplight on the automatic. Instantly he ducked his head, "covering up" with his helmet and arms, and charged like a bull at a gate. A moment before the impact, there came a shattering pang in his left shoulder and the clap of the pistol deafened him; then Raught was down, fighting like a maniac to throw off the weight of Mavor's thirteen stone, and to free the right arm to whose wrist Mavor was clinging with the only hand he now could use.

All was over in the space of a few seconds. Before the first policeman could reach the scene of the wild-cat scramble, and while windows and doors were being flung open all the length of the street, the rising tumult of shouts and screams was cloven by a fourth report.

Helmetless, breathless, white from the pain of his broken bone, and with blood running into his eyes from a cut on the forehead, Constable Mavor rose on his knees and looked down at the ugly sight before him.

"—the—!" He panted, while his right hand pressed his wounded shoulder. "He's done himself in after all!"

18

INFORMATION RECEIVED

When Raught had taken his leave after the secret interview in Trent's studio, it was already midnight; and for more than an hour afterwards Trent had sat smoking and gazing into the fire as his mind played vehemently with the new train of ideas called into being by the story to which he had listened. The fire was nearly cold when he knocked out the last pipe and went to his bedroom. Sleep, when it came at last, was broken and unrefreshing; but a clear view and a testing purpose had already begun to shape themselves after so much fumbling in the dark.

It was late in the following morning when, at work in his studio, he was called to the telephone and heard, to his surprise, the clear voice of Verney inquiring for him.

"I rang you up," Verney said, "about something I am sure you would like to hear, and besides that, you are the only person I can think of who might be able to do something about it. It's about Dr Fairman. I know you are a friend of his. It is a rather long story for telling over the phone. Can I see you about it sometime today?"

"Yes, of course." Trent thought swiftly a few moments. "I think you told me you spend most of your time at the Randolph Institute. If you are going to be there this evening, how would it suit you if I were to call there somewhere about six o'clock. I've never seen the place, you know, and I should like to if I may. I can't make it earlier, because I shall be working here as long as the light lasts."

"That will be just the thing," Verney said heartily. "It is just about then that we begin to get busy, and you will get some idea of what the Institute means to this part of the world. You know where it is—Marigold Street; anyone in the neighbourhood can tell you the way. I shall be about the place, and shall be delighted to see you."

"Right. I'll be there."

It was a few minutes past six that evening that Trent, driving his car, invaded the territory of the Randolph Institute. He pulled up and asked his way of an aged loafer who was buttressing the wall of a public house. The man painstakingly removed a battered pipe from his mouth, spat ritually, and made a jab with this thumb over his right shoulder.

"First to the right, second to the left. You'll see the lights, and hear them damned boys a-playing ball."

He replaced his pipe and turned again to his Atlantean task with a finality that dried up any further inquiries on the tongue of Trent, who felt curious to know how any boys, whatever their spiritual state, could be playing ball in those narrow and crowded streets.

The answer came to him as soon as he had reached the second to the left. There was a blaze of light from the top of a high building. Its flat roof was covered by a vast wire cage, brilliantly illuminated, and the thuds of footballs, kicked violently against walls, mingled with short bursts of applause, told that several games of "fug soccer" were proceeding at once in the upper air of London.

The entrance of the building was as easily to be seen. A powerful arc-lamp cast a pool of light round a large doorway, by which four or five youths were at the moment passing in. Trent left his car by the curb and followed them into a tile-paved lobby from which half a dozen doors opened, with a stairway ascending from the opposite end. Addressing himself to a wiry-looking youth who was regarding him inquisitively, Trent asked if he knew where Verney could be found.

"Upstairs, I expect," was the answer. "I'll find him for you if you wait here. Any name?"

Trent confessed to having a name, and mentioned what it was. The helpful youth fled up the stairs and left the visitor standing in the centre of the lobby, savouring the faint aroma of the place, which seemed to be compounded of soft-soap, coconut-fibre, leather and other elements less readily identifiable—a not displeasing, indeed a confidence-inspiring smell, as Trent thought.

At one side of the lobby, some distance from him, a wall lamp shed its beams upon a green baize board, and before it a small group of youths stood examining notices displayed.

"Somebody left his ticker lying about," one of them announced. "Found in the upstairs changing-room, it says here. Any claimants?"

"Does it say a platinum bracelet wrist-watch, jeweled in forty-nine holes?" another asked with affected anxiety. "I couldn't think what I'd done with it. I was up there last night."

"Funny ass!" the first youth remarked dispassionately. "It can't be much good, anyway, or you'd have pinched it. Hullo! Here's Ginger. Wiry ain't you murdering mice at South Kensington, Ginger, this fine evening? Lost your interest in science? Or has the supply of pore dumb animals run out?"

"I wish some of you could be dumb animals for a change," rejoined a tall youth with rebellious red hair and spectacles, who had just joined the group. "Lord knows I can't afford to waste time, with my biology final coming on in a fortnight, but it's the library committee this evening."

"Liar!" another youth said. "The library committee's tomorrow, like it always has been."

"My God!" the spectacled one exclaimed. "I thought today was Friday." He swore fervently, and there was a burst of hearty merriment from his sympathizing friends.

"You'll forget your name's Ginger next," one of them said.

"You ain't a professor yet, you know, Ginger," another said. "When you are, it will be all right to do that absent-minded stuff—like the old bloke who buttered his newspaper and read his toast."

"Ginger's drunk, I believe," another said.

"Drunk with the blood of pore dumb animals," amended the youth who had already raised this humanitarian point.

"All right; you can laugh!" the young man called Ginger grumbled. He grinned drily himself; and Trent, listening unobtrusively to the conversation, could realize something of the amiability in Ginger which his companions were recognizing in their peculiar way. "Talk about me being absent-minded!" he pursued, scratching his nose with a large notebook, "A pithed frog has got more mind that you have among the lot of you. And look here! If this is Thursday, why isn't young Peters out in the streets in his underwear, doing his seven and a half miles with the rest of the circus, instead of playing upsy-daisy all by himself?"

"Hark at him!" said young Peters, who, dressed in shorts and a sweater, and with one leg held out straight in front of him, was going repeatedly and rapidly through the motions of sitting on an imaginary stool and rising from it. "Wednesday's the day for the grind now, you old fathead, and has been for the last month," he went on, without a pause in his invigorating exercise. "Getting out of touch—that's what you are, Ginger. You ought to give the rabbits a rest oftener than what you do, and come here and give us something to laugh at." He changed to the other leg.

"Your wind seems to be all right, that's one thing," Ginger observed. "If you're as good at sucking as you are at blowing, I might get you a job as an air-pump in the physics lab." Here the conversation was broken off as Verney appeared running down the stairway from the upper regions, and was greeted cordially by all the group.

"I hope you haven't been waiting long," he said to Trent. "Hullo, Ginger! We don't often see you here nowadays. Trent, let me make you acquainted with Ginger Stimpson, the best goalkeeper we have ever had—now a man of science. Come along, we'll go up to my office—it's on the first floor." He led the way up the lino-covered stairs to a big reading-room, having at one end of it a bar-like counter presided over by an elderly woman engaged in darning a sock. Here a number of youths were sitting round the long table occupied with papers and magazines, and enjoying refreshments among which cocoa had a popular place. From overhead came faintly the noise of ping-pong, mingled with stampings and thuddings that told of some more robust forms of exercise—boxing and gymnastics, as Trent could guess.

Verney opened a door half-way down the reading-room, disclosing a small room of strictly utilitarian aspect, with a roll-top desk, a plain table and a filing-cabinet of green-painted metal for its principal furniture. As they entered, a tall and lean old man with a neat white beard and gold-rimmed spectacles rose alertly from the table, where he had been busy with a ruler and a fountain pen.

"This is Mr Bowes, who is kind enough to take a lot of the work of this place off my shoulders," Verney said. "This is the friend I told you about, Bowes—Mr Trent."

The expression of Mr Bowes's pink face was open and generous. "Pleased to meet you," he said, shaking hands vigorously. "It was you who were to have done a portrait of the governor for us, I believe. A terrible business that, sir—terrible.

I was out of town when it happened, and heard nothing about it until I saw the headlines in the paper. I never had such a shock. I came back to London at once—not that I could do anything or be of any use; but you know how it is. I take a great interest in the Randolph Institute, and I wanted to hear what was likely to happen about that, and to talk the thing over with our friend Verney. I did hope that the inquest would throw some light on the mystery of the murder; but it was adjourned—I suppose you saw that—as soon as they had taken the doctor's evidence, which didn't tell you any more than was in the papers at first."

"It is what usually happens," Trent said, "when the police are still busy with their inquiries."

"So I am told," Mr Bowes said. "Well, we don't know what it is going to mean for us here, if it is true that Randolph left no will, as Verney believes. But the Lord will provide; that is what I always say. Anyhow, we carry on, sir, even in the shadow of death. I am busy with the scheme for the boxing tournament, Verney; it ought to have been ready sooner. You were quite right about my needing a holiday, my dear boy; I am feeling twice the man I was; but it has got me a little behindhand with some of the jobs. I will get on with it in the library, and stick it up before I go. I know you two have something private to talk about."

"Thanks very much, Bowes," Verney said, as the old gentleman gathered his papers together and went out. "That is one of the Institute's best friends," Verney went on. "A wealthy man, retired from business, and unmarried, who devotes himself to church work and practical philanthropy. He has been kindness itself to me personally, too. Bowes is a man with few friends, in spite of his having a heart of gold, and I think this is about the only social life he has. He spends half his time here, and I don't know what I should do without him." He motioned Trent to the bentwood armchair just vacated by Mr Bowes, and, gently expelling a curled-up black kitten from the one which stood before the desk, took it himself.

"You are a cat-lover?" hazarded Trent as he seated himself.

"Not in a general way," Verney said. "I haven't got a horror of cats, as some people are said to have; but I would rather have their room than their company if I had any choice in the matter. It makes all the difference, though, when a black kitten walks into your room and makes itself at home, as this one did about a week ago. Some good luck is what I need just now, by way of a change." He handed over a box of cigarettes. "Please help yourself, and excuse me if I don't join you. That one I had at your place was my only smoke in two years or thereabouts, and in any case I should never smoke here. It's a habit that doesn't do boys any good—they always overdo it. I know I used to."

"You are quite right." Trent took and lighted a cigarette. "If any of them see me at it, you can always tell them I am a broken-down debauchee with one foot in the grave, and that it all began with smoking."

Verney smiled grimly. "You don't look the part, I'm afraid. Well, I suppose I need not worry about such things now—perhaps that is what you're thinking too. I shall very likely not be here much longer. Just how long I don't know. There are a few friends of the Institute, men of means, who have got together and guaranteed the expenses for some time ahead. Dear old Bowes was the leading spirit in that. It is generally believed that some person or persons will turn up claiming to be next-of-kin—may have turned up already, for all I know; and we hope that whoever does ultimately inherit Randolph's money will decide to keep the place going. But the future is absolutely uncertain. We can but wait and see.

"And now about your friend, Dr Fairman. The position really is amazing. To begin with, we know he was arrested on the day after the murder and charged with attempting suicide; and as the newspapers have published the fact that he had lost his job at the Randolph Hospital, it is generally assumed that he is suspected of the murder as well. Now that is simply incredible to me. I don't know him intimately, and you do; but I have had a good deal to do with him when I was attending to the Randolph Hospital's affairs, and I cannot believe this. I should put him down as a man of principle and rather unusually strong character, the last in the world to have any hand in such a crime. Why he was discharged from his position at the hospital I haven't the least idea, but if the suggestion is that it made a murderer of a man like Fairman, I should say it was absolute nonsense."

"I agree with you entirely," Trent said. "For my part, I am quite convinced that he is innocent. Perhaps you have heard, too, that he has had a bad break-down, and is in the prison infirmary."

"No, I hadn't heard that. I am very sorry to hear it now. We shall learn a lot more, no doubt, when he is well enough to be taken into court." Verney paused, as if inviting more information from one evidently better posted than himself; but Trent decided to leave the subject of Fairman's proceedings there. At all times he had been scrupulously careful to avoid the least breach of confidence in his friendly relations with Mr Bligh and other officers of the law. Fairman's confession, he knew, was still a well-kept official secret, and that was equally true of other details of the crime beyond the bare statement which had been given out at the outset.

"Well, it will take a lot to persuade me that he did it," Verney said at length. "However, that is not the point I wanted to tell you about. It's this. Two days after Randolph was murdered, and before anyone knew that Fairman was the man who had been arrested, I had a letter from Dr Dallow, who is the medical superintendent of the hospital. He knew me, of course, as the old man's personal representative in dealing with the hospital's business; and he began by saying how deeply shocked he and all the staff had been when they heard of the crime. Then he went on to say something that didn't surprise me, because I knew it had been in the wind for some time. He said he had been given to understand that if the position of the hospital should ever become difficult for any reason—I suppose he meant Randolph's dying, and some trouble arising about his estate—the West Riding County Council were prepared to take over the entire responsibility of the hospital just as it stood, including himself and the rest of the staff, and run it themselves as a part of their own mental service, if that could be arranged."

"I see," Trent said thoughtfully. "The county had been getting the advantage of a perfectly good institution for nothing, and the council had no objection to taking it over as a going concern. I dare say it is doing indispensable work."

"So it is, and of a very special kind—this is the point. Well, that is what Dallow had been told, and what I had heard unofficially myself. But what he went on to say did surprise me. He asked if I was in touch with Dr Fairman, or knew where he could be found. When he wrote this, remember, he didn't know that Fairman had been arrested. He said that Fairman's leaving the staff had been due to a most regrettable misunderstanding, which he was only too anxious to set right without delay if it was possible. Fairman had been doing invaluable work, he said, and if he could' be prevailed upon to come back upon the old footing everybody would be delighted, and no one more so than mine very truly Maxwell Dallow. That was his letter. I must say I was astonished. Wouldn't you have been?"

"I should. I am," Trent said. "One can't help wondering what lies behind it. You don't deprive yourself of the services of a man like Bryan Fairman without having very good reasons indeed. If there had been a misunderstanding, I should say that yours very truly, Maxwell Dallow, ought to be bally well ashamed of himself."

He paused, reflecting that that probably was Dr Dallow's own feeling, if the joint surmises of Mr Bligh and himself were at all well-founded. To have done an act of injustice in submission to a threat could not be agreeable to any man's self-esteem. If Randolph's sudden death had meant, for Dallow, liberation from a secret yoke, and if he had at once set about trying to undo what had been forced upon him, there was at least some merit in that; for to restore Fairman would be to humiliate himself.

"If Dallow really means that—" he began.

"Oh, he means it," Verney said. "His letter could leave no one in any doubt about that. I have quoted it from memory, but I have got it at my rooms, and you can see it if you like; so can Fairman. And it is right enough, too, about the future position of the hospital. The council intend to save it, if it needs saving; the medical officer has told me that, privately but quite definitely, more than once, and Dallow probably got it from the chairman, Sir Norman Connors, who is an old friend of his. No; if Fairman gets out of this trouble he is in now, without any reflection on his character, it looks as if it will be open to him to go back to the job if he chooses. Dallow is evidently ready to eat humble pie if required. But I shouldn't think Fairman is the sort of ass to demand written apologies and all the rest of it. The work he was doing on the invasion of the brain by toxins was all he seemed to care about, and if he is able to get back to it with all the honours, I should think he would."

"So should I," Trent said. "I will see that he hears all this as soon as may be. Getting him out of the hole he is in at present may not be so easy, but I have hopes of that too."

"How on earth he got into it what puzzles me. The whole thing looks—" Here Verney checked himself, and began playing with a pen on the desk.

"You were going to say," Trent suggested.

"Why, I was going to say"—Verney spoke reluctantly—"it looked perfectly mad. That is just a phrase, of course; but it does happen to fit in with a possibility that has occurred to me. Isn't it conceivable that Fairman may have gone out of his mind, and that he did, after all, murder Randolph when he was not responsible for his actions? Much as I hate the idea, I cannot help thinking there may be something in it; and what you told me just now about his having had some sort of a collapse seems rather to bear it out."

Trent rose to his feet. "Yes; as you say, it is conceivable. In fact, I don't mind saying that I conceived it myself at quite an early stage of the affair. Probably a lot of people have done the same. Still, it is not much use speculating about that, is it? We shall get at the facts in due course. And now, before I go, I must congratulate you on the work you are doing in this place. It must have simply changed the face of life for most of these young fellows, I should think."

A shade came over Verney's face. "The man who deserves to be congratulated is the man who made it possible," he said, "and James Randolph is gone beyond the reach of our-goodwill."

Trent drummed lightly with his fingers on the window-pane. "You know, Verney," he said, looking out on the dismal street below, "this business is telling on you to much. One can see it in your face. It must have been ghastly for you, of course, but you mustn't let it get you down. Look here"—he turned to face the other—"I have a suggestion to make. I remember you saying you enjoyed a round of golf from time to time; in fact, you spoke of it like a true devotee. If you really do feel that way about the game, I believe a little of it is just the treatment for you. How about a match with me at Molesworth one afternoon—next Monday, say? I could drive you down, and we could have lunch at the club."

Verney's eyes had lighted up unmistakably at the proposal. "I can't think," he said, "of anything I should like better. I know Molesworth of old, though it is long since I played there." He caught Trent's inquiring eye, and added a little awkwardly,

"I used to be a good deal better off than I am now, you see; I have played on a good many famous courses, and I know what good golf is. Molesworth! I should say the fifth at Molesworth is one of the finest holes I know. It is like a combination of the Gadget's Hough at Strathinver with the seventeenth at Kempshill. There's the double-twisted stream that you want to carry with your second, and then there's the narrow green with the road bunker in the face of it, and all sorts of horrors behind it."

Trent laughed aloud. "I can see I have bitten off rather more than I can chew. What handicap do you confess to?"

"Five."

"Then I shall want—let's see—three strokes. And Monday afternoon will suit you?"

"Yes; but," Verney said, "I can't go down there to lunch, I'm sorry to say. The morning will be a pretty busy one, and I expect I shall not be able to get away before two o'clock. How would it do if I run down in my own ancient car, and join you there as early as I can? I should get some food from the canteen here while I'm working—I often do."

"No, no," Trent said. "We will go together. I'll have lunch early, and call for you here about two. That right? Very well then; I'll be on my way."

Trent, as he descended the stairway to the now deserted lobby, was busy with thoughts. His glance fell on the green notice-board, and he went to inspect it more closely. There was a schedule of weekly committee meetings. There were intimations of articles lost and articles found. There was a list of the fixtures of the Institute's Soccer team. There was a plan of the route of the Athletic Club's weekly long-distance run—a beautifully neat piece of work, with the names of streets and landmarks done in red ink; the work, Trent felt sure, as he studied it, of the excellent Mr Bowes. There were some advertisements of Saturday motor-coach tours, with the football ground of a famous club as the objective in each case. There were two announcements from places of worship in the neighbourhood, giving the subjects with which their respective pastors proposed to deal in addressing their congregations during the present and the following months; and Trent noted with interest that while the one list led off sternly with the question "What Do We Mean by a Sacrament?" the other began by asking, with tenderly reproachful irony, "Only a Bob Each Way?" The draw for the boxing tournament had not yet made its appearance.

When he left the building, Trent found another and a larger car standing at the roadside, and a pleasant-faced chauffeur, with hands behind him, closely examining his own.

"Nice little car, sir," the man said, as Trent made to open the door.

"You know this make?" Trent asked. "You are a better judge than I am."

"I had one, an older model, to look after two years ago," the chauffeur said, evidently relieved at the prospect of a little conversation. "There's no better value in the trade, to my way of thinking. If they have a fault—" Here the chauffeur became immersed in technicalities, until Trent, expressing his substantial agreement on the points raised, offered him a cigarette.

"You don't know if my boss is ready to go—Mr Bowes, that is?" the man asked. "Thank you, sir; I'll risk it."

"You know Mr Verney, I expect, if you are here often," Trent said as he lighted the chauffeur's cigarette and his own. "What sort of a car has he got?"

"A Ludford Comet," the chauffeur said. "She's old, but she's a nice-looking bus still, and got plenty of work in her, makes very little noise if she ain't shoved, good acceleration—" The catalogue of details ended with, "Mr Verney told me what he gave for her, second hand, and I told him he had a bargain."

"You seem to know all about the car."

"I did ought to," the chauffeur said. "I have been looking after it for more than a year. It's kept in our garage, where there is space for two big cars, and Mr Bowes has only got the one. Mr Verney has regularly got on the right side of the boss, both of them being as keen as what they are about this here place. I don't say they ain't right to be, mind you. I only wish I'd had any of them advantages in Bermondsey, when I was a young chap. When Mr Verney got his car, the boss insisted on his keeping it at our place, and he didn't say no, which you might say it would be wicked waste if he had done, the space being going begging, and him living quite near at hand in Purvis Crescent. Besides, it's a pleasure to do anything for a gentleman like him."

"Where does Mr Bowes live, then?" Trent asked. "It's a queer thing about this part of London, that a well-to-do district joins on to a district like this so suddenly as it does."

"That's right, it does," the chauffeur said. "Our place, which Silkwood is the name of the house, is less than a minute's run up the main road, corner of Pilbeam Road. Mr Bowes comes here nearly every day of his life, all but a fortnight in Torquay now and again."

"You have been there lately, haven't you?" Trent asked. "I don't know it myself, but I know a lot of people make a habit of going there."

"We only came back a week ago," the chauffeur said. "No, it ain't so bad. Give me Margate for a blow of sea air; Torquay makes me feel like I was in Kew Gardens of a Whit Monday. But anything for a change, I say. You can't help liking the boss, but the life here is a bit one-sided. Might as well be a goldfish in a bowl, almost. He couldn't take more interest in these lads, not if they were all his own sons. If we don't come here, we go to a football or cricket match when the Randolph team is playing; or if it's the day for one of these here steeplechases through London that Mr Verney is so keen about, the boss will sit at his window at home and watch them a-trotting past. There'd be a bit more variety, if I had my way. But there! It's a good job, and you can't have everything, can you?"

"It doesn't seem to have damaged your health or happiness, anyway," Trent said as he took his seat in his own car, and started the engine.

"Yes, I'm still up and about," the chauffeur grinned. "Goodnight, sir."

As the chauffeur had estimated, it was less than a minute later that Trent checked his car and drove slowly past the house Silkwood. This pleasing, even poetic, name turned out to be attached to a large, glum-looking, early-Victorian double-fronted mansion, its frowning portico approached by a flight of stone steps, and a cockatoo in a gilded cage gravely surveying the busy traffic of the Willesley Road from one of the front windows. In an earlier day, it could be guessed, Silkwood had afforded accommodation for a large family and a commensurate domestic establishment. The fact that it was now the residence of one unmarried old gentleman of a retiring nature was, Trent thought, among those facts with which the foreign student of English character and customs is doomed to wrestle in vain.

The entrance to the garage was round the corner in Pilbeam Road, a smaller and much more quiet thoroughfare, with the wall of a row of tennis courts running along its opposite side. Turning into this backwater of the traffic stream, Trent stopped his car and made a brief reconnaissance. The garage, converted from its use as coach-house and stable for some Thackerayan business magnate, was entered by a high wooden double door; and one leaf of this being at the moment left open, it could be seen that it gave inwards upon a small paved yard. At the other end of the yard was the garage itself, also open-doored, clean, dry and, as the chauffeur had said, spacious enough.

In the farther corner of it stood a car—a smaller car than Mr Bowes's—a car that Trent sincerely wished could be endowed with the power of speech divinely conferred on Balaam's donkey, or the horse of Patroclus.

But if the car was dumb, the garage and its situation had plenty to say for themselves; fully as much, indeed, as Trent had dared to hope.

When Trent pulled up, a little later, before the vast red pile of the Woburn Hotel, it was nearly half-past seven. He was. told at the reception office that no one of the name of Randolph was staying in the place; but when, recollecting himself, he inquired for Mr J. B. Waters, of Salisbury, he found that he was fortunate. Mr Waters was still staying at the hotel; he had, as it chanced, come in some ten minutes before, and was probably in his room.

James Randolph, when he came down with Trent's card in his hand, did not appear displeased with life, but he owned to being a little tired of his own company, and immediately suggested that anything Trent wished to talk to him about could be more comfortably discussed over a drink in the lounge. "It was lucky," he remarked when he had given his order to the waiter, "you thought of asking for me by the name of Waters. I have used it for so many years now that it's hard for me to remember what my right name is; but even if I had done, I should not have put up here as James Randolph. The news would have been all over the place in a minute, and I shouldn't have had any peace till the papers had got the whole story. I don't want to be bothered more than I can help, and it will all come out soon enough, when my application comes before the Court. I suppose I can speak to you in confidence, Mr Trent, as the inspector said. You are here about something connected with the police inquiries, I take it."

"Connected with them—yes," Trent said. "I am busy on a line of inquiry which I don't believe the police have been giving attention to. But it has got to the point now where I am going to put all my results, such as they are, before Inspector Bligh. In fact, my intention is to put it in writing and post it to him tonight; only I wanted to see you first if I could find you."

Randolph looked at him warily. "I'll be hanged if I see where I come in," he observed.

"You don't come in if you would rather not; but if you decline, Mr Randolph, it is going to make it much more difficult to prove what I believe to be the truth about your father's death. I have a plan in my head which I should like to lay before you. It depends entirely on your co-operation."

"You can have that, and welcome," Randolph said; adding cautiously, "That's to say, if the plan seems to me as good as it seems to you. It's not my way to go into anything blindfold, you know; but I suppose you wouldn't suggest that."

"No, of course not," Trent said. "My idea is to put all my cards on the table, Mr Randolph, and to tell you, first, everything I have discovered, and next, the method we can try for getting proof of what I am convinced is the truth. Then, if you think I am wrong, or if you don't like my proposal, you have only to say so."

"Well, you can't say fairer than that," Randolph admitted. "I'm not the sort of chap that can't say no, if he feels that way. Tell you what, Mr Trent; this looks like being a yarn that will take some time, and besides that, we might as well be quite sure we are not overheard. How about having a bit of dinner with me here—it's none too early for me, I can tell you—and afterwards we can go into the matter in my room? I have driven up to Cambridge and back today, to look into a business there which I have some idea of taking over, and I am as sharp-set as I ever expect to be in my life. I hope you're the same. What do you say?"

Trent, who felt himself confirmed in his first instinctive liking for Randolph's very direct and unornamented personality, said yes, and said it with cordiality. They found a table for themselves in the large, fully-populated dining-room. Trent had never yet tested the reputation the hotel possessed, in a quiet way, for cookery of the more substantial sort; and he now found it to be very well deserved. James Randolph declared his conviction that, when you were hungry, there was nothing to touch the right kind of beefsteak done in the right way; and he mentioned the details of rightness with an assurance that told of careful thought as well as experience. He spoke highly too of boiled cabbage with a dash of vinegar. Trent, who since his schooldays had indulged a prejudice against precisely these two articles of diet, declared in favour of saddle of mutton; but he joined his host with enthusiasm in drinking what Randolph described as the best beer he had ever found in London.

"This beer reminds me," Trent said, "of all that the poets have ever said about beer. It is more than you might think, Mr Randolph. You may not care about poetry; I like it myself. This stuff makes me think of what one of them calls it—'that mild, luxurious, and artful beverage, beer.' "

"It isn't only the beer; it's the way it's looked after," Randolph answered thoughtfully. "As for poetry, you are quite right, it isn't much in my line; but any poet that understands beer is a poet I can understand—anyhow, when he's on that subject. I am going to be a rich man now, by what I can see of it; but I don't reckon I shall ever give up beer till it gives up me. Some chaps have to knock it off, you know, in their old age; I only hope I shan't be one of them."

"When you say you are going to be a rich man," Trent hazarded, "you mean that there isn't any difficulty about your claim to your father's estate."

"Nought to speak of," Randolph answered. "Muirhead & Soames say they have ought to have old Mrs Waters's evidence about my identity, and she is laid up with a sprained ankle, so they can't get it till she is able to travel. But they treat me as if it was all settled. They know there isn't a will, you see. The old man made it quite plain to them, before his death, that there wasn't one, and never had been one, and that he was for the first time in his life thinking about making one. In fact, he even told them the name of the person who would probably come in for most of the money. It would surprise you to hear who it was, if I was at liberty to tell you."

"I don't think it would, really," Trent said. "You see, your father told her himself, just before his death."

"Did he, by gum?" exclaimed Randolph.

"Yes; and she told me, only two days ago. I know her very well. In fact, I thought it was right for me, as a friend, to advise her that she had nothing to expect as a result of your father's death, because the idea of her being his nearest living relative was not correct."

James Randolph shot a queer glance at his guest, the while he helped himself prodigally to toasted cheese. "So that was your advice to her," he remarked after a slight pause. "Well, we were going to keep private matters for our talk upstairs, now I come to think of it." He turned the conversation back to the subject of food, mentioning the curious substances that many people nowadays preferred to eat. One of his best mechanics, he said, a man who earned good money, insisted on having a pound of tinned salmon for his evening meal every day of his life.

Trent wanted to know if this epicure had ever tried the fresh variety of salmon. "He told me," Randolph said, "he had tried it now and again, but it hadn't got any taste, and it was waste of money to have it, costing so much more, not to mention the Worcester sauce it needed to make it eatable at all. Then there is another fellow I know who never has but one meal a day, which he takes at lunch-time. There might be some sense in that, perhaps, if it had been something like what we have been having this evening; but all he ever has is porridge and apples and nuts."

"What does he do for a living?" Trent inquired.

"It's nought that requires much hard labour, you may depend," Randolph said. "He is a quantity-surveyor, if you know what that is."

"I don't," Trent admitted. "But I remember reading of another famous one-meal-a-day man who might be said to have surveyed quantities, in a sense—Dr Fordyce, a professor of chemistry, who lived in days when people dined at four o'clock. You never heard of him? For more than twenty years he always had his one meal at the same chophouse in the City, beginning with half a chicken and a gill of brandy, then a pound and half of grilled rumpsteak with a quart of strong beer, and finally a bottle of port. Afterwards he used to stroll down to Essex Street and lecture to his chemistry class."

"I should think the chemistry of his inside would have made a lecture worth hearing," Randolph observed. "And now, Mr Trent, if you feel like a bottle of port on top of your beer, say the word—though you must excuse me from joining you. No? Then let us go upstairs and make ourselves comfortable while you tell me about this business of yours." He led the way to the lift, and thence to a large bedroom on the third floor.

They sat facing each other in the two armchairs after Randolph had produced a box of cigars. "Before you start," he said, "there's something I should like to tell you, as you say you are a friend of Miss Faviell's. It's this way. When I heard from the lawyers about all the mess and trouble that was going to result from the old man not having put his affairs in order, I made up my mind that if the money came to me I should do what he ought to have done. Don't think I mean sharing it all out among other people—no fear! I can use a big fortune myself; I have got my business ideas, and I mean to try them out. But it's these hospitals and charities and that, which he founded himself, and called by his name, and used to finance entirely out of his own pocket, from hand to mouth, as you might say. My notion is to make a sufficient settlement on each of them, so as they will know where they are."

Trent began to say what he thought of this intention, but Randolph cut him short impatiently. "That's nought to make a fuss about. They have got a claim, which any chap that wasn't a hog would be bound to respect. Besides, they stand in my name, like. As for the others—the charities that had my father on the list of their supporters—they will have to take their luck. I don't consider myself bound to anything, as far as they go; I haven't even inquired what they are. What I contribute to charity will be off my own bat, whoever it goes to. But there is one other thing. It is quite certain that the old man meant to do your friend Miss Faviell a bit of good; and now I have stepped into her place." Here Randolph showed some signs of embarrassment, and the trace of Yorkshire in his speech became something more apparent. "Now this is the point, Mr Trent. I hear from you—I didn't know it before—that she was informed by the old man of his intention to leave her the residue of his estate, which would have been a lot of money. Now she is a near relation; she had been led to expect something; and I think my father's intentions ought not to be disregarded altogether. When things are all settled up, I should wish her to accept something substantial, which she could regard in the light of a legacy—and there you have it." Randolph leant back in his chair, drew long at his cigar, and gazed through half-closed eyes at Trent.

"It is most generous of you to think of such a thing," Trent said.

"It's nowt o' t'sort," Randolph said atavistically and abruptly. "What I mean is, Mr Trent, it's her having been told about it that makes the difference to me. It she hadn't been, I shouldn't have thought of it, I dare say. It's my own credit I am thinking about."

"Put it how you like," Trent said laughing. "It's quite possible she would refuse to accept anything, from what I know of her. She can support herself well enough—and if she did accept anything," he added a little bitterly, "it wouldn't stay in her possession long, probably." He was thinking of the insatiable Wetherill; for the news of the death of that ornament of English letters had not yet reached him.

"If you mean that she is a brass-finisher, she is not the only one of her sex, by what I hear," Randolph remarked. "Anyhow, that's her business. Well, keep all this to yourself, Mr Trent, if you please. I only mentioned it to you in the hope of hearing what I have just heard—I mean, what sort of a position she is in. We'll see what she says about my notion when the time comes. And now, what was it that you were wanting to put before me?"

Trent put it before him.

James Randolph listened with close attention, his face grown set and harsh. Now and then he shot out a question, but he made no comment.

"There!" Trent said in conclusion. "That's my case, as the lawyers say. What do you think about it?"

Randolph's answer was brief and blasphemous, but it made very clear his conviction that Trent's case was a sound one. He rose to his feet, squared his shoulders, and thrust his hands deep into his pockets. "Now, Mr Trent," he said, "let's hear what you propose. There's nought much I wouldn't do, after what you've told me; so fire away."

As Trent set forth his scheme, Randolph's features relaxed into a grim smile. "It's a rum notion, sure enough," he said at last, "but it might come off, and it's well worth trying, if what you say about me is correct. Come to think of it, Inspector Bligh said the same, that day I turned up at Newbury Place; and he put it pretty strong, too. All right; you can count me in. It's not as if you had given me much to do—what they call a walking-on part, and short at that. It's lucky it is, because I'm no actor."

"You haven't got to act at all," Trent assured him. "You have only got to be yourself. Now about the arrangements. Tomorrow is Saturday, and I have to see Dr Fairman—in the prison infirmary, you know, as I told you. But we have got to look over the scene of action and get it all properly planned out; so on Sunday morning, if it's convenient, we can do that. Then on the Monday morning we can see about getting your own little adornments; and then—"

"And then the balloon will go up," James Randolph said, with a frosty gleam in his hard blue eye. "All right, lad; that suits me."

19

RESURRECTION

In a small room opening out of a ward in the Newhaven prison infirmary Trent sat facing Bryan Fairman, who lay back, enveloped in a dressing-gown, in a somewhat timeworn armchair. Trent had last seen his friend, and then for a few moments only, on the evening when he had so narrowly escaped missing the boat-train at Victoria. Fairman had then looked wildly excited as well as white and drawn with illness—in both respects unlike the austerely composed and vigorous personality known to Trent since student days in Paris. Today he appeared depressed and languid; his movements were listless and his voice, as he greeted his visitor, was apathetic. At the first glimpse of him Trent's mind was made up as to the best means of broaching his business.

"Look here, Bryan," he said lightly. "Before we speak of anything else, I want to give you a piece of news about yourself; good news too—at least I hope you'll think so."

Fairman's brow contracted slightly. "Good news about me would be a nice change. I can't guess what you mean."

"Don't try," Trent advised him. "You wouldn't succeed. The news is that old Dallow has repented in sackcloth and ashes. He says that it was all a mistake, and that he is sorry he made such a fool of himself, or words to that effect. He says that if you can get out of this jam you are in now, and go back to your job, and forget that there was ever any sundering of your loves, he will be devilish glad to see you again."

The effect upon Fairman of these words was instant and transforming. His eyes opened and lit up, his cheeks flushed, his expression lost all its rigidity, a deep inspiration raised his chest and threw back his drooping shoulders. He sat up in his chair, his hands grasping the arms of it, and looked at his friend with all the well-remembered keenness. His voice had a new strength in it as he said, "I know you too well, Phil, to think you would tell me a thing like this unless you were sure of it. You understand what it means to me. Will you give me the details?"

Although Trent had counted upon something of the kind, the extent of the change in Fairman astonished him. Wasting no words on that, however, he proceeded at once to give, as fully as he could, the sense of what Verney had told him at their last interview. Fairman listened eagerly, and when the story was told he lay back in his chair and again drew a long breath.

"Good Lord!" he said, pressing his hands to his ribs. "This ought to wake up my metabolism properly, Phil. I believe I shall really be able to look lunch in the face for the first time in weeks. Now I will tell you something. There is another side to this business about Dallow, and you shall hear it presently; but first, what am I to do about escaping from what you so poetically call the jam I'm in? To begin with, there is a lot for you to explain—"

"For me to explain?" Trent exclaimed.

"Yes, you. I feel interested at last, thank God! What you tell me has put a new heart in me."

"Stimulated the activity of the cardiac functions, I suppose you mean," Trent said reproachfully. "And you accuse me of using lyrical expressions. A new heart! Why, you ought to be kicked out of the Royal College of Surgeons, his Majesty having no further use for your services. Well, I will explain as much as you like when I know what needs explaining."

Fairman smiled a tight-lipped smile. "That's all right. First of all, then, I wish you would answer one or two plain questions. Had you anything to do with the murder of Randolph—anything at all, even indirectly?"

"Absolutely nothing whatever, Bryan. Will that do for you? But what put this notion in your head? Not thrice your branching limes have blown since I beheld that person dead; but why the devil should you imagine I had anything to do with it? Never shake thy gory locks at me, old man; thou canst not say I did it. I mean, can you? Or do you? Or did you?"

"I can't say you did it," Fairman answered gravely. "I know you didn't do it, if you tell me so. But you remember you wrote to me about Randolph making himself a nuisance to Eunice Faviell, and said you were going to see him, and you knew how to put a stop to it. When I saw him lying dead that came back to me. Still, if I had been in my proper senses at the time I shouldn't have imagined you had actually shot him. But the important question is, Phil, does anyone else think you did it?"

Trent stared at him for some seconds. "Do you remember," he inquired at length, "what the Frenchman said when St. Peter told him he could enter into heaven? He said, '*Je vous entends* la *bouche bée*.' That is how I feel now. Does anybody think I did it? Who do you mean?"

"I mean the police," Fairman said quietly.

Again Trent stared at him, and his face flushed. "Oh! The police," he said slowly. "Does this mean, Bryan, that you know something that—but no; that's impossible, of course. Still, you must have had some sort of reason for imagining that I might be suspected?"

"That you might be—yes, I had. And it seemed a good reason to me."

"Well, it didn't work, that's all," Trent said. "And I will tell you why. I did call on Randolph that evening, at six; but I was let in by his manservant, Raught, and let out again by him about a quarter-past. I told the police so myself, without waiting to be asked; and Raught told them the same, before I saw them. Another point is that the surgeon put the earliest time that Randolph could have been shot as seven o'clock, whereas by 6:30 I was in the Cactus Club with Major Robert Sellick Patmore, D.S.O. He didn't get rid of me until it was time for me to drive to Victoria, where I ostentatiously bought some flowers, saw someone off by the 8:20, and watched you just failing to miss it. Ten minutes later I was helping to start the Oastlers' housewarming party in Bloomfield Terrace, and stayed there until midnight. So there you are. Philip Trent, the well-known prison-visitor, left the Court without a stain on his character, amid deafening cheers which the magistrate made no attempt to suppress."

"My reason was a good one, all the same," Fairman said. "You'll say so when I tell you what it was. But if you are not suspected, there is one other question. Is someone else—someone we both know?"

"You are making my brain reel," Trent complained. "I wish you wouldn't; I hate the feeling. No, and no, and no; in other words, the answer is in the negative. As far as I can say, the only person who has been suspected up to now, my dear friend, is your mysterious self—also for a very good reason, written in your own hand, and posted to Scotland Yard."

"Ah!" Fairman said. "So you know about that. It is part of the story, of course."

"I guessed that it might be."

"Well," Fairman said, "now the ground is cleared of all that, I will tell the story, and you can let me know what you make of it.

"It begins on the morning of the day Randolph was shot, when I got a note from Dallow—my chief, you know—telling me, without any beating about the bush, that he was not satisfied with my work and that I was discharged with a half-year's salary. Of course, you don't know Dallow. I wasn't astounded so much at his putting it like that, curtly and without preliminary. Dallow is like that. If he had caught any of the staff doing something discreditable, or if he was satisfied a man was slacking on the job, he would sack him in just that way. What did amaze me was his treating me in that style. It wasn't only that I knew there was absolutely nothing against me—he had often said nice things about my work, in fact, and I knew it was sound work myself. But Dallow, you see, has always been a scrupulously fair man, and a good fellow generally in his dry way—though for all I personally cared he could have been what sort of man he liked so long as he was the very great alienist that he undoubtedly is.

"So I was completely taken aback at hearing this from him. Still, I assumed there had been some mistake, which could easily be cleared up in a personal interview. But not a bit of it. When I saw him, he simply stuck to it that I had got to go, and that there was no more to be said; and when I realized that there wasn't, in fact, any more to be said, I simply went to pieces. As you know, Phil, I was in no condition at that time for standing a shock. I had had 'flu badly on top of months of overwork, and I had known well enough I was due for a serious break-down if I couldn't get away for a rest. Dallow himself had told me I would have to, only the week before, and had urged me to knock off. I would have done it, if I hadn't been at the critical stage of a controlled experiment—the sort of thing you can't wash out and start all over again.

"I don't remember much of what I said to Dallow when it became clear that it was a settled thing, and I had got to go; but I know it was not polite. Then I went back to my quarters and—you are the only man I would tell this to, Phil—I shed tears for the first time since I was a little boy. You don't know what acute nervous fatigue is. It is bad enough when you haven't really got anything to worry about; when you are merely at the end of your strength. Even in that condition you can get the feeling, a purely causeless feeling, that life is not only not worth living, but unbearable. It's the state in which many a man has done away with himself without any ostensible reason whatever. But when you get, on the top of that, the abrupt removal of the only thing that was keeping you more or less balanced—well, that is the end. Or so it seems to you. When I left Dallow I felt that it was impossible to go on living; and at the same time I felt, with the last relics of sense I had left, a horror of the idea of suicide—of the painful and repulsive sort of circumstances that go with suicide.

"But it's no use, I know, trying to explain to you what my sensations were. They were completely morbid, and if you haven't had them yourself you can't possibly understand. I will just go on to tell you what came into my mind as I sat there having the horrors. I thought of my old friend Raoul d'Astalys, that I used to share rooms with when we were both students at the Salpêtrière. I don't think you met him."

Trent, who knew the time allowed to him for his visit to Fairman to be limited, had already decided to waste none of it in describing his fruitless journey to Dieppe. He therefore said, "I have met him, though. The Comte d'Astalys—a tall fellow with large, melancholy eyes."

"That's the man. He was not the ordinary student by any means. I don't believe anyone else knew as much as I did about the work he was doing, and especially about his study of euthanasia. He had the idea, you see, that a time was coming when getting rid of life by agreeable means would be a legally recognized thing; not a crime at all, but a part of the regular apparatus of civilization. Now I knew that d'Astalys had kept up his researches. The last time I had been in touch with him, a few years ago, he had read a paper on Eastern methods of analgesia, at the *Académic de Médecine*, that started a big discussion. I had written to him then, and he had replied from an address in Dieppe—he said in his letter it was a house that had belonged to his family for generations, but was now officially known by the good republican name of 7A, *Impasse de la Chimère*. I gathered that he was not very deeply attached to the Republic. The *Impasse de la Chimère!* That is," Fairman said with conviction, "a God-forsaken spot if there ever was one."

"Is it?" Trent inquired innocently.

"Yes—but never mind that. I was going to say that, some time after getting his letter, I happened to hear some vague gossip about a scandal in which d'Astalys was mixed up; something that had been kept very dark by the authorities. I heard it from a French doctor who had come over to see what we were doing at the hospital. It was a story about orgies of drug addicts being held at a place in Dieppe with the queer name of the *Pavilion de l'Ecstase*, which belonged to d'Astalys. I didn't really believe, when I heard it, that d'Astalys would ever have had anything to do with that sort of thing; but when the blow fell on me as I have told you, it was enough for me that there was even a chance of d'Astalys having become an unscrupulous character. I knew he approved of euthanasia in principle, and I hoped now that he would not mind breaking the law. I resolved then and there that I would look him up, and get out of him some means of putting myself away comfortably and happily, and so as to look as if I hadn't done it on purpose. I felt sure he could do that, and I hoped he would do it, if I undertook to keep him out of it. But I didn't really think about any snags there might be; I just wanted to get going, to be doing something, and I routed out my passport and began packing a bag at once.

"It was while I was doing so that I had another idea. It struck me suddenly that this sacking me was almost certainly not Dallow's work at all, but Randolph's. More than once he had made it pretty clear that he had taken a dislike to me; I couldn't imagine why, and I didn't bother, because it never occurred to me he would go the length of ruining my life just for a whim. But now, the more I considered it the more sure I became that this must be the explanation, whatever Dallow's reason might have been for lending himself to such an outrage.

"I went down at once to the telephone and got through to Brinton Lodge. They told me Randolph was in London, and gave me the address. I thought, all the better; I'm going through London anyhow. I determined to see if I could find him, and make an appeal to him—I didn't care what I did if only I could get back to my work. I say, Phil, I'd like a cigarette if you've got one. They'll let me smoke in here."

Trent gave him what he wanted, standing over him while he gratefully drew the smoke into his lungs. "Poor old Bryan!" he said, laying a hand on the other's shoulder. "What an awful time you have been through! I suppose it's all right for you to go on yarning away like this. As a doctor, I mean, you know what suits you."

"Do me good!" Fairman said. "I have had a long rest; and if I know anything about psychology, letting loose all this that I've had bottled up inside me is the very thing for my complaint. Besides, what I have heard from you this morning has undone the worst of the knots I was tied up in. You don't know!" He reached up and pressed for a moment the hand on his shoulder as he resumed his tale.

After obtaining Randolph's address (he said) he took the next train to London, arriving there with nearly an hour to pass before the departure of the boat-train from Victoria. From Euston he took a cab to Newbury Place. He was feeling exhausted and ill, but he was determined to go on with the program he had vaguely mapped out for himself. He rang once; then, hearing no sound in the little house, rang again. Still nobody came, and he stepped out from the doorway to look at the upper floor. He could see that there was a light in the upper front room. The window was thickly curtained, but there was a thin pencil of light where the curtains had not been drawn together completely. While ringing a third time, he happened to place his hand on the door, and found to his surprise that it was not latched.

He pushed it open, stepped into the lighted passage, and called out asking if anyone was at home. There was no answer; and Fairman, who in his state of mental disturbance cared for nothing but his purpose of coming face to face with Randolph, put down his bag and began hastily to search the place. The rooms on the ground floor were in darkness, and he proceeded to mount the stairs. Turning to the left, he came to the open door of a brightly lighted room, and the first glance within showed him the dead body of the man he sought lying where he had fallen.

Fairman hurried into the bedroom. As a doctor, he needed no more than a moment's examination to make sure that Randolph was past all help, and he left the body undisturbed. The shock of surprise had for the moment a steadying effect, and the plain fact that murder had been done produced its natural reaction of horrified interest. His attention was attracted at once by a litter of papers, wrappings and string on the floor before the open safe, and he went over to look more closely at what lay scattered there.

At this point in his story Fairman was checked by an exclamation from Trent.

"Papers! Do you mean written papers, Bryan—written or printed; not only brown-paper wrappings?"

"Yes; a number of small packets of papers—seven of them, to be precise—I counted afterwards. Each packet was secured with an elastic band. I could see at once that the outside sheet of each packet was headed by a name in large letters, with lines of close, neat writing underneath it. There was also a thick budget of manuscript in a parchment cover."

"Documents! This is getting interesting, Bryan; because the police—I happen to know this—didn't find anything of that sort."

"No," Fairman said. "Like you, I happen to know they didn't find anything of that sort; because nothing of that sort happened to be there when they looked. I will tell you how it was."

Fairman had bent down to look more closely at the papers on the floor (he said) and immediately his eye was caught by a name on one of the packets. It was the name DALLOW.

Fairman took the packet in his hand. It was thin and light, consisting apparently of a few letters on ordinary note-paper—as was the case, he found afterwards, with most of the packets. He looked then at the writing on the covering sheet, which was in Randolph's characteristic hand; and as soon as he had read the first paragraph he understood very well the nature of the compulsion under which Dr Dallow had been brought to act as he had done that morning.

"I am not going to tell you what it was," Fairman said. "You wouldn't, Phil, if you were in my place. All I need say is that it was something which meant utter ruin for Dallow if ever it was disclosed. I might add, too, that it was something he had done, very probably, out of kindness of heart. It's only fair to him to say so.

"Well, there I stood for a minute or two, taking in this discovery. It didn't make me feel any happier; it made no difference to my position, that I could see. Randolph had done his worst for me. Someone else that he had had under his thumb, I imagine, had paid him back with a bullet, and had gone off with the papers relating to himself. But as for me, I was no better off; and the wave of unbearable depression came over me again as I stood there. I was sweating at the palms, my ears were singing, and my feet felt as if I was shod with cotton wool. One thing occurred to me to do. I looked rapidly over the notes written on the other packets. They were quite evidently all of the same character. Although none of the names was known to me, I decided to do those unfortunates the kindness of destroying the evidence of their indiscretions in the past; and I stowed away the lot of them, including Dallow's, in my coat pockets.

"And then, Phil, I looked at the first page of the bundle of manuscript. Can you imagine what I found it to be? You can't, of course; yet it was the text of a book you have told me about more than once. It was that thing of Wetherill's."

"What!" Trent exclaimed. "Do you mean *The Broken Wing?* And he had it in that safe—of course, that is just where it would be. And what happened to that, Bryan? Did you take it? The police didn't find it."

Fairman nodded with a lowering face. "I took it—yes. Stole it, if you like, for that at least was Randolph's legitimate property, I suppose, though how he came by it I cannot think. Or perhaps he had borrowed it from the repulsive brute who wrote it. I didn't care. I only knew I wasn't going to leave that infamous thing lying about for anyone else to see. So I put it under my arm and carried it off; and at the present moment it is at the bottom of the Channel, tied up in a bundle along with the other papers."

"Good!" Trent said with keen satisfaction. "And what then, Bryan?"

"Why then, handling those packets of letters, as most of them were, I was reminded of something. I thought I would send a farewell note to yourself, Phil, as my best friend, saying a few of the things that one leaves unspoken as a rule, before I took the final step. I meant to write it in the boat-train. I had pen and pencil on me, stamps in my note-case; but I had no paper. There was none to be seen in the bedroom, and I hurried downstairs thinking I would forage for some in the living-room before I left the place."

Fairman had entered the front room on the ground floor, and switched on the lights. He saw the writing-table at once, and upon it the open-fronted cabinet with its ample choice of what he was seeking. He helped himself to a number of sheets of blank paper and some envelopes; and as he was doing so, his eye was caught by the names written on the visible leaf of the engagement-block that stood on the top of the cabinet. He gazed in bewilderment at the neatly pencilled record that would speak so plainly to those looking for light on the matter of Randolph's death.

"1:15, Eunice, Porter's," he read. "6, Trent." And at the bottom of the page, "7:45, Tabarders'," followed by a printed sentence from one of the *Epistles*.

The name of Eunice in this context was quite unmeaning to Fairman. The mere name was a stab to his sensibilities; and for an instant he wondered hazily how this note of an appointment with Randolph could be reconciled with what he had heard of her resentment at the old man's attempts to win her favour. But, what fixed his attention was the name of his friend, put down for a visit that had preceded by little more than an hour his own unappointed appearance on the scene of a fatal crime.

"You can see for yourself, Phil," Fairman said, "how it might look to anyone in a state of mental incoherence. Muzzy as I was, I simply wasn't capable of thinking straight. The nearest I could get to putting my ideas together was something like this:—'Here is Randolph shot dead—Phil was here with Randolph only a short time ago—Phil came here intending to have a row with Randolph—Phil may be suspected, whether he did it or not.' And at that point, you see, I had my brilliant inspiration."

Trent looked fixedly at his friend. "Yes," he said slowly. "I begin to see."

"If I was going to make an end of myself, as I very certainly meant to do in any case, here was the chance of doing it to some purpose. You have saved my life, which is the sort of thing a man doesn't forget—"

"A man might try," Trent said impatiently. "Anyone who happens to be a good swimmer is not a hero because he rescues someone who isn't; if he didn't, he ought to be drowned himself. I would have done the same for anybody; you know that."

Fairman laughed gently. "Yes, I know that. But it happened to be me, through no fault of yours, and it is one of those little trifles that stick in one's memory, as I was saying. And so, when I saw your name written there, inviting the attention of anyone looking into the matter of Randolph's murder, my mind was made up in a moment. Then I just did the first things that came into my head. I tore off the leaf from the block and stuck it in my pocket. I went out into the passage and ripped the label with my name on it off the bag, and chucked it into a corner. Then, just as I was going, I thought about fingerprints; so I went upstairs again to the bedroom, where I had noticed the water-bottle and glass, and took a drink.

"After that I cleared out as quick as I could, and hailed a taxi in Bullingdon Street. I had been much longer at Randolph's than I had ever anticipated, and I had only just time to book a passage and catch the train—as you saw. That was another little jolt for me." Fairman closed his eyes with a reminiscent smile. "There you were, as cool as Christmas, and evidently with not the least idea of fleeing the country—in fact, looking a little bit bored, I thought—and there was I, flustered and feverish and right at the end of my tether, feeling far worse than I should have done if I had shot the old man myself."

After this brief glimpse of his friend, Fairman said, he had taken his seat at the table in the Pullman and begun to consider what he should do. He had already settled it with himself that he would leave behind him a letter to the police stating that he was guilty of the murder of Randolph. Deciding on the form of the letter was not so easy. He began and then abandoned first one, then another; in the end he came to see that the more of detail he put into the story, the more chance there was of its being discredited by some small, unrealized error. The final letter satisfied him as being the barest possible form that could be given to his false confession; and he had posted it at the station office at Newhaven.

One disconcerting thing had happened during the change from the train to the steamer at Newhaven. Without his perceiving it, the leaf torn from Randolph's engagement-block had dropped from among his papers to the floor of the carriage; and it had been picked up by an old lady, who afterwards tried to restore it to him. Confused at first, he had quickly reflected that there was nothing on the leaf that could tell a story, and had simply denied all knowledge of it. In mid-Channel he had watched his opportunity to go to the side of the vessel, unseen, and drop overboard the parcel he had made of the documents taken from Randolph's bedroom.

Arriving at Dieppe about two in the morning, he took a room at a hotel, and passed a few hours in drug-induced, yet broken, sleep. He then rose, and asked to be directed to the *Impasse de la Chimère*. After several times renewing his inquiries, he came at length to that remote neighbourhood. There was no mistaking the house when he came to it—a typical *château*—but it was, to all appearance, deserted. Repeatedly he rang the bell at the somewhat dilapidated outer gateway without result, and no sign of habitation was to be seen about the house itself. The smaller house whose grounds adjoined those of the d'Astalys mansion, and which bore the name of which he had heard—*Pavilion de l'Ecstase*—was silent and deserted too.

Worn out and distraught as he was, Fairman had not failed to notice that he was being curiously observed from the windows of the large, old-fashioned inn that occupied the end of the *Impasse*. This was evidently the place to yield information about the whereabouts of the people of the big house; and thither. Fairman now betook himself, ordering coffee and brandy to be served to him in the room looking out on the quiet street. But he found there was nothing to be learned at the *Hôtel du Petit Univers*. The huge man who kept the place avoided his eye when questioned, and mumbled that he had enough to occupy him without keeping watch on the comings and goings of his neighbours—if the comte was not at home, that was none of his, the innkeeper's business; nor did he know of any other address at which the comte might be found.

After such a reception, Fairman had not energy enough for any further pursuit of his attempt to regain touch with the Comte d'Astalys. Weary, sick, and engulfed in the blackest despair of the soul, he had dragged his footsteps back to the harbour and booked a passage by the one o'clock boat back to Newhaven. "It was," he said to Trent, "the only thing I could think of. I meant to destroy myself; and by that time I was too far gone to think of anything the least little bit out of the way. Do you know what I mean? I mean that I had crossed over by sea, and naturally I had thought about drowning when I looked into the water, and when I threw those papers overboard; and now, after failing in the crazy business I had set out on, I came back to that, and never thought of anything else.

"And what happened afterwards I expect you know. I did try to jump overboard, when I thought nobody was paying the slightest attention to me; and the first move I made, a large and powerful man, whom I had been watching scratching his head over a cross-word puzzle, was on me like a cat on a mouse. If I hadn't been such a wreck as I was," Fairman added regretfully, "I would have given him a lesson against interfering with other people's private business."

"You didn't do so badly, at that," Trent assured him. "I am told that Sergeant Hewitt's appearance has been simply ruined for the time being."

"Oh, well!" Fairman said. "If I did anything of that sort, I'm sorry. I didn't really mean what I said about giving him a lesson—it's the sort of thing one says without thinking. Of course I soon found that he was a police-officer, doing his infernal duty; but at the time when he tackled me, I would have torn his heart out with all the pleasure in the world."

"Never mind," Trent said. "I don't suppose Sergeant Hewitt minds. The sort of marks you gave him don't last long, and the sort he has got added to his record for pinching you will do him plenty of good. And so you were run in as a suicide; and then, according to what I hear, you crumbled into ruins. Now, look here, Bryan; we have got to think about the best way of getting you let loose again. The only thing for you to do if you will take my advice, is that whenever anybody asks you, you give the whole story, without any reservation whatever—including your reason for stacking it all up against yourself."

"All right," Fairman said. "I was thinking I would do that in any case. If you are out of it, there's no point in keeping my mouth shut any longer. But they won't believe me. There is a good enough case against me."

"Though you say it as shouldn't, eh? Well, never mind about that; it may not be as good as you think. You haven't been tried for murder yet, you know, and if you ever are, it may not be in the precise form that you expect. You know what they are holding you for at present, of course."

"Of course. Suicide."

"So I thought; but I am told that the official way of putting it is rather more ornamental. A captious critic might even call it laboured. The way the law looks at it is that when you tried to jump overboard, you did it with intent then feloniously, wilfully, and of your malice of aforethought, to kill and murder yourself. It is possible that that is the only murder charge you will have to meet, and I don't think it should worry you. When you are taken to court again, which will be quite soon, the evidence as to your state of health, both before and after the rash act that didn't come off, should be quite enough. What will happen—

so I am told—is that if you consent to be dealt with summarily, you will be bound over to come up for judgment when called upon; which will be never, if you behave yourself. And now I must leave you, Bryan, before they throw me out. The next time I see you, I hope and believe, you will be at liberty again—at liberty to dine with me, in the first place."

Trent got up to go, then checked himself. "Oh, I forgot one thing," he said. "You have heard me mention my aunt, Miss Yates, haven't you? I had a letter from her this morning, to say she is returning soon from Rome, where she has been making a short stay with friends. She describes an odd experience she had on the way there, between London and Dieppe."

Fairman looked a little mystified. "Well?" he said.

"She enclosed a little document which she thought would interest me. I thought it would interest you." He drew from his letter-case a slip of thin paper, which he handed to his friend—a printed leaf, with a few words of handwriting upon it as follows:

APRIL 12.

1.15 Eunice – Porter's
6 Trent
7.45 Tabarders'

"Henceforth there is laid up for me a crown of righteousness,
which the Lord, the righteous judge, shall give me at that day."—2 Tim., iv. 8.

At Scotland Yard a few hours later, Inspector Bligh succeeded, after several attempts, in getting speech by telephone with Trent at his house. His words were brief and guarded. "I've got your letter," he said, "and I believe you have got hold of the right end of the stick. As for what you propose, I'm willing to try it. But we can't talk about these things over the wire. How soon can you see me here?"

"In about half an hour."

"Right. Come along."

"There's one thing," Trent said, "that I didn't mention in my letter. You might think it over while I am on my way. Those fingerprints on the razor-blade—you haven't traced them, have you?"

"No."

"I thought not. They were mine." And Trent hung up the receiver.

20

A GOLF MATCH

It was a bright and lively April afternoon when Verney travelled in Trent's car to the scene of their pre-arranged golf match at Molesworth. The secretary was a different man indeed from the distressed and shaken being of the day after the murder of his employer; in better trim, too, than he had seemed to be when Trent had seen him at the Randolph Institute four days ago. The fresh, clean air, and the prospect of a little freedom from the bonds of duty, had put some colour in his firm, aquiline face. If it looked still a little drawn, and if in his clear blue eyes there was still something of a brooding expression that had not been there when Trent met with him first at Brinton Lodge three months before, he was certainly in better spirits as he talked of indifferent things, or discussed golf with that earnest gravity which Trent always found so impressive in the true votaries. He noted that Verney never said a word about his own game, or any successes that might have fallen to him; but Trent had never placed him among the numskulls of the fraternity.

Verney enlarged upon his happy memories of the course they were about to visit, the details of which he seemed to recall as readily as if it had been not years, but days, since he last played there. As the car cleared the remoter northern outskirts of London, he took off his cap, breathed deep, and came nearer than Trent had yet seen him to looking satisfied with the world we live in.

The prospect for the Institute, he said in answer to a discreet inquiry, was quite uncertain still; but he had received more than one offer which showed him that there were better opportunities than he had thought for one of his peculiar experience. The administration of charity seemed not to be an overcrowded profession; which was fortunate, he said simply, as he had come to care for nothing else.

"Not only fortunate, but natural," Trent suggested, "as there is no more than a bare living to be made by it as a paid job, I suppose. And it leads to nothing, does it?"

"Only to itself," Verney said.

He began to talk of the work to which he had devoted himself; and Trent was an interested listener. Verney had inside knowledge of the working of almost every known kind of organized philanthropy, from the maintenance of Nonconformist pastors' retiring funds to the provision of lifeboats; and he showed himself to have a keen, if cold, eye for the absurdities occasionally to be met with when those concerned have least idea of being amusing. There was, he assured Trent, a small fund, recently created by will, for the annual provision of twelve pairs of knickerbockers for poor little boys in a certain parish; it being carefully laid down by the testator that the knickerbockers should be fastened below the knee, so as to avoid the repulsive impropriety of the garments known as shorts.

He mentioned also the case of an elderly benefactor who had, at great expense, presented a certain orphanage with an up-to-date gymnasium. This gentleman, being invited to perform the ceremony of opening the building, had been transported with rage on finding that no arrangement had been made for his being presented with a golden key in honour of the event; and this had had to be provided for him, by a committee struggling with money difficulties, under the threat of his removing his name from the list of the institution's supporters.

By this time they were nearing their destination; and Trent noted with relief, as they passed by the opening of a lane leading towards the course, that a small canary-coloured car was parked some distance down it.

"I never have a caddie—d'you mind?" Verney said in the dressing-room, as they prepared themselves for the fray. "I can't allow myself any luxuries, for one thing; and for another, the work I do among boys doesn't make me much in love with any employment of that kind."

"I think you mentioned it before," said Trent, who in fact had borne this principle of Verney's very clearly in mind. "It makes no difference to me. I won't have one either. Shall we have anything on the game? Some people always like to. I am just as happy whether we do or not."

"I'd rather not," Verney said. "If one's always carrying on a fight against betting among other people, I think one ought to avoid it oneself. It's a good enough game without that, if one's at all keen."

It was close on three o'clock when they went to the first tee, and Verney, who was giving three strokes, opened the match. He swung with an easy perfection of style, and there was a sting in his drive that moved Trent's admiration. There were no other players near them, before or behind; for Trent had deliberately chosen the day of the week when the average attendance at the course was least. The conditions were in every way ideal; and both gave themselves up to the pure pleasure of a keenly contested game. During the first half of the round the match was an even one, and the position as they quitted the ninth green was all square.

"A man I know," Trent said as they walked towards the tenth tee, "is fond of calling golf the silliest of games."

"If he plays golf," Verney said, "it's excusable in a way. It's only a sort of swearing. It would probably mean that he was playing below his form, and couldn't make out what he was doing wrong. You get the extreme form of it in the man who chucks his clubs into the sea, and swears he will never touch one again, and then turns up at the first tee next morning with a new outfit. But if the man you mention doesn't play, I should think he was the silliest of your friends."

"No," Trent said, "he is far from that. He has a very fine mind. But he believes it is his duty to lash the age, modern life being made up entirely, in his view, of follies and corruptions. So when he sees nine out of ten of the people he knows doing any particular thing, he assumes it must be wrong or idiotic, and he feels he has to castigate it."

"Well, golf will survive it, I daresay," Verney said. "If it has survived all the silly fuss that has been made about it by the golfmaniacs, it isn't likely to be hurt by the golfophobes. Especially as so many of them get unexpectedly converted, and drive everybody frantic by talking about their own performances. Anyhow, people who lash the age don't get too much attention paid to them, as a rule, do they?—even when what they say is perfectly right."

"I wouldn't quite say that," Trent answered, as he teed his ball. "They get attention enough, I think—in fact, they are quite popular, and are expected to say the most amusing things. Like comic colonels when they get into bunkers."

Trent was sincere in his compliments upon the brilliant three which gave Verney the lead at the eleventh hole. At the next, Trent drew level again, and on the thirteenth tee the honour was his.

This was an uphill beat, with a belt of thick wood flanking the fairway on the left side, and a high hedge on the right. Half-way up the slope could be seen white posts on either side, marking the direction of a public footpath which led straight across the fairway from a gate in the fence to an opening in the wood; and it was at this gate that Trent was glancing with the tail of his eye as he teed his ball.

"It's a funny thing about the number thirteen," he remarked, "that though the superstition about it is so strong, you never find a golf course without a thirteenth hole. It is often left out when houses are being given numbers, or almost anything else, except golf-holes. Perhaps they are immune because somebody has got to lose the hole anyhow, and that may count as the bad luck. All the same, lots of people don't like the thirteenth, simply because of the number."

Verney heard this with a clouded brow. "I know," he said briefly; and Trent turned to grounding the club behind his ball.

"Hold hard!" Verney said, suddenly. "You can't go yet. Someone's crossing the fairway. You might easily hit—" Here he broke off with a sharp catching of the breath, and the bag of clubs that he was holding fell to the ground with a clatter.

Trent, staring at him, then up the slope before them, was the picture of bewilderment and concern. "Someone crossing!" he repeated blankly. "You must be dreaming, my dear chap! Aren't you well?"

The question needed no answer; for Verney, supporting himself against a tree-trunk, was the colour of paper. His eyes still fixed ahead, he passed a hand across his bare forehead and seemed to breathe with difficulty. At length he turned a lamentable look upon Trent, and attempted to rally himself.

"No, not quite well," he panted. "Nothing really wrong, though." He pressed a hand over his heart. "I get taken—this way—sometimes. Fancying things—and feeling pretty sick. It soon passes off."

Trent spoke words of sympathy. "Well, it's a bad finish to a good game," he ended, picking up his ball. "You don't feel like going on, I'm sure."

"I couldn't do it," Verney declared with vehemence, his eyes still turned fearfully towards the distant opening in the wood. "I can't go on, really—not up that hill. I dare not try. These attacks—they leave me in a devil of a state. I'm terribly sorry."

He wetted his handkerchief with water from the tee-box, and pressed it to his forehead. "Do you mind if we walk back now?"

"It isn't far," Trent said. "I'll carry your clubs." But this Verney would not allow. He grew more composed as they made their way towards the clubhouse, but he still looked shaken, and made brief and disjointed replies to Trent's efforts to make conversation. He refused a drink at the bar, though evidently not without an inward struggle; but he thankfully accepted a cup of coffee, and he seemed to be almost restored when he took his seat beside Trent for the run back to town.

A glance told Trent that the yellow car was gone from its halting-place in the lane near the course. It was five minutes later, as they passed a crossroads inn, that he had another glimpse of it drawn up beside the building. He saw with satisfaction that it was empty. The affair was going according to plan.

A long, straight stretch of houseless country road now opened before them, a few pedestrian figures dotting its length. A moment later there came a strangled exclamation of terror from the man at his side.

"He's there!" Verney gasped in a dreadful voice. "He's there—again!"

"Where do you mean?" Trent asked in a carefully casual tone, as though resolved to discourage any outbreak of hysteria in his companion.

"On the footpath—right on ahead there—walking with his back to us. Good heaven! Can't you see?"

"I see two women," Trent replied, grimly staring before him, "with a dog on a lead." And this was true.

"The old man—with his bag. We're going to pass him. I won't see his face!" Verney bent down and covered his eyes with his hands, shuddering violently.

Trent slackened the pace of the car, and said nothing while Verney gradually recovered himself. He sat crouched in his corner, a hand still shading his eyes, and never looking out of the car, right, left or ahead. When the yellow car presently overtook and passed them with a nerve-racking screech, he did not glance at it.

"I'm sorry," he said at last in a low tone, "for giving such a performance. I've never been as bad as this before—can't understand it."

"You'll have to see a doctor at once, won't you?" Trent said conversationally. "It isn't any use letting yourself get worked up about it; there can't be anything much that's wrong. Why, you were the picture of health an hour ago. You'll be ordered a rest, I expect, and in a short time you'll be as fit as the proverbial flea. But now, we shall be passing my place in a minute, and you must come in and have a restorative—anything you like, from tea to sal volatile, not to mention Christian drinks. You know," he added seriously, "you seemed to be a little more upset after that second—er—attack than you were after the first. I really think you need a bracer of some sort." And Verney, with genuine gratitude, agreed to the suggestion.

The car came to rest before Trent's little house and studio in Grove End Road. "Here we are," he said, as he opened the front door and made way for Verney to enter. "On the right is the door of my mean and virtually uninhabitable sitting-room, as Kai Lung would say. Inside it you will find a few characterless armchairs, a very commonplace fire, and waiting ready for us, a few drinks guaranteed to sting like an adder and bite like a serpent. For you, perhaps, a brandy and—Why, what the devil's wrong now, man?"

For Verney, entering the room first, had fallen back against Trent with a cry. "There!" he gasped. "It's there!"

"What d'you mean? Where? For the Lord's sake, get a hold on yourself, Verney," Trent said roughly, and shook the trembling wretch by the shoulders. "Tell yourself it isn't real, whatever it is. Tell yourself it's fancy. Go and shove your fist through it. There's no ghost there, Verney; it's just your imagination—no ghost at all. Nerves out of order, that's all that's the matter; or tummy gone wrong—like the chap in Kipling, don't you remember? When he saw what he thought he saw, it got up out of the chair and walked into the back room; but there was nothing there really."

"That's what it's doing! That's what it's doing!" Verney sobbed, clutching his arm. "Getting up from that chair at the writing-table—going into the other room—always with its back to me. There! It's shut the door—didn't you see? It's in there—in there, I tell you! My God! If it comes out, and I see the face—Let me go, damn you! Stand away from that door, get out of my way, or I'll kill you too! Let me out!" And he grappled furiously with Trent, whose broad shoulders were planted now against the door by which they had entered the room.

"Not till you tell me what you saw—who it was you saw," Trent panted, his grip locked round the other's arms and body.

"James Randolph, you devil!" Verney screamed. "Old James Randolph! Let me out!"

"James Randolph is dead, Verney. James Randolph was murdered. How could you see a dead man? Why should he come for you, Verney? Why should he come for you, Verney? Why should he—"

"Because I did it, because I killed him! Now will you let me go? Ah! You won't, because I tried to put it on to you—Yes, I did, I confess it, only let me go, for pity's sake, Trent. Have mercy! I'll tell everything, I'll give myself up for the murder, I'll do anything you ask, only let me—Oh God!" For he had caught a slight sound from the direction of the door leading to the studio. "Look! The door's moving, it's opening!" And again he struggled madly to escape.

A horrible sound broke from Verney's lips as he felt a light touch on his shoulder. But the figure that met his starting eyes as he whirled round was no phantom. A tall, ungainly man with a basilisk eye stood there: and he said, "Henry Malcolm Verney, I am a police-officer, and I arrest you for the murder of James Randolph by shooting him on the twelfth of this month."

Inspector Bligh then administered the usual caution.

21

AUNT JUDITH KNITS

Chief-Inspector Bligh lowered himself by sections into an armchair in Trent's studio, on the evening of the day following that of Verney's arrest and removal. Bryan Fairman, who had been "bound over" at Newhaven that morning, and Miss Yates, just returned from her visit to Rome, were already there. They had been Trent's guests at dinner; and the old lady's fingers were actively busy with some kind of knitting that seemed not to prevent her taking the keenest interest in all that passed.

"He went quietly enough," Mr Bligh told them. "In fact, he was pretty well prostrated by what he had been put through. But he had got enough hold on himself, by the time he was charged at Marlborough Street this morning, to refuse to say anything at all. He'll need to do a lot of thinking to get himself out of the fix he's in. He's the kind that will very likely try to short-circuit the case by doing himself a mischief; but they'll see after that at Brixton. As it is, we shall have everything in order very nicely for the adjourned inquest on Friday. You're a clever dog," he added, turning a thoughtful eye on his host.

"If rather a dirty one, you mean," Trent suggested, clasping his fingers behind his head. "It's true, I didn't feel disposed to deal very gently with a man who had been plotting for weeks to get me hanged for a murder he did himself. Verney is a dangerous, treacherous beast, but there wasn't enough evidence for you to go on, as you said yourself, and I had to try and get what was wanted, simply in self-defence. To tell the truth, it worked out better than I ever hoped."

"Same here," said Mr Bligh succinctly; then he laughed a little. "I wish you could have seen Bloom's face—that's my shorthand man—when Verney got as far as saying he would give himself up for the murder. I started for the door when we heard that, and Bloom cocked his eye at me, grinning, as much as to say, 'Don't you wish we could put over these sort of games?' "

"And why can't you?" Miss Yates inquired.

"Because, ma'am," the inspector explained stiffly, "if a person in authority induces a suspected person to make a statement, it isn't evidence. That was why Bloom grinned. But there wasn't much grin about Mr Randolph," he added reflectively. "Why, when he came in to us through that door, what with the farmer's hat, and the little bag, and the set look on his face, he was so exactly like his father that it almost made me jump. He slung down the hat and bag, and he says to me, 'If you need any assistance in taking him, Officer, I'm your man. If it was legal,' he says, 'I'd handle him myself, and be glad of the chance.' "

"Well, you and he might have liked the job: I didn't," Trent said, "I simply wanted that engaging young fellow put in a safe place, where he couldn't get at me or anyone else he happened to take a dislike to. I shall be stiff for a week, I think. As for what the law will do to him now, it is no business of mine, but he will deserve it a lot more than many men do who have to face the same thing."

Fairman confirmed this with a judicial nod. "He ought to have been content with shooting Randolph," he said severely.

"Just so; there ought to be moderation in all things," Trent agreed.

Miss Yates, still knitting composedly, observed without looking up, "I know very well what it is that Inspector Bligh has very nearly taken out of his pocket half a dozen times in the last five minutes. Philip knows I haven't the least objection, so will you all please smoke?"

Mr Bligh thankfully accepted this suggestion, and Fairman, being supplied with a long cigar, did likewise. Miss Yates's faintly-clicking needles now seemed to signal expectation in a code of their own, and Trent responded to it.

"I had been telling them all about the case before you came," he said to the inspector, "and I had just finished speaking of the visit paid to me by that poor devil Raught."

"That dangerous criminal Raught, you mean," Mr Bligh growled. "When I think of that fellow lying up all that time under our very noses, where I could almost have put out my hand and touched him—"

"Now I think," Miss Yates interposed, "we ought not to talk of the poor wretch like that now he is dead—even if he did shoot a man nobody is likely to miss."

"Never mind," Trent soothed the disconcerted inspector. "You'll get over it in time. As I was saying, I had been telling them all about how he came here, and all that he said, just as I told you last week—including the strange story of the man that he caught sight of going into No. 5 a little after seven o'clock on the night of the crime. And I was going to tell them how it was that that story put me, for the first time, definitely on the track of Verney."

"You didn't tell me that," the inspector observed.

"No; because it wasn't of any immediate importance just then. I told you the material points of the case that built itself up against Verney, once I began to take him seriously as a suspect. But I thought all of you might find it interesting to hear what it was that turned my nose in his direction, so to speak, because it shows how useful luck is in matters of this sort. Inspector Bligh would admit that, if he ever admitted anything. He would tell you that he would rather have a good fat slice of luck in any investigation than the most brilliant piece of sleuthing work."

The inspector, apparently rapt in contemplation of the toe of his left boot, made no remark.

"In this case," Trent resumed, "it was just a chance recollection that came to me while listening to Raught; something that I hadn't remembered for years until then. It started from Raught's saying that the man he saw going into Randolph's place looked like what he called a gentleman. He explained that by saying that the man carried himself well, and was in evening dress, and was, he thought, not a short man. Now you remember that all he saw was the fellow's back-view, and that for only a few seconds; so I got him to revise his impressions, and he then added that the man was wearing an overcoat, a white scarf and a tall hat."

"Well, naturally," Fairman interjected. "A coat and scarf and a tall hat—it's a sort of uniform when you're in evening dress. But I don't see how that could help you to spot the wearer. For all you could tell from Raught's account, it might have been one of hundreds who would be about at that hour of the evening in the West End."

Trent waved him a cordial assent. "O wild West End, thou breath of London's being, as the poet sings. As you say, there might have been hundreds of them. Put the figure higher if you like. Ten thousand times ten thousand, in sparkling raiment bright, may have been thronging up the slopes of Piccadilly or any neighbouring thoroughfare at the time. But I was thinking about the rather smaller number of people who were more or less mixed up in the Randolph affair, and I was wondering which of them this rear elevation described by Raught might have belonged to."

"There seem to have been enough of them, at that," Fairman observed grimly. "And as for the description, the visitor might have been any of us in this room, as far as I can see."

Miss Yates, still knitting, remarked tranquilly: "It couldn't have been me."

The sniff evoked by this frivolity was not quite suppressed by Fairman; but the sound of it was lost in Trent's immediate comment.

"There you are! That's the point, or one of the points. If you remember, Inspector, once in the dim damned days beyond recall there was some morbid idea—which you refrained from mentioning to me—about a lady being in the case. But the mysterious visitor wasn't a woman."

Mr Bligh, challenged, eyed him with severity. "So you say now," he remarked. "We all know who it was now. But how could you be sure *then* that what Raught saw wasn't a woman masquerading as a man?"

Trent laughed. "Oh well! You can argue that. It might have been the Mayoress of Bruddersfield dressed up as the Ruritanian *Chargé d'Affaires*. But really the only woman who was in question at all was Eunice Faviell, wasn't it? We all know what she looks like. We all know that, however she was dressed, and from whatever angle she was regarded, she couldn't possibly suggest the idea of a gentleman. No gentleman would suggest such an idea. If she impersonated a man at all, she would look like something that— "

"Never mind that," Miss Yates said firmly. "You were going to say something objectionable, Philip, I know. You were sure that the man Raught saw must be a man; that's enough."

Mr Bligh stirred in his chair a little impatiently. "All right," he said. "I'll concede that. Let us get to the point. This interests me. Mr Trent says that Raught's tale put him definitely on the track of Verney. That means, I suppose, that he was able to convince himself that the tale ruled out everybody else but Verney."

He looked at Trent, who contented himself with a polite inclination of the head.

"Then," the inspector went on, "I *should* like to know, certainly, why it ruled out everybody else, and especially why the devil—sorry!—It didn't rule out Verney, who at the time of the mysterious visit was supposed to be prancing about the streets with only just enough on to prevent him being arrested for indecency. I mean, that's what you supposed, just as other people did. Taking the story at its face value, we can admit that it ruled out Raught himself. And I'm willing to agree that it ruled out Miss Faviell. Well, who else was there mixed up in the affair who the visitor might have been? It might have been yourself, to begin with. It might have been Dr Fairman here. It might have been Wetherill, who you tell me had been threatening him. It might have been Randolph junior. And of course it might have been Verney, because we know it was."

"Very well put," Trent said. "Only, by parity of reasoning, it couldn't have been me, because I know it wasn't. As for the others you mention: let us start with Randolph junior. Now I knew very well what he looked like; he looked just like his father; whereas the unknown man looked like Raught's idea of how a gentleman looks. Sir Walter Scott, I remember, put the same thing another way when describing the celebrated Claver'se; he said he had the air of one whose life had been spent among the noble and the gay. I told myself, then, that even from behind, and in a bad light, neither Randolph *père* nor Randolph *fils* would make exactly that impression on a casual observer.

"And I thought there was a good case for ruling out Wetherill. It was true that I had met him in the Cactus Club, not far from Randolph's place, shortly after the unknown man was seen by Raught; and it was true that when I met him Wetherill had on much the same sort of rig that Raught described. But there was one exception—the hat. Wetherill, when I saw him, was wearing a broad-brimmed, black, soft hat. He always did. It was a vital element in his personal make-up. I mean, Eugene Wetherill had been giving his impersonation of Eugene Wetherill all his life, and he always dressed the part very carefully. I felt certain he didn't own such a thing as a tall hat of any description; and so I didn't believe the visitor had been Wetherill.

"Then again, I didn't see much sense in the idea that it had been Fairman, because I had seen Fairman catch the boat-train at Victoria at 8:20; and at Victoria he was wearing a brown hat and brown overcoat, terminating in brown trouser-legs and brown shoes—quite a colour-scheme, really. Of course, I knew Fairman *had* been at Randolph's that evening; but it was some time after the man Raught saw. The time Fairman's train from Claypoole got to London settled that. But suppose, I thought, Raught had been wrong about the time. Well, I still didn't see why Fairman should have called on Randolph in evening clothes; and even if he did, how or where could he have changed out of them rapidly enough to get to Victoria and catch the 8:20? That seemed to me an impossibly rapid transformation-scene." Trent turned to Fairman. "So you see why I thought, after hearing what Raught had to tell me, that the man he had caught sight of couldn't have been you.

"And then, quite suddenly, while I was giving that wretched fellow a cigarette and a drink—"

"Aiding and abetting," Inspector Bligh remarked gloomily.

"Is that what they call a cigarette and a drink at Scotland Yard?" Trent inquired with interest. "Well, I gave the poor devil what I could see he wanted. And just then, as I was saying, a notion suddenly came to me that was altogether new. While I was considering whether Fairman could have changed his clothes, the phrase 'transformation-scene' had come into my mind, as I've just been telling you; and there it stuck, somewhere in the background. My thoughts kept catching sight of it again and again—and then, in a flash, I saw why."

Trent paused; and Inspector Bligh, staring at him in a slightly dazed manner, observed, "I'll be damned if I know what you're talking about."

"So will I," Miss Yates said, continuing to knit; and Mr Bligh stiffened for an instant in his chair.

Dr Fairman coughed instructively. "What Trent means," he said, "is, to put it quite simply, that a certain concept had planted itself in his subconsciousness, where an association of ideas had taken place which abruptly emerged, quite spontaneously and unsought, in the sphere of consciousness."

The inspector gazed grimly at the speaker for some moments. "Oh! If that's all he means," he said at last, "why couldn't he say so? You *have* relieved my mind." He turned to Trent. "You had a brain-wave—is that it?—started somehow by the idea of a transformation-scene."

"That's it," Trent said. "You see, I suddenly remembered Charles Hawtrey."

His three hearers looked at each other dazedly.

"In *A Message from Mars*," Trent hastened to explain. "Didn't any of you ever see it?"

"I saw it," Miss Yates said, now keenly interested. "I went to it with the Pethertons—you remember them, Philip; their second daughter, Juliet, had very nearly married an Oriental of some sort just before that, and they were both in such spirits, I recollect, because the thing had been broken off. There was a man who came down to earth from Mars in the play, a kind of magician, who made all the furniture jump about when he got annoyed. And Hawtrey had the part of a useless rich man, very lazy and selfish. The Martian changed him into a homeless tramp, very ragged and without a shirt."

Trent laughed. "That was it—the transformation-scene. It couldn't be better described. And do you remember, Aunt Judith, how he was dressed before he was changed into a tramp?"

"Why, of course!" Miss Yates exclaimed. "He was in evening dress, just going out to a dinner-party or somewhere."

"You are quite clear about the evening dress, Aunt?"

Miss Yates considered. "Dear me, yes! I can see him now. A very shiny top hat—"

"And a very patrician black overcoat," Trent added quickly, "and round his neck, inside the coat collar, a white muffler hiding everything up to his chin. That was all you saw of his evening dress. In fact, you didn't see it at all, except two ends of black trouser below the coat; his feet were hidden by some small obstacle or other—do you remember? You just knew he must be in evening dress, because of the uniform, as Bryan calls it."

At this point Fairman ejaculated "Ha!" Miss Yates, allowing her knitting to relapse into her lap, met her nephew's eye. "Yes," she said thoughtfully. "I see now what you're driving at, Phil." Inspector Bligh smiled a sphynx-like smile.

"And then," Trent went on with animation, "as he stood backed up against the scene, facing you, the hat, scarf and coat were all twitched off him together from behind; all done in the twinkling of an eye, wasn't it?—so that you could hardly see that they disappeared through an open-and-shut trap in the scene."

"I didn't see how they disappeared at all," Miss Yates said. "They just went—and there he was, a ragged, shivering poor wretch."

Again Trent took up the tale. "And when he stepped forward, shivering and hugging himself against the cold, you could see the tattered ends of his trouser-legs and his aerated boots. There you are, then; that was the eye-opener for me. I saw it was, at any rate, on the cards that the somebody seen by Raught had been wearing the simplest and most effective of camouflage clothing. All that was needed was a pair of dress trousers—with braces ready adjusted, no doubt—an overcoat, muffler and hat.

"But though I saw that much, and also that it might lead to something, it didn't lead me at once to the idea of Verney. What I did began to wonder was whether the man might not have been Bryan after all, as an uncommonly quick change now seemed to be possible. He would have had to change only the trousers and shoes and hat, if the other clothes were simply being worn all the time under the camouflage. It could have been done in a taxi. Only where was the sense of it, even then? A taxi-man would certainly notice it, and remember it, if he took up a fare in one kind of clothes and set him down a few minutes later, at Victoria, in a totally different costume. Besides, if there was any humbug about the evening dress get-up, it was hard to account for that humbug except on the assumption that somebody, being about to shoot Randolph, was trying to cover his tracks in some way. And of course that was exactly what Bryan never attempted to do; quite the contrary. He simply did a public bunk, in addition to leaving his traces all about the place, and making a confession afterwards. That was what I told myself; and it was just then that another little point occurred to me."

Mr Bligh, who had been listening so closely that he had forgotten to smoke, now sighed gently, and began abstractedly searching his pockets.

"He knows not where is that Promethean heat," Trent murmured. "Your matchbox is on the table at your elbow, Inspector, where you put it."

"Ha! Thanks," Mr Bligh grunted, and attended to his relighting.

"You two can be cold-blooded if you like," Fairman exploded. "I want to hear the rest." Miss Yates knitted on in ostentatious patience.

"It wasn't me, please," Trent said. "It was him—letting his pipe go out just when I was coming to the part that will make your six eyes, like stars, start from their spheres. The new point that occurred to me was this. Raught had mentioned that it surprised him to see a man at the door of No. 5, because he had heard no footsteps, although the window that he peeped out of was open at the top—and Raught had sharp ears, too. Now, if that was so, the visitor must have been walking with most unnatural noiselessness; and the idea presented itself to me that he was perhaps wearing rubber-soled shoes.

"As soon as that notion came to me, things began to explode quite rapidly in my imagination. That is the way it works; the moment a match is really put to the train, off go the fireworks. It isn't at all logical or scientific, I suppose; but that is how it happens. The order of ideas was something like this: 'Rubber-soled shoes are not commonly worn in the streets of London during the evening hours; but they are worn at that time by Verney and his lads when leaping about the highways and byways. I have not hitherto considered Verney, just because he was supposed to be on the run at the time when the mystery-man appeared. It is known that he started and finished the run, because he did so in the presence of witnesses; but is it at all possible that he could have fallen out for some time while the run was in progress? If so, could he have got to Newbury Place and away from it in the interval?

"So there I was, fairly started on the proposition that Verney might be, after all, the man we were after. Then, as always does happen when you have got hold of the right idea at last, a lot of things began to fall into their places of their own accord. First, it occurred to me that rubber-soled shoes were not only suitable for roadway athletics, but would be just as useful for entering a house quietly—if one had a latch-key—and pussyfooting up the stairs without being heard by the occupier of the premises. It had been thought at first, you see, that the man who shot Randolph had had an appointment with him; that Randolph had been expecting him, and had opened the door to him himself—being alone in the place at the time. That was what he did sometimes do, according to what Raught told the police; but there was also the possibility that he had been taken quite by surprise, in the way I have described. And you see it was important for Verney that he should be taken by surprise. He didn't want to have the old man making any resistance, or yelling for help. There was no telling what might happen if he wasn't taken unawares.

"Then I realized that, as far as changing clothes went, Verney would not have had to change at all. What he was wearing for the run was simply the equivalent of the lightest of summer underclothing, and he would have had merely to put on the camouflage over that, and, later on, peel it off again. He wouldn't take off his shoes at any point in the performance. They would be black shoes, you see; suitable for wearing with evening dress. By the way, Inspector, have you got them?"

Mr Bligh turned to the others with a curt nod. "That was what he advised me to look for," he said. "A pair of black, rubber-soled gym-shoes. They were almost the first things I found when searching Verney's rooms this morning. I didn't find the weapon, though," he added, addressing Trent. "That would be doo much to expect. It may be anywhere in the Home Counties, as he has had nearly a fortnight for putting it out of sight."

"Well, it doesn't matter, fortunately," Trent said. "To go back to what I was saying: once I got started, there were a lot of things that came to me. Especially, some details from a conversation I had with Verney on the evening of the day after the murder, when he came to see me. His pretence was, of course, that he had not even known that Randolph was in London; that he had heard of Randolph's death for the first time that morning when Inspector Bligh had called on him in quest of information. Verney said to me then that the inspector had told him nothing beyond the bare fact of Randolph's having been murdered."

"Naturally," Mr Bligh put in. "It wasn't for me to be giving anything away."

"I know. It was for him to give himself away."

"Which he didn't," the inspector said. "He handled the situation beautifully, I will say. Quite cool at first; curious to know what I wanted. Then his distress when he heard the news—why, it was a treat to watch him."

Trent turned to Miss Yates. "He isn't such a brute, really," he assured her. "He only means it would have been a treat if he had known Verney was the guilty man. That's the police idea of a bit of fun—watching the criminal tie himself in knots, thinking he's going to get away with it." Mr Bligh's austere features relaxed into a grin. "You see; that's when they smile a smile more dreadful than their own dreadful frown. But as I was saying—Verney told me he had learnt practically nothing from the inspector; and when the evening paper appeared, it gave merely the fact that Randolph had been shot through the heart, and had been found lying dead on the bedroom floor. And yet when Verney called on me, he was full of indignation about the cowardly atrocity of shooting a defenceless old man in the back. And that 'in the back' really was a blunder. It puzzled me when I came to think about it, after he had gone. All the same, at that time the notion of Verney really knowing something about the crime seemed to me ridiculous; and I came to the conclusion, I regret to say, that Inspector Bligh had been a little more communicative than he need have been when putting Verney through it."

Mr Bligh directed a withering stare at the speaker; and Miss Yates, still knitting, placidly inquired, "Through what, Philip?"

"The mangle," Trent explained. "An apparatus used by the police for making people come clean. Of course I was wrong to come to that conclusion, and this case will always be a lesson to me to think only beautiful thoughts about officers of the law. If I had done so then, I might have got properly on to Verney sooner. But there were some other things in what he had said to me that seemed odd, though I took no more than a passing notice of them at the time. For instance, his professing not to have known the old man was in London on that day. Even I knew, from the way Randolph had talked while he was sitting to me, that he was particularly pleased with himself as an important figure in the Worshipful Company of Tabarders, and never missed their dinners on any account. It was strange, I had thought at the time, that Verney should not have known about that engagement.

"Then again, he had spoken repeatedly of the late Randolph as if he had been a totally unspotted saint upon earth—said he had a veneration for him, and that he didn't know of the old man having an enemy in the world. Now I didn't know much about Randolph then—less than I do now—but I did know enough to take him out of the class of prodigies of spiritual loveliness; and I didn't quite believe that Verney, after two years of him at close quarters, could genuinely take that view of him.

"One thing more I recalled about that talk I had with Verney on the day after the crime. He had said one or two things that sounded like fishing to find out whether I had or hadn't been at Randolph's place that Wednesday evening. I didn't rise to it, because I had gone there on purpose to give Randolph an unpleasant quarter of an hour; not to talk about doing a job for him, as Verney believed. My purpose was no business of Verney's, so I just left him guessing whether I had kept the appointment or not. He couldn't ask me straight out, because he was pretending not to know that Randolph had made any appointment with me. It must have been maddening for Verney; because my going there was necessary to his little plan. If I had stayed away for any reason, I should probably be able to prove an alibi if I was ever suspected at all. You see, he had come round to call here in the confident expectation of finding that I had already been scooped in by the iron talons of the law. Then he saw me grinning out of the window as if nothing at all had happened; and being already, no doubt, a bit edgy—he must have been having a pretty anxious day—it made him jump as if he had been shot. So he came in, to try and find out how the land lay, and work off a lot of lies about how broken up he was by Randolph's death. I thought at the time that he was rather more shattered than was altogether natural in a healthy young fellow in first-class condition. What was really the matter with him was a very nasty jar on top of a murderer's conscience.

"Verney isn't cut out for a murderer, really. He is a daring man, and like a good gambler, he doesn't mind taking risks that the average man would funk. But he has another of the gambler's traits: he is devilish superstitious. I could tell that from several things I had noticed in him; and when the time came, I played on it without any hesitation.

"Well, I have told you what were the points that I recalled from that conversation, while I was turning over the idea that Verney might be the guilty man. And then, apart from all that, I remembered one little reason I had already for thinking that Verney might not be an absolutely flawless mirror of sincerity."

Fairman raised his eyebrows. "How was that?" he asked. "Most people, I believe, thought he was as guileless as an infant. I only met him a few times, quite casually, when he came to Claypoole on the business of the hospital; but he always struck me as just the sort of person one could trust—open, and frank, and a little severe; one might even say high-minded."

Trent shook his head. "That comes of being a psychological expert," he remarked.

"Oh! I know I was wrong," Fairman said testily. "I never had him under observation, of course. And I know there is a class of pretenders who have the secret of making just that kind of impression. How was it you diagnosed his weakness?"

"I'll tell you. Verney has, you know, a rather unusual face—beaky and chinny and fine-drawn in structure, with that wide-eyed and my-spirit-beats-its-mortal-bars sort of look. Did it ever strike you, Bryan, that the least little contraction of the muscles—just a touch of the brush between the eyebrows and at the mouthcorners—would turn that expression into something rather more than severity?"

"Ha!" Fairman exclaimed. "You mean cruelty—yes!"

"Ruthlessness," Trent said, "is rather the idea, I think. A cruel man has a positive taste for inflicting pain. Old James Randolph had that, I'm afraid; complicated with what he thought was religion—a depressing mixture. But a ruthless man will inflict pain for a purpose, and without necessarily getting any fun out of it. Now, I had seen Verney just once before I became acquainted with him. I mentioned it to you, Inspector; it was when I saw him playing roulette at Monte Carlo—and he didn't see me. I hadn't a notion who he might be, of course, but the look of him interested me. He had a seat at the table, and he was intent on the game."

Miss Yates sighed gently. "Sitting at the table," she remarked to her needles, "is such a bad sign."

"Yes," Trent said. "But at least he didn't have a beastly little notebook, and jot down the results after every whirl. He knew he was playing a game of chance, and he didn't want it to be anything else. It was easy to see he was an old hand, and his gambling face, like many other people's, was not quite his vicarage tea-party expression. It attracted me as a portrait-painter. I thought that as a cross between Cardinal Manning and Lucretia Borgia—"

"My dear Phil!" Miss Yates interjected.

"That's to say, I thought it was a head that I was bound to recognize if I ever met it again. Then, a few years later, I did meet it again, wearing a rather more saintly expression, at Randolph's place at Brinton; and when I said, in the tentative sort of way we polite creatures have, that I believed I had seen it before at Monte, it answered, without the flicker of an eyelash, that it had never been anywhere near the place. So that's why Verney was filed away in my mind among those who might not, at a pinch, admit that they did it with their little hatchets.

"So there you are. I had Verney before me now as a man who was capable of telling a thumping lie without the least hesitation or trace of nervousness. A man with a taste for an amusement that often gets people into tight places, and doesn't fit in very well with the character of a fundamentally puritanical, if cheerful, social worker. A man who, when off his guard, could look more than a little sinister. A man who had seemed to me to know a trifle too much about the details of the Randolph crime, and not to know enough about Randolph's movements before the crime. And a man who could have been, so far as height and figure went, the mysterious visitor seen by Raught. In fact, before Raught left the studio that night I was turning over in my mind quite seriously the idea that Verney might be the murderer of James Randolph.

"Before I went to bed that night I had turned it over a lot more. Once I had him in mind, I saw that nothing could have been easier than for him to get hold of a razor-blade with my finger-marks on it—the thing which, as I told you, was so unaccountable to me that it nearly drove me silly. Like an ass, I never thought of its having been kept in cold storage weeks before it was planted; though in fact such marks will stay on metal for years if they aren't messed about, and I ought to have remembered it. He must have done it when I was staying at Brinton; probably during my second visit.

"What had happened, I guess, was that after my making that indiscreet remark about seeing him at Monte, which Randolph heard, the old man must have done a little thinking on the subject. He may have decided to look into the accounts more carefully at the Institute and elsewhere; and if he did that, and found that there had been any funny business going on in that quarter—"

"Funny business!" Mr Bligh exclaimed. "Why, what the auditors have found out already, since I arrested Verney, would be enough to get him two years. He had been helping himself for seventeen months, up to the middle of last January; after that the accounts are quite straight. Where the money went we don't know yet; but a man who is in the know can always get the kind of amusement that Verney liked in London. It was the usual thing, no doubt—he meant to put things straight again when his luck changed. It's very likely, too, that the people who ran the gaming-house got on to who he was, and threatened to inform on him to the old man, and get him prosecuted, if he didn't dig up more money. That sort of thing often happens."

"That wouldn't matter to Verney," Trent observed, "if once the old man had found out for himself. The point is that he stopped stealing shortly after I had unconsciously given Randolph the tip. Randolph, as I say, must have investigated after that; and then the game was up for Verney. He would be just where Randolph liked to have people—under his thumb, where he could keep them; not for any sordid pecuniary motive, but just for the pure pleasure of making them squeak. Also, everything points to his having treated Verney as he treated Raught—made him sign a confession, which could be filed away for use when required. If Randolph did all that, Verney was not the sort of young man to accept the situation without any effort to change it; and if he meant to kill Randolph, he would naturally prefer that someone else should be suspected of the crime, as well as faking an alibi for himself. What more suitable object of suspicion than the interfering fool whose remark had so completely and disastrously upset the applecart?

"As for the blade, all he had to do was to visit my bedroom—while I was in my bath, say—find what blade I was equipped with, get a packet of them for himself, and then next day steal the one I had been using and fingering, and substitute another. Then—this is a point I got from Raught—he must have advised Randolph to give up his out-of-date razor, and to take to the razor and blade that I prefer, as countless multitudes of other shavers do—see advertisements. We know that Randolph did take advice from Verney about some things. For instance, from what Raught said, we know that it was Verney who persuaded him to get me to paint a replica of his portrait; whereas Verney pretended it was Randolph who had originated that very praiseworthy idea.

"Anyhow Randolph certainly did change his type of razor; and once he had done that, Verney's little bit of framework was all in readiness to go merry as a marriage bell. The man who murdered Randolph would, to all appearance, have proceeded to take the blade out of Randolph's razor to cut the strings of the packets, and then left it lying about with his fingerprints—mine—all over it.

"Then there was another thing that occurred to me while I was meditating in here after Raught had gone. I told you, Aunt Judith, how the engagement-block was found standing on the table in Randolph's sitting-room, with the leaf for the day torn off."

"Yes," Miss Yates said, smiling gently. "The leaf which I picked up in the boat-train, and which Dr Fairman had never seen before when I suggested that he had dropped it."

"Oh well! The leaf's adventures don't matter now," Trent went on hurriedly, observant of Fairman's reddening face. "All it did, when you enclosed it in your letter to me, was to clinch the fact that I was the only visitor Randolph was expecting at Newbury Place before his dinner engagement. The block was left in sight for the purpose of letting the police know that very important fact; and Bryan tore it off so as to prevent them knowing it. But who, I asked myself while thinking it over, could have left it in that position? Raught had declared, and there was no reason to doubt him, that it never was left out, but kept in a locked drawer. Who else would be likely to know of its existence, and where to find it, besides Raught? Only Verney, so it seemed to me; and so it seems still."

Trent paused to light a cigarette; and Inspector Bligh observed meditatively, "I've often heard of chaps who could talk the hind leg off a donkey."

Miss Yates, shooting a glance at him between stitches, said precisely, "That is all very well, Mr Bligh, but you have heard all this before, perhaps, and Dr Fairman and I have not. We find it most interesting."

The inspector handsomely acknowledged the hit. "You are quite right, ma'am," he said. "I was forgetting. Yes, I have not only heard it before, but I have filed a note of all these points which Mr Trent was good enough to draw up for me. It is in rather more official language, in some places; that's all."

Bryan Fairman made a sound of slight impatience. "None the better for being in that language, I should think," he said. "I know, if anybody does—all research workers know—how much is missed that really matters because reports have to be written in officialese. They have to be, because a lot of us can't take anything seriously unless you make it dull for them. But what Miss Yates and I would like to hear, Phil, is how Verney managed the carrying out of the crime. You have made it clear that he could change himself in half a minute from an athlete with hardly anything on to a diner-out in complete evening dress, and back again. But how did he do it at the same time that he was running round London with the boys, and where did he change, and how did he get to Newbury Place and get away again?"

Trent and the inspector regarded one another with some amusement. "Exactly what I asked him," Mr Bligh remarked, "when he explained to me about the quick-change dodge."

"And exactly what I asked myself," Trent said. "I could see, I thought, that it was possible, or perhaps easy, for him to dodge out of the procession at some point, and to rejoin it again later, without its being spotted. They run in little groups of twos and threes, you may have noticed if you have seen them at it; so as not to impede traffic, I suppose. And none of them has much energy to spare for keeping an eye on the others. Fairly easy, I should think, for one of them to fall out to tie a shoe-lace or something, at some favourable spot; and he could join in again later, when the run was nearly at an end, by falling in at the tail of one of the groups, without his absence ever having been noticed."

"That's right," the inspector said. "It never was noticed. All the lads who were out that night have been interrogated. It can be proved that he started and it can be proved that he finished; but there isn't one of them who can say he had Verney in sight at any time except the beginning and the end. They never gave it a thought till they were asked."

"Good! Of course, the place where he dropped out would have to be out of sight. So it was, as I shall tell you. But when he had done his disappearing act, Verney had to get to Randolph's, and spend some time there—ten minutes at the very least, I figured it out—and get away again; because though the line of the run goes not far from Newbury Place, it doesn't pass it.

"The only answer that I could think of was a car; and it would have to be a car that was standing all ready at some convenient place; and that place would be the place where Verney dropped out of the company."

"How clever!" Miss Yates exclaimed.

"It's very good of you to say so, Aunt."

"It was Verney I meant, my dear Phil. He thought of it first," Miss Yates pointed out.

"That's true," Trent admitted. "In fact, now you put it that way, I'm dashed glad I wasn't the criminal and he the sleuth. He would probably have had the salt on my tail much quicker than I got it on his. However—when I got to that point in my musings, the next thing obviously was to scout round for some information bearing on these matters; so when Verney rang up saying he wanted to see me about Bryan, I had the devilish cunning to say I would go round and see him at the Randolph Institute, where I hoped I might be able to pick up a thing or two. And so I jolly well did!

"I won't go into all the details about how I got at the facts, because that would be a long story. It was just by listening to some of the lads at the Institute chatting back and forth, and talking to one or two people who were there. But I came away with quite a bagful of useful knowledge. To begin with, I had had a careful look at the track of the weekly run, stuck up on the notice-board. I had also learnt that the evening for the run had recently been changed from the usual day to Wednesday, the day of the murder. I knew already that Verney possessed what he called an ancient car; and I found out now that it was a very good and reliable car, old as it was. Also, I learnt that he was allowed the free use of the garage attached to the house of a very nice old man, who was helping Verney to run the Institute. Also, that this garage was in a nice, quiet place, not far from the Institute, and just round a corner which was right on the track of the run. Also, that the nice old man had been persuaded by Verney to go away to Torquay for a rest and change, taking his own car and chauffeur with him; so that Verney had the garage all to himself on the night of the crime. And I think that was about all."

"Enough too, I should think," Mr Bligh grumbled. "I wish I ever had such luck."

"Perhaps you often have, and took it to be the result of dazzling detective genius," Trent suggested amiably. "You wouldn't think it to hear him now, Aunt Ju, but he was quite pleased when I told him all this a few days ago. It gives you the raw material of the crime, so to speak. Verney had the car waiting for him in the garage before they started on the run. In the car were the hat and the clothing and a loaded revolver, probably with a silencer on its nose. He dropped out and dodged in there, shut the garage door, slipped on the camouflage—not forgetting a pair of gloves—then took out the car and was off and away to the West End, looking the complete swell. He left the car at the entrance to Newbury Place, stepped across to

No. 5 in his rubber-soled shoes, opened the door quietly with his key, slipped upstairs, and very likely shot Randolph without the old man ever hearing or seeing him. Then he pocketed the revolver, took Randolph's keys from the table, opened the safe, and took out the packets. He could tell at once which was the Verney packet, as they were all docketed on the outside; so Bryan has told us. Probably he shoved that in his pocket straight away, unopened. Then he took the blade out of Randolph's razor and pocketed that; got out my blade that he had been saving up for me, and used that—very delicately, so as not to blur my fingermarks—to cut the strings of the remaining packets."

"Why did he take the trouble to do that?" Fairman wanted to know.

"Because there had to be a reason for the blade being taken from the razor and left on the floor. So he just cut them all open and left them there, where Bryan found them and walked off with them."

"Abominable!" Miss Yates remarked with emphasis. "Other people's disagreeable secrets left lying about for the police to find!"

Mr Bligh grunted expressively. "A fat lot he cared about that! Of course," he added a little wistfully, "they would have been very interesting."

"But why," Fairman persisted, "did he use your blade for cutting the strings, when he had to take pains not to blur the marks? He could have used Randolph's blade for that, and made a quicker job of it, not having to be careful."

"Verney is clever, as my aunt says. He knew that a very fine edge which has been used for sawing through a lot of string bears very plain traces of having been misused in that way. Even with the naked eye you can see them. The blade with my marks on had to bear those traces. Well, when that job was done, he took the keys again, went downstairs, got out the engagement-block from the drawer where he knew Randolph usually kept it when he was at Newbury Place, and stuck it up where it could be seen."

"That wasn't so clever," Mr Bligh observed. "I should have found it soon enough without that; and its being left out like that wasn't quite natural. He ought to have realized that."

"Yes; it was a slip," Trent agreed. "You wouldn't have done it yourself, Inspector. But Verney hadn't had your experience, you see. Now I come to think of it, it seems likely that all the really perfect crimes are committed by officers of the C.I.D. However, that was what he did; and then, I think, all he had to do was to make his exit and get back to his car. One thing he did was to leave the front door not quite shut, as Bryan found it later on. He didn't want to make any unnecessary noise, you see. To walk in an unhurried manner from the door to the spot just outside the archway, where I think he must have left his car, takes about ten seconds—I've timed it myself."

"Why, Phil!" Miss Yates exclaimed. "Ten seconds! That is no time at all!"

"A very generous allowance, I assure you," Trent said. "So many people think a second is the sort of time it takes to blink your eye. But a man can run a hundred yards in ten seconds—some men can, anyhow. And in America it has been proved that a good murderer can shoot up six people in one second."

"Well, but suppose," Fairman said, "he had met somebody coming in by the archway as he went out. His face would have been seen and remembered."

"Not if he had been blowing his nose at the moment, which he would have been, if he is the man I take him for. So now, Verney returned to his car, ran back to the garage in North London, put away the car, and then waited behind the garage doors until the first of the returning runners showed up. All he had to do then was to shed the outer clothing, and step out and attach himself to the tail of one of the little groups. It was all over!"

The brief but thoughtful silence which ensued was broken by Inspector Bligh. "And a very nice bit of work too," he remarked appreciatively, pressing down a new charge of tobacco in his pipe. "It was more by accident than anything else that it came unstuck."

"You mean the accident of my mind being engaged on the case," Trent suggested. "There is something in that, no doubt."

"What I mean," Mr Bligh answered with a shade of truculence, "is the pure and simple accident of Raught having seen a man in what looked like evening dress going into the place at the time he did." He lighted the refilled pipe.

"Which, you were about to say, provided a starting-point for the operations of my flame-like intelligence. Yes: true," Trent said. "The accompanying fact that the man seen was wearing silent shoes was no accident, of course. It was just because Verney was so jolly careful; and it gave him away, as happens so often in this vale of tears. There was another large-scale accident, though."

"What was that, Phil?" Miss Yates inquired.

"I mean Raught not going out until some hours later than he usually did on his half-day off. Verney's idea was, you see, that the old man would be alone in the house when I called, and that I couldn't possibly prove that he was alive and well when I left. But its being such beastly weather kept Raught at No. 5, not only to let me into the place, instead of Randolph admitting me himself, but to see me off the premises afterwards. And as I had a solid mass of coagulated alibi for the rest of the night, that accident completely ruined the part of the plan that was intended for my benefit. And so, one thing leading to another, not even my old friend Inspector Bligh dreamed of connecting me with the crime, and I was left at large to go nearly off my head worrying about the case, and finally to get on the track—as I fully and freely admit, the fact being obvious—entirely by accident."

"Well, if you come to accidents, Phil," Fairman observed, "the whole of this hideous business came of those few casual words you let drop to Verney, as you were telling us, when you first met him. Those words cost Randolph his life in the end. They will cost Verney his, I suppose. He certainly meant that they should cost you yours."

"You might take it a step farther back," Trent said, "and make the trouble date from the day when the Prince of Monaco leased the gambling concession to M. Louis Blanc. It's an endless chain. Still, it can't be denied that what I said so carelessly at Brinton was a link in it. The awful power of a chance remark! But listen! I see the inspector pricking up his ears. What is that faint musical sound—as if some seraph hand, with touch of fire, were arranging glasses on a tray in the pantry? Inspector Bligh, the hour is nigh, the sun has left the lea."

"Yes: some time ago," said that officer, now amiably expectant. "But I don't see what it has to do with me."

"The nark, his lay who trilled all day, sits hushed—"

"You sit hushed," suggested Inspector Bligh.

III
TRENT INTERVENES

1

THE GENUINE TABARD

It was quite by chance, at a dinner party given by the American Naval Attache, that Philip Trent met the Langleys, who were visiting Europe for the first time. During the cocktail time before dinner was served, he had gravitated towards George D. Langley, because he was the finest looking man in the room—tall, strongly built, carrying his years lightly, pink of face, with vigorous, massive features and thick grey hair.

They had talked about the Tower of London, the Cheshire Cheese, and the Zoo, all of which the Langleys had visited that day. Langley, so the attaché had told Trent, was a distant relative of his own; he had made a large fortune manufacturing engineers' drawing-office equipment, was a prominent citizen of Cordova, Ohio, the headquarters of his business, and had married a Schuyler. Trent, though not sure what a Schuyler was, gathered that it was an excellent thing to marry, and this impression was confirmed when he found himself placed next to Mrs Langley at dinner.

Mrs Langley always went on the assumption that her own affairs were the most interesting subject of conversation; and as she was a vivacious and humorous talker and a very handsome and good-hearted woman, she usually turned out to be right. She informed Trent that she was crazy about old churches, of which she had seen and photographed she did not know how many in France, Germany, and England. Trent, who loved thirteenth-century stained glass, mentioned Chartres, which Mrs Langley said, truly enough, was too perfect for words. He asked if she had been to Fairford in Gloucestershire. She had; and that was, she declared with emphasis, the greatest day of all their time in Europe; not because of the church, though that was certainly lovely, but because of the treasure they had found that afternoon.

Trent asked to be told about this; and Mrs Langley said that it was quite a story. Mr Gifford had driven them down to Fairford in his car. Did Trent know Mr Gifford—W. N. Gifford, who lived at the Suffolk Hotel? He was visiting Paris just now. Trent ought to meet him, because Mr Gifford knew everything there was to know about stained glass, and church ornaments, and brasses, and antiques in general. They had met him when he was sketching some traceries in Westminster Abbey, and they had become great friends. He had driven them about to quite a few places within reach of London. He knew all about Fairford, of course, and they had a lovely time there.

On the way back to London, after passing through Abingdon, Mr Gifford had said it was time for a cup of coffee, as he always did around five o'clock; he made his own coffee, which was excellent, and carried it in a thermos. They slowed down, looking for a good place to stop, and Mrs Langley's eye was caught by a strange name on a signpost at a turning off the road—something Episcopi. She knew that meant Bishops, which was interesting; so she asked Mr Gifford to halt the car while she made out the weatherbeaten lettering. The sign said SILCOTE EPISCOPI ½ MILE.

Had Trent heard of the place? Neither had Mr Gifford. But that lovely name, Mrs Langley said, was enough for her. There must be a church, and an old one; and anyway she would love to have Silcote Episcopi in her collection. As it was so near, she asked Mr Gifford if they could go there so she could take a few snaps while the light was good, and perhaps have coffee there.

They found the church, with the parsonage near by, and a village in sight some way beyond. The church stood back from the churchyard, and as they were going along the footpath they noticed a grave with tall railings round it; not a standing-up stone but a flat one, raised on a little foundation. They noticed it because, though it was an old stone, it had not been just left to fall into decay, but had been kept clean of moss and dirt, so you could make out the inscription, and the grass around it was trim and tidy. They read Sir Rowland Verey's epitaph; and Mrs Langley—so she assured Trent—screamed with joy.

There was a man trimming the churchyard boundary-hedge with shears, who looked at them, she thought, suspiciously when she screamed. She thought he was probably the sexton, so she assumed a winning manner and asked him if there was any objection to her taking a photograph of the inscription on the stone. The man said that he didn't know as there was, but maybe she ought to ask Vicar, because it was his grave, in a manner of speaking. It was Vicar's great-grandfather's grave, that was; and he always had it kep' in good order. He would be in the church now, very like, if they had a mind to see him.

Mr Gifford said that in any case they might have a look at the church, which he thought might be worth the trouble. He observed that it was not very old—about mid-seventeenth century, he would say—a poor little kid church, Mrs Langley commented with gay sarcasm. In a place so named, Mr Gifford said, there had probably been a church for centuries farther back; but it might have been burnt down, or fallen into ruin, and been replaced by this building. So they went into the church; and at once Mr Gifford had been delighted with it. He pointed out how the pulpit, the screen, the pews, the glass, the organ-case in the west gallery, were all of the same period. Mrs

Langley was busy with her camera when a pleasant-faced man of middle age, in clerical attire, emerged from the vestry with a large book under his arm.

Mr Gifford introduced himself and his friends as a party of chance visitors who had been struck by the beauty of the church and had ventured to explore its interior. Could the vicar tell them anything about the armorial glass in the nave windows? The vicar could and did; but Mrs Langley was not just then interested in any family history but the vicar's own, and soon she broached the subject of his great-grandfather's gravestone.

The vicar, smiling, said that he bore Sir Rowland's name, and had felt it a duty to look after the grave properly, as this was the only Verey to be buried in that place. He added that the living was in the gift of the head of the family, and that he was the third Verey to be vicar of Silcote Episcopi in the course of two hundred years. He said that Mrs Langley was most welcome to take a photograph of the stone, but he doubted if it could be done successfully with a hand-camera from over the railings—and of course, said Mrs Langley, he was perfectly right. Then the vicar asked if she would like to have a copy of the epitaph, which he could write for her if they would all come over to his house, and his wife would give them some tea; and at this, as Trent could imagine, they were just tickled to death.

"But what was it, Mrs Langley, that delighted you so much about the epitaph?" Trent asked. "It seems to have been about a Sir Rowland Verey—that's all I have been told so far."

"I was going to show it to you," Mrs Langley said, opening her handbag. "Maybe you will not think it so precious as we do, I have had a lot of copies made, to send to friends at home." She unfolded a small, typed sheet, on which Trent read:

Within this Vault are interred
the Remains of
Lt.-Gen. Sir Rowland Edmund Verey,
Garter Principal King of Arms,
Gentleman Usher of the Black Rod
and
Clerk of the Hanaper,
who departed this Life
on the 2nd May 1795
in the 73rd Year of his Age
calmly relying
on the Merits of the Redeemer
for the Salvation of
his Soul.
Also of Lavinia Prudence,
Wife of the Above,
who entered into Rest
on the 12th March 1799
in the 68th Year of her Age.
She was a Woman of fine Sense
genteel Behaviour,
prudent Oeconomy
and
great Integrity.
"This is the Gate of the Lord:
The Righteous shall enter into it."

"You have certainly got a fine specimen of that style," Trent observed. "Nowadays we don't run to much more, as a rule, than 'in loving memory,' followed by the essential facts. As for the titles, I don't wonder at your admiring them; they are like the sound of trumpets. There is also a faint jingle of money, I think. In Sir Rowland's time, Black Rod's was probably a job worth having; and though I don't know what a Hanaper is, I do remember that its Clerkship was one of the fat sinecures that made it well worth while being a courtier."

Mrs Langley put away her treasure, patting the bag with affection. "Mr Gifford said the clerk had to collect some sort of legal fees for the crown, and that he would draw maybe seven or eight thousand pounds a year for it, paying another man two or three hundred for doing the actual work. Well, we found the vicarage just perfect—an old house with everything beautifully mellow and personal about it. There was a long oar hanging on the wall in the hall, and when I asked about it the vicar said he had rowed for All Souls College when he was at Oxford. His wife was charming, too. And now listen! While she was giving us tea, and her husband was making a copy of the epitaph for me, he was talking about his ancestor, and he said the first duty that Sir Rowland had to perform after his appointment as King of Arms was to proclaim the Peace of Versailles from the steps of the Palace of St. James's. Imagine that, Mr Trent!"

Trent looked at her uncertainly. "So they had a Peace of Versailles all that time ago."

"Yes, they did," Mrs Langley said, a little tartly. "And quite an important Peace, at that. We remember it in America, if you don't. It was the first treaty to be signed by the United States, and in that treaty the British government took a licking, called off the war, and recognized our independence. Now when the vicar said that about his ancestor having proclaimed peace with the United States, I saw George Langley prick up his ears; and I knew why.

"You see, George is a collector of Revolution pieces, and he has some pretty nice things, if I do say it. He began asking questions; and the first thing anybody knew, the vicaress had brought down the old King of Arms' tabard and was showing it off. You know what a tabard is, Mr Trent, of course. Such a lovely garment! I fell for it on the spot, and as for George, his eyes stuck out like a crab's. That wonderful shade of red satin, and the Royal Arms embroidered in those stunning colours, red and gold and blue and silver, as you don't often see them.

"Presently George got talking to Mr Gifford in a corner, and I could see Mr Gifford screwing up his mouth and shaking his head; but George only stuck out his chin, and soon after, when the vicaress was showing off the garden, he got the vicar by himself and talked turkey.

"Mr Verey didn't like it at all, George told me; but George can be a very smooth worker when he likes, and at last the vicar had to allow that he was tempted, what with having his sons to start in the world, and the income tax being higher than a cat's back, and the death duties and all. And finally he said yes. I won't tell you or anybody what George offered him, Mr Trent, because George swore me to secrecy; but, as he says, it was no good acting like a piker in this kind of a deal, and he could sense that the vicar wouldn't stand for any bargaining back and forth. And anyway, it was worth every cent of .it to George, to have something that no other curio-hunter possessed. He said he would come for the tabard next day and bring the money in notes, and the vicar said very well, then we must all three come to lunch, and he would have a paper ready giving the history of the tabard over his signature. So that was what we did; and the tabard is in our suite at the Greville, locked in a wardrobe, and George has it out and gloats over it first thing in the morning and last thing at night."

Trent said with sincerity that no story of real life had ever interested him more. "I wonder," he said, "if your husband would let me have a look at his prize. I'm not much of an antiquary, but I am interested in heraldry, and the only tabards I have ever seen were quite modem ones."

"Why, of course," Mrs Langley said. "You make a date with him after dinner. He will be delighted. He has no idea of hiding it under a bushel, believe me!"

The following afternoon, in the Langleys' sitting-room at the Greville, the tabard was displayed on a coat-hanger before the thoughtful gaze of Trent, while its new owner looked on with a pride not untouched with anxiety.

"Well, Mr Trent," he said. "How do you like it? You don't doubt this is a genuine tabard, I suppose?"

Trent rubbed his chin. "Oh yes; it's a tabard. I have seen a few before, and I have painted one, with a man inside it, when Richmond Herald wanted his portrait done in the complete get-up. Everything about it is right. Such things are hard to come by. Until recent times, I believe, a herald's tabard remained his property, and stayed in the family, and if they got hard up they might perhaps sell it privately, as this was sold to you. It's different now—so Richmond Herald told me. When a herald dies, his tabard goes back to the College of Arms, where he got it from."

Langley drew a breath of relief. "I'm glad to hear you say my tabard is genuine. When you asked me if you could see it, I got the impression you thought there might be something phony about it."

Mrs Langley, her keen eyes on Trent's face, shook her head. "He thinks so still, George, I believe. Isn't that so, Mr Trent?"

"Yes, I am sorry to say it is. You see, this was sold to you as a particular tabard, with an interesting history of its own; and when Mrs Langley described it to me, I felt pretty sure that you had been swindled. You see, she had noticed nothing odd about the Royal Arms. I wanted to see it just to make sure. It certainly did not belong to Garter King of Arms in the year 1783."

A very ugly look wiped all the benevolence from Langley's face, and it grew several shades more pink. "If what you say is true, Mr Trent, and if that old fraud was playing me for a sucker, I will get him jailed if it's my last act. But it certainly is hard to believe—a preacher—and belonging to one of your best families—settled in that lovely, peaceful old place, with his flock to look after and everything. Are you really sure of what you say?"

"What I know is that the Royal Arms on this .tabard are all wrong."

An exclamation came from the lady. "Why, Mr Trent, how you talk! We have seen the Royal Arms quite a few times, and they are just the same as this—and you have told us it is a genuine tabard, anyway. I don't get this at all."

"I must apologize," Trent said unhappily, "for the Royal Arms. You see, they have a past. In the fourteenth century Edward III laid claim to the Kingdom of France, and it took a hundred years of war to convince his descendants that that claim wasn't practical politics. All the same, they went on including the lilies of France in the Royal Arms, and they never dropped them until the beginning of the nineteenth century."

"Mercy!" Mrs Langley's voice was faint.

"Besides that, the first four Georges and the fourth William were Kings of Hanover; so until Queen Victoria came along, and could not inherit Hanover because she was a female, the Arms of the House of Brunswick were jammed in along with our own. In fact, the tabard of the Garter King of Arms in the year when he proclaimed the peace with the United States of America was a horrible mess of the leopards of England, the lion of Scotland, the harp of Ireland, the lilies of France, together with a few more lions, and a white horse, and some hearts, as worn in Hanover. It was a fairly tight fit for one shield, but they managed it somehow—and you can see that the Arms on this tabard of yours are not nearly such a bad dream as that. It is a Victorian tabard—a nice, gentlemanly coat, such as no well-dressed herald should be without."

Langley thumped the table. "Well, I intend to be without it, anyway, if I can get my money back."

"We can but try," Trent said. "It may be possible. But the reason why I asked to be allowed to see this thing, Mr Langley, was that I thought I might be able to save you some unpleasantness. You see, if you went home with your treasure, and showed it to people, and talked about its history, and it was mentioned in the newspapers, and then somebody got inquiring into its authenticity, and found out what I have been telling you, and made it public—well, it wouldn't be very nice for you."

Langley flushed again, and a significant glance passed between him and his wife.

"You're damn right, it wouldn't," he said. "And I know the name of the buzzard who would do that to me, too, as soon as I had gone the limit in making a monkey of myself. Why, I would lose the money twenty times over, and then a bundle, rather than have that happen to me. I am grateful to you, Mr Trent—I am indeed. I'll say frankly that at home we aim to be looked up to socially, and we judged that we could certainly figure if we brought this doggoned thing back and had it talked about. Gosh! When I think—but never mind that now. The thing is to go right back to that old crook and make him squeal. I'll have my money out of him, if I have to use a can-opener."

Trent shook his head. "I don't feel very sanguine about that, Mr Langley. But how would you like to run down to his place tomorrow with me and a friend of mine, who takes an interest in affairs of this kind, and who would be able to help you if anyone can?"

Langley said, with emphasis, that that suited him.

The car that called for Langley next morning did not look as if it belonged, but did belong, to Scotland Yard; and the same could be said of its dapper chauffeur. Inside was Trent, with a black-haired, round-faced man whom he introduced as Superintendent Owen. It was at his request that Langley, during the journey, told with as much detail as he could recall the story of his acquisition of the tabard, which he had hopefully brought with him in a suitcase.

A few miles short of Abingdon the chauffeur was told to go slowly. "You tell me it was not very far this side of Abingdon, Mr Langley, that you turned off the main road," the superintendent said. "If you will keep a lookout now, you might be able to point out the spot."

Langley stared at him. "Why, doesn't your man have a map?"

"Yes; but there isn't any place called Silcote Episcopi on his map."

"Nor," Trent added, "on any other map. No, I am not suggesting that you dreamed it all; but the fact is so."

Langley, remarking shortly that this beat him, glared out of the window eagerly; and soon he gave the word to stop. "I am pretty sure this is the turning," he said. "I recognize it by these two haystacks in the meadow, and the pond with osiers over it. But there certainly was a signpost there, and now there isn't one. If I was not dreaming then, I guess I must be now." And as the car ran swiftly down the side road he went on, "Yes; that certainly is the church on ahead—and the covered gate, and the graveyard—and there is the vicarage, with the yew trees and the garden and everything. Well, gentlemen, right now is when he gets what is coming to him. I don't care what the name of the darn place is."

"The name of the darn place on the map," Trent said, "is Oak-hanger."

The three men got out and passed through the lych-gate.

"Where is the gravestone?" Trent asked.

Langley pointed. "Right there." They went across to the railed-in grave, and the American put a hand to his head. "I must be nuts!" he groaned. "I know this is the grave—but it says that here is laid to rest the body of James Roderick Stevens, of this parish."

"Who seems to have died about thirty years after Sir Rowland Verey," Trent remarked, studying the inscription; while the superintendent gently smote his thigh in an ecstasy of silent admiration. "And now let us see if the vicar can throw any light on the subject."

They went on to the parsonage; and a dark-haired, bright-faced girl, opening the door at Mr Owen's ring, smiled recognizingly at Langley. "Well, you're genuine, anyway!" he exclaimed. "Ellen is what they call you, isn't it? And you remember me, I see. Now I feel better. We would like to see the vicar. Is he at home?"

"The canon came home two days ago, sir," the girl said, with a perceptible stress on the term of rank. "He is down in the village now; but he may be back any minute. Would you like to wait for him?"

"We surely would," Langley declared positively; and they were shown into the large room where the tabard had changed hands.

"So he has been away from home?" Trent asked. "And he is a canon, you say?"

"Canon Maberley, sir; yes, sir, he was in Italy for a month. The lady and gentleman who were here till last week had taken the house furnished while he was away. Me and Cook stayed on to do for them."

"And did that gentleman—Mr Verey—do the canon's duty during his absence?" Trent inquired with a ghost of a smile.

"No, sir; the canon had an arrangement with Mr Giles, the vicar of Cotmore, about that. The canon never knew that Mr Verey was a clergyman. He never saw him. You see, it was Mrs Verey who came to see over the place and settled everything; and it seems she never mentioned it. When we told the canon, after they had gone, he was quite took aback. 'I can't make it out at all,' he says. 'Why should he conceal it?' he says. 'Well, sir,' I says, 'they was very nice people, anyhow, and the friends they had to see them here was very nice, and their chauffeur was a perfectly respectable man,' I says."

Trent nodded. "Ah! They had friends to see them."

The girl was thoroughly enjoying this gossip. "Oh yes, sir. The gentleman as brought you down, sir"—she turned to Langley—"he brought down several others before that. They was Americans too, I think."

"You mean they didn't have an English accent, I suppose," Langley suggested drily.

"Yes, sir; and they had such nice manners, like yourself," the girl said, quite unconscious of Langley's confusion, and of the grins covertly exchanged between Trent and the superintendent, who now took up the running.

"This respectable chauffeur of theirs—was he a small, thin man with a long nose, partly bald, always smoking cigarettes?"

"Oh yes, sir; just like that. You must know him."

"I do," Superintendent Owen said grimly.

"So do I!" Langley exclaimed. "He was the man we spoke to in the churchyard."

"Did Mr and Mrs Verey have any—er—ornaments of their own with them?" the superintendent asked.

Ellen's eyes rounded with enthusiasm. "Oh yes, sir—some lovely things they had. But they was only put out when they had friends coming. Other times they was kept somewhere in Mr Verey's bedroom, I think. Cook and me thought perhaps they was afraid of burglars."

The superintendent pressed a hand over his stubby moustache. "Yes, I expect that was it," he said gravely. "But what kind of lovely things do you mean? Silver—china—that sort of thing?"

"No, sir; nothing ordinary, as you might say. One day they had out a beautiful goblet, like, all gold, with little figures and patterns worked on it in colours, and precious stones, blue and green and white, stuck all round it—regular dazzled me to look at, it did."

"The Debenham Chalice!" exclaimed the superintendent.

"Is it a well-known thing, then, sir?" the girl asked.

"No, not at all," Mr Owen said. "It is an heirloom—a private-family possession. Only we happen to have heard of it."

"Fancy taking such things about with them," Ellen remarked. "Then there was a big book they had out once, lying open on that table in the window. It was all done in funny gold letters on yellow paper, with lovely little pictures all round the edges, gold and silver and all colours."

"The Murrane Psalter!" said Mr Owen. "Come, we're getting on."

"And," the girl pursued, addressing herself to Langley, "there was that beautiful red coat with the arms on it, like you see on a half crown. You remember they got it out for you to look at, sir; and when I brought in the tea it was hanging up in front of the tallboy."

Langley grimaced. "I believe I do remember it," he said, "now you remind me."

"There is the canon coming up the path now," Ellen said, with a glance through the window. "I will tell him you gentlemen are here."

She hurried from the room, and soon there entered a tall, stooping, old man with a gentle face and the indescribable air of a scholar.

The superintendent went to meet him.

"I am a police-officer, Canon Maberley," he said. "I and my friends have called to see you in pursuit of an official inquiry in connection with the people to whom your house was let last month. I do not think I shall have to trouble you much, though, because your parlourmaid has given us already most of the information we are likely to get, I suspect."

"Ah! That girl," the canon said vaguely. "She has been talking to you, has she? She will go on talking for ever, if you let her. Please sit down, gentlemen. About the Vereys—ah yes! But surely there was nothing wrong about the Vereys? Mrs Verey was quite a nice, well-bred person, and they left the place in perfectly good order. They paid me in advance, too, because they live in New Zealand, as she explained, and know nobody in London. They were on a visit to England, and they wanted a temporary home in the heart of the country, because that is the real England, as she said. That was so sensible of them, I thought—instead of flying to the grime and turmoil of London, as most of our friends from overseas do. In a way, I was quite touched by it, and I was glad to let them have the vicarage."

The superintendent shook his head. "People as clever as they are make things very difficult for us, sir. And the lady never mentioned that her husband was a clergyman, I understand.

"No, and that puzzled me when I heard of it," the canon said. "But it didn't matter, and no doubt there was a reason."

"The reason was, I think," Mr Owen said, "that if she had mentioned it, you might have been too much interested, and asked questions which would have been all right for a genuine parson's wife, but which she couldn't answer without putting her foot in it. Her husband could do a vicar well enough to pass with laymen, especially if they were not English laymen. I am sorry to say, Canon, that your tenants were impostors. Their name was certainly not Verey, to begin with. I don't know who they are—I wish I did—they are new to us and they have invented a new method. But I can tell you what they are. They are thieves and swindlers."

The canon fell back in his chair. "Thieves and swindlers!" he gasped.

"And very talented performers too," Trent assured him. "Why, they have had in this house of yours part of the loot of several country-house burglaries which took place last year, and which puzzled the police because it seemed impossible that some of the things taken could ever be turned into cash. One of them was a herald's tabard, which Superintendent Owen tells me had been worn by the father of Sir Andrew Ritchie. He was Maltravers Herald in his day. It was taken when Sir Andrew's place in Lincolnshire was broken into, and a lot of very valuable jewelry was stolen. It was dangerous to try to sell the tabard in the open market, and it was worth little, anyhow, apart from any associations it might have. What they did was to fake up a story about the tabard which might appeal to an American purchaser, and, having found a victim, to induce him to buy it. I believe he parted with quite a large sum."

"The poor simp!" growled Langley.

Canon Maberley held up a shaking hand. "I fear I do not understand," he said. "What had their taking my house to do with all this?"

"It was a vital part of the plan. We know exactly how they went to work about the tabard; and no doubt the other things were got rid of in very much the same way. There were four of them in the gang. Besides your tenants, there was an agreeable and cultured person—I should think a man with real knowledge of antiquities and objects of art—whose job was to make the acquaintance of wealthy people visiting London, gain their confidence, take them about to places of interest, exchange hospitality with them, and finally get them down to this vicarage. In this case it was made to appear as if the proposal to look over your church came from the visitors themselves. They could not suspect anything. They were attracted by the romantic name of the place on a signpost up there at the corner of the main road."

The canon shook his head helplessly. "But there is no signpost at that corner."

"No, but there was one at the time when they were due to be passing that corner in the confederate's car. It was a false signpost, you see, with a false name on it—so that if anything went wrong, the place where the swindle was worked would be difficult to trace. Then, when they entered the churchyard their attention was attracted by a certain gravestone with an inscription that interested them. I won't waste your time by giving the whole story—the point is that the gravestone, or rather the top layer which had been fitted onto it, was false too. The sham inscription on it was meant to lead up to the swindle, and so it did."

The canon drew himself up in his chair. "It was an abominable act of sacrilege!" he exclaimed. "The man calling himself Verey—"

"I don't think," Trent said, "it was the man calling himself Verey who actually did the abominable act. We believe it was the fourth member of the gang, who masqueraded as the Vereys' chauffeur—a very interesting character. Superintendent Owen can tell you about him."

Mr Owen twisted his moustache thoughtfully. "Yes; he is the only one of them that we can place. Alfred Coveney, his name is; a man of some education and any amount of talent. He used to be a stage-carpenter and property-maker—a regular artist, he was. Give him a tub of papier-mache, and there was nothing he couldn't model and colour to look exactly like the real thing. That was how the false top to the gravestone was made, I've no doubt. It may have been made to fit on like a lid, to be slipped on and off as required. The inscription was a bit above Alf, though—I expect it was Gifford who drafted that for him, and he copied the lettering from other old stones in the churchyard. Of course the fake signpost was Alf's work too—stuck up when required, and taken down when the show was over.

"Well, Alf got into bad company. They found how clever he was with his hands, and he became an expert burglar. He has served two terms of imprisonment. He is one of a few who have always been under suspicion for the job at Sir Andrew Ritchie's place, and the other two when the Chalice was lifted from Eynsham Park and the Psalter from Lord Swanbourne's house. With what they collected in this house and the jewelry that was taken in all three burglaries, they must have done very well indeed for themselves; and by this time they are going to be hard to catch."

Canon Maberley, who had now recovered himself somewhat, looked at the others with the beginnings of a smile. "It is a new experience for me," he said, "to be made use of by a gang of criminals. But it is highly interesting. I suppose that when these confiding strangers had been got down here, my tenant appeared in the character of the parson, and invited them into the house, where you tell me they were induced to make a purchase of stolen property. I do not see, I must confess, how anything could have been better designed to prevent any possibility of suspicion arising. The vicar of a parish, at home in his own vicarage! Who could imagine anything being wrong? I only hope, for the credit of my cloth, that the deception was well carried out."

"As far as I know," Trent said, "he made only one mistake. It was a small one; but the moment I heard of it I knew that he must have been a fraud. You see, he was asked about the oar you have hanging up in the hall. I didn't go to Oxford myself, but I believe when a man is given his oar it means that he rowed in an eight that did something unusually good."

A light came into the canon's spectacled eyes. "In the year I got my colours the Wadham boat went up five places on the river. It was the happiest week of my life."

"Yet you had other triumphs," Trent suggested. "For instance, didn't you get a Fellowship at All Souls, after leaving Wadham?"

"Yes, and that did please me, naturally," the canon said. "But that is a different sort of happiness, my dear sir, and, believe me, nothing like so keen. And by the way, how did you know about that?"

"I thought it might be so, because of the little mistake your tenant made. When he was asked about the oar, he said he had rowed for All Souls."

Canon Maberley burst out laughing, while Langley and the superintendent stared at him blankly.

"I think I see what happened," he said. "The rascal must have been browsing about in my library, in search of ideas for the part he was to play. I was a resident Fellow for five years, and a number of my books have a bookplate with my name and the name and arms of All Souls. His mistake was natural." And again the old gentleman laughed delightedly.

Langley exploded. "I like a joke myself," he said, "but I'll be skinned alive if I can see the point of this one."

"Why, the point is," Trent told him, "that nobody ever rowed for All Souls. There never were more than four undergraduates there at one time, all the other members being Fellows."

2

THE SWEET SHOT

"No; I happened to be abroad at the time," Philip Trent said. "I wasn't in the way of seeing the English papers, so until I came here this week I never heard anything about your mystery."

Captain Royden, a small, spare, brown-faced man, was engaged in the delicate—and forbidden—task of taking his automatic telephone instrument to pieces. He now suspended his labours and reached for the tobacco-jar. The large window of his office in the Kempshill clubhouse looked down upon the eighteenth green of that delectable golf course, and his eye roved over the whin-clad slopes beyond as he called on his recollection.

"Well, if you call it a mystery," he said as he filled a pipe. "Some people do, because they like mysteries, I suppose. For instance, Colin Hunt, the man you're staying with, calls it that. Others won't have it, and say there was a perfectly natural explanation. I could tell you as much as anybody could about it, I dare say."

"As being secretary here, you mean?"

"Not only that. I was one of the two people who were in at the death, so to speak—or next door to it," Captain Royden said. He limped to the mantelshelf and took down a silver box embossed on the lid with the crest and mottoes of the Corps of Royal Engineers. "Try one of these cigarettes, Mr Trent. If you'd like to hear the yarn, I'll give it you. You have heard something about Arthur Freer, I suppose?"

"Hardly anything," Trent said. "I just gathered that he wasn't a very popular character."

"No," Captain Royden said with reserve. "Did they tell you he was my brother-in-law? No? Well, now, it happened about four months ago, on a Monday—let me see—yes, the second Monday in May. Freer had a habit of playing nine holes before breakfast. Barring Sundays—he was strict about Sunday—he did it most days, even in the beastliest weather, going round all alone usually, carrying his own clubs, studying every shot as if his life depended on it. That helped to make him the very good player he was. His handicap here was two, and at Undershaw he used to be scratch, I believe.

"At a quarter to eight he'd be on the first tee, and by nine he'd be back at his house—it's only a few minutes from here. That Monday morning he started off as usual—"

"And at the usual time?"

"Just about. He had spent a few minutes in the clubhouse blowing up the steward about some trifle. And that was the last time he was seen alive by anybody—near enough to speak to, that is. No one else went off the first tee until a little after nine, when I started round with Browson—he's our local padre; I had been having breakfast with him at the vicarage. He's got a game leg, like me, so we often play together when he can fit it in.

"We had holed out on the first green, and were walking onto the next tee, when Browson said: 'Great Scot! Look there. Something's happened.' He pointed down the fairway of the second hole; and there we could see a man lying sprawled on the turf, facedown and motionless. Now there is this point about the second hole—the first half of it is in a dip in the land, just deep enough to be out of sight from any other point on the course, unless you're standing right above it—you'll see when you go round yourself. Well, on the tee, you are right above it; and we saw this man lying. We ran to the spot.

"It was Freer, as I had known it must be at that hour. He was dead, lying in a disjointed sort of way no live man could have lain in. His clothing was torn to ribbons, and it was singed, too. So was his hair—he used to play bareheaded—and his face and hands. His bag of clubs was lying a few yards away, and the brassie, which he had just been, using, was close by the body.

"There wasn't any wound showing, and I had seen far worse things often enough, but the padre was looking sickish, so I asked him to go back to the clubhouse and send for a doctor and the police while I mounted guard. They weren't long coming, and after they had done their job the body was taken away in an ambulance. Well, that's about all I can tell you at first hand, Mr Trent. If you are staying with Hunt, you'll have heard about the inquest and all that, probably."

Trent shook his head. "No," he said. "Colin was just beginning to tell, me, after breakfast this morning, about Freer having been killed on the course in some incomprehensible way, when a man came to see him about something. So, as I was going to apply for a fortnight's run of the course, I thought I would ask you about the affair."

"All right," Captain Royden said. "I can tell you about the inquest anyhow—had to be there to speak my own little piece, about finding the body. As for what had happened to Freer, the medical evidence was rather confusing. It was agreed that he had been killed by some tremendous shock, which had jolted his whole system to pieces and dislocated several joints, but had been not quite violent enough to cause any visible wound. Apart from that, there was a disagreement. Freer's own doctor, who saw the body first, declared he must have been struck by lightning. He said it was true there hadn't been a thunderstorm, but that there had been thunder about all that weekend, and that sometimes lightning did act in that way. But the police surgeon, Collins, said there would be no such displacement of the organs from a lightning stroke, even if it did ever happen that way in our climate, which he doubted. And he said that if it had been lightning, it would have struck the steel-headed clubs; but the clubs lay there in their bag quite undamaged. Collins thought there must have been some kind of explosion, though he couldn't suggest what kind."

Trent shook his head. "I don't suppose that impressed the court," he said. "All the same, it may have been all the honest opinion he could give." He smoked in silence a few moments, while Captain Royden attended to the troubles of his telephone instrument with a camel-hair brush. "But surely," Trent said at length, "if there had been such an explosion as that, somebody would have heard the sound of it."

"Lots of people would have heard it," Captain Royden answered. "But there you are, you see—nobody notices the sound of explosions just about here. There's the quarry on the other side of the road there, and any time after seven a.m. there's liable to be a noise of blasting."

"A dull, sickening thud?"

"Jolly sickening," Captain Royden said, "for all of us living near by. And so that point wasn't raised. Well, Collins is a very sound man; but as you say, his evidence didn't really explain the thing, and the other fellow's did, whether it was right or wrong. Besides, the coroner and the jury had heard about a bolt from a clear sky, and the notion appealed to them. Anyhow, they brought it in death from misadventure."

"Which nobody could deny, as the song says," Trent remarked. "And was there no other evidence?"

"Yes, some. But Hunt can tell you about it as well as I can; he was there. I shall have to ask you to excuse me now," Captain Royden said. "I have an appointment in the town. The steward will sign you on for a fortnight, and probably get you a game too, if you want one today."

Colin Hunt and his wife, when Trent returned to their house for luncheon, were very willing to complete the tale. The verdict, they declared, was tripe. Dr Collins knew his job, whereas Dr Hoyle was an old footler, and Freer's death had never been reasonably explained.

As for the other evidence, it had, they agreed, been interesting, though it didn't help at all. Freer had been seen after he had played his tee-shot at the second hole, when he was walking down to the bottom of the dip towards the spot where he met his death.

"But according to Royden," Trent said, "that was a place where he couldn't be seen, unless one was right above him."

"Well, this witness was right above him," Hunt rejoined. "Over one thousand feet above him, so he said. He was an R.A.F. man, piloting a bomber from Bexford Camp, not far from here. He was up doing some sort of exercise, and passed over the course just at that time. He didn't know Freer, but he spotted a man walking down from the second tee, because he was the only living soul visible on the course. Gossett, the other man in the plane, is a temporary member here, and he did know Freer quite well—or as well as anybody cared to know him—but he never saw him. However, the pilot was quite clear that he saw a man just at the time in question, and they took his evidence so as to prove that Freer was absolutely alone just before his death. The only other person who saw Freer was another man who knew him well; used to be a caddy here, and then got a job at the quarry. He was at work on the hillside, and he watched Freer play the first hole and go on to the second—nobody with him, of course."

"Well, that was pretty well established then," Trent remarked. "He was about as alone as he could be, it seems. Yet something happened somehow."

Mrs Hunt sniffed sceptically, and lighted a cigarette. "Yes, it did," she said. "However, I didn't worry much about it, for one. Edith—Mrs Freer, that is: Royden's sister—must have had a terrible life of it with a man like that. Not that she ever said anything;—she wouldn't. She is not that sort."

"She is a jolly good sort, anyhow," Hunt declared.

"Yes, she is; too good for most men. I can tell you," Mrs Hunt added for the benefit of Trent, "if Colin ever took to cursing me and knocking me about, my well-known loyalty wouldn't stand the strain for very long."

"That's why I don't do it. It's the fear of exposure that makes me the perfect husband, Phil. She would tie a can to me before I knew what was happening. As for Edith, it's true she never said anything, but the change in her since it happened tells the story well enough. Since she's been living with her brother she has been looking far better and happier than she ever succeeded in doing while Freer was alive."

"She won't be living with him for very long, I dare say," Mrs Hunt intimated darkly.

"No. I'd marry her myself if I had the chance," Hunt agreed cordially.

"Pooh! You wouldn't be in the first six," his wife said. "It will be Rennie, or Gossett, or possibly Sandy Butler—you'll see. But perhaps you've had enough of the local tittle-tattle, Phil. Did you fix up a game for this afternoon?"

"Yes; with the Jarman Professor of Chemistry in the University of Cambridge," Trent said. "He looked at me as if he thought a bath of vitriol would do me good, but he agreed to play me."

"You've got a tough job," Hunt observed. "I believe he is almost as old as he looks, but he is a devil at the short game, and he knows the course blindfolded, which you don't. And he isn't so cantankerous as he pretends to be. By the way, he was the man who saw the finish of the last shot Freer ever played—a sweet shot if ever there was one. Get him to tell you."

"I shall try to," Trent said. "The steward told me about that, and that was why I asked the professor for a game."

Colin Hunt's prediction was fulfilled that afternoon. Professor Hyde, receiving five strokes, was one up at the seventeenth, and at the last hole sent down a four-foot putt to win the match. As they left the green he remarked, as if in answer to something Trent had that moment said: "Yes; I can tell you a curious circumstance about Freer's death."

Trent's eye brightened, for the professor had not said a dozen words during their game, and Trent's tentative allusion to the subject after the second hole had been met merely by an intimidating grunt.

"I saw the finish of the last shot he played," the old gentleman went on, "without seeing the man himself at all. A lovely brassie it was, too—though lucky. Rolled to within two feet of the pin."

Trent considered. "I see," he said, "what you mean. You were near the second green, and the ball came over the ridge and ran down to the hole."

"Just so," Professor Hyde said. "That's how you play it—if you can. You might have done it yourself today, if your second shot had been thirty yards longer. I've never done it; but Freer often did. After a really good drive, you play a long second, blind, over the ridge, and with a perfect shot you may get the green. Well, my house is quite near that green. I was pottering about in the garden before breakfast, and just as I happened to be looking towards the green a ball came hopping down the slope and trickled right across to the hole. Of course, I knew whose it must be—Freer always came along about that time. If it had been anyone else, I'd have waited to see him get his three, and congratulate him. As it was, I went indoors, and didn't hear of his death until long afterwards."

"And you never saw him play the shot?" Trent said thoughtfully.

The professor turned a choleric blue eye on him. "How the deuce could I?" he said huffily. "I can't see through a mass of solid earth."

"I know, I know," Trent said. "I was only trying to follow your mental process. Without seeing him play the shot, you knew it was his second—you say he would have been putting for a three. And you said, too—didn't you?—that it was a brassie shot."

"Simply because, my young friend"—the professor was severe—"I happened to know the man's game. I had played that nine holes with him before breakfast often, until one day he lost his temper more than usual, and made himself impossible. I knew he practically always carried the ridge with his second—I won't say he always got the green—and his brassie was the only club that would do it. It is conceivable, I admit," Professor Hyde added a little stiffly, "that some mishap took place and that the shot in question was not actually Freer's second; but it did not occur to me to allow for that highly speculative contingency."

On the next day, after those playing a morning round were started on their perambulation, Trent indulged himself with an hour's practice, mainly on the unsurveyed stretch of the second hole. Afterwards he had a word with the caddymaster; then visited the professional's shop, and won the regard of that expert by furnishing himself with a new midiron. Soon he brought up the subject of the last shot played by Arthur Freer. A dozen times that morning, he said, he had tried, after a satisfying drive, to reach the green with his second; but in vain. Fergus MacAdam shook his head. Not many, he said, could strike the ball with yon force. He could get there himself, whiles, but never for certainty. Mr Freer had the strength, and he kenned how to use it forbye.

What sort of clubs, Trent asked, had Freer preferred? "Lang and heavy, like himsel'. Noo ye mention it," MacAdam said, "I hae them here. They were brocht here after the ahccident." He reached up to the top of a rack. "Ay, here they are. They shouldna be, of course; but naebody came to claim them, and it juist slippit ma mind."

Trent, extracting the brassie, looked thoughtfully at the heavy head with the strip of hard white material inlaid in the face. "It's a powerful weapon, sure enough," he remarked.

"Ay, for a man that could control it," MacAdam said. "I dinna care for yon ivorine face mysel'. Some fowk think it gies mair reseelience, ye ken; but there's naething in it."

"He didn't get it from you, then," Trent suggested, still closely examining the head.

"Ay, but he did. I had a lot down from Nelsons while the fashion for them was on. Ye'll find my name," MacAdam added, "stampit on the wood in the usual place, if yer een are seein' richt."

"Well, I don't—that's just it. The stamp is quite illegible."

"Tod! Let's see," the professional said, taking the club in hand. "Guid reason for its being illegible," he went on after a brief scrutiny. "It's been obleeterated—that's easy seen. Who ever saw sic a daft-like thing! The wood has juist been crushed some gait—in a vice, I wouldna wonder. Noo, why would onybody want to dae a thing like yon?"

"Unaccountable, isn't it?" Trent said. "Still, it doesn't matter, I suppose. And anyhow, we shall never know."

It was twelve days later that Trent, looking in at the open door of the secretary's office, saw Captain Royden happily engaged with the separated parts of some mechanism in which coils of wire appeared to be the leading motive.

"I see you're busy," Trent said.

"Come in! Come in!" Royden said heartily. "I can do this any time—another hour's work will finish it." He laid down a pair of sharp-nosed pliers. "The electricity people have just changed us over to A.C., and I've got to rewind the motor of our vacuum cleaner. Beastly nuisance," he added, looking down affectionately at the bewildering jumble of disarticulated apparatus on his table.

"You bear your sorrow like a man," Trent remarked; and Royden laughed as he wiped his hands on a towel.

"Yes," he said, "I do love tinkering about with mechanical jobs, and if I do say it myself, I'd rather do a thing like this with my own hands than risk having it faultily done by a careless workman. Too many of them about. Why, about a year ago the company sent a man here to fit a new main fuse-box, and he made a short- circuit with his screwdriver that knocked him right across the kitchen and might very well have killed him." He reached down his cigarette-box and offered it to Trent, who helped himself; then looked down thoughtfully at the device on the lid.

"Thanks very much. When I saw this box before, I put you down for an R.E. man. Ubique, and Quo fas et gloria ducunt. H'm! I wonder why Engineers were given that motto in particular."

"Lord knows," the captain said. "In my experience, Sappers don't exactly go where right and glory lead. The dirtiest of all the jobs and precious little of the glory—that's what they get."

"Still, they have the consolation," Trent pointed out, "of feeling that they are at home in a scientific age, and that all the rest of the army are amateurs compared with them. That's what one of them once told me, anyhow. Well now, Captain, I have to be off this evening. I've looked in just to say how much I've enjoyed myself here."

"Very glad you did," Captain Royden said. "You'll come again, I hope, now you know that the golf here is not so bad."

"I like it immensely. Also the members. And the secretary." Trent paused to light his cigarette. "I found the mystery rather interesting, too."

Captain Royden's eyebrows lifted slightly. "You mean about Freer's death? So you made up your mind it was a mystery."

"Why, yes," Trent said. "Because I made up my mind he had been killed by somebody, and probably killed intentionally.

Then, when I had looked into the thing a little, I washed out the 'probably.' "

Captain Royden took up a penknife from his desk and began mechanically to sharpen a pencil. "So you don't agree with the coroner's jury?"

"No: as the verdict seems to have been meant to rule out murder or any sort of human agency, I don't. The lightning idea, which apparently satisfied them, or some of them, was not a very bright one, I thought. I was told what Dr Collins had said against it at the inquest; and it seemed to me he had disposed of it completely when he said that Freer's clubs, most of them steel ones, were quite undamaged. A man carrying his clubs puts them down, when he plays a shot, a few feet away at most; yet Freer was supposed to have been electrocuted without any notice having been taken of them, so to speak."

"H'm! No, it doesn't seem likely. I don't know that that quite decides the point, though," the captain said. "Lightning plays funny tricks, you know. I've seen a small tree struck when it was surrounded by trees twice the size. All the same, I quite agree there didn't seem to be any sense in the lightning notion. It was thundery weather, but there wasn't any storm that morning in this neighbourhood."

"Just so. But when I considered what had been said about Freer's clubs, it suddenly occurred to me that nobody had said anything about the club, so far as my information about the inquest went. It seemed clear, from what you and the parson saw, that he had just played a shot with his brassie when he was struck down; it was lying near him, not in the bag. Besides, old Hyde actually saw the ball he had hit roll down the slope onto the green. Now, it's a good rule to study every little detail when you are on a problem of this kind. There weren't many left to study, of course, since the thing had happened four months before; but I knew Freer's clubs must be somewhere, and I thought of one or two places where they were likely to have been taken, in the circumstances, so I tried them. First, I reconnoitred the caddymaster's shed, asking if I could leave my bag there for a day or two; but I was told that the regular place to leave them was the pro's shop. So I went and had a chat with MacAdam, and sure enough it soon came out that Freer's bag was still in his rack. I had a look at the clubs, too."

"And did you notice anything peculiar about them?" Captain Royden asked.

"Just one little thing. But it was enough to set me thinking, and next day I drove up to London, where I paid a visit to Nelsons, the sporting outfitters. You know the firm, of course."

Captain Royden, carefully fining down the point of his pencil, nodded. "Everybody knows Nelsons."

"Yes; and MacAdam, I knew, had an account there for his stocks. I wanted to look over some clubs of a particular make—a brassie, with a slip of ivorine let into the face, such as they had supplied to MacAdam. Freer had had one of them from him."

Again Royden nodded.

"I saw the man who shows clubs at Nelsons. We had a talk, and then—you know how little things come out in the course of conversation—"

"Especially," put in the captain with a cheerful grin, "when the conversation is being steered by an expert."

"You flatter me," Trent said. "Anyhow, it did transpire that a club of that particular make had been bought some months before by a customer whom the man was able to remember. Why he remembered him was because, in the first place, he insisted on a club of rather unusual length and weight—much too long and heavy for himself to use, as he was neither a tall man nor of powerful build. The salesman had suggested as much in a delicate way; but the customer said no, he knew exactly what suited him, and he bought the club and took it away with him."

"Rather an ass, I should say," Royden observed thoughtfully.

"I don't think he was an ass, really. He was capable of making a mistake, though, like the rest of us. There were some other things, by the way, that the salesman recalled about him. He had a slight limp, and he was, or had been, an army officer. The salesman was an ex-serviceman, and he couldn't be mistaken, he said, about that."

Captain Royden had drawn a sheet of paper towards him, and was slowly drawing little geometrical figures as he listened. "Go on, Mr Trent," he said quietly.

"Well, to come back to the subject of Freer's death. I think he was killed by someone who knew Freer never played on Sunday, so that his clubs would be—or ought to be, shall we say?—in his locker all that day. All the following night, too, of course—in case the job took a long time. And I think this man was in a position to have access to the lockers in this clubhouse at any time he chose, and to possess a master key to those lockers. I think he was a skilful amateur craftsman. I think he had a good practical knowledge of high explosives. There is a branch of the army"—Trent paused a moment and looked at the cigarette-box on the table—"in which that sort of knowledge is specially necessary, I believe."

Hastily, as if just reminded of the duty of hospitality, Royden lifted the lid of the box and pushed it towards Trent. "Do have another," he urged.

Trent did so with thanks. "They have to have it in the Royal Engineers," he went on, "because—so I'm told—demolition work is an important part of their job."

"Quite right," Captain Royden observed, delicately shading one side of a cube.

"Ubique!" Trent mused, staring at the box-lid. "If you are 'everywhere,' I take it you can be in two places at the same time. You could kill a man in one place, and at the same time be having breakfast with a friend a mile away. Well, to return to our subject yet once more; you can see the kind of idea

I was led to form about what happened to Freer. I believe that his brassie was taken from his locker on the Sunday before his death. I believe the ivorine face of it was taken off and a cavity hollowed out behind it; and in that cavity a charge of explosive was placed. Where it came from I don't know, for it isn't the sort of thing that is easy to come by, I imagine."

"Oh, there would be no difficulty about that," the captain remarked. "If this man you're speaking of knew all about H.E., as you say, he could have compounded the stuff himself from materials anybody can buy. For instance, he could easily make tetranitroaniline—that would be just the thing for him, I should say."

"I see. Then perhaps there would be a tiny detonator attached to the inner side of the ivorine face, so that a good smack with the brassie would set it off. Then the face would be fixed on again. It would be a delicate job, because the weight of the club-head would have to be exactly right. The feel and balance of the club would have to be just the same as before the operation."

"A delicate job, yes," the captain agreed. "But not an impossible one. There would be rather more to it than you say, as a matter of fact; the face would have to be shaved down thin, for instance. Still, it could be done."

"Well, I imagine it done. Now, this man I have in mind knew there was no work for a brassie at the short first hole, and that the first time it would come out of the bag was at the second hole, down at the bottom of the dip, where no one could see what happened. What certainly did happen was that Freer played a sweet shot, slap onto the green. What else happened at the same moment we don't know for certain, but we can make a reasonable guess. And then, of course, there's the question what happened to the club—or what was left of it; the handle, say. But it isn't a difficult question, I think, if we remember how the body was found."

"How do you mean?" Royden asked.

"I mean, by whom it was found. One of the two players who found it was too much upset to notice very much. He hurried back to the clubhouse; and the other was left alone with the body for, as I estimate it, at least fifteen minutes. When the police came on the scene, they found lying near the body a perfectly good brassie, an unusually long and heavy club, exactly like Freer's brassie in every respect—except one. The name stamped on the wood of the club-head had been obliterated by crushing. That name, I think, was not F. MacAdam, but W. J. Nelson; and the club had been taken out of a bag that was not Freer's—a bag which had the remains, if any, of Freer's brassie at the bottom of it. And I believe that's all." Trent got to his feet and stretched his arms. "You can see what' I meant when I said I found the mystery interesting."

For some moments Captain Royden gazed thoughtfully out of the window; then he met Trent's inquiring eye. "If there was such a fellow as you imagine," he said coolly, "he seems to have been careful enough—lucky enough too, if you like—to leave nothing at all of what you could call proof against him. And probably he had personal and private reasons for what he did. Suppose that somebody whom he was much attached to was in the power of a foul-tempered, bullying brute; and suppose he found that the bullying had gone to the length of physical violence; and suppose that the situation was hell by day and by night to this man of yours; and suppose there was no way on earth of putting an end to it except the way he took. Yes, Mr Trent; suppose all that!"

"I will—I do!" Trent said. "That man—if he exists at all—must have been driven pretty hard, and what he did is no business of mine anyway. And now—still in the conditional mood—suppose I take myself off."

3

THE CLEVER COCKATOO

"Well, that's my sister," said Mrs Lancey in a low voice. "What do you think of her, now you've spoken to her?"

Philip Trent, newly arrived from England, stood by his hostess within the loggia of a villa looking out upon a prospect of such loveliness as has enchanted and enslaved the Northern mind from age to age. It was a country that looked good and gracious for men to live in. Not far below them lay the broad, still surface of a great lake, blue as the sky; beyond it, low mountains rose up from the distant shore, tilled and wooded to the summit, drinking the light and warmth, visibly storing up earthly energy, with little villages of white and red scattered about their slopes—like children clustered round their mothers' knees. Before the villa lay a long, paved terrace, and by the balustrade of it, from which a stone could be dropped into the clear water, a woman stood looking out over the lake and conversing with a tall, grey-haired man.

"Ten minutes is rather a short acquaintance," Trent replied. "Besides, I was attending rather more to her companion. Mynheer Scheffer is the first Dutchman I have met on social terms. One thing about Lady Bosworth is clear to me, though. She is the most beautiful thing in sight, which is saying a good deal. And as for that low, velvety voice of hers, if she asked me to murder my best friend I should have to do it on the spot."

Mrs Lancey laughed.

"But I want you to take a personal interest in her, Philip; it means nothing, I know, when you talk like that. I care a great deal about Isabel, she is far more to me than any other woman. That's rather rare between sisters, I believe; but when it happens it is a great thing. And it makes me wretched to know that there's something wrong with her."

"With her health, do you mean? One wouldn't think so."

"Yes, but I fear it is that."

"Is it possible?" said Trent. "Why, Edith, the woman has the complexion of a child and the step of a racehorse and eyes like jewels. She looks like Atalanta in blue linen."

"Did Atalanta marry an Egyptian mummy?" inquired Mrs Lancey.

"Not by any means—priests of Cybele bear witness!"

"Well, Isabel did, unfortunately."

"It is true," said Trent, thoughtfully. "That Sir Peregrine looks rather as if he had been dug up somewhere. But I think he owes much of his professional success to that. People like a great doctor to look more or less unhealthy."

"Perhaps they do; but I don't think the doctor's wife enjoys it very much. Isabel is always happiest when away from him—if he were here now she would be quite different from what you see. You know, Philip, their marriage hasn't been a success—I always knew it wouldn't be. It's lasted five years now, and there are no children. Peregrine never goes about with her; he is one of the busiest men in London—you see what I mean."

Trent shrugged his shoulders.

"Let us drop the subject, Edith. Tell me why you want me to know about Lady Bosworth having something the matter with her. I'm not a physician."

"No, but there's something very puzzling about it, as you will see; and you are clever at getting at the truth about things other people don't understand. Now, I'll tell you no more. I only want you to observe Bella particularly at dinner this evening, and tell me afterwards what you think. You'll be sitting opposite to her, between me and Agatha Stone. Now go and talk to her and the Dutchman."

"Scheffer's appearance interests me," remarked Trent. "He has a face curiously like Frederick the Great's, and yet there's a difference—he doesn't look quite as if his soul were lost for ever and ever."

"Well, go and ask him about it," suggested Mrs Lancey. "I have things to do in the house."

When the party of seven sat down to dinner that evening, Lady Bosworth had just descended from her room. Trent perceived no change in her; she talked enthusiastically of the loveliness of the Italian evening, and joined in a conversation that was general and lively. It was only after some ten minutes that she fell silent, and that a new look came over her face.

Little by little all animation departed from it. Her eyes grew heavy and dull, her red lips were parted in a foolish smile, and to the high, fresh tint of her cheek there succeeded a disagreeable pallor. There was nothing about this altered appearance in itself that could be called odious. Had she been always so, one would have set her down merely as a beautiful and stupid woman of lymphatic type. But there was something inexpressibly repugnant about such a change in such a being; it was as though the vivid soul had been withdrawn.

All charm, all personal force had departed. It needed an effort to recall her quaint, vivacious talk of an hour ago, now that she sat looking vaguely at the table before her, and uttering occasionally a blank monosyllable in reply to the discourse that Mr Scheffer poured into her ear. She helped herself from the dishes handed to her; some she refused; she made a fairly good dinner in a lifeless way. It was not, Trent told himself, that anything abnormal was done. It was the staring fact that

Lady Bosworth was not herself, but someone wholly of another kind, that opened a new and unknown spring of revulsion in the recesses of his heart.

Mrs Stone, with whom he had been talking uninterruptedly as he watched, caught his eye.

"We don't notice it," she murmured, quickly.

An hour later Mrs Lancey carried Trent off to a garden seat facing the lake.

"Well?" she said, quietly, glancing back into the drawing-room.

"It's very strange and rather ghastly," he answered, nursing his knee. "But if you hadn't told me it puzzled you, I should have thought it was easy to find an explanation."

"Drugs, you mean?" He nodded. "Of course everybody must think so. George does, I know. It's horrible!" declared Mrs Lancey, with a thump on the arm of the seat. "Agatha Stone began hinting at it after the first few days. I told her it was a sort of nervous attack Isabel had been subject to from a child, which was a lie, and of course she didn't believe it. Gossiping cat! She loathes Isabel, and she'll spread it round everywhere that my sister is a drug fiend. How I hate her!"

"But you do believe it isn't that?"

"Philip, I don't know what to believe. Listen, now! The morning after the second time it happened, I asked her what was the matter with her. She said she didn't know; she began to feel stupid and strange soon after dinner began. It had never happened to her before until she came to us here. It wasn't either a pleasant or an unpleasant feeling, she said; she just felt indifferent to everything, and completely lazy. Then I asked her point blank if she was taking anything that could account for it. She was much offended at that; told me I had known her long enough to know she never had done and never would do such a thing. And it is certain that it would be utterly against all

I ever knew of her. Besides, she denied it; and, though Isabel has her faults, she's absolutely truthful."

Trent looked on the ground. "Yes, but you may have heard—"

"Oh, I know! They say that kind of habit makes people lie and deceive who never did before. But you see, she is so completely herself, except just at this time. I simply couldn't make up my mind to disbelieve her. And besides, why should she ever start such a practice? I don't see how she would have been drawn into it. If Bell is peculiar about anything, it's clean, wholesome, hygienic living. She was always that way as a girl, but she was studying to be a doctor, you know, when she met her husband, and that made her ever so much worse. She has every sort of carbolicky idea. She never uses scent or powder or any kind of before-and-after stuff, never puts anything on her hair; she is washing herself from morning till night, but she always uses ordinary yellow soap. She never touches anything alcoholic, or tea, or coffee. You wouldn't think she had that kind of fad to look at her and her clothes, but she has; and I can't think of anything in the world she would despise more than dosing herself with things."

"Not any kind of cosmetic whatever? That is surprising. Well, it seems to suit her," Trent remarked. "When she isn't like this, she is one of the most radiant creatures I ever saw."

"I know, and that's what makes it so irritating for women like myself, who look absolute hags if they don't assist nature a little. She's always been as strong as a horse and bursting with vitality, and her looks have never shown the slightest sign of going off. And now this thing has come to her, absolutely suddenly and without warning."

"How long has it been going on?"

"This is the seventh evening. I entreated her to see a doctor, but she hates the idea of being doctored. She says it's sure to pass off and that it doesn't make any difference to her general health. It's true that she is quite well and lively all the rest of the time; but even if that is so, of course you can see how serious it is for a woman. It means that people shun her. She hasn't realized it yet, but I can see our friends are revolted by the sight of these fits of hers, which they naturally account for in the obvious way. And Bella hasn't any pleasure in life without society—especially men's. But it's come to this, that George, who has always been devoted to her, only talks to her now with an effort. Randolph Stone is just the same; and two days before you arrived the Illingworths and Captain Burrows both went earlier than they had intended—I'm certain, because this change in Isabel was spoiling their visit for them."

"She seems to get on remarkably well with Scheffer," remarked Trent.

"I know—it's extraordinary, but he seems more struck with her than ever."

"Well, he is, but in a lizard-hearted way of his own. He and I were talking just now after you left the dining-room. I had said something about the art of primitive peoples, and he took me aside soon afterwards and gave me more ideas on the subject in ten minutes than I'd ever heard in all my life. Then he began suddenly to speak of Lady Bosworth in a queer, semiscientific sort of way, saying she was the nearest approach to a perfect female physiology he had ever seen among civilized and educated woman; and he went on to ask if I had noticed her strangeness during dinner. I said: 'Yes,' of course; and he said it was very interesting to a medical man like himself. You didn't tell me he was one."

"I didn't know. George calls him an anthropologist, and disagrees with him about the races of farther India. George says it's the one thing he does know something about, having lived there twelve years governing the poor things. They took to each other at once when they met last year, and when I asked him to stay here he was quite delighted. He only begged to be allowed to bring his cockatoo, as it could not live without him."

"Strange, pet for a man," Trent observed. "He was showing off its paces to me this afternoon. It's a mischievous fowl, and as clever as a monkey. Well, it seems he's greatly interested in these attacks of hers. He has seen nothing quite like them. But he is convinced the thing is due to what he calls a toxic agent of some sort. As to what, or how, or why, he is absolutely at a loss."

"Then you must find out what, and how, and why, Philip. I'm glad Scheffer isn't so easily upset as the other men; it's so much better for Isabel. She finds him very interesting, of course; not only because he's the only man here who pays her a lot of attention but because he really is a wonderful person. He's lived for years among the most appalling savages in Dutch New Guinea, doing scientific work for his government, and according to George they treat him like a sort of god; he's somehow got the reputation among them that he can kill a man by pointing his finger at him, and he can manage the natives as nobody else can. He's most attractive and quite kind really, I think, but there's something about him that makes me afraid of him."

"What is it?"

"I think it is the frosty look in his eyes," replied Mrs Lancey, drawing her shoulders together in a shiver.

"You share the public opinion of Dutch New Guinea, in fact," said Trent. "Did you tell me, Edith, that your sister began to be like this the very first evening she came here?"

"Yes. And it had never happened before, she declares."

"She came out from England with the Stones, didn't she?"

"Only the last part of the journey. They got on the train at Lucerne."

Trent looked back into the drawing-room at the wistful face of Mrs Stone, who was playing piquet with her host. She was slight and pretty, with large, appealing eyes that never lost their melancholy, though she was always smiling.

"You say she loathes Lady Bosworth," he said. "Why?"

"Well, I suppose it's mainly Bella's own fault," confessed Mrs Lancey, with a grimace. "You may as well know, Philip—you'll soon find out, anyhow—the truth is she will flirt with any man that she doesn't actively dislike. She's so brimful of life she can't hold herself in—or she won't, rather; she says there's no harm in it, and she doesn't care if there is. Before her marriage she didn't go on in that way, but since it turned out badly she has been simply uncivilized on that point. And her being perfectly clear-headed about it makes it seem so much worse. Several times she has practised on Randolph, and, although he's a perfectly safe old donkey if there ever was one, Agatha can't bear the sight of her."

"She seems quite friendly with her," Trent observed.

Mrs Lancey produced through her delicate nostrils a sound that expressed a scorn for which there were no words. There was a short silence.

"Well, what do you make of it, Philip?" his hostess asked at length. "Myself, I simply don't know what to think. These queer fits of hers frighten me horribly. There's one dreadful idea, you see, that keeps occurring to me. Could it, perhaps, be"—Mrs Lancey lowered her already low tone—"the beginning of insanity?"

He spoke reassuringly. "Oh, I shouldn't cherish that fancy. There are other things much more likely and much less terrible. And there are some things we can do, too, and do at once. Look here, Edith, you know I hate explaining my own ideas until I'm sure there's something in them. Will you try to arrange certain things for tomorrow, without asking me why? And don't let anybody know I asked you to do it—not even George. Until later on, at least. Will you?"

"How exciting!" Mrs Lancey breathed. "Yes, of course, mystery-man. What do you want me to do?"

"Do you think you could manage things tomorrow so that you and I and Lady Bosworth could go out in the motorboat on the lake for an hour or two in the evening, getting back in time to change for dinner—just the three of us and the engineer? Could that be worked quite naturally?"

She pondered. "It might be. George and Randolph are playing golf at Cadenabbia tomorrow. I might arrange an expedition in the afternoon for Agatha and Mr Scheffer, and let Bella know I wanted her to stay with me. You could lose yourself after breakfast with your sketching things, I dare say, and return for tea. Then the three of us could run down in the boat to San Marmette—it's a lovely little place—and be back before seven. In this weather it's really the best time of day for the lake."

"That would do admirably, if you could work it. And one thing more—if we do go as you suggest, I want you privately to tell your engineer to do just what I ask him to do—no matter what it is. He's an Italian, isn't he? Yes, then he'll be deeply interested."

Mrs Lancey worked it without difficulty. At five o'clock the two ladies and Trent, with a powerful young man of superb manners at the steering-wheel, were gliding swiftly southward, mile after mile, down the long lake. They landed at the most picturesque, and perhaps the most dilapidated and dirtiest, of all the lakeside villages, where in the tiny square above the landing-place a score of dusky infants were treading the measures and chanting the words of one of the immemorial games of childhood. While Mrs Lancey and her sister watched them in delight Trent spoke rapidly to the young engineer, whose gleaming eyes and teeth flashed understanding.

Soon afterward they strolled through San Marmette, and up the mountain road to a little church, half a mile away, where a curious fresco could be seen.

It was close on half past six when they returned, to be met by Giuseppe, voluble in excitement and apology. It appeared that while he had been fraternizing with the keeper of the inn by the landing-place a certain triste individue had, unseen by anyone, been tampering maliciously with the engine of the boat, and had poured handfuls of dust into the delicate mechanism. Mrs Lancey, who had received a private nod from Trent, reproved him bitterly for leaving the boat, and asked how long it would take to get the engine working again.

Giuseppe, overwhelmed with contrition, feared that it might be a matter of hours. Questioned, he said that the public steamer had arrived and departed twenty minutes since; the next one, the last of the day, was not due until after nine. Their excellencies could at least count on getting home by that, if the engine was not ready Sooner. Questioned further, he said that one could telephone from the post office, and that food creditably cooked was to be had at the trattoria.

Lady Bosworth was delighted. She declared that she would not have missed this occasion for anything. She had come to approve highly of Trent, who had made himself excellent company, and she saw her way to being quite admirable, for she was in dancing spirits. In ten minutes she was on the best of terms with the fat, vivacious woman of the inn. Trent, who had been dispatched to telephone their plight to George Lancey, and had added that they were enjoying it very much, returned to find Lady Bosworth in the little garden behind the inn, with her skirts pinned up, peeling potatoes and singing "*Il segreto per esse felice*," while her sister beat up something in a bowl, and the landlady, busy with cooking, laughed and screamed cheerful observations from the kitchen. Seeing himself unemployable, Trent withdrew; sitting on a convenient wall, he took a leaf from his sketchbook and began to devise and decorate a menu of an absurdity suited to the spirit of the hour.

It was a more than cheerful dinner that they had under a canopy of vine-leaves on a tiny terrace overlooking the lake. Twilight came on unnoticed. It was already dark when Trent, returning from an inspection of the boat, advised that they should return by the steamer if they would make sure of getting home that night; it would take an hour, but it would be safer. And presently there was a long-drawn hoot from down the lake, and a great black mass crowned with a galaxy of yellow lights came moving smoothly through the darkness.

It was as they sought for places on the crowded upper deck that Mrs Lancey put her hand on Trent's arm. "There hasn't been a sign of it all evening," she whispered. "What does that mean?"

"It means," murmured Trent, "that we got her away from the cause at the critical time, without anybody knowing we were going to do it."

"Whom do you mean by 'anybody'?"

"How on earth should I know? Here comes your sister."

It was not until the following afternoon that Trent found an opportunity of being alone with his hostess in the garden.

"She is perfectly delighted at having escaped it last night," said Mrs Lancey. "She says she knew it would pass off, but she hasn't the least notion how she was cured. Nor have I."

"She isn't," replied Trent. "Last night was only a beginning and we can't get her unexpectedly stranded for the evening every day. The next move can be made now, if you consent to it. Lady Bosworth will be out until this evening, I believe?"

"She's gone shopping in the town. What do you want to do?"

"I want you to take me up to her room, and there I want you to look very carefully through everything in the place—in every corner of every box and drawer and bag and cupboard—and show me anything you find that might—"

"I should hate to do that!" Mrs Lancey interrupted him, her face flushing.

"You would hate much more to see your sister again this evening as she was every evening before last night. Look here,

Edith, the position is simple enough. Every day, about seven, Lady Bosworth goes into that room in her normal state to dress for dinner. Every day she comes out of it apparently as she went in, but turns queer a little later. Now is there any other place than that room where the mischief, whatever it is, could happen?"

Mrs Lancey frowned dubiously. "Her maid is with her always."

"I suppose so; but it doesn't make any difference to the argument. That room is the only place where Lady Bosworth isn't with the rest of us, doing what we do, eating the same food, breathing the same air, exposed to all the same influences as we are. Does anything take place in that room to account for those strange seizures?"

Mrs Lancey threw out her hands. "I cannot bear to think that Isabel should be deceiving me. And yet I know—it's a dreadful thing—and what else could happen there?"

"That is what we may find out, if we do as I. say. You must decide. But remember that you must think of Lady Bosworth as one whom you are trying to save from a subtle evil. You can't shrink from a step merely because you wouldn't dream of taking it in the ordinary way."

For a few moments she stood carefully boring a hole in the gravel with one heel. Then: "Come along," she said, and led the way toward the house.

"Unless we take the floor up," said Mrs Lancey, seating herself emphatically on the bed in her sister's room twenty minutes later, "there's nowhere else to look. I've taken everything out and pried into every hole and corner. There isn't a single lockable thing that is locked. There isn't a bottle or phial or pillbox of any sort to be found. So much for your suspicions. And all the time I have been working like a Negro slave you have done nothing but stare about you, and play with brushes and combs and manicure-things. What interests you about that nail-polishing pad? You must have seen one before, surely?"

"This ornamental design on hammered silver is very beautiful and original," replied Trent, abstractedly. "I have never seen anything quite like it."

"The same design is on the whole of the toilet set," Mrs Lancey observed tartly, "and it shows to least advantage on the manicure-things. You are talking rubbish, Philip. Put the pad away and shut the case as you found it. We shall do no good here, I am sure; you will have to guess again. And yet," she added, slowly, "you are looking rather pleased with yourself."

Trent, his hands in his pockets, was balancing himself on his heels as he stared out of the window of the bedroom. His eyes were full of animation, and he was whistling almost inaudibly.

He turned round slowly. "I'm only guessing again—that's my guessing face. Whose are the rooms on each side of this, Edith?"

"This side, the Stones'; that side, Mr Scheffer's."

"Then I will go for a walk all alone and guess some more. Goodby."

"Yes," declared Mrs Lancey, as he went out, "it's plain enough you have picked up some scent or other."

"It isn't scent exactly," Trent replied, as he descended the stairs.

"Guess again."

Trent was not in the house when, three hours later, a rousing tumult broke out on the upper floor. Those below in the loggia heard first a piercing scream, then a clatter of feet on parquet flooring, then more sounds of feet, excited voices, other screams of harsh, inhuman quality, and a lively scuffling and banging. Mr Scheffer, with a volley of guttural words of which it was easy to gather the general sense, headed the rush of the company upstairs.

"Gisko! Gisko!" he shouted, at the head of the stairway. There was another ear-splitting screech, and the cockatoo came scuttling and fluttering out of Lady Bosworth's room, pursued by three vociferating women servants. The bird's yellow crest was erect and quivering with agitation; it screeched furious defiance again as it leapt upon its master's outstretched wrist.

"Silence, devil!" exclaimed Mr Scheffer, seizing it by the head and shaking it violently. "I know not how to apologize, Lancey," he declared. "The accursed bird has somehow slipped from his chain away. I left him in my room secure just before we had tea."

"Never mind, never mind!" replied his host, who seemed rather pleased than otherwise with this small diversion. "I don't suppose he's done any harm beyond frightening the women. Anything wrong, Edith?" he asked, as they approached the open door of the bedroom, to which the ladies had already hurried. Lady Bosworth's maid was telling a voluble story.

"When she came in just now to get the room ready for Isabel to dress," Mrs Lancey summarized, "she suddenly heard a voice say something, and saw the bird perched on top of the minor, staring at her. It gave her such a shock that she dropped the water-can and fled; then the two other girls came and helped her, trying to drive it out. They hadn't the sense to send for Mr Scheffer."

"Apologize, carrion!" Commanded Gisko's master. The cockatoo uttered a string of Dutch words in a subdued croak. "He says he asks one thousand pardons, and he will sin no more," Mr Scheffer translated. "Miserable brigand! Traitor!"

Lady Bosworth hurried out of her room.

"I won't hear the poor thing scolded like that," she protested. "How was he to know my maid would be frightened? He looks so wretched! Take him away, Mr Scheffer, and cheer him up." So Gisko was led away to bondage, and the episode was at an end.

It was half an hour later that Mrs Lancey came to her husband in his dressing-room.

"I must say Bella was very decent about Scheffer's horrid bird," she began. "Do you know what the little fiend had done?"

"No, my dear. I thought he had confined himself to frightening the maid out of her skin."

"Not at all. He had been having the time of his life. Bella saw at once that he had been up to mischief, but she pretended there was nothing. Now it turns out he has bitten the buttons off two pairs of gloves, chewed up a lot of hairpins, and spoiled her pretty little manicure-set. He's torn the lining out of the case, the silver handles are covered with beak marks, two or three of the things he seems to have hidden somewhere, and the polishing pad is a ruin. When Hignett saw him perched on the mirror he had the pad in one hand—I mean, foot—and was busy tearing away the last rags of the leather."

"It's too bad!" declared Mr Lancey, bending over a shoe.

"I believe you're laughing, George," said his wife, coldly.

He began to do so audibly. "You must admit it's funny to think of the bird going solemnly through a program of mischief like that. I wish I could have seen the little beggar at it. Well, we shall have to get Bell a new nail-outfit. I'm glad she held her tongue about it just now."

"Why?"

"Because, my dear, we don't ask people to the house to make them feel uncomfortable—especially foreigners."

"Bella wasn't thinking of your ideal of hospitality. She held her tongue because she's taken a fancy to Scheffer. But, George, how do you suppose the little pest got in? The window was shut, and Hignett declares the door was too, when she went to the room."

"Then I expect Hignett deceives herself. Anyway, what does it matter? What I am anxious about is your sister's little peculiarity. As I've told you, I don't at all like the look of her having been quite normal yesterday evening, the one evening when she was away from the house by accident. I wish I wasn't so fond of her, Edith. If it was another woman, she could do what she liked to herself for all I cared."

Mrs Lancey sighed. "If she had married you she would have been a very different woman."

"I know. It's awful to think of what we've all missed. If you had married Scheffer, Gisko would have been a very different cockatoo. For of all sad words of tongue or pen—I really am feeling miserably depressed, Edith. What I'm dreading now is a repetition of the usual ghastly performance tonight."

But neither that night, nor any night after, was that performance repeated. Lady Bosworth, free now of all apprehension, renewed and redoubled the life of the little company. And the lips of Trent were obstinately sealed.

***

Three weeks later Trent was shown into the consulting-room of Sir Peregrine Bosworth. The famous physician was a tall, stooping E. man of exaggerated gauntness, narrow-jawed and high-nosed. His still black hair was brushed backward, his eyes were deep-set and ' glowing, his mouth at once sensitive and strong. He was courteous of manner and smiled readily, but his face was set in unhappy lines.

"Will you sit down, Mr Trent?" said Sir Peregrine. "You wrote that you wished to see me upon a private matter concerning myself. I m at a loss to imagine what it can be, but, knowing your name, I had no hesitation in making an appointment."

Trent inclined his head. "I am obliged to you, Sir Peregrine. The matter is really important, and also quite private—so private that no person whatever knows the material facts besides myself. I won't waste words. I have lately been staying with the Lanceys, whom you know, in Italy. Lady Bosworth was also a guest there. For some days before my arrival she had suffered each evening from a curious attack of lassitude and vacancy of mind. I don't know what it was. Perhaps you do."

Sir Peregrine, immovably listening, smiled grimly. "The description of symptoms is a little vague. I have heard nothing of this, I may say, from my wife."

"It always came on at a certain time of the day, and only then. That time was a few minutes after eight, at the beginning of dinner. The attack passed off gradually after two hours or so."

The physician laid his clenched hand on the table between them. "You are not a medical man, Mr Trent, I believe. What concern have you with all this?" His voice was coldly hostile now.

"Lots," answered Trent, briefly. Then he added, as Sir Peregrine got to his feet with a burning eye, "I know nothing of medicine, but I cured Lady Bosworth."

The other sat down again suddenly. His open hands fell upon the table and his dark face became very pale. "You—" he began with difficulty.

"I and no other, Sir Peregrine. And in a curiously simple way. I found out what was causing the trouble, and without her knowledge I removed it. It was—oh, the devil!" Trent exclaimed in a lower tone. For Sir Peregrine Bosworth, with a brow gone suddenly white and clammy, had first attempted to rise and then sunk forward with his head on the table.

Trent, who had seen such things before, hurried to him, pulled his chair from the table, and pressed his head down to his knees. Within a minute the stricken man was leaning back in his chair. He inspired deeply from a small bottle he had taken from his pocket.

"You have been overworking, perhaps," Trent said. "Something is wrong. I think I had better not—"

Sir Peregrine had pulled himself together. "I know very well what is wrong with me, sir," he interrupted, brusquely. "It is my business to know. That will not happen again. I wish to hear what you have to say before you leave this house."

"Very well." Trent took a tone of colourless precision. "I was asked by Lady Bosworth's sister, Mrs Lancey, to help in trying to trace the source of the disorder which attacked her every evening. I need not describe the signs of it, and I will not trouble you with an account of how I reasoned on the matter. But I found out that Lady Bosworth was, on these occasions, under the influence of a drug, which had the effect of lowering her vitality and clogging her brain, without producing stupefaction or sleep; and I was led to the conclusion that she was administering this drug to herself without knowing it."

He paused, and felt in his waistcoat pocket. "When Mrs Lancey and I were making a search for something of the kind in her room, my attention was caught by the fine workmanship of a manicure-set on the dressing-table. I took up the little round box meant to contain nail-polishing paste, admiring its shape and decoration, and on looking inside it found it half-full of paste. But I have often watched the process of beautifying fingernails, and it seemed to me that the stuff was of a deeper red than the usual pink confection; and I saw next that the polishing-pad of the set, though well worn, had never been used with paste, which leaves a sort of dark encrustation on the pad. Yet it was evident that the paste in the little box had been used. It is useful sometimes, you see, to have a mind that notices trifles. So I jumped to the conclusion that the paste that was not employed as nail-polish was employed for some other purpose; and when I reached that point I simply put the box in my pocket and went away with it. I may say that Mrs Lancey knew nothing of this, or of what I did afterwards."

"And what was that?" Sir Peregrine appeared now to be following the story with an ironic interest.

"Naturally, knowing nothing of such matters, I took it to a place that called itself 'English Pharmacy' in the town, and asked the proprietor what the stuff was. He looked at it, took a little on his finger, smelt it, and said it was undoubtedly lipsalve.

"It was then I remembered how, when I saw Lady Bosworth during one of her attacks, her lips were brilliantly red, though all the colour had departed from her face. That had struck me as very odd, because I am a painter, and naturally I could not miss an abnormality like that. Then I remembered another thing. One evening, when Lady Bosworth, her sister, and myself were prevented from returning to the house for dinner, and dined at a country inn, there had been no signs of her trouble; but I had noticed that she moistened her lips again and again with her tongue."

"You are observant," remarked Sir Peregrine, dispassionately, and again had recourse to his smelling-bottle.

"You are good enough to say so," Trent replied, with a wooden face. "On thinking these things over, it seemed to me probable that Lady Bosworth was in the habit of putting on a little lipsalve when she dressed for dinner in the evening; perhaps finding that her lips at that time of day tended to become dry, or perhaps not caring to use it in daylight, when its presence would be much more easily detected. For I had learned that she made some considerable parade of not using any kind of cosmetics or artificial aids to beauty; and that, of course, accounted for her carrying it in a box meant for manicure-paste, which might be represented as merely a matter of cleanliness, and at any rate was not to be classed with paint and powder. It was not pleasant to me to have surprised this innocent little deception; but it was as well that I did so, for I soon ascertained beyond doubt that the stuff had been tampered with and drugged.

"When I left the chemist's I went and sat in a quiet corner of the Museum grounds. There I put the least touch of the salve on my tongue, and waited results. In five minutes I had lost all power of connected thought or will; I no longer felt any interest in my own experiment. I was conscious. I felt no discomfort, and no loss of the power of movement. Only my intelligence seemed to be paralyzed; and that did not trouble me in the least. For upwards of an hour I was looking out upon the world with the soul of an ox, utterly placid and blank."

Trent now opened his fingers and showed a little round box of hammered silver, with a delicate ornamentation running round the lid. It was of about the bigness of a pillbox.

"It seemed best to me that this box should simply disappear, and in some quite natural, unsuspicious way; merely to remove the salve would have drawn Lady Bosworth's attention to it and set her guessing. She did not suspect the stuff as yet, I was fully convinced, and I thought it well that the affair of her seizures should remain a mystery. Your eyes ask why. Just because I did not want a painful scandal in Mrs Lancey's family—we are old friends, you see. So the problem was to make the box and its contents disappear in a manner which would appear completely accidental, and suggest no ideas of any sort to Lady Bosworth or anyone else. That I managed to do; and now here I am with the box, and neither Lady Bosworth nor any other person has the smallest inkling of its crazy secret but you and I."

He stopped again and looked in Sir Peregrine's eyes. They remained fixed upon him with the gaze of a statue.

"It was plain, of course," Trent continued, "that someone had got at the stuff immediately before she went out to Italy, or immediately on her arrival. The chemical operation of combining the drug with the salve would hardly have been performed during the journey. But the attacks began on the first evening there, two hours after her reaching the house. Therefore any tampering with the salve after her arrival was practically impossible. When I asked myself who should have tampered with it before Lady Bosworth left this house to go out to Italy, I was led to form a very unpleasant conjecture."

Sir Peregrine stirred in his chair. "You had been told the truth—or a part of the truth—about our married life, I suppose?"

Trent inclined his head. "Three days ago I arrived in London, and showed a little of this paste to a friend of mine who is an expert analyst. He has sent me a report, which I have here." He handed an envelope across the table. "He was deeply interested in what he found, but I have not satisfied his curiosity. He found the salve to be evenly impregnated with a very slight quantity of a rare alkaloid body called purvisine. Infinitesimal doses of it produce effects on the human organism which he describes, as I can testify, with considerable accuracy. It was discovered, he notes, by Henry Purvis twenty-five years ago; and you will remember, Sir Peregrine, what I only found out by inquiry—that you were assistant to Purvis about that time ago in Edinburgh. Where he had the Chair of medical jurisprudence and toxicology."

He ceased to speak, and there was a short silence. Sir Peregrine gazed at the table before him. Once or twice he drew breath deeply, and at length began to speak with composure.

"I shall not waste words," he said, "in trying to explain fully my State of mind or my action in this matter. But I will tell you enough for your imagination to do the rest. My feeling for my wife was an infatuation from the beginning and is still. I was too old for her. I don't think now that she ever cared for me greatly; but she was too strong-minded ever to marry a wealthy fool, and I had won a high position and a fortune. By the time we had been married a year I could no longer hide from myself that she had an incurable weakness for philandering. She has surrendered herself to it with less and less restraint, and without any attempt to deceive me on the subject. If I tried to tell you what torture it has been to me, you wouldn't understand. The worst was when she was away from me, staying with her friends, and I could not know what was happening. At length I took the step you know. It was undeniably an act of baseness, and we will leave it at that, if you please. If you should ever suffer as I do, you will modify your judgment upon me. I knew of my wife's habit, discovered by you, of using lip-salve at her evening toilette. On the night before her departure I took what was in that box and combined it with a preparation of the drug purvisine. The infinitesimal amount which would pass into the mouth after the application of the salve was calculated to produce for an hour or two the effects you have described, without otherwise doing any harm. But I knew the impression that would be produced upon normal men and women by the sight of anyone in such a state. I wanted to turn her attractiveness into repulsiveness, and I seem to have succeeded. I was mad when I did it. I have been aghast at my own action ever since. I am glad it has been frustrated. And now I should like to know what you intend to do."

Trent took up the box. "If you agree, Sir Peregrine, I shall drop this from Westminster Bridge tonight. And so long as nothing of the sort is practised again, the whole affair shall be buried. Yours is a wretched story, and I don't suppose any of us would find our moral fibre improved by such a situation. I have no more to say."

He rose and moved to the door. Sir Peregrine rose also and stood with lowered eyes, apparently deep in thought. Suddenly he looked up.

"I am obliged to you Mr Trent," he said formally. "I may say, too, that your account of your proceedings interested me deeply. I should like to ask a question. How did you contrive that the box should disappear without its owner seeing anything remarkable in its absence?"

"Oh, easily," Trent replied, his hand on the doorknob. "After experimenting on myself, I went back to the house before tea-time, when no one happened to be in. I went upstairs to a room where a cockatoo was kept—mischievous brute—took him off his chain, and carried him into Lady Bosworth's room. There I put him on the dressing-table, and teased him a little with the manicure-things to interest him in them. Then I took away one of the pairs of scissors, so that the box shouldn't be the one thing missing, and left him shut in there to do his worst, while I went out of the house again. When I went he was ripping out the silk lining of the case, and had chewed up the silver handles of the things pretty well. After I had gone he went on to destroy various other things. In the riot that took place when he was found the disappearance of the little box and scissors became a mere detail. Certainly Lady Bosworth suspected nothing.

"I suppose," he added, thoughtfully, "that occasion would be the only time a cockatoo was of any particular use."

4

THE VANISHING LAWYER

What made the Gayles affair such an especially bad business was the culprit's standing in his profession and in the eyes of the world. The firm of Gayles & Sims had a position as family solicitors that was second to none, and its head was a very important person indeed.

So it was that John Charlton Gayles, after the fact of his disappearance became known, was one of the most badly wanted men who had ever attracted the attention of the police. According to the information furnished by his partner, he had always had the sole control of the firm's accounts and financial business. An enormous amount of property entrusted to his care could not be traced; and neither could Mr Gayles, of whom nothing had been seen or heard since he retired to his bedroom one Tuesday night in May. During the following two days matters had been brought to the notice of Mr Sims which made it clear that there was a great deal requiring explanation from the senior partner; and on the Friday it was decided to give information to the police of his disappearance and of the firm's predicament.

Philip Trent, at the opening of his first article as the *Record's* special investigator of this unusual case, dwelt upon the rock-ribbed respectability of the missing man.

"It is a safe statement," he wrote, "that no lawyer has ever enjoyed a more spotless reputation. He has for some years been chairman of the Law Society's Disciplinary Committee, whose duty is to examine and act upon cases of professional misconduct. In his own life he has always been a model of probity and high principle.

"On Tuesday last Mr Gayles returned by an early train after a long weekend at Preakness, and drove from Victoria to his office in Lincoln's Inn Fields. This, at least, was his own account of how he had spent his time; but it is now established that nothing was seen of him that weekend at the hotel where he always stayed in Preakness. He did a normal day's work, and a little after six o'clock went home to his house in Castle Terrace, Knightsbridge. At 9:30, as usual, he went to bed; for Mr Gayles believed in very early hours both night and morning.

"He was not called next day, as he preferred to rise at his own time, and often did so before the servants were stirring. But at eight, his hour for breakfast, he did not appear; and when his butler went to call him, he found no sign anywhere of Mr Gayles. His bed had been slept in, and he had washed and shaved in the bathroom opening out of the bedroom. It would seem that he left the house before seven, the servants' time for rising, and that he did not go out by either of the house doors, which were still bolted inside. Mr Gayles had his bedroom on the ground floor; it opens on the garden by way of a French window, and through this, it is surmised, he went to the end of the garden and out by a door in the wall, which was found unlocked with the key in its place. This door gives on a narrow blind alley leading into Knightsbridge, where an early bus or cab could have been taken. Mr Gayles, an old-fashioned man in many ways, did not own a car and had never learnt to drive one.

"His partner, Mr Sims, when told of his disappearance, was completely mystified. Why Mr Gayles, the sanest of men, should have chosen so to absent himself without a word to anyone was quite incomprehensible; but Mr Sims was naturally unwilling to take any hasty action which might prejudice the reputation of the firm. When facts came to light, however, which made Mr Gayles's presence desirable, to say the least, the police were called in. After a day of investigation they are believed to be still at a loss.

"Mr Gayles recently drew from his bank a large sum in cash, being the whole of the amount standing to his credit."

The photograph accompanying this article showed a firm, grave face, of which the most striking details were the bushy brows over dark-rimmed glasses, the rather heavy jowls, and, by contrast, the hair not yet at all receded from the forehead. This was from a press picture of the high table at a City banquet; for Gayles, as far as could be discovered, had never been photographed on his own account.

Trent had added little to the bare facts given to the newspapers from Scotland Yard. He set out now to follow his own hunting nose; and on the morning of the appearance of this article he had an interview at the firm's office with the junior partner. Mr Sims was a man in the forties, smart, worldly, and with competence stamped on his hard, clean-shaven face. He looked jaded and harassed.

"You want to hear about Gayles as a personality?" Sims said. "Well, I thought that if anybody knew John Gayles, I did. I would have trusted him with every shilling I had in the world. And now we find he has gambled away his own fortune and God knows how much of other people's money. So much for being a very reserved character! Gayles was always that; and after his wife's death he became very much more so. He was devoted to her—even he couldn't help showing that—and it wasn't until after she died, as far as we can make out, that this Stock Exchange mania got hold of him. It was a distraction, perhaps; anyhow, it seems to have begun the year after she died."

"I am told he was a Cambridge man," Trent said. "Did you ever hear of his doing any gambling in those days? It's one of the tastes that can be acquired at the universities, I know."

"Oh no! Far from it. His father—the founder of the firm—was very proud of Gayles's Cambridge record. He carried off two prizes, I remember, and got an excellent degree, besides being President of the Union. I never heard of his making a bet in his life."

"Did he take any interest in sport or games?"

'"Not the faintest. He never seemed to need exercise himself."

"Was his health good, then?" Trent asked.

"Why, he never looked healthy, because of that pale face of his," Sims said. "But as a matter of fact, I never knew him to have an illness until the time he took a holiday five years ago. He used always to go abroad for a month in the summer, not having letters forwarded. Well, this time, when the month was up, instead of Gayles came a post card from him saying he was obliged to prolong his holiday for a week or two. There was no address on the card, but it was postmarked Freiburg in Breisgau. This was very unlike Gayles, because he had always been keen to get back to his work—that and his garden at home. When he did return, it came out that he had travelled straight to Freiburg, arrived there feeling very ill, and been sent straight into the Heiliggeist Hospital with scarlet fever."

"Then was he there all by himself all that time?"

"Absolutely. He only sent me that one disinfected post card, and remained there till he was out of quarantine. He had had it badly, and all his hair had fallen out. He was wearing a wig, a very expensive one he said it was, but it never looked like his own hair. He was evidently feeling very disgusted about it; and he said he wished never to have it referred to again. It wasn't, either; it didn't do to annoy Gayles. I suspect he had been rather proud of having a thick crop of dark hair at his age."

"And didn't the illness mark him in any other way?"

"Only that it had affected his eyes—he had to wear tinted glasses all the time. But his health recovered completely, in spite of the fact that he never took a proper holiday after that. He had had enough of long holidays, he said; and he made up for it by spending most of his weekends inhaling the sea-air at Preakness."

"Why at Preakness?" Trent wondered. "I barely know its name, and I've never met anyone who has been there."

Sims made a grimace. "You wouldn't. It's on a branch off the main line to Mewstone, and once when I was there I ran over in my car to have a look at Preakness. Gayles always said it was the quietest spot on the South Coast, and I should say he wasn't far wrong. Five minutes of it was ample for me. I believe the inn Gayles stayed at is good enough, though—people go there for the trout-fishing. Anyhow, it did Gayles good. The only thing he has ever had wrong with him since that illness is neuralgia, which he began to suffer from intermittently some time ago. Now and then he would come to the office with his jaws tied up in a scarf—he was that way the last time he was here."

Trent considered a few moments. "His hair was entirely gone, you say. I suppose you never saw him without his wig."

"No, not I. Some of the staff have done, though. There's Willis, the clerk who went to his room to take letters at eleven each morning. Once or twice he has caught Gayles with his wig off at the glass over by the window. Of course, Willis had the sense to pretend not to have seen, and Gayles had shoved it on again in a moment. Then there's the office boy who had to take in Gayles's cup of tea at 4:30. He caught him once in just the same way, Willis told me."

Trent smiled. "Would you describe Gayles as at all an eccentric man?" he said as he got up to go.

"Oh no," Sims said, rising also to his feet. "He was much like a hundred other lawyers of fifty-five to look at—more old-fashioned and black-coated than some, perhaps but that's all. And he was a perfect devil for punctuality and system in the office. But many of us are like that, and all of us ought to be. And it is just that, you see, Mr Trent, that makes this affair so completely bewildering. Gayles was almost inhumanly correct. It's what makes me wonder"—Sims lowered his voice impressively here—"if there can have been anything wrong with him mentally after all. Well, goodbye. Look me up again if you want to ask about anything more."

Trent had no difficulty, later in the day, in prevailing on Perfitt and his wife, the butler and cook-housekeeper in the Gayles household, to talk about their employer's disappearance, and to allow an inspection of the bedroom from which the bird had so mysteriously flown. They found a gloomy enjoyment in their connection with fraud on such a scale, and the collapse of such a reputation. None of the four servants had had much liking for Gayles, but they had esteemed him a just man and a tower of respectability. It was, Mrs Perfitt said, like as if the world had turned upside down to think of Mr Gayles having took money, and being in hiding from the police.

The bedroom was a large, airy, rather monastic apartment, with a small shelf of bedside books as its only humane feature. This, thought Trent, would be Gayles's idea of light reading. His roving eye fell upon *Serjeant Ballantine's Experiences; Anomalies of the Law of England; Stories from the Law Reports; Life in the Law.* Fiction was represented by *The Pilgrim's Progress*, with the excellent illustrations of J. D. Watson.

A little chilled by this glimpse into the mental privacy of John Gayles, Trent turned to the French window, still open upon a beautifully tended garden. Beds of tulips in luxuriant variety flanked the smooth lawn. Gayles, it could be seen, was an enthusiast. Companies of different blooms were arrayed in a carpet-work of diagonal stripes. Mr Gayles, said the butler, did most of the work himself, in the early morning or after office hours; when he was not planting and trimming he would just sit and look at them.

A garden-book lay open on a table by the window, and Trent looked down on a list of tulips, in the order of the time of their flowering. Albino; Bronze Knight; Sieraad van Flora; Mewstone Glory; Rijnland; Pollux; Mr Zimmerman; Malicorne—so the list went on. With what a wrench must Gayles have torn himself away from all this! In a corner of the room stood a strange-looking standard lamp, topped by a metal cowl with wires attached, and stamped with a maker's name and the words ULTRA-VIOLET RAY. Gayles used it, the butler said, for his neuralgia.

There was a bathroom, with the usual outfit of toilet accessories, opening out of the bedroom. None of these things, nor, as far as Perfitt could say, any clothing or requisites of travel, had been taken away by Gayles. He seemed to have taken nothing but the clothes he stood up in—those he had worn the day before. This was as much as an inquirer without authority could gather from the household of the much-wanted man.

Three days later Trent was closeted with Chief Inspector Murch in his bare little office at Scotland Yard; a room which the visitor knew well. He had even contributed to its scanty decoration a charcoal sketch of Mrs Murch, which beamed from above the fireplace.

"Yes," Mr Murch said as he stuffed tobacco into a pipe. "We have been in communication with the police at Freiburg. What to make of it I don't know; and I can't think what put you onto suggesting this line. Nor how it's going to help us, either.

But the fact, for what it's worth, is that the whole story about Gayles's having scarlet fever in Freiburg is simply a lie."

Trent jumped to his feet. "Three ringing cheers! And just what did you hear from the police there?"

Mr Murch got his pipe going, then said, "They're very thorough; very anxious to be helpful, too. They say there was no Englishman, or any other foreigner, in that hospital with scarlet fever or with anything else all that summer. Not only that, but there wasn't a single case of scarlet fever in the town all that year. So there you are—Gayles cooked up the whole thing. Presumably he did go there, because of the post card; but nobody calling himself Gayles stayed at any of the hotels at that time. And now, what about it?"

"It depends," Trent said, "on the answer to another question. Do you know when he began helping himself to his clients' money?"

The inspector took up some typewritten sheets from a wire basket. "I can give you an outline of what has been found out so far. He started speculating on a large scale about nine years ago, and at first he made a lot of money. After that he had a run of serious losses, and he appears to have got through the whole of his private fortune four years after he began; anyhow, it was then that he took his first fatal step. He was a trustee of various settlements and other funds. He started with one of £17,000, which he converted for his own use and benefit; lost that, and went on going deeper and deeper, in the hope of getting square again. All the victims received their incomes regularly, so they naturally never suspected they were being paid out of stolen capital. You can see how easy it is, when every one has absolute confidence in a man's integrity. First and last, nearly £200,000 had gone by the time Gayles did his disappearing act. Some of it, no doubt, he had Stowed away somewhere where he could get at it under another name. The rest went down the drain. That's the story, put short. It has taken some getting at, because he employed a number of different brokers."

"Thank you," Trent said. "It is just as I expected."

"You mean about the time when he went wrong?"

"Yes, first we hear that he had scarlet fever five years ago. Now we hear that he began gambling nine years ago, and that ruin was Staring him in the face after four years of it. You see? The Freiburg .trick was staged just about the time when he had yielded to temptation, or was just going to, perhaps."

Mr Murch looked at Trent consideringly. "Well, if you will tell me why," he said slowly. "I suppose you are not suggesting he could have lost his hair any other way than by having a severe illness somewhere. And why should that have had anything to do with his starting out as a wrong 'un? I agree that he had been preparing his getaway a long time. The Perfitts say it was some years ago—they don't remember exactly—that he took to sleeping in that convenient ground-floor room. And we know now why he never took a holiday apart from weekends—a show-up might come at any time, if he wasn't on the spot to stave it off. I must say he managed very well. He knew Sims wouldn't have any grounds for calling us in at first, so that the trail was stone-cold by the time we started. We don't know when he left the house, and we haven't a clue to where he went, and the watch-out for him at home and abroad has been absolutely fruitless so far."

"Yes, he certainly showed good judgment. But I should keep Freiburg in mind if I were you. Did you find anything out of the way when you went through Gayles's place?"

"Nothing—except that in the bathroom, among the little bottles over the basin, there was one of spirit gum. And I don't see what he could have wanted with that. He couldn't have imagined he could get away with a false beard or moustache."

"Perhaps he put it there to make it more difficult. You must have been meant to find it."

"That's just the kind of thing," the inspector said, "you can't be so sure about. A criminal will often mess up the cleverest plan by some idiotic piece of carelessness—you know that as well as I do."

"Just so. Well, I hope the Freiburg myth seems to you worth pondering about—it does to me. Now I must be off—and I say, if I should manage to beat you to Gayles, I will let you know at once. The word will be Snowdrop."

"Well, it's nice to see you again, Phil," Eunice Faviell said. "I wish it happened oftener. What did you want to see me about? You aren't here on account of my beautiful eyes, I know."

She was receiving Trent in her dressing-room at the Siddons Theatre, after the first act of that vivacious comedy *Beautiful Soup*, and she was delicately adjusting, before her glass, the coronet she was to wear in the second act.

"It was to get some advice about beauty treatment, at least," Trent said.

"Beauty treatment!" she stared at him. "My dear, do you want to have your face lifted, or your silhouette improved? I can put you onto a friend of mine who has just had ten pounds carved off below the waistline—or perhaps I hadn't better, as no one is supposed to know. But really, Phil, you will do as you are for a few years yet. You mustn't lose heart about your figure."

"I don't. I want to know about something quite different. The question is whether a man can disguise his complexion in such a way that it will look natural by daylight and not be detected at all."

Eunice reached to a row of small bottles on a shelf by the mirror. "You could do it with this wash," she said. "It will change that light gingerbread colour of yours to an interesting paleness, and if you renew it two or three times a day it will look all right to anyone who doesn't know you. But with anyone who does, it would be very hard to change your complexion so that he couldn't tell it was faked. And now will you tell me why you should be thinking of trying to look like a turnip?"

"But I wasn't thinking of myself at all. I never do—you know that. The man I have in mind is a white-faced man."

"If that's his type," Eunice said, "you can get lotions which claim to give you a healthy tan that you haven't deserved. But it never looks as good as the real thing, and, like the other, it wouldn't deceive his friends. The only convincing way for a pale man to get brown is nature's way."

"I see. Well, that clears up my uncertainties, Eunice; and you have given me something to think about."

"Miss Faviell, please," came a yelp and a knock at the door.

One evening a week later Inspector Murch was much moved on receiving a telegram in these words:

> SNOWDROP WHAT TRAIN SHALL I MEET TOMORROW PRINCES STREET REPLY TRENT NORFOLK HOTEL MEWSTONE.

Mr Murch, knowing Trent well enough to be sure that this meant business, consulted a timetable and replied at once. Next morning at 10:45, on the platform of the Prince's Street Station at Mewstone, he was greeted by Trent.

"I can see by the look in your eye that you have got something," the inspector said as they went through the barrier.

"When I say Snowdrop, I mean Snowdrop."

"All right. Where do we go from here? And why Mewstone?"

"We go to the Botanic Gardens," Trent said as they went briskly up the station approach. "They are said to be among the finest in the country—and Gayles, you know, loved flowers. You may not know that he had among his tulips one named after this place. It's famous for them, I find. Then there is the immortal question, 'Where does a wise man hide a leaf?' Answer, 'In the forest.' And where does a retired—or retiring—professional man hide himself? In Mewstone, of course—it's swarming with them. Above all, Mewstone is not very far from Preakness, and you take the same train from Victoria for both of them. So I decided to pay a visit to Mewstone; and yesterday I saw Gayles in the Botanic Gardens. When he went off to his hotel for lunch, I went there too, and took a room. I have made a few discreet inquiries there; also at Preakness.

"Now I will tell you a few things I guessed about Gayles. The first is that, during that long holiday five years ago, wherever he spent it, he employed his time learning to drive a car."

"Ha!" Mr Murch ejaculated.

"Anyhow, he drives quite well now. He went on improving, I dare say, during those solitary weekends of his, most of which he did not spend at Preakness, as you'll find if you look up the register at the Pitt's Head Inn there, where he was supposed to stay. It's true he went there fairly often; but Mewstone is the place for hiring cars.

"In other ways he got ready for the smash, if it should become inevitable. For five years he wore his wig and his conspicuous glasses. He took to sleeping on the ground floor.

"In time things went from bad to worse, and at last exposure was very near. So Gayles took his final measures. He developed neuralgia, and bought an ultra-violet sun-ray lamp to cure it. It is true that the deep infra-red is what they use for neuralgia; but the ultra-violet is excellent for another thing—it cures you of being pale. Gayles used it, I imagine, each morning before breakfast. In a fortnight, say, he had a fine natural brown-red colour. As soon as it began to appear, he took to whitening his face with liquid powder or some such stuff, and he kept it on till bedtime.

"Then he went for his last long weekend. Early on the Friday evening he took a taxi from the office, with his suitcase, to Victoria. We know that; what follows is guesswork. At the station he took a dressing-room, perhaps, washed his face, shed his wig and glasses, and changed into different—very different—clothes. Also he trimmed his eyebrows close, and put the loose hair in an envelope. Then he left Victoria, when the rush-period was on, and nobody paid any attention to him. He proceeded to make a call on Mr H. T. Wyman, of 37 Yarborough Place, who performed on him the simple and swift operation of lifting his face."

"What!" shouted Mr Murch, exploding in a laugh; then added soberly, "Well, go on."

"I got the idea of it," Trent said, "from a chance remark made by a friend whom I was consulting about changing one's complexion. Then I inquired for the names of the principal experts who do that operation, and started to look them up; and at the second shot I found Wyman. He will tell you that at 5:30 that day he did the job for a man named Davies, who had made the appointment by phone some days before—an elderly sportsman with a very brown face, in light grey tweeds and a rather larky striped tie.

"Gayles returned to the station and took the dining-car express, not to Preakness, but to Mewstone. He had nothing to show on him but some stitches behind his ears, and he looked about half his age. On arriving, he went to the Norfolk Hotel and took a room in the name of E. G. Fairhurst, saying that he would probably be staying some months if he liked the place. He has stayed there ever since."

"That's wrong, anyhow," snapped the inspector. "On the following Tuesday—"

"Let me tell you what he did on the following Tuesday. He left for London by the 7:35 a.m., on which he had booked a compartment for himself. He said he was going to bring his car down to Mewstone, and took a place for it in the hotel garage. In the compartment he changed into the Gayles outfit, whitened his face, and resumed his wig; also he stuck on his eyebrows the clippings he had kept, using that spirit gum which he afterwards left about to keep you guessing. Before reaching London he tied up his jaws in a scarf because of his neuralgia, which had taken the unusual form of much improving the shape of his face. Then he was ready for what was to be positively the last appearance of J. C. Gayles. After his day at the office he went home, and retired at 9:30. As soon as he was in the room, he floundered about in the bed for a little, then changed back into the personality of E. G. Fairhurst, put the Gayles clothes into his suitcase, walked out with it through the garden, and went off to some garage where he had been keeping a car for some time—under his new name, no doubt.

"And so, you see, he drove straight down to Mewstone, arriving, according to the night porter, about 1:30, saying he had had a breakdown; garaged the car, went up to bed, and had six or seven hours of refreshing slumber after a busy day. He had been in regular residence at the hotel for five days before Gayles was missed from his home, and a week before his disappearance was reported in the papers. Looking as if he had never put his nose inside an office in his life, too. He must have thought the position fairly safe."

"Devil doubt it," agreed Mr Murch. "He had worked hard enough."

By this time they had arrived at the Botanic Gardens, and Trent led the way to a seat in that well-wooded, smooth-turfed and gorgeous-bedded park. "That is how the fake was managed, I believe," he said. "Some of it is conjecture, of course; but does it seem to you to hang together?"

The inspector lay back with his arms along the top of the seat, and reflected. "If you have really got Gayles, it would account for everything. If you have got him, it's a fine piece of work, and you can say I said so."

"I said Snowdrop," Trent reminded him. "Take a look at the man over there." His glance indicated a typical Mewstone resident, brown-red of face, leisurely of mien, rather gaily plus-foured and stockinged, on a seat about twenty yards from them on the opposite side of the walk. This person had bared his head to the gentle breeze, and was contentedly eying the great bank of tulips that faced him beyond the path. Mr Murch stared, then turned to Trent.

"I don't see it," he said curtly. "Why, that man's hair is as genuine as your own. Dammit, look at it! And he isn't more than forty at the outside—I'd say thirty if he wasn't going grey."

"That," Trent said, "is what Wyman does for you. As for his hair, of course it's genuine, because he never lost it. He wore a wig on top of it for those five years."

The inspector snorted. "Then you haven't heard that Gayles has been seen without his wig, and that he is as bald as a coot."

"Oh yes; Sims told me that. But on those occasions, you see, Gayles was wearing a sham bald head, such as you've often seen on the stage. Now and then, when he meant to be caught that way, he would wear his bald pate, and the wig over that. He was seen so only for a moment, with the light behind him, and the effect was quite convincing. All the same, it was just that that gave me my first idea about the whole fraud. He was always seen by people whose duty it was to come into his room at that precise moment. You know that he insisted on the strictest punctuality. When I realized that he would naturally be most careful to have his wig in place at those times, the great idea began to dawn on me. At last I saw that he had planned to disappear by shedding a few things that were not genuine, and giving himself an entirely new appearance that anyone could see was genuine. Quite a good notion, I thought."

The inspector sighed. "All right; you win. But how am I going to arrest a man I can't identify? I have only known him as he was before he absconded. The real hair, and the eyebrows, and the shape of the face—they make all the difference."

Trent took from his pocket an envelope, and drew out two slips of paper. "Here are two portraits cut from unmounted group-photographs of the Committee of the Cambridge Union Society, taken in Gayles's third year, before his eyebrows began to thicken. I had them sent to me by Hurst & Bingham, the firm who took them; they keep negatives of that kind in case they're wanted for memoirs or biographies. The serious-looking person in this print is the Librarian of the Union. In the other, taken six months later, you see him again as President. Pretty good likenesses, don't you think?"

Mr Murch gazed at the young-old face in the two prints, then at the old-young face of the man on the neighbouring seat. He shook hands with Trent in silence, then rose, walked over to his unsuspecting victim, and touched him lightly on the shoulder.

Two months later John Charlton Gayles, found guilty on all counts of the indictment, was sentenced to fourteen years' penal servitude.

5

THE INOFFENSIVE CAPTAIN

"Inspector Charles B. Muirhead. Introduced by Chief Inspector W. Murch." Trent was reading from a card brought to him as he sat at breakfast. "I had no idea," he remarked to his servant, "that Mr Murch was introducing a new kind of policeman. What does he look like, Dennis?"

"He might be anything, sir. A very ordinary-looking man, I should say."

"Well, that's the highest compliment you could pay a plainclothes officer, I suppose."

Trent finished his coffee and stood up. "Show him into the studio. And if he should happen to arrest me, telephone to Mr Ward that I am unfortunately detained and cannot join him this evening."

"Certainly, sir."

The two men who came together in Philip Trent's studio looked keenly at each other. The police-officer, who did not much approve of the mission on which he had been sent, was not reassured by what he saw. Trent was at this time—it was a few years before the unravelling of the Manderson affair came to change his life—a man not yet thirty, with an air of rather irresponsible good humour and an easy, unceremonious carriage of his loose-knit figure that struck his visitor as pleasing in general, but not in keeping with great mental gifts. His features were regular; his short, Curling hair and moustache, and, indeed, his whole appearance, suggested a slight but not defiant carelessness about externals.

Mr Muirhead, knowing nothing of modern painters, thought this quite right in an artist, but he wondered what could have led such a man to interest himself in police problems.

As for Inspector Muirhead, he was a lean, light-haired, upstanding man with a scanty yellow moustache, dressed in an ill-fitting dark suit, with a low collar much too large for his neck. The only noticeable things about him were an air of athletic hardness and a pair of blue eyes like swords. He looked like a Cumberland shepherd who had changed clothes with a rent-collector.

"I am very glad," said Trent, "to meet any friend of Inspector Murch's. Sit down and have a cigar. Not a smoker? So much the worse for the criminal class—you look as if your nerves were made of steel wire. Now, let me hear what it is you want of me."

The hard-featured officer squared his shoulders and put his hands on his knees. "Inspector Murch thought you might be willing to help us unofficially, Mr Trent, in a little difficulty we are in. It concerns the escape of James Rudmore from Dartmoor yesterday afternoon."

"I hadn't heard of it."

"It's in the papers today—the bare fact. But the details are unusual. For one thing, he's got clear away, which has happened only in a very few cases at Dartmoor. Rudmore did what others have done—made a bolt from one of the gangs doing outdoor labour, taking advantage of a mist coming on suddenly. But instead of wandering on the moor till he was taken again, as they mostly a do, he got on a road some miles from the prison, where he had the luck to meet a motor-car going slowly in the mist. He jumped out in front of the car, and when the chauffeur stopped it Rudmore sprang at him and gave him a knock on the head with a stone that stunned him. The car belongs to an American gentleman and his wife, by name Van Sommeren, who were touring about the country."

"Gratifying for them," remarked Trent. "They will feel the English are not making strangers of them—that we are taking them to our bosom, as it were."

"Mr Van Sommeren drew a revolver," pursued the detective stolidly, "and shot twice before Rudmore closed with him. He managed to get hold of the weapon after a struggle, and so had them at his mercy. He was hurt slightly in the arm by one of the shots, Mr Van Sommeren thinks. Rudmore made him give up his motor-coat and cap, and all he had in his pockets; also the lady's purse. Then he put on the coat and cap over his convict dress and drove off alone, going eastward. The others waited till the chauffeur was all right again, then made the best of their way along the road on foot. It was hours before they got to Two Bridges and told their story."

"He managed it well," Trent observed, lighting a pipe. "Decision and promptitude. He ought to have been a soldier."

"He was," returned Mr Muirhead. "He had been, at least. But the point is, where is he now? We now know that he drove the car as far as Exeter, where he abandoned it outside the railway station, taking with him two large suitcases and a dressing-bag. There can be no doubt that he came on by train to London, arriving last night. He has particular business here, as well as friends who would help him. Do you remember the Danbury pendant affair, Mr Trent? It's nearly two years ago now."

"I don't. Probably I was not in England at the time."

"Then I may as well tell you the story of it and the Rudmores. You must know it if you're to assist us. Old John Rudmore was for many years a doctor in very good practice in Calcutta—had been an army doctor at first. He was a widower, a man of good family, highly educated, very clever and popular. His only son was James Rudmore, who was a lieutenant in a Bengal cavalry regiment, very much the same sort of man as his father. There was a daughter, too—a young girl. Six years ago, when James was twenty-three, something happened—something to do with old Rudmore, it is believed. It was kept dark quite successfully, but the word went out against the Rudmores. The old man threw up his practice, and the son sent in his papers. All three of them came home and settled in London. The Rudmores had influential connections, and Jim got a soft job under the Broad of Trade. His sister went to live with some relatives of her mother's. The father made his head- quarters in bachelor chambers in Jermyn Street. He travelled a good deal and was interested in mining properties. He seemed to have amassed a great deal of money, and it was believed he made his son a considerable allowance."

"Was there supposed to be anything wrong about the money?"

"That we don't know; but what happened afterward makes it seem likely. Well, James Rudmore went the pace considerably. He got into a gambling, dissipated set, and wasn't particular about what friends he made. He was intimate with some of the shadiest characters in sporting circles—people we'd had an eye upon more than once. He was a reckless, desperate chap, with a dangerous temper when roused, and he was well on his way to being a regular wrong 'un when the affair of the pendant happened; but he was very clever and amusing, and had a light-hearted way with him; a gentleman all over to look at, and hadn't lost caste, as they say."

Trent nodded appreciatively. "You describe him to the life. I should like to have known him."

"One day there was a big garden party at Danbury House, and he was there helping with some sort of entertainment. Lady Danbury was wearing the pendant, which was a famous family jewel containing three remarkable diamonds and some smaller stones. It was late in the afternoon before she found that the chain it was attached to had broken and the pendant was gone. By that time many of the guests had gone, too, and James Rudmore among them. A search was begun all over the grounds, but it hadn't gone far when one of the maids, hearing of the loss, came forward with a statement. It seemed she had been philandering with one of the men servants in a part of the grounds where she'd no business to be; the countess had been receiving people there, but it was deserted at the time. The man's eye was caught by something on the grass, and the girl, going nearer to it, recognized the pendant. Just as she was hurrying forward to pick it up, they heard steps on the path, and thinking it might be one of the upper servants, who would make trouble about her being out there, they both stepped behind a clump of shrubbery. They saw James Rudmore come round the corner of the path. He was alone and seemed to be looking for something on the ground. He caught sight of the pendant and stood gazing at it a moment. Then he picked it up and, holding it in his hand, went on toward the place where the company were. That was all that the two saw. Naturally, they thought he was carrying the thing straight to the countess; it never occurred to them that a man of young Rudmore's appearances would steal it."

"It was a silly thing to do," Trent remarked.

"He was in a tight place," explained the detective. "It came out afterward that he was deeply in debt and had just dropped a good sum on the Stock Exchange. He wanted money desperately."

"He had one resource," suggested Trent. "I have heard it described as tapping the ancestor."

"The ancestor," said Mr Muirhead with a hard smile, "was away on his travels, looking into some East African mining proposition, and apparently couldn't be got at. Besides, as you'll see, tapping him might not have been much good; and James no doubt knew that, for their relations were always very close and confidential. But as I was saying: The two witnesses told their story about the finding of the pendant. An hour afterward I was out after James with a warrant in my pocket. About nine o'clock I arrested him as he walked into the hotel where he lived. He denied the charge with a show of astonishment and indignation, but he made no resistance. The pendant was not on him then, and it was never found. I took him away in a taxicab. In Panton Street he gave me a blow on the jaw that knocked me out, jumped from the cab, and darted round the corner into Whitcomb Street. There he ran into the arms of a constable, who held him; he fought savagely, and was only secured by the help of two men. He didn't get away again."

"Until yesterday," Trent observed. "Where had he been between leaving Danbury House and returning to his hotel?"

"Apparently at a club in the Adelphi, where he played billiards for an hour and then dined. His story was that he'd walked there straight from Danbury House and gone straight from there to his hotel. It couldn't be shown that he'd been anywhere else; but nobody knew exactly when he had left Danbury House. His line at the trial was that he knew absolutely nothing of the pendant and that it was a plot to ruin him. The case against him was unanswerable and the assaults on the police, of course, made the matter much worse. He was sent to penal servitude."

"Then you think he has his booty hidden somewhere, waiting him to take it when he comes out?"

"Sure of it," the detective replied. "Doesn't it stand to reason? He was ruined anyway, and the assaults which his temper had led in into made a heavy sentence certain. He might as well have something to show for it when it was all over."

"Just so. Well, then, Inspector, where do I come in?" Mr Muirhead drew out a pocketbook.

"Three weeks before his escape James Rudmore, who had been a model prisoner from the first, was allowed the privilege of writing a letter, in accordance with the regulations. He wrote to his father. Now it so happened that old Rudmore had then been himself in jail six months or more. I had arrested him, too. The charge was fraudulent bankruptcy, and it was as clever a piece of crooked work as ever came into court, I should think. I took him at his rooms, and he went like a lamb; pleaded guilty and took his dose without any fuss."

"A philosopher," said Trent. "So he never got the letter from James."

"Certainly not. James Rudmore was informed, in accordance with the regulations, that his letter could not be forwarded, the reason being withheld. He then asked to have it back; and that was a mistake, for the governor of Dartmoor had already taken it into his head that there was something more than met the eye in the letter, and that made him certain of it. He believed it contained a secret message telling old Rudmore where the pendant was. Why he thought so I don't myself know; but it was likely enough, of course. The letter was forwarded to Scotland Yard and has been gone over carefully by the experts. They can make nothing of it."

"That is probably just because they are experts," Trent commented. "You want a really scatter-brained man—or shall we call him a man of tropically luxuriant mental gifts?—such as myself, for example, to deal with the little dodges of people like the Rudmores. I know now what it is your people want of me. They think the hiding-place of the jewel is described in that letter, and that if they can discover it, and mount guard over it, they will soon get James. I am to give an opinion on the letter. There is nothing I should like better. Where is it?"

The inspector, without reply, drew a folded paper from his pocketbook and handed it to Trent. He read the following, written in a firm and legible handwriting:

My dear Dad:

I am writing to you, the first time I am allowed, to say how sorry I am for all the misery my disgrace must have caused you. When I was made a scapegoat, it was the thought of how you would feel the dishonour to our name that hurt me most.

I wish I could have seen you just once before I was put away here. But you, at least, will never have doubted my innocence, know. It would be the end for me, indeed, if when I were free again I should find even your door closed against me.

I am strong and well; in better health than I have been for years. Most of the time I have been set to what is really navvy's work in the open air, reclaiming waste land. At first it was fearfully hard work, and I used to wish I had a hinge in my back, and as many arms as the idol, whose name I forget, on your mantelshelf. But I soon got hardened. I have not lived an out-of-door life regularly for some years, and it has made me a new man. I feel trained to a hair. I did have one bad bout of fever, though, before I got fit. I fancy the climate here is rather hard on one if one has malaria in one's system, and isn't up to the mark; the country looks and smells rather like the Gelderland country round Apeldjik, where you remember I was laid up three years ago. But this was a much worse attack. I was light-headed for days, and felt like dying. Isn't it somebody in Shakespeare who talks about "the wretch whose fever-weakened joints buckle under life?" I felt exactly like that.

I would like to tell you about the life we lead here, and my opinion of the system, but all I write has to pass under the officials' eyes, and "sie würden das nicht so hingehen lassen," as old Schraube used to say.

I send this to the old rooms in Jermyn Street, trusting it will reach you. Goodby.

Your loving son,

Jim.

Trent read this through carefully once. Then he looked at Inspector Muirhead with a meditative eye. "Well?" demanded that officer.

"This," said Trent, "is what judges in lawsuits call a very proper letter; meaning, usually, a letter with a faint flavour of humbugging artificiality about it. I don't like the note of its pathos and I think there's some hanky-panky about it somewhere. It contains one passage which must be an absolute lie, I should say."

"I don't know which you mean," the inspector replied, "but all the statements about himself in prison are true enough. He did have a bad illness—"

"Yes, naturally all those are true; he knew the letter would be read by the authorities, of course. I didn't mean anything of that sort. Look here, I should like to spend some time with this in a reference library. Will you meet me outside the British Museum one hour from now?"

"Right, Mr Trent!" The detective rose quickly. "You'll find me waiting. There may be no time to lose."

But it was the inspector who found Trent awaiting him fifty minutes later, with a taxicab in attendance.

"Jump in," said Trent. "The man knows where to go. I didn't take very long after all. I even had time to dash up into Holborn and buy this." He produced a stout screwdriver from his pocket.

"What on earth for?" inquired Mr Muirhead blankly as the cab rushed westward. "Where are we going? What have you made of the letter?"

"Inquisitive!" Trent murmured, shaking his finger at him gravely. His eyes were shining with suppressed elation and expectancy.

"What is the screwdriver for? Well, you surely will admit that it is prudent to be armed when going after a dangerous man. I got it of Lake and Company, so I am going to call it Excalibur. Come, Inspector, I ask you as a reasonable man, what else could one call it? Then, as to where we are going—we are going to Jermyn Street."

"Jermyn Street!" Mr Muirhead was staring at his companion as at some strange animal. "You think the stuff is there?"

"I think the letter says it is—or was—hidden in old Rudmore's rooms."

"But I told you, Mr Trent, old Rudmore was hundreds of miles away when the theft took place. His rooms were locked up."

"Yes, but isn't it likely James had a key to them? You told me they were on terms of great mutual confidence. The father was quite likely to leave a key with his son, in case it should prove useful—and a latch-key to the front door, too, I dare say."

The inspector nodded gloomily. "Yes—it's quite likely. Then I suppose your idea is, he just walked round to Jermyn Street with the pendant, let himself in, went upstairs to his father's rooms, tucked the thing away, and then strolled on to the club... Certainly it's possible. Only nobody happened to think of it."

"I don't know that anything would have been found if anybody had, with all regard and reverence to you and your friends, Inspector, I doubt if anything could have been done without the indications in this letter."

"Well, what does—"

"No! Here we are in Jermyn Street. What number, Inspector? 230—right!" Trent leaned out of the window and instructed the driver. The cab drew up before a shoemaker's shop of such supreme distinction that only three unostentatious pairs were placed, as if they had been left there by accident, in the window. To the left of the shop was a closed private door for the use of those living in the chambers above.

The inspector's ring was answered by an extremely corpulent, mulberry-faced man with snowy side-whiskers and smooth, white hair. His precision of dress and manner, with a certain carriage of the body, proclaimed the retired butler.

"Well, Hudson, have you forgotten me?" asked the detective pleasantly, stepping into the well-kept but gloomy little hall. The stout man hesitated, then said, "Bless my soul! It's the officer who came to take Mr Rudmore." His face lost something of its over-ripe appearance, and he added, as he closed the door, "I do hope it's not another business of that sort. My house will be getting the name of—"

"Now don't you worry yourself," the man of authority advised him. "I'm not after anybody in your house. I only want to know if the rooms that old Rudmore had are occupied at present."

"They are, Inspector. They were taken, shortly after that unfortunate affair, by Captain Ainger, who has them still—a military gentleman, invalided home from India, I believe; a very pleasant, quiet gentleman—"

"Is he at home now?"

"Captain Ainger never goes out until luncheon time."

"Then we want to see him. Don't you trouble to come up, Hudson; stairs don't agree with you, I can see that. It's the second floor, I remember."

"Second floor, and the door on the left. And I do hope, gentlemen—" Hudson withdrew, murmuring vague apprehension, and ponderously descended to the basement floor as Mr Muirhead, followed by Trent, went up the narrow stairs.

"I thought it better," said the inspector, pausing on a stair, "to go up unannounced. He can't say he won't see us if we just walk in and make ourselves pleasant."

As the two men reached the first landing they heard the sound of a door closed gently on the one above and of light-stepping feet. A tall girl, in neat and obviously expensive tailermade clothes, appeared at the head of the short stairway and, apparently not seeing them, stood for a moment adjusting her hat and veil. Mr Muirhead uttered a growling cough from below, at the noise of which the young lady started slightly and hurried down the stairs. In the half light on the landing, they received, as she passed them, an impression of shining dark hair and barely perceptible perfume. Trent looked after her meditatively as she went swiftly along the groundfloor passage and let herself out.

"Smart woman," observed the inspector appreciatively, as the front door slammed.

"A fine example of healthy modern girlhood," Trent agreed. "Did you see the stride and swing as she went to the door? From the cut of her clothes I should say she was American."

There was a note in his voice which made the other look at him sharply.

"And," pursued Trent, returning his gaze with an innocent eye, "I suppose you noticed her feet and ankles as she stood up there and as she came downstairs."

"I did not," returned Mr Muirhead gruffly. "What was there to notice?"

"Only the size," said Trent. "The size—and the fact that she was wearing a man's shoes."

For an instant the inspector glared at him wild-eyed; then turned and plunged without a word down the stairway. He reached the door and tore at the handle.

"It's locked! Double-locked from outside! Here, Hudson!" bellowed, and swore loud and savagely as the fat man was heard shuffling across the passage in the basement below and labouring heavily up the stairs. "Give me your latch-key!" he commanded, as Hudson, with a staring housemaid in his wake, appeared, trembling and gasping. For a few moments, filled with vivid language by the enraged officer, the man fumbled at a trousers pocket. At last he produced his key. Mr Muirhead seized it and endeavoured to thrust it into the keyhole. After half a dozen vain attempts he resigned the key to Hudson, who grasped the situation at the first try.

"I'm afraid whoever double-locked it has left the key in on the other side," he panted. "This'll never go in till the other's taken out."

Mr Muirhead suddenly recovered his calm and stuck his hands in his pockets. "He's done us," he announced. "He could reach Piccadilly in fifteen seconds from here, without hurrying. It's a clean getaway. Probably he's bowling off in a taxi by now. Hudson, why the devil didn't you say there was a lady with the captain? I'd never have let him pass me if I'd known he was coming from these rooms."

"I never knew there was anyone with him, indeed, Inspector," quavered the old man, his mind wrestling feebly with the confusion of genders. "I expect it was this girl let her in."

"How was I to know there was anything wrong?" cried the domestic, bursting into tears. "She spoke like a perfect lady and sent me up with her card and all. I never thought till this minute—"

"All right, all right, my girl," said the inspector brusquely, "You'll get into no trouble if you're straight. Hudson, I want your telephone. In the back room here? Right! And you'd better hail somebody next door and get your door opened."

The detective disappeared into the room and Hudson shuffled down the passage to the back of the building, still in a dazed condition. "What, I don't see," he mumbled, "is where she, or he, or whoever it was, got the key from." And as he said it, Trent, who had been leaning against the wall with a face of great contentment, suddenly turned and fled lightly up the stairs.

Captain Ainger's door opened easily. Captain Ainger himself, a Small, crop-headed man, lay upon a sofa near the window of his tastefully furnished sitting-room. As Trent burst in a look of relief came into the captain's bewildered eyes. The rest of his face below them was covered by an improvised gag made out of a tobacco pouch and a tightly-knotted silk scarf.

His ankles were tied together and his arms lashed to his sides with box cord.

He looked wretchedly uncomfortable.

Five minutes later, in answer to a call from Trent, Mr Muirhead closed his conversation with Scotland Yard and came upstairs. He found Captain Ainger sitting in an armchair, restoring his physical tone with a deep glass of whisky and soda. To Trent's account of how he had found that ill-used officer the detective answered only with a grim nod. Then, "I suppose it was your latch-key, sir," he said to the victim.

"Yes," replied the little captain, "she took my latch-key—he did, I mean. Tell you just how it was. She sent up her card—his, I should say—well, it was a woman's card, anyhow. I put it up here." He rose and took a card from the mantelshelf.

Mr Muirhead glanced at it with curiosity. "Of course!" he exclaimed.

"Mrs Van Sommeren's card, is it?" asked Trent from his chair by the window.

"It is."

"And Mrs Van Sommeren's clothes and hat, and Mrs Van Sommeren's little bag, and Mrs Van Sommeren's own particular perfume—they all went by us just now," Trent remarked, "in company with (I expect) Mr Van Sommeren's shoes and Mr James Rudmore's wig. Probably he was a little excited at seeing you, Inspector, awaiting him at the bottom of the stairs. It needed some nerve for him to stand there fixing his veil without a quiver, and to trip downstairs right into your yearning embrace, as one may say."

Annoyance, self-reproach, menacing resolve, and appreciation of the comic side of the episode—all these things were in the inspector's eloquent answering grunt.

"If only he had remembered to walk along the lower passage like a lady, instead of like a champion lightweight," Trent resumed, "I don't believe the meaning of the shoes would have burst upon me as it did. I dare say his hold on himself began to go when he saw the street door and safety six steps in front of him. Yet that latch-key business was pretty coolly done. Jim is certainly a gifted amateur. But you were telling us"—he turned to the obviously mystified captain—"how she made her appearance."

"The message with the card," resumed Captain Ainger who still preserved his pained expression, "was that she would be obliged if I would answer an inquiry on a family matter. It made me feel curious, so I said I would see her. She had on a very thick veil—he had, I mean."

"Why not stick to 'she,' Captain," Trent suggested. "We should get on quicker, I think."

"Thank you," said the veteran gratefully, "I believe we should. The whole thing is so confusing, because she talked just like a woman from beginning to end. Where was I? Ah yes! I couldn't see her face very well, but her voice and style were those of a well-bred woman. She told me that a year ago she had lost a brother who was very dear to her, and that in his deathbed he had laid what she called a sacred charge upon her. It seemed he had been befriended at some critical time, when he was in India, by an English officer of my name, of whom he had lost sight for many years. He wished her, if possible, to find out that officer and place in his hands a memento, something which had belonged to himself, in token of his undying gratitude. She had made inquiries and had found me in the first place, but understood there were others of my name in the army list."

"How did Rudmore get hold of your name, I wonder?" mused the inspector. "He only got away from Dartmoor yesterday."

"That wouldn't have been difficult for his sort of man," Trent replied. "Very likely he got it out of the housemaid who opened the door, before sending up the message."

The captain cursed the absent malefactor feebly and took another drink from his tumbler. "I confess I was rather touched.

Of course, I've usually done a man a good turn when it lay in my power, but I couldn't remember having played Providence to an American at any time. So I asked what his name was. She said their name was Smith. Well, you know, I must have run across about fifty Smiths, and I told her so. Then she said she had a photograph of him with her. She took it out of her bag. It was a picture of a good-looking, youngish chap, with the name of a Philadelphia firm on the mount."

"Van Sommeren's photograph," murmured Trent. "She carried it about with her. You didn't tell me they were on their honeymoon, Inspector."

"I felt sure I'd never seen the man," continued Captain Ainger, "but I took it to the window to have a good look. And the moment my back was turned she leaped on me and garotted me. There wasn't a chance for me. She was as strong as a tiger, and I'm pretty shaky from a long illness. When I was about at my last gasp she gagged me with that infernal thing, then dragged me into the bedroom and tied me up with my own cord. When I was trussed properly she went through my pockets and took my latch-key, then she carried me back to the bedroom door. She said she was so sorry to be giving me all this trouble and that she always wished women were not so dependent upon men for everything. She put her veil up a little way and helped herself to a whisky and soda and lighted one of my cigars. After that she took a screwdriver out of her bag and went to work at something behind me. I don't know in the least what she was doing; I couldn't move. It took about five minutes, I should say. Then she skipped to the window with something that looked like a wad of cotton wool in her fingers and began gloating over something I couldn't see. She stood there a long time, smoking and looking out, and then all at once she gave a start and stared down into the street. Just after that I heard the front doorbell ring. And then she—well, she went." The captain's bronzed face went slowly scarlet to the roots of his hair.

"She said goodby, surely," murmured Trent, looking at him attentively.

"If you must know," burst out the captain with his first show of fierceness, "she said she didn't know how to thank me, and that I was a dear, and might she give me a kiss? So she—she did it." Here his narrative dissolved into unchivalrous expressions. "And then she went out and shut the door. That's all I can tell you." He wearily resorted to his tumbler again.

Trent and the inspector, who had prudently avoided catching each other's eyes during the last part of the story, now conquered their feelings. "What I want to know now," the detective said, "is where the stuff was hidden here. Can you go straight to the place, Mr Trent, or should we have to search?"

Trent took the convict's letter from his pocket. "Let me tell you how I got at it first," he said. "You will be interested, Captain, you read it." He handed the document to the soldier and gave him a brief account of the circumstances regarding it.

The captain, now highly interested, read it through carefully? twice, then handed it to Trent again. "I don't believe I should make anything out of it in a thousand years," he said. "It seems straight enough to me. I should call it an interesting letter, that' all."

"This letter," said Trent, regarding it with a look of unstinted appreciation, "is the most interesting, by a long way, that I have ever read. It tells us, not, I think, where the pendant was hidden, but where the diamonds of the pendant were hidden by Jim Rudmore before his arrest. What Jim did with the setting I don't know, nor does it matter much. But the diamonds were concealed here; and they are now again, I am afraid, in the possession of Jim."

Inspector Muirhead made an impatient movement. "Come to the point, Mr Trent," he urged. "What did you pick up from that letter? Where was the stuff hidden?"

"I will tell you first the things I picked up, and how. The first time I read the letter—in your presence, inspector—I checked at the statement that 'the country looks and smells like the Gelderland country around Apeldjik.' When one reads that, it naturally occurs to one's mind that Dartmoor is practically a mountain district, whereas Gelderland is a part of Holland, most of which country is actually below the sea level."

"It didn't occur to my mind," observed Captain Ainger.

"Therefore," pursued Trent, unconscious of him, "any similarity of look or smell would be rather curious, don't you think? Possibly that was what struck the governor of the prison and aroused his suspicions of the letter. Well, the next thing that pulled me up was the Shakespearean reference. I knew I'd read it in Shakespeare, and yet I felt it was wrong somehow. There were some words missing, I thought. Besides, it didn't look like a prose passage; yet it didn't fit into the decasyllabic form, or any other metre... The only other notion that occurred to me at first glance was that it was an odd thing to quote a German phrase where an English one would have been just as good.

"Then I took the letter to the British Museum library and sat down to the problem in earnest. I said to myself that if there was any cipher in it, it was probably impossible to get at it. But I thought it more *likely that the message, if any, was conveyed in the words as they stood. So I asked myself* what were the signals that it hung out to a man who would be trying to read some inner Waning into it. What things in it were, by ever so little, out of common, so that the reader would say to himself, 'This may be a pointer'? And I had to remember that both the Rudmores were said to be clever and cultivated men, who understood each other well.

"Now, to begin with, I thought that 'the idol, whose name Is forget, on your mantelshelf,' was the sort of thing Rudmore pere would have pondered over. Of course we've all seen those little images of the Hindu goddess with ten arms. Jim Rudmore, who had lived in India for years, said he had forgotten her name. That might possibly be meant to draw attention to the name."

"It's Parvati—heard it thousands of times," the captain interjected.

"Yes, I found that name when I looked up the Hindu mythology. But there's another, by which she is known in Bengal, where the Rudmores had had their experience of India. There, my book told me, the people call her Doorga. So I noted down both names... Very well; now the next passage that seemed out of the ordinary was that about 'the Gelderland country round Apeldjik.' The first thing I did was to look up Apeldjik in the gazeteer. It mentioned no such place; the nearest thing to it was a town called Apeldoorn, which was in Gelderland sure enough. Then I got a big map and went through Gelderland from end to end. As I expected, it was as flat as a board, and there was no sign of Ateldjik. But I found several towns in Holland ending in 'djik,' which shows you what a conscientious artist Jim is. Now if he had really been ill at Apeldoorn, as I expect he had been, his father would have got a hint at once. I wrote down Apeldoorn, and then I began to see light."

Mr Muirhead rubbed his nose with a puzzled air. "I don't see—" he began.

"You will very soon. Next I turned to the odd-looking quotation from Shakespeare. On looking up 'joints' in the Cowden-Clarke Concordance, I found the passage. It's in Henry IV, where North-umberland says:

"And as the wretch, whose fever-weaken'd joints,
Like strengthless hinges, buckle under life...

"What do you think of that?"

The inspector shook his head.

"Well, then, look at the German phrase. Sie würden das nicht so hingehen lassen means 'They would not allow that,' or 'They would not pass that over,' or something of that sort. Now suppose a man looking for a suggestion or hint in each of those German words."

Mr Muirhead took the letter and conned the words carefully. "I'm no German scholar," he began, and then his eyes brightened. "Those missing words—" he said.

"Like strengthless hinges," Trent reminded him.

"Well, and here"—the inspector tapped excitedly upon the word *hingehen*—"you've got 'hinge' and 'hen' in English."

"You're there! Never mind the hen; she's not there on business. Lastly, I'll tell you a thing you probably don't know. *Schraube* is the German word for 'screw.' "

Mr Muirhead gave his knee a violent blow with his fist.

"Now then!" Trent tore a leaf from his notebook. "I'll put down the words we've got at that were hidden." He wrote quickly and handed the paper to the inspector. Both he and Captain Ainger read the following:

Boorga.

Doorn.

Hinges.

Hinge.

Screw.

"Also," Trent added, "the word 'door' occurs twice openly in the body of the letter, and the word 'hinge' once. That was to show old Rudmore. He was on the right track, if he succeeded in digging out those words. 'Good!' says he to himself. 'The loot is hidden under a screw in a hinge on a door somewhere. Then where?' He turns to the letter again and finds the only address mentioned in it is 'the old rooms in Jermyn Street.' And there you are!"

Trent took his screwdriver from his pocket and went to the open door leading into the captain's bedroom. "Naturally it wouldn't be the outer door, as to get at the hinges one would have to have it standing open." He glanced at the hinges of the bedroom door. "*These screws"—he pointed to those on the door-*

post half of the upper hinge—"have had their paint scratched a little."

In a minute or two he had removed all three screws. The open door sank forward slightly on the lower hinge and the upper one came away from its place on the door-post. Beneath it was a little cavity roughly hollowed out in the wood. Silently the inspector probed it with a penknife.

"The stones are gone, of course," he announced gloomily.

"Certainly, gone," Trent agreed. "The stones were in that little piece of cotton wool the captain saw him handling."

Mr Muirhead rose to his feet. "Well, I don't think they'll go far." As he took up his hat there was a knock at the door and Hudson entered panting, a sharp curiosity in his eyes.

"A messenger boy just brought this for you, Inspector," he wheezed, handing a small package to the detective. It was directed in a delicate, sloping handwriting to "Inspector C. M. Muirhead, C.I.D., care of Captain R. Ainger, 230 Jermyn Street."

Hastily the inspector tore it open. It contained a small black suède glove, faintly perfumed. With this was a scrap of paper, bearing these words in the same writing:

"*Wear this for my sake.*—J.R."

6

TRENT AND THE FOOL-PROOF LIFT

One of the commonest forms of fatal accident in the life of the town is falling down a lift shaft. Every coroner of large urban experience has dealt with cases by the score, whether due to short sight, negligence, faulty construction, or defective safety mechanism. And there is another possibility.

One perfect day in June M. Armand Binet-Gailly, who held an important agency in the wine trade, left his office in Jermyn Street rather earlier than usual, and strolled homewards through the Parks to his bachelor flat at 42 Rigby Street. This was a tall old house, "converted" from the errors of its pre-Victorian youth. There were five flats, and M. Binet-Gailly's was the second above the ground level. About 5:30—so went his statement to the police—he entered by the front door, which always stood open during the daytime, and went to the lift at the end of the hall. The lift was not at the ground floor, as he could see through the lattice gate; and he pressed the button which should bring it down. But nothing happened.

M. Binet-Gailly was very much annoyed. A portly man, he did not relish the prospect of climbing two flights of stairs on a warm day when he had paid for lift service. He aimlessly seized and shook the handle of the lattice gate. To his amazement, the gate slid aside as if the lift were in place. It should, of course, have been impossible to move it unless the lift were there. The whole system was out of order, he thought. He put his head into the shaft and looked upwards. There was the lift; so far as he could judge, at the top floor. Then, as he drew back his head, his eye was caught by something at the bottom of the shallow well in which the lift shaft ended. There was a strong electric ceiling lamp always alight at this dark end of the hall; and it showed M. Binet-Gailly quite enough.

Like most of his countrymen, he had served in arms, and things of this kind did not upset him. Plump though he was, he began to clamber down into the well; then he bethought himself. Certainly there could be no life in that crumpled bundle of humanity. The thing to do was to leave it untouched until the arrival of the police. M. Binet-Gailly went to the door communicating with the basement, and bellowed downstairs for Pimblett, the caretaker. Forty-two Rigby Street, though distant by little more than the breadth of Oxford Street from the elegance of Mayfair, did not rise to the luxury of a uniformed porter, and neither Pimblett nor his wife was usually to be seen after the morning job of cleaning the hall and staircase was done.

Pimblett, who also had served in arms, and had seen more dirty work than had M. Binet-Gailly, took in the situation at a glance. Wasting no words, he strode to the hall telephone and rang up the police station. Both men then mounted the stairs to find which gate it was through which the unknown—for the face of the corpse could not be seen—had plunged to his death. On the floor immediately above M. Binet-Gailly's they found the gate drawn back. On this floor was the flat occupied by Mr Anthony Villiers Maxwell—a young man of sporting tastes—and his valet. M. Binet-Gailly proposed ringing the bell of the flat to make inquiries; but Pimblett remarked that the police would prefer to have all that left to them.

An hour later M. Binet-Gailly, sipping a glass of Campari in his own rooms, discussed with his own servant, by name Aristide, what he had just learnt of this mysterious affair. The dead man had turned out to be his own landlord, Mr Stephen Havelock Hermon, who had bought the house a few years before, and had installed his nephew, Anthony Maxwell, in the flat above-stairs on its falling I vacant soon afterwards. There had been some slight lack of sympathy between M. Binet-Gailly and Mr Hermon, owing to the fact that Mr Hermon had among his eccentricities a passionate hatred of liquor in every form, and when he purchased the place had not concealed his chagrin on finding that one of the sitting tenants was engaged in the wine trade, which Mr Hermon preferred to call the drink-traffic.

No one in the building had seen Mr Hermon enter it that afternoon. No one had seen him at all before the finding of his body. No one had known of his intention to come to the house. Mr Clayton Haggett, the famous surgeon, who had the top flat, had not been at home; his housekeeper had heard no ring. Anthony Maxwell also had been out, and his valet had had the afternoon off. Aristide could vouch for it, as he had already informed the police that no one had called at M. Binet-Gailly's. Mr Lucian Corderoy, the eminent dress designer, and his wife had both been at his shop in Malyon Street, and their "daily" servant was never in the place after twelve noon. As for Sir George Stower, the Keeper of Phoenician Antiquities at the British Museum, he was enjoying a hard-earned holiday at Margate, and his flat on the ground floor had been shut up for some days past.

"But naturally," remarked Aristide, fingering a swarthy chin, "the old gentleman wished to call upon his nephew."

"It is very probable," M. Binet-Gailly agreed. "He was devoted to that young animal, and they say he had no other relative living. The nephew will be his heir, no doubt, and he will make the money roll a little faster than the uncle ever did."

"Ah! When one is young," observed Aristide sentimentally.

"And when one is a waster by nature," M. Binet-Gailly added. "Well, Aristide, it is time for me to dress."

Philip Trent, in his first outline of the case for the readers of the *Record*, had given these facts about the other tenants of the building. "It is naturally assumed (he wrote) that Mr Hermon had called, as he often did, to see his nephew, to whom he is said to have been much attached. His ringing at the door had been resultless, and he had turned away to go down by the way he had come. He had opened the gate, believing the lift to be in position there—and stepped out into emptiness. He was known to be extremely short-sighted. His neck, so says the police surgeon, was broken, and there were other injuries that must have been immediately fatal. When his body was found, he had been dead not more than an hour.

"This is very simple; but it leaves all the important questions unanswered.

"Why was not the lift where he expected it to be? He had only just left it; and according to the information gathered by the police there had been no one leaving or entering any of the flats since the early afternoon, when Mr Clayton Haggett and Mr Maxwell went out.

"Why was it at the top floor?

"How was it that he had been able to open the gate, which should have been locked automatically the moment the lift moved from that floor?

"Why was the gate on the ground floor unlocked? Why indeed? Conceivably the mechanism of the upstairs gate had gone wrong, so that Mr Hermon could open it; but the gate at the bottom could not be opened by a dead man.

"Why were all the other gates in working order—the top gate, where the lift was, unlocked; the other two locked?

"On this very vital point I have had some conversation with the expert who was sent to investigate by the firm which built and installed the lift. The mechanism, he told me, was tested by the makers at monthly intervals, and had been in perfect order at the last examination, ten days before. The system was as nearly foolproof as it could be. 'But,' he added, 'it isn't toolproof. Any engineer could see with half an eye that both those locks have been forced.'

"Here are the elements of a very sinister mystery. Someone who was not Mr Hermon forced the groundfloor gate. Presumably he forced the other. The only persons known to have been in the house from three o'clock onwards were the caretaker in the basement, the French manservant in M. Binet-Gailly's flat, and the housekeeper in Mr Haggett's. Did someone enter the house before Mr Hermon; or did someone accompany him? To this point the inquiries of the police are being directed—so far, I believe, without result.

"If Mr Hermon was a victim of violence, it is hard to think that any feeling of ill-will could have been at work. It is true that he was a man of strong opinions, often violently expressed in public controversy—the hard knocks exchanged between him and his tenant, Mr Clayton Haggett, in their dispute over vivisection last year will be remembered. But he was always a fair and even a chivalrous fighter, on the friendliest footing with opponents to whom he was personally known. His nature was kindly and generous, his great wealth was largely devoted to works of benevolence; the hospital endowments made by him as memorials to his late wife are but a part of his service to humanity."

Trent did not try to intrude on the sorrow of Anthony Maxwell; but he had from the young man's valet, Joseph Weaver, some material information. He learned that the nephew felt his loss very deeply indeed; that he did not look like the same man. He had, Weaver said, a feeling heart. A little wild he might have been—young gentlemen would be young gentlemen—but he had what they call a nice nature. He owed everything to Mr Hermon, who had been a father to him after his parents died when he was a child. Naturally he was very much upset.

Trent reflected privately on the deceitfulness of appearances; for he knew Anthony Maxwell by sight, and would not have said that either his eye, his mouth, or his bearing proclaimed the niceness of his nature. Perhaps Weaver was being loyal to his employer. He did not look particularly loyal; but then he did not look anything to speak of. He had the expressionlessness of his calling. His quiet voice, neat clothes, and sleek black hair suggested nothing but discretion. Trent asked a question.

Mr Hermon, Weaver said, came up fairly often on business from his place in Surrey, and when he did so always visited his nephew. Sometimes he came on purpose to see him. No; Mr Maxwell had not been expecting him on the day of the accident; he had given no notice that he was coming. If he had done so, Mr Maxwell would naturally have been at home. Weaver thought it unlikely that Mr Hermon had been intending to call on any of the other tenants. He did do so from time to time, to talk about some matters of repairs or other landlord's business; but that would always be by appointment, and not during the working day. All the tenants, Weaver pointed out, were busy men, with the exception of Mr Maxwell; they would seldom be at home until the evening.

Yes; Mr Hermon attended personally to the management of all his house property in the West End. There was a good deal of it, and it gave him occupation. No; he was not what they call a hard landlord; quite the contrary, Weaver would say. Mr Hermon liked to do things for people, being a very generous man, as Weaver had good reason to know.

"You mean that he was generous to you," Trent suggested. "A present for you when he called here—that sort of thing?"

"Mr Hermon always behaved like a gentleman," Weaver said demurely. "But I meant more than that, sir. You see, I was two years in his service before I came to Mr Maxwell; that is how I came to know so much about his habits, and to appreciate his kindness. Then when Mr Hermon went on a tour round the world, he suggested I should go to Mr Maxwell, who was not satisfied with the valet he had then; and I have remained in his service since then—about nine months ago it would be."

When Trent went to talk it over with his friend Chief-Inspector Bligh, he found that officer cheerfully interested in what he described as a very nice case.

"There's nothing easy," he said, "about it so far. Of course, it's a murder—that's certain. You have heard what the lift company's man says. And, of course, it was meant to look as if it might be an accident."

"Then how about the groundfloor gate being forced as well as the other? That doesn't look like an accident."

"Well, what does it look like?" Mr Bligh wanted to know.

"It looks to me as it looks to you, I suppose. When the old man had been pushed into the lift shaft, the murderer realized that something had gone wrong with his plan. Hermon had had something on him that might give the murderer away if it was found on the body. The only thing for him to do was to run downstairs, prize open the bottom gate, and take what he wanted off the body. If Pimblett or anybody appeared while he was doing so, he could say he had seen the old man open the gate and fall down the shaft, and had rushed down and forced the gate to see if he was still alive."

The inspector nodded. "Yes; that's the idea. And he did get what he wanted, presumably; and nobody did see him. Of course, it's the sort of place where nobody is about most of the time, and the man who did the job knew that."

"Well, how about the people who live here? Are they all above suspicion?"

"There is no such thing," Mr Bligh declared, "as being above suspicion—not if I do the suspecting. And it just happens that most of them haven't an alibi. The Museum man has, of course; his flat was shut up, and is still. And the Corderoys were at their dress shop till after six. But the Frenchman was alone when he came in and reported having found the body; and his story of how he found it, and what time he entered the house, is quite unsupported. Maxwell says he lunched at his flat, went out immediately afterwards, and spent all the afternoon at Lord's watching Lancashire take a licking from Middlesex; then went to his club with some other bright boys, had drinks, and came home to dress for dinner. But Lord's is a place you can dodge out of and return to later, and it's no distance for a car to Rigby Street. Then there's Clayton Haggett, the surgeon. He had lunch in his flat too, after a morning at the hospital; went down to his car at 2:30, had an operation at a nursing-home and another at a private house; finished by 4:15, had a cup of tea, and then spent two hours driving about down Richmond way—just to take the air, and nobody with him all that time, which is a pity."

"He didn't like Hermon," Trent remarked. "He was very bitter in that tussle they had over vivisection."

"Yes, and he's got a naughty temper when he's crossed. Loses his self-control. He had to resign from the Hunter Club for knocking a man down in the smoking-room. Nobody would have anything to do with him if he wasn't such a wizard with the knife."

"And what about the servants in the building? Do they come into the picture at all?"

"All I can tell you is that none of their stories can be checked. Pimblett says he was in the basement all the afternoon until the Frenchman shouted for him; his wife was away calling on her sister in Highbury. The French manservant and Haggett's housekeeper say they never opened the doors of their flats until the police looked them up after the finding of the body. Maxwell's man says he had the afternoon off, went out after his master had gone, and sat through the cinema program at the Byzantine, getting back a little before Anthony did. Well, what good's that? Like the other three, he can't prove anything at all about where he was for some hours before the police were called in."

"Any of them ever been in trouble?"

"Nothing known against any of them. Ex-Sergeant Pimblett—excellent record. Mrs Hargreaves, the housekeeper—ditto. Weaver used to be employed at Harding's, the big barbershop in Duke Street, where old Hermon used to go when he was in town. He always had Weaver to attend to him, and at last he took him on as his valet. Afterwards—"

"Yes, he told me; he was switched onto Anthony. Perfectly respectable. And the French domestic?"

"All I know about Aristide Recot is that he has a wooden face and side-whiskers, and doesn't mind being seen in an apron. What I'm told by his master is that he has been with him for some years, and given every satisfaction. But what's the use? We had to consider the servants, of course; but what motive could any of them have had? It's a different thing when you come to their employers. Haggett, for instance."

Trent looked the inspector in the eyes. "You were talking about motive," he said gently. "Is Haggett's resentment really the strongest you can think of? I don't like being teased."

"All right; I was coming to it," Mr Bligh responded with a faint grin. "Yes, I suppose the expectation of coming into the greater part of a very large fortune might operate as a motive. That is what Maxwell will do, according to our information. Unless something happens to him. His uncle made him a very generous allowance, and he lived rent-free, and Weaver's wages were paid by the old man. Maxwell ought to have been grateful, and perhaps he was; but there you are—he's a vicious young brute, and always in debt; and though Hermon wasn't strong, he might have lived to any old age. Now then! Will that do for you?"

"Something of the sort had crossed my mind," Trent admitted. "Certainly it will do—until something better comes along."

Mr Bligh raised an impressive finger. "And now," he said, "I'll tell you something that hadn't crossed your mind. It's information received. If it's right, the coroner will hear it at a later stage, but at present we would rather the murderer didn't know about it. You remember I mentioned that Clayton Haggett left his flat at 2:30 that afternoon. Well, he had more to tell us than that. He went down by the lift, he said. It's rather a slow-motion lift. As it passed down by the floor below—Anthony's floor—Haggett heard some words spoken. He could see as he passed that the door of the flat was just being opened from inside, and as it opened he heard a loud, bullying voice call out, 'You do what I say, and look sharp about it. If you get on the wrong side of me, you know what to expect.' That is as near as Haggett can go to the actual words he heard—I asked him to be particular."

Trent stared at the inspector with kindling eyes. "You do like saving up the best bit to the last, don't you? And you had this—this!—simply handed to you. On a plate."

"With parsley round it," added Mr Bligh, unashamed.

"I have heard you use that phrase before," Trent said thoughtfully. "It meant, I think, that you were rather mistrustful of good things that came so easily. But now, what about this remarkable addition to the record? Did Haggett recognize the voice? Did he see anybody?"

"No. Haggett says it might have been Maxwell he heard talking; but he only knows Maxwell by sight, has never spoken to him, and has no idea what his voice would sound like if it was raised. And, of course, it might have been anybody else in the world. Then I asked him what class of voice it was—like a curate's, or a dustman's, or what. All he could tell me was that it was not a coarse voice, and not a refined one; just middling. Very useful! But that isn't all. As the lift got to the bottom, he heard a door above slam violently, which he assumed to be the one he had just seen being opened; and as he was getting into his car, Maxwell came out of the street door, with his hat on, looking furiously angry and very red in the face, and walked away rapidly."

Trent considered this. "So this is Haggett's information. And what does Maxwell say about it?"

"He hasn't been asked—yet. He is being given a little more time to make mistakes. But, of course, it may all be a lie. Yes, you may look surprised; but Haggett isn't out of it yet, as I told you. There's another piece of news I've got for you, which certainly isn't a lie. When Jackson did the post mortem, he found something that wants a lot of explaining."

"What! Another thing you are keeping dark?"

"For the present. He noticed that the fingernails of the right hand looked as if they had been scratching hard at something, and there was a very faint odour that he couldn't place; so he took some scrapings from the nails to be analyzed. They found some tiny scraps of human skin; also traces of some things with hydrocarbo scientific names that don't seem to tell you much, and one thing that I have heard of quite often before."

"Yes. What?"

"Chloroform."

Thinking it over in his studio, Trent could make no more of this at first than Mr Bligh and he had made between them. If there had been a struggle, and if chloroform had been used, it did seem to point to the one resident in the house who might be presumed to know all about chloroform and what could be done with it. And Haggett was known to be a hot-tempered man and a good hater, as well as a very able and successful professional man—not an unknown combination of qualities. But Trent found it hard to believe in such a character expressing its dislike in murder done by tricky and treacherous means. A quarrel; yes. An assault; possibly. As assault with a fatal result, legally a murder; such things did happen. But a planned and cold-blooded crime, with the murderer scheming to avoid detection by means of a trumped-up tale—Trent did not see it. In his experience, trained faculties, high responsibility, and professional distinction did not go with dirty actions and circumstantial lying.

But if Raggett's story of what he had heard and seen was true, how could it be fitted to the known facts? Maxwell's own statement about the time at which he had left the building agreed with Haggett's. Weaver's statement was that he had, as was natural, gone out a little later. Both of them had said nothing of this loud-voiced unknown who had used threatening language in Maxwell's flat. It might have been Maxwell himself. Could it have been Hermon? But Hermon had been fond, even foolishly fond, of his nephew. Unless—and here opened a new vista of ugliness—both Maxwell and his servant had been concealing the truth on that point, building up the fiction of a generous benefactor whom for worlds Maxwell would not have injured. There might be purpose enough in their doing so. The inspector had not thought of that; at least (Trent reflected with a wry smile) he had not mentioned it. Hermon's visit, by the way, had been a surprise visit, according to Weaver.

Trent, at this point in his meditations, rose and began to pace the studio. Soon he went across to the model's dressing-room and examined his appearance in the mirror there. His hair had been cut fairly recently, but another trimming would not upset the balance of nature, he thought. Within the hour he was one of a dozen sheeted forms, sitting in a strange chair before a tall mirror, and had met the attendant's opening comment on the warmth of the day with the due rejoinder that it looked like rain later on.

Trent, like many other men, found his thoughts the clearer for being written down, and would often prepare for the drafting of a dispatch that could be published by a private memorandum including all that could not. That evening he sat at his bureau, and did not rise until the account of what he had discovered, and the conclusions drawn, was complete in black and white.

"Starting with the belief that Haggett's story was true" (he wrote), "I had to make out who the person in Maxwell's flat was who gave some order, in offensive words, coupled with a vague threat; and who the person ordered about and threatened was. As Bligh said, it might have been anyone who used those words; someone who had not as yet come into view in the case. But it was as well to consider first those who were known to have been in the place; and one of these was Hermon. But the accounts we had of Hermon made this seem unlikely; and they were not only the accounts given by Maxwell and his valet. Hermon's general reputation was that of a man who would be the last in the world to bully and threaten. As for the others who had been in the other flats, there was no visible shadow of a reason for suspecting any one of them.

"There remained Maxwell and his valet.

"Maxwell might be capable of bullying and threatening. He is not a nice young man. Could he have been the speaker, and either Hermon or Weaver the man spoken to?

"Well, is it likely? Maxwell is not a lunatic. No man in his senses would talk like that to his rich uncle, whose fortune he expected to inherit; nor to his valet unless he was prepared for the man leaving him on the spot, and for being obliged to do his own valeting and cooking and housework until he could get another servant. Unless, of course, he had got either of them under his thumb in some way. Has Hermon, or Weaver, a guilty past, known to Maxwell?

"I had got as far as this when a new point occurred to me. Weaver, when I saw him, had told me that Maxwell had not been expecting his uncle's visit. As this looked very much like a plain lie, I thought some attention paid to Weaver might be worth the trouble; and so I went and had my hair cut at Harding's.

"The man who cut it was as ready for conversation as barbers usually are. I spoke of the fatal accident to Mr Hermon, and the barber, who may have been reading my own remarks on the subject, said that it was a funny sort of accident, giving his reasons for that view. Then I mentioned that I knew Mr Hermon's former valet had once had a job at Harding's. The man remembered both of them very well. He only wished he had the chance of bettering himself as Weaver had done. He had not known that Weaver had become Mr Maxwell's valet; but he had known that Weaver had done very well for himself. Besides that, Weaver had come into a bit of money of his own; he had mentioned it confidential. He was quite the gentleman now, especially in the last six months. He had taken to having his hair done at Harding's once a fortnight, probably just to show off a bit among his old pals. Gold wristwatch, diamond tie-pin, quite the swell. Liked to do himself well, too, in his time off; and why not if you could run to it? Sometimes he would have my barber and other friends from Harding's to meet him after hours, and would stand drinks like a lord; and you could always see he had had a few beforehand.

"So far, my visit to Harding's had yielded more than I had any right to expect. But this was not all. My man came at length to that stage of the proceedings at which it is usual for the barber to hint delicately that the condition of one's scalp is not all that could be wished, and that this could be remedied by the use of some sort of hair-wash. With a flash of inspiration, I asked what Weaver was in the habit of buying for himself. The best hair-tonic there is, said my barber with enthusiasm; Harding's own preparation, Capillax—just the thing for me; and I would understand that Weaver knew, as a hairdresser, how excellent it was. I thought, when I was told the price of it, that Weaver also knew how impressively costly it was. I was shown a bottle of Capillax; a green, fluted bottle, with NOT TO BE TAKEN stamped in the glass. Why, I asked my barber, should I be forbidden to take Capillax, if I should choose to buy Capillax?

"He turned the bottle over, and showed me on the back a tiny pasted label. It read:

This preparation, containing among other valuable ingredients a small amount of Chloroform, is in accordance with the Pharmacy Act hereby labeled POISON.

"I ordered a bottle, of course. I thought my barber had earned his commission on the sale. And I asked him if he could tell me why chloroform should be used in a tonic for the hair, because I had thought it was for putting people to sleep. He said, yes, but that was only the vapour of chloroform; in solution it acted as a stimulant to the skin, and had cleansing properites.

"My reconstruction of this crime is that Weaver planned the murder of Hermon. He had found out something that Maxwell did not dare have known about himself; he put the screw on him and bled him for every shilling he could raise. A servant who knows too much about his employer is a figure common enough in the odorous annals of blackmail. Weaver had 'come into money' indeed! Probably he got rid of a lot of it by betting. Anyhow, the more he got, the more he wanted. He had tasted easy money; he could not do without it; and there was no more in sight. But he knew that Maxwell, when his uncle died, would be a rich man. Weaver thought it over; and he formed a plan, to be carried out the first time that opportunity offered.

"On the morning of Hermon's death Maxwell heard, by letter or telephone, that his uncle intended to call that afternoon.

Weaver's tale, that the old man had given no notice of his coming, was hardly credible. It was the height of summer, and it was utterly unlikely that Maxwell would be staying indoors that afternoon unless he was expecting a visitor. Hermon would certainly have let him know he was coming. This was what Weaver had been waiting for. After lunch he told Maxwell to leave the flat, go somewhere where he could mix with friends, and stay away until dinnertime. I do not believe Maxwell knew what was intended, because Haggett's story makes it plain that he protested against this. He did not see why he should deliberately absent himself when his uncle had asked him to be at home; why should he affront the old man? Weaver then went to the door of the flat, and as he opened it he raised his voice in the bullying words that Haggett caught as the lift went down. Maxwell, in a furious temper, did as he was told.

"When Hermon arrived, coming up by the lift, Weaver opened the door to him. He framed some lie to account for Maxwell's absence, and asked him to come in, perhaps for a rest and a cup of tea. Hermon did so; and while he was alone in the sitting-room, Weaver slipped out, took the lift to the floor above, and forced the lift gate on Maxwell's floor. When the old man went, Weaver saw him to the lift, opened the gate, and thrust him into the empty shaft. He knew better than most people how bad Hermon's sight was, and how little strength he had for a struggle. And here the plan went wrong. Hermon realized at the last instant that the lift was not there, and grabbed at Weaver as he felt the push given him. His right hand clutched Weaver's hair, tearing some of it out as he fell to his death, and lacerating the man's scalp.

"Weaver had seen instantly that if hair was found in the dead man's hand there would be an end of the theory that he had met with an accident. The police would be looking for a man with black hair and a scratched head; and they would not have far to look. There was only one thing for it. Weaver ran down to the ground floor, forced the gate there, stepped into the well, and carefully removed the hair he found in the dead man's grasp. There was nothing else he could do. He must simply stick to the story he had already made up, and trust to luck. After all, as far as he knew, there had been no witness whatever to anything that had passed."

It was late by the time Trent had finished his memorandum. He read and reread it; then slipped it into an envelope, addressed it to Mr Bligh at Scotland Yard, went out and registered it at the district post office.

Trent was at work in his studio next morning when the telephone bell called him.

Mr Bligh, not an effusive man by nature, said that Trent's report had reached him. "There's no doubt but what you're right," he went on. "It's a pity, though, that we shall never hear what it was Weaver knew about Maxwell. It might very well have been a job for us."

"Well, you called him a vicious young brute," Trent said. "With my morbid imagination and your fund of horrid experience, we ought to be able to guess a few of the things that it might have been. But why do you say you will never know? If you bring the murder home to Weaver, he will probably give Maxwell away, having no further use for his secret. It would be just like him."

"Weaver won't do that." There was a note of grimness in the inspector's voice. "At 8:15 last night Weaver was on his way down Coventry Street. He had been drinking, and couldn't walk straight. A dozen people saw him stumble off the curb and into the road, right under a passing bus. He was killed instantly. His injuries—"

"Thanks, I don't want to hear about his injuries." Trent wiped his brow. "They were fatal—that's enough for me."

"Yes, but there were some that weren't fatal. On the head, concealed by the hair, there were four deep scratches, not completely healed, and the signs of some hair having been torn out by the roots. I thought you'd like to know."

7

THE OLD-FASHIONED APACHE

When Dr Francis Howland was attacked and left for dead in Stark Wood, near his house at Wargate, none of his many friends could imagine an explanation of the apparently motiveless crime. Among them was Sir James Molloy, editor of that powerful morning newspaper the Record, who often made one of the little company that welcomed Dr Howland whenever he appeared at the Russell Club; and it was at Sir James's request that Philip, Trent went down to Wargate next day "to see what he could make of the mystery" for Sir James's paper.

Trent, once on the spot, could make little enough of it at the outset; and the police, so far as he could discover, were equally at a loss. But he was able to add to the few bare facts reported in the first accounts of the crime, and to supply from his own knowledge, as Sir James had suggested, some details of the victim's unusual career. Sitting in his room at the Packhorse and Talbot Inn, he drew up a dispatch to reach London by train that evening.

"Dr Howland (he wrote) has lived for some two years in this charming corner of Sussex at his little house Fairfield, his establishment consisting of a secretary, a housekeeper, and a domestic servant. Fairfield lies on the outskirts of Wargate village, and it has been his habit to take an hour's walk, usually alone, each evening before dinner in the surrounding country. Yesterday (Sunday) he went out as usual about 5:30.

"At about 6:15 Mr Derek Scotson, walking on the main road from Wargate to Bridlemere with his spaniel, heard the dog barking excitedly behind him, and turning back he was guided by the sound to a spot, not far from the road, in Stark Wood, which lies to the left of it. He found the dog standing by a man's body, lying prone on the footpath, but with the right side of the face visible; and he at once recognized Dr Howland, who was well known to him. He could see that the back of the head was terribly injured, and at first he believed that Dr Howland was dead; but a movement of the features told him that it was not so, and Mr Scotson, ordering his dog to stand guard over the victim, hurried off to the roadside telephone-box which he knew to be not far away.

"He rang up the police in Bridlemere, reporting the facts and asking them to send a doctor, as there is none living in Wargate; then rang up Dr Howland's, intending to ask that Mr Gemmell, the secretary, should bring first-aid equipment to Stark Wood immediately. Neither Mr Gemmell nor the maid, however, was in the house at the time, and the housekeeper, who is very deaf, did not hear the bell. Mr Scotson had therefore to leave the unconscious man still in charge of his dog while he stood at the Roadside to halt the police car when it should arrive. Fortunately Kit was soon on the spot, accompanied by a motor-ambulance. The doctor, after attending to the wounded man, removed him to the cottage hospital at Bridlemere, while the police, in the now failing light, made such beginning as they could in the search for traces.

"Dr Howland's injuries were found to be serious enough, though probably not fatal. He had been struck more than once on the back of the head with some heavy weapon, possibly an iron bar, and at 4 p.m. today he was still unconscious. Detective-Inspector Clymer, continuing his investigation this morning, found a number of footprints in the damp soil of the path. He formed the opinion that Dr Howland had been followed into the wood from the open field beyond it by his assailant, who had afterwards gone off at a run by the way he came. It seems likely that Dr Howland owes his life to Mr Scotson's dog, whose barking may well have frightened of the ruffian before his brutal work was done.

"From my own knowledge I may recall some leading facts about the career of Dr Howland, which is better known to the French public than to his countrymen. Before his retirement, he had for many years a remarkable place in the legal world. He was born and brought up in Paris, where his father was the correspondent of an important newspaper. He was educated in England. At Oxford he studied law with brilliant success, and took, later, his doctorate in that school. After being called to the Bar, he returned to Paris, where he qualified as an advocate, and built up a practice among British subjects engaged in litigation, or faced with prosecution, in the French courts. This was soon extended to other foreigners in Paris; for Dr Howland was a notable linguist, having mastered half a dozen continental tongues with extraordinary facility, and speaking them as readily as English and French. It was said of him (untruly) that if a client applied to him whose language he did not know, Dr Howland would make an appointment with him for the following day, by which time he would be ready to discuss his case with him fluently and idiomatically in his own native speech.

"In this corner of his profession the doctor made for himself a unique and very profitable place. He was best known to the public as a defender of accused persons, and as the deadliest cross-examiner of his day. At the same time he had won distinction among legal scholars with a few volumes on comparative jurisprudence. When I was living in Paris I met Dr Howland more than once, and was struck by the gravely handsome presence and splendid voice which were so effective in the French tribunals.

"Dr Howland had certainly made at least a moderate fortune at the French Bar, but much of it, according to rumour, had been sunk for ever in the financing of a new health resort in the Puy-de-Dôme which came to nothing. Then one day an aunt of the King of Annam, in French Indo-China, was accused by a mandarin, her enemy, of attempting to poison M. de Choiselle, the Resident-Superior, and Dr Howland was offered an enormous fee by the king to leave his practice and go out to defend the lady. He spent six months in Hué, routed a dozen bought witnesses, saved his client, and at once decided to retire on his gains and settle down in England.

"So he came to Wargate, an elderly bachelor in easy circumstances. There he has lived in scholarly peace, working at another book, entertaining a few friends, and running up frequently to town for luncheon at the Russell Club, where his wit and his fund of curious experience have made him the centre of an admiring circle. No man could be more liked and respected, and his being made the subject of a murderous attack has been heard of with no less amazement than concern."

At breakfast next morning Trent had the coffee-room to himself. As he was filling a pipe he heard a car draw up at the inn, and presently Inspector Clymer, whose acquaintance Trent had already made, ushered in to him a slim, hard-looking man who, Trent decided privately, would be at his best on horseback in a weatherbeaten scarlet coat. After this personage came young Mr Gemmell, Dr Howland's secretary, with whom also Trent had had some talk the day before.

"Can I have a word with you, Mr Trent?" the slim man said. "My name's Hildebrand—Captain Hildebrand—Chief Constable in these parts."

Trent, who asked nothing better than this, said he would be glad if he could be of any use, and drew out chairs for Captain Hildebrand and the two others.

"Well, you may be of more use than any of us are, as it happens," the captain said, biting off the end of a cigar. "You understand our work, I know, and it seems you have lived in Paris and knew something of Dr Howland. I read that article with your name at the top of it in the paper this morning."

"What is the news of the old gentleman?" Trent asked.

"Pretty good. They feel sure now that he'll get over it. I saw him last night. He was getting his wits back, and I think he knew me. Well now, I made this an early call, because I wanted to be sure of finding you, and I picked up Mr Gemmell on my way, thinking he might be able to throw some light on the subject. I'll tell you what it is. When Inspector Clymer was going over the ground yesterday, he found two bits of paper, pieces of a torn-up letter, lying near the footpath through Stark Wood and close to where you come into it from the field—that's to say about thirty yards from where the doctor was found. Is that right, Clymer?"

"That's the measurement I made," said the inspector.

"Now, what is written on these pieces of paper seems to be in some sort of French. I can read French pretty well, and I've shown them to one of my superintendents who knows the language thoroughly, and neither of us can make head or tail of some of it. I've got them here, and I should like to hear what you think about it."

Captain Hildebrand produced from his pocket a letter-case, and extracted from it two battered scraps of notepaper which he handed to Trent. They bore a few lines written in a sprawling but sufficiently legible hand.

oici le flambeau, Vous savez
tobre tombe sur un dimanche
vez ce quil laufeme, la

en sorte du village
ire suer le lieuvème
praudra se payer notre

Trent frowned over the sordid-looking scrawl for a few minutes. He held the bits of paper up to the light, while Captain Hildebrand and the inspector exchanged significant glances.

"There are some curious points about all this," Trent said at last. "Whoever wrote it knew French well enough—"

"Damned queer French too," the captain interjected.

"Almost too queer," Trent agreed. "But what I was saying is that he didn't know it thoroughly. You see this about some date ill October falling on a Sunday—possibly that refers to the day of the crime, Sunday the fourteenth. Well, I can't see any Frenchman writing, or saying, 'tombe sur un dimanche.' He would write 'tombe un dimanche,'—that is the universal idiom, as far as know. I doubt if this man is a Frenchman at all."

"Ha!" The captain exclaimed. "Now we're getting somewhere. What else?"

"The puzzling words here"—Trent laid the scraps on the table—"are queer French, as you say. They belong to a sort of thief patter, the same sort of thing as the old back-slang in the English underworld—only not so simple. You take a word, cut off the first letter and stick it onto the end, then put an L at the beginning, and finish off the job by tacking on the final syllable 'eme.' Louchébème, it's called—because the butchers of the Paris abattoirs invented it before the apaches took it up. You see: boucher—ouchéb—louchéb—louchébème."

"Golly, what a lingo!" Captain Hildebrand observed. He was keenly interested. The inspector's face expressed a certain bewilderment; Mr Gemmell's nothing whatever. "Well then, what about 'laufème' and 'lieuvème'? I don't seem to get it."

"Why, that's another point, and an important one. You see, louchébème was a spoken secret language; it was meant to keep k anybody guessing who heard you talking about your private affairs—not for letter-writing. That being so, any silent letters would be dropped out. Well then, 'laufème' gives you 'fau' and 'lieuvème' gives you 'vieu.' "

Captain Hildebrand bent over the writing. "Yes, of course—'vieu' is 'vieux,' the old man. We're getting on! But what do you make of 'fau,' then? Oh yes, I see! He must have written, 'Vous something-or-other ce qu'il faut.' It would be, 'You know what is necessary,' I dare say."

"Yes, probably. But what is odd about all this is that it's a good many years since I lived in Paris, and learnt about louchébème. Half my friends there knew about it too. We used to use louchébème words for fun. And of course that meant that the crooks had given it up; a slang that everybody understands is no good to them. I did hear, in fact, that they had got another called javanais; and the mere fact that I heard of it probably meant that it was already disused. So you see how strange it all is—a man apparently trying to write like a French crook, and not, I think, succeeding.

"You see the same thing in that word 'flambeau.' He seems to written 'Voici le flambeau.' That used to be thieves' slang for is the affair,' or 'the business'—I've come across it in novels as Les Misérables, as old as Dickens. It's like a modern English crook talking about 'cly-faking,' or calling the police 'slops.' And you can say the same about the word 'suer.' If he wrote 'faire suer le lieuvème'—make the old man sweat—it would mean in slang of the Bill Sikes vintage 'kill the old man.' Which somebody tried to do. There you are, Captain Hildebrand." Trent handed the pieces of paper to him. "I'm sure I hope you enjoy hearing lectures.

"Some lectures." The captain had a pleasant smile. "Then what it comes to is that this is just a blind, planted near the scene of the crime for us to pick up. Somebody being clever, in fact. And we had already come to the conclusion that it's in a disguised hand. Now, what about the watermark? I saw you spotted that. You can see on the long slip the end of a word, 'KOLAJ.' "

"Or a name. Well, you know as much about that as I do. Words ending with a J don't belong at this end of Europe; at the other end they're as common as blackberries. Our friend couldn't have faked that, anyhow."

"Just so. It's another point for us to think about. Now, I told you I thought Mr Gemmell here might be able to help us possibly, with you in support, as it were, Mr Trent—knowing all you do about the doctor's life abroad. You attended to his correspondence, Mr Gemmell, I suppose?"

Mr Gemmell's tight-lipped Scottish mouth opened for the first time since he had entered the room. "I made yesterday a full statement about myself and my recent movements to Inspector Clymer," he said. "Perhaps you have not seen it, Captain Hildebrand."

"Not yet."

"Well, I mentioned in it the fact that I have been only three weeks in Dr Howland's employment. Until I came, he had done without a secretary. So it's not much that I can tell you about his correspondence."

"Hm! That's a pity," the captain said. "What I was going to ask is whether he had ever received anything in the nature of threatening letters, or ever answered anything of that kind."

"I cannot say what he may have received or what he may have answered personally," said Mr Gemmell with caution. "From my brief experience I would say that his correspondence was not large. Since I came, he has dictated only a few letters to me, all of a business or formal character. My work was principally in connection with his legal studies and the book that he was writing." Mr Gemmell produced a notebook from his breastpocket. "I have here my shorthand notes of the letters I took. The addresses were E. L. Chambers & Son, booksellers, 92 Ermine Street, London; Mr H. T. Saltwell, tailor, 143 Jermyn Street, London; the Manager, Henson's Bank, Bridlemere; Messrs. Quin & Barnard, stockbrokers, 54 Copthall Avenue, London; the Editor of The Deipnosophist, 11 Henrietta Street, London; the Secretary of the Cassowary Club, Singapore; Mr L. G. Minks, antique dealer, 38 Godden Street, Maidstone. And the Bridlemere Gas Company, Bridlemere. That's all."

"None of them any use to us, I should think," Captain Hildebrand said. "Well, Clymer, you and I must be getting along. Sorry to have brought you here for nothing, Mr Gemmell. We shan't be going by Fairfield again, or I'd offer you a lift back. Very many thanks for your help, Mr Trent—your very valuable help. Good morning."

The captain and his satellite went briskly out. Mr Gemmell rose and began to follow them at a more leisurely pace, paying no attention to Trent; but at a word from him the young Scotsman paused.

"I am thinking about one of those names you read out to us, Mr Gemmell," Trent said. "Chambers & Son, of Ermine Street. You have your note of the letter. As it is only a business letter, would it be in order for you to tell me what was in it? It has just occurred to me that there might be something worth following up."

Mr Gemmell regarded him with a wooden face for a few moments. "In my opinion," he then said, "it would be highly irregular. It is no part of my duty to give such information to any private individual. Good morning to you." And he walked out.

Trent, not at all discomposed by a snub which he had fully expected, set off for London in his car a little later. During the hour's run, he gave more thought to the question he had broached so unsuccessfully to the faithful Gemmell, and decided in favour of a little scouting. He had never had any dealings with the firm of Chambers & Son; but he happened to know—most people interested at all in the book world knew—that they specialized in foreign literature, stocking the books of the day in half a dozen languages, and would produce for a purchaser any foreign book that was still on sale. And was there not a foreign flavour about the whole business, about all of Dr Howland's record, about the relic of French or pseudo-French script on which his advice had been sought? It was, he thought, a trail worth following. He would assist the police, and incidentally the Record, and satisfy his own inquisitive taste, by following it himself.

A little before noon he visited Chambers's establishment. The only shopman visible was attending to a customer, and Trent wandered among the neatly-kept shelves and tables, with their array of paper-covered volumes, until a little man wearing pincenez, and radiating consciousness of his own importance, came down a staircase at the back and asked if there was anything he required. Trent, visited by an inspiration, wondered if a copy of Victor Hugo's Quatre-Vingt-Treize was to be had; the shopman, with the negligent air of a conjurer producing a rabbit from a hat, at once fished out the book from the recesses of a deep drawer.

Trent, showing himself properly impressed, talked with the little man, who seemed to have read, or to know all about, everything in the shop, and was very willing to display his erudition. When at length Trent asked if his friend Dr Howland was a customer of Chambers's, the man shook his head. He did not know the name, he said; though anyone, of course, could buy books without the person who served him knowing who he was.

Trent, presuming on his having made a purchase, next asked to see the manager, whose name, he was told, was Mr Nauck, and whom he saw in a little office on the first floor. Mr Nauck was a tall and bulky person, shaven-faced and crop-headed, whose correct and fluent English was marred only by a slight difficulty with the letters W and V. He knew Dr Howland by name, but not as a client of Chambers's; he had been shocked to read of the brutal assault made upon him.

Had no letter been received from Dr Howland? None, said Mr Nauck. The firm dealt with a very large correspondence, both home and foreign; but Mr Nauck had an excellent memory, and he was sure that there had been no such letter. In any case, if the letter had been received, it could easily be traced through the firm's files. Could Trent give the date of it?

Trent knew only that it had been dictated at some time during the past three weeks. Mr Nauck, after a reference to his filing cabinet, declared positively that no letter from any one of the name of Howland had been received for a clear month past. It was clear that if the letter had been written, it had somehow gone astray. He was sorry to have been of no assistance to Trent, and took leave of him with a Nordic bow.

The little shopman was putting on his hat and overcoat, it being no doubt his time for lunch, as Trent passed through the shop his way out. He returned to his house in Grove End Road, and passed an hour in mental review of the facts; then wrote and posted a letter to Inspector Clymer at Bridlemere.

The inspector met Trent the next morning, as he had suggested in his note, at a tea-shop in Ermine Street at the hour of noon. From a table by the window, Chambers's shop, on the other side of the way, was well in view; and they sat down to cups of coffee.

"I don't know what to make of your letter, Mr Trent," Inspector Clymer began. "You say you think you may have got a line. You don't say much more and if it wasn't that you have a reputation, and the way you dealt with those bits of writing, I don't know that I should be justified in leaving my investigation on the spot. Not that it's led to anything yet. It isn't easy to trace a man that you know nothing about but the size of his foot. Nobody in the Wargate neighbourhood noticed any stranger about the place that evening. He could have got away by car, or cycle, or train from Bridlemere, or any of three coach-services that halt near the station. Nobody there could give me anything—why should they? There's plenty of traffic on Sunday evenings."

"And I suppose Dr Howland has not been able to say anything yet. Is he doing as well as they expected?"

"Making a wonderful recovery, they say. He is conscious, and able to speak, but not much. The doctor allowed me to see him early this morning, and stood over me while I put a question or two on the main point—whether he saw anything of the man who attacked him. Nothing at all, the old man whispered—I could barely make out what he was saying. But he had heard the man talking to himself after he coshed him—something about 'smash you,' 'trying to smash me,' and then 'think nobody's a swell but yourself.' Which doesn't seem to make much sense. After that, he says, he heard Edward barking—that's the dog, we all know him in Bridlemere—and then he passed out. That was all I got; they wouldn't let me question him any further. But it does tell us something. If those bits of a letter were dropped by the criminal on purpose, which I think is a moral certainty, they were dropped by a man who spoke English, and what you might call colloquial English at that, when he thought he had knocked a man silly, and fully intended to finish him off properly."

Trent nodded. "And a man who talks to himself in English—"

"Is not a Frenchman, anyway; or any other kind of foreigner. It shows you we're right about those scraps being a blind, Mr Trent, and that somebody was being clever, as the captain says. And now about that letter you wanted a copy of. I saw Gemmell this morning, and asked him to type it out for me from his shorthand note. He thought it over, and then said that in his opinion the proper procedure would be for me to take his carbon copy of the letter as sent. When I thanked him, he said it was his duty to assist the police, and that he would require a receipt. Well, I thought, Lord knows what will happen to the West Sussex force if we lose this precious document; so I had it copied at the station, and here's one that you can keep—have it framed, if you like."

Trent took the envelope from him, and glanced over the contents. "You shouldn't let Gemmell annoy you. He is the slave of duty, and he isn't one of the glad hearts, without reproach or blot, who do its work and know it not. Well, Inspector, I am glad you got this. I think it is going to be helpful. Let me just go through it again."

The letter ran as follows:

FAIRFIELD,
WARGATE,
SUSSEX.
24th *September*, 19—

Messrs. E. L. Chambers & Sons,
92 Ermine Street
London, W.1.

Dear Sirs,

Some weeks ago I asked your firm to procure for me the following books:

Darstellung der *Leibnitzschen Philosophie*
By Ludwig Feuerbach
Die Grundformen der *Gesellschaft*
By Eugen Eschscholz

When I visited your shop to give this order, I took the trouble, in order to prevent mistakes, to spell carefully the titles and the authors' names to the person who took the order.

After about a fortnight, having heard nothing from you, I wrote to a friend of mine in Leipzig, who sent me the books required. They arrived this morning.

I think that if it is not worth your while to make inquiry for books not published recently, and possibly seldom asked for, I should have been told so.

Yours faithfully,

Trent looked up at the inspector. "A very nasty letter indeed," he remarked approvingly. "Clear, precise, not a word wasted, and yet calculated to make Chambers & Son foam at their respective mouths. Did you ask, as I suggested, if it was quite certain the letter had been signed and posted?"

"Yes. Gemmell was quite sure of it."

"All right. Now, Inspector, I am going to explain to you what my notion is, but time presses, it's nearly 12:30.1 want to confront Chambers's manager with this letter, and I want to do so while his chief assistant is not within call. The assistant goes out to lunch, unless I'm mistaken, just about now, and if you will take it on trust from me, you ought to have a look at him while I am interviewing the boss. If you will do that, and meet me here in half an hour, say, I'll tell you the whole thing." Trent paused, his eye on Chambers's doorway. "I may say it's possibly a chance for you, if you care about that."

"You bet I do!" said Inspector Clymer fervently. "Here! Is that him coming out now—the cocky little chap?"

"That's the man. Is it a cosmic law, d'you think, that conceited men's hats are always too small?" But the inspector, in no mood for probing the mysteries of the universe, was already at the door, bent on not losing sight of the little man.

"Vell, Mr Trent," the manager said, as he took the copy from its envelope, "I shall be interested to see this letter. If it is as you say, I ought to see it, as I deal with the firm's correspondence, and it should haf been delivered here—" he glanced at the date—"nearly three weeks ago."

Mr Nauck read; and as he did so his broad, bland face was transfigured to a mask of rage. As he finished the last paragraph, he struck the table with an enormous fist and exploded in a seven-syllable German oath; then, curbing his emotion with obvious difficulty, he turned to his visitor.

"I beg you to excuse me, Mr Trent. Perhaps you don't see vot a bad business this is. It comes to this: that I am being deceived by a man I haf trusted. It is evident that my chief assistant, Mr Votkin, took that order, and nefer passed it on to me, as he should haf done, for the sending of the necessary letters."

"But he might have mislaid it and then forgotten it," Trent suggested.

"Yes, that vas going to be his story," Mr Nauck said grimly. "If Dr Howland had inquired further about his order, that is vot Votkin could haf said, and he might expect to get off with a sharp reprimand and a caution. But he did not reckon on Dr Howland doing vot he did, and then writing this—" here Mr Nauck appeared to swallow something; probably, Trent thought, a vivid German epithet—"this letter. Vot does this letter mean, Mr Trent? It means that the firm has lost an order—a small matter, yes, but it also means that ve haf lost an important client, and that our reputation is compromised. Think vot Dr Howland may haf been saying about us! If I had seen this letter, I should haf sacked Votkin on the spot and veil he knew it!"

Trent considered a moment. "But how could he know anything about it? You say the letter was never delivered."

"Oh yes, it vos! I know now vot happened. You see, Mr Trent, my assistants come here in the morning a little earlier than I do, and it is Votkin's job to open the letters and sort them for my attention ven I arrive. He read that letter. He saw vot it meant for him, and he simply suppressed it."

"You think that was it? I see." Trent was, in fact, beginning to see somewhat further than did Mr Nauck. "But what could have induced the man to act in this way? Why, I mean, should he have ignored that order in the first place?"

"Vy? Because Votkin is a puffed-up mass of conceit, Mr Trent, and because he has a violent temper. I gif him his due; he is an excellent linguist and a valuable man for our business. His conceit is nothing to me, nor is his temper. He got nasty with me vonce, but he didn't do it again," said Mr Nauck with significance. "But I vouldn't have his touchiness interfering with business, and more than vonce I haf censured him severely for being disrespectful to clients. Veil, you see vot Dr Howland says here." He tapped the letter. "He took the trouble to spell the names carefully to the man who took his order. He treated him like some commonplace, ignorant fellow, perhaps."

Trent called on his memories of the Doctor in past years. "He had rather a crushing manner at times. Eminent barristers often have."

"There you are!" Mr Nauck exclaimed. "He must haf got Votkin into such a raving passion that he would do anything to spite him, and the only thing he could do was to keep him vaiting for his order. It vas an idiotic trick, of course; but it's just the sort of thing these irritable, vindictive fools do. Veil, I don't lose my temper often, but I am going to haf it out with Mr Votkin as soon as I see him."

Trent took leave of the seething Mr Nauck, and went out to wait for Inspector Clymer.

"He went to the St. Alban's buffet," the inspector reported, "having a drink at the bar first. I sat near him at the counter. He had a ham sandwich for lunch, which he didn't finish, and two more double whiskies, which he did. That's a badly frightened man if I ever saw one, his nerves are all to pieces. I left him there when I thought I had seen enough. And now, perhaps, Mr Trent, you will let me know what all this means, and why you wanted me to join you here."

Trent let him know. He told how the name of a foreign bookseller, where half-sheets from foreign letters with foreign watermarks would be easily come by, had caught his attention. He told of Mr Watkin's innocent display of his familiarity with French authors, and of his failure to remember Dr Howland's name, although he had ordered books to be sent to him at his address. He told what Mr Nauck had said of Watkin's disposition, and the story that Mr Nauck had pieced together from the evidence. Finally, Trent told what he himself now guessed to be a later chapter of that story.

The inspector listened keenly, his face full of a restrained eagerness. "One thing's clear," he said. "It is my business to interrogate this Mr Watkin, and the sooner the better. Look! There he comes now." And with Trent in attendance he left the tea-shop and hurried after his unconscious prey.

They entered the book-shop, and saw Mr Watkin hanging up his hat and coat in a cupboard under the stairs at the back of the shop. He turned at the sound of their footsteps and came towards them; but the polite inquiry was checked on his lips, and his face turned white and frightened as he recognized Trent and took in the unmistakable appearance of Inspector Clymer.

"You are Mr Watkin, I believe," the inspector said. The terrified man only stared at him in silence, putting a hand to his throat. "I am a police officer, and—" Here he broke off, for Watkin had turned and made as if to rush to the stairs.

But coming down them at that moment appeared Mr Nauck, wearing a tigerish scowl and holding out in a hand shaking with fury the paper which Trent had given him.

"Votkin!" Roared the big man. "Vot does this mean? I hear this morning that you haf concealed from me a letter addressed to the firm, and not only that, but you haf—"

"Oh, let me alone, for God's sake!" Watkin staggered to a table and collapsed onto a chair beside it. For a moment he dropped his head on his arms; then looked up with a ghastly face at the inspector. "All right," he said. "You can take me. I shan't resist."

"Now, now! Pull yourself together!" Inspector Clymer snapped.

"I haven't asked you anything yet, you know."

Again Watkin hid his head on his arms. "That be damned!" He said in a muffled voice. "I've had enough of it, I want to get it over, a little more of what I've been going through would drive me raving mad." He got to his feet. "If you won't take me in charge, I'm going round to the police-station to give myself up."

"I'm taking him down to Bridlemere this evening," Inspector Clymer said as they left the station in Chapman Row an hour later. "I'm sorry I had to ask you to wait, Mr Trent, but I couldn't tell what sort of a statement he was going to make, and as it happens, there is a point I would like your opinion on. He has told all about how he went down there, and hung about watching for the old man, and followed him, and how he did it, and how he got away afterwards; but he never said a word about why he did it. As you know, we aren't allowed to put any questions about a voluntary statement. It seems a large order to try to murder a man because you didn't like his manner."

"It depends on how much insane vanity you have got crammed into your carcass," Trent said. "That wretched little fellow is stuffed to the gills with it, I should say, and when people like that take offence, they can hate to an extent that's impossible for nice men like you and me, Inspector. But Watkin had another motive, I think. The first time I talked to him it was plain that he was devoted to his job, revelled in it, and fancied himself hugely in it. When he read that letter of the doctor's he saw it meant his being sacked without a character, and that even if he destroyed it he could never feel safe unless the writer was destroyed too."

"I see. That was what he meant when the old man heard him talking about 'trying to smash me.' Yes. But what about 'think nobody's a swell but yourself?"

"The doctor heard him imperfectly, I believe. The words were 'think nobody can spell but yourself.' That was the thing that rankled."

8

TRENT AND THE BAD DOG

At the very outset of Trent's investigation of the Headcorn murder he came to realize that no tears were being shed about the death of James Beadle Hoyt. Americans, as a rule, make themselves very well liked in England; but Hoyt was a marked exception. Plausible at first, he went off rapidly on further acquaintance. He drank too hard to be popular outside drinking circles. He was short-tempered, apt to turn sulky, and appeared to be really interested in nothing but whisky, gambling, and himself. Nothing whatever was known about him but his name, that he had been staying at a very expensive hotel in London, that he had had good clothes and plenty of money.

Hoyt had been one of two guests brought down by Gerald Shelley to his father's house, South Court, near Headcorn, in the depths of the garden of England. General Shelley, who in his latter years had suffered one domestic tragedy, could refuse nothing to his son and to Helena, his daughter. He had been delighted to receive Gerald's friends, the American Hoyt and a superbly mannered Italian gentleman, Signor Giulio Capazza, who was understood to be engaged in some form of commerce—to judge from his appearance and style, a profitable form.

Gerald Shelley, as junior partner in a flourishing business, lived the life of the City and acquitted himself well in it. He had weakness for high play at cards; but as he won—by his own account—more than he lost, it had led to no trouble hitherto.

Gerald had come down from London for a short holiday, with Hoyt and Capazza for company; and for the first time in his life he had looked seriously worried and depressed. There had been an interview with his father which had left the general in no better condition.

The three men had travelled down to Headcorn in Gerald's car on a Tuesday. The next Saturday afternoon had been fixed for a Garden Fete at a country house close by; one of those junketings to which District Nursing Associations, Women's Institutes, or Church Funds look for occasional support. After luncheon the servants at South Court, being given leave to attend the Fete, had all left the house. Miss Shelley and Signor Capazza had gone off soon afterwards with the same purpose. Gerald Shelley, before joining them at the Fête, had driven over to Maidstone to borrow an extra fishing-rod from a friend, for Capazza, whom everyone liked, had begged to be instructed in the sport which was Gerald's favourite. General Shelley had retired as usual to his study for a rest, which meant as a rule a good two hours of refreshing slumber; and Hoyt had gone to sleep off his potations in a room on the ground floor, known as the gunroom, which Gerald Shelley and his friends used as a sitting-room of their own. The American and his host were thus the only persons left in the place that pleasant summer afternoon.

At six o'clock the servants had returned, and the parlourmaid had gone to put on a table in the gunroom some letters which had arrived for Gerald during their absence. She had been heard to shriek wildly; and the others, crowding into the room, had seen the dead body of Hoyt lying on its face in the middle of the floor, a knife driven into the back below the left shoulder-blade.

When, an hour later, the Shelleys and Capazza returned from the Fête, the police were already well advanced in the first stage of investigation. A statement had been taken from the general, who had seen or heard nothing unusual, and had not left his study until the house was roused by the parlourmaid's screams. No traces whatever appeared to have been left by the murderer. The weapon was of the hunting-knife type, bearing the mark of a Pittsburgh firm. Its blade, some ten inches long, was straight and single-edged, curving on the sharp side to a dangerously fine point; the handle was of coarsely cross-cut deerhorn, on which no fingermarks could show.

As for the means by which the murderer could have gained admission to the house, the matter was simple enough. The doors at the front and back were locked only at night, and could be opened by turning a handle. Any prowling thief who had seen the servants and the others leave, and might have assumed that the place was deserted, could have got in without any difficulty. But nothing had been taken from any room; Hoyt's watch and well-filled note-case were in his pockets. The mystery was complete, and the Italian's suggestion of a murder for hatred or revenge—he called it a *vendetazzia*—seemed as reasonable a guess as any.

These facts, which appeared in an expurgated form in Trent's first dispatch to the *Record*, were gathered by him partly from the police, largely from Miss Shelley, who was very ready to give information, as she said, where it was likely to do any good. She was a handsome, self-possessed brunette, who had just been, in her own words, "having a shot at her Mus. Bac." at Oxford, and was now at home waiting to learn her fate at the examiners' hands. She had talked to Trent as they paced a narrow lawn at the back of the house, separated from it by a gravel path and a flower-bed that skirted the wall. Miss Shelley was escorted by a recently barbered black poodle.

"It's no use to pretend," she said, "that any of us liked Mr Hoyt. I couldn't stand him myself. He began by paying me offensive compliments; and when I let him see I didn't like it, and especially after I took Signor Capazza for a run in the car without asking him to join us, he was like a bear with a sore head. He drank more whisky in a day than father gets through in a month. He was insolent to the servants; and once when he wanted to go out in Gerald's car by himself, and our chauffeur told him plainly he wasn't in a fit state to drive, he shouted at him in the most disgusting language I have ever heard. Then again, I knew he had been illtreating my dog Harlequin, beating him or kicking him on the sly; because after the first day Hoyt was here, Harlequin was scared to death of him—you know, dumb and shivering whenever he was about, though Harlequin is naturally a spirited and friendly I sort of dog.

"Another thing—Hoyt was often rude to my brother; and when I spoke to Gerald about it he confessed that he had lost much more than he could pay to Mr Hoyt, playing poker with him and Signor Capazza. Gerald said Hoyt had won a lot from Capazza too, but he had paid up, being quite well-off, apparently. Gerald admitted, too, that he had asked father to help him; and that must have been a dreadful shock to father, because he can only just make ends meet keeping up this place. You see," Miss Shelley went on with the candour of her generation, "my poor mother went out of her mind two years ago, and keeping her in a home over at Smeeth costs more than you would believe. Father has never been the same man since that disaster, because he was devoted to her; and now this new trouble over Gerald, with a man murdered in the house to follow it up, has simply broken him, poor dear."

Trent hoped he did not look his embarrassment at being so frankly taken behind the family scenes. He had suggested that Helena Shelley should tell him all the details she could think of about the crime; and she was taking him at his word. He spoke some words of the sympathy that he felt; then added, "I believe you and Signor Capazza were the last members of the household to see Hoyt alive."

"I was going to tell you about that. About an hour after lunch, Capazza and I came out into the garden, because I was going to take him over to the Garden Fete in Sir Gilbert Tregelles's meadow, which is just next to father's land—only two minutes' walk from here. Capazza was interested, because I had entered Harlequin for the Bun Race at the Fete, and it was a new idea to him."

"So it is," Trent said, "to me."

"It's rather fun. The owners run with their dogs on the lead, and when they get to a point a hundred yards away each owner and each dog has to eat a bun, and when both buns are finished—not before—run back to the starting-place. The first couple to get back wins the prize. As Harlequin is the greediest dog I know, and I can bolt my food when I like, I hoped we should win; and so we did, by a short head, amid fearful excitement. It was a great day for Harlequin, because he also won the prize in the Dog-with-the- Most-Pathetic-Eyes class at the Comic Dog Show. You can see if you look at him... Now where," Miss Shelley broke off, perching a pair of thick-lensed spectacles on her pretty nose, "has that animal got to?"

Trent pointed. "There he is, straight in front of you, in the middle of that flower-bed, looking at you—very pathetically indeed."

"Come here, sir!" His owner called. "How dare you go in that bed? Well, as I was saying—bad dog!—We came out through the drawing-room, and were walking over this lawn to get to the other end of the garden, where there is a gate leading towards the Tregelles's place."

She took a few steps and paused before a small circular bed of rose trees in the midst of the lawn.

"That window just opposite us now is the window of the room where Hoyt was at the time. It was open, and as we came near it, Capazza asked if he might have a flower for his coat. I said yes, of course, and at that moment Hoyt appeared at the window. He gave a sneering sort of laugh and said, 'That's right, Miss Shelley, the white flower of a blameless life for him, he surely has it coming to him,' or something like that; and he added, looking at Capazza, 'I'm going to keep my promise.' His manner was most offensive, and I was so disgusted I turned my back on him and began cutting a rose with the scissors out of my bag. After I had pinned it in Capazza's buttonhole we went on our way."

"And that was the last you saw of Hoyt?"

"Well, very nearly. When we got to the gate—you can see it down there, in the holly hedge—he shouted after us, and as I glanced back he waved his arm. Harlequin began barking and dragging at the lead, trying to run back, and I thought the noise might wake my father, so I said something peevish about the way Hoyt was behaving, and Capazza said in his quaint accent, 'I think he wish us to return. Poor fellow, he dooes not know what he doos. Do you wish to return, Miss Shelley?" I said certainly not, that I shouldn't dream of it; and we went on to the Fête.

"That was actually the last that any of us saw of Hoyt before he was murdered. The police asked us if it sounded as if he was shouting for help—hoping to fix the time of the murder, I suppose. Well, it didn't sound like that. He certainly didn't shout 'Help!' It was just a 'Hi!' As if he was trying to attrack our attention; and I believe that's all it was."

Trent looked down to the gate in the hedge, some seventy yards, "Yes; if he had shouted anything articulate I suppose you must have heard it. And your father, I understand, heard nothing at all."

"No; he wouldn't—what with being rather deaf, and asleep too, as he would be at the time, and the study being on the other side of the house. But he is terribly distressed that he did not—I think he persuades himself that he is to blame in a way. The whole thing has been quite shattering for him."

Trent considered for a few moments of silence. "And at the Fete you met your brother?"

"Yes; he came there straight from Maidstone. It is only a twenty-minutes' run, and he probably got there before we did. He had been there some time, he said, when we ran into him in the crowd. After that the three of us were together until we returned here, and heard what had happened."

Trent found Gerald Shelley and Signor Capazza in the middle of a meadow that sloped down to a stream bounding the general's property on one side. They had rods in their hands, and it was evident that the Italian was being given a dry-land initiation in the art of casting a fly. "There! You've got the trick of it," Trent heard Shelley say. "I've never known a beginner so quick at picking it up." "*Aha! Sono molto pescatore!*" The other laughed. "Watch out, you feesh, when I get-a-going!"

Shelley, a slight, fair young man with a distraught and worn-out look, made a striking contrast with his friend, a tall, swarthy and solidly built man of about thirty, with health and vigour in every athletic line of him.

Shelley had quite agreed with his sister, he said, that Trent should be told all they could tell him, because he and his paper had a name for not printing anything the family wouldn't like. He supposed she had already told him what she and Signor Capazza knew about it, which was more than anyone else knew, as no one else had seen Hoyt between lunch-time and the time when he was found murdered.

Shelley dwelt upon this point, and volunteered a particular account of his own doings on the afternoon of the crime, mentioning several persons who had seen him in Maidstone, and appealing to the Italian to bear out his statement that the two of them and Miss Shelley had not been out of each other's sight during the time spent at the Fête. Trent, who could think of one period when, by the girl's account, she had not been with the other two, turned to Signor Capazza.

"Eet ees true," Capazza said. His voice was deep and soft. "Togezzer all-a time, and so he tell-a da police. But my friend ees afraid they suspect-a heem," he added with a dazzling smile. "Ees allbunk, eh? Ees-a not likely he keel a man een hees own house, and among hees own-a famiglia, and for no reason. You theenk?"

Trent agreed that it did not seem probable.

"Oh, they suspect everybody, of course," Shelley said gloomily. "They suspect my father, for instance, just because he happened to be in the house when this murderer got in—which only shows you, because the governor would as soon shoot himself as do violence to a guest under his roof, to say nothing of stabbing him in the back."

"Well, they have to work to their system, you know," Trent said. "Will you tell me, Signor, about that time when you and Miss Shelley saw Hoyt at the window? He said something, did he, about keeping his promise? What could he have meant by that?"

A shade of embarrassment passed over Capazza's expressive face. "I do not like to speak of eet, Mr Trent; but of course everything must be explain, I know eet. What you ask, I tell-a da police-inspector already. You see, Hoyt would make-a fun of me often, because I drink always water. That day when he was keel he had drink-a much whisky, and after lunch he start on me again, why I not get souse once in a while and enjoy myself. Then I say to heem, 'These friend of ours do not enjoy themself when you are souse, you know. They ought to be consider, when you are guest. Why do you not go easy on da liquor while you are here, so they like you better?' And Hoyt say, 'I believe you give-a me good advice, and I show you I can lay off da booze when I want. After- thees I am on the water-cart while

I am here, and that ees a promise.' So you see what he mean when he tell-a Mees Shelley about my blameless life, and that he will keep-a da promise."

Trent nodded. "Yes, I see. And a little later he shouted after you when you and Miss Shelley were at the gate. Why was that, I wonder?"

Capazza shrugged lightly. "How can I tell? I think he weesh us to return, but Mees Shelley say no, he is not sober, let us go on. And that ees the last time we see him alive."

"And when you heard of the murder, you could not form aid idea of who did it, or why? I suppose you have not thought of anything since then, Signor Capazza. I mean, Hoyt was a friend of yours, and you knew something of his life and his circumstances, no doubt."

Capazza wagged a forefinger in a Latin gesture of emphatic denial. "No, no, Mr Trent; make-a no mistake. I know no more of heem than Mr Shelley knows. We all meet for da first time at da Greville Hotel, where Hoyt and I are both staying to visit your wonderful London. We sit in a bridge game a few times after dins' ner, and so we become acquaint. One evening Hoyt came to me in da smoke-room, and Mr Shelley with heem, and Hoyt say, 'Thees gentleman and I have meet in da cocktail bar and got-a talking, and we think we would like to have a spot of poker. Will you join us?' I say, I will be very please indeed; so we play in Hoyt's sitting-room, and we are all pretty good players, and we have a good time. After that we meet some more times; and then we are so friendly that Mr Shelley invite the two of us here to thees charming house. And now eet is all come to thees terrible end." Signor Capazza, sighing deeply, rolled his fine eyes heavenward.

At the inquest next day, before the customary adjournment at the request of Chief-Inspector Jewell, in charge of the inquiry, the medical evidence was taken. Describing the wound, the witness said the knife had penetrated the left lung and the left ventricle of the heart. Such an injury must have been instantly fatal, and the victim had probably died without uttering a cry. The blow could not possibly have been self-inflicted. It would not have required any great strength, because the point of the weapon was as sharp as a knife-point could be.

Trent, after hearing this evidence, was seen no more that day. He had driven back to London, and had spent an afternoon hour at the office of a friend of his, in the neighbourhood of Leicester Square. He had then written a carefully considered letter to Inspector Jewell, who received it duly the next morning.

"I have (Trent wrote) a few suggestions to make which you may think it worth while to follow up. Some of the points, perhaps all of them, will have occurred to you already, but for the sake of clearness I will put down all that I think, and something that I know.

"Gerald Shelley believes that he is under suspicion of having committed the crime; and so no doubt he is. Everything points to his having lost more money than he could pay to Hoyt and having applied to his father for help, probably at Hoyt's suggestion. It may well be that General Shelley's financial position was already not an easy one, and that Gerald was told so by him. If Hoyt's antecedents could be traced, it might turn out that he was a professional sharper and swindler. In any case, if he had got Gerald in a desperate difficulty, Hoyt's death would be very convenient for Gerald—and. for his father also, who therefore falls under suspicion too, the more so as he was admittedly in the house when the murder was done. That is not the case with Gerald; but his alibi is no good. He could easily have called at the house, without being seen by" anyone, on returning from Maidstone; and then proceeded at once to the Fête.

"You will have considered that, of course; but you may not be as confident as I am that that is precisely what Gerald did do. What happened was, I believe, that he drove back to South Lodges for some purpose, went to the gun-room, and there found Hoyt lying dead with the knife in his back. At the same time he saw through the open window Miss Shelley and Signor Capazza walking towards the gate in the hedge. He ran to the window, shouted to them, and waved his arms, before he knew what he was doing. He saw them turn and glance towards him, while the poodle barked, recognizing him, and leapt about in sympathy with his excitement, as dogs will. When they went on without paying any further attention to him, he was naturally astonished, for although he knew his sister was too short-sighted, even with glasses, to recognize him at that distance, he had no reason to suppose that Capazza was short-sighted too. Still, he could only think that neither of them, in fact, had recognized him; and when he began to realize his position, he was glad indeed to think so.

"He saw that if he was known to have been in the room where the murdered man lay, before the body was found by any other person, he would be in the gravest danger. He knew what motive would be imputed to him, and he could not imagine, then or afterwards, who else could possibly have murdered Hoyt. He was in the position of an innocent man who fears to tell the truth because it points directly at his own guilt.

"He determined to do his best to fabricate an alibi, weak though he must have seen it to be; and his statement to you was the result.

"I was led to this conclusion by noting some curious details in the account given to me by Miss Shelley of what happened on that same occasion. In the first place, she said that when she heard Hoyt shouting, she glanced back and saw him waving his arm. Now I knew from my own observation that Miss Shelley could not see well enough to have made out, at a glance and at that distance, who it was at the window. What she actually did was to assume that it was Hoyt; and quite naturally, having really seen him at that Window a minute before. She said, too, that she was annoyed by the dog trying to run back, and making a noise that might disturb her father's siesta. I was struck by that, because she had already told me that the dog was terrified of Hoyt, and could only shiver and cringe when he was about. But if she had had the least un- certainty about its being Hoyt at the window, it must have been banished by Signor Capazza recognizing him as Hoyt, and asking her if she wished to go back at the invitation of a tipsy man.

"That was quick and clever of Capazza, for if it was really Gerald at the window, as I believe, Capazza would have recognized him instantly. His sight is exceptionally keen. I know that now; and I had got that impression before, when I heard how quickly he had mastered the art of throwing a fly, which is a difficult combination of the work of wrist and eye.

"There was another thing which struck me about Miss Shelley's story of what happened when Hoyt spoke from the window to herself and Capazza. She said that his manner had been offensive and sneering—and she is, I think, a perfectly honest witness. But Capazza, telling me of the same facts, put an entirely different colour on them. He represented Hoyt as being in a rather chastened temper, after having sworn off drink at Capazza's suggestion, and as having merely repeated his promise made a short time before. That would have been quite a plausible explanation of the words Hoyt had said, but for Miss Shelley's description of the way he had said them. And she was very sure about that, because she had been so much offended that she turned her back on him and gave her attention to cutting a rose.

"It was that final detail which put an idea into my head. It was an idea which might be wild, but which provided an answer, at least, to some curious questions.

"Why had the dog behaved in that way, if the man who shouted from the window had been Hoyt?

"If the man was not Hoyt, why had Capazza pretended to Miss Shelley that he was Hoyt? And why had he reminded her that Hoyt had been drinking, if he believed Hoyt to be at that time in a penitent mood, and anxious not to make himself objectionable?

"Lastly, had something happened, unseen by Miss Shelley, while her back was turned; while she was taking the scissors from her bag and cutting a rose?

"Perhaps you see the direction that my ideas were taking. I waited for the inquest, to hear what the doctor would say about the cause of death; and it did not dispose of my suspicion. A few hours later I paid a visit to Mr Hyman Weingott, of 247 Green Street, who has a theatrical and vaudeville agency, and knows all there is to know about the business. I described Signor Capazza to him, and I asked him a question. Mr Weingott went to a book-case filled with cardboard folders, arranged alphabetically, and took down one from among the B's. The name on the cover was Briccione. He took out some papers and three photographs, which he handed to me. They were excellent likenesses of Signor Giulio Capazza.

"Then I told Mr Weingott the whole story, and my guess as to how Hoyt had met his death. He was keenly interested. He said there were many people in London who could identify Briccione, but he would like to do it himself. He will travel to Headcorn tomorrow afternoon by the train which gets in at 3:28, and will report to you when he arrives.

"Tito Briccione was born at Calascibetta in Sicily. He is an American citizen, his parents having emigrated when he was an infant; and he was brought up amongst the poor Italians in New York. Briccione is the most eminent knife-thrower in that small and highly-paid profession, having learnt his art from the celebrated Leo Latti. He can hit the ace of spades at 20 feet, and has never been known to miss. He has toured all over Europe and America for years, and in England his minimum fee has been for a ten-minute turn. He is said to have made a good money, in spite of his career having been interrupted by two terms of imprisonment in New York State. In both cases his offence was aggravated assault as the result of a quarrel. Owing to his ferocious temper and readiness to use the knife he always carried (under his left arm), he is reputed a dangerous man, and credited with several murders and stabbings that were never brought home to him. He is rigidly abstemious, because knife-throwers have to be; but he is a confirmed gambler, and associates a good deal with professional card-sharks.

"So there you have a brief history of Signor Capazza. I don't know what you thought about his story of how he became acquainted with Hoyt, and afterwards with Gerald Shelley. It sounded to me at the time just like a card-sharping variation of the confidence trick, and I think it fits in—as also does the sort of English Capazza talks—with what Mr Weingott told me. Probably the two of them had conspired to fleece Gerald, and Capazza would not leave Hoyt until the money had been collected and divided.

"I suggest that Capazza murdered Hoyt by throwing his knife at a moment when Hoyt turned away from the gun-room window, Miss Shelley having her back to it; that he did so while standing close to Miss Shelley, but between her and the window, and at a distance from it of about 16 feet. Gerald Shelley entered the room while they were walking to the gate in the hedge, and as they reached it he shouted after them. Briccione—Capazza is a Snan who can think and act very swiftly. He saw instantly that Miss Shelley took the man at the window to be Hoyt, and that if they both gave evidence to that effect his alibi would take a lot of breaking; so he played up to her belief.

"Why he killed Hoyt can be matter of guesswork only. My own guess is that Hoyt, who resented Miss Shelley's preferring Capazza's company to his own, had threatened to tell the

Shelley family the story of Capazza's 'blameless life' unless he gave up cultivating Miss Shelley's society; that when Hoyt heard him asking for a rose he determined to 'keep his promise,' and he said so; that this was too much for Briccione's fiendish temper, and that en Hoyt turned from the window he seized his chance with a gambler's boldness."

On the afternoon of the day on which Inspector Jewell received this letter, Trent was at home in his studio. He had plenty to do there, and on the scene of the murder there was no more, he thought, to be discovered. A representative of the Record, who remained on the spot, was to telephone him the result of Mr Weingott's visit; and Trent had already drafted, in advance of the facts, a message announcing the latest action taken by the police, and revealing the true indentity of Giulio Capazza. At 4:15 the call came through, and Trent had little to add to his story before dispatching it to Fleet Street.

An official version of what had happened came to Trent by the first post next morning. The letter ran as follows:

Dear Sir,

I have to acknowledge your favour of the 22nd inst., and to thank you for the contents of same.

Mr Weingott arrived here this afternoon as per your letter, and we then proceeded to South Court. In view of your information re the criminal record of Briccione, alias Capazza, I thought it best that we should be accompanied by a uniformed constable. We found Briccione with Mr Gerald Shelley fishing in the stream, and they did not observe our approach until Mr Weingott said to me, "That is the man. I should know him anywhere." Briccione looked up and appeared to recognize Mr Weingott, to whom he applied an obscene epithet. Acting with such rapidity that for a moment we were unable to intervene, Briccione then flung himself upon Mr Weingott, seized him by the hair with both hands and attempted to bite him in the throat. Mr Weingott struck Briccione a heavy blow over the ear, and another below the belt, while we were pinioning him from behind, so that the arrest was effected without further difficulty. Subsequently Briccione was charged before the magistrate in Maidstone, and committed for trail at the next assizes.

Mr Gerald Shelley has confessed that his statement made to us on the day of the crime was an incomplete account of his movements, which were substantially as suggested in your letter. As he appears to have had no knowledge of the identity of the murderer of Mr Hoyt, and no motive but to avoid being implicated in the crime, we have decided as at present advised to bring no charge against him.

I am,

Yours faithfully,

C. M. Jewell

(CHIEF-INSPECTOR)

9

THE PUBLIC BENEFACTOR

Colonel White drifted gently out from the enormous portal of the Hotel Artemare, and relapsed into a chair on the veranda over-looking the sunlit picture of Monte Carlo, with the wall of mountain majesty that made a sublimely unconscious background for its trivial charm. With his long, slim fingers he lighted a long, slim cigar, and his heavy-lidded eyes roamed slowly over the scene. Presently he rose to his feet as a tall, fair young woman came from the hotel and took a chair near his.

"You are looking fine this morning, Mrs Ashley," the colonel said. He knew that an allusion to her appearance was what this lady expected from every man, and he wanted to get it over, for the subject bored him.

Mrs Ashley blinked her sandy eyelashes at him, taking no notice of what she regarded as an observation forced from him by the spectacle of herself. She was fully satisfied with the two hours' work which she and her maid had lately completed at her toilet; and she believed that insolent manners were a mark of social distinction.

"How is your father this morning?" the colonel asked.

"Bad," Mrs Ashley said briefly. "Something has upset him again—I don't know what. He is more shaky and depressed than ever and I have phoned for Dr Cole to see him again. He may be here any minute."

Colonel White fingered his neat black moustache. "I suppose," he said, "I ought not to butt in, but as a friend of your father's I may perhaps ask if you are quite satisfied with Dr Cole."

"Well, I ought to be," Mrs Ashley said a little sharply. "I've known him for years, and he is wonderful with nervous cases. It was great luck his being here when Father had this trouble. Oh! Here he is."

A robustly handsome man, who looked as if his study of nervous disorders had been entirely unassisted by personal experience, came up the steps and joined them on the veranda. "I was sorry to get your message, Mrs Ashley," he said. "Morning, Colonel. Mrs Ashley has told you, I suppose, that she thinks her father is not so well today."

"She didn't tell me that," Colonel White answered. "She told me he was worse than ever." Something in his tone brought a flush to the doctor's face, but he turned to Mrs Ashley coolly enough.

"I met someone you know on my way here," he said. "Philip Trent—he's staying with friends at the Cluny. He knew you were here, and he was going to call, but he hadn't heard of Mr Somerton being ill, of course. I told him it would do your father nothing but good to see him, and the sooner the better—he wants taking out of himself as much as anything. So Trent is coming this afternoon. Shall I go up to Mr Somerton now? He is in your sitting-room, I suppose."

Mrs Ashley rose, and the doctor followed her to the hotel entrance. As they reached it, Colonel White heard Dr Cole say, in a tone of contempt obviously intended to reach his ears, "Your American friend is very polite this morning."

The colonel smiled. "Like hell he is!" He murmured to the landscape.

When Trent was shown up to Mr Somerton's suite that afternoon, he was astonished at the change in his appearance. Somerton, a few months ago, had been carrying his sixty-odd years lightly. With his short, thick-set figure and square, snub-nosed countenance, he had never been a beauty; but he had been the picture of health and vitality. Now he looked an old man and a sick one. His face was white and drawn, his eyes were tragic, he was stoop-shouldered, his whole being bespoke distress and haunting fear.

"I am devilish glad to see you, Trent," he said. "You may be able to help me—this break-down of my health has come at an awkward time. I am in a fix, my boy. Here, have a cigar." He pushed over a box. "I've had to give them up myself, but even the' smell of a good cigar will be something."

Trent helped himself, and through the blue haze looked thoughts-fully at Somerton. "What do you mean by being in a fix?" he asked. "You aren't being hunted by mad cannibals in an African jungle. There are doctors enough in Monte Carlo to sink a battleship. You've got your daughter here to look after you. And that American colonel I met just now would be a useful friend, I should think."

"Yes, White is a good fellow," Somerton said. "I don't know what I should have done without him. I met him here last year, and we got very friendly then; but since this trouble of mine began he has been kindness itself."

"He is young for a colonel," Trent observed.

"Oh, he's not a soldier; it's only an honorary title, he told me. He is immensely rich, and when he began life he hadn't a shilling. As for Jo being here to look after me—well, I'm sorry to say that is why the position is so bad. You see, when my—my nerves began to go wrong, a week ago, she sent for this man Cole. She knew he was staying here, and she believes in him. Well, I think he's a fool, and I know he has done me no good at all."

"Then why not get rid of him? You've never been afraid of telling people what you thought of them."

"It isn't that, it's Jo. Look here, Trent, if I want you to help me I must tell you the truth. Jo is an only child and a spoilt one, she is hard and selfish, but I'm devoted to her and can't bear to give her any cause for resentment. I couldn't, even if she was sweet-tempered, but the fact is she gets furious if she is crossed in anything, and in the state I am in now I simply dare not face one of her scenes. I can't suggest going home before she wants to. I can't tell her Cole is no use to me. On the contrary, I'm expected to like him." Somerton wiped his forehead with a shaking hand, then resumed, "You may as well know it all. I believe she's in love with him. They are always about together. It was Cole who attended Hugh Ashley when he went to pieces; and since his death she and Cole have been bosom friends."

Trent reflected over his cigar. "You don't think Cole is a wrong 'un, do you?" he asked at length.

"Oh no, nothing of the sort. After being a beak for nearly twenty years, and having had half the rascals in London up before me, I know dishonesty when I see it. Cole doesn't understand me, that's all, and he won't realize it. Now, Trent, can't you do something for me? You see how it is. You might say a word to Jo about getting another opinion, perhaps. She might listen to you; and any-how she can't make you suffer as she can make me. White has dropped a hint or two, he tells me, but she pays no attention."

"I will do anything I can, of course," Trent said. "But, Somerton, what exactly is the matter with you? You speak of your nerves going wrong; that might mean anything. You certainly don't look well; but how does it take you?"

Somerton held up a weary hand. "For God's sake, don't tell me I don't look well! I'm sick of hearing that. People I've never met come up to me in the street and tell me I look ill, and ask if they can do anything. How does it take me?" Somerton leaned forward in his chair and stared miserably into Trent's eyes. "I'll tell you. I believe I'm going out of my mind—dying at the top."

Trent showed nothing of the shock he felt. "Oh, come!" He said with a smile. "You're as sane as I am, Somerton. You haven't said a word yet that wasn't perfectly rational."

"All the same, there's something desperately wrong. I'll tell you how it began. One evening, about a week ago, Jo suggested we might run over to Mentone and take the mountain railway to Sospel, which we'd never seen, and come back by Nice. We made up a small party in the hotel, to go next day. Well, next morning I was down before the others, and Gaston, the head porter, came up to me and said he had got the timetable I asked for, with the service to Sospel. I was astounded, because I could have taken my dying oath I had ever asked him for any timetable, or even thought of doing so.

"I said nothing about this to the others, because, of course, they would have thought I had simply forgotten asking for the time-table; but it kept coming back into my mind all day. Then in the evening, when I was dressing in my room here, there was a knock at the door, and a man came in saying he was the valet. I said I hadn't rung for the valet, or for anybody. The fellow looked surprised. He said the bell had rung in the valets' room; and the little blue light over the bedroom door, which goes on when you ring, had been showing when he knocked, and he had only that moment switched it off. I said there must be something wrong with the electrical arrangements, and he went off, looking at me queerly. After what had happened that morning, I didn't like this. I hadn't rung, or wanted anything to ring for—but could I have rung all the same? I felt worried; and at dinner Jo asked me what I had got on my mind. Of course, I said there was nothing; and I worried all the more, and slept badly afterwards.

"The next morning, when I was shaving, exactly the same thing happened. The valet knocked, asked what monsieur desired; and do you know, Trent, rather than have him look at me again as if I was crazy, I told him I wanted some cigarettes. That shows you how shaken I was; for I hadn't the faintest recollection of having rung, and I felt by now that there must be something wrong mentally.

"The following day some of us went down to the front to watch a regatta, and I had a bet with a man on a crew I fancied in a boat race. I lost, and found I was short of money to pay him; so I went on to the Lyonnais where I have a credit, and drew ten *milles* and some smaller notes. I rejoined our party, and we had a few more bets. When I took out my case to settle what I owed, I found I had twenty *milles* in it.

"I said nothing about it, I was too much upset. I went back to the bank and asked how much I had drawn. The cashier showed me my cheque—10,500 francs. I said they had given me twenty milles, and produced my case to show him. There were only ten *milles* in it. The man looked at me exactly as the valet had done. I could have screamed.

"The next day White and I were out for a stroll, and we stopped at Madame Joubin's stall, as we often did, to buy papers. I got the *Times* of the day before—Tuesday, February 2nd; it was too early for that day's issue. When we sat down to look at our papers, I caught sight of the date on the front page of mine, which I hadn't unfolded. It was the Times for Monday, February 2nd—of last year!

"I said to White, 'Here's a curious thing. Look at the date on my paper.' He took it and said, 'Why, what's wrong with it?' I said 'Can't you see? It's a year old.' White stared at me, with that look I had got to dread so much. He only said, 'No, it's yesterday's paper all right'; and when I looked again, it was so.

"As soon as we got back to the hotel, I told Jo I must see a doctor at once, that for the first time in my life my nerves had gone wrong. I didn't say anything about mental trouble. She said she was sure it would be wise, that I had been looking queer for some days past; and she sent off for this fellow Cole. Well, you know what I think of him. I told him all that I've told you—I've never told any one else until now. He wagged his head and thought a little, then he asked me if I hadn't been in Monte Carlo about this time last year. I said I always came here at this time. Then Cole said that probably I had done last year all these things which I had done again unconsciously this year, or imagined myself doing this year; that I had got a kink in my memory, or something like that; that I had drawn 20,000 francs one day a years ago, and bought a *Times* on February 2nd a year ago, and so on. Well, I couldn't say it wasn't so; but you can imagine that it didn't altogether relieve my mind. It's not a good sign when your memory takes to turning somersaults. Besides, it didn't explain the time-table incident. Well, Cole said I must take a sedative, which he Ascribed, and on no account let myself get tired, and give up smoking and stimulants."

Trent, who had listened in silence while Somerton set out all these strange facts, or fancies, in their due order, now crushed out his cigar-butt and spoke. "I don't know anything about it, but I agree it looks as if nerve trouble, in the ordinary sense, hardly covers the facts. And yet, you know, Somerton, you're not a bit like a mental case, as far as my small experience goes."

Somerton uttered an impatient exclamation. "That's just it! I feel absolutely sane—and all the same there's the fact that I don't know what I'm doing sometimes. And you haven't heard the worst, either—the thing that bowled me over this morning. You see, a week ago I sent my wife a birthday present. She is at our flat in Brook Street just now; she hates Monte Carlo. I sent her a small Chinese statuette in white jade—got it at Grangette's little shop in the Rue de la Scala, and wrote down the name and address for him to send it to.

"This morning I had a letter from Mary thanking me warmly for the present, but at the same time asking whether the address

I had sent it to was some sort of joke. Fortunately the people at that address knew where we live now, but even so it had taken three days to reach her. She enclosed the label with the address written on it. Have a look at it, will you?"

Trent took the paper from Somerton's quivering hand, and read what follows:

Mrs J. L. Somerton,
23, Taiford Street,
London, S.W.7.
ANGLETERRE.

"I don't wonder she was puzzled," Trent observed, looking up at the other. "What is this address?"

"23 Talfourd Street—there ought to be a U after the O—is the house where we lived from the time we were married. We left it in 1912—fourteen years ago." Somerton lay back in his chair with closed eyes. "I've never seen it since, or given it a thought during most of that time. So there you are. A nice thing to be faced with when I was already afraid—" he left the sentence unfinished and covered his face with his hands.

Trent looked at him in silence a few moments; then stared again at the label. He rose and took it to the window, where he studied it with his back to the stricken figure in the chair. Then, looking out over the sunlit *Escalier des Fleurs*, he began to whistle almost inaudibly.

"And you had no thought of this address in your mind when you were giving Grangette his instructions.

Somerton looked up irritably. "I told you. Why, I had almost forgotten I had ever lived there until I read that label this morning. You see how it fits in with the rest. But to my mind going back to a year ago, without my being conscious of it, is one thing; fourteen years is another."

Trent left the window and laid a hand on Somerton's shoulder. "Don't you lose heart," he said. "It seems bad, I know, but I believe I may be able to help you. In fact, I am quite confident you can be put right if you'll leave it to me." And Trent, slipping the label into his pocket, took a hasty leave of his friend.

An hour later Trent found Colonel White in his favourite seat on the veranda, turning the lively pages of The New Yorker.

"I have just been having an interesting talk, Colonel," he said without preliminary, leaning back on the railing as he faced the other. "I have been to Grangette's little antique shop—you know the place."

Colonel White laid aside his paper. "Sure I know it," he said. "I have done business with Grangette a few times."

"Yes, I know you have done business with him," Trent said with an acrid smile. He drew from a pocket the label which he had taken away from Somerton's room, and tossed it on the small table at the colonel's elbow.

"That is a pretty good address, as they go," Trent went on. "There are only two things wrong with it. The name of the street is spelt the way an American would spell it. It ought to be T-A-L-F- O- U- D."

The colonel, inspecting the label with languid interest, nodded. "Pronounced T-A-L-F-O-R-D," he remarked. "Yes, I see."

"Also," Trent continued, "that postal direction, 'S.W.7.,' is a little too modern. The post office didn't begin putting a numeral after the district letters until long after Somerton had left that address. I am not sure when they started doing so, but I know it was during the war."

Colonel White sighed. "Now isn't that just too bad?" he commented.

"I took that label to Grangette," Trent went on, "and I told him I was making inquiries on behalf of Somerton, and

I wanted to know how his packet came to be sent to that address. I said that it was a situation grave. Grangette is not a reliable tool, Colonel. He began to go to pieces at once. He swore Somerton had given him the address; but the next moment he was declaring that he hadn't meant any harm, and that anyhow there was nothing illegal. So I said that was a matter for the Correctional Court to decide. I think Grangette must have been in trouble before, because as soon as I mentioned the Court he broke down and began to beg to be let off, and told me the whole thing. He even told me how much you paid him to address the packet wrongly. What I should like to know is how you got hold of that address."

The colonel smiled amiably. "Anything else you would like to know?" he inquired.

"I can imagine," Trent said, "how some of this malicious persecution was carried out. It was easy to bribe the porter and the floor-valet to pretend that Somerton had asked for a timetable and that he had rung his bedroom bell. It was easy to pay people to speak sympathetically to him in the street about how ill he was looking. But I don't see how the trick with the newspaper was done; and that business of changing the banknotes in Somerton's note-case puzzles me. Not that it matters very much; because the thing is going to stop now, and Somerton is going to be told that all this trouble of his was due to a heartless fraud. What he will do about it is for him to say. Probably he will prosecute you, for Somerton can be a very hard man when he likes."

Colonel White rose from his chair and approached Trent. "I know he can. I know he can." He stared into Trent's eyes and tapped him lightly on the chest. "You don't have to tell me that. And I can be hard too, when I like. Now, Mr Trent, I am not sorry you have found all this out. I wanted it to be known; it was part of my plan that it should be known. You have speeded matters up by a day or two, that's all. I had very nearly finished with Somerton, and my intention was to go away suddenly, without a word to him, leaving a letter for him in which I reminded him of certain matters between ourselves. What I am now going to do is this. I shall write you a letter about this heartless fraud of mine—I have no objection to that way of putting it—because since you have found out so much, I should prefer you to know just why I did it. You shall have the letter today and you can show it to Somerton when you've read it. But I will tell you one thing now—the way the banknote trick was worked." The colonel paused a moment, then asked, "Have you got a cigarette?"

Trent put his hand mechanically to his handkerchief pocket, looked surprised, then searched several other pockets in vain. "I'm sorry. I must have mislaid my case somewhere."

"No," Colonel White said. "It was in that outside pocket of yours all right. I noticed this afternoon that you carry it there. I've got it now. Here it is." He held out the case to Trent, who took it with a slightly bewildered air. "I took it when I faced right up to you a minute ago, and emphasized my remarks by poking you in the upper vest. That was how I attended to Somerton's note-case—only with him it was much easier, because he has the reckless habit of carrying his money in his hip-pocket. Now that is all I'm going to say before I leave you, and I don't suppose we shall meet again."

"I hope not, most sincerely," Trent said. "I look forward to reading the explanation of your proceedings; but on the facts, as far as I know them, you seem to be a dangerous and unscrupulous rascal. Do you make a living out of that little accomplishment you were giving me a display of just now?"

Colonel White shook his head. "On the contrary," he said, "playing off that little accomplishment on our friend Somerton has cost me some thousands of dollars, one way and another. And don't try to make me lose my temper, Mr Trent—you can't do it. I am feeling perfectly satisfied. I have done what I came to Monte Carlo to do and I leave for Paris tonight. The Hotel Meurice will find me for the next ten days, in case Somerton should want to start anything; but he won't. You will receive my letter in the course of the evening." The colonel turned away with a slight bend of the head, and, looking more distinguished than ever, faded away into the hotel.

While Trent was dressing for dinner at his own hotel, two hours later, Colonel White's letter was brought to him. The neat, clear handwriting covered a number of sheets of Artemare notepaper. There was neither date nor signature, and the document began without preliminary as follows:

"I was born in Islington, London, 38 years ago. My mother, who was an Italian, was a good woman, and brought me up well; but my father was an English pickpocket, as his father was before him, and I took after him, especially in having the right sort of hands. It is not highly thought of as a profession, but my father was at the top of it and made a decent living out of it. He was very seldom caught, I believe; never in the ten years that I remembered him. Before he died I had learnt all he could show me, and he said I as better than he was, but probably that was parental pride.

"I always worked alone, as he did. It is much more difficult than when you work with stalls, and as regards class there is all the difference in the world. I had had a fair education; I could pass anywhere as far as appearance and dress and speaking good English went. I spoke as my father did, it was natural to me; how he got his quiet, unaffected upper-class way of talking I don't know, I never met another man who could do it without being born to it.

"When I was seventeen I was caught in the act, by a piece of bad luck. I came up before the North London magistrate, Mr Somerton. He was a recent appointment, and he wasn't popular with the crooks. I knew that, but I was surprised at the way he treated me. As it was my first appearance, I thought I might be bound over, or get off with a month at the very worst. But it was clear from the start that he had taken a dislike to me. When the police had told him that I associated with criminals and was a bad influence, and I said it was a lie, he kept a vicious eye on me, and finally said he could not take a lenient view of this case, and gave me three months.

"Not long after I came out, I came before Somerton again. There had been a jewelers' window smashed and a lot of stuff taken, and a policeman, a man with whom I had had some unpleasantness, gave evidence. There were three men in it, and he had come up just as they were making off. He gave chase, and they got away, but he swore that he recognized one of them, and that I was that one. Actually I had been nowhere near the place at the time, but I couldn't prove it, and when I said the cop was trying to frame me because we were not on good terms, the magistrate got to drumming with his fingers and looking more and more sour. He gave me six months. I didn't like being punished harshly, on insufficient evidence, for something I never did—a spite sentence—and being treated as if my word against the cop's wasn't worth a damn, but the worst was what he said before passing sentence. He need not have said it, it was simply meant to hurt, you could see that by the way he glared at me as he said it. He told me I thought I looked like a gentleman, but what was I but a common thief, who could never enter a decent house or mix with decent people. There was more, but those words were what I never forgot. What I decided Somerton should pay for one day, and what he has paid for, was using his position to insult and browbeat me.

"Every day while I was serving that sentence I was thinking about Mr James Lingard Somerton, and what I would do to one day. I'm not what you would call a vindictive man in the ordinary way, I think; but all my life when I have got set on a thing I have kept that thing before me and fixed my will on it, and I was very much set on making Somerton pay.

"I knew it was going to be a very long job. I meant it to be. I meant to make good, in the first place. I didn't mind his telling me I was a thief, because I was, but I objected to his saying I thought I looked like a gentleman, because I knew I looked like -gentleman, and a lot more like a gentleman than Somerton did, or does now. In my business it was necessary to look that way—all first-class dips do. And I wasn't going to be told I could never mix with decent people, either. That was telling me I didn't have character enough to become a good citizen—and the consequence was that I got set on becoming just that thing; which was very far from what Somerton intended.

"When I came out of prison I knew just what I meant to do. I went to my mother's brother, who was a fruit merchant, and toId him I was going to go straight for the future. I asked him if would pay my passage to America, so I could begin life again. He agreed to do that, and I emigrated. There was no difficulty about getting into the United States in those days. I soon found employment clerking. To make a short story of it, in five years' time I had a good position with a firm in Harrison, Colorado, and S saving money. When I was twenty-eight, some land I had bought near the town for a speculation turned out to be mostly copper-ore under the surface, and the first thing I knew I was a millionaire.

"After that I engaged in all kinds of business, and prospered 11 more. I donated a library and a hospital to Harrison, founded professorships at Denver and Boulder, subscribed liberally to charities. I was a prominent citizen and a public benefactor. The governor of the state appointed me a member of his personal staff the rank of colonel. That was just an honour, I didn't have do a thing for it. I liked being a colonel, for I thought it might useful when I got after Somerton. I had plenty else to think about, but I never forgot him.

"Three years ago I put a private inquiry agency onto Somerton, ad reports of his position, his health, his way of life. I got the addresses he had lived at during the years since I last saw him. I found he had come into a lot of money and resigned from the bench; and among other things I heard he had the habit of spending month in Monte Carlo after Christmas, staying at the Artemare.

"Well, the next time he went there, last year—I went there too. We became acquainted, we got on well together. When I left to attend to my business interests at home, we both hoped we should meet again next year—that is to say, this year. During those few weeks I learnt a lot more about him than I knew before, I had spied out the land for my enterprise, and I had my little scheme ready for a year ahead. The hotel staff knew me as a man who tipped extravagantly. I was on the best of terms with Madame Joubin at the paper-stand and I had wasted a lot of money with old Grangette.

"When Somerton arrived at the Artemare a fortnight ago I was already here. He was delighted to see me, and I spent all my time with him and his daughter and their friends. After a few days I started on him, in the way you know. The hotel servants, who disliked him, entered thoroughly into the spirit of the thing. The people who spoke to him in the street would have done a lot more than that for a 100-franc bill.

"I have told you, in part, how I managed the matter of Somerton's billfold. I expected he would be going to the bank for money some time, and I had been practicing for months till my hands had got the old dexterity. I was with him when he went to the Crédit Lyonnais, saw him draw his ten bills, returned with him to the crowd watching the regatta. Lifting a wallet from a hip pocket is one of the easiest things an expert dip ever does. I put in ten more milles, returned the case, watched him turn white when he made the discovery. That was good! A minute later I had the case out again, removed my own ten, put it back. It all went over very smoothly.

"The newspaper trick was done in this way. Passing through London I had obtained from the Times back-date department copies of the paper covering a fortnight of this time last year. Madame Joubin willingly agreed, for a consideration, to help me work a practical joke on Somerton. She was to hand him a year-old paper the first time we both came to her stand together. I timed that for the day after the billfold incident. I already had in my coat pocket a Times of the right date, which I had provided myself with an hour before. When he took his paper from Madame Joubin I bought a copy of Esquire, which is a large-size American magazine, and I held my own *Times* ready underneath it. When he did notice the date on his paper, and exclaimed about it, I very naturally held out my hand for it. Looking him in the eyes—as I did with you, you may remember—I changed the papers in an instant, and then remarked that the date was all right. His ghastly face as I handed it to him was well worth all my trouble and expense, believe me.

"What I had in mind when I got Somerton's old address was this. The year before, he had sent his wife a birthday present, which I had helped him choose, from Grangette's. I gambled on his doing the same again, and he did; but if he didn't, I thought I would be able to make a good use of that address some way. As it happened, he actually asked me to go with him to Grangette's again, for the same purpose; he had confidence in my judgment. As you know, I didn't make the mistake of offering Grangette too little; he would probably have done it for much less, but I wanted that thing done.

"Of course, it went wrong because the inquiry agent made a couple of errors in giving me that old address. I do not blame him, at that. No man could have thought of the slight change in the postal direction since Somerton lived there, and the misspelling of Talfourd was a very natural slip. I am not worrying, anyway. I got the effect I wanted. And I have found it quite a pleasure telling this story to an intelligent person who can appreciate it.

"I believe that is all. I have had a very interesting and happy time. Somerton will miss me, I am afraid. He can put in the time thinking about all the pleasant little talks we have had together, beginning in his own police court twenty years ago."

"A very interesting and happy time!" Trent repeated to himself, "Monte Cristo in miniature!" He turned back a few sheets. "A prominent citizen and a public benefactor, was he? And a private malefactor in his spare time. Well, Somerton won't like this; but I dare say he will like it better than being driven out of his mind. All the same, I don't think I'll deliver it by hand."

He telephoned to the porter's office for a chasseur.

10

THE LITTLE MYSTERY

It was early on a Saturday afternoon that Philip Trent, passing through Cadogan Place, caught sight of a trim figure in the portico of one of the tall old houses. The girl came down the steps as he stopped his car.

"How goes it, Marion?" he said. "It must be all of a year since I saw you last."

"Why, Phil! What a surprise!" She glanced back at the door she had just left. "Have you come to see the doctor? But no, you can't do that without an appointment—and besides, he's just going out himself."

Trent got out of the driving seat and shook hands with Marion Silvester, whom he had known for most of her twenty-two years. "So this is the doctor's. Ah yes, I see—brass plate so tiny you don't notice it's there. A great man, evidently—the smaller the plate the bigger the doctor. Still, *I* don't want to see him. I have just been lunching in Chelsea, but it wasn't as bad as all that."

"Well, you will see him, whether you want to or not," she said in a low tone as the door opened, and a tall, gaunt man, black-bearded, came out. He took off his hat to Marion, with a swift glance at Trent as he returned the salutation, and passed on his way.

"He's not a doctor, really, he's a surgeon," Marion explained. "But he is a Pole, and it seems that whatever degree you take in his country, you're called a doctor."

Trent examined the brass plate. "Dr W. Kozicki. There is something very tragic about the look of your Dr W. Kozicki, Marion. An interesting, cultured face. And he has very small ears, with hardly any lobes. Beautiful hands; and he has had the left one badly bitten by a dog, or possibly a patient—some years ago by the look of the scar. No baldness, though he must be over fifty. Short nose, long upper lip—he wouldn't look nearly so handsome if he was clean-shaven."

She laughed. "Isn't that just like you! You see a person for a split second, and you've got him photographed. Well, I'm his secretary, and as Saturday's a short day, I get off after lunch."

"Is there anywhere I can take you? I am free for the next hour."

She thought for a moment. "You know, Phil, meeting you like this is really rather lucky. Several times I've wished I could tell you about something that's been annoying me, because I can't understand it, and perhaps you could, though it's not one of your crime problems. If you could take me home, I could explain it best there. I suppose you don't know Reville Place."

"I know where it is."

"Then you know it's where a quite nice neighbourhood shades off into a dingy one. I've got a cheap top floor at number 43." Trent opened the door of the car, and she took her place. "It's not a very cheery spot, but my flatlet is all right once you're inside the door. Mother let me have some decent furniture and things, and it's airy and comfortable."

The car started, and Marion continued, "Yes, I am on my own now. Of course, we haven't met since father died. We weren't left any too well-off, as you may imagine, knowing him as you did."

Trent nodded. He had indeed known Colin Silvester well enough to be surprised that he had left anything at all. Probably, he reflected, Mrs Silvester had her own income. Silvester had made money easily and abundantly, but he had loved entertaining on a generous scale, and loved yet more anything in the nature of a gamble for high stakes. He had been well-known and popular in the social world, though a malicious wit had made him not everyone's friend; which had added a spice to the news that, at his death, he had left behind him the material for a volume of memoirs, to be published in due time.

"Mother has the house in Wallingford," Marion said, "and not too much to run it on, when Fred's school bills have been paid. I had a little capital of my own, enough to keep me while I was learning to make a living, so I decided to come to London and train for a secretary's job. I took this place we're going to, and started a course at Needham's."

Trent asked when she had finished her course.

"Why, I never did finish it," Marion said. "I hadn't been at it three months when Paula Kozicki looked me up. You wouldn't know her—she's my boss's daughter, of course, and she was my greatest friend at school. She had all her education in England, and you would never know she was a Pole. She's lived with her father since he came to London. He had a son who went to the devil, Paula told me, and since then the old man has been entirely devoted to her. Well, when she called on me, she told me her father wanted a new secretary, and nothing would do but that he must have me for the job.

"I was astonished. I had only seen him once in my life, when Paula brought him to tea in Reville Place. I had heard about him sometimes from father, who for some reason didn't like him, and I had always imagined he was very disagreeable; but when he came I quite took to the old chap, he so evidently doted on Paula. But of course I hadn't ever dreamed of an offer like this. Well, she made me come round and see him; and he was most charming—said he had been so much touched by Paula's story of me and my doings—he laid it on rather thick, really. You know the sort of thing men say when a girl doesn't merely curl up and collapse when things get difficult."

"Yes, I do know," Trent said with feeling. "Your pluck, your self-reliance, your—"

"All right, I see you've got it by heart," interrupted the girl of the period. "So when we had got over that part, he asked if I could come to him, as his secretary was leaving him for a better position—which I knew from Paula; only she also told me the doctor had got her another post because he wanted to have me. I said how gratified I was, but that I had had very little training and no experience; and he said any fool could do the work—though he didn't put it quite that way—as it was just keeping a list of appointments with patients, and receiving them when they came, and taking some correspondence, and noting up the fees. And then he offered me about double what I should have expected for my first job.

"Well, I took it. There was absolutely nothing wrong with it; and there still isn't, after a month of it. The work's not hard, and in fact there's often not much to do, so that I can get a little work done on Father's book. Oh! I didn't tell you that I was putting his rough notes for his memoirs into shape for the publishers. They're very rough ones, and I have to write the whole thing out myself. I take some of the stuff to the doctor's every day. There's quite a lot of it—I haven't read it all yet, in fact; but a good deal of what I have read is pretty scandalous, believe me."

Trent, with a vivid memory of Silvester's vein of unexpurgated anecdote about people of importance, said that this was easy to believe. "But you say there's still nothing wrong with this heaven-sent job of yours. Marion, you blast my hopes. I thought I was going to hear that Kozicki had made dishonourable proposals to you, or that he drinks laudanum, or that he has a private delusion that he is a weasel. Well, it's all very capital for you, and I am gladder than I can say—and here we are at 43 Reville Place."

This was an old-fashioned, high-roofed, stucco-fronted house with a basement and three other floors; like all its neighbours, slightly dingy in appearance, though not dilapidated. They mounted the steps, and Marion opened the door with a latch-key. It could be seen, as they went up the stairs, that each floor had been partitioned off to form a self-contained flat; and Marion's own door, like the front door, was fitted with a Yale lock.

"Well, here's my top floor," she said as they entered. There were four rooms opening off the landing, all fairly lofty and well lighted.

"And a very good top floor," Trent observed when he had been shown the living-room, bedroom, bathroom and kitchen. "Much better than the top floor in my own place; and furnished, as I think you said, with faultless taste. If ever you want to get rid of that little tallboy you might let me know. And that mahogany writing-table—it was a spinet when it was young, wasn't it? You want to keep that, I suppose."

Marion laughed. "Are you setting up an antique shop? But now, let me tell you what it was I wanted your advice about. To begin with, look at the top of that table."

He bent over it. "You mean these faint scratches here and there—as if something hard and heavy had been shifted about on it. Curious? The scratches are in four lots—making the four corners of a square. Was it done when the furniture was moved here from Wallingford?"

"No, it was done fairly lately—three weeks ago, say; perhaps more. That table was as smooth as glass till then. I rub it over with a duster every day, so I noticed it at once. And it wasn't done by the charlady who comes in two mornings a week.

She is a very careful, neat-handed woman; and besides, I first saw the scratches on a Thursday, and her days are Tuesday and Friday. Of course, I don't like having my table scratched, but what I like much less is not knowing who did it, and how anyone could have been here to do it. The entrance door is locked when I'm out, of course; and the street door always is. And don't look as if you thought I was worrying about a trifle. There are other things that tell me plainly someone comes into this place when I'm not here.

"You see the velvet cushion in that armchair? It's embroidered a prettier pattern on one side than on the other, and I always leave it showing that side, as it is now. But several times I have come in and found it turned the other way round. Anyone who had been sitting in that chair, and had punched the cushion into shape again before going away, would be as likely as not to leave it wrong way round. Then again there is that old writing-table you covet so much. There is nothing of value in either of the drawers—I keep Father's notes for his memoirs in the left-hand one, and as much as I have done of the fair copy in the other—but three times someone has been at them."

"They are not locked?" Trent asked.

"No—nothing in the place is locked except the door of the flat. Now, look at these drawers. You see"—she opened both and shut them again—"they both push in a little too far when you close them, and I always pull them back so as to be just level with the woodwork round them. I'm fussily particular, perhaps you think; anyhow, I am absolutely certain I have never left those drawers pushed right in as I found them three days running not long ago. And now here"—she led the way into the kitchen—"I'll show you the thing that makes me quite certain, and that is this sink. When I've washed up after breakfast I leave it not only perfectly clean, but quite dry, bottom and sides as well."

"Why?" Trent wondered.

"Because I've been well brought up," Marion said conclusively. "Well, every day for some time past I have come home and found it perfectly clean, but not dry—drops of water on the sides, which you get from the splashes when you're running the tap. Look! You see those drops? A man wouldn't, I suppose, unless they were pointed out to him. They weren't here when I left this morning." Marion and her guest looked at one another in silence for some moments; then Trent remarked, "You say nothing about having missed anything—jewelry, or any other sort of portable property."

"No," she said. "Absolutely nothing has ever been stolen, I am sure. I often leave money in my dressing-table drawer, and my jewelry, such as it is, is kept there, too, and nothing has been taken. What food I have had in the place has never been touched, nor any of the household things—unless you count those matches, which I suppose came from my box."

Trent rose and paced the floor. "It all sounds pretty mad, I must say," he observed. "And it doesn't make it seem any saner to suggest that one of the people on the lower floors may be your visitor, as they haven't got your private key."

"Yes, and besides, why should they? As for my keys, they are always in my handbag, which is with me all the time. The only duplicates are a pair I keep in the dressing-table drawer, and a pair the charwoman has; and if you ever saw Mrs Kinch you would know she was incapable of doing anything eccentric or not respectable. She worships the vicar of St. Mark's, just round the corner, and she sings hymns while she is doing out the place, as she calls it; and she has a son in a solicitor's office, and likes to let you know it. There have been other things, too, which you can't possibly connect with Mrs Kinch. There's that window you saw me shut when we came in. She knows I always leave it open, to air the room. Well, several times I have come home and found it shut. You see?"

Trent went to the window and opened it for a moment. "Yes, there might be a draught that anyone sitting in this armchair would feel. I agree; it does look as if somebody has been coming in here while you were away—in particular, sitting in your armchair, and plumping up the cushion when he leaves the place."

An exclamation of disgust came from Marion Silvester. "And that's a nice thing to think of, isn't it? I prefer to know something about people who visit my flat and sprawl in my armchair. And it's no use going to the police about it, as you can see. What have I got to tell them? The place hasn't been broken into, nothing has been stolen. I've no actual proof that anyone has been making themselves at home here. They'd only grin, and say—or think—I was fancying things."

Trent considered. "Yes, I suppose they would. By the way, what time do you leave here in the morning?"

"Nine-fifteen; and get back about seven, usually."

"Much at home during the weekends?"

"No, not a lot. I spend a good deal of the time with friends—Paula Kozicki and other people I know in London. On Sundays I get out into the country if the weather's decent, and have a day in the open air, with or without a companion. I don't have at all a dull life, Phil. The one bad spot is this silly little mystery."

"Perhaps," Trent said, "the best thing you can do, Marion, is to leave it to me. I must be on my way now, but I will let my giant intellect play round the subject, and make a few inquiries and see you again very soon."

She jumped up. "Heaven bless you, Phil! That's what I hoped you would say."

"And before I go, would you like to trust me with those spare keys of yours?"

She fetched them from the bedroom. "If you use them, you must promise not to pilfer anything, or smash up the furniture."

Trent expressed the hope that he would be able to overcome his lower nature. Before he left the house, he tried each of the keys in its lock, and found that they fitted easily.

In the Cactus Club most ways of life are represented, and there are few subjects on which some information cannot be gleaned from fellow-members whenever there is a large muster. Lunching there next day, Trent was able to draw upon more than one source for facts about Dr Kozicki. He was an orthopaedic specialist with certain methods of his own devising and a fancy for making his own surgical appliances. He had built up a large practice in his native city of Posen, and made a European reputation. The afflicted grandson of Jason B. Rhodes, the sulphur magnate, had been brought across the ocean to him for treatment, and had been cured.

An ex-patient of the doctor, who had attended him at his own house, gave some more intimate details. Kozicki was a widower. His son and daughter had been sent to school in England, so as to escape the influence of German culture, of which the doctor disapproved, for he had been an ardent Polish patriot under the German rule. This had not been a success in the case of the son, who had turned out a hopeless waster.

Some ten years ago Dr Kozicki had, it was vaguely known, "got into trouble" with the German authorities, and had found it advisable to transfer himself to London, where he had resumed his practice, and was doing more than well. The son, going from bad to worse, had turned his attention to forgery, and had been sent to penal servitude. The doctor was entirely wrapped up in his daughter, who was a Slade art student. He had not succeeded in spoiling her, and every one thought her charming.

Besides his liking for Marion Silvester, Trent had another motive for taking up her "little mystery." He thought there might be something more in the affair than she imagined, and his curiosity was awake. It might be worth while to look further into the affairs of Dr Kozicki; and there was one line, at least, that could be followed up. After leaving the Cactus Club, he spent a fruitless hour searching the files in the offices of the Record for a report of the trial of the younger Kozicki; and he was still at this task when Homan, the paper's regular crime expert, came into the library.

"If you're hunting for the name Kozicki," Homan said, "you won't find it. I remember the case. He was prosecuted under the name of Jackson, by which he was known to the police as being mixed up with a bad lot. He had forged a stolen cheque and collected the money. It didn't come out till afterwards that he was the doctor's son, and the fact was never made public. He was informed on by a man he had quarrelled with, and his evidence got Jackson five years."

Thus put on the right track, Trent soon turned up the report of the case. It was colourless enough; but Trent noted that the name of the informer was given as Whimster, that he had been on intimate terms with Jackson before their quarrel, and that his going to the police had the air of an act of treachery rather than of dauntless public spirit. A public house called the Cat and Fiddle, in the Harrow Road, had figured in the evidence as a rendezvous of Jackson, Whimster, and their associates. A comparison of dates showed that Jackson-Kozicki's sentence had still six months to run; but as Homan pointed out, it might be shortened considerably as the reward of good conduct.

The landlord of the Cat and Fiddle, whose beer Trent found to be in excellent condition, had known Whimster very well. Jackson had been before his time. When the landlord first came to the place, three years ago, Whimster had been using the Cat and Fiddle regularly. He was a racing tipster, and seemed to do pretty well out of it, taking good times with bad. Last year Whimster had left the district, saying nothing to nobody; but

Joe Chittie, being over in Woolwich not long ago, had seen him in the street. Joe could swear it was Whimster; but when he spoke to him he said that wasn't his name, and he had never seen Joe in his life—quite nasty about it he was, Joe said. Well, what could you make of it?

Funny, but Trent was not the first to be asking after Whimster, the landlord said. There had been a gent in not long ago wanting to get in touch with the same party, and the landlord had told him the same as he had told Trent.

"Would you know that man again?" asked Trent.

Yes, the landlord would; it was a face that gave you a funny feeling, you couldn't easily forget it. But what, the landlord wondered, was the reason for all this interest in Whimster?

Trent could only tell him that he thought Whimster might have some information that would be useful to him. What was the landlord having? The landlord's was a toothful of old Jamaica—good stuff this chilly weather. Happy days, sir!

Chief Inspector Bligh, receiving Trent in his little office at Scotland Yard, pushed the cigarette-box across the table.

"Yes, I can tell you something more about Ladislas Kozicki, alias George Jackson," Mr Bligh said, when Trent had set forth the extent of his own information. "I'm glad you got the landlord of the Cat to talk; his evidence will be useful. We hadn't got onto that line, because, you see, the man you know as Whimster has called himself Barling since he went to live in Woolwich. They must be the same man; I can see that. We have got plenty on Jackson as it is, but you can't have too much."

"Why, is he in trouble again?"

"You might call it that," the inspector said grimly. "He came out of prison five weeks ago. He's wanted now for attempted murder. Last Tuesday night Barling passed two men who knew him walking up Foxhill Street, where he lives. There was nobody else about. They exchanged greetings as they passed;

and then the two chaps met another, whose face they say they didn't like. This fellow was staring after Barling, and looked as if he was following him. Well, out of curiosity they turned and followed too.

"Just as Barling was approaching a pub called the Red Cow, which he was probably on his way to, they saw the follower catch him up and take him by the arm. They were too far behind to hear what was said, but the other man seemed to steer Barling into the entry of a builder's yard at the side of the pub. Then they heard Barling yelling for help, and as they ran up, the other man came bolting out of the entry and made off in the opposite direction, towards the main road.

"They found Barling lying in his blood, apparently dead; he had been stabbed twice. His injuries were serious, but not fatal. Next day he was able to state that the man who had knifed him was George Jackson, who had done time for forgery. We looked him up in the Rogue's Gallery, and showed the two witnesses his picture, which they recognized at once. Barling refuses to say anything more."

Trent, his elbows on the table, had followed this terse narrative with kindling eyes. "And Jackson is still on the run?"

"He is. He probably slowed down when he got to the main road, seeing he wasn't being pursued; and he could have boarded any one of a dozen buses or trams. It was easy for him to vanish. His description has gone out, of course, with his prison photo; but there's no trace of him as yet. As we knew his real name and history, Dr Kozicki was called on and interrogated; but he could tell us nothing—didn't even know his son was at liberty, he says. He had had six months knocked off his sentence, you see, for being a good boy. He shed his virtue with his convict's uniform—they often do—"

Trent eyed the inspector thoughtfully for a few moments, then looked away. "It all fits in," he said as if to himself. "I don't like it, but it can't be helped."

"What's on your mind?" Mr Bligh demanded. "Is it another of your bright ideas? They are usually worth something, so let's have it."

"Well, I have an idea—I don't know if you'll call it a bright one—about where you can lay hands on your man. But it means more tragedy for someone, if I'm right."

"It'll mean tragedy for you, my lad, if you connive at the escape of a dangerous criminal," the inspector said briskly, drawing his chair up to the table. "Come on; let's hear it."

Trent let him hear it.

At the corner of Reville Place next morning Trent met Mr Bligh, who was followed at some distance by another plain-clothes officer, already known to Trent as Sergeant Borrett. A closed car was waiting there, and as they passed it the inspector and its driver exchanged almost imperceptible nods.

"You've told her what to do?" Mr Bligh asked.

"She will have got my letter this morning," Trent said. "As we arranged, I didn't tell her anything—only asked her to leave at her usual time, not to take any notice of us when she sees us at the door, and to go straight off to her job as if nothing was happening."

"Right."

They came to the door of No. 43, and Trent opened it with Marion's latch-key. When the sergeant had joined them in the entry, they went quickly up to the top floor and waited before the entrance to the flat. "Probably nothing will happen until she's been gone some time," the inspector remarked, "but we don't want to have this door opening and shutting more than it usually does."

At nine-fifteen precisely. Marion, equipped with hat and handbag, opened the entrance door and came out. She was flushed and bright-eyed as she took in the sight of the three tall figures waiting on the stair-head. "I got your note," she murmured to Trent; then hurried down below.

The three men entered quietly, shutting the door behind them, however, not so quietly. Mr Bligh, after a glance into each of the four rooms that opened upon the landing, led the way into the largest, the living-room in which Trent had listened to Marion's story; and there they waited in silence with the room door open, for what seemed to Trent the longest half-hour his watch had ever told.

At last a sharp, slight noise came from without, and the inspector motioned the others to stand farther back from the door. Other faint sounds followed; and then there came into view through the doorway an object which was slowly descending from the ceiling outside the room. It was a small suitcase, dangling from a cord fastened to its handle. This came noiselessly to rest on the landing; the cord dropped beside it; and then with a dry rattle, a rope ladder with rungs of cane unrolled itself swiftly from above until its end just cleared the floor.

The ladder began to thresh about and to creak, and two feet appeared. A man was feeling his way down by this awkward means; a short, strongly-made man with disproportionately broad shoulders. But just before the head on the shoulders came into the watchers' field of vision the two officers were out of the room with a rush.

The man was instantly dragged from the ladder. There followed a furious and wordless struggle, during which a small hall table and the bowl of flowers upon it were smashed to pieces, and a panel of the entrance door was cracked by a boot heel. At last the handcuffs snapped, and George Jackson was formally acquainted with the reason for his arrest as he stood glowering and panting in the secure grasp of Sergeant Borrett.

Jackson's broad, high forehead and over-developed jaws made his face almost square; his lips were thin, his chin was short, his narrow-lidded eyes were much too far apart, and he was villainously unshaven.

Mr Bligh jerked an automatic pistol from the captive's breast pocket.

"You see," he remarked to Trent, "there couldn't have been a better way of getting him. If he'd had his hands free, somebody might have been hurt with this Betsy before he could be stopped. If we had tried to get him in that loft, somebody would have been killed pretty certainly, and he could have stood the whole force off up there, so long as he had food and ammunition. But if he was making use of the flat, there had to be a rope or a ladder of some kind; and while he was coming down he was helpless."

He went to the window opening on the street, put his head out and waved a hand. The car at the corner rolled gently up to No. 43.

"Take him along, Borrett," Mr Bligh said, opening the entrance door. "I'll be over when I have had a look round up above."

The sergeant twined one fist scientifically into Jackson's collar, the other into a sleeve, and propelled him at arm's length through the doorway and down the stairs. From first to last he had not spoken a word.

"First we'll have a look at his travelling outfit," Mr Bligh said, as he slipped the catches of the suitcase on the floor. "Good idea, that—saved a lot of climbing up and down. What have we here? Toothbrush, soap, and towel, brush and comb—he has nice, clean habits, anyhow, and didn't like to use anything of Miss Silvester's more than he had to. He was able to wash regularly and leave no traces—have a bath, too. No shaving tackle—as you might expect from the look of him."

"That was the notion, I think," Trent said. "To lie low—or rather high—until the hunt for him had cooled off, and meanwhile grow a beard and moustache that would be a better disguise than anything else. What's that you've got there?"

The inspector held it up, eying it appreciatively. "Boned chicken in glass—none of your vulgar tins. Tomato soup in bottle. Biscuits, butter—his old man was doing him well, I must say. Salt and pepper, packet of tea. Two cloths—for washing up, I suppose, so as not to use Miss Silvester's. He must have made free with her plates and knives and forks and kitchen things, though; there's none of them here. By the way, she may notice a rise in her gas bill, if Jackson has been using the cooker as well as the kitchen and bathroom geysers, and the gas-fire in the sitting-room. I should say he was very comfortable here, making himself quite at home for eight hours or so a day."

"And at intervals the doctor would look in with fresh supplies," Trent remarked. "That would be when he was supposed to be attending patients at their own homes, no doubt."

The inspector closed the suitcase and rose from his knees. "I'm glad his old man supplied a ladder. It will be easier than a rope for anybody my size."

"It will certainly be easier than the way Jackson first got up into the loft," Trent remarked, "if I am right in thinking they dragged the living-room table onto the landing and put a chair on top of it. Jackson would only just be able to push up the trapdoor with his fingers, and hauling himself up required some strength. The scratches made by the feet of the chair gave me an idea almost at the start."

"But that wasn't all you had to go on?" suggested the inspector.

"No. Before that I thought the doctor must have some reason for manufacturing a job for a girl he didn't know, and keeping her safe in his own house all day. What he did know was that she lived in a top-floor flatlet; and he visited her once to see if the usual loft and trapdoor were where they could be made use of. When she started work with him, he borrowed the keys from her bag at the first opportunity, took a squeeze of them, and filed duplicates from a couple of Yale blanks—he's quite a craftsman, I'm told. Then he laid in the necessary stores, and one evening when Miss Silvester was at the theatre with his daughter he met Ladislas, brought him here, and left him settled in under the roof. That's my story, anyhow. I've thought over it a lot since yesterday, and that's how I fill in the outlines."

Mr Bligh grunted. "It must have been something like that. Of course he knew his son was released as soon as it happened. Probably he got the doctor on the phone and arranged a meeting somewhere. He may have told him what he meant to do to Whimster. He must have told him he was going to be wanted by the police again, and must have a safe hideout. Then the doctor was struck by a notion, and he began working on the plan for making a hideout of the loft over his daughter's friend's place. A good plan, too."

"Perhaps he didn't need to be told what a lad like that was going to do to the man who put him away," Trent suggested. "If you're a Pole, as well as a wrong 'un, you are not apt to have a forgiving nature. If it was a question of saving his son from a hanging, I suppose he was ready for anything."

"Well, he'll get plenty, I dare say—though there'll be sympathy for him, too. Now will you hold onto the foot of this ladder while I go up? If you want to come, you'll have to manage by yourself, as Jackson did."

"If I want to come?"

By the light of the inspector's big electric torch they surveyed the sleeping quarters of the soi-disant George Jackson. Between two of the roof beams a light canvas hammock was slung, folded blankets within it. Some sheets of pasteboard had been laid over the ceiling joists in one corner, and on them stood an array of preserved foods, a tin of biscuits, a carton of eggs, a packet of candles, and other household necessaries. In another corner was a pile of newspapers.

"Nothing to sit on," Trent observed. "You can't carry a chair about the streets without exciting remark—besides, there's nowhere for a chair to stand. No wonder he had a fondness for that armchair below."

"It must have taken the doctor several visits to get this place furnished," the inspector said. "Well, I've seen enough. I'll have all this removed before Miss Silvester comes home. I wonder how she'll like it when you tell her the story. It'll be something for her to talk about for the rest of her life—how she had a young man staying in her flat for a fortnight without knowing it."

When they had made the descent, Trent turned to gathering up the wreckage on the floor and stowing it in a corner of the kitchen.

"I shall have to get Marion a new table and bowl," he remarked. "I promised her I wouldn't smash up the furniture." He laughed suddenly.

Mr Bligh inquired what the joke was.

"Why, I just remembered," Trent said, "that she told me this wasn't one of my crime problems."

11

THE UNKNOWN PEER

When Philip Trent went down to Lackington, with the mission of throwing some light upon the affair of Lord Southrop's disappearance, it was without much hope of adding anything to the simple facts already known to the police and made public in the newspapers. Those facts were plain enough, pointing to but one sad conclusion.

In the early morning of Friday, the 23rd of September, a small touring-car was found abandoned by the shore at Merwin Cove, some three miles along the coast from the flourishing Devonian resort of Brademouth. It had been driven off the road over turf to the edge of the pebble beach.

Examined by the police, it was found to contain a heavy overcoat, a folding stool, and a case of sketching materials with a sketching-block on the back seat; a copy of Anatole France's Mannequin d'Osier, two pipes, some chocolate, a flask of brandy, and a pair of binoculars in the shelves before the driving-seat; and in the pockets a number of maps and the motoring papers of Lord Southrop, of Hingham Blewitt, near Wymondham, in Norfolk. Inquiries in the neighbourhood led to the discovery that a similar car and its driver were missing from the Crown Inn at Lackington, a small place a few miles inland; and later the car was definitely recognized.

In the hotel register, however, the owner had signed his name as L. G. Coxe; and it was in that name that a room had been booked by telephone early in the day. A letter, too, addressed to Coxe, had been delivered at the Crown, and had been opened by him on his arrival about 6:30. A large suitcase had been taken up to his room, where it still lay, and the mysterious Coxe had deposited an envelope containing £35 in banknotes in the hotel safe. He had dined in the coffee-room, smoked in the lounge for a time, then gone out again in his car, saying nothing of his destination. No more had been seen or heard of him.

Some needed light had been cast on the affair when Lord Southrop was looked up in Who's Who—for no one in the local force had ever heard of such a peer. It appeared that his family name was Coxe, and that he had been christened Lancelot Graham; that he was the ninth baron, was thirty-three years old, and had succeeded to the title at the age of twenty-six; that he had been educated at Harrow and Trinity, Cambridge; that he was unmarried, and that his heir was a first cousin, Lambert Reeves Coxe. No public record of any kind, nor even any "recreation" was noted in this unusually brief biography, which, indeed, bore the marks of having been compiled in the office, without any assistance from its subject.

Trent, however, had heard something more than this about Lord Southrop. Sir James Molloy, the owner of the Record, who had sent Trent to Lackington, had met everybody, including even the missing peer, who was quite unknown in society. Society, according to Molloy, was heartily detested and despised by Lord Southrop. His interests were exclusively literary and artistic, apart from his taste in the matter of wine, which he understood better than most men. He greatly preferred Continental to English ways of life, and spent much of his time abroad. He had a very large income, for most of which he seemed to have no use. He had good health and a kindly disposition; but he had a passion for keeping himself to himself, and had indulged it with remarkable success. One of his favourite amusements was wandering about the country alone in his car, halting here and there to make a sketch, and staying always at out-of-the-way inns under the name he had used at Lackington.

Lord Southrop had been, however, sufficiently like other men to fall in love, and Molloy had heard that his engagement to Adela Tindal was on the point of being announced at the time of his disappearance. His choice had come as a surprise to his friends; for though Miss Tindal took art and letters as seriously as himself, she was, as an authoress, not at all averse to publicity. She enjoyed being talked about, Molloy declared; and talked about she had certainly been—especially in connection with Lucius Kelly, the playwright. Their relationship had not been disguised; but a time came when Kelly's quarrelsome temper was no longer to be endured, and she refused to see any more of him.

All this was quite well known to Lord Southrop, for he and Kelly had been friends from boyhood; and the knowledge was a signal proof of the force of his infatuation. On all accounts, in Molloy's judgment, the match would have been a complete disaster; and Trent, as he thought the matter over in the coffee-room of the Crown, was disposed to agree with him.

Shortly before his arrival that day, a new fact for his first dispatch to the *Record* had turned up. A tweed cap had been found washed up by the waves on the beach between Brademouth and Merwin Cove; and the people at the Crown were sure that it was Lord Southrop's. He had worn a suit of unusually rough, very light-grey homespun tweed, the sort of tweed that, as the headwaiter at the Crown vividly put it, you could smell half a mile away; and his cap had been noted because it was made of the same stuff as the suit. After a day and a half in salt water, it had still an aroma of Highland sheep. Apart from this and its colour, or absence of colour, there was nothing by which it could be identified; not even a maker's name; but there was no reasonable doubt about its being Lord Southrop's, and it seemed to settle the question, if question there were, of what had happened to him. It was, Trent reflected, just like an eccentric intellectual—with money—to have his caps made for him, and from the same material as his clothes.

It was these garments, together with the very large horn-rimmed spectacles which Lord Southrop affected, which had made most impression on the headwaiter. Otherwise, he told Trent, there was nothing unusual about the poor gentleman, except that he seemed a bit absentminded-like. He had brought a letter to the table with him—the waiter supposed it would be the one that came to the hotel for him—and it had seemed to worry him. He had read and reread it all through his dinner, what there was of it; he didn't have only some soup and a bit of fish. Yes, sir; consommé and a nice fillet of sole, like there is this evening. There was roast fowl, but he wouldn't have that, nor nothing else. Would Trent be ordering his own dinner now?

"Yes, I want to—but the fish is just what I won't have," Trent decided, looking at the menu. "I will take the rest of the hotel dinner." An idea occurred to him. "Do you remember what Lord Southrop had to drink? I might profit by his example."

The waiter produced a fly-blown wine-list. "I can tell you that, sir. He had a bottle of this claret here, Chateau Margaux 1922."

"You're quite sure? And did he like it?"

"Well, he didn't leave much," the waiter answered. Possibly, Trent thought, he took a personal interest in unfinished wine. "Were you thinking of trying some of it yourself, sir? It's our best claret."

"I don't think I will have your best claret," Trent said, thoughtfully scanning the list. "There's a Beychevelle 1924 here, costing eighteenpence less, which is good enough for me. I'll have that." The waiter hurried away, leaving Trent to his reflections in the deserted coffee-room.

Trent had learned from the police that the numbers of the notes left in the charge of the hotel had been communicated by telephone to Lord Southrop's bank in Norwich, the reply being that these notes had been issued to him in person ten days before. Trent had also been allowed to inspect the objects, including the maps, found in the abandoned car. Lackington he found marked in pencil with a cross; and working backwards across the country he found similar crosses at the small towns of Hawbridge, Wringham, and Candley. The police, acting on these indications, had already established that "L. G. Coxe" had passed the Thursday, Wednesday and Tuesday night respectively at inns in these places; and they had learned already of his having started from Hingham Blewitt on the Monday.

Trent, finding no more to be done at Lackington, decided to follow this designated trail in his own car. On the morning after his talk with the waiter at the Crown he set out for Hawbridge. The distances in Lord Southrop's progress, as marked, were not great by the most direct roads; but it could be guessed that he had been straying about to this and that point of interest—not, Trent imagined, to sketch, for there had been no sketches found among his belongings. Hawbridge was reached in time for lunch; and at the Three Bells Inn Trent again found matter for thought in a conversation—much like the chat which he had already enjoyed at the Crown Inn—with the headwaiter. So it was again at the Green Man in Wringham that evening. The next day, however, when Trent dined at the Running Stag in Candley, the remembered record of Lord Southrop's potations took a different turn. What Trent was told convinced him that he was on the right track.

The butler and housekeeper at Hingham Blewitt, when Trent spoke with them the following day, were dismally confident that Lord Southrop would never be seen again. The butler had already given to the police investigator from Devon what little information he could. He admitted that none of it lent the smallest support to the idea that Lord Southrop had been contemplating suicide; that he had, in fact, been unusually cheerful, if anything, on the day of his departure. But what, the butler asked, could a person think? Especially, the housekeeper observed, after the cap was found. Lord Southrop was, of course, eccentric in his views; and you never knew—here the housekeeper, with a despondent head-shake, paused, leaving unspoken the suggestion that a man who did not think or behave like other people might go mad at any moment.

Lord Southrop, they told Trent, never left any address when he went on one of these motoring tours. What he used to say was, he never knew where he was going till he got there. But this time he did have one object in mind, though what it was or where it was the butler did not know; and the police-officer, when he was informed, did not seem to make any more of it. What had happened was that, a few days before Lord Southrop started out, he had been rung up by some one on the phone in his study; and as the door of the room was open, the butler, in passing through the hall, had happened to catch a few words of what he said.

He had told this person he was going next Tuesday to visit the old moor; and that if the weather was right he was going to make a sketch. He had said, "You remember the church and chapel"—the butler heard that distinctly; and he had said that it must be over twenty years. "What must be over twenty years?" Trent Wanted to know. Impossible to tell: Lord Southrop had said just that.

The butler had heard nothing further. He thought the old moor might perhaps be Dartmoor or Exmoor, seeing where it was that Lord Southrop had disappeared. Trent thought otherwise, but he did not discuss the point. "There's one thing you can perhaps tell me," he said. "Lord Southrop was at Harrow and Cambridge, I believe. Do you know if he went to a preparatory school before Harrow?"

"I can tell you that, sir," the housekeeper said. "I have been with the family since I was a girl. It was Marsham House he went to, near Sharnsley in Derbyshire. The school was founded by his lordship's grandfather's tutor, and all the Coxe boys have gone there for two generations. It stands very high as a school, sir; the best families send their sons there."

"Yes, I've heard of it," Trent said. "Should you say, Mrs Pillow, that Lord Southrop was happy as a schoolboy—popular, I mean, and fond of games, and so forth?"

Mrs Pillow shook her head decisively. "He always hated school, sir; and as for games, he had to play them, of course, but he couldn't abide them. And he didn't get on with the other boys—he used to say he wouldn't be a sheep, just like all the other something sheep—he learned bad language at school, if he didn't learn anything else. But at Cambridge—that was very different. He came alive there for the first time—so he used to say."

In Norwich, that same afternoon, Trent furnished himself with a one-inch Ordnance Survey map of a certain section of Derbyshire. He spent the evening at his hotel with this and a small-scale map of England, on which he marked the line of small towns which he had already visited; and he drew up, not for publication, a brief and clear report of his investigation so far.

The next morning's run was long. He had lunch at Sharnsley, where he made a last and very gratifying addition to his string of coffee-room interviews. Marsham House, he learnt, stood well out-side Sharnsley on the verge of the Town Moor; which, as the map had already told him, stretched its many miles away to the south and west. He learnt, too, what and where were "the church and chapel," and was thankful that his inquiring mind had not taken those simple terms at their face value.

An hour later he halted his car at a spot on the deserted road that crossed the moor; a spot whence, looking up the purple slope, he could see its bareness broken by a huge rock, and another less huge, whose summits pierced the skyline. They looked, Trent told himself, not more unlike what they were called than rocks with names usually do. Away to the right of them was a small clump of trees, the only ones in sight, to which a rough cart-track led from the road; and from that point, he thought an artist might well consider that the church and chapel and their background made the best effect. He left his car and took the path through the heather.

Arrived at the clump, which stood well above the road, he looked over a desolate scene. If anyone had met Lord Southrop there, they would have had the world to themselves. Not a house or hut was in sight, and no live thing but the birds. He looked about for traces of any human visitor; and he had just decided that nothing of the sort could reasonably be expected, after the lapse of a week, when something white, lodged in the root of a fir tree, caught his eye.

It was a small piece of torn paper, penciled on one side with lines and shading the look of which he knew well. A rapid search discovered another piece near by among the heather. It was all that the wind had left undispersed of an artist's work; but for Trent, as he scanned the remnants closely, it was enough.

His eyes turned now over a wider range; for this, though to him is spelt certainty, was not what he had been looking for. Slowly following the track over the moor, he came at length to the reason for its existence—a small quarry, to all appearance long abandoned. A roughly circular pond of muddy water, some fifty yards across, filled the lower part of it; and about the margin was a confusion of stony fragments, broken and rusted implements, bits of rotting wood and smashed earthenware—a typical scene of industrial litter. With his arm bare to the shoulder Trent could feel no bottom to the pond. If it held any secret, that opaque yellow water kept it well.

There was no soil, to take a footprint near the pond. For some time he raked among the débris in which the track ended, finding nothing. Then, as he turned over a broken fire-bucket, something flashed in the sunlight. It was a small, flat fragment of glass, about as large as a three penny piece, with one smooth and two fractured edges. Trent examined it thoughtfully. It had no place in his theory; it might mean nothing. On the other hand ... he stowed it carefully in his note-case along with the remnants of paper.

Two hours later, at the police headquarters in Derby, he was laying his report and maps, with the objects found on the moor, before Superintendent Allison, a sharp-faced, energetic officer, to whom Trent's name was well known.

It was well known also to Mr Gurney Bradshaw, head of the firm of Bradshaw & Co., legal advisers to Lord Southrop and to his father before him. He had, at Trent's telephoned request, given him an appointment at three o'clock; and he appeared at that hour on the day after his researches in Derbyshire. Mr Bradshaw, a courteous but authoritative old gentleman, wore a dubious expression as they shook hands.

"I cannot guess," he said, "what it is that you wish to put before me. It seems to me a case in which we should get the Court to presume death with the minimum of difficulty; and I wish I thought otherwise, for I had known Lord Southrop all his life, and I was much attached to him. Now I must tell you that I have asked a third party to join us here—Mr Lambert Coxe, who perhaps you know is the heir to the title and to a very large estate. He wrote me yesterday that he had just returned from France, and wanted to know what the position was; and

I thought he had better hear what you have to say, so I asked him for the same time as yourself."

"I know of him as a racing man," Trent said, "I had no idea'he was what you say until I saw it in the papers."

The buzzer on the desk-telephone sounded, and Bradshaw put it to his ear. "Show him in," he said.

Lambert Coxe was a tall, spare, hard-looking man with a tanned, clean-shaven face, and a cordless monocle screwed into his left eye. As they were introduced he looked at the other with a keen and curious scrutiny.

"And now," Bradshaw said, "let us hear your statement, Mr Trent."

Trent put his folded hands on the table. "I will begin by making a suggestion which may strike you gentlemen as an absurd one. It's this. The man who drove that car to Lackington, and afterwards down to the seashore, was not Lord Southrop."

Both men stared at him blankly; then Bradshaw, composing his features, said impassively, "I shall be interested to hear your reasons for thinking so. You have not a name for making absurd suggestions, Mr Trent, but I may call this an astonishing one."

"I should damned well think so," observed Coxe.

"I got the idea originally," Trent said, "from the wine which this man chose to drink with his dinner at the Crown Inn before the disappearance. Do you think that absurd?"

"There is nothing absurd about wine," Mr Bradshaw replied with gravity. "I take it very seriously myself. Twice a day, as a rule," he added.

"Lord Southrop, I am told, also took it seriously. He had the reputation of a first-rate connoisseur. Now this man I'm speaking of had little appetite that evening, it seems. The dinner they offered him consisted mainly of soup, fillet of sole, and roast fowl."

"I am sure it did," Bradshaw said grimly. "It's what you get nine times out of ten in English hotels. Well?"

"This man took only the soup and the fish. And with it he had a bottle of claret."

The solicitor's composure deserted him abruptly.

"Claret!" he exclaimed.

"Yes, claret, and a curious claret too. You see, mine host of the Crown kept a perfectly good Beychevelle 1924—I had some myself, But he had also a Margaux 1922; and I suppose because it was an older wine he thought it ought to be dearer, so he marked it in his list eighteen pence more than the other. That was the wine which was chosen by our traveller that evening. What do you think of it? With a fish dinner he had claret, and he chose a wine of a bad year, when he could have had a wine of 1924 for less money."

While Coxe looked his bewilderment, Mr Bradshaw got up and began to pace the room slowly. "I will admit so much," he said. "I cannot conceive of Lord Southrop doing such a thing if he was in his right mind."

"If you still think it was he, and that he was out of his senses," Trent rejoined, "there was a method in his madness. Because the night before, at Hawbridge, he chose one of those wines bearing the name of a chateau which doesn't exist, and is merely a label that sounds well; and the night before that, at Wringham, he had two whiskies and soda just before dinner, and another inferior claret at an excessive price on top of them. I have been to both the inns and got these facts. But when I worked back to Candley, the first place where Lord Southrop stayed after leaving home, it was another story. I found he had picked out about the best thing on the list, a Rhine wine, which hardly anybody ever asked for. The man who ordered that, I think, was really Lord Southrop."

Bradshaw pursed up his mouth. "You are suggesting that someone in Lord Southrop's car was impersonating him at the other three places, and that, knowing his standing as a connoisseur, this man did his ignorant best to act up to it.

Very well; but Lord Southrop signed the register in his usual way at those places. He received and read a letter addressed to him at Lackington. The motor tour as a whole was just such a haphazard tour as he had often made before. The description given of him at Lackington was exact—the clothes, the glasses, the abstracted manner. The cap that was washed up was certainly his. No, no, Mr Trent. We are bound to assume that it was Lord Southrop; and the presumption is that he drove down to the sea and drowned himself. The alternative is that he was staging a sham suicide, so as to be able to disappear, and there is no sense in that."

"Just so," observed Lambert Coxe. "What you say about the wine may be all right as far as it goes, Mr Trent, but I agree with Mr Bradshaw. Southrop committed suicide; and if he was insane enough to do that, he was insane enough to go wrong about his drinks."

Trent shook his head. "There are other things to be accounted for. I'm coming to them. And the clothes and the cap and the rest are all part of my argument. This man was wearing Lord Southrop's tweed suit just because it was so easily identifiable. He knew all about Lord Southrop and his ways. He had letters from Lord Southrop in his possession, and had learnt to imitate his writing. It was he who wrote and posted that letter addressed to L. G. Coxe; and he made a pretence of being worried by it. He knew that Lord Southrop's notes could be traced; so he left them at the bureau to clinch the thing. And, of course, he did not drown himself. He only threw the cap into the sea. What he may have done is to change out of those conspicuous clothes, put them in a bag which he had in the car, and which contained another suit in which he proceeded to dress himself. He may then have walked, with his bag, the few miles into Brademouth, and travelled to London by the 12:15—quite a popular train, in which you can get a comfortable sleeping-berth."

"So he may," Bradshaw agreed with some acidity, while Lambert Coxe laughed shortly. "But what I am interested in is facts, Mr Trent."

"Well, here are some. A few days before Lord Southrop set out from his place in Norfolk, someone rang him up in his library. The door was ajar, and the butler heard a little of what he said to the caller. He said he was going on the following Tuesday to visit a place he called the old moor, as if it was a place as well known to the other as to himself. He said, 'You remember the church and the chapel,' and that it must be over twenty years; and that he was going to make a sketch."

Coxe's face darkened. "If Southrop was alive," he sneered, "I am sure he would appreciate your attention to his private affairs. What are we supposed to gather from all this keyhole business?"

"I think we can gather," Trent said gently, "that some person, ringing Lord Southrop up about another matter, was told incidentally where Lord Southrop expected to be on that Tuesday—the day, you remember, when he suddenly developed a taste for bad wine in the evening. Possibly the information gave this person an idea, and he had a few days to think it over. Also we can gather that Lord Southrop was talking to someone who shared his recollection of a moor which they had known over twenty years ago—that's to say, when he was at the prep school age, as he was thirty-three this year. And then I found that he had been at a school called Marsham House, on the edge of Sharnsley Town Moor in Derbyshire. So I went off there to explore; and I discovered that the church and chapel were a couple of great rocks on the top of the moor, about two miles from the school. If you were there with your cousin, Mr Coxe, you may remember them."

Coxe was drumming on the table with his fingers. "Of course I do," he said aggressively. "So do hundreds of others who were at Marsham House. What about it?"

Bradshaw, who was now fixing him with an attentive eye, held up a hand. "Come, come, Mr Coxe," he said. "Don't let us lose our tempers. Mr Trent is helping to clear up what begins to look like an even worse business than I thought. Let us hear him out peaceably, if you please."

"I am in the sketching business myself," Trent continued, "so I looked about for what might seem the best view-point for Lord Southrop's purpose. When I went to the spot, I found two pieces of torn-up paper, the remains of a pencil sketch; and that paper is of precisely the same quality as the paper of Lord Southrop's sketching-block, which I was able to examine at Lackington. The sketch was torn from the block and destroyed, I think, because it was evidence of his having been to Sharnsley. That part of the moor is a wild, desolate place. If someone went to meet Lord Southrop there, as I believe, he could hardly have had more favourable circumstances for what he meant to do. I think it was he who appeared in the car at Wringham that evening; and I think it was on Sharnsley Moor, not at Lackington, that Lord Southrop—disappeared."

Bradshaw half rose from his chair. "Are you not well, Mr Coxe?" he asked.

"Perfectly well, thanks," Coxe answered. He drew a deep breath, then turned to Trent. "And so that's all you have to tell us. I can't say that—"

"Oh no, not nearly all," Trent interrupted him. "But let me tell you now what I believe it was that really happened. If the man who left the moor in Lord Southrop's car was not Lord Southrop, I wanted an explanation of the masquerade that ended at Lackington. What would explain it was the idea that the man who drove the car down to Devonshire had murdered him, and then staged a sham suicide for him three hundred miles away. That would have been an ingenious plan. It would have depended on everyone making the natural assumption that the man in the car was Lord Southrop, and how was anyone to imagine that he wasn't? '

"Lord Southrop was the very reverse of a public character. He lived quite out of the world; he had never been in the news; very few people knew what he looked like. He depended on all this for maintaining his privacy in the way he did when touring in his car—staying always at small places where there was no chance of his being recognized, and pretending not to be a peer. The murder knew all about that, and it was the essence of his plan. The people at the inns would note what was conspicuous about the traveler; all that they could say about his face would be more vague, and would fit Lord Southrop well enough, so long as there was no striking difference in looks between the two men. Those big horn-rims are a disguise in themselves.

Bradshaw rubbed his hands slowly together. "I suppose it could happen so," he said. "What do you think, Mr Coxe?"

"It's just a lot of ridiculous guesswork," Coxe said impatiently. "I've heard enough of it, for one." He rose from his chair.

"No, no, don't go, Mr Coxe," Trent advised him. "I have some more of what you prefer—facts, you know. They are important, and you ought to hear them. Thinking as I did, I looked about for any places where a body could be concealed. In that bare and featureless expanse I could find only one: an old, abandoned quarry in the hillside, with a great pond of muddy water at the bottom of it. And by the edge of it I picked up a small piece of broken glass.

"Yesterday evening this piece of glass was shown by a police-officer and myself to an optician in Derby. He stated that it was a fragrant of a monocle, what they call a spherical lens, so that he could tell us all about it from one small bit. Its formula was not a common one—minus 5; so that it had been worn by a man very short-sighted in one eye. The police think that as very few people wear monocles, and hardly any of them would wear one of that power, an official inquiry should establish the names of those who had been supplied with such a glass in recent years. You see," Trent went on, "this man had dropped and broken his glass on the stones while busy about something at the edge of the pond. Being a tidy man, he picked up all the pieces that he could see; but he missed this one."

Lambert Coxe put a hand to his throat. "It's infernally stuffy in here," he muttered. "I'll open a window, if you don't mind." Again he got to his feet; but the lawyer's movement was quicker. "I'll see to that," he said; and stayed by the window when he had opened it.

Trent drew a folded paper from his pocket. "This is a telegram I received just before lunch from Superintendent Allison, of the Derbyshire police. I have told him all I am telling you." He unfolded the paper with deliberation. "He says that the pond was dragged this morning, and they recovered the body of a man who had been shot in the head from behind. It was stripped to the underclothing and secured by a chain to a pedal bicycle.

"That, you see, clears up the question how the murderer got to the remote spot where Lord Southrop was. He couldn't go there in a car, because he would have had to leave it there. He used a cycle, because there was to be a very practical use for the machine afterwards. The police believe they can trace the seller of the cycle, because it is in perfectly new condition, and he may give them a line on the buyer."

Bradshaw, his hands thrust into his pockets, stared at Coxe's ghastly face as he inquired, "Has the body been identified?"

"The superintendent says the inquest will be the day after tomorrow. He knows whose body I believe it is, so he will already be sending down to Hingham Blewitt about evidence of identity. He says my own evidence will probably not be required until a later stage of the inquest, after a charge has been—"

A sobbing sound came from Lambert Coxe. He sprang to his feet, pressing his hands to his temples; then crashed unconscious to the floor.

While Trent loosened his collar, the lawyer splashed water from the bottle on his table upon the upturned face. The eyelids began to flicker. "He'll do," Bradshaw said coolly. "My congratulations, Mr Trent. This man is not a client of mine, so I may say that I don't think he will enjoy the title for long—or the money, which was what really mattered, I have reason to believe. He's dropped his monocle again, you see. I happen to know, by the way, that he has been half-blind of that eye since it was injured by a cricket ball at Marsham."

12

THE ORDINARY HAIRPINS

A small committee of friends had persuaded Lord Aviemore to sit for a presentation portrait, and the painter to whom they gave the commission was Philip Trent. It was a task that fascinated him, for he had often seen and admired, in public places, the high, halfbald skull, vulture nose, and grim mouth of the peer who was said to be deeper in theology than any other layman, and all but a few of the clergy; whose devotion to charitable work had made him nationally honoured. It was not until the third sitting that Lord Aviemore's sombre taciturnity was laid aside.

"I believe, Mr Trent," he said abruptly, "you used to have a portrait of my late sister-in-law here. I was told that it hung in the studio."

Trent continued his work quietly. "It was just a rough drawing I made after seeing her in Carmen—before her marriage. It has been hung in here ever since. Before your first visit I removed it."

The sitter nodded slowly. "Very thoughtful of you. Nevertheless, I should like very much to see it, if I may."

"Of course." Trent drew the framed sketch from behind a curtain. Lord Aviemore gazed long in silence at Trent's very spirited likeness of the famous singer, while the artist worked busily to capture the first expression of feeling that he had so far seen on that impassive face. Lighted and softened by melancholy, it looked for the first time noble.

At last the sitter turned to him. "I would give a good deal," he said simply, "to possess this drawing."

Trent shook his head. "I don't want to part with it." He laid a few strokes carefully on the canvas. "If you care to know why, I'll tell you. It is my personal memory of a woman whom I found more admirable than any other I ever saw. Lillemor Wergeland's beauty and physical perfection were unforgettable. Her voice was a marvel; her spirit matched them; her fearlessness, her kindness, her vigour of mind and character, her feeling for beauty, were what I heard talked about even by people not given to enthusiasm. She had weaknesses, I dare say—I never spoke to her. I heard her sing very many times, but I knew no more about her than many other strangers. A number of my friends knew her, though, and all I ever gathered about her made me inclined to place her on a pedestal. I was ten years younger then; it did me good."

Lord Aviemore said nothing for a few minutes. Then he spoke slowly. "I am not of your temperament or your circle, Mr Trent. I do not worship anything of this world. But I do not think you were far wrong about Lady Aviemore. Once I thought differently. When I heard that my eldest brother was about to marry a prima donna, a woman whose portrait was sold all over the world, who was famous for extravagance in dress and what seemed to me self-advertising conduct—I was appalled when I heard from him of this engagement. I will not deny that I was shocked, too, at the idea of a marriage with the daughter of Norwegian peasants."

"She was country-bred, then," Trent observed. "One never heard much about her childhood."

"Yes. She was an orphan of ten years old when Colonel Stamer and his wife went to lodge at her brother's farm for the fishing. They fell in love with the child, and having none of their own, they adopted her. All this my brother told me. He knew, he said, just what I would think; he only asked me to meet her, and then to judge if he had done well or ill. Of course I asked him to introduce me at the first opportunity."

Lord Aviemore paused and stared thoughtfully at the portrait. "She charmed everyone who came near her," he went on presently. "I resisted the spell; but before they had been long married she had conquered all my prejudice. It was like a child, I saw, that she delighted in the popularity and the great income her gifts had brought her. But she was not really childish. It was not that she was what is called intellectual; but she had a singular spaciousness of mind in which nothing little or mean could live—it had, I used to fancy, some kinship with her Norwegian landscapes of mountain and sea. She was, as you say, extremely beautiful, with the vigorous purity of the fair-haired Northern race. Her marriage with my brother was the happiest I have ever known."

He paused again, while Trent worked on in silence; and soon the low, meditative voice resumed. "It was about this time six years ago—the middle of March—that I had the terrible news from Taormina, the day after my return from Canada. I went out to her at once. When I saw her I was aghast. She showed no emotion; but there was in her calmness the most unearthly sense of desolation that I have ever received. From time to time she would say, as if she spoke to herself, 'It was all my fault.' "

At Trent's exclamation of surprise Lord Aviemore looked up. "Few people," he said, "know the whole of the tragedy. You have heard that a slight shock of earthquake caused the collapse of the villa, and that my brother and his child were found dead in the ruins; you have heard, I suppose, that Lady Aviemore was not in the house at the time. You have heard that she drowned herself afterwards. But you have evidently not heard that my brother had a presentiment that this visit to Sicily would end in death, and wished to abandon it at the last moment; that his wife laughed away his forebodings with her strong common sense. But we belong to the Highlands, Mr Trent; we are of that blood and tradition, and such interior warnings as my brother had are no trifles to us. However, she charmed his fears away; he had, she told me, entirely lost all sense of uneasiness. On the tenth day of their stay her husband and only child were killed. She did not think, as you may think, that there was coincidence here. The shock had changed her whole mental being; she believed then, as I believed, that my brother inwardly foreknew that death awaited him if he went to that place." He relapsed into silence.

"I know slightly," Trent remarked, "a man called Selby, a solicitor, who was with Lady Aviemore just after her husband's death."

Lord Aviemore said that he remembered Mr Selby. He said it with such a total absence of expression of any kind that the subject of Selby was killed instantly; and he did not resume that of the tragedy of the woman whom the world remembered still as Lillemor Wergeland.

It was a few months later, when the portrait of Lord Aviemore was to be seen at the show of the N.S.P.P., that Trent received a friendly letter from Arthur Selby. After praising the picture, Selby went on to ask if Trent would do him the favour of calling at his office by appointment for a private talk. "I should like" (he wrote), "to put a certain story before you, a story with a problem in it. I gave it up as a bad job long ago, myself, but seeing your portrait of A. reminded me of your reputation as an unraveller."

Thus it happened that, a few days later, Trent found himself alone with Selby in the offices of the firm in which that very capable, somewhat dandified lawyer was a partner. They spoke of the portrait, and Trent told of the strange exaltation with which his sitter had spoken of the dead lady. Selby listened rather grimly.

"The story I referred to," he said, "is the Aviemore story. I acted for the countess when she was alive. I was with her at the time of her suicide. I am an executor of her will. In the strictest confidence, I should like to tell you that story as I know it, and hear what you think about it."

Trent was all attention; he was deeply interested, and said so. Selby, with gloomy eyes, folded his arms on the broad writing-table between them, and began.

"You know all about the accident," he said. "I will start with the 15th of March, when Lord Aviemore and his son were buried in the cemetery at Taormina. That was before I came on the scene. Lady Aviemore had already discharged all the servants except her own maid, with whom she was living at the Hotel Cavour. There, as I gathered afterwards, she seldom left her rooms. She was undoubtedly overwhelmed by what had happened, though she seems never to have lost her grip on herself. Her brother-in-law, the present Lord Aviemore, had come out to join her. He had only just returned from Canada"—Selby raised a finger and repeated slowly—"from Canada, you will remember. He had gone out to get ideas about the emigration prospect, I understand. He remained at the hotel, meaning to accompany Lady Aviemore home when she should feel equal to the journey.

"It was not until the 18th that we received a long telegram from her, asking us to send some one representing the firm to her at Taormina. She stated that she wished to discuss business matters without delay, but did not yet feel able to travel. At the cost of some inconvenience, I went out myself, as I happen to speak Italian pretty well. You understand that Lady Aviemore, who already possessed considerable means of her own, came into a large income under her husband's will."

"She was a client who could afford to indulge her whims," Trent observed. "If you were already her adviser, she probably expected you to come."

"Just so. Well, I went out to Taormina, as I say. On my arrival Lady Aviemore saw me, and told me quite calmly that she was acquainted with the provisions of her late husband's will, and that she now wished to make her own. I took her instructions, and prepared the will at once. The next day, the British Consul and I witnessed her signature. You may remember, Trent, that when the contents of her will became public after her death, they attracted a good deal of attention."

"I don't think I heard of it," Trent said. "If I was giving myself a holiday at the time, I wouldn't know much about what was going on."

"Well, there were some bequests of jewelry and things to intimate friends. She left £2,000 to her brother, Knut Wergeland, of Myklebostad in Norway, and £100 to her maid, Maria Krogh, also a Norwegian, who had been with her a long time. The whole of the rest of her property she left to her brother-in-law, the new Lord Aviemore, unconditionally. That surprised me, because I had been told that he had disapproved bitterly of the marriage, and hadn't concealed his opinion from her or anyone else. But she never bore malice, I knew; and what she said to me at Taormina was that she could think of nobody who would do so much good with the money as her brother-in-law. From that point of view she was justified. He is said to spend nine-tenths of his income on charities of all sorts, and I shouldn't wonder if it was true. Anyhow, she made him her heir."

"And what did he say to it?"

Selby coughed. "There is no evidence that he knew anything about it before her death. No evidence," he repeated slowly. "And when told of it afterwards he showed precious little feeling of any kind. Of course, that's his way. But now let me get on with the story. Lady Aviemore asked me to remain to transact business for her until she should leave Taormina. She did so on the 27th of March, accompanied by Lord Aviemore, myself, and her maid. To shorten the railway journey, as she told us, she had planned to go by boat first to Brindisi, then to Venice, and so home by rail. The boats from Brindisi to Venice all go in the daytime, except once a week, when a boat from Corfu arrives in the evening and goes on about eleven. She decided to get to Brindisi in time to catch that boat. So that was what we did; had a few hours in Brindisi, dined there, and went on board about ten o'clock. Lady Aviemore complained of a bad headache. She went at once to her cabin, which was a deck-cabin, asking me to send someone to collect her ticket at once, as she wanted to sleep as soon as possible and not be awakened again. That was soon done. Shortly before the boat left, the maid came to me on her way to her own quarters and told me her mistress had retired. Soon after we were out of the harbour, I turned in myself. At that time Lord Aviemore was leaning over the rail on the deck onto which Lady Aviemore's cabin opened, and some distance from the cabin. There was nobody else about that I could see. It was just beginning to blow, but it didn't trouble me, and I slept very well.

"It was a quarter to eight next morning when Lord Aviemore came into my cabin. He was fearfully pale and agitated. He told me that the countess could not be found; that the maid had gone to her cabin to call her at seven-thirty and found it empty.

"I got up in a hurry, and went with him to the cabin. The dressing-case she had taken with her was there, and her fur coat and her hat and her jewelry-case and her handbag lay on the berth, which had not been slept in. The only other thing was a note, unaddressed, lying open on the table. Lord Aviemore and I read it together. After the inquiry at Venice, I kept the note. Here it is."

Selby unfolded and handed over a sheet of thin ruled paper, torn from a block. Trent read the following words, written in a large, firm, rounded hand:

> "Such an ending to such a marriage is far worse than death. It was all my fault. This is not sorrow, it is complete destruction. I have been kept up till now only by the resolution I took on the day when I lost them, by the thought of what I am going to do now. I take my leave of a world I cannot bear any more."

There followed the initials "L. A." Trent read and reread the pitiful message, so full of the awful egotism of grief, then he looked up in silence at Selby.

"The Italian authorities found that she had met her death by drowning. They could not suppose anything else—nor could I. But now listen, Trent. Soon after her death I got an idea into my head, and I have puzzled over the affair a lot without much result. I did find out a fact or two, though; and it struck me the other day that if I could discover something, you could probably do much better."

Trent, still studying the paper, ignored this tribute. "Well," he said, "what is your idea, Selby?"

Selby, evading the direct question, said, "I'll tell you the facts I referred to. That sheet, you see, is torn from an ordinary ruled writing-pad. Now I have shown it to a friend of mine who is in the paper business. He has told me that it is a make of paper never sold in Europe, but sold very largely in Canada. Next, Lady Aviemore never was in Canada. And there was no paper-pad in her dressingcase or anywhere in the cabin. Neither was there any pen or ink, or any fountain pen. The ink, you see, is a pale sort of grey ink."

Trent nodded. "Continental hotel ink, in fact. This was written in a hotel, then—probably the one where you had dinner in Brindisi. You could identify her writing, of course."

"Except that it seems to have been written with a bad pen—a hotel pen, no doubt—it is her usual handwriting."

"Any other exhibits?" Trent asked after a brief silence.

"Only this." Selby took from a drawer a woman's'handbag of elaborate bead-work. "Later on, when I saw Lord Aviemore about the disposal of her valuables and personal effects, I mentioned that there was this bag, with a few trifles in it. 'Give it away,' he said. 'Do what you like with it.' Well," Selby went on, smoothing the back of his head with an air of slight embarrassment, "I kept it. As a sort of memento—what? The things in it don't mean anything to me, but you have a look at them." He turned the bag out upon the writing-table. "Here you are—handkerchief, notes and change, nail-file, keys, powder-thing, lipstick, comb, hairpins—"

"Four hairpins." Trent took them in his hand. "Quite new ones, I should say. Have they anything to tell us, Selby?"

"I don't see how. They're just ordinary black hairpins—as you say, they look too fresh and bright to have been used."

Trent looked at the small heap of objects on the table. "And what's that last thing—the little box?"

"That's a box of Ixtil, the anti-seasick stuff. Two doses are gone. It's quite good, I believe."

Trent opened the box and stared at the pink capsules. "So you can buy it abroad?"

"I was with her when she bought it in Brindisi, just before we went on board."

Again Trent was silent a few moments. "Then all you discovered that was odd was this about the Canadian paper, and the note having obviously been prepared in advance. Queer enough, certainly. But going back before that last day or two—all through the time you were with Lady Aviemore, did nothing come under your notice that seemed strange?"

Selby fingered his chin. "If you put it like that, I do remember a thing that I thought curious at the time, though I never dreamed of its having anything to do—"

"Yes, I know, but you asked me here to go over the thing properly, didn't you? That question of mine is one of the routine inquiries."

"Well, it was simply this. A day or two before we left Sicily I was standing in the hotel lobby when the mail arrived. As I was waiting to see if there was anything for me, the porter put down on the counter a rather smart-looking package that had just come—done up the way they do it at a really first-class shop, if you know what I mean. It looked like a biggish book, or box of chocolates, or something; and it had French stamps on it, but the postmark I didn't notice. And this was addressed to Mlle. Maria Krogh—you remember, the countess's maid. Well, she was there waiting, and presently the man handed it to her. Maria went off with it, and just then her mistress came down the big stairs. She saw the parcel, and just held out her hand for it, and Maria passed it over as if it was a matter of course, and Lady Aviemore went upstairs with it. I thought it was quaint if she was ordering goods in her maid's name; but I thought no more of it, because Lady Aviemore decided that evening about leaving the place, and I had plenty to attend to. And if you want to know," Selby went on, as Trent opened his lips to speak, "where Maria Krogh is, all I can tell you is that I took her ticket in London for Christiansand, where she lives, and where I sent her legacy to her, which she acknowledged. Now then!"

Trent laughed at the solicitor's tone, and Selby laughed too. His friend walked to the fireplace, and pensively adjusted his tie. "Well, I must be off," he announced. "How about dining with me on Friday at the Cactus? If by that time I've anything to suggest about all this, I'll tell you. You will? All right, make it eight o'clock." And he hastened away.

But on the Friday he seemed to have nothing to suggest. He was so reluctant to approach the subject that Selby supposed him to be chagrined at his failure to achieve anything, and did not press the matter.

It was six months later, on a sunny afternoon in September, that Trent walked up the valley road at Myklebostad, looking farewell at the mountain far ahead, the white-capped mother of the torrent that roared down a twenty-foot fall beside him. He had been a week in this remote backwater of Europe, seven hours by motorboat from the nearest place that ranked as a town. The savage beauty of that watery landscape, where sun and rain worked together daily to achieve an unearthly purity in the scene, had justified far better than he had hoped his story that he had come there in search of matter for his brush. He had worked and he had explored, and had learnt as much as he could of his neighbours. It was little enough, for the postmaster, in whose house he had a room, spoke only a trifle of German, and no one else, as "far as he could discover, had anything but Norwegian, of which Trent knew no more than what could be got from a traveller's phrase-book. But he had seen every dweller in the valley, and he had paid close attention to the household of Knut Wergeland, the rich man of the valley, who had the largest farm. He and his wife, elderly and grim-faced peasants, lived with one servant in an old turf-roofed steading not far from the post office. Not another person, Trent was sure, inhabited the house.

He had decided at last that his voyage of curiosity to Myklebostad had been ill-inspired. Knut and his wife were no more than a thrifty peasant pair. They had given him a meal one day when he was sketching near the place, and they had refused with gentle firmness to take any payment. Both had made on him an impression of complete trustworthiness and competency in the life they led so utterly out of the world.

That day, as Trent gazed up to the mountain, his eye was caught by a flash of sunlight against the dense growth of birches running from top to bottom of the steep cliff that walled the valley to his left. It was a bright blink, about half a mile from where he stood; it remained steady, and at several points above and below he saw the same bright appearance. He perceived that there must be a wire, and a well-used wire, led up the precipitous hill-face among the trees. Trent went on towards the spot on the road whence the wire seemed to be taken upwards. He had never been so far in this direction until now. In a few minutes he came to the opening among the trees of a rough track leading upwards among rocks and roots, at such an angle that only a vigorous climber could attempt it. Close by, in the edge of the thicket, stood a tall post, from the top which a wire stretched upwards through the branches in the same direction as the path.

Trent slapped the post with a resounding blow. "Heavens and earth!" he exclaimed. "I had forgotten the saeter!"

And at once he began to climb.

A thick carpet of rich pasture began where the deep birch-belt ended at the top of the height. It stretched away for miles over a gently sloping upland. As Trent came into the open, panting after a strenuous forty-minute climb, the heads of a score of browsing cattle were sleepily turned towards him. Beyond them wandered many more; and two hundred yards away stood a tiny hut, turf- roofed.

This plateau was the saeter; the high grass-land, attached to some valley farm. Trent had heard long ago, and never thought since, of this feature of Norway's rural life. At the appointed time, the cattle would be driven up by an easier detour to the mountain pastures for their summer holiday, to be attended there by some peasant—usually a young girl—who lived solitary with the herd. Such wires as that he had seen were kept bright by the daily descent of milk-chums, let down by a line from above, received by a farmhand at the road below.

And there, at the side of the hut, a woman stood. Trent, as he approached, noted her short, rough skirt and coarse, sack-like upper garment, her thick grey stockings and clumsy clogs. About her bare head her pale-gold hair was fastened in tight plaits. As she looked up on hearing Trent's footfall, two heavy silver earrings dangled about the tanned and careworn face of this very type of the middle-aged peasant women of the region.

She ceased her task of scraping a large cake of chocolate into a bowl, and straightened her tall body. Smiling, with lean hands on her hips, she spoke in Norwegian, greeting him.

Trent made the proper reply. "And that," he added in his own tongue, "is a large part of all the Norwegian I know. Perhaps, madam, you speak English." Her light blue eyes looked puzzlement, and she spoke again, pointing down to the valley. He nodded; and she began to talk pleasantly in her unknown speech. From within the hut she brought two thick mugs; she pointed rapidly to the chocolate in the bowl, to himself and herself.

"I should like it of all things," he said. "You are most kind and hospitable, like all your people. What a pity it is we have no language in common!" She brought him a stool and gave him the chocolate cake and a knife, making signs that he should continue the scraping; then within the hut she kindled a fire of twigs and began to boil water in a black pot. Plainly this was her dwelling, the roughest Trent had ever seen. He could discern that on two small shelves were ranged a few pieces of chipped earthenware. A wooden bed-place, with straw and two neatly folded blankets, filled a third of the space in the hut. All the carpentering was of the rudest. From a small chest in a corner she drew a biscuit-tin, half full of flat cakes of stale rye bread. There seemed to be nothing else in the tiny place but a heap of twigs for fuel.

She made chocolate in the two mugs, and then, at Trent's insistence in dumb show, she sat on the only stool at a rude table outside the hut, while her guest made a seat of an upturned milking-pail. She continued to talk amiably and unintelligibly, while he finished with difficulty the half of a bread-cake.

"I believe, madam," he said at last, setting down his empty mug, "you are talking simply to hear the sound of your own voice.

In your case, that is excusable. You don't understand English, so I will tell you to your face that it is a most wonderful voice. I should say," he went on thoughtfully, "that you ought to have been one of the greatest sopranos that ever lived."

She heard him calmly, and shook her head as not understanding.

"Well, don't say I didn't break it gently," Trent protested. He rose to his feet. "Madam, I know that you are Lady Aviemore. I have broken in on your solitude, and I ask pardon for that; but I could not be sure unless I saw you. I give you my word that no one else knows or ever shall know from me, what I have discovered." He made as if to return by the way he had come.

But the woman held up a hand. A singular change had come over her brown face. A lively spirit now looked out of her desolate blue eyes; she smiled another and a much more intelligent smile. After a few moments she spoke in English, fluent but with a slight accent of her country.

"Sir," she said, "you have behaved very nicely up till now. It has been an amusement for me; there is not much comedy on the saeter. Now, will you have the goodness to explain?"

He told her in a few words that he had suspected she was still alive, that he had thought over such facts as had come to his knowledge, and had been led to think she was probably in that place. "I thought you might guess I had recognized you," he added, "so it seemed best to assure you that your secret was safe. Was it wrong to speak?"

She shook her head, gazing at him with her chin on a hand. Presently she said, "I think you are not against me. I can feel that, though I do not understand why you wanted to search out my secret, and why you kept it when you had dragged it into the light."

"I dragged it because I am curious," he answered. "I have kept it and will keep it because—oh well, because it is your own, and because to me Lillemor Wergeland is a sort of divinity."

She laughed suddenly. "Incense! And I in these rags, in this hovel, with what unpleasantness I can see in this little spotty piece of cheap mirror!... Ah well! You have come a long way, curious man, and it would be cruel not to gratify your curiosity a little more. Shall I tell you? After all, it was simple.

"It was very soon after the disaster that the resolve came to me. I never hesitated. It was my fault that we had gone to Sicily—you have heard that? Yes, I see it in your face. I felt I must leave the world I knew, and that knew me. I never really thought of suicide. As for a convent, unhappily there is none for people with minds like mine. I meant simply to disappear, and the only way to succeed was to get the reputation of being dead. I thought it out for some days and nights. Then I wrote, in the name of my maid, to an establishment in Paris where I used to buy things for the stage."

"Ha!" Trent exclaimed. "I heard of that, and I guessed."

"I sent money," she went on, "and I ordered a dark-brown transformation—that is a lady's word for wig—some stuff for darkening the skin, various pigments, pencils, et tout le bazar. My maid did not know what I had sent for; she only handed the parcel to me when it came. She would have thrown herself in the fire for me, I think, my maid Maria. When the things arrived, I announced that I would return to England by the route you have heard of, perhaps."

He nodded. "The route that gave you a night passage to Venice. And you disguised yourself in your cabin at Brindisi, and slipped off in the dark before the boat started."

"Indeed, I was not such a fool!" she returned. "What if my absence had been discovered somehow before the boat left Brindisi? That could easily happen, and then goodby to the fiction of my suicide. No; when we reached Brindisi, we had, as I knew, some hours there. We left our things at a hotel, where we were to dine, and then I put on a thick veil and went out alone. At the office near the harbour I took a second-class passage to Venice for myself, in the name of Miss Julia Simmons, in the same boat I had planned to take. It would be at the quay, they told me, in an hour. Then I went into the poorer streets of the town, and bought some clothes, very ugly ones, some shoes, toilet things—"

"Some black hairpins," Trent murmured.

"Naturally, black," she assented. "My own gilt pins would have looked queer in a dark-brown wig, and I had to have pins to fasten it properly. I bought also a little cheap portmanteau-thing, and put my purchases in it. Then I took a cab to the quay, found the boat had arrived, and gave one of the stewards a tip to show me the berth named on my ticket, and to carry my baggage there. After that I went shopping again on shore. I bought a long mackintosh coat and a funny little cap, the very things for Miss Simmons; took them to the hotel and pushed them under the things my maid had already packed in my big case.

"On the steamer, when Maria had left me and I had locked the cabin door, I arranged a dark, rather catty sort of face for myself, and fitted on Miss Simmons's hair. I put on her mackintosh coat and cap. When the boat began to move away from the quay, I opened my door an inch and peeped out. As I expected, everyone was looking over the rail, and so—the sooner the better—I just slipped out, shut the cabin door, and walked straight to Miss Simmon's berth at the other end of the ship... . There is not much more to say. At Venice, I did not look for the others, and never saw them. I went on to Paris, and wrote to my brother Knut that I was alive, telling him what I meant to do if he would help me. Such things do not seem so mad to a true child of Norway."

"What things?" Trent asked.

"Things of deep sorrow, malady of the soul, escape from the world… . He and his wife have been true and good to me. I am supposed to be her cousin, Hilda Bjoernstad. In my will I left them money, more than enough to pay for me, but they did not know that when they welcomed me here."

She ceased, and smiled vaguely at Trent, who was considering her story with eyes that gazed fixedly at the skyline.

"Yes, of course," he remarked presently in an abstracted manner. "That was it. As you say, so simple. And now let me tell you," he went on with a change of tone, "one or two little details you have forgotten.

"At Brindisi you bought, just before going on board with the others, a box of the stuff called Ixtil, because it looked as if there might be bad weather. You took a dose at once, and another a little later, as the directions told you. You might have needed more of it before reaching Venice, but as Mr Selby was with you when you bought it, you thought it wiser to leave it behind when you vanished. Also, you left behind you four new black hairpins, which had somehow, I suppose, got loose inside your handbag, and were found there by Selby. You see, Lady Aviemore, it was Selby who brought me into this. He told me all the facts he knew, and he showed me your bag and its contents. But he didn't attach any importance to the two things I have just mentioned."

She raised her eyebrows just perceptibly. "I cannot see why he should. And I cannot see why he should bring in you or anybody."

"Because he had some vague notion of your brother-in-law having either caused your death, or at least having known of your intention to commit suicide. He never told me so outright, but it was plain that that was in his mind. Selby wanted me to clear that up, if I could. You see, your brother-in-law stood to benefit enormously by your death, and then there was the matter of the note announcing your suicide."

"It announced," she remarked, "the truth; that I was leaving a world I could not bear any longer. The words might mean one thing or another. But what about the note?"

"The perfectly truthful note was written with pen and ink, of which there was none in your cabin. It was written on paper which had been torn from a writing-pad, and no pad was found. Also that make of paper is sold in Canada, never in Europe. You had never been in Canada. Your brother-in-law had just come back from Canada. You see?"

"But did not Selby perceive that Charles is a saint?" inquired the lady with a touch of impatience. "Surely that was plain! More Dominic than Francis, no doubt; but an evident saint."

"In my slight knowledge of him," Trent admitted, "he did strike me in that way. But Selby is a lawyer, you see, and lawyers don't understand saints. Besides, your brother-in-law had taken a dislike to him, I think, and so perhaps he felt critical about your brother-in-law."

"It is true," she said, "he did not care about Mr Selby, because he disliked all men who were foppish and worldly. But now I will tell you. That evening in the hotel at Brindisi I wanted to write that note, and I asked Charles for a sheet from the block he had in his hand and was just *going to* write on. That is all. I wrote it in the hotel writing-room, and took it afterwards in my bag to the cabin."

"We supposed you had written it beforehand," Trent said, "and that was one of the things that led me to feel morally certain you were still alive. I'll explain. If, as we thought, you had written the note in the hotel, your suicide was a premeditated act. Yet it was afterwards that Selby saw you buying that Ixtil stuff, and it was plain that you had taken two doses. And it struck me, though it didn't seem to have struck Selby, that it was unlikely any one already resolved to drown herself at sea would begin treating herself against seasickness.

"Then there were those new black hairpins. The sight of them was a revelation to me. For I knew, of course, that with that hair of yours you had probably never used a black hairpin in your life."

The countess felt at her pale-gold plaits, and gravely held out to him a black hairpin. "In the valley we use nothing else."

"It is very different in the valley, I know," he said gently. "I was speaking of my world—the world that you have left. I was led by those hairpins to think of your having changed your appearance, and I even guessed at what was in the parcel that came for your maid, which Selby had told me about."

She regarded her guest with something of respect. "It still remains," she said, "to explain how you knew it was in Norway, and here, as a poor farm servant, that I should hide myself. It seemed to me the last thing in the world—your world—that a woman who had lived my life would be expected to do."

"All the same, I thought it was a strong possibility," he answered. "Your problem, you see, was just what you say—to hide yourself. And you had another—you had to make a living somehow. Everything you possessed—except some small amount in cash, I suppose—you left behind when you disappeared. And a woman can't go on acting and disguising herself for ever. A man can grow hair on his face, or shave it off; for a woman, disguise must be a perpetual anxiety. If she has to get employment, and especially if she has no references, it's something very like an impossibility."

She nodded gravely. "That was how I saw it."

"So," he pursued, "it came to this: that the world-famous Lillemor Wergeland had to come to the surface again somewhere, and in no long time—Lillemor Wergeland, whose type of beauty and general appearance were so marked and unmistakable, whose photographs were known everywhere. The fact is that for some time I couldn't see for the life of me how it could possibly have been done. There were only a few countries, I supposed, of which you knew enough of the language to attempt to live in any of them; and if you did, you would always be conspicuous by your physical type and your accent. If you attracted attention, discovery might follow at any moment. The more I thought of it, the more marvellous it seemed that you had not been recognized—assuming you were still alive—during the six years or so that had passed before I heard the full story and guessed at the truth.

"And then an idea came. There was one country in which your looks and speech would not betray you as a foreigner—your own country. And if there were any corners of the world where you could go with a fair certainty of being unrecognized, the remoter villages of Norway would be among them. And at Myklebostad, on the Langfjord, which the map told me was one of the remotest, you had a brother, who was two thousand pounds richer by your supposed death. You see how it was, then, that I came to this place on a sketching holiday."

Trent stood up and gazed across the valley to the sunlit white peaks beyond. "I have visited Norway before, but never had such an interesting time. And now, before I return to the haunts of men, let me say again that I shall forget at once all that has happened today. Don't think it was merely a vulgar curiosity that brought me here. There was once a supreme artist, whose gifts made me her debtor and servant. Anything that happened to her touched me; I had a sort of right to go seeking what it really was that had happened."

She stood before him in her coarse and stained clothes, her hands clasped behind her, with a face and attitude of perfect dignity. "Very well—you stand on your right, and I on mine—to arrange my own life, since I am alone in it. I will spend it here, where it began. My soul was born here before it went out to have adventures, and it has crept home again for comfort. Believe me, it is not only that, as you say, I am safe from discovery here. That counts for very much; but also I felt I must go and live out my life in my own place, this faraway, lonely valley, where everything is humble and unspoilt, and the hills and the fjords are as God made them before there were any men. It is all my own, own land!

"And now," she ended suddenly, "we understand one another, and we can part friends." She extended her hand, saying, "I do not know your name."

"Why should you?" he asked. He bent over the hand, then went quickly from her. At the beginning of the descent he glanced back once; she waved to him.

Halfway down the rugged track he stopped. Far above a wonderful voice was singing to the glory of the Norse land.

> " *Ja, herligt er mil Fodeland*
> *Dei ewig trodser Tidens Tand*"

sang the voice.

Trent looked out upon the wild landscape. "Her fatherland!" he soliloquized. "Well, well! They say the strictest parents have the most devoted children."